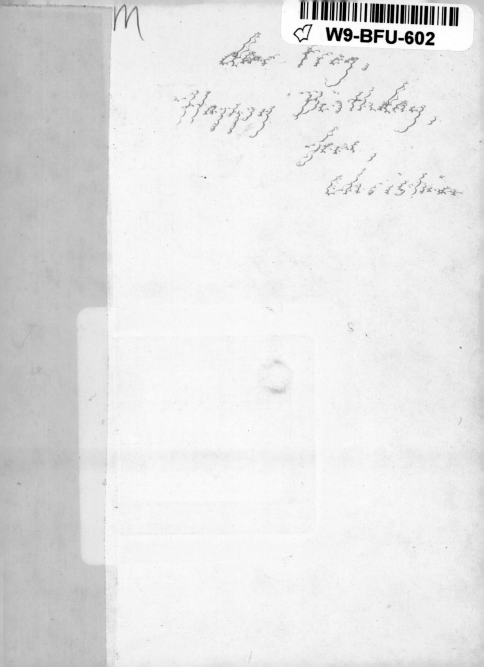

FROG

by
Stephen Dixon

British American Publishing

Portions of FROG have appeared in the following publications: Agni Review, Ambit, American Letters & Commentary, Another Chicago Magazine, Asylum, Beloit Fiction Journal, Boston Review, Boulevard, Caprice, Confrontation, Denver Quarterly, Fiction International, Florida Review, Frank, Gettysburg Review, Kansas Quarterly, Kennesaw Review, The Literary Review, Nebraska Review, New American Writing, North American Review, Northwest Review, Other Voices, Paris Transcontinental, Pequod, Quarterly West, Redstart, Satchel, South Carolina Review, Southern California Anthology, Story Quarterly, Threepenny Review, Triquarterly, Western Humanities Review, Witness, and as the stories "On the Beach," "Mom in Prison," and "Joe," in the story collection *All Gone*, Johns Hopkins University Press.

British American Publishing
19 British American Boulevard
Latham, New York 12110
Typesetting by C. F. Graphics Inc.
Manufactured in the United States of America

95 94 93 92 91 5 4 3 2 1

Library of Congress Cataloging-in-Publication Data

Dixon, Stephen, 1936–
    Frog / by Stephen Dixon.
        p.   cm.
    ISBN 0-945167-41-5 :
    I. Title.
PS3554.I94F76   1991
813'.54—dc20

91-12639
CIP

FROG

Other Works by Stephen Dixon:

FRIENDS

ALL GONE

LOVE AND WILL

THE PLAY

GARBAGE

FALL & RISE

TIME TO GO

MOVIES

14 STORIES

QUITE CONTRARY

TOO LATE

WORK

NO RELIEF

DEDICATION

To my wife, Anne
and daughters, Sophia and Antonia
with love and thanks

Contents

Frog in Prague

They stand still. "And Kafka?" Howard says.

"Kafka is not buried here."

"No? Because I thought—what I mean is the lady at my hotel's tourist information desk—the Intercontinental over there—and also the one who sold me the ticket now, both told me—"

The man's shaking his head, looks at him straight-faced. It's up to you, his look says, if you're going to give me anything for this tour. I won't ask. I won't embarrass you if you don't give me a crown. But I'm not going to stand here all day waiting for it.

"Here, I want to give you something for all this." He looks in his wallet. Smallest is a fifty note. Even if he got three-to-one on the black market, it's still too much. He feels the change in his pocket. Only small coins. This guy's done this routine with plenty of people, that's for sure, and he'd really like not to give him anything. "Come, come," the man said.

"You understand?" Howard said. "For Kafka's grave. Just as I told the lady at the ticket window, I'm sure the other parts of this ticket for the Old Synagogue and the Jewish Museum are all very interesting—maybe I'll take advantage of it some other time—but what I really came to see—"

"Yes, come, come. I work here too. I will show you."

Howard followed him up a stone path past hundreds of gravestones on both sides, sometimes four or five or he didn't know how many of them pressed up or leaning against one another. The man stopped, Howard did and looked around for Kafka's grave, though he knew one of these couldn't be it. "You see," the man said, "the governor at the time—it was the fourteenth century and by now there were twelve thousand people buried here. He said no when the Jewish elders of Prague asked to expand the cemetery. So what did the Jews do? They built down and up, not outwards, not away. They kept inside the original lines of the cemetery permitted them. Twelve times they built down and up till they had twelve of what do you call them in English, plateaus? Places?" and he moved his hand up in levels.

"Levels?"

"Yes, that would be right. Twelve of them and then the ground stopped and they also couldn't go any higher up without being the city's highest cemetery hill, so they couldn't make any levels anymore."

"So that accounts for these gravestones being, well, the way they are. All on top of one another, pressed togetherlike. Below ground there's actually twelve coffins or their equivalents, one on top of—"

"Yes, yes, that's so." He walked on about fifty feet, stopped. "Another governor wouldn't let the Jews in this country take the names of son-of anymore. Son of Isaac, Son of Abraham. They had to take, perhaps out of punishment, but history is not clear on this, the names of animals or things from the earth and so on." He pointed to the stone relief of a lion at the top of one gravestone. "Lion, you see." To a bunch of grapes on another stone: "Wine, this one. And others, if we took the time to look, all around, but of that historical era."

"So that's why the name Kafka is that of a bird if I'm not mistaken. Jackdaw, I understand it means in Czech. The Kafka family, years back, must have taken it or were given it, right? Which?"

"Yes, Kafka. Kafka." Howard didn't think by the man's expression he understood. "Come, please." They moved on another hundred feet or so, stopped. "See these two hands on the monument? That is the stone of one who could give blessings—a Cohen. No animal there, but his sign. Next to it," pointing to another gravestone, "is a jaw."

"A jaw?" The stone relief of this one was of a pitcher. "Jar, do you mean?"

"Yes. Jaw, jaw. That is a Levi, one who brings the holy water to wash the hands of a Cohen. That they are side by side is only a coincidence. On the next monument you see more berries but of a different kind than wine. Fertility."

"Does that mean a woman's buried here? Or maybe a farmer?"

"Yes. Come, come." They went past many stones and sarcophagi. All of them seemed to be hundereds of years old and were crumbling in places. Most of the names and dates on them couldn't be read. The newer section of the cemetery, where Kafka had to be buried, had to be in an area one couldn't see from here. He remembered the photograph of the gravestone of Kafka and his parents. Kafka's name on top—he was the first to go—his father's and mother's below his. It was in a recent biography of him he'd read, or at least read the last half of, not really being interested in the genealogical and formative parts of an artist's life, before he left for Europe. The stone was upright, though the photo could have been taken many years ago, and close to several upright stones but not touching them. The names and dates on it, and also the lines in Hebrew under Kafka's name, could be read clearly. It looked no different from any gravestone in an ordinary relatively old crowded Jewish cemetery. The one a couple of miles past the Queens side of the Fifty-ninth Street Bridge where some of his own family were buried.

The man walked, Howard followed him. "Here is the monument of Mordecai Maisel. It is much larger than the others because he was a very rich important man. More money than even the king, he had. The king would borrow from him when he needed it for public matters. Later, after he paid it back, he would say to him 'Mordecai, what can I give you in return for this great favor?' Mordecai would always say 'Give not to me but to my people,' and that did help to make life better in Prague for the Jews of that time. He was a good wealthy man, Mordecai Maisel. Come, come."

They stopped at another sarcophagus. Hundreds of little stones had been placed on the ledges and little folded-up pieces of paper pushed into the crevices of it. "Here is Rabbi Löw. As you see, people still put notes inside his monument asking for special favors from him."

"Why, he was a mystic?"

"You don't know of the famous Rabbi Löw?"

"No. I mean, his name does sound familiar, but I'm afraid my interest is mostly literature. Kafka. I've seen several of his residences in this neighborhood. Where he worked for so many years near the railroad station, and also that very little house on Golden Lane, I think it's translated as, across the river near the castle. A couple of places where Rilke lived too."

"So, literature, what else am I talking of here? *The Golem*. A world famous play. Well? Rabbi Löw. Of the sixteenth century. He started it. He's known all over."

"I've certainly heard of the play. It was performed in New York City—in a theater in Central Park—last summer. I didn't know it was Rabbi Löw who started the legend."

"Yes, *he, he*. The originator. Others may say other rabbis might have, but it was only Rabbi Löw, nobody else. Then he knocked the Golem to pieces when it went crazy on him. Come, come."

They went on. The man showed him the grave of the only Jewish woman in medieval Prague who had been permitted to marry nobility. "Her husband buried here too?" Howard said. "No, of course not. It was out-of-religion. The permission she got to marry was from our elders. He's somewhere else." The stone of one of the mayors of the Jewish ghetto in seventeenth-century Prague. The stone of a well-known iron craftsman whose name the man had to repeat several times before Howard gave up trying to make it out but nodded he had finally understood. Then they came to the entrance again. After the man said Kafka wasn't buried here and Howard said he wanted to give him something for all this, he gives him the fifty note, the man pockets it and Howard asks if he might know where Kafka is buried.

"Oh, in Strašnice cemetery. The Jewish part of it, nothing separate anymore. It isn't far from here. You take a tube. Fifteen minutes and you are there," and he skims one hand off the other to show how a train goes straight out to it. "It's in walking distance from the station. On a nice day unlike today the walk is a simple and pleasant one. And once you have reached it you ask at the gate to see Kafka's grave and someone there will show you around."

Frog Remembers

He was once somewhere. On a rooftop. Looking out. He saw
many mountains and sky. He saw lots of things. What else? Birds.
Sunrise. Low-hanging clouds. That's not where he was. He was
home. In bed. That's where he is. Now. Thinking of the time. Now
he has it. Time when he first met her. Where was that? When? No
rooftop or mountains, birds or sunrise. From where he met her. One
of the windows out of. Oh, he supposes they could have seen some
of those if they'd looked out the window—not mountains or
sunrise—and maybe one to more of them did. But where was he?
There were several people there. He had it before. Suddenly the
thought disappeared. The memory of it. Here once, now gone. It'll
come back. Always has. No it doesn't, or not necessarily. This is the
first time, in fact, he's thought of this particular memory since it
happened. Can't be true. Must have thought of it a couple of times
soon after it happened. At least once. Had to. Then several to many
times when they were together all those years. Then after they split
up and certainly while they were splitting up. But the first time for
a long time. Now that's true. A fact. At least he thinks it is. That
it's true. Anyway—

6

Anyway, she was somewhere, he was somewhere. They met, somehow met. They immediately took to one another, or almost immediately. That's what they both later said. Said a number of weeks later. Three to be exact. Three on the nose. They met on a Saturday night. Now he's got it. And three Saturday nights later—and he knows it was three. Because they often said to one another, starting from that night. Maybe not often but almost. That good things come in threes. And it's been, they said to one another that night, three weeks from the time they first met to the time they first went to bed. Later, after they'd made love, said it. Made love three times. How's he remember that? Because she later said to him that same night "Good things might come in threes"—said it in so many words—"but this was too much of a good thing. I hurt." Anyway—

Anyway, after they'd made love—maybe after the first time. Maybe after the second. Probably one of those for he doubts it was after the third. For after the third she said what he just said she said. But after one of the other two times, they said to one another "I love you." Exact words. He doesn't remember which one said it first, but what of it? Just that they both said the same thing. He said it or she said it but right after one of them said it the other said it. Then, after they'd made love the third time—actually, only he'd made love that third time. She just let him use her. That's what she later said in so many words too. "It hurt. It really stung. I wasn't involved in it anymore. I was still probably very slippery inside from the previous two times, which is how you were able to do it so easily." Anyway—

Anyway, where were they and when was it? Don't lose it now. It was years ago. Twenty-five. More. They were somewhere. On a rooftop. In a tree. Flying on a cloud. Sliding down a rainbow. Standing on top of such a tall mountain that they saw a sunrise and sunset at the same time. It was at a friend's house. Her cousin's, to be exact, and his friend's. He'd been invited for dinner. They'd been. Separately of course. Sandy. She's dead now. Stroke. She was there when he got there. Denise. He looked at her while he took off his coat and rubber boots and thought "Now she's quite something, that

gal. This a setup? If so, I like it. But first let's see how she thinks
and speaks. She looks like someone who does both very well." But
time out for Sandy. Or Sandra, as she was called at her funeral. They
went to it. With their eldest child. She was a good friend, cousin
and friend-cousin-pampering-aunt to their children and always, far
as they could tell and everyone else said, big spirited, even-tempered,
well-meaning and up till her split-second death, in excellent health.
Anyway— Poor Sandra. Anyway— They once made love. They were
both dead drunk and long before Denise. He just remembered it,
after about thirty years, and that he never told Denise and she'd never
asked him if anything like that had ever happened between them.
Nothing much did, did it? He thinks at best they each tore off his
and her own clothes, stroked and poked a part or two and passed
out till morning. Anyway—

Anyway, he told Denise what he first thought about her when
he first saw her that night. Not that night told her. A week or so
later. A month. After he told her she said "You know, when you came
in"—in so many words, just as his thoughts and talk were—"and
started taking off your outerclothes, I thought 'Nice-looking enough,
that guy. This prearranged? If it is, good going, Sandy. For once you
might come close to hooking me up. He looks fairly intelligent too.
No dresser though. Almost a slob. Not a big problem for now. So,
we'll see what we'll see, OK?' " He doesn't remember saying anything
to her over drinks. Maybe "Hello, my name's Howard," and then she
might have given hers. Of course she did if he gave his. They were
seated opposite one another at dinner. Sandy said, after she said
dinner was ready, who should sit where. There were about ten
guests. "Nobody object. I know what I'm doing. I've been running
over this network of seating places all week. The single and multiple
conversations will just sizzle." The living room window was behind
her chair. The view was of another apartment building's wall. He
probably made a reference or two to it. And to the snow, which had
been predicted but not in such abundance and had just begun to
fall and became one of the city's biggest storms for that or any other

year. Certainly for that year, since that was another thing they later referred to about that night and their children, usually over dinner, liked them to remember for them: the record snow the night they met and how each got home. He thinks he walked and she bused. One of the children would know. He thinks he even offered her cab fare to get home. He lived about ten blocks uptown and she about sixty blocks down. "Just as a loan then if that's the only way you'll accept it," he thinks he said, but she refused: "I'll make do with a subway" or "bus." Did he walk her to a station or stop? Doesn't remember. They talked at the table to each other and others. Of course. But much more than "Please pass the peas and tuna and cheese casserole." Though the main dish was turkey with all the traditional trimmings. Sandy asked him to carve it. She'd seen him do it at his parents' home once or twice. What's he talking about? She was his cousin only by marriage and he doesn't believe she met his parents till the wedding. If she saw him carve a turkey or goose anyplace outside of her home it was later: when Denise and he had her over for a holiday feast, which he thinks they did invite her for once or twice. She must have said something like "Anyone here know how to carve a turkey?" and he volunteered, since he'd carved a turkey and capon at his parents' home several times. Was it a holiday eve or night at Sandy's? Around November or December, so could have been one of many. And someone else walked Denise to the station or stop. Or a group of guests walked together or she went alone. He might have offered, she might have said not to bother, but he stayed with Sandy—was the last to leave, in fact—to talk about Denise. Did it matter much that Sandy and he had once made love? Probably not. That was two years before, and the morning after they agreed it had been a big drunken mistake and to just forget it ever happened, if much, they said, really had—they didn't want to go any deeper into what actually did happen since that was part of their starting to forget it—if they wanted to continue their friendship. Anyway—

Anyway, wine. He brought some. That's not important. He's brought wine to just about every dinner party at someone's home for the last thirty-five years. For a while he was bringing two and a few times three bottles of very good wine to a dinner party. That was when he was a more serious wine drinker and just a bigger drinker and also a lot more flush than he is now. Denise refilling his glass. That's why he brought up the wine. First she asked. He said thanks and she poured. But what he remembers most about it was that this woman he hardly knew and was already very attracted to would want to pour him another glass. First hers, then his? Doesn't remember and what's the difference? Perhaps there's some significance, and she might have felt "How can I get away with refilling my glass without refilling his?" but "That was nice," he remembers thinking. "I like it. She's bold, free-going, present-time, doesn't see wine as just a formality at dinner and linger over a single glass, and also doesn't mind a man who drinks, after he's probably had two or three predinner drinks, a number of glasses of wine and might even be encouraging me to," though he doesn't see how he could have assumed all that. She refill the glass of the person on her right? Denise and he sat at the end of the long table and each had a person seated next to him and her. Doesn't remember, thinks not. Memory he has of it—really just a vague picture—is of that person talking mostly to the person on the other side of him and the one directly across the table next to Howard. Twenty-nine years ago to be exact. He just tallied it. He remembers dates that long ago by the age of his first child. So all he has to do is remember how old Olivia is and he always seems to. She's twenty-five. They were married almost to the day a year before she was born and they got married three Januaries after the November or December night they met. That would make it twenty-eight years ago to be exact. They had three children, two girls and then a boy. They're all grown up, out of college or never entered it, professionals or on his or her way to becoming one, but on their own. They had the children quickly, three in four years. That was very tough on Denise in a number of ways. Olivia alone seemed to cry from birth onward for three straight years. Now she's remarried. Denise is. Actually, Olivia is too. Her first marriage lasted a year. Had a fourth child, Denise did, by her second husband, who already had three by his first two wives. Olivia doesn't ever want to have a child. "In this world?" she's said. Her husband's just about said the same thing. Her second husband. "By war, riots, famine or nuclear accidents, the kid would never live till middle age." Her first husband wanted desperately to have a child. That was the main reason she divorced him. But he helped her with the children—Howard did—helped Denise—as much as possible in every way he could. That's what he remembers and also remembers her saying at the time. Later she said he had hardly ever helped her with the children. But there was practically no letup in childwork for both of them for seven or eight years. That wasn't why Denise divorced him: that he had hardly ever helped her with the children. "Incompatibility," she said, "principally," and that it just wasn't a marriage anymore. To her it wasn't. To him it still was. Very much still was. Not just that they continued to make love. *He* continued, she said, but who was she kidding? Even if she wanted to be rid of him at the time, when it came to their lovemaking she continued to be into it as much as he. Let's face it: sometimes she forgot what she wanted too. Anyway—

Anyway. . .anyway. "That's OK," one of his daughters—Eva—used to say when she was three and did something she thought one of her parents would scold her for. "It's not so bad." Always worked. But where was he? In his room. Where he is. Wasn't his question—an answer too—but that's OK. Lying in bed. Light on above. Ceiling light. All his clothes on. Shoes on. Only light on and only light in the room and his only room. What he's come to. That's OK. Things could improve. Doesn't really care if they don't. So? Thinking of Denise. *There.* Where he was. Called her a year ago. Good. Get right into it. No more whatever they are. Diversions, discursions, ramblings, roundabouts. On Olivia's birthday called, which is how he remembers it so well: when it was. First Olivia—"Happy birthday, darling"—then, long as he had the receiver in his hand and was thinking family, Denise. That day's—Olivia's birthday—coming up in less than a week, so it's been almost a year exact. Last time he spoke to her but not the last time he heard her voice. Why be cryptic when he knows better? Denise's. His wife for nineteen-and-a-half years. She said "Nice to hear from you. How are you? How's work?" Things like that. Finally: "Awful," he said. Good. No more diversions or detours. "I wish you hadn't told me that," she said. "I really don't, if you'll excuse me, want to hear how bad off you are in a mental, emotional, professional or even in a physical kind of way." "Mean, mean. You once wanted to or at least didn't object." "One more remark like that and I swear I'm hanging up," she said. "Please don't," he said, "even if I know you've every reason to or just about. I'll come right out with it: I called to hear your voice. If Phil had answered—" "Bill," she said. "Or your child Annette—" "Anita." "I would have hung up. No, if Anita had answered I would have said 'Oh, must have got the wrong number.' No, I would have said 'Hello, young lady. Could you put your mommy on please?' Then when you got on and said hello and then maybe 'Hello, hello, who is this? Is anyone there?' I would have hung up. If Bill had got on I would have said nothing. Or just 'Excuse me, must have got the wrong number,' and hung up. Then I would have called the next day or two later." "Why are you telling me all this?" she said. "No, forget I asked." "I would have called the next day or two later just to hear your voice. That is, if I hadn't heard it the first time I called, since not only might Anita not have been able to get you but you might not have been home. But if you had got on the first time without Bill or Anita first getting on, I would have just said nothing. I would have just listened to you saying hello or whatever you would have said, but that's not what I did or what happened. I mean, you did get on, but I'm talking to you. You're listening to me. I mean, you are still there and perhaps still listening to me?" "Yes," she said. Anyway—

Anyway, what? Well, that that phone call wasn't a year ago. It was last week. No, last week he called and only heard her voice. She got on, he heard it and hung up. Not as quick as that but he'll get into it. Last year he spoke to her on the phone. So last week when he called she must have known, if she remembered what he'd said in his phone call a year ago, who it was who hung up a minute or so after she said "Hello, who is it, anyone there?" a couple of times. She knew. Had to. He called. Anita got on. He said "Hello, little girl, your mother home?" She said "Just a minute please," and yelled "Mommy." Denise got on, said hello. He said nothing. She said "Hello, who is it, anyone there?" He heard in the background "Who is it, honey?" That was Bill. Or maybe another man. Maybe Bill isn't around anymore. Maybe he's dead, run off or they've separated, divorced. Maybe this man was a new lover. Called her honey. Had to be close to her. Or maybe Bill was on a business trip and the lover was with her only for the night or for the entire time Bill was away. No, couldn't be. She wasn't like that and would never be. Have a lover over while her husband was away and her daughter was home? No. Maybe he was her new husband. But she said to this man— probably Bill—"I don't know, nobody's answering. Maybe it's a crank. Hasn't hung up though. Was it a man or a woman, Anita?" and Anita said "A man." "What did he say to you—exactly, do you remember?" and Anita said "To get you." "Hello, who is it? Is anyone still there?" she said into the phone. Then "That you, Howard? I've a sneaking suspicion it is." He waited a few seconds, she said nothing else, he hung up. That was last week. A year ago on the phone he told her why he had called. Not only about wanting to hear her voice. About his life. How lonely he was with all their children grown up and gone. With just about nobody around. No woman in his life for years now, years, since she left him, he told her. "Oh please," she said. "You? No women? With your emotional needs and sexual drive? Come off it. Anyway—"

Anyway, twenty-eight years ago was it? He took her in his arms. She took him in hers. They took, they took. She was on top, he was on top. They held each other all night. That's the way he remembers it. Most of the night, then. Part of—what's the difference? They held, held. Exactly three weeks after they first met. Saturday, Saturday.

13

They said "I love you, I love you," many times. She can't deny that, any of that, now, but so what and why would she? All in the past for her. He kissed her whole body. Tell it. He said "I don't want any part of your body to feel left out." She said "I like that line, I like it a lot." She kissed most of his body soon after. Slowly: here, there. Not just pecks either. Some of them big kisses, long. He turned over: here, there. She did what he'd done, he did what she'd done. Remembers it, so much of it, as if it were happening. Next morning she said her vagina still hurt. He said he just had a tough time peeing too. "No, my vagina," she said, "not the hole where I pee. It's sore. Hurts something terrible. I think I need an aspirin. Two." That first night on her big bed in the dark room her hair hung long and loose when she was on top of him. Hung all around his face, covered his head and neck completely. Looking through its thin vertical slats, just a little light filtering in from he can't remember where—street? bathroom right outside her bedroom?—it seemed as if he was looking out of what? Tent, he thinks he thought then. Tent with thin vertical slats? Hair like thin vertical slats? Filtering in? Trickling in? He looked out of hair, that's all, long fine loose hair that covered his head. He kissed her breast when she was on top of him. Kissed and then grasped it with his lips till she said "Please, that's not the spot now; stop." She was on top the first time, he the second time, they were side by side, she with her back to him, the third. "Only way I can possibly do it," she said. "No energy to get on top again, and you get on top again and I'll burst." He kept slipping out that third time and kept putting it back in. He just wanted to do it three times with her that first night. Adolescent, he knows, he didn't think then, but so what? He wasn't excited anymore. Erection, yes, but didn't get excited till the end, and even then not so much. But it was as if with three she was his, or something. One was normal, two could be accidental but wasn't atypical, but three was difficult, intentional and maybe memorable. Three clinched it. After a brief sleep he thought of trying for four but felt he might fail at it, and that might somehow undo the ones they'd done and the memorableness of their number.

14

Four would be pushing it, would be pushy. He might have been physically able to do it if she'd got down on all fours and he got behind her. That had usually been the most exciting way for him and usually still is, but it would have been too much to ask of her, it seemed. Maybe too early too. Though doing it that way the first night for either that second or third time might have done something toward clinching it too. But she was tired, she'd said, and sore, and keeping herself in that position for the time it would have had to take to do it wouldn't have been easy. "What are you trying to prove?" she might have asked him. "Once can say it all," she once said to him a year, maybe two later. They did it seventeen straight nights. Just once and sometimes twice each night. The eighteenth night, when they were in bed and he started to kiss and rub her, she said "What are we trying to prove by doing it every night? It's getting silly. Let's prove we can go to sleep once without screwing." He's never done it five times in one night with anyone. Four, just with Denise once, and once with some woman he forgets now. He was probably never physically able to do it that often or knew a woman who let or wanted him to. Both. All three. Six. That would be something. What would it feel like after? Would he feel anything but pain or irritation during? Would six be physically damaging? He might be able to do it five or six times—might have been, rather—in one night if he'd had two or more women to do it with. Seven would probably have been impossible no matter how many women he'd had to do it with. Eight, impossible, period. So he called it quits that night with three. It's not something he'd do now or even be physically able to do in one night with one woman: three. Certainly not something he has the chance to do now. Maybe in a whorehouse, if he knew where there was one and he had the money for it and the woman let him. But he hasn't been to one since a few months before he met Denise and wouldn't go to one now for a number of reasons. Anyway—

Anyway. Anyway. He wishes he were young. Twenty-two. Twenty-three. Around the age he was when he first met Denise. That she were young. Around the age she was then too. That he could meet her for the first time. That they had no children, had never been married. Married, what's the difference? But no children. That they were at a dinner party. Any kind of party. That she was sitting in the living room or standing there or in the foyer when he first got to the party. Or that he was sitting or standing in one of those rooms or the kitchen when she walked in soon after she got to the party or the public hallway right outside the crowded foyer when she was coming upstairs. That they'd look at each other for the first time. Speak, all of that, a first time. Ask the other to pass something at the dinner table or across the bar. Salt, pepper. A bottle of wine, plate of canapés. Smile, say thank you, you're welcome, not know each other's last names yet. Know nothing about the other's family and very little what each has done educationally or does professionally or wants to do in either or both. That the scene would suddenly jump to three Saturdays later. Sundays. Fridays. Two weeks later. It didn't have to take so much time. He was hedging then. Didn't know, though he knew he was very attracted to her and she seemed to be attracted to him, whether he wanted to see her again. Knew he'd get involved. Didn't know if he wanted to. Thought he might want to play around with several women at one time. They're in bed. Hers, his. She had actually called him after he didn't call for a week and said "I thought you were going to call. Anything wrong? Tell me and I won't bother you again." Just remembered that. They'd met for coffee a few days after the party, took a long walk, had a good time together, laughing, joking, telling each other deep and personal things about themselves, and a week after that was when she called. Blanket, sheet over them. Nothing over them, no clothes. She's on top of him first, he's on top of her first, later holding each other through some to most of the night. Outside, a thunderstorm. Lightning. Went on for a long time. She asked if he was frightened— "I am." Storm had wakened them. He said "No, but it's wonderful having thunder, lightning, rain batting the windows and you with me all at the same time for our first night. Sort of enshrines it, or something." Just remembered that. The electric storm and almost exactly what he'd said. He's thought of it before but not for years. She said that was sweet. They probably then kissed, covers must have been back over them, and maybe it was then when they started to make love a third time. He started to. She just turned onto her right side and let him put it in. Now on a single bed. One small room with a kitchenette. Had a large studio then, much better furnished. She had two rooms with a full-sized kitchen and a backyard. She was making lots of money, for more than a year she was one of the leads in a very successful play. It's been a bad year for him. Several bad years in a number of ways. He doesn't have a phone. Called her from a booth that last time. From his phone in his previous apartment a year ago. She can't call him even if she wanted to. Why would she want to, except maybe to say one of their children is sick. She could send him a letter. A telegram, if it was an emergency, though she'd have to get his address from one of the children. It wouldn't be the same thing, a letter. Remembers hers. The good ones, ardent ones, ones that said—only one did—"So bus the 450 miles to see me, but see me, for I need and want you now." Not like the letters after they split up. "Please don't call—*don't* call, that's all—or ring my downstairs buzzer, wait for me at work, send me anymore gifts, telegrams or letters, bother me in any kind of way again." Anyway—

Anyway, should go to sleep now. He's tired enough. Has to be at work early tomorrow. Isn't: end of job. Odd that he's making less now, in what the money buys, and gets less respect at work, mainly because of the kind of job he had to take at his age just to survive, than when he first met her. Probably not so odd, but then was he ever on his way. Turns off the light, turns over on his side—right side, but don't make anything of it—cups his hands under his cheek, wishes he had two pillows. They always slept with two each. Her habit. He got to like it. She had two for herself when he met her and wanted two for herself when he moved in. They went to a store to buy two more, but the same kind she had in case their pillows got mixed up on the bed. But enough of that. Shuts his eyes. Thinks of himself sitting on a rooftop. Climbing a tree. Sailing a boat. He never sailed. Hasn't climbed a tree since he was a young man. He was sitting cross-legged when he never does. She sailed before she met him—with the man who played her father in the play: just friendship; they'd never made love—and liked to sit cross-legged in her short nightie while reading on their bed, but that doesn't have to be the explanation why. They're naked in bed. Image just entered. He didn't do anything to bring it on. Nothing immediate he means; *now*. It's that first time again. He remembers her body so well. For those twenty or so years it only imperceptibly changed. Maybe a little more. She studied dance for years, continued to as an actress, during their marriage always ran, swam, did dance warmups, kept in shape. Waist, breasts, hips, arms, legs—all like a dancer's. Muscular buttocks, calloused feet, delicate hands. The neck. Strong stomach. Her face. Long blond hair usually brushed straight back with a barrette on top or pinned into a chignon. Dirty blond hair to almost brown by the time they divorced. Always so soft. Covered his face. Sucked her nipples when it did. Right one was the one he preferred, maybe because it was the easiest to reach. That make sense? Could. Ran his hand down her long hard deep back crack. She's on top of him now. Grabbed her ass and squeezed and rubbed. Pressed it into him. Steered their movements just like she did. They came, one of them first. Rolled over. Soon started doing it again. They said "You know, I love you." "And you know I love you." "And I love you." "And I love you, my darling." "And you're my darling too and I love you." "And I love you, my darling sweetheart, I love you, just you." "And I love you too, my darling darling sweetheart, I love you, just love you, I do." "Love love love," one said. "Love love love love," the other said. They came, slept, sometime after that started doing it again. He did. She let him. All that's been said. If that hasn't been said then should have been assumed. Long kisses, all kinds of kisses. Telephone rings. Must be ringing in the apartment across from his or is in his head. Listens. Ringing stops. "Rachel, thought it was you," a woman says. He imagines her speaking on the phone to him. "My darling, I haven't changed and I'm coming right over." Her clothes, body, feelings toward him? "My sweetheart, I've changed somewhat, but who doesn't in ten-some years at our age, and I'm coming right over. I'm going to jump right into bed with you when I get there. How could we have let it go on like this so long? I let it. But enough talk. I'm on my way." She comes. Rings the vestibule bell. He opens his door while she's running upstairs. "As you can see," she says, "I'm still in pretty good shape." He pulls her down on him. First closes the door. First tears off her clothes. First hurries with her to the bed. He had waited naked for the half-hour it took her to get there. He raises the top part of his body to hers. Their heads meet, chests. They open their mouths. Kiss for a minute like that without stopping. He's inside her now. Just happened. Corresponding parts found their way. For the time being he doesn't feel much down there; it's all in the kiss. Her hair around him. Still soft and fine. Used to frizz up a bit when she took a hot shower or the air was damp. Then he falls back on the bed because he can't keep himself up like that any longer and she falls on him, clip their teeth and almost chip them, and they start kissing again and holding each other as tight as they can without hurting the other, she with her arms under him till she has to pull them out because, she later tells him, they were beginning to hurt.

Frog's Nanny

This is how he remembers it. He shits in his pants. Actually, it starts with him coming up to her—his memory of it always starts with him coming up to her and pointing between his legs. She says something like "Did you make doody in your pants?" He nods. Remembers nodding, not speaking. "Doody in your pants again?" Nods. Next thing he remembers she's pulling him into the bathroom, then that he's in the bathroom, long pants are off his legs, she slips his underpants off with the shit inside it, and holding the clean part of the underpants pushes the shit into his face. Then she picks him up by his underarms, holds him in front of the medicine chest mirror and tells him to look at himself. He doesn't want to. He's crying. "Look, I'm telling you to look!" He looks. Shit all over his face. Looked like hard mud. Just then he hears his father's voice. "Hello, anyone around?" He starts squirming in her arms to be let down. He wants to run to his father to show him what she did. He knows what she did was wrong. She lets him down. He runs out of the bathroom, through what they called the breakfast room into the kitchen where his father is. He points to his face. His father starts laughing very hard. That's all he remembers. Scene always goes blank then.

"Frieda's coming today," his mother said on the phone. "She particularly asked me to see if you could be here. I'd love for you to be here too." "I don't know if I can make it," he said. "Please do though. She'll be here at noon. She's always very punctual, to the point most of the times of getting here ten to fifteen minutes early. I'm taking her out to lunch. Would you like to join us?" "Now that I know I can't do." "Dobson's—for fish. She was thrilled with it the last time. Raved and raved. Even had a glass of wine." "No, thanks, Ma. If I come I can only spare an hour. Getting there and back will take another hour, which is really all I can spare. Two. Total."

He tells his wife that his mother called before. "Frieda's visiting her for the day. Both want me to be there. For lunch too, but that I'm definitely not doing."

"Your old nanny? What was the story you told about her—what she did to you?"

"What? Every morning rolling down my socks in a way where I could just hop out of bed and roll them up over my feet? Actually, she did that the night before. Left them at the end of my bed along with my—"

"Not the socks. The feces in your face. How'd that go again? I remember your father was in on it too. In the story."

"He laughed when he saw me."

"What do you think that was all about?"

"More I think of it, maybe he really did think it was funny. Here's this kid of his running up to him with shit all over his face. He had a great sense of humor. —No, he did. And for all he knew I might have tripped and fallen into it and maybe that's what he thought was so funny. His kid tripped head first into shit."

"But later he knew. You told him, didn't you? You were pointing, crying. And you told your mother later—you must have, or he did— but they still kept her on."

"Frieda was a gem, they thought. She ran the house. Kept the kids disciplined, quiet when necessary and out of the way. Three boys too, so no easy task. She gave them the time to do what they liked. Work, play, go off for two-week or weekend vacations whenever they wanted. Cruises, and once all summer in Europe. And she wasn't well paid either. None of the nannies then were."

"But she did lots of cruel things like that feces scene. She beat you, hit your face. Smacked your hands with a spatula that you said stung for hours later."

"That was Jadwiga, the Polish woman who replaced Frieda when Frieda married."

"Sent you to bed without your dinner several times."

"Both of them."

"Twisted your wrists till they burned. Right? Frieda?" He nods. "Face it, she was a sadist, but your parents permitted it."

"Look, you have to understand where she came from and the period. As for my parents, who knows if they didn't think that discipline—her kind—and it probably wasn't an uncommon notion then—attitude, belief, whatever—was what we needed. The kids. And OK, since they didn't want to discipline us like that themselves—didn't have the heart to, or the discipline for it or the time—she got anointed. *Appointed*. That wasn't intentional. I'm not that smart. Or just was tacitly allowed to. Anyway, Frieda came from Hanover. 1930 or so. A little hamlet outside. My father hired her right off the boat. Literally, almost. She was here for two or three days when he got her from an employment agency. And that had to be the way she was brought up herself. Germany, relatively poor and little educated, and very rigid, tough, hard, disciplined years."

"What did your father do after he stopped laughing? Did he clean your face?"

"I don't remember, but I'm sure he didn't. He would never touch it. The shit? That was Frieda's job. On her day off, my mother's."

"Can you remember though?"

"Let me see." Closes his eyes. "She put me down. I'd asked her to. Your know all that. I ran into the kitchen. I see him coming, and then he's there. He's got on a business suit, white shirt and a tie. His office was in front of the building, you know."

"Yes."

"So it could have been around lunchtime. He came back to the apartment for lunch every workday. Did it through a door connecting the office and apartment."

"The door's not there now, is it?"

"On my mother's side it is—in the foyer—but she had that huge breakfront put up in front of it. On the other side it was sealed up when he gave up the office. I don't know why they didn't have the door sealed up on their side. Would have been safer from break-ins and more aesthetic. Maybe he thought he'd start up his practice again when he got well enough to. But after he gave up the office it was rented by another dentist. A woman. He sold her most of his equipment. And he wouldn't have been in a business suit then. White shirt and tie, yes. He wore them under his dental smock on even the hottest days. So now it makes me wonder. It was definitely a business suit I saw. A dark one. He must have come into the apartment through the front door, not the office door. It was probably a Sunday. Frieda got her day off during the week and a half day off on Sunday right after lunch. So I don't know. Maybe it was one of the Jewish holidays. He could have just come back from *shul*. But where were my brothers? They could have gone with him and were now playing outside. And my mother? She would have been in the kitchen cooking if it was a Jewish holiday. That was the time—the only time, just about, except for Thanksgiving and I don't know what—my father's birthday? her father visiting? which he did every other week till he died when I was six, through I don't ever remember seeing him, there or any other place—when she really went at it in the kitchen. The other times it was fairly quick and simple preparations and, occasionally, deli or chow mein brought in. Maybe we were going to my father's sister's—Ida and Jack's—in Brooklyn for dinner that night. We did that sometimes. She cooked kosher, if that's the right expression, and my father, raised on it, still fancied it, especially on Jewish holidays. Anyway, he approached. I was around three or four at the time. So if it was a nursery school day and not a serious Jewish holiday and I wasn't home from school because I was sick—but she never would have put shit in my face if I were sick—then it was the afternoon. My nursery school for the two years was always in the morning. But what about my father's business suit? Let's just say he closed the office for the day and had a suit on because he'd just come back from a dental convention downtown. He's there though. I see him coming through the living room into the kitchen. I run through the breakfast room—where we never had breakfast, except Sunday morning, just dinner—to the kitchen. The kitchen was where we had breakfast and lunch. Frieda's behind me. I don't remember seeing her, just always sensed she was. I hold out my arms to him. I'm also crying. I don't remember that there, but how could I not be? I think a little of the shit was getting into my mouth. I don't remember smelling it but do tasting it a little. All this might sound like extrapolation, exaggeration—what I didn't smell but did taste. But I swear it's not. Anyway, to it. Arms are out. Mine. I've a pleading look. I know it. I had never felt so humiliated, soiled, so sad, distressed—you name it. Dramatic, right? I'm telling you," opening his eyes, "I felt absolutely miserable and this had to be evident to him. So maybe when he saw me he took that kind of defense—laughter—rather than deal with it, try to comprehend it. But maybe not. Maybe he did think I tripped into it. So even though I was so distressed his first reaction might have been 'Oh my God, Howard's tripped into shit.' Maybe he thought it was our dog Joe's. Or dirt. That I'd been playing in one of the backyard planters, or that it was paint on my face. Clay. But no play clay's that color. Maybe it does get that way when you mix all the colors up. Anyway, my arms are out. Let me try to get beyond what I've so far can't remember about it. Past the blank." Shuts his eyes. "Arms. He's there. Kitchen. I run to him. Frieda's behind me. Sense that. I'm crying. Have to. Pleading look. He laughs. Blank. Blank." Opens his eyes. "No, didn't work. Most of my real old memories end like that. Like a sword coming down. Whop! Maybe hypnosis would get me past, but I tend to doubt those aids. Or can't see myself sitting there, just submitting."

"But your mother. Didn't she say it never happened?"

"To me, yes. She says it happened to Alex. He says it did happen to him but nothing about a kitchen or pair of pants, which she seems to remember hearing he did it in, or my dad. That he was in a bathtub by himself—one of the first times. Till then he had always bathed toe-to-toe with Jerry, but Frieda throught they were too grown-up for that so had it stopped—when he suddenly shit. Two big—"

"Come, on, spare me."

"So he called out that he'd just made kaka in it. Frieda came, grabbed some of it out of the water and put it in his face. He said he never kakaed again in the tub or anywhere but in the potty, or at least that he doesn't remember being anything but toiletized after that."

"How about you?"

"I don't know if what Frieda did to me stopped me from having kaka accidents or even was the last time she put it in my face. I do think it happened to me. For sure. Memory of it's too vivid for it not to have happened, but I guess that doesn't have to be the case."

"So, are you going to see her?"

"Yes, I think so, you mind? I had Olivia two hours today, so I've at least done part of my daily share. When I come back I'll take her to the park or something and you can get back to work."

He goes to his mother's. Has the keys, lets himself in. "Hi, hi, it's me," he says walking through the living room. They're having coffee and cookies in the kitchen. Frieda sees his mother look up at him and smile and turns around. "Oh my, look who's here," she says. "What a nice thing to do," and holds out her arms. He bends down and kisses her cheek while she hugs him around the waist. Still that strong scent of that German numbered cologne she always wore. He wondered on the subway if he should bring the shit incident up. If it did happen to him or has he been imagining it all this time? If he has been imagining it, that'd say something about something he didn't know about himself before. But he'd never bring it up. It would embarrass her, his mother, ultimately him. Or immediately him, seconds after he asked it.

"You didn't bring the little one," Frieda says. "Or your wife. I never met them and was hoping."

"I'm sorry, I didn't even think of it. Maybe no time to. When my mother called you were coming, I just ran right down."

His mother asks if he wants coffee. "Black, I remember, right?" Frieda says.

"Always black," his mother says.

Frieda talks about her life. He asked. "As I told Mrs. T., we're still living in the same small house in Ridgewood and we'll probably die there. That's Ridgewood Brooklyn, you know, not Queens. There, just over the line, it's always been very different. But our area's been much improved. Young people are living in. Excuse me, moving. Many good whites, blacks, Spanish—hard-working people, with families, and honest. You'd like this: some artists, even. For years we couldn't go out on the streets after six. Even during the days it was dangerous sometimes. We needed escorts—you had to pay for them; they simply didn't volunteer—just to go shopping." The same high reedy voice, trace of a German accent. Must be a more accurate way—a better way—to describe the distinctiveness of it, but will do for now. "Martin is as well as can be expected for someone his age." He asked. "He still does all the baking at home. Breads, rolls, pies, cakes—he does one from the first two and one from the second two every other day. I don't understand how we stay so thin, and he still only uses real butter, a hundred percent. The baking company gave him a good pension, and with the Social Security we both get—Dr. T. helped set it up for me. I really wasn't eligible to be paying for it at the time, but oh my god, could he finagle. For good reasons mostly, I'm saying, for he knew we'd need it later. So, we live all right and have no complaints other than those every old person has. But Mrs. T. looks wonderful, thank God," and she knocks twice on the table. "Such a tough life, but she never changes, never ages. She'll always be a beautiful bathing beauty and a showgirl, which she only stopped being, you know, a few years before I came to work for her. She's amazing," and squeezes his mother's hand. "The parties you gave then—I still see them in my head."

"That's what I just told you about yourself," his mother says. "Look at her. Everything's the same. She doesn't age."

"No no no no." She closes her eyes modestly. Those stove hoods for eyelids. Not stove hoods but something like them. Roll tops of roll-top desks. Her sister is very sick. He asked. "She lives with us now. She has since Fritz died. I don't want to say this, but it's possible she won't live out the year. Age is awful, awful, when it gets like that."

"Awful," his mother says. "No matter how good you feel one day; at our age, the next you could snap, go."

Her nephew married and moved to Atlanta and bought a house. He asked. "They want to have children. Buy a house after you have a child, Martin and I told them, but they wanted one first. He's an air controller, went to a special school for it. Six to six for months. We loaned him five thousand dollars of our savings for the house. After all, he's our only nephew and we love him, and his wife is like our only niece. So he's like our only son in many ways. You were like one of my children when I worked here. I can still see you pulling your wagon down the street. Red, do you remember?"

"I do if he doesn't. It said Fire Chief on the sides."

"I don't remember that," Frieda says, "but it probably did, since it was that color red. A very fine wagon—very sturdily made—and with a long metal handle he pulled. You were so small you couldn't even carry it up to the sidewalk."

"It was even almost too heavy for me," his mother says. "We got it from our friends the Kashas. It was their son Carl's."

"They were so old then they must be both dead now."

"He did about fifteen years ago. Bea—Mrs. Kasha—moved to Arizona and I never heard from her again."

"Too bad. Nice people. But I'd do most of the carrying up the steps for his wagon. The neighborhood was very safe then so we'd—your mother and I—let you go by yourself to the stores you could get to without crossing the street. Think of anyone letting their child do that today. He wasn't even four."

"He was so beautiful that today he'd be kidnapped the first time."

"You'd have a note in your hand. It would say this, when he went to Grossinger's, which is where he wanted to go most: 'Three sugar doughnuts, three jelly doughnuts,' and perhaps some Vienna or their special onion rolls and a challah or seeded rye. You had a charge there, didn't you?"

"At all the stores on Columbus. Gristede Brothers. Hazelkorn's kosher butcher. Al and Phil's green grocers. Sam's hardware and so on. But sometimes we gave him money to buy. Shopkeepers were honest to a fault then, and when he did carry money I think the note always said to take the bills out of his pocket and put the change back in."

"It would have had to. So you'd go around the corner with your wagon and park it outside the store. Then you'd go inside and give the note to the saleslady, who was usually Mrs. Grossinger—"

"She passed away I think it was two years ago. She had a bad heart for years but never stopped going in every day."

"Oh, that's too bad; a very nice lady. I hope the store was kept up. There aren't any good home bakeries where we are."

"Her son runs it and even opened a branch store farther up Columbus."

"Good for him. So Mrs. Grossinger or the saleslady would give you whatever was on the note and you'd put the bags in your wagon one by one and start home. But sometimes I got so worried for you, or your mother did where she'd send me after you, that I'd follow you all the way there and back—maybe he was around five when he did this, what do you say?"

"I'd think at least five," his mother says.

"But this was how I was able to see all this. Not worried you'd be kidnapped. Just that you might cross the street. You never did. He was a very obedient boy, Howard. But once I found you sitting on the curb—you must have done this a few times because more than a few times a doughnut or roll was missing from a bag—eating one. Then he'd come home. I used to watch you from the street. You know, sneak up from behind car to car so you wouldn't see me following you. If someone saw me doing this with a boy today they'd think I was trying to kidnap him and I'd be arrested, no questions asked. But everyone around then knew I was your nanny. Then you'd leave your wagon out front and go into the building and apartment—the doors were always unlocked during the day—and ask me or one of your brothers or your mother to help you bring the wagon downstairs."

"What a memory you have."

"I don't remember most of that," he says. "Going into Grossinger's for sugar and jelly doughnuts I do, but no note or wagon. Sitting on the curb eating a roll or doughnut I've no mental picture of, I think, other than for what other people's accounts of it have put into my head."

"Believe me," Frieda says. "If you did it once, shopping with your wagon, you did it a dozen times. And when you got home, first thing you always asked for was one of those doughnuts or rolls or the end slice of the rye bread if it was rye. With no butter on it—no spread. Just the bread plain."

"I remember liking the end slice then. The tiny piece—no bigger than my thumb—but which was usually left in the bakery's bread slicer. In fact, I still have to fight my wife for it. At least for the heel of the bread, since it seems all the bread we get comes unsliced."

"How is Denise?"

"Fine."

"She's wonderful," his mother says. "As dear to me as any of my children, that's the way I look at her, terrible as that might be to say."

"It isn't. I'm sure Howard loves to hear it. And your daughter?" she says to him. "Olivia? You really should have brought her."

"Next time, I swear."

His mother asks Frieda about her trip to Germany this summer, her first time back there is about forty-five years. Then she starts talking about the European trip she took with his father more than twenty years ago and especially the overnight boat ride their tour took down the Rhine. It was in this room. His father walked in from there, he ran up to him from there, arms out. From where he's sitting—different table and chairs but same place, the small kitchen alcove—he sees it happening in front of him as if onstage. Two actors, playing father and son. "Frieda" must still be offstage or never gets on. He's in the first row, looking up at them, but very close. Or sitting level with them, three to four feet away, for it's theater-in-the-round. The two actors come from opposite directions—the father from stage left if that's the direction for Howard's left, the son from stage right. They stop, the father first, about two feet from each other. He points, with his arms still out, to his face. The young actor playing him does. He's asking for help, with his pointing and expression. He wants to be picked up or grabbed. The shit doesn't smell because it's makeup. The young actor gives the impression he just tasted a little of it. But he's not going to throw up. Howard didn't then, far as he can remember, and that's not what the young actor's face says, though he does look as if he'd just gagged. The father bursts our laughing. He's wearing the same clothes his father wore that day. Dark suit, white shirt, tie. Howard doesn't recognize the son's clothes. The father continues to laugh but now seems somewhat repelled by him. Scene goes blank. Curtain comes down. He's left looking at the curtain. Or if it is theater-in-the-round, which it resembles more: blackout, and when the house lights come on thirty seconds later, the actors have left the stage. "Frieda," he says.

"Excuse me," she says to his mother. "Yes?"

"I'm sorry, I didn't mean to break in like that, but there's something I've often wanted to ask you about from the time when I was around five."

"You wanted to ask me it since you were five?"

"No, I mean, what I want to ask you about happened, or I think it did, when I was around five."

"Howard," his mother says, as if saying, since they had talked about it a few times, not to ask it.

"What is it?" Frieda says. To his mother: "What's the big mystery?"

"No mystery," Howard says. "Just that your memory's so good—phenomenal, really—that I wondered if you could remember it for me from that time."

"Why don't we keep it for lunch," his mother says. "I want you to join us. Frieda already told me she wants you to come too. Have anything you want."

"Let me just finish this, Mom. I don't think, if I'm gauging her right, she wants me to ask this, Frieda. Thinks it might offend you. Believe me, that's not my purpose. Whatever happened so long ago is over and past, period. We all—anyway, if it did happen, you were probably doing something—I know you were—that you thought right or necessary. Or just required for what you were hired for, or something. I'm not getting this out right—and I meant by that nothing disparaging about you, Mom—but just know I'm not asking this with any harm in mind whatsoever. None."

"What could it be? The mystery gets bigger and bigger. That I slapped you a few times? I'm sorry for that. I never wanted to. But sometimes, sweet and darling as you were, and beautiful—he was such a beautiful child, everyone thought so—you got out of control, like all children can. Out of my control."

"That's true. They could be something."

"I had three very wild boys to take care of sometimes, so sometimes I had to act like that. Rough. Mean. Slap one or the other. I always tried for the hands or backside first—to get control or they'd run over me. I had a lot of responsibility taking care of you all. Your mother understood that."

"I did. I wouldn't have accepted outright slaughter, but certainly corporal punishment is needed sometimes. You must do it with Olivia from time to time, spank her," she says to him. "Later, against your better judgment, you might even slap her face a couple of times. You'll see. Children can get to you."

"I don't know. If I did, I'd have Denise to deal with."

"She too. Calm as she is, and reasonable, she'd—"

"No, never. Not her, take it from me."

31

"But with Howard," Frieda says, "I just hope you'll have forgiven me by now. But if it had to be done sometimes, it had to be done."

"Of course. I'm not saying. But I was talking of once when you— at least my second-rate memory tells me this—when you pulled my hair and a big chunk came out. Did it? Where I walked around with a big bald spot for about a month?"

"I don't remember that."

"Neither do I," his mother says.

"To be honest, I do remember once putting filth in Alex's face. He was in the bath. He made in it. Number two. I felt I had to teach him somehow not to. I don't like it now. But that was about the worst I ever did, I think. In ways I don't like most of it now, but then I was so much younger, a new foreigner here—well, you know. Also, since your parents didn't object, and I always told them later what I did, I felt I had their approval. Am I wrong, Mrs. T.?"

"You had it. I'm not going to deny it now. Not for putting filth in their faces—this is the first I can remember hearing of that—but as Howard said, it's past, finished. But no matter what happened, all my boys couldn't have turned out better."

"Did anything like that ever happen in my face?" he asks Frieda. "In the bathtub? Anyplace?"

"No, you? You were toilet-trained earlier than the others, so it never got necessary. A year earlier than either of them. By the age of eighteen months, if I'm not wrong. Two years at the most, and that's for both things. You probably had the advantage of seeing them go to the potty on their own, and maybe even scolded or punished for doing it in their pants. So you followed them, did what they did or were supposed to—going to the toilet."

"That's the way it usually is," his mother says.

"He was ahead of the other two in many ways like that. Reading. Writing. Manners at the table. It could be just the reverse with the youngest, but wasn't with him. Dressing himself. Almost everthing. Remember how you let him eat at the adult table, rather than here in the kitchen with me, two years before you let the other two?"

"Maybe because he was the last, and to give you a break from it finally, we let him join our table."

"No, I remember. Because he ate. Because he didn't drop things on the floor or talk loudly and interrupt at the table. He was a dream child. Active and a bit of a rascal at times, yes, but that's not so bad if it's not too often. But sweet, good-natured, helpful most times—a real young gentleman with a much older head than his age. If I had had children, boys or girls, I would have wanted them to be the way you were more than like your brothers. They were good, but you were almost perfect to bring up. You listened and watched. And what I did to Alex in the tub was the only time I think I ever did anything like that. I can't really remember it happening another time, before or after."

"I don't remember being toilet-trained so early. Well, of course I wouldn't, but it's interesting to know."

"He *was* a dream child," his mother says. "You never said it before, but I always knew you had a special place for Howard over the others."

"I did, but not by much, you understand. They were all wonderful. I felt very lucky with the family I ended up in. But maybe Howard was just a little more wonderful. A little." She smiles at him, reaches out to touch his cheek and then kisses it. He hugs her.

On the subway ride home he tries to remember the incident again. First of all, it happened. He knows it did or is almost a hundred percent sure. He runs to his father. First he walks bowlegged to Frieda, points to his crotch. She knows what it is, takes his hand and pulls him into the bathroom. She takes down his pants. His shoes—she takes them off, socks with them. Then she takes off the underpants carefully so the shit stays in them. She says "This will teach you never to do it in your pants again." That's new, but he thinks he just imagined she said it. Her face is angry. It was probably a thick shit, not messy. She puts it into his face. He cries—screams— and she picks him up and holds him in front of the mirror. He sees his face with the shit on most of it. Just then he hears his father.

"Hello, anyone around?" Something like that. He squirms to get down, is let down, runs to him. She says "Go on, show him, and don't forget to tell him what you did." That's also new, but he really seems to remember it. His father's coming into the kitchen from the living room. Is in the kitchen, he is too. His arms are out. His father looks at him and bursts out laughing. He continues to look at him and laugh very hard.

Frog Dances

He's passing a building in his neighborhood, looks into an apartment window on the second floor and sees a man around his age with a baby in his arms moving around the living room as if dancing to very beautiful music—a slow tragic movement from a Mahler symphony, for instance. The man seems so enraptured that Howard walks on, afraid if the man sees him looking at him his mood will be broken. He might feel self-conscious, embarrassed, leave the room or go over to the window with the baby to lower the shade or maybe even to stare back at Howard. Howard knows it can't always be like this between the man and his baby. That at times the man must slap the wall or curse out loud or something because the baby's screaming is keeping him from sleep or some work he has to do or wants to get done—but *still*. The man looked as happy as any man doing anything with anyone or alone. He wants to see it again. He goes back, looks around to see that nobody's watching him, and looks into the window. The man's dancing, eyes closed now, cheeks against the baby's head, arms wrapped around the baby. He kisses the baby's eyes and head as he sort of slides across the room. Howard thinks I must have a child. I've got to get married. At my age—even if I have the baby in a year—some people will still think I'm its grandfather.

But I want to go through what this man's experiencing, dance with my baby like that. Kiss its head, smell its hair and skin—everything. And when the baby's asleep, dance with my wife or just hold her and kiss her something like that too. Someone to get up close to in bed every night for just about the rest of my life and to talk about the baby, and when it and perhaps its brother or sister are older, when they were babies, and every other thing. So: settled. He'll start on it tomorrow or the day after. He looks up at the window. Man's gone. "T'ank you, sir, t'ank you," and walks to the laudromat he was going to, to pick up his dried wash.

Next day he calls the three friends he thinks he can call about this. "Listen, maybe I've made a request something like this before, but this time I not only want to meet a woman and fall in love but I want to get married to her and have a child or two. So, do you know—and if you don't, please keep your ears and eyes open—someone you think very suitable for me and of course me for her too? I mean it. I had an experience last night—seeing a man holding what seemed like a one- to three-month-old baby very close and dancing around with it as if he were in dreamland—and I felt I've been missing out, and in a few years will have completely missed out, on something very important, necessary—you name it—in my life."

A friend calls back a few days later with the name of a woman she knows at work who's also looking to find a mate, fall in love and marry. "She's not about to jump into anything, you know. She's too sensible for that and already did it once with disastrous results, but fortunately no children. Her situation is similar to yours. She's thirty-four and she doesn't want to wait much longer to start a family, which she wants very much. She's extremely bright, attractive, has a good job, makes a lot of money but is willing to give it up or just go freelance for a few years while she has her children. Besides that, she's a wonderful dear person. I think you two can hit it off. I told her about you and she'd like to meet you for coffee. Here's her office and home numbers."

Frog Dances

He calls her and she says "Howard *who?*" "Howard Tetch. Freddy Gunn was supposed to have told you about me." "No, she didn't mention you that I can remember. Wait a second. Are you the fellow who saw a man dancing on the street with his baby and decided that you wanted to be that man?" "I didn't think she'd tell you that part, but yes, I am. It was through an apartment window I saw him. I was just walking. Anyway, I'm not much—I'm sure you're not also—for meeting someone blind like this, but Freddy seemed to think we've a lot in common and could have a good conversation. Would you care to meet for coffee one afternoon or night?" "Let's see, Howard. This week I'm tied up both at work and, in the few available nonwork hours, in my social life. It just happens to be one of those rare weeks—I'm not putting you on. Or putting you off, is more like it. Would you mind calling me again next week—in the middle, let's say?" "No, sure, I'll call."

He calls the next week and she says "Howard Tetch?" "Yes, I called you last week. Freddy Gunn's friend. You said—" "Oh, right, Howard. It's awful of me—please, I apologize. I don't know how I could have forgotten your name a second time. Believe me, it's the work. Sixty hours, seventy. How are you?" "Fine," he says, "and I was wondering if there was some time this week, or even on the weekend, we could—" "I really couldn't this week or the weekend. What I was doing last week extended into this one, and maybe even worse. Not the socializing, but those sixty-seventy-hours-a-week work. I'm not stringing you along, honestly. But I do have this profession that's very demanding sometimes—" "What is it you do?" "Whatever I do—and I wish I had the time to tell you, but I haven't. We'll talk it over when we meet. So you'll call me? I can easily understand why you wouldn't." "No, sure, next week then. I'll call."

He doesn't call back. A week later another friend calls and says he's giving a dinner party Saturday and "two very lovely and intelligent young women, both single, will be coming and I want you to meet them. Who can say? You might get interested in them both. Then you'll have a problem you wish never started by phoning

37

around for possible brides and mothers for your future kids, right?"
"Oh, I don't know," Howard says, "but sounds pretty good so far."

He goes to the party. One of these two women is physically beautiful, all right, but unattractive. Something about the way she's dressed—she's overdressed—and her perfume, makeup, self-important air or something, and she talks too much and too loudly. She also smokes—a lot—and every so often blows smoke on the person she's talking to, and both times she left her extinguished cigarette smoldering. He just knows—so he doesn't even approach her—he could never start seeing or not for too long a woman who smokes so much and so carelessly. The other woman—seems to be her friend—is pretty, has a nice figure, more simply dressed, no makeup or none he can make out, doesn't smoke or isn't smoking here, talks intelligently and has a pleasant voice. He introduces himself, they talk about different things, she tells him she recently got divorced and he says "I'm sorry, that can be very rough." "Just the opposite. We settled it quickly and friendly and since the day I left him I've never felt so free in my life. I love going out, or staying in when I want to, and partying late, meeting lots or people, but being unattached." She has a six-year-old son who lives with his father. "One child, that's all I ever wanted, and now I think even one was too many for me, much as I love him. Since his father wanted to take him, I thought why not? I see him every other weekend, or every weekend if that's what he wants, but he so far hasn't, and get him for a month in the summer. Lots of people disapprove, but they're not me. Many of them are hypocrites, for they're the same ones who feel so strongly that the husband—so why not the ex-husband who's the father of your child?—should take a much larger if not an equal role in the partnership. Well, it's still a partnership where our son's concerned, or at least till he's eighteen or twenty-one, isn't it? Do you disapprove too?" He says "No, if it works for you all and it's what you want and no one's hurt. Sure. Of course, there's got to be some sadness or remorse in a divorce where there's a child involved," and she says "Wrong again, with us. Having two parents was just too confusing for Riner. He thinks it's great having only one at a time to answer to, and another to fall back on just in case."

He takes her phone number, calls, they have dinner, he sees her to her apartment house after, shakes her hand in the lobby and says he'll call again if she doesn't mind, "for it was a nice evening: lively conversation, some laughs, many of them, if fact, and we seem to have several similar interests," and she says "So come on up. Even stay if you want; you don't seem like a masher." They go to bed and in the morning over coffee she says "I want to tell you something. I like you but don't want you getting any ideas about my being your one-and-only from now on. You should know from the start that I'm seeing several men, sleeping with three of them—they're all clean and straight, so don't worry. And you can be number four if you want, but I'm not for a long time getting seriously connected to anyone. You don't like the arrangement—no problem: here's my cheek to kiss and there's the door." He says he doesn't mind the arrangement for now, kisses her lips just before he leaves, but doesn't call again.

He sees a woman on a movie line waiting to go in. He's alone and she seems to be too. She's reading quite quickly a novel he liked a lot and never looks up from it at the people in front and behind her, at least while he's looking at her. Attractive, intelligent looking, he likes the casual way she's dressed, way her hair is, everything. He intentionally finds a seat two rows behind hers, watches her a lot and she never speaks to the person on either side of her. On the way out he does something he hasn't done in about twenty years. He gets alongside her and says "Pardon me, Miss, but did you like the movie?" She smiles and says "It was a big disappointment, and you?" "Didn't care for it much either. Listen, this is difficult to do—introducing myself to a woman I've never met—like this, I mean, and something I haven't done in God knows how many years. But would you—my name is Howard Tetch—like to have a cup of coffee someplace or a beer and talk about the movie? That book too—I read it and saw you reading. If you don't, then please, I'm sorry for stopping you—I already think you're going to say no, and why shouldn't you?" "No, let's have coffee, but for me, tea." "Tea, yes, much healthier for you—that's what I'll have too."

They have tea, talk—the book, movie, difficulties of introducing yourself to strangers you want to meet, something she's wanted to do with a number of men—"I can admit it,"—but never had the courage for it. He sees her to a taxi, next day calls her at work, they meet for tea, meet again for lunch, another time for a movie, go to bed, soon he's at her place more than his own. She's thirty-three and also wants to get married and have a child, probably two. "With the right person, of course. That'll take, once I meet him, about six months to find out. Then once it's decided, I'd like to get married no more than a month after that, or at least begin trying to conceive." The more time he spends at her place, the bossier and pettier she gets with him. She doesn't like him hanging the underpants he washes on the shower curtain rod. He says "What about if I hang them on a hanger over the tub?" but she doesn't like that either. "It looks shabby, like something in a squalid boardinghouse. Put them in the dryer with the rest of our clothes." "The elastic waistband stretches. So does the crotch part to where after a few dryer dryings you can see my balls. That's why I hand-wash them and hang them up like that." Problem's never resolved. He wrings his underpants out and hangs them on a hanger, with a few newspaper sheets underneath, in the foot of closet space she's set aside for her clothes. A couple of times when he does this she says the drops from the hanging underpants might go through the paper and ruin the closet floor. He puts more newspapers down and that seems to assuage her. She thinks he should shave before he gets into bed, not when he rises. He says "But I've always shaved, maybe since I started shaving my entire face, in the morning. That's what I do." "Well try changing your habits a little. You're scratchy. It hurts our lovemaking. My skin's fair, much smoother than yours, and your face against it at night is an irritant." "An irritant?" "It irritates my face, all right?"

"Then we'll make love in the morning after I shave." "We can do that too," she says, "but like most couples, most of our lovemaking is at night. Also, while I'm on the subject, I wish you wouldn't get back into bed after you exercise in the morning. Your armpits smell. You sweat up the bed. If you don't want to shower after, wash your arms down with a wet washrag. Your back and chest too." "I only exercise those early times in the morning when I can't sleep anymore, or am having trouble sleeping. So I feel, long as I'm up, I should either read or do something I'm going to do later in the day anyway, like exercising. But from now on I'll do as you say with the washrag whenever I do exercise very early and then, maybe because the exercising's relaxed or tired me, get back into bed." She also thinks he hogs too much of the covers; he should try keeping his legs straight in front of him in bed rather than lying them diagonally cross her side; he could perhaps shampoo more often—"Your hair gets to the sticky level sometimes." And is that old thin belt really right for when he dresses up? "If anything, maybe you can redye it." And does he have to wear jeans with a hole in the knee, even if it is only to go to the corner store? "What about you?" he finally says. "You read the *Times* in bed before we make love at night or just go to sleep, and then don't wash the newsprint off your hands. That gets on me. Probably also gets on the sheets and pillowcases, but of course only on your side of the bed, and your sheets and pillowcases, so why should I be griping, right? And your blouses. I'm not the only one who sweats. And after you have into one of yours—OK, you had a tough day at work and probably on the crowded subway to and from work and your body's reacted to it—that's natural. But you hang these blouses back up in the closet. On your side, that's fine with me, and I'm not saying the smell gets on my clothes. But it isn't exactly a great experience to get hit with it when I go into the closet for something. Anyway, I'm just saying." They complain like this some more, begin to quarrel, have a couple of fights where they don't speak to each other for an hour, a day, and soon agree they're not right for each other anymore and should break up. When he's packing his things to take back to his apartment, she says "I'm obviously not ready to be with only one man as much as I thought. I'm certainly not ready for marriage yet. As to having a child—to perhaps have *two*? I should really get my head looked over to have thought of that." "Well, I'm still ready," he says, "though maybe all this time I've been mistaken there too."

He meets a woman at an opening at an art gallery. They both were invited by the artist. She says she's heard about him from the artist. "Nothing much. Just that you're not a madman, drunk, drug addict or letch like most of the men he knows." He says "Gary, for some odd reason I don't know why, never mentioned you. Maybe because he's seeing you. Is he?" "What are you talking about? He's gay." "Oh. He's only my colleague at school, so I don't know him that well. I know he's divorced and has three kids, but that's about it. May I be stupidly frank or just stupid and say I hope you're not that way too? Wouldn't mean I'd want to stop talking to you." "I can appreciate why you're asking that now. No, as mates, men are what I like exclusively. I didn't come here to meet one, but I've been in a receptive frame of mind for the last few months if something happens along." They separate at the drink table, eye each other a lot the next fifteen minutes, she waves for him to come over. "I have to go," she says. "The friend I came with has had her fill of this, and she's staying with me tonight. If you want to talk some more, I can call you tomorrow. You in the book?" "Hell, here's my number and best times to reach me," and he writes all this out and gives it to her.

She calls, they meet for a walk, have dinner the next night, she takes his hand as they leave the restaurant, kisses him outside, initiates a much deeper kiss along the street, he says "Look-it, why don't we go to my apartment—it's only a few blocks from here?" She says "Let's give it more time. I've had a lot of rushing from men lately. I'm not boasting, and I started some of it myself. It's simply that I know going too fast, from either of us, is no good, so what do you say?" They see each other about three times a week for two weeks. At the end of that time he says he wants to stay at her place that night or have her to his, "but you know, for bed." She says "I still think it'd be rushing. Let's give the main number some more time?" Two weeks later he says "Listen, I've got to sleep with you. All this heavy petting is killing me. I've got to see you completely naked, be inside you—the works. We've given it plenty of time. We like each other very much. But I need to sleep with you to really be in love with you. That's how I am." She says "I don't know what's wrong. I like you in every way. I'm almost as frustrated as you are over it. But something in me says that having sex with you now still wouldn't be sensible. That we're not ready for it yet. That what we have, in the long run, would be much better—could even end up in whatever we want from it. Living together. More, if that's what we ultimately want—if we hold out on this a while longer. It's partly an experiment on my part, coming after all my past involvement failures, but also partly what I most deeply feel will work, and so feel you have to respect that. So let's give it a little more time then, please?" He says "No. Call me if you not only want to see me again but want us to have sex together. From now on it has to be both. Not all the time, of course. But at least the next time if there's nothing—you know— physically, like a bad cold, wrong with one of us. I hate making conditions—it can't help the relationship—but feel I have to. If I saw you in one of our apartments alone again I think I'd tear your clothes off and jump on you no matter how hard and convincingly you said no. It's awful, but there it is." She says "Let me think about it. Either way, I'll call."

She calls the next week and says "I think we better stop seeing each other. Even if I don't believe you would, what you said about tearing off my clothes scared me." "That's not it," he says. "I don't know what it is, but that's not it. OK. Goodbye."

He misses her, wants to call her, resume things on her terms, dials her number two nights in a row but both times hangs up after the first ring.

He's invited to give a lecture at a university out of town. His other duty that day is to read the manuscripts of ten students and see them

43

in an office for fifteen minutes each to discuss their work. The man who invited him is a friend from years ago. He says "What'd you think of the papers I sent you? All pretty good, but one exceptional. Flora's, right? She thinks and writes like someone who picked up a couple of postdoctorates in three years and then went on to five years of serious jounalism. Easy style, terrific insights, nothing left unturned, everything right and tight, sees things her teachers don't and registers these ideas better than most of them. She intimidates half the department, I'm telling you. They'd rather not have her in their classes, except to look at her. That's because she's brilliant. I can actually say that about two of my students in fourteen years and the other's now dean of a classy law school. But hear me, Howard. Keep your mitts off her. That doesn't mean mine are on her or want to be. Oh, she's a honey, all right, and I've fantasized about her for sure. But I don't want anyone I'm inviting for good money messing with her and possibly messing up her head and the teaching career I've planned for her. Let some pimpleface do the messing; she'll get over it sooner. I want her to get out of here with top grades and great GREs and without being screwed over and made crestfallen for the rest of the semester by some visiting horn. Any of the other girls you'll be conferencing you can have and all at once if they so desire." "Listen, they all have to be way too young for me and aren't what I've been interested in for a long time, so stop fretting."

He sees two students. Flora's next on the list. He opens the office door and says to some students sitting on the floor against the corridor wall "One of you Ms. Selenika?" She raises her hand, stands, was writing in a pad furiously, has glasses, gold ear studs, medium-length blond hair, quite frizzy, little backpack, clear frames, tall, rustically dressed, pens in both breast pockets, what seem like dancer's legs, posture, neck. "Come in." They shake hands, sit, he says "I guess we should get right to your paper. Of course, what else is there? I mean, I'm always interested in where students come from. Their native areas, countries, previous education, what they plan to do after graduation. You know, backgrounds and stuff; even what their parents do. That can be very interesting. One student's father was police commissioner of New York. Probably the best one we had there in years. Another's mother was Mildred Kraigman. A comedian, now she's a character actress. Won an Academy Award? Well, she was once well known and you still see her name around, often for good causes. But those are my students where I teach. When I've time to digress, which I haven't with every student here. You all probably don't mind the fifteen minutes with me, but that's all we've got. So, your paper. I don't know why I went into all of that, do you?" She shakes her head, holds back a giggle. "Funny, right? But you can see how it's possible for me to run on with my students. As for your paper, I've nothing but admiration for it. I'm not usually that reserved or so totally complimentary, but here, well—no corrections. Not even grammatical or punctuational ones. Even the dashes are typed right and everything's before or after the quote marks where it belongs. Honestly, nothing to nitpick, even. I just wish I had had your astuteness—facility—you know, to create such clear succinct premises and then to get right into it and with such writing and literary know-how and ease; had had your skills, intelligence and instincts when I was your age, I mean. Would have saved a lot of catching up later on. Sure, we could go on for an hour about what you proposed in this and how you supported what you claimed, and so on. Let me just say that when I come across a student like you I just say 'Hands off; you're doing great without me so continue doing what you are on your own. If I see mistakes or anything I can add or direct you to, to possibly improve your work, I'll let you know.' And with someone like you I also say, which isn't so typical for me, 'If you see something you want to suggest about my work, or correct: be my guest.' In other words, I can only give you encouragement and treat you as my thinking equal and say 'More, more.' But your paper's perfect for what it is, which is a lot, and enlightened me on the subject enormously. But a subject which, if I didn't know anything about it before, I'd be very grateful to you after I read it for opening me up to it. You made it interesting and intriguing. What better way, right? Enough, I've said too much, not that I think compliments would turn you."

He looks away. She says something but he doesn't catch it. Something like "I'm no different than anyone else." He actually feels his heart pounding, mouth's parched, fingers feel funny. Looks at her. She's looking at him so seriously, fist holding up her chin, trying to make him out? Thinks he's being too obvious? "I'm sorry, you said something just now?" he says. "Oh nothing. Silly. Commonplace. I also tend to mumble." "But what?" "That I can be turned too, that's all." Smiles, big beautiful bright teeth, cute nose. Button pinned to her jacket, children in flames, caption in Chinese or Japanese. Or Korean or Vietnamese. What does he know? And turned how? That an oblique invitation? He once read a novel where the literature teacher took his student on the office floor. She willingly participated. In fact, she might have come to his office to make love. It was their first time. The teacher was married. He always thought that scene exaggerated—the author usually exaggerated or got sloppy when he wrote about sex—but the feeling the narrator had is the same he has now. Her brains, looks, body, little knapsack. He'd love right now to hold her, kiss her, undress her right here—hell with his friend. Hell with the rest of the students. They'd do it quickly. She'd understand. Even if it was their first time. He doubts it'd take him two minutes. Another minute for them both to undress. He bets she likes that kind of spontaneity. "I have got to make love to you," he could whisper. "Let's do it right now." He'd lock the door if it has a lock from the inside—he looks. Hasn't and he doesn't have the key. Now this would be something: opening the door to push the lock-button with all those students in the hall waiting for him. Instead he could put a chair up against the doorknob. They'd be quiet; to save time, just take their pants and shoes off and make love on the floor. Carpet seems clean. He could put his coat down. He wonders what such a young strong body like that looks and feels like. He looks at her, tries to imagine her naked. She says "Thanks for reading my paper and everything, but now I must be wasting your time. It's a rigorous day for you: all those conferences and papers to read and your lecture later on." "You're not wasting it." She opens the door. "Oh, maybe you won't go for this, but another student and I—my housemate—would like to invite you to a student reading after dinner." "Listen, maybe I can even take you both to dinner before the reading." "You're eating at the club with Dr. Wiggens, aren't you?" "Right; that's a must. Sure, tell me where to be and when. I haven't been to a good student reading in years." "This might not be good." "Even more fun. I like to see what goes on at different campuses. And after if, you'll be my guests for food and beer." "If he wants to and we're up to it, fine."

She sits at the back of his room during the lecture, laughs at all the right lines, claps hard but doesn't come up after.

"So how'd everything go today?" Wiggens asks at dinner. "Great bunch of kids," Howard says. "Incredibly keen and bright. Wish I had some like them in my own classes." "None of the girls made a pass at you?" his wife says. "Nah, I let them know I don't come easy." Wiggens says "That's the best approach. Why get all messy in a day and possibly go home a father-to-be with a social disease?" "What nonsense," she says. "One-night stands with students is the safest sport in town." They drop him off at his hotel, he goes inside the lobby, waits till their car leaves the driveway and runs to the building of the reading. He's already pretty tight. He sleeps through most of the stories and poems and the three of them go to a pizza place later. The housemate downs a beer, puts on his coat and says to Flora "Maybe I'll see you home." "Why'd he think you might not be home?" Howard says. "He meant for himself. He has a lover who occassionally kicks him out before midnight." They finish off the pitcher, have two brandies each, he says "This is not what I'm supposed to be doing here according to Wiggens, so don't let on to him, but may I invite you back to my room?" She says "I'm really too high to drive myself home and you're too high to drive me, so I guess I'll stay the night if you don't mind. You have twin beds?" "Sure, for twins. —No, OK," when she shakes her head that his humor's bad, "anything you want." When she takes off her clothes in his room he says "My goodness, your breasts. I had no idea they were so large. Why'd I think that?" "It's the way I dress. I'm extremely self-conscious about them. They've been a nuisance in every possible way." "I love large breasts." "Please, no more about them or I'm going to bed in my clothes." They shut off the lights. He's almost too drunk to do anything. In the morning he doesn't know if they even did anything. He says he wants to stay another night. "At my expense, in this same or a different hotel if you can't or don't want to put me up in your house. Take you to lunch and dinner and even a movie and where we'll start all over and do the whole thing right. The heck with Wiggens and his proscriptions." She says "My vagina hurts from last night. You were too rough. I couldn't do it again for a day." "So we did something? I was afraid I just passed out." "To be honest," she says, "it was horrendous. Never again when I and the guy I'm with are that stoned." "It'll be better. I can actually stay for two more nights, get some work done in your school library simply to keep busy and out of your hair all day, and we'll both stay relatively sober throughout." "No, it isn't a good idea. Where's it going to land us?" "Why, that you're way out here and I'm in New York? I'll fly out once a month for a few days." "Once a month." "Twice a month then. Every other week. And the entire spring break. Or you can fly to New York. I'll pay your fare each time. And in the summer, a long vacation together. Rent a house on some coast. A trip to Europe if that's what you want. I don't make that much, but I can come up with it." "Let's talk about it again after you get to New York, but you go this afternoon as scheduled."

He calls from New York and she says "No, everything's too split apart. Not only where we live but the age and cultural differences. You're as nice as they come—sweet, smart and silly—but what you want for us is unattainable." "Think about it some more." He calls again and she says he got her at a bad moment. He writes twice and she doesn't answer. He calls again and her housemate, after checking with her, says she doesn't want to come to the phone. Howard says "So that's it then. Tell her."

Frog Dances

He's invited to a picnic in Riverside Park for about twelve people. He doesn't want to go but the friend who's arranged it says "Come on, get out of the house already, you're becoming a hopeless old recluse." He meets a woman at the picnic. They both brought potato salad. "It wasn't supposed to happen like this," he says. "I was told to bring the cole slaw. But I didn't want to make the trip to the store just to buy cabbage, had a whole bag of potatoes around, so I made this salad. Anyway, yours is much better. You can see by what people have done to our respective bowls." "They're virtually identical," Denise says. "Eggs, celery, sweet pickles, fresh dill, store-bought mayonnaise, maybe mustard in both of them, and our potatoes cooked to the same softness, but I used salt." She gives him her phone number and says she hopes he'll call. He says "I wouldn't have asked for it if I didn't intend to. Truly."

He was attracted to her at the picnic but after it he thinks she was too eager for him to call. Well, that could be good—that she wants him to call, is available—but there were some things about her looks he didn't especially like. More he thinks of them, less he likes them. Nice face, wasn't that. But she seemed wider in the hips, larger in the nose, than he likes. Were her teeth good? Something, but nothing he can remember seeing, tells him they weren't. She was friendly, intelligent, no airs, good sense of humor. But if she's wide in the hips now, she's going to get wider older she gets. And noses, he's heard, and can tell from his own, grow longer with age. Everything else though...

He doesn't call her that week. On the weekend he bumps into a friend on the street who's walking with a very pretty woman. She can't be his girlfriend. The friend's married, much in love with his wife. And he has two young sons he dotes on and he'd never do anything that could lead to his being separated from them, but then you never know. Howard and the woman are introduced, she has a nice voice, unusually beautiful skin, and the three of them talk for a while. Her smile to him when they shake hands goodbye seems to suggest she wouldn't mind him contacting her. He calls his friend the next day and says "This woman you were with—Francine. If she's not married or anything like that, what do you think of my calling her?" "Fine, if you like. She's a great person, stunning looking as you saw, cultured, unattached—what else? One hell of a capable lawyer." "Why didn't you tell me about her before?" "You mean you're still searching for that ideal lifemate? I thought you gave that up." "No, I'm still looking, though maybe not as hard as I did. Went out with several women—a couple you even met. Nearly moved in with one, but nothing materialized beyond that with any of them, which has sort of discouraged me a little. But if I haven't found someone marriageable after a year, that's OK too, right? I've still plenty of time." "Then call Francine. She's been divorced for two years, no children, and from what she's let on in certain unguarded moments, I think she's seriously shopping around for a new lifemate herself." "What do you mean 'unguarded'? Is she very secretive, uncommunicative, cool or distant—like that?" "Hardly. Just that some things about herself she keeps inside."

Howard calls her. They make a date to go out for beers. He feels she's not right for him the moment she opens her apartment door. Something overdone in the way she's dressed for just beers at a local place. Also her apartment, which is practically garish. The books on the shelves say she isn't much of a serious reader, and same with the music on the radio, records on the shelf, prints on the walls. During their walk to the bar and then in the bar he finds she's interested in a lot of things he isn't: money matters, big-time professional advancement, exercise classes, gossip about famous people, the trendy new restaurants, art exhibitions, movies, shows. They walk back to her building. She asks if he'd like to come up for a drink or tea. "No thanks, I've still plenty of work to do for tomorrow, but thank you." "If you'd like to phone me again, please do." "No, really, I don't think it would work out, but thanks for suggesting it. It's been a nice evening." "Actually, I doubt it has been for you, nor in many ways for me either. We're a bit different, that's easy to see, but I thought after a few times together we'd find much in common.

Something told me that. What do you think?" "I don't think so, honestly. It's all right to say that, isn't it?" "I suppose, but it's probably not something we should go too deeply into," and she goes inside. He's walking uptown to his apartment when he sees a pay phone. Call Denise, he thinks. It's been two weeks since he said he would. He'll give a good excuse if he feels from what she says that he ought to. That he's been so steeped in his work that he didn't want to call till now just to say he'd be calling again to go out with her once he's done with this work. Or that he simply lost track of time with all the work he's been doing and also some personal things that are now over. He puts the coin in, thinks no, don't start anything, she isn't right for him. Her looks. The teeth. Something. Plump. Not plump but wider in the hips and he thinks heavier in the thighs than he likes, and her nose. And so sweet. Almost too damn too—even meek. He doesn't like meek and overly sweet women either who let the man do most of the speaking and decision making and so on. That's not what he wants. He wants something else. So he won't call her. He continues walking, passes another pay phone. Why not call her? Because he's a little afraid to. Already his stomach's getting butterflies. What would he say? Well, he'd say "Hello, it's Howard Tetch, and I know it's a bit presumptuous thinking you'd agree to this at the spur of something or another, but. . ." "But" what? Have a drink first. He goes into a bar, has a martini. After he drinks it he feels relaxed. One more. Then he should go home and, if he still wants to, call her tomorrow. He has another. Two, he tells himself, is his limit. Three and he's had it, not good for anything but sleep. But he doesn't want to be on the street with three. When he gets off the stool he feels high. He feels sexy when he gets to the street. He wants to have sex with someone tonight. He hasn't had sex with anyone since Flora and that was around three months ago and what does he remember of it? Her large breasts, that's all, which was before they had sex. He thinks of the man in the window holding the baby. The baby must be a month or two past a year old. It was April, right after his mother's birthday, so it was almost twelve months ago. Today or some

51

day this or last week might be the baby's first birthday. The man might still be dancing with it at night, but by now the baby's probably saying words. "Hi. 'Bye." The man might have slept with his wife 350 times since that night, made love with her about 150 times. That would be about the number of times Howard thinks he'd make love to his wife in that time. But there is that period, maybe a month or two after the birth, maybe longer for some women if it was a particularly difficult delivery—a Cesarean, for instance—when you don't have sex, or not where the man penetrates her. So, 100, 125. The woman he ends up with will have to be receptive to sex. As much as he, in her own way, or almost. If more so, fine. And sometimes do it when he wants to and she doesn't especially. That isn't so bad. It isn't that difficult for a woman to sort of loan her body like that, turn over on her side with her back to him and let him do it without even any movement on her part, and he'll do as much for her if it comes to it. And if the baby was a month or two old when he saw it in the window, then the man and his wife might have just around that time started to make love again, and even, for the first time in months, that night. For all he knows, that might account for the loving way the man danced with his child. No. But call her. He goes through his wallet, thought the slip with her number on it was inside, can't find it, dials Information, dials the number he gets and she says hello. "Hello, it's Howard Tetch, from that picnic in the park, how are you?" and she says "I'm all right, and you?" "Fine, just fine. Thank you. Listen, I called—well, I wanted to long before this but something always came up—to suggest we get together tonight. But I now realize it's much too late to. I'm sorry. This is an awful way to call after two weeks, but tomorrow?" "Tomorrow?" "Yes, would it be possible for us to meet sometime tomorrow or any day soon as we can? Evening? Late afternoon for a cup of something?" "Excuse me, Howard. This certainly isn't what I wanted to speak about first thing after enjoying your company at the picnic, but am I wrong in assuming you've had a bit to drink tonight which is influencing your speech and perhaps what you have to say?" "No, you're right, I have, and right in saying it to me. I shouldn't have called like this. But I was somewhat anxious about calling you, and just in calling any woman for the first time I'm not that . . . I get nervous, that's all. It's always awkward for me, no matter how anxious I was in wanting to call you. So I thought I needed a drink to brace me, you can say, and had two, at a bar just now, but martinis. I'm calling from the street, by the way." "I can hear." "What I meant by that is I have a home phone but was on the street, saw a phone, wanted to call, so called. Anyway, two martinis never hit me like this before. Never drink three martinis and think you'll have your head also, I always say. What am I saying I always say it? I'm saying it now, but probably have thought of it before. But I also had a drink at my apartment before I went out, so it was accumulative. Wine, gin. I'm not a problem drinker though." "I didn't say or think you were." "Little here, there, but only rarely in intoxicating quantities. Just that I didn't want that to be the reason you might not want us to meet." "All right. Call tomorrow if you still want to. Around six. We'll take it from there, OK?" "Yes." "Good. Goodnight."

He calls, they meet, have coffee, take a long walk after, the conversation never lulls, lots of things in common, no forced talk, good give and take, mutual interests, laughs, they touch upon serious subjects. Her teeth are fine. Her whole body. Everything's fine. Profile, full face. Some bumps, bulges, but what was he going on so about her hips and nose and so on? Scaring himself away maybe. They're right, all part of her, fit in just fine. She's also very intelligent, not meek, weak, just very peaceful, thoughtful, subdued, seemingly content with her life for the most part. They take the same bus home, he gets off first and says he'll call her soon, she says "That'll be nice," waves to him from the bus as it passes. He doesn't call her the next week. First he thinks give it a day or two before you call; see what you think. Then: this could get serious and something tells him she's still not exactly right for him. She's a serious person and would never have anything to do with him in any other way and maybe playing around is what he really wants right now. She may even be too intelligent for him, needing someone with larger ideas, deeper thoughts, better or differently read, a cleverer quicker way about him, smooth-spoken; she'd tire of him quickly.

He calls a woman he used to go out with but was never serious about more than a year ago and she says "Hello, Howard, what is it?" "Oops, doesn't sound good. Maybe I called at a wrong time." "Simply that you called is a surprise. How is everything?" "Thank you. Everything's fine. I thought you might want to get together. Been a while. What are you doing now, for instance?" "You're horny." "No I'm not." "You only used to call when you were horny. Call me when you're feeling like a normal human being. When you want to have dinner out, talk over whatever there's to talk over, but not to go to bed. I'm seeing someone. Even if I weren't. I could never again be around for you only when you have your hot pants on." "Of course. I didn't know you thought I was doing that. But I understand, will do as you say." The phone talk makes him horny. He goes out to buy a magazine with photos of nude women in it. He buys the raunchiest magazine he can find just from the cover photo and what the cover says is inside, sticks it under his arm inside his jacket, dumps it in a trash can a block away. He really doesn't like those magazines. Also something about having them in his apartment, and why not do something different with the rutty feeling he's got. A whorehouse. He buys a weekly at another newsstand that has articles on sex, graphic photos of couples, and in the back a couple of pages where they rate whorehouses, single bars, porno flicks, peep shows and sex shops in the city. He goes home to read it. There's one on East Fifty-fourth that sounds all right. "Knockout gals, free drink, private showers, classy & tip-top." He goes outside and waits at a bus stop for a bus to take him to West Fifty-seventh, where he'll catch the crosstown. He has enough cash on him even if they charge a little more than the fifty dollars the weekly said they did, plus another ten for a tip. He wants to do it that much. He gets off at Sixty-fifth—butterflies again—will walk the rest of the way while he thinks if what he's doing is so smart. The woman could have a disease. One can always get rid of it with drugs. But some last longer than that. You have to experiment with several drugs before one works. And suppose there's one that can't be cured with drugs or not for years? No, those places—the expensive ones—are clean. They have to be or they'd lose their clients. He keeps walking to the house. Stops at a bar for a martini just to get back the sex feeling he had, has two, heads for the house again feeling good. No, this is ridiculous. His whoring days are over. They have been for about ten years. He'd feel embarrassed walking in and out of one; just saying what he's there for to the person at the front desk, if that's what they have, and then making small talk or not talk with the women inside, if they just sit around waiting for the men to choose them—even looking at the other men in the room would be embarrassing—and then with the woman he chooses. "What do you like, Howard?" or whatever name he gives. Howard. Why not? No last one. "You want me to do this or that or both or maybe you want to try something different?" It just isn't right besides. He still wants very much to have sex tonight—with a stranger, even—but not to pay for it. A singles bar? What are the chances? For him, nil, or near to it. He doesn't feel he has it in him anymore to approach women there or really anywhere. To even walk into one and find a free place at the bar would be difficult for him. Maybe Denise would see him this late. Try. If she doesn't want him up, she'll say so quickly enough. Or just say to her "You think it's too late to meet for a beer?" If she says something like "It's too late for me to go outside, why don't you come here," then he'll know she wants to have sex with him. She wouldn't have him up this late for any other reason. And if he comes up at this hour, she'll know what he's coming up for. If she can meet at a bar, then fine, he'll start his approach from there. Suppose she gets angry at him for calling so late and being so obvious in what he wants of her, expecially after he said a week ago he'd call her soon? Then that's it with her then, since he doesn't feel there'll be anything very deep between them, so what he's really after is just sex. But don't call from pay phone on the street. She may think he always walks the streets at night and get turned off by that.

He goes into a bar, buys a beer, tells himself to speak slowly and conscientiously and watch out for slurs and repeats, dials her number from a pay phone there. She says "Hello," doesn't seem tired, he says "It's Howard, how are you, I hope I'm not calling too late." "It's not that it's too late for me to receive a call, Howard, just that of the three to four calls from you so far, most have come this late. Makes me think...what? That your calls are mostly last-minute thoughts, emanating from some form of desperation perhaps. It doesn't make me feel good." "But they're not. And I'm sorry. I get impulsive sometimes. Not this time. You were on my mind—have been for days—and I thought about calling you tonight, then thought if it was getting too late to call you, but probably thought about it too long. Then, a little while before, thought 'Hell, call her, and I'll explain.' So some impulsiveness there after all." "All right. We have that down. So?" "So?" "So, you know, what is the reason you called?" "I wanted to know if you might like to meet at the Breakers for a drink, or maybe it's too late tonight for that too." "It probably is. Let me check the time. I don't have to. I know already. Way too late. If you want, why not come here." "That's what I'd like much better, really. You mean now, don't you?" "Not two hours from now, if you can help it." "Right. Is there anything I can pick up for you before I get there?" "Like what?" "Wine, beer? Anything you need? Milk?" "Just come, but without stopping for a drink along the way." "I already have. But so you won't get the wrong idea, it was because my phone wasn't working at home. Just tonight, which was a big surprise when I finally picked up the receiver to call you. So I went out to call from a public phone. But I didn't want to call from the street. Too noisy, and I also didn't want to give you the wrong idea that I'm always calling from the street. So I went into this bar I'm in to call but felt I should buy a beer from them first, even if I didn't drink it—though I did—part of it—rather than coming in only to use their phone. That's the way I am. I put all kinds of things in front of me." "Does seem so. Anyway, here's my address," and gives it and what street to get off if he takes the bus. "If you take the Broadway subway, get off at a Hundred-sixteenth and ride the front of the train, but not the first car, so you'll be right by the stairs. The subways, or at least that station at this hour, can be dangerous, so maybe to be safer you should take the bus or a cab." "A cab. That's what I'll do." "Good. See you."

He subways to her station, runs to her building. If she asks, he'll say he took a cab. They say hello, he takes off his jacket, she holds out her hand for it, probably to put it in what must be the coat closet right there. He hands it to her and says "I took the subway, by the way. Should have taken a cab, but I guess I'm still a little tight with money. I'm saying, from when I wasn't making much for years. I don't know why I mentioned that. It was a fast ride though—good connections—and I'm still panting somewhat from running down the hill to your building," has moved closer to her, she says "I didn't notice—you ran down the hill here?" he bends his head down, she raises hers and they kiss. They kiss again and when they separate she says "Your jacket—excuse me. It's on the floor." "Don't bother with it." "Don't be silly—it's a jacket," and picks it up, brushes it off and hangs it in the closet. He comes behind her while she's separating some of the coats, jackets and garment bags hanging in the closet, turns her around by her shoulders and they kiss. She says "Like a nightcap of some sort—seltzer?" "Really, nothing, thank you." "Then I don't know, I'm enjoying this but we should at least get out of this cramped utilitarian area. The next room. Or maybe, if we want, we should just go to bed." "Sure, if it's all right with you." "I'll have to wash up first." "Same here." "And I wouldn't mind, so long as you'd come with me, walking my dog." "You've a dog?" "It'll be quick, and I won't have to do it early in the morning."

They walk the dog, make love. They see each other almost every day for the next few weeks. Museums, movies, an opera, eat out or she cooks for them in her apartment or he cooks for them in his, a party given by friends of hers. They're walking around the food table there putting food on their plates when he says "I love you, you know that, right?" and she says "Me too, to you." "You do? Great." That night he dreams he's being carried high up in the sky by several party balloons, says "Good Christ, before this was fun, but now they better hold," wakes up, feels for her, holds her thigh and says to himself "This is it, I don't want to lose her, she's the best yet, or ever. Incredible that it really happened. Well, it could still go bust." He takes her to meet his mother, has dinner at her parents' apartment. He sublets his apartment, moves in with her. He can't get used to the dog. Walking it, cleaning up after it, its smells, hair on the couch and his clothes, the sudden loud barks which startle him, the dog licking his own erection, and tells her that as much as he knows she loves the dog, the city's really no place for it. She says "Bobby came with me and with me he stays. Sweetheart, think of it as a package deal and that Bobby's already pretty old." When his lease expires he gives up his apartment to the couple he sublet it to. He begins insisting to Denise that Bobby's long hair makes him sneeze and gives him shortness of beath, which is keeping him up lots of nights, and that the apartment's much too crowded with him. "If we ever have the baby we've talked about maybe having, it would mean getting an apartment with another bedroom at twice the rent we pay now, which we couldn't afford, or disposing of the dog somehow and staying with the baby here." She gives Bobby to a friend in the country. "If one day we do get a larger apartment," she says, "and Bobby's still alive, then I don't care how sick and feeble he might be then, he returns. Agreed?" "Agreed."

They marry a few months after that and a few months later she's pregnant. They planned it that way and it worked. They wanted to conceive the baby in February so they could spend most of the summer in Maine and have the baby in October, a mild month and where he'd be settled into the fall semester. He goes into the delivery room with her, does a lot of things he learned in the birth classes they took over the summer, to help her get through the more painful labor contractions. When their daughter's about a month old he starts dancing with her at night just as that man did three years ago. He has two Mahler symphonies on record, buys three more and dances to the slow movements and to the last half of the second side of a recording of Sibelius's Fifth Symphony. Denise loves to see him dancing like this. Twice she's said "May I cut in?" and they held the baby and each other and danced around the living room. Dancing with the baby against his chest, he soon found out, also helps get rid of her gas and puts her to sleep. He usually keeps a light on while he dances so he won't bump into things and possibly trip. Sometimes he closes his eyes—in the middle of the room—and dances almost in place while he kisses the baby's neck, hair, even where there's cradle cap, back, ears, face. Their apartment's on the third floor and looks out on other apartments in a building across the backyard. He doesn't think it would stop him dancing if he saw someone looking at him through one of those windows. He doesn't even think he'd lower the blinds. Those apartments are too far away—a hundred feet or more—to make him self-conscious about his dancing. If his apartment were on the first or second floor and fronted on the sidewalk, he'd lower the living room blinds at night. He'd do it even if he didn't have a baby or wasn't dancing with it. He just doesn't like people looking in at night from the street.

Frog Fears

His daughter's asleep upstairs, his wife's out. After his wife left he got his daughter to sleep by giving her a bath (very brief; small portable plastic tub in the kitchen into which he poured three parts hot water to two parts cold), reading to her for about fifteen minutes, then in the dark telling her another part of the "Mickey and Donald Go Fishing" story he's been making up for her just about every other night for the past year, and finally singing a few nursery rhymes in a low voice to his own impromptu tunes. His wife went to a movie in the nearest big town from here. Seventeen miles along mostly curvy country roads. She wanted him to go with her, he would have but not enthusiastically (doesn't especially like movies, and especially in theaters and in the evening when he has to drive a good ways to one), but they couldn't get a babysitter. "You go," she said. "No, you go, since you're really the one who wants to." A new Russian movie she's been eager to see since they saw the trailer of it in a Manhattan theater last year and she read a couple of reviews. Being shown in the town hall meeting room, on hard fold-up chairs, so not the most comfortable place to see a relatively long and, from what the trailer suggested and she told him the reviews said, slow, dark, dense movie. About two-and-a-half hours. That's what someone at the town hall said tonight when she called up about it. It's been almost an hour since she said she'd be home. The movie might have started late. The organizer of the event, Denise has said, tends to wait till the last possible customer has bought his ticket, decided if he wants anything at the refreshment table, sat down and taken off his sweater or shawl and hung it over the back of the chair, before she starts the movie. The single showing of the only movie being shown in that town this week, other than a nature movie at the library, let's say. There's no real movie theater there. White Hill. The nearest real theater (marquee, box office, refreshment stand and soft movie seats), which shows a movie two to three times a day once a week, is in an even larger town twenty-one miles past White Hill. Elksford. It's twelve on the dot now. Takes a half-hour to drive back from White Hill under normal driving conditions. There may be a thick fog on the road and she's driving very slowly. The route from their village to about five miles from White Hill is along one peninsula. Or even stopped for a while when the driving became too hazardous for her because of the fog. He's never seen a movie in that hall. She's been to two this summer, both times with a friend of theirs who couldn't go tonight, and came back around when she said she would. He did see one in the Elksford theater, only because she'd wanted to see it even more than this one and he didn't want her driving that far alone at night or even walking back to her car after the movie was over. Elksford's about ten miles from a national park and can get rowdy at night. Motorcycles; campers filling up on food, booze and gas and getting drunk or high. White Hill has no bars or stores open past nine. Only times he's been inside the town hall have been in the basement once a summer for the last few years when they take their cats there for their annual shots. Cheaper and easier than in New York. An Elksford vet who sets up a clinic every Monday night. Even puts a desk nameplate out, probably so the pet owners can spell his name right on their checks. Dr. Hugh van Houtensack or von Hautensack. There have been accidents on the roads around here because of the fog, most of them early morning or late at night. He reads about them happening every other week or so in the local weekly. One man lost a leg last summer. In a rented car, visiting his daughter and son-in-law for a few days, so probably wasn't familiar with the area and also might not have known how to drive in fog. Denise knows the roads and what to do with the headlights in fog. She's more than seven months pregnant. Maybe she shouldn't have been driving. Her stomach's already pressed up against the steering wheel. If she pushes the seat back any farther she can't reach the floor pedals. Maybe she suddenly got labor pains or false labor pains she took for the real ones and went to the White Hill hospital. Should he call? His daughter snores upstairs. She sleeps in a crib in the one room upstairs, their own bed behind a screen. Don't call. Denise knows the difference between the two pains, and he's sure she'd try to call him before she went to a hospital, but definitely have someone at the hospital call him once she got there. Maybe she met someone she knows at the movie and they talked after, wanted to continue the talk so went for coffee or ice cream at the sandwich and ice cream shop a couple of miles past White Hill. She would have called, from the town hall if it had a phone, but definitely from the shop. She might be driving along the secondary road to their private road right now. Or driving down the private road any second now. He'd see the headlights thirty seconds or so before she reached the house. My worries are over he'd say if he saw the lights now. He'd go outside to greet the car, open the door for her, help her out, kiss her and walk back to the house holding her shoulder and hand. The headlights would only be from her car. Maybe twice a summer someone's driven down their road by mistake—none so far this summer, far as he knows—and for some reason almost always in the day. Not many people around here leave their grounds after dark. And so few unusual things happen around the cottage that he thinks they've always told one another when someone's driven down their road by mistake. Olivia snores. Loves to see her sleep. He goes upstairs to see if she's OK. He knows she is but goes upstairs just to do something but also, he just now thinks, to pull the covers back over her if they've slid off and to push her left leg back in if it's sticking through the crib bars. That's the one that recurrently comes out; the other side of the crib's against the wall.

She's OK, everything in place, in the same position, far as he can tell, she was in when he last looked in on her an hour ago. About an hour and fifteen minutes now. Nobody to call. The town hall, but he's just about sure nobody's there to answer. Looks outside the bedroom window that faces the front. Doesn't seem to be any fog around. Bug light above the front door and the living room floor lamp he was sitting under give off enough light to tell. But the roads always get the fog worse than their house. Denise would also have called, if she was going anywhere but home after the movie, to make sure everything was all right with Olivia. Something's wrong. He's almost sure of it. There's just no reason for her not to be home by now. He thinks that even if there was an accident on the road that prevented her car and others from going around it—on one of the two narrow bridges, for instance—she would have got the trooper to somehow call him or gone into someone's home to call herself. No, that's going too far—both those. Olivia stirs, turns her head over to the other side. She probably did that several times in the last hour, stuck her foot out of the crib and brought it under the covers too. He hopes she wakes up. He'd love to pick her up, wrap a baby blanket around her and hold her to him till she fell asleep again. Maybe singing to her; probably just quietly. Maybe she has to pee. She doesn't wake up. He pulls the covers back, feels inside her diapers. Dry. if they were wet he'd go downstairs to run warm water over her washrag, change her in the crib.

He goes downstairs, sits in the living room chair under the lamp, picks up the book he's been reading, stares outside. Mosquito buzzes his ear. He jerks his head back, looks around for it, sees it, holds his hand and the book out on either side of it and slaps. Got it, but nothing's there when he looks at the book and his hand. Spreads his fingers wide, looks at his lap and the floor, stands and brushes off anything that may be on his chest. Doesn't see how he could have missed it, since he didn't see it fly away, but it's sometimes happened. It'll be back. He goes to the window. Private road leading to the secondary road roughly a quarter of a mile up the hill. Right on that road to the general store and main country road 2.3 miles away. Mosquito again, once around his head, and when he holds out his hands to slap it, though there's much less light here, it darts away and seems to go up the fireplace chimney, but he's lost it in a darker part of the room for a few seconds, so that could have been another one. Right on that road to White Hill. Movie's probably been over an hour and three-quarters by now, longer if it started on time. So it's been almost an hour and a half since she should have been home, and longer if she left the movie early because she didn't like it, let's say, or wasn't feeling well. He can see only a few feet of road going up the hill. Can see some sky through the trees. A dark blue with a streak of bright light. Good. Must be a clear night and full moon or no more than a day before or after one. Better for driving. Some full-moon nights, which they don't get the effect of in front of the house because of the tall trees, it's almost as if streetlights lit the road. They usually say something about the moon when it's full. Just that there is one and it looks nice over the bay from their deck and lights the path and garden behind the house as electric overhead lights would and maybe something about its face. But it's rained or has been cloudy or misty the last three days. Slippery roads? No, they were dry this afternoon when they drove to the lake to swim, though some puddles on the road when the culverts under them must have got clogged. Denise, get home now, come on, will you? Oh shit, where is she? Way past midnight. She's been tired lately because of the pregnancy. Quiet upstairs. Very quiet inside this room and around the house. Baby inside kicks hard now. It could have kicked so hard she lost control of the car for a few seconds and crashed. He should have gone with her. Of course he couldn't. Then convinced her to stay home. "If the movie's that good and been reviewed so much," he should have said, "it'll be coming around New York for the next year." Some men could have stopped her car. The old trick of pulling alongside her car and pointing to the back wheel as if something were wrong with it—just the driver visible, the others lying on the seat or floor—and she should stop. He's warned her about it, but a while ago, so she may have forgotten it or only remembered it once she got out of the car. Read about it happening to a woman in New York, another somewhere else, and that's *just* what he's read. They'd stop, if she did, and jump out after she stepped out to look at her wheel or just rolled down her window, and do who knows what to her. "I'm pregnant," she could say and that might work with some of them but excite one of them even more. "You'll kill the baby," she could say and they could get so guilty or just want her out of the way so she can't identify them that they'd kill her and dump her into a ditch along the road or drive into the woods along an old quarry or clammer's road and dig a hole and bury her or cover her up with brush and leaves. It's happened. It could happen. He hasn't heard of it happening around here, but no area's exempt, especially one with so many transients. Campers from the national park who were out for a good time and got carried away. Maybe it has happened around here, since he doesn't know what's in the local papers between Labor Day and July 1. He can't hear any cicadas, or whatever are the summer's last noise-making insects of that kind. Maybe the phone's dead or off the hook. Goes into the kitchen and picks up the receiver. Working. He looks outside. No lights coming down the road. Thinks he heard something outside—an animal walking, or a person, or falling tree branch hitting the ground. He goes out the kitchen door and looks. Nothing. "Anybody here?" Holds his breath to listen. Not even car sounds from far off. If a car were approaching their road from either way, he'd be able to hear it from here even if it were a half-mile away. Thinks so. Or maybe just from the top of the road. Very few cars on it at this time. Maybe none. Maybe there won't be one till five o'clock or so when the lobstermen drive past their road to the point a mile away. Who to call? No one. The phone's ringing and he runs to the kitchen to get it. Olivia cries. Oh God, he thinks, what to do?

"Mommy Mommy, Daddy," she screams. Phone rings probably scared her. He picks it up. "Denise?" "No," a woman says. "Is it something immediately urgent?" "Well. . ." "Anyway, please, whoever it is, hold for ten seconds—a minute at the most. I have to see to my daughter. OK?" "I guess."

He runs upstairs. "Where's Mommy? I want Mommy," Olivia says. "She'll be home very soon. She went to a movie. You knew; we told you. Listen, I have to get the phone downstairs. Someone's on it. It's very important. That's what woke you up—the phone ringing. Stay here, sweetheart." "No." "I'll be right back up." She holds out her arms. "Carry me." "I can't. Stay in bed." "Carry me downstairs. I don't want to be here alone." He picks her up, grabs a blanket out of the crib and throws it around her, goes downstairs, sits at the table with Olivia on his thigh, picks up the receiver and says "Excuse me, you still there?" "Yes," the woman says. "Is this Mr. Tetch?" "What is it, my wife?" "I'm Officer Ragnet, state police. There's been an auto accident and your wife's been hurt." "Is she seriously hurt?" "Yes, I'm sorry."

That can't have happened, he tells himself later. Impossible. Never, and he shakes it off. He's sitting in the same chair. Olivia's asleep upstairs. Denise shouldn't have gone to the movie, period. He didn't think it would be a good movie no matter what anyone said. The trailer they saw made it seem as if it would be a terrible movie, very slow paced, trite plot, too heavily acted, that's what it'll be, he remembers thinking then, and then, he thinks, telling her. "Derivative. The way the people are dressed and look. The background darkness. The long camera shots out into space. Bergman," he said in the theater after the trailer was over. "All that rain." He remembers a Bergman movie he'd seen that resembled the little they saw in the trailer. The listless way the people spoke and moved. Their depressed, estranged looks. "Bad Bergman, that's what it'll be," he said after they left the theater. "Even the actors look as if they were picked because they look like some of the more well known actors in the Bergman repertory company." Olivia was with his mother-in-law. The movie they saw that afternoon was what? Funny to remember the trailer but not the movie it was with. All the movies they've seen together the last two-and-a-half years have been in the afternoon. That's when his mother-in-law can take care of Olivia, or prefers to. Besides, they like to get Olivia to bed by eight so she'll be asleep by nine. The movie only stayed around for a week, despite the good reviews. They thought it would be around for a month or two. He would have seen it with her. He likes going to movies with her when his mother-in-law takes care of Olivia. It seems the only itme they're out of the house alone together in New York. So far they haven't got anyone else to babysit for them there. For a while they were reading about a number of babysitters in and out of New York who killed or mutilated or molested the children they sat, and it spooked them. They decided they'd only start hiring sitters when Olivia was clearly able to tell them if the sitter had done anything wrong to her or had left her alone in the apartment for even a minute or anything like that. His mother-in-law will only sit at her apartment, which would have meant, if she had agreed to sit for them at night, getting Olivia out of sleep to take her home. He likes walking out of his in-laws' building with Denise, just after they've left Olivia there. And taking her hand and holding it all the way to the theater, even if they take a subway or bus, though most of the movie threaters they go to are in walking distance of his in-laws'. Also holding her hand through the movie, kissing it a few times, pressing it to his cheek, maybe kissing her once or twice and whispering things to her he never seems to say anywhere else, other than at a party or some social gathering like a wedding when he's a little tight, or in bed when he thinks he hasn't said anything like that for a long time and maybe he should. Even waiting on the movie line with her is nice, except when it's cold. Actually, when it's very cold or raining they usually go to another theater that doesn't have a long line. Most of the movie theaters near his in-laws' are pretty good. If that movie had had a good New York run she wouldn't have gone to see it tonight. Now that he thinks of it, the newspaper review she told him about was only so-so. The two magazine reviews she read parts of to him were ecstatic, but they came out after the movie was gone. The telephone call was a wrong number. The caller was very apologetic. Howard didn't think anyone called anyone around here so late—long after midnight. Maybe it was silly to think that, but that's what he thought. He wishes it were possible to think that and it had been a wrong number. Tonight's a year after Denise was killed coming back from the movie. If was foggy. Year to the day. She lost control of the car, it seems, and she and the baby she was carrying died. He screamed "Oh nooo" when the officer on the phone told him. Olivia started crying upstairs. He didn't know what to do, called friends and told them what had happened and if one of them could stay here with Olivia while the other drove him to the hospital where the police wanted him to identify Denise. He sits in the same chair he sat in that night. Almost to the minute a year ago when the officer called. He's drinking brandy straight. He wants to get drunk. He is getting drunk. He raises his glass and says "Denise, my love, where in God's name are you? Please come back," and drinks. It's actually the night she went to the movie. Almost one now. If there was fog or slow traffic in front of her—a tractor, but there wouldn't be one on the road that late. So just someone in front of her driving very slowly—she still should have been home two hours ago. The fog slows you down fifteen minutes from White Hill, maybe a half-hour if it's thick. Same with a slow driver no matter how slow. And then only if he's going the whole way, White Hill to the country-road cutoff at their village, and she can't pass him, something she doesn't like to do, but does if he urges her to, on these roads even during the day. Anyway, her trip home, if it were one of those, would take no more than an hour and fifteen minutes at the most. He did hear the phone ring when he was outside before. He ran in. Olivia was crying. Phone rings must have woke her. He said into the receiver "Denise?" "No." He told the woman to hold, his daughter was crying, and ran to the bedroom, brought Olivia downstairs, apologized to the woman for keeping her waiting and asked what she wanted. "Is this the Drickhoff residence?" "No, we share a party line. They're four rings and we're three." "I'm almost positive I dialed right. How terrible at this hour." "You had to have dialed right. I was outside when I heard the phone ring. I must have missed the first ring, so thought it was three I was hearing. Then I ran in and picked it up on the third ring of the second series, when there no doubt would have been a fourth. You see, I was anxious to pick up the phone—I thought it was my wife calling—that 'Denise' name I said before—that I answered it by mistake. Excuse me, but you'll have to dial again. I hope you're not calling from out of state." "No, from Bellsport—not far. OK. Sorry." "May I also say, because this is a party line and we hear the Drickhoff rings, that it might be a bit late to call?" "I know and I'm sorry. I wouldn't call if I didn't have to. But it is rather a little urgent, as I'm sure your wife's call to you must be." "That's right. Look what I get for sticking my nose in. Excuse me. Goodnight." Right after that the phone rings four times, twice. Maybe one of the Drickhoffs picked it up or the woman thought that was enough times to ring. He gave Olivia water, brought her upstairs, she said "Where's Mommy?" he said she'll be back soon, sang to her, she fell asleep in his arms and he put her down. He rolled the mosquito netting over her crib and went downstairs, poured a brandy, drank it quickly, poured another and sat in the living room chair and opened the book. Can't read, he thought, and shut it and sipped the brandy while he stared out the window. A mosquito flew out of the fireplace. He watched it hover above his knee and then go across the room. Must be a male.

Flash of light outside. Lightning? No, sky was too clear before, but weather could have changed. He goes to the window. Headlights. Sounds of a car coming down the dirt road. He goes outside. Their car. She drives it as far forward as it can go without hitting the parking log, stops to shift it into reverse, sees him and waves. He holds up his hand. She backs into the parking space he cut out of the woods this summer. Hand brake, lights off and she steps out of the car as he come around the front of it. "I was worried, where were you?" he says. "Say hello first, say hello." "Hello. *So?*" "Grief, what a reception after so many hours. I tried to get you several times but our phone was always dead. There, now don't you feel bad?" and she puts up her face and they kiss. "I was just on the phone—thirty minutes ago, and it was working." "Who called so late? I hope not my father." "Wrong number." "Then it must have started working again around that time till up to an hour and a half ago, because that was the last time I tried to call." "Actually, it was for the Drickhoffs. I picked it up impulsively, so could be our phone still isn't working fully. We can worry about it tomorrow. But why were you so late in getting back?" "Can't we go inside first? It's getting cold for me." They start for the house, his arm around her shoulder, other hand holding her hand. She looks straight up. "See any shooting stars tonight?" "I didn't look." "You didn't even go on the deck for a minute? That's all it would have taken. The first clear night in three and the best week for it." "I was only interested in the front of the house—our car coming down and you driving it." "I met Rick and Arlene at the movie and went for tea with them." They go inside. "That's what I tried to call you about." "What place would be open now?" "Not now—before. Little past eleven. We got to the Frigate as it was closing. They didn't mind us having coffee and tea—we also wanted desserts but they were all out—because they were cleaning up around us. They do unbelievably well there and have a good menu. We should go. Hire a babysitter a few days in advance and make it an early dinner." "OK. But why a little past eleven? Why'd it take so long to get there, is what I mean? When did the movie end?" "At eleven." "Why so late?" "Why so many questions?" "Because I was worried. I imagined all sorts of awful things happening to you." "Maybe you wanted them to." "That's silly. Where'd that come from?" "I don't know. Interrogating me. I did try calling you though." "But when you couldn't reach me, what did you think I'd think was happening to you?" "I thought you'd know everything was all right even if I didn't call you. I just thought, well, that you'd at least wouldn't get worried. Truth is, I thought you'd

70

be asleep by now. That you'd read and have some wine and then get so tired from the reading and wine or maybe even television, that you'd go to sleep long before I came back. In other words, that you wouldn't even be in a mental state to worry. It's past one. What are you doing up? You usually get to sleep at ten—eleven, the latest." "I was worried. Just never do it again, OK?" "What?" "If you can't reach me, then come straight home." "Why? If I can't reach you and it's getting to where I was expected back much earlier, check the phone to see if it's working. If it isn't, assume I'm trying to get you but can't because the phone's not working." "I tried the phone. I just remembered. I got a dial tone." "Probably long after I stopped trying to call you, right? Because you don't think I'd call past twelve, do you? Not even past eleven-thirty. You'd be sleeping, I'd think. Or the Drickhoffs would, and the phone would wake them. I even asked the operator—you forgot to tell me something, I forgot to tell you this—and she said our connection wasn't working. And since there were no reports of lines being down, to try again in fifteen minutes. Well, fifteen minutes was eleven forty-five, so I wasn't going to try again. But that's it, all right? How was Olivia?" "She woke up crying before—the Drickhoff's call—but it was quick. Gave her water, sang a song, she went back to sleep. Actually, I carried her downstairs because I had to get back to the caller; I'd asked her to hold so I could attend to Olivia." "That person say why she called so late?" "She said 'pretty urgent.' " "It should have been very urgent. Extremely. Anyway, I'm sorry for the confusion and that you worried so much. I am." "I thought you had a car crash. I even imagined it. Worse, I saw myself alone with Olivia for the rest of my life. At least the next fifteen years of it, and the two of us always sad that you had died. That the fetus died also so late in its development made me sad too. I thought people would feel sorry for me. I saw myself at your funeral. I saw myself not teaching classes this fall. Just grieving, mourning, going a little crazy, but taking care of Olivia for the next year best as I could. Real self-pity. I don't know why I went so far with these thoughts. That I'd never love any woman again as I did

71

you. Like that. It's possible I took some pleasure in all the attention I got—but real sadness. I actually sat here crying for about a minute over my imagined loss of you." "Maybe it was from the drink over there. How many you have?" "That only came after I started thinking about it. Could be you're right though. Brandy can do that." "Brandy?" "I felt I needed something stiff to relax me. I even saw myself sitting here a year later drinking brandy from the same juice glass and staring out the window, remembering the night of the crash exactly a year before. Olivia was again upstairs. In my thoughts. I'd rented the cottage for the summer. Everyone said I shouldn't. That it would bring up old stuff better left where it was, but I said it was my final farewell to you. Of my mourning. That I had to come back here to get through the next few years. That's what I said, but I don't quite know now what I meant. Olivia wanted to come back too. She liked it that the Hahn kids were just around the loop. I did too. And another practical reason: that it was the one place around here I could afford. Maybe I'm nuts for having gone so far in these thoughts, and the crying. What do you think?" "I think that I'm glad to be back. And that I didn't die. Very glad of that. Also, that I probably shouldn't go to movies alone at night. Anywhere far alone. It's become too uncomfortable to drive, and what if the baby started? Oh, I could take care of that. But that if we go to White Hill or any long distance, for you to do all the driving from now on. That puts a big strain on you when we go back to New York, but what else can I do? I'll be even bigger then." "I definitely should have had more control over myself before. Thought what you said I should have. Such as picking up the phone around eleven or so, or anytime when it's more than a half-hour after you said you'd be home. Next time I'll do that." "There won't be a next time for months." "With the next baby then." "What next baby?" "Or if you change your mind one afternoon soon and go out alone and aren't back a half-hour after you said you'd be." "Wait, whoa. What's with this next baby business? Not only that it came out of nowhere and doesn't much relate to what we were talking about, but who's having one?" "Don't you want to have three?" "Only if I'm carrying twins, which I'm not." "Maybe if it's relatively easy having two, we'll want to have another. We should leave it open. I've always wanted—imagined having—three." "First time you've said that." "I'm sure I have before. I love it when you're pregnant. That's not why I want three. I just love having one and know I'll love, or very much think I will, having two, and want a third because I think it'll be the right number for us and for the first two. They can play off one another, and other things." "I don't understand. Maybe it's your brandy, or me. Anyway, it's not something to think or talk seriously about now." "You don't want to have some brandy—can't have any, right? Why do I ask? I know you can't." "Truth is, it's probably late enough to. Just about all the damage that can be done to it has been done. Still, best to play safe. I'm going to get some milk." She kisses him. "Somehow I really enjoy all the attention I didn't know you were giving me before, morbid as it was. I just wish, my sweetie, it hadn't hurt you so." Kisses him again and goes to the kitchen. He follows her. "How was the movie?" he says.

Frog's Break

A break. Olivia's watching the one hour a day of TV they allow her to. Denise is in the bedroom nursing their three-week-old baby. He pours coffee out of the thermos—this morning's, but doesn't want to spend time making fresh coffee—and goes into his room and shuts the door. What to do? An hour, but only if Eva falls asleep right after she's fed. She doesn't, then if Denise doesn't ask him to walk her to get her to sleep or gently bounce her to bring up the bubble. First a postcard to get started.

"dear jack: sorry for not writing sooner. please excuse my now writing a pc but it forces me to be brief. also excuse that i leave just a 10th of an inch margin on both sides and start at the very top and will end at the very bottom, with maybe the bottom half of my last line left on the platen, but this way i can get in as much as i do. of course all i usually manage to get in is this explanation and the preceding excuses. look, your rt about what you said. remember what that was? i doubt ive room to go over it here. it was in your last letter. you say you keep copies of all yours, so you mt want to check it to find out. as for summer rental you want to take, we plan to be in that area also, so if thats whats stopping you—are not being there— excuse me: 'our'—dont let it. of course—so many of courses; why,

74

when im so concerned about this pc's limited space?—of course if it ends up where we cant afford the house we want and hv to go to cheaper pastures—browner ones—just hv to go elsewhere—what can i say? also, youre rt about my work (at the end of your letter; other 'rt' was in the middle). so what if—oops, out of space. best to m, your pal, h. ps: no time to correct thi"

He should also write his mother. No, quicker to call. Goes into the kitchen and dials. "I knew it was you," she says. "How? When I heard the ring I thought 'That has to be Howard; it can't be anyone else.' Crazy, right?" "Well it isn't Howard. It's Jerry." "Don't tell me. I know my sons' voices. Jerry talks faster, higher, and he only calls Monday, from work, between one and two, which must be his lunch hour. So I'm always here then, because one time he called later in the day and gave me an argument why I wasn't here between one and two when I ought to know by now that's when he calls. He's never called from his home once. Has he ever called you from there?" "I don't know." "Four times he's called from a hospital, all the other times from work. Once each when his three children were born and once when he was in one after his heart attack, which he still denies he got. Gas, he says, but a paralyzing attack of it. He called that day to say don't visit because he was getting his clothes on now to go home, but they convinced him to stay two more weeks." "Good. Listen, I've the train schedule for this weekend." "I don't know—you don't think you'll be too busy and tired from it all?" "We can manage it, believe me. And I want you to see Eva before she's grown up." "I know I mentioned this before, but where'd you ever get that name? I mean, some names, even with just the initial, one could say it stands for somebody in the family. But Eva? Nobody in our family had a first name with E in it in anyone's memory, and your father-in-law says nobody in his or Vela's either." "It's a nice name. Dark, eve, feminine. Or near dark. We also wanted it to be as strong as the name Olivia -- but also to contrast with it -- which we thought of as airy, light. And she is dark—her skin coloring and hair." "That's now. Her skin might not get lighter but her hair could all fall out and come in as blond as Olivia's. And you chose the name before you had her, didn't you?" "Even if she turns out to be light in everything—hair, skin and weight—still, we like the sound of the name. But what are you saying, you don't want to see her because you don't like her name?" "Don't be silly." "Only kidding. But look, I'm really in a hurry, so what about this weekend?" "Why you rushing so? Keep on like that and you'll get as sick as Jerry. Take it easy; you now have two babies to take care of." "OK. But how about the nine o'clock on Saturday and I'll pick you up at the station at 11:47?" "I can take a cab when I get there." "Please, don't argue, Ma. I really don't have the time. And it's easy—not like New York. Always a parking spot at the station. Or the ten o'clock and I'll pick you up at 12:35." "Why is one ten minutes longer than the other?" "Probably an extra stop. Metropark or someplace. So, either of those okay?" "Ten o'clock. That way I won't have to rush. What do you want me to bring?" "Nothing. No, if I say nothing, you'll go over an endless list of things, so bring bread and cheese. A good slab of parmesan would be nice, and smoked mozzarella. Anything you want. A corn bread and seeded rye unsliced. But don't overload yourself. Take a cab to Penn Station. Call for one—Love Taxi, for instance—and they'll pick you up at the door. And keep your pocketbook closed when you're there and your hand on the clasp. We're all looking forward to seeing you." "Thank you." "Before I forget. Get a special senior citizen round-trip ticket. The regular round-trip discount fare isn't good for Sunday, but the senior citizen one is." "I hate going up to the ticket counter—" "Do it, don't be ridiculous. You're fifteen years into your senior citizenship, so take advantage of it when you can really save. If I could get away with it, I'd do it too. No I wouldn't—I mean, illegally—but do what I say." "All right." "Much love from Denise and me."

He goes into his room, sits back and thinks. I should do one of my projects now. I should start retyping it. I should get it going and finish the first page in the forty minutes or so I've left or maybe if I come back to it tonight when the kids are asleep or Olivia's asleep and Eva's feeding and work on it every day like that and finish the whole thing in about two weeks. I never feel good unless I've a project going. End one, begin one, work on one, end one, and so on.

He takes off the typewriter cover, picks up the first draft of a manuscript, bounces it on the table till it's stacked and squared, puts it down, reads the title page—OK, nothing much, but he'll make it better, turn it into something—puts paper into the typewriter and sits back and thinks. Why did I shake the baby like that yesterday? I could hurt its brain. Bleeding in the brain. I could kill it. Some kind of hematoma. Subdural. Read about it in the paper last week. Mother's lover did it to her four-month-old baby. "She was crying," she said. "We couldn't sleep. He didn't mean to harm it." Something like what I did. I was trying to work and she wouldn't sleep even during the time she usually does, even after I walked her a lot and two diaper changes. Why am I such a cruel prick sometimes? She was crying. Babies cry. I also squeezed her too tight. In anger. I could hurt her kidneys. One of her inner organs—she's so small: several of them at one time—by squeezing her like that. Why did I also drop her on the bed from so high up? Why from any height? I was actually mad at her. For keeping me from my work. She was taking up too much of my time. But I could have hurt her back. Broken it. Maybe done something to her head. I still might have. I said to her but very low so Denise wouldn't hear: "I'm mad, you little bastard, can't you see? Why are you crying so much? Stop it." People will find out. Denise will. That's not the problem. Problem is why I do it. She cried for about a half-hour straight. Denise was napping in our bedroom at the other end of the hall. I didn't want her to get up and say something like "She's not hungry, I just fed her, so maybe she needs her diapers changed or you're not walking her right. Or she could have developed a diaper rash. You check? But I can't get up every time. I need some rest." The baby's cries are penetrating, but so what? When I held her to my chest and walked her, she screamed in my ear. I said "Damn, must you do that?" and reamed my ear with my finger, though it wasn't in any way bad as that. I was doing that for her. It's stupid. She also slobbered on my neck and on my shoulder right through the shirt, but what of it? If it gets to me—any of it—admit it and wake Denise and say "Much as I know you need the rest and I hate doing this, I have to have a ten-minute break. If you can't get her to sleep, I'll take over and you go back to bed." I did the same with Olivia. Denise never found out. One time she said from the next room "What's happening—why's she screaming?" and I said "I don't know, suddenly started, must be gas." Treated her cruelly sometimes. Sometimes bordering on violence. A few times, violently. The first three months were the worst with her and when I lost control most often. She wouldn't sleep for more than an hour or two at a time and usually cried when she wasn't sleeping. When she was around two months old I held her upside down by her legs and said "Stop crying," and swung her back and forth: "Stop crying I said." A few times when I was alone with her and not even when she was crying—I was just frustrated at not having time to do what I wanted—I slammed the bed with my fists and screamed as loud as I could and just hoped the neighbors, if any were in, wouldn't say anything to Denise about it. I scared the hell out of Olivia then with my rage and screams. This happened over about two years. She'd burst out crying, and when she learned to say the word, called for her mommy, and I'd have to hold and comfort her till she stopped. I'm sure I've traumatized her. She gets scared when I raise my voice about anything, even when I'm just joking about something or on the phone with someone. Runs out of the room whenever one of the puppets or cartoon characters on that hour-a-day TV program acts threateningly or angrily. Won't let me read "The Three Bears" to her because Father Bear speaks in a loud gruff voice. Eva sleeps better than Olivia did and doesn't cry as much. If I hurt her—I didn't Olivia, at least physically, but could have the way I treated her sometimes—I know I'll pay for it always or pretty close. They get hungry. Gas. They cry when they're wet or tired. For a number of reasons when they're in pain or uncomfortable, and sometimes two or three of them combined. The bubbles hurt. The rash. They may also cry for reasons people can't be aware of. What's in their dreams perhaps. But none of that should get to me, or surely not as much.

The night he got down on his knees, when Olivia was around one and sleeping in a crib, and he practically prayed his apologies to her. Closed his eyes, clasped his hands, said "I'm sorry, my sweetheart, for acting so horribly to you. I don't know what gets into me sometimes, I swear. Please forgive me." Cried. Then for another year continued to treat her badly, though maybe less so and not as cruelly. He doesn't want it to be like that with Eva. Wants to stop now. This moment, the end. Has to tell himself that yesterday was the last time he'll treat her like that, squeeze and shake her hard and drop her on the bed and so on. Also has to tell Denise what he's done with both children. That he knows he won't do. But if he stops, he won't have to tell her anything, unless he later finds out Olivia or Eva has been physically damaged in a way he could have been responsible for. Then, since it's possible if the doctors know how it happened they might have a better chance of correcting it, he thinks he'd admit what he's done, but isn't sure. Probably not.

He looks at the manuscript. Doesn't like the title now. Needs one before he can start completing a piece. It's part of its completeness. That's always been the case and he doesn't want to start changing his work habits now. Maybe by the time he gets to the bottom of the page he'll have come up with a title. But he's never done it that way. Just call it "Jobs," that's all, "Just Jobs" is even better, for that's what it's about. A man's jobs. Just about an endless series of them for forty years with no end in sight. Just tired old age in sight, with maybe some savings and pension for him and his wife to get by but little energy left to start or complete any creative work anymore. He writes "Just Jobs" at the top and starts typing. It starts: "I start, deliver, come back, sort, pack, box, wrap, deliver, get a little tip, back, sort, pack, box, wrap, again and again for a couple-years. My first job. I'm ten." Awful, and he tears it out of the typewriter and throws it into the wastebasket, rips the manuscript up and dumps it into the basket. A ripped piece stays on the basket lip and just as he reaches over to tip it in, drops on the floor on the other side. Always something sometimes; where it never goes just right. He leans over. Paper's just out of reach and he doesn't want to get up to get it. Too tired. But he likes a neat room, always has, everything in its place, something about visual aesthetics and also if things look too chaotic, which doesn't take much for him, he gets disoriented and begins thinking he can't find anything and even starts typing the wrong keys. Won't even put up with a small paperclip or piece of paper the size of a small paperclip on the floor. Maybe a staple or two, pulled out of paper with his thumbnail or that had been jammed in the stapler, is about all the disorder he can put up with on his floor or desk. Stands, picks up the paper and puts it in the basket. "Now don't try to climb out. You do—" Why's he talking like that? Fun, that's all, having some, but suddenly it sounded too strange to him. Not that if Denise overheard him through the door he couldn't explain it to her. "I was having a heart-to-heart with my heart." No, that would make it worse. But to himself, he just doesn't like it. Wasting time too. Sits.

Never ripped up a first draft of anything and felt regret after. If a piece doesn't feel good—if he's not excited by it after he's done the first draft—it's just no good or not worth working on to finish it. Something will replace it. Always has. Either something new, which he'd try now if he had the time, or the other first-draft manuscript.

He puts that one on the table where the first one was, paper into the typewriter, likes the title, types it at the top and starts typing from the manuscript. It starts: "So he goes down. Went down. That's the right expression. Babies are 'put down,' which has nothing to do with it, just what he's been doing lately. The expression we always used about him and is most common. Quite common. Just very common. His brother Lon. Twenty years ago and more. Much more. Twenty-five. Twenty-six to be exact. But here he is, back. Just rang the bell downstairs. I said into the intercom 'Yes?' He said 'Lon.' I pressed the button to let him in and he came up. 'Lonathan, Lonald,

Lonnie, why hello. I want you to meet my family. That's what I've regretted most about your not being here all these years and having gone down in that ship. Is that the right expression, I mean, term?' 'It'll do,' he says. 'That you never met my wife, my first child and now my second. I'm not saying my first child is my second but that I have one. Two to be exact. Daughters. You always said you wanted sons. Lonsons, you called them. Oh Lon, I've missed you so, which goes way beyond any regrets I've had that you never met my wife and kids.' I take his hand and kiss it. It's made of sand, falls apart while I'm spitting."

Rips it out of the typewriter. No good and never will be, and throws it into the basket. Where was his mind when he did it? Worries him. Never did anything this bad, so maybe something's now missing. He rips up the manuscript and drops it into the basket. Never ripped up two first drafts at one sitting before. They were written back to back shortly after he finished the last piece, so maybe something's been missing awhile without him knowing it. Maybe the last finished piece is nothing what he thinks it is. No, don't overdo it. These two as first drafts and possible finished manuscripts, stank and should have been dumped right after he did them. All he needs is some time to do a good one, but maybe the next sitting.

He writes on the back of a thank-you card. "Dear Aunt Louise. Thank you for the lovely"— What did she give Eva? The acetate stretchie they gave a few days later to their super for his daughter's baby? He'd ask Denise now but doesn't want to waste even more time. Because he really could still begin a new piece. A quick first draft of a very short one or the beginning of a longer one. Puts the thank-you aside, paper into the typewriter, thinks who else hasn't he thanked yet whom he's supposed to? Denise writes all the thank-yous for presents from her friends and family, he does the ones from his, and friends they both have but didn't come into the relationship with, she'll write or ask him to. Lily and Ruben. "Dear Lily & Ruben," he types. "You know how I hate these printed thank-you cards. Know from the note I inserted in the thank-you card for the gift you gave

Olivia. But Denise felt, and I kind of go along with, that as long as we had them for O, we should for E, or else she might take it as some sort of rejection slip. Blip that slip. Just: Eva will feel quilty—what am I talking 'guilty'? Rejected if she happens to find out later on. When she's 4, 14, even 24. Anyway, thanks for the silver baby cup. I hope it lasts longer than the one someone got Olivia when she was born. Hope it wasn't you, by the way. Be an awful way to find out what happened to it. Like all good silver, it wasn't indigestible. Indestructible. Unintentional. Trying to write this too fast. It was soft silver. That one I stepped on in the dark and squashed. The dark unlit room at night. I wasn't in the dark figuratively. Meaning, my figure was but my mind wasn't. Some thank-you. But really, thank you. This cup I'll keep off the floor, or at least when it's on the floor, the room in light. And I know the last cup didn't come from you. You gave that nice tartan wool crib blanket that Olivia sucked a few fringes off of but which Eva can still now use. See what a memory I gots?" Xes out the last sentence. "Both gifts were very generous of you. But you know, when we had the birth announcements made, something Denise also wanted and I only eventually went for, I wanted to have printed on them 'Please, no gifts. Our apartment's one filled closet just from the gifts we got for Olivia's birth. At the most, have a cedar planted in Lebanon in Eva's name or give what you would've spent on a gift to your local right-to-abort clinic, no slur, smear, swipe, sneer or stigmata intended to our kids or any national or natal strife.' Should I also X those three sentences out? And the last plus this? Denise vetoed it. Not the Xing or to get gifts but because—lots of reasons. Smothering natural good-naturedness, for one thing. Maybe making those, who hadn't planned to give gifts, self-conscious that they hadn't planned to, for another. More. That it might seem like a hidden signal, for those who were wavering or hadn't planned to, to give gifts. How? Some way. People know me by now? But Denise is well, Olivia's taking baby and banishment (her own room for the 1st time in 15 months) pretty well, and I'm barren and wasted but fare-thee-well. What the hell's he mean by that? Time will tell. This's becoming a no-note. Beg-pardons, thanx, loves & bests from us all around, H." Pulls it out, folds it up and sticks it in the card and looks for his address book. Not on the table where it usually is, so he'll look for it later, and puts the card on Aunt Louise's.

Now, and sticks paper into the typewriter. But a student paper. Should have it done with comments for a conference with the student day after next. If he gets all his school work out of the way he'd really feel free, if not for today then tomorrow, to do his own work. Gets the paper out of his briefcase, reads it quickly, types. "How can I begin to judge the content of your work when I can barely wade thru the poor punctuation, spelling, grammar, paragraphing, you name it? Plus, why the very skimpy margins, making it doubly difficult to read, 18–19 words to a line, 29–30 lines to a page? Save it for letters to friends or notes to yourself but not lit papers which the teacher, whose eyes are lousy to begin with and his glasses a year too old, has to read some 15 of at a time." No, much too tough and self-something. Stupid, wrong, that's what it is. Try a gentler approach, but can't think how to do that with this paper now. Later, and puts the paper and what he's written about it on the cards.

Student recommendation. Tacked to the wall facing him. She said last week it should be sent out by this Friday if it's to be of any use for her grad school application. He told her "Then you should've given it to me weeks ago, because I'm too busy with a zillion other things, not to mention my own stinking work, to be rushed. But OK." Took it from her, didn't smile, might have even snarled. She said thanks, looked angry or hurt, left without saying goodbye. He wanted to yell out after her "Oh by the way, you're welcome." He should have called out to her "Wait, I'm sorry. It's the new baby, so not much sleep." Or when she first came into his office: "Sure, no problem, we're all running behind, but I'll make it." Even added: "You sure a reference from me won't hurt your chances? Only kidding." He should call her now to explain. Better when he next sees her. Takes the form off the wall, fills in the first side, turns it over and puts it into the typewriter. It starts: "One of the smartest, most articulate, pleasant and mature students to have come my way in years." Used that several times before, but doesn't think for the English Department of this grad school. "I also got to know Felicia a little better than I have most of my students, simply because she was extremely interesting and has a magnetic personality and for some reason we'd periodically bump into each other on campus. During these encounters she would tell me what she was doing, pursuing, books she's read, and so on, and I was never anything but deeply impressed by the range of her interests, consistency of her goals and values, depth of her thinking. . ." Won't do. They might think he was carrying on with her. Starts it again, on university stationery. "I'm afraid I've misplaced your reference form. I hope this letter will do, since I don't want to jeopardize Ms. Sollenberg's chances by requesting another official form and possibly returning it long past the deadline." Repeats the first sentence he wrote on the form, changes the next part he thought might be misunderstood. "Let me add that from time to time Ms. Sollenberg would come to my office during office hours. . ." Seems he's trying too hard to show he hasn't had an affair with her. He does think she's very attractive. Maybe that's what's screwing up the reference. Likes to look at her face, chest and legs when she isn't looking, her behind when she leaves his office, but never thought of starting anything with her. Never has with any of his students. Though some of them over the years—not Felicia—have made what could be interpreted as verbal or visual passes at him. But suppose, suppose, one of the students he's attracted to said "I want to screw you, Mr." or "Dr." or "Professor Tetch," or just "Howard," which he prefers them calling him but so many can't do. "Would you like to screw me, but right here and now, I'm saying?" What would he do? He'd say no. If he had a condom on him maybe he'd say yes. For suppose she also reached for his fly—he knows he'd have an erection by then—what would he do? He'd slide his chair back and say Stop. He'd put his hand inside her skirt or open her fly or just pull down her pants and sit her on top of him. He'd make sure the door was closed and locked. Would not. Door always stays open. That's his protection in case a student—it's happened here and in other schools—wanted to accuse him of making a pass at her or even of fondling when he never did anything. She could still accuse him, with the door open, but less chance of it. He has an erection. He touches and then grabs it through the pants, shakes it, thinks "Can't do it here, can in the bathroom, but why waste it? We haven't made love in three days. We'll probably do it tonight." But if Felicia—probably the student he's most attracted to—said something like that, what would he do? If she said what? "Let's fuck right now on your chair or the floor." It's ridiculous. He'd say the floor's filthy, the chair would never hold them. Suppose she said "Put a sign on your door next time you're to have office hours, saying Office Hours Canceled Today. Then come to my apartment. I'll see that my roommate's out, but I won't tell her who for. I never will. Just our secret for as long as you like." Or "We'll do it here or in my bed as quickly as you like. And if you like, just this once." What would he do? He'd do it with a condom. Wouldn't want to give Denise a disease. He'd do nothing. He'd say "I'm complimented, honestly. You're great in every way and if I weren't married I certainly would have started something with you, or tried to, long before now." Or "You don't understand. I'm not saying this to hurt or chastise you or anything like that, but my sex life with my wife is pretty near perfect and I don't want or need, nor do I think I'd have the energy for it, anything extra. The urge to make love with her hasn't abated since I met her. Sure, I've an erection now, but I also get one when my oldest daughter or one of our cats or even a heavy book sits in my lap. Or maybe it's more. Say it's because I'm aroused by you. Very much so, let's say, but what of it? Also say I've thought of making love with you. Many times, or at least a pass. But what of that too? It's all in the head. To entertain myself, maybe. Or to arouse myself for my wife when things are a little slack when I don't want them to be or she doesn't. When I'm having trouble getting it up—let's say it right out. But I'll do nothing to screw up my relationship with

85

my wife. In other words, I've taken a long time to say that much as I might have thought of starting up something with you, now or in the future, I can't and won't carry it through and never will. Thank you." No, he'd do it. He wouldn't. But if she closed the door, made sure it was locked, said she won't make any noise, will be very quick, will never say a thing to anyone about it, touched his penis through his pants, unzipped him, went down on him, while she was doing this put his hand inside her panties and held it there and even stuck his finger inside her and even began rubbing herself with it, what would he do? It'd never happen. He'd have to tell her to stop somewhere along the line. Maybe he couldn't. The blinds would have to be dropped and shut. Would she do it, he? It'd have to be she, since if he did it there'd be complicity. It's ridiculous. He puts in another sheet of paper, starts. "This is a letter of. . ." Maybe he'd only kiss. Kiss hard, open mouths and tongues, then pull back and say "I think that's far enough." Tears out the sheet, sticks in another. But if they kissed like that and she began touching him, maybe even pulling at it through the pants, how could he stop? Repeats the opening sentence about her being one of his best students in years, then "Listen, why beat around the bush about Ms. Sollenberg? *Felicia.* I'll put it right to you—straight forward, rather than straitlaced, as I can be. OK, enough of that too. Just showing off and no doubt making a damn ass of myself. But this is it. I've work up to my ears now, from teaching, homebodying (one three-year-old, another brand-new) and my own writing, so I'll be as brief as I can. She's the most intelligent, personable, mature, perceptive, attractive, diligent, reliable and hardworking student I've ever had. Check check check on all the top-2 percent-of-my-students boxes (that's to take care of side one of your reference form, which I spilled coffee on so am not sending). If there were a 1 percent category I'd check all those instead. Take her, she's great, tops, first-rate, so grave mistake if you lose her." Would never do. Rips the paper out and dumps it. Write it tonight when the kids are asleep, blaming yourself for being late. "I'm incorrigible but predictable that way. For their own sakes

Frog's Break

I wish students wouldn't ask me for references, not only because of my tardiness but because I've never turned one down even when I thought very poorly of the student and his work." Just write for another form and only say sorry you're late. Now your own work. Still time. Try for a quick first draft of a very short piece. Who knows what'll come? Sometimes when he's very short of time a two-to-three-pager pops out, which in later drafts becomes six-to-seven pages. And maybe Denise, hearing him pounding away in here, will wait till he stops typing or typing hard before she knocks and says his hour's long over. She knows when he's hot into a first draft, and he never types that hard and fast for anything else except maybe a personal letter, and if suddenly stopped, he can lose it. He's described it. In a few interviews and in his classes and classes and groups he's visited in other schools. Maybe repeated it so much with only slight variations that word's got around he only has one way of describing it. Champagne cork in his forehead which when he unplugs or uncorks, it flows out or spills or gushes out till the bottle's empty. "But you know, champagne will turn" or "spoil if you don't finish it in one sitting, since you can't recork it as you can other wines." Recently a student of his said his father bought a gadget that puts the champagne cork back into the bottle, keeping it fresh for a week or more. So he won't use that analogy again, if he can remember not to or can come up with one almost as good. "Ejaculation, once it's started, for example," but maybe only in his graduate class.

He sticks paper in, little raps on the door. Must be Olivia. "Yes, what is it!" he says. "It's me. Can I have a Gummy Bear?" "Oh come on, don't bother me with that now, and you know I don't like you having candy." "Mommy says I can have one if you also say I can." "OK, have one, but see if Mommy can get it. I'm busy; working. Let me alone for a few more minutes." "Mommy says to ask you to help me. She's with baby." "Oh Jesus, damnit, all right." He opens the door. "But only one." "Two." "One or none. Which is it? I don't want you taking all day." "One. I want to pick the color."

He gets the container of Gummy Bears out of the kitchen cupboard, holds it open for her. She looks inside, holds her hand over it. "Come on, pick it quickly. Red, green, orange, yellow or white." "Not white. It's light, like light. But not like that light," pointing to the ceiling fixture. "All right, light. And oh, poetry. But quick, which?" She looks in the container, hand over it again. "Orange is your favorite color. Why not choose orange?" "Orange," and she picks one out and puts it into her mouth. "OK now. This is my one big hour to do some important work at home. So please be my little sweetheart and let me use it? Go back to your program." "It's over." "Then into your room. Look at your books. Put on a record." "I don't want to." "I'll put one on for you. Maybe it's still too hard. "Sleeping Beauty. The beluga whale song by whoever sings it." "I want you to play doctor and nurse with me." "Not now. I haven't time. That's final. I'll take care of all your bears later." "Not all of them." "Then just some. But go in your room and line them up and dress them in paper towels if you want. That'll look like hospital gowns," and he gives her the roll of paper towels from the shelf over the sink. "And tell them I'm—" She drops the roll on the floor. "I want someone to play with now." "You shouldn't drop things like that. Especially paper towels. We use them to clean things." He picks it up and puts it back on the shelf. "I want you to play with me, or someone." "Olivia, haven't I been patient with you and clear? This is my break, my free time. So give me ten minutes longer. That isn't much. Ten is little. So go into—" "No!" "I said go into your room," and grabs her shirt at the shoulder and starts pulling her to her room. She screams, starts crying. "Shit ole-bitching-mighty," he yells. "Why you doing that? You've nothing to cry about. I'm the one. Oh the hell. And I didn't mean to pull at you so hard, or yell. I didn't hurt you—you know that." She backs away and cries harder. "What's wrong?" Denise says from the baby's room. "What? Speak louder." "I said why's she crying?" "I was just telling her—that's all—telling her—" "It sounded like shouting." "Well, shouting to myself mostly that an hour-a-day break is just too little." "First try to comfort Olivia. I'm trying to get the baby to sleep." He moves toward Olivia with his arms out. She's sobbing now, backs off to a corner. "Sweetheart, please come to me. I'm sorry. Don't make Daddy feel bad." Gets on one knee. "Honestly, I'm sorry. I apologize. Your Daddy's frustrated. You know what frustrated means?" She shakes her head, still sobbing. "It means I want to work more than I have the time to. And when I can't, then for some dumb reason I get mad. But it's OK. It wasn't your fault. Here, you want another Gummy Bear? I don't like bribing you to make you feel better, but maybe you deserve it." "I don't want anything," and she runs out of the kitchen. "Ah, fuck it," he says low to himself. "When does it ever go right? Plenty, plenty. But me and my goddamn fucking breaks. Stop it, stop it." Oh for once, he thinks, just go back to your room and do what you were doing and maybe neither of them, because of the mood they know you were in, will bother you for another half-hour. It's cheating but it'll be worth it to them in the long run.

He goes into his room, shuts the door and says "So let's have a first line. Give me a first. Give me a second. But first a first. Any first line that leads straight through to a quick first draft of something I really like."

"Da-da," Olivia says through the door.

"Da-da," he types. "Da-da, I want—"

"Mommy says you should—"

"Today Mommy says I should, definitely should, do what?" he types. "I should go—"

She raps on the door. He rips out the paper, a piece of it gets caught in the roller. If he doesn't get it out now he might forget about it and later it could jam the machine. He starts pulling it out with the tweezers he keeps in a utility box on the desk. He has a magnet in the box for retrieving paperclips that fall through the keys, a brush and sewing needles for cleaning the typefaces. "Da-da, I have to go pee-pee." "You can't do it yourself?" "No, and Mommy's busy. She says—" "Damn," he shouts, and slams his fist down on the table. An eraser pencil and his fountain pen jump up and fall to the floor. Probably busted the pen's point. Should always keep it capped. When did he uncap it? Probably been there like that since last night.

He jotted down a note and in his compulsion for neatness he must have put the paper the note was on back in the pile of scrap paper or dumped it into the basket. He forgets what he wrote. Can't be important then. But it could be a good starting line, one he intended for that. Did he? Was it? Heck with it. She's probably peed in her pants by now. Denise will love that. Heck also with trying to squeeze in minutes, thanking God for a free half-hour. She jiggles the doorknob, had been trying to turn it to get in but this door gets stuck. He gets up. Tweezers are still in his hand. She might think he's going to do something to her with them. He puts them in the box. Opens the door. She looks sad, a little frightened. "Did you pee in your pants, sweetheart?" "No. Can I sit at your typewriter?" "Let's just concentrate on your pee-pee. I also don't want to be washing the floor and your pants." He picks up the eraser pencil and pen, point's OK, caps it, sets them side by side on the desk. Picks her up, kisses her forehead a few times as he carries her to the bathroom. Stands her up, unhitches her overalls, pulls them down and her panties and sits her on the toilet. She pees and shits. "Good," he says. "A double success."

Frog Blahs

Can't sleep, can't eat. Goes to the bathroom. Can't pee. Sits on the seat. The same. Something's wrong. Feeling queasy inside, bit of a headache. Goes back to bed to rest and think. So what did you do today to feel this way? For instance? Food. Ate very little, no alcohol. Yesterday? A repeat. How come? Didn't feel like doing anything but that. Why not? Don't know. Up till now it hadn't affected my stomach or head, so just did or didn't do those things without thinking I guess. Think about it now? Just one of those periods when I didn't feel like drinking alcohol, eating very much or anything but bland. Also not cooking up a storm, cleaning a slew of dishes, going out for the extra ingredient—things like that. No need for alcohol, not even a beer. Wasn't warm enough for one, if that could be a reason. One reason it could be. Another is a need for a beer sometimes, or for its taste, if that's not saying the same thing. Something cool or quenching or that tastes like beer, but no. Booze? I don't do much. Sometimes a hefty straight one to calm myself or mixed with a mixer to help get me to sleep, but no feeling for any of that yesterday or today. Why? Thought I said. Or don't have to because it's all so no-relate. I'm just not a big drinker, what can I say? Then what do you think's causing your physical queasiness, lethargy, inability to sleep, pee, shit, or eat or drink much? Can't say. Maybe the start of a flu. Something's in there though, my bladder and bowels. Have the feeling to go but nothing comes out. The day before last? What about it? What you drank, ate, did that might have contributed to how you feel today. Too much exercising perhaps? Some older men don't know how or when to stop. No, it was just another normal day I think. Or who can remember the details that far back? I might have had a beer. I bought a six-pack that day, along with some other things, that I can remember, so if one's gone from the refrigerator you know that that day I drank a beer. Also might have had something more to eat than I did yesterday or today. Sure I did. Far as I can remember, I just about felt fine that day. But that was two days ago—a full two. I peed that day I'm sure. And yesterday—remember now lifting the toilet seat to do it—and shit both days too. So I got rid of whatever waste was in me for two days, and probably a lot from yesterday. Well, that leaves me stumped; what do you make of it then? Nothing. I make nothing. I wish I could make more, but that's all there is in my head now. I'll try for sleep again. Who knows? Maybe it'll work this time and when I wake up everything will be fine.

He lies on his side, shuts his eyes, pictures come. Mother. Looking radiant and beautiful, as so many people used to say in just about the same words, standing in a bright light. Theater spots, sunlight—she did both. This is something he's making up. Or a memory stored away for thirty to forty years and just now emerged from its little hole and came to the top. But so what? Mother, so glad to see her. Great, that's what it is, since she's rarely appeared so clearly in his dreams or thoughts: light on her, serene smile, about to speak. What, Mother? Holding a closed umbrella, slowly closes her mouth. No, please, speak. It's really more a movie scene, though she never did anything but stage. Right: couple of silents, she said, but ones she was only a chorus girl in and he's never seen. Even her clothes now are from another century, one she wasn't in. Goodbye, Mother, I know you're aching to go. She seems to be fading. Goodbye. Then Father. Drill in his hand, patient in his chair, white dental smock, dental lamp overhead. "Open wider," he says. Or mouths that to his patient. Patient opens wider. Patient's he. He's in his father's operatory, hands clutching the armrests. His father hated to treat him. Also hated sending him to another dentist. Never resolved that. So he got bad teeth from it. When by the time he got to his office the tooth was often gone or the cavity very deep. Root canal needed. But he hated doing root canal on him, so drilled deeper. Oh the pain. "Novocaine isn't working," he'd say. "I gave you a shot big enough to knock out a horse. Sit still, keep your mouth open." Oh the pain. Later when he was old enough he went to another dentist but didn't tell his father. Saved the money to pay for it by working as a delivery boy. His father found out. Bill came to the house by mistake. Called him into a room alone. "What's this?" "Why'd you intercept it? It was addressed to me." "Don't worry, I didn't open it. What's it for though? Don't give me a cock-and-bull story either." "I went for a root canal." "I'm not good enough to do it for you?" That what your mother says too? She lead you up to it?" "She doesn't know. Besides, she says all the time you're a fine dentist, a terrific dental surgeon, but that what you're best at is plates and false teeth. But my tooth got so bad I didn't want to bother you. I know you hate giving me pain in your chair." "You still should've come to me. If I couldn't do it myself, or didn't have the heart to, I would've sent you to a dentist friend who wouldn't have charged you. Or if he did, only for the x-rays and lab work, which I would've taken care of for you. What's this guy charging you? I bet too much." "Two hundred." "For one tooth? Is that with a complete set of x-rays and some fillings and a cleaning?" "No." "He's robbing you blind." "But he's a good dentist, and there was almost no pain. Who would you have sent me to, Hirsch?" "Sure, Dr. Hirsch, why not?" "Because I've heard you yourself say he's a cheapskate with x-rays and giving shots and even his lights. He just digs till you scream and then says 'spit.' " "He's an expert dentist, been at it for more than forty years." "Maybe that's his trouble then. His hands shake. He's half-blind and never seems to clean his glasses. I bet he doesn't even wash his hands, as you do, before he works on a patient. I wouldn't have gone to him even if you paid me to." "Then Dr. Wachtel." "Same. I don't want your cronies. Excuse me, but I want real careful professionals who don't skimp on anything." "You want dentists just out of college. You want fancy equipment and degrees all over the office. You want to pay through the nose. Well good, go ahead, since whatever I tell you to do, you always do the opposite anyway." "So what are we arguing about then? In the end, it's my money." "But I hate seeing you waste it. You should have at least come to me for advice. It's true I don't like working on my kids. But I could've found you excellent treatment—not Hirsch or Wachtel if you didn't want—and for a lot less money. I would've paid for it all, in fact. Now you won't get a dime from me for it." "It's okay. I didn't want any. I know how hard you work for your money." "Good. Then we're settled."

He opens his eyes. That actually happened much like that. He was fourteen, he was sixteen. What's bothering him though? Maybe he should force himself to eat, get back into life. He goes into the kitchen, opens the refrigerator, takes out cheese. Cuts a slice and puts it into his mouth. Can't bite down on it. Do. Shuts his eyes and tries. Spits it into his hand and dumps it. Milk. He pours a glass but doesn't drink it. It's not sour; just suddenly he doesn't like the milk smell. Too what? Milky, creamy, something. A carrot. Always a carrot. No, enough with carrots. Chump chump chump, that's all he ever does with them, four to five times a day, and mostly out of nervousness. Bad letter or phone call, he'd quickly go to the refrigerator, get out a carrot, scrape it and chump on it. It used to be: he'd want to call a woman or for a job but too many jitters to: chump on a carrot. Celery. Doesn't want to cut off the leaves, clean the stalk, anything like that. Then don't cut or clean: eat it all. Not hungry. You don't have to be hungry to eat celery. Water. Drink water. Maybe he's too dry inside. What's the word that's used? Evaporated, desiccated, something else but which could lead to the body's electricity going awry. Just dry, very dry inside. Gets a glass of water but doesn't want to drink. Feels he'll gag. Sips a little and spits most of it out. Get on the toilet then. Sit on it till something comes out of one of those holes. He used to have to do that as a kid? Thinks sometimes his mother or one of the women who took care of him made him do it, but that was probably for his own good.

He goes into the bathroom, sits, nothing. Read then, on or off the toilet. Goes into the living room, sits, opens a book. Doesn't want to read. Read. Reads the opening line a dozen times, two dozen. He could read it a hundred times and it still might not make any sense. Maybe it's the book. Opens another. Same thing. A dozen times, quits. The newspaper. They're easy. But he's not interested in anything in the news. Yesterday's story a little changed today. Today's story not much different from one a month ago, a year. Reviews of books, movies and plays he won't want to read or see. Masturbate then. Maybe that'll help. He lies on the bed, lowers his pants, tries getting an erection by pulling and caressing himself, can't. Vaseline. Gets some from the bathroom, rubs it on his penis, tries again, using all the tricks he knows; nothing. Stomach pain and headache are gone though. Not thinking of them probably got rid of them. Maybe that says something. What? Just that if he does or thinks of other things—well, what he just said.

He goes into the living room, sits in the armchair and stares at the wall. Nothing comes. Shuts the light. Now it's dark. Closes his eyes. Denise. Pushing a stroller down a street. Which baby was inside? He's had this memory of her doing this several times before. But thinking about the image like that has made him lose it. Bring it back. Opens and closes his eyes. It's back. He isn't often successful doing that. Denise. In a blue parka with the hood up, outfit she had on when his mind took this image. Pushing the stroller down the street they lived on when their girls were infants. One of those harmless light memories that stayed. He doesn't know why. Glad it did. Maybe that's what he should think about. Image is gone again. Bring it back. Does. That's never happened that he can remember. But stick with it now, think of nothing else. Loves the image, picture, of her pushing the stroller with one of their babies inside. It was a much better time for him, no doubt about that. One of the best times. Maybe the best. Still got angry then, often got sour. Often was dissatisfied with lots of things, etcetera, but for the most part, or a great deal of the time, or just some of the time—enough of the time to make him think things were going reasonably well for him— he was OK. He was relatively content. Image is long gone and he doubts he'll be able to bring it back. That's never happened. Try. Tries. Opens and closes his eyes. Nothing but quick pictures of sparkling lights, an opened window moving diagonally down to the left, a picture frame with nothing inside. And very often he was very content. They talked a lot, made love several times a week. Laughed, kidded, traded observations about people, news items, books. They kissed on the lips just about every day. How about an image of that? Isn't one, or not one he unwittingly took. Not even at the door? Opens and closes his eyes. Can't even picture it, doesn't know why. Then making love. There too. She on top, he on top—nothing resembling them comes through. First two planks, then a double-decker bed, then two dark masses of gas, twitching. She usually let her long hair down before they began, sometimes where it covered their heads. If they hadn't kissed that day and it was late and they were in bed, let's say, he'd say something about it and they'd kiss, usually twice, a long and short. So: every day unless one of them fell asleep before he could say something about it. If it were she, he'd kiss her shoulder and head, since one on the lips, no matter how lightly, would wake her. That was then. Time of the stroller. For about three years. If it was his youngest girl in that stroller image, then that was around the time he was taking the oldest girl to the playground once or twice a week. Talked to her as they walked. Carried her if she asked. Kissed her as he carried her. Blew or sputtered into her cheek, which she found fun. Pushed her on the swings, sometimes for a half-hour straight. See if he can picture it. Sort of: man, holding out his hands, standing behind a deadpan girl swinging back and forth. Man's not he, girl's not she. Told her stories before she went to sleep. Which were her favorites? Then what were some of the things she loved to say? Then some of the more memorable one-time things she said? One then. Closes his eyes. Gives up. Turns on the light, takes a piece of paper from the secret pocket in his wallet and reads. " 'When I grow up I want to meet a man, get married, have babies and live happily ever after.' 'Like your mommy and daddy?' I asked. 'Yes, but with a different man.' 'When baby sister is in the country I'm going to teach her how to smell flowers and pet cats.' 'Will the dandelions like the water we put them in?' Regarding any body of water she sees: 'Would a whale be happy in there?' 'The moon is a ball which you hit till it falls. That rhymes. So does shines.' " Where's she now? Go to the phone and call. Puts the paper back into the wallet, wallet into his pocket. If you get a forwarding number, call that. Never, she'll hang up. Just to hear her voice. Do it with the youngest too. Or in a fake voice and accent if you speak. "Hello, hello," say; "is Alexander P. Snappin in?" That relates to a private joke betwe n them he's forgotten. Suppose she says "Is that you, Daddy?" If she does, she'll then say "If it is, I already told you." Same with the youngest. "No more communications," she wrote. "No anonymous letters, impetuous phone calls, telegrams telling of your love, power of the blood, remorse." "Please dear," he wrote back, or something like it. He gets the letter out of the table drawer and reads. "I'm your father; I'm sorry for everything I've done to hurt or anger you, even the things I'm not aware I should be sorry for, even this letter; I love you both more than I could ever say in any way, so please, please; gesundheit."

He crumples up the letter, shuts the light, puts his hands over his eyes, would like a complete—whatever it is—total cry. Pulls at the hair on his arms. Stamps the floor with his feet till it sounds as if he's running fast. Raps his temples with his knuckles. Digs into his temples with them. Pounds his thighs with his fists. Presses a fist into his palm and squeezes, squeezes hard as he can till he's out of breath. Scratches his face with his hands and wants to cut through the skin, can't get himself to do it. Grabs his penis and shakes and pulls it hard, imagines it coming off in his hand and shudders, stops. Goes to the kitchen, gets cheese from the refrigerator and stuffs it into his mouth, swallows it. Opens a bottle of beer and drinks it down in several gulps. Opens another beer and pours himself a tall brandy and drinks the two alternately till he's finished them. Pulls the cork out of the half-filled bottle of wine, empties the bottle into a water glass and drinks it down. Stuffs bread and more cheese into his mouth, swallows them. Opens a new bottle of wine and fills up the water glass with it. Gets a plate out of the refrigerator, cuts up meat left from a few nights ago, smells it, it smells OK and stuffs it into his mouth and washes it down with the wine. Bites off most of the baked potato from that same dinner a few nights ago, shoves in his mouth a handful of lima beans and dressed leftover salad from that plate, swallows everything. Goes to the bathroom and pees, shits. Wipes himself. Is pulling up his pants when he has to shit again. He just sits there till he shits a third time, gets a bunch of tissues out of a tissue box and soaks them in warm water and pats himself.

He goes into the bedroom with another glass of wine, reads while he drinks. He gets through paragraph after paragraph, several pages. The book isn't interesting but he is reading. He feels sick, tired, turns off the light and shuts his eyes, sees pictures, flashing. Watch out, and he runs to the toilet and throws up into it. Drinks some more wine and throws up some more. He rinses his mouth, throws water on his face, pats his face, slaps it, pulls his head hair till a couple of patches come out, scratches his arms till blood comes, grabs his cheeks and squeezes hard as he can, but they don't hurt. Bangs the dresser top till his hands hurt. Kicks the door till his foot hurts. Screams "Screw it, hell with it, all of it, damnit, rage, goddamn rage, goddamn crazy rage, page, inexplicable, indespicable, indesquickable, immicterial, bloody, ruddy, fuddy doo-dah income, nincom splage. Something else, schmelse, belsh." He feels dizzy, just makes it to bed, falls on it, reaches for the phone on the night table, doesn't know whom he'll call if anyone or what he'll say if anything, passes out.

Frog Going Downstairs

He's walking down the stairs in his apartment building when he hears voices on the first floor. He sees two policemen and a priest. "Is anything wrong?"

"No," one of the policemen says and turns back to the priest. "I thought it might be one of the people living here. Is it Carl?"

"Carl?"

"The superintendent. He's been ill, hasn't looked well for months. Emphysema, for one thing, besides working too hard for a guy his age and smoking, to make it even worse."

"I don't know about your Carl, but nothing's wrong here. We're just talking to the father."

"Only because—I mean I know I'm probably overdramatizing this—but suddenly seeing a priest and two policemen in your building—"

"I'm having dinner here," the priest says. "And these officers, who are my friends, happened to see me enter the building and stopped to speak to me."

"Oh. Sorry for interrupting you then. Have a good dinner," and nods to the policemen as he passes them, and leaves the building.

He's walking downstairs when he hears voices coming from the ground floor. Men. Laborers? Something wrong? It's the tone.

Burglars? A mugging going on? He goes down slowly. Two policemen and a priest, talking low to one another. "I say no," the priest says. "And we, with all due respect, but we make no apologies for asking this, think you should go along with it," one of the policemen says. "Well, that's what we're here to discuss then, right? That we can be frank and civil about it is even better," and he slaps both policemen on the arm.

"Excuse me," Howard says.

"Yeah, what is it? the other policeman says and they all look at him as if they only just noticed him, though he's been on the bottom step for almost a minute, five feet from them.

"Is anything the matter?"

"What? Between us? Nothing. Thank you," and looks at the other two.

"I meant, two policemen and a priest in the building. I thought it could be one of the tenants."

"One of the tenants what?"

"Sick, in trouble—dead, even; I didn't know. Just, it was very startling to see you."

"I'm sure all the tenants are fine," the priest says. "I'm looking in on someone here, and the two policemen wanted to speak to me."

"We saw him walking in here and had something to say to him," the first policeman says. "Nothing about any of your tenants, so don't worry none."

"It's just that, well...one can't help thinking that...Mrs. Harlan on the top floor is very old and never gets out—"

"It's Mrs. Harlan whom I'm looking in on," the priest says. "But she's OK, I spoke to her a short while ago, so my visit is only routine, all right?" and he looks at the police and takes an envelope out of his jacket pocket.

"Maybe we shouldn't have a look at it after all," the first policeman says.

"That's what I've been telling you all along. We could have saved ourselves ten minutes arguing about it here, and a few phone calls before this," and he laughs and puts the envelope back into his pocket.

"Well, good afternoon," Howard says and smiles at them and leaves the building.

He's rounding the second floor when he hears voices downstairs. He stops.

"Definitely we should have acted sooner," a man says.

"And if we did, what then?" a second man says. "It wouldn't've changed things. It all ends up at Pickle Creek."

"One's either too early or too late but never on time," a third man says. "Nothing we can do about it though, and nothing we learn from it will help us the next time around."

He continues downstairs and sees two policemen and a priest. "Hello."

"How do you do, sir," the priest says and the policemen nod at Howard and resume talking almost at once.

"If, if, if," one says. "I'm sick of it." "Then let's drop the whole freaking thing," the other says.

"You boys really mean that?" the priest says. "Because if you do, then at least we came to something constructive today."

"Excuse me, but is anything wrong in the building?" Howard says.

"What could be wrong?" one of the policemen says.

"I don't know. Two policemen and a priest standing, midafternoon, in the hallway of a small apartment building? The priest dressed all in black—"

"This is the way I always dress outside."

"But also the two policemen here. When you're all together like that—"

"We're friends of Father Keiser," the other policeman says. "And we've official business to discuss with him."

"So it's not Mr. Spady in that apartment? He's been rushed to the hospital twice in the last couple of months—maybe more, I'm not quite sure."

101

"It isn't Mr. Spady," the priest says. "I was on my way to the mall, the policemen saw me from their car and wanted to talk. It was too hot to stand on the street or sit in the car and talk—"

"We would've given you a lift, Father. We still could."

"No, I need the exercise badly. —So, when we saw someone entering your building, we said 'Why don't we do that too?' and we came in here. That's the only reason—to get out of the sun. Now if it's all right with you, sir, thanks for your interest, but these men are very busy and we have to finish our little talk."

"Yes of course, I'm sorry," and he leaves the building.

He's walking downstairs, thinking of the work he wants to do and how he might start it, when the sight of three men stops him. A priest in a black suit and two policemen in white shirts with no jackets. Something about the bright light on them from the hallway window, making the shirts seem illuminated and the suit look as if it has a white outline around it. They're talking low, stop, look at him a few seconds and continue talking low. He can't make out what they're saying, but by their looks he can see it's something very serious to them. Then the priest slaps his hands, keeps them clenched and says "Don't worry, leave it to me. It'll turn out aces, I guarantee it."

"There's never a guarantee with something like that," one of the policemen says.

"Excuse me," Howard says. "Is anything going on in the building that I can be of some assistance to or that as a tenant here I should perhaps know about?"

"What could be going on?" the policeman says.

"Just that you three men here. It's not the kid—maybe I shouldn't say this."

"No no, go on, what?"

"The young man above us—our apartment. I mean, I don't want to start anything, but it's only that he has been in trouble with the police before that made me bring it up. They've been here a couple of times the last year, so I thought— Just that, well, when you live in a building with your family—even alone, if that's the case—and there's one guy who occasionally acts like a punk and once or twice has been one too—"

"Wait, you mean the Huffman kid?" Howard nods. "Right, for a moment I didn't realize what building we were in. —Drugs, selling them," he says to the priest, "and supposedly ripping off a bike in this or the next building a few months ago."

"The next one, which is the sister one to ours," Howard says.

"Anyway, all straightened out now, I heard. —You know the Huffman kid, don't you?" he says to the other policeman.

"No, who?"

"Long hair, kind of stringy, dirty. Tall, hefty, really fat-faced kid we came here or the next building to see about that bike, and maybe last year also, winter."

"You probably came here for him but to the next building for the bike owner," Howard says.

"I wasn't on with you either time," the other policeman says.

"I don't know the young man either," the priest says. "But he has nothing to do with our being here," to Howard, "nor does anyone in the building, far as I can tell. And we do have to finish our talk . . ."

"Sure, certainly. And I'm sure I shouldn't have said anything about the Huffman kid."

"Why not? Neighbors should look after neighbors, so long as they're not being nosy; and if there's wrongdoing, to do what they can to discourage it. That's all you were doing."

"I suppose. Thank you," and he goes past them.

He's walking downstairs when he hears men on the first floor and then sees two policemen and a priest. "Excuse me, is anything wrong?"

"No, we're just talking," the priest says.

"It's only that you all look so grave. For a moment I thought it could even be my daughter at nursery. She goes to the one over there at First Lutheran Church."

"I'm a Roman Catholic priest."

"Of course, I'm sorry. Also, I didn't really think it seriously, that something was wrong about my daughter. It was just something that came all of a sudden when I saw you."

"It isn't your daughter, don't worry," one policeman says.

"I know; but someone here?"

"Nobody regarding anything grave," the priest says. "I was returning something to a member of my church," and he nudges a shopping bag on the floor with his foot, "and the officers were talking to me outside when it began to rain."

"Oh, it's raining? I better go up and get an umbrella. Excuse me," and he goes upstairs.

He's walking downstairs when he sees two policemen and a priest. Priest is in a black suit, clerical collar, has white hair. Police are jacketless and in long-sleeved white shirts, black ties held down by clips, no hats. One's leaning against the radiator, other's against the wall, both with their arms crossed, listening to the priest. The priest stops talking when Howard approaches them. "Good afternoon," he says.

"Afternoon," the priest says. The policemen nod, arms stay crossed, look at him, he thinks, as if he may be the one they've come to see.

"Something wrong in the building?"

"Nothing's wrong, everything's right, thank you."

"But having the police and you—"

"We're just—"

Walking downstairs. Hears voices from the second floor. Men's. Three to four, it sounds like. Stops halfway down to listen. Garbled, can't make out a word. Maybe it's a foreign language. But he knows a few foreign languages, or two fluently and parts of others. Nothing. He goes all the way down. Two policemen and a priest. Priest is gesticulating with his hands and head. Police are shaking their heads animatedly. "But we have to," the priest says. "Not on your life," one policeman says. "I also have serious reservations," the other policeman says. "No, we have to, that's all there is to it," the priest says.

"Anything wrong?" Howard says.

"Wrong, how?" one policeman says.

"In this building. Maybe on this floor. Is anything the matter?"

"Yes, now that you mentioned it," the priest says.

"Father. It's supposed to be strictly official," the policeman says.

"Why? Maybe this man knows something. —You live here, don't you?"

"On the second floor. Howard Tetch. With my family. What is it?"

Suddenly he sees two policemen and a priest. They look at him, come straight toward him. "What? Is it my wife?"

"No, why would it be?" one policeman says.

Two policemen and a priest. "May I help you?" Howard says. They hurry past him. "Excuse me, but is anything wrong?" They keep going, don't look back at him, he starts after them upstairs. They go down the hall, stop at his door and ring the bell. "That's my door. The bell doesn't work. And you don't have to knock. I'll let you in if you want. Nobody's home though. My wife's out with our kids. Is it something about them? She took the car." The priest says something to the policemen, walks toward him, the policemen stay behind.

Priest and two policemen. "Yes?" he says. "Well, tell me."

"It's true," the priest says. "I've some news for you, very bad news. Give me your hand, sir."

"No."

"Perhaps one of the officers can stand beside you while I tell you." One of them does. Howard steps away, looks at the priest who's now telling him something, runs out the building.

Two policemen and a priest. "Hello," he says. They nod. He snaps his fingers, says "Excuse me, I think I forgot something," and goes back upstairs and unlocks his door.

"Leave something behind?" his wife says.

"No, nothing. Then what am I doing back here, right? Oh, I don't see why I shouldn't tell you. One of the oddest things just happened to me downstairs. I was on my way out—well, you know. Going to the mall. All very innocent. When I heard male voices and then saw two policemen and a priest on the ground floor and I didn't want to pass them. I actually made up an excuse to them to get back here."

"Did they come to see you?"

"I don't know. I don't see why they would. No, of course they didn't. I think something terrible's happened to someone in the building and I didn't want to know. Maybe not even that's it, but here I am and I still don't want to go downstairs till I'm sure they're gone."

"You should have left the building without saying anything to them and it all would have been past you by now."

"I knew I couldn't. Something told me. And I felt if I had tried to push myself to get past them, I would have acted even stranger than I did."

"You make me curious though. Maybe something did happen. I'm going to see. Olivia's fine, playing in her room by herself. If Eva gets up and she's not wet, just hold her for a while and she's sure to go back to sleep," and she leaves the apartment.

Frog's Brother

He thinks about his brother. Puts the book down, drink down, lowers the pillows with the back of his head and then lowers his head to them, remembers the night he first heard the news. Shuts the light. His older brother called him over. Called him up to come over. Both brothers were older. Alex was three years older than he and four years younger than Jerry, the oldest child. Three years almost to the day. They sometimes—neither liked it much—celebrated their birthdays on the same day. Closest brother or sister in age, day of birth and closeness. Jerry called him at their parents' apartment where Howard was staying then. "I got word today"—it went something like that—"word that Alex's ship is missing." "What do you mean missing?" Howard said. "I spoke to the ship's shipping company. Asking what's the status of his ship, when will it be in, and so forth. It's been overdue four days. You knew that." "I knew but thought it could be natural. A small freighter. It doesn't travel as fast or run on the tight time schedule of one of the big liners." "It could be it sunk." "What do you mean?" "I'm saying sunk, went down. Everything. In the ocean. Word is another freighter got a distress signal a week ago in the area Alex's ship was in." "But lots of ships were probably in that area." "That's what I told this man, but he says no. None on any company's log, anyway. They've checked. His ship was the only one known to be there, or at least from what's been graphed as its position, comes closest to being there at that time, and we're talking about something like a hundred square miles. Nothing came of the distress signal. It went on for a short time and stopped. It could even have been a portable transmitter from a lifeboat, it was so weak. Then a short time again—maybe three minutes, maybe less—and stopped. The radioman tried making contact with it to pinpoint it, but couldn't." "Oh come on, how thoroughly could one company check? Did it contact every ship company in the world that has ships crossing that part of the Atlantic, and did every one of these companies radio their ships that traveled this route? Are they also in touch with the ship companies of the Communist countries, especially the ones that won't have anything to do with us?" "Apparently the shipping world's very much in touch when something like this happens. And every ship that could have been in that sea lane was contacted in the last two days or had got in contact with its company or some weather ship out there." "How do they know another ship didn't go off its normal route and send that signal? Or sent it, then corrected its troubles on its own, and now isn't saying anything about the signal because it wasn't supposed to be in that sea lane." "Look, I can understand why you're taking this attitude, but Alex's ship hasn't made contact with anything for seven days. Two might be normal. Seven is practically unheard of unless their radio's down, but even there, they should have been spotted long before now." "So that's it. No radio, can't make contact, no other ship's seen them because of so few ships in their lane around this time or some kind of heavy mist or cloud cover all the way west, storm's held them up several days, maybe two storms, maybe three, and they sail into Boston Harbor tomorrow or the day after." "OK, maybe you're right—we can certainly hope so." "I have to be right, right? Have to. No two ways about it."

Jerry didn't tell him it over the phone. Called and said to come over. He lived a few blocks away with his wife and infant son. "What's wrong?" Howard said. "By your tone, it seems very bad. Is it Dad? Something Mom didn't want to tell me herself?" "No, Dad's in awful shape, but no worse than a month ago. Just come over." He did. They sat in the living room. Howard said "So?" "Have a drink first. Take a few sips, then we can talk. Simply to hold one will be good." Doesn't remember if he had one. Probably did. Any excuse at night to have a drink—today, same with twenty-five years ago. Probably scotch. That was Jerry's drink. Good stuff too. Ballantine's. Chivas. And listened to Jerry about the tremendous storm in the North Atlantic eight days ago, ship could have split in two and gone down fast. It's happened with other freighters of the same make and class. "And from what I found out through just a few simple phone calls, the ship's owners weren't known for keeping their ships in great shape, having enough lifeboats, going over the maximum weight, things like that. It doesn't look good, that's all I can say. It looks hopeless, quite honestly. Hate to be so blunt, but believe me, if I'm proven wrong I'll shout from a rooftop admitting it and fast for a week. Coast Guard planes—British ones too—have been combing the area for two days. But that's standard operating procedure, I was told, and that if the ship did sink, just about every trace of it, except the slick, would have disappeared in a day. Twenty-two men on board, most of them Cubans. Water so cold that anyone not in a lifeboat couldn't last in it for ten minutes, and the sea so rough that the lifeboats wouldn't survive for a few hours. The captain was a son of an old patient of Dad's, which is how Alex happened to get a free ride on the ship. That's one bargain we all could have missed. . ." Howard just sat there, drink in both hands probably, said nothing, stared without seeing anything, body numb.

He's got the place all wrong. He got a call. Jerry was living in Washington, D.C. then. He said "Dad called with some very bad news. He didn't have the heart to tell you himself, so he asked me to." "But I just saw him and he looked fine. An hour ago, for dinner, he and Mom." "And he didn't say anything? You didn't pick up on how they both looked?" "Nothing. We talked about what I was doing, her work, some big tooth he suddenly had the strength to extract today, baseball, etcetera." "Maybe because they knew I'd call you later. It's Alex, his ship. It's way overdue. We think it went down. They do—the authorities, the shipping company, the Coast Guard, everyone. Hit by an iceberg, knocked over by a bad storm, ship simply splitting in half, they don't know. But it hasn't transmitted or answered any radio signals or been sighted or anything like that for eight days. It's a little too unusual. There was something like the worst storm in ten years in the area his ship would have been in seven days ago. Sometimes these small old freighters can go a couple of days without being able to make known their positions. Their signals or receivers aren't strong enough sometimes or its frequency interferences or whatever they're called, and caused by God knows what, besides their shitty equipment. But never this long. There were also what one guy I spoke to called A-grade distress signals the night of that tremendous storm..."

He read about it in the papers. He would have liked to. Liked to have read that the ship was found, or all the men were found alive in lifeboats, ship down. Didn't happen. He imagines Alex going down. Ship splits in two, he's sleeping, water's in his cabin, tries to get out, ship's mostly underwater by now, it happens very fast, he struggles, slips, lights are going on and off, he tries swimming to the door, gives up, water in his lungs, can't keep himself from swallowing too much, doesn't give up, tries keeping his chin above water, stands on a berth, a washstand, grabs a chain strung along the ceiling and pulls himself up, but the water fills up the cabin almost to the ceiling, he holds his breath, maybe the room will burst and the water all at once will gush out, some pain, suffocation, he's dead. Eyes closed, his head bobs against the ceiling a few times, then his body rolls over when the half of the ship he's in does. He sinks. Fish are already inside.

Alex was the only passenger on the freighter. His father's patient called his son in England and asked as a favor to the man who's treated his family's teeth for forty years if he could take Alex aboard free. Alex was in London then, wanted to get back home, had little money, could have borrowed plane or ocean liner fare from his parents or Jerry, wanted the experience of being on a freighter during a long crossing. Though he got free passage, he asked to work without pay at any job the captain wanted him to. He'll clean latrines, even, he said in his last letter to Howard. Anything the lowest-grade seaman does, just to get the full feel of it and perhaps seaman's papers for a paid trip later. He was a newsman turned fiction writer. Two months after the ship disappeared a parcel of manuscripts arrived at their parents' apartment from England by surface mail. Maybe the manuscripts he didn't much care about. Maybe the ones he cared most about he took with him on the ship. Howard read the stories and vignettes soon after and then some of them every three or four years till about ten years ago. He never found them very good, but Alex was just starting. Two diaries and some oriental figurines in the parcel also, and lots of letters from his parents, brothers, friends. He'd traveled around the world. Saved up for three years to do it. Did it for a year. A prostitute in a dilapidated hut in a small village outside Bangkok. Why's that experience come to mind first? It was in a letter to Howard, not the diaries. He searched the diaries for it, thinking an elaboration of it might be interesting, revealing, sexually exciting. She was fourteen years old. That made Alex sad. She asked him to marry her. She said she'd be devoted, would learn to cook and make love American, bear him many children if he wanted, all boys if he wanted (she knew how), would return to grade school. He gave her his silver ID bracelet, pleaded with her to give up prostitution. Then he did it a third time with her the same day and came back the next. Talk about hypocrisy! he said. What's the trick of turning a customer into a suitor? he asked. But one who'll be good to her and an adequate provider. If he knew, he'd give it to her. Sent her a pearl necklace from Manila. If he got a venereal disease from her he'd worry more about her than himself. He might go back for her before he leaves for India, or send for her once he gets back to America, and maybe even marry her when she comes of age. Keep this between them just in case it does happen. Taught English to Malaysian businessmen for a month. Met two old men in New Guinea—Canadians—who were living the primitive jungle life. They were good friends of his till they tried to drug and rape him. He's afraid he had to kick them both in the balls to get out of there and then steal their canoe to get back to town. Fell in love with a witch. Read Proust's *Remembrances* in five nearly sleepless days, an experience that's left him dreaming of the books every night for the last six weeks. A Goan fortuneteller told him his trip would end badly. He said to go home by plane, don't sail. Remind him when the time comes, for the man wouldn't take any money. Had a fifteen-year-old girl in Nairobi. What can he tell Howard?—he likes young girls. It's more than just the way their hair blows and breasts point and bellybuttons dimple and thighs are so even. Maybe it's because of all the girls who barely let him pet them when he was a teenager. Rode a camel through part of the Sahara. Ate lizard, locusts, grasshoppers, grubs. Never felt very Jewish before till he started hitting all the old synagogues and Jewish cemeteries he could find in the Orient and Middle East. Wait'll he gets to Poland and Prague and also tries to look the old families up. He's afraid it's converted him, but not to the point of wearing a skullcap. Hitchhiked with a sixteen-year-old sabra through Turkey and Yugoslavia, though she might have been younger. When she had to go back she said she thinks he got her pregnant—her device wasn't put in right a few times, she was so new at it. He told her he's heard that one before, but if she has the baby and the calendrical configurations fix it as his, or just if she still says it is, he'll love and provide for it, adopt it if she wishes and take it to America with or without her or emigrate to Israel if she prefers, marry her if that's what she wants—she's quite striking and clever and potentially very artistic and smart. He's written what he thinks is fairly decent work recently, he said in his last letter. He's glad he's found something he wants to do for the next twenty to thirty years, has Howard?

He's on the deck. It's his watch. Suddenly there's a crash. Bells, sirens. Someone's shouting orders that you have to put your ear to his mouth to hear. They've only minutes. Lots of running around, tying shoelaces and vests. Lifeboats are unhitched. It's late in November. The 27th, 28th. Three days past Ireland. Can't see five feet in front of him because of the rain. They get in two boats. Both are overloaded. Should be a third, but that davit was empty when they sailed. His turns over when it hits the water. He tries swimming to it. Water's too cold and rough. His head's splitting, as if he cracked it on something, but it's the icy water. Tries to tread to stay above it. No control over his legs. Arms feel gone. The flag was Panamanian. Ship was owned by Greeks. Captain was American. Most of the crew's families and the captain's lived in the same Havana housing project. Other lifeboat hit the water well. But something happened. Nobody was found. Only a single life preserver with the ship's name. The Ardy. Arty. Ardie. One of those. Something close. Preserver washed up on the Irish coast two weeks later. Doesn't mean the ship sank, authorities said. Preservers come loose from ships plenty of times in heavy storms and sometimes are thrown off by drunken or angry seamen. And there was definitely a heavy storm at the time. Even preservers from the *Queen* get washed ashore. Even a lifeboat from the *Queen* a couple of times and once even a tender, if that's what it's called. He emerges from a wave and tries to take a deep breath. He couldn't take in much. Feels frozen all over. His chest's killing him. Knows he's going to die but can't fathom it. Can't fathom it. Now that's rich. Think like that some more. Great distraction. Die laughing. Scream some more. Other lifeboat may be right over there. Tries to scream. Maybe he did. Can't hear much with the wind and waves. Tries again. Blacks out. Bobs around awhile, once even bumping into another body.

In the galley eating with some seamen. Soup, bread, potted meat, cheese, coffee. A dinner, lunch, breakfast. It'd be dinner. Distress signal was picked up late at night, or early morning. But ship hours are all hours. While some sleep, others watch. Possibly divided into thirds, engine down there always going. The galley. Food's almost beginning to taste good after three days and lots of work. When big crash. Men and chairs fall, breakage. Sirens, bells, shouts, alarms. Told to get life vests on, over heavy sweaters, heavy socks if they got them in their pockets, but no one return to his cabin. Everyone including the engineers on top deck. Whatever the deck's called. Flight deck because they're in flight. He's especially confused because he's so new at this and doesn't recognize all the signals. Follow someone. He's climbing the hatchway stairs when a ton of water comes down it. Someone's near the top, someone behind, all climbing when the water knocks them to the floor. Ship seems to be shivering, then turning over. They don't know what to do, can't do much. Decks below filling up fast. Water's pouring down the hatchway, preventing them from swimming to it, getting up it. Men struggle around him. One can't swim and is held up by a man who can. The current carries Alex back to the galley. He treads water, looking for something high up to hang on to or something floating to hold him up. Two chairs, which he tries pulling together to make a float, but one flips out of his hand and goes out the galley. A table, which keeps rolling over when he tries climbing on top of it. Can't feel his feet anymore. Lights go. Several of them yelling help from different rooms. No strength left to climb on top of the table anymore so just holds on. Maybe the ship will turn rightside up. Surely the radioman's sent signals. Maybe some men above will do something to help get them up. A line's all he needs with a loop at the end of it. Ships are always near, aren't they? Even fifty miles away, a hundred, they'd be here—at least one would—in hours. Stick it out till then. More than try. Water's so cold. He's going to die, what's there to do about it? Someone shouts something about the aft exit. At the other end, may as well be a mile from him. Table rolls over and he loses it. Reaches out, can't feel anything but blank wall and water. Fingers the wall for a hook. Tries treading while doing this but forgets how to. Dear God, save me. Takes a deep breath, loses most of it, huge rumble from someplace, then a sound like spouting. No use, hasn't got thirty seconds. Puts his arms straight up, opens his mouth wide, says to himself as he sinks "Dear Mother," tries not to squirm and kick but for a few seconds has to.

Sleeping. Top bunk of a double- or triple-decker. Weren't that many men aboard, so maybe they all had single bunks, two or three to a cabin. Dreaming he's back home, having coffee in the kitchen with his mother, when three men run in with tommyguns and start shooting at the ceiling. His younger brother and sister are in the bedroom right above. Blood pours through the holes the bullets made. He lunges at the men when they aim the guns at his mother. Alarm clock goes off in the upstairs bedroom. To wake the kids for school. Ship alarm. He wakes up, says "Huh, what's wrong?" "Emergency, man," his bunkmate says in English or Spanish. "Big one. Only goes off like that when it's the most serious. All-hands-on-deck kind of thing, ship going down, could be. Hurry." Can't be as bad as the guy's saying. Where are his shoes? Gets his sweater and pants from the end of his bunk. Socks are in his shoes. Lights go on and off, alarm continues, men running past their cabin, someone throws open the door and shouts "Out, up." Suddenly the ship's being shoved back and forth. Way it's been for days, but side to side while now it's fore to aft, motion he's never heard of on so large a ship. "My damn shoes, where are they?" "Forget them, man. We could be sinking this minute," and runs out, clothes and vest on. Alex gets two pairs of socks out of his locker and pockets them, vest off the wall, last look under and around his bunk, runs to the stairs putting the vest on. On deck everyone's dressed for very cold weather and rain. "Ship's being abandoned," the first officer says. "We caught something, no time to find out what it is. Nobody fret. We're still radioing and we've time to lower boats and get extra provisions and equipment in." Alex says "I'll freeze without shoes. I'm freezing now." His feet are in an inch of water. "Anyone have extra shoes for this man?" the officer says. Shaking of heads, some say no, wish they did, sorry. "I'll be right back," Alex says. "I'm sure I'll find them this time, or someone's." Runs to the stairs. "Come on back," someone shouts. "You'll hold us all up." Has to hold on tight to get below, brace his hands against the corridor walls as he runs to his cabin. Two to three inches of water already. Shoes are on the unused bunk above his. Doesn't remember putting them there. Someone must have while he slept. Or he did just before he fell asleep exhausted, though he doesn't know why he'd do it. Grabs them. Also another sweater and a watch cap out of his locker. Starts for the stairs. His manuscripts. Hell with them. If any are worth it he'll remember them and rewrite them. Water pours down the stairs. Crunching sound from the deck below his. Ship tips straight up and he falls on his back. Tries crawling upstairs. Ship's righted somewhat, then tips up again. He's thrown downstairs, thinks he hurt badly or broke a leg. Can't stand on it. Ship's also shaking too much. Then vibrating, and a few places in the walls crack. Shoes are gone. Sweater and cap he held on to without knowing it and lets them float away. Lights have gone but he can see the hatchway hole as they may be shooting off flares up there. Enough water below now to swim in. He tries to get to the stairs. Lots of pain but screw it, he's able to swim if he digs in hard and doesn't kick. Orders from above, shouting, constant stack blasts, crunching noises from the sides now too. Ship seems to be rolling over, then tips up but from the other end, dropping him by the stairs. Water's up to the middle steps. He grabs the stair rail, tries pulling himself upstairs, is thrown against the wall, head banging it so hard he's knocked out. He awakes underwater, at the other end of the corridor, water in his lungs, spits out a mouthful, tries to swim, can't, cough up water, can't. Can hardly breathe it seems. Tries, takes in a little water stuck in his nose. Corridor wall rips open and he's sucked out.

Eating dinner with Len, the captain. A good wine. Better food by far than they get from the galley. Len cooked it on a hot plate. He offers Alex a black cigar. "No thanks." "Havanas. You soon won't see these in America anymore." "Ah, why not? You mind if I don't smoke it but give it to my dad when I get home?" "You bet. Anything for your old man. He took care of my teeth when I was a kid, you know. Maybe why I have so few, but that's all right." Holds up his glass. Alex holds up his. "To my precious wife and kids in Cuba and six teeth, at last count, I didn't have to pay for," and they drink. "To my parents and sister and—oh, I don't know how to toast," Alex says, when the intercom buzzes. "Yes? Holy shit," and some nautical terms, sounding like instructions. Tells Alex to quickly get his warmest clothes on, several pairs of socks, cap that fits over his ears, gloves if he has. "Ship might be sinking. Don't worry. We've plenty of time to get into the boats if we have to, and I got to get you back alive and well or I'll never hear the end of it from my old man." Alex runs to his cabin. Bells sounding. Gets his coat, sweater, hat, socks, scarf, fountain pen, ballpoint pens, memobook, sticks what he thinks are his best new manuscripts inside his shirt, picks up his typewriter in its case and wonders if he should try to take it. For the trip he borrowed Howard's portable in exchange for his standard. "Hustle," someone says. "Worse than they thought. Forget all that crap. Just the sweater and cap. Len sent me down to get you in one minute." Entire crew's upstairs. Len says to them "Unbelievable as this is to believe, believe it: the ship's splitting apart. For real. Right down the middle. We didn't hit anything nor I think do anything that wicked or impious on this crossing to whip up the cussedness of the gods. It happens to about one transoceanic ship a year and we seem to be this year's catch. But our boats are in good order, sturdily built and well stocked right down to the prescriptive quart per man of hundred-proof rum. We'll get ten in one, eight in another, five plus oversize me in the smallest. We'll stay close together but not that close to risk ramming one another. Each boat's equipped with an emergency distress signal," or whatever it's called. "Because of the signals we're still putting out and the heavy traffic of this sea lane, I'm reasonably cheerful a ship, even if we haven't pinpointed our location"—or whatever's the expression—"in two days, will pick us up in ten to twelve hours. So hold out, don't start cannibalizing or throwing one another overboard just yet. If we survive the killer wind, rain and cold that's in store for us out there, we'll have come through something almost unheard of, whatever good that'll do us. Good luck. I love you all and loved sailing with you. Alex, you come with me," and they get in the boats and lower them or lower them

117

and get in, Alex's last. His is overturned a few minutes after it's in the water. He tries reaching the boat but the waves keep moving it farther away, or him away from it. Water so cold he can hardly use his limbs a minute into it. "Over here," he yells. "Save me, please get me, it's Alex," just as others are yelling to be saved; most in Spanish. "Where are you, we can't see you, keep yelling so we can find you," other men yell to them, most in Spanish. Then so numb he can't do anything to keep himself up or yell he's there, and sinks. Held his breath and tries getting his head out of the water, but nothing he does pushes it through. His breath breaks, water rushes into his nose and mouth, spits our some, more than what he spit comes in, tries kicking and flapping to get above water, chokes, gags, retches.

Assisting the cook with the ship's supper when the ship jolts, then an explosion. Alarms, bells, the cook says "They say 'Emergency, straight to deck, no stopping in your cabin.'" He's assigned to one of the boats. It's lowered and breaks apart when it hits the water. Or they can't lower it. They cut lines, clip chains, boat still won't lower. Or the boat's in the water and he tries climbing down to it but falls into the water. Or dives in to reach another boat, since none's left on ship, and water's so cold his heart stops, or he has a cardiac arrest or shock, or whatever happens in a heart failure or attack, when he hits the water. Or water so cold he can't come up from the dive. Paralyzes him and he just sinks. Or he's underwater, swimming up. Holds his breath long as he can, but he dove too deep and his mouth bursts.

Huge iceberg hits the ship while he's climbing an outside stairway and knocks him into the water. Or while he's leaning on a stern railing, smoking a cigarette and looking at the water. Or hits the ship while he's sleeping. Cuts right through it to his cabin. There might have been emergency sirens and bells warning of the approaching iceberg, but he slept right through them. He doesn't wake up or feel anything. Slams through so hard and fast he's killed instantly or knocked unconscious while he's reading in bed or further unconscious in his sleep, and drowns without waking. Or wakes for a second or two underwater, goes into shock or coma from the freezing water and drowns without coming out of it. Or wakes while he's thrown from the stairs or his bunk or over or through the railing into the water, blacks out a few seconds after he hits the water and drowns almost instantly or is dead from the impact of the iceberg or being thrown through the railing, before he hits the water.

Ship splits apart just where he's sleeping. Happens so fast he never even senses it. Sleeping, suddenly ship's in two. Ship might have hit something. Or it was some unseen or neglected flaw in its structure that took ten to twenty years to materialize this way. He drops several decks, never wakes up. Is dreaming while he's in bed and while the bunk drops with him in it to the ocean. Of the city, night, stars, flying, gliding, then drowning. In the dream he tries swimming to the surface, then is one of the other crew members on watch seeing his head emerge from the water.

He was sitting on a kitchen chair in Jerry's small living room. Jerry's wife Iris nursed their first child on a couch across from him. Suckling and smacking sounds irritated him. Been irritated by certain repeated or oral or eating sounds like that long as he can remember. Finger drumming. Watermelon and carrot crunching. Couples doing some heated kissing in theaters. Soup-slurping, fingernail clipping, gum-snapping, nervous foot-tapping, snoring, dripping faucets, heavy breathing in sleep (even his kids'). Jerry sat in the rocker Iris usually nursed in, said the ship was long overdue and it didn't look good. "It stinks to be honest. I hate thinking the worst but I'm thinking it. Some emergency distress signals—I forget the exact technical term the Coast Guard spokesman used; in fact that could have been it—were heard in that general area, but briefly. —You OK?" Howard nodded. "That doesn't mean their ship sent them. Another freighter in the same general area could have been testing out its signal-making machine. Any kind of ship. A Coast Guard cutter, for instance, though of course this spokesman would have mentioned if one had been in the area at the time. God, that would have been a miracle, wouldn't it?" Howard looked up. "For one to have been there, on a routine cruise, let's say—east, going west, out there to spy on Soviet submarines, who the hell cares, so long as it saved them. Not a cutter but a regular-sized Coast Guard or Navy ship just miles away—fifty to a hundred miles, even, for those babies move fast. Anyway, the signals were so weak, the spokesman said, that they more than likely came from a much smaller windup crank-type version of this machine on a lifeboat." Howard looked confused. "I'm saying it could have come, these weak distress signals, from a lifeboat launched from Alex's ship. From his lifeboat, even—why not? The machine was battery operated, probably. Though maybe not. Maybe the manual cranking does the operating. I wish I knew more about boats. It could have been a practice drill, everyone to his station and so on, with designated men testing all the ship's emergency distress signals. The spokesman doubts that. He said there would have been an all-clear signal immediately after the distress run. But it was a terrific storm they were in, one of the worst there in years, so maybe Len wanted to be extra cautious and tried out all the distress-signal machines, or just the ones on the lifeboats, and the all-clear signal was never heard by anyone. It's something he might do, from what Dad's said about him. He's an iconoclast, goes his own way always. He once ran guns for Nationalist or Red China; supposedly fought against and then bought off his execution by Thai pirates. But a great captain, I was told—something in our favor. One of the youngest ever to get his master's license for that size ship. He could have been a doctor, a physicist, Dad days. Chose water. But you can see why I think the situation's getting almost hopeless. Since we're talking here about several weak emergency distress signals most likely sent from a lifeboat, one out of who knows how many on that ship, during an unbelievably terrible storm seven, maybe eight days ago."

After the first sip, when Jerry held up his glass of scotch and they silently toasted as they just about always did with their first drink, Howard didn't touch it. After awhile he wasn't even aware he was holding it. He was surprised, when he later walked downstairs, the drink hadn't dropped out of his hand. He could hardly speak. Tried a couple of times, couldn't. Said a few times to himself while Jerry told him about Alex "I don't believe this, I just don't. It can't be happening, couldn't have happened." His throat was a lump. Maybe that was why he couldn't speak or didn't want to. He knew what his voice would sound like and that he'd start crying while he spoke or right after, when what he wanted was to sit calmly as he could and hear everything Jerry was telling him. He was looking for something hopeful in what Jerry was saying. That the storm hadn't been so bad, or if it had, that the ship hadn't gone down, or if it had, that Alex had got on a lifeboat and had already been saved or had survived on the lifeboat till now and would be saved in a day. His fingers felt cold, tingled; chest as if a cold wind whirled around in it. That was what came to him then. Except for a few quick looks at Jerry, he stared into space, at the floor, window, wall of lithos, maybe his glass without realizing it, the baby, Iris. She continued to nurse, sounds of it no longer irritated him. Probably because he told himself a few minutes into Jerry's account "Worrying about some stupid nursing sounds now? That's ridiculous." She took the baby off her breast and held him on her shoulder to burp. Her exposed nipple was erect, fat, very red, wet. It looked like a worm coming out of sand. That also came to him then. Because it glistened he thought it must be the one just sucked. Hadn't seen. Only looked at her breast when she wasn't looking at him and Jerry was looking somewhere else. First he looked at Jerry to see he wasn't looking at him, then at Iris's face and then quickly back to Jerry and if he still wasn't looking at him, quickly at her breast. He was probably caught looking at it by one or both of them a few times, but didn't think of it then. What might they have said later? "Fucking guy, at a time like this, trying to sneak a peak?" "It's natural, he's curious, and it certainly doesn't bother me." If Iris was looking at him when he looked at her face, he nodded or shook his head and looked away. Breast was big and full. Before she got visibly pregnant she seemed, from seeing her in a swimsuit and T-shirt several times, almost flat chested. He'd once looked down one when she didn't have a bra on, didn't see much but bumps. He pictures his lips kissing and tugging at the tip of it, fingers gently pinching the nipple and finger circling its rim. He'd dreamt of making love with her, or starting to, both times both of them naked on the couch and floor and playing with each other when the door banged open and a gruff voice bawled "Virus," but didn't think anything of that then. Baby burped. "That-a-boy," and she put her breast to his mouth which quickly latched on to it. She mostly gazed at his head while he sucked, played with his fingers. Light in the room seemed dimmer than when Howard had come in. Jerry might have dimmed it with a new kind of light switch device he'd recently installed himself that had a name like a heat regulator. Alex had been the handiest, Jerry next, Howard far behind. Alex could take apart and reassemble clocks and radios when he was seven. Just opened them up and went right at it. Maybe Jerry dimmed the lights whenever she started nursing. He remembers her once talking at length about the sensitivity of babies' eyes to sunlight and high-wattage bulbs and fluorescent lights and how even a little of these lights could later lead to color or night blindness. Nobody spoke for about ten minutes, maybe twenty. Solo piano music on the record player. Chopin, Schubert, Schumann, someone like that, inclined toward the high keys and feathery, which Howard just heard but it could have been on since he got there. For all he knew Jerry might have turned the record over a few minutes ago. "You all right?" Jerry said. "Hmm?" "So silent. I can imagine. Listen, it's still not that absolutely hopeless. Even better than that. Did you see the looks Iris was giving me before?" "Nuh." "Well she was, because I'm sure she thinks I made things out to be much worse than she knows even I believe. There's still some hope. Possibly even plenty. We're both sure—Iris and I—there is." Good moment to look at her even while Jerry was looking at him. Few minutes the feeding would be done and blouse buttoned. Doesn't know why he wanted to look so much then. Just young and horny perhaps, sometimes overcoming everything, or he wanted to take his mind off what Jerry was saying.

Both. Maybe deeper, more complicated. When he got home he probably looked out his bedroom window as he did almost every night in hopes of seeing the woman in the next building's back apartment undressing or walking to and from another room nude. Nipple was in the baby's mouth, blouse somehow hid the rest of her breast, either unknowingly or something new. "It's got to turn out all right," Howard said to Jerry. "Ships just don't suddenly disappear in the middle of the North Atlantic like that." "It wasn't in the middle. It was estimated to be about three days past the Irish coast which, weatherwise, is a real trouble area." "Whatever. But to get even a little irrational about it, ships with Alex on them just don't disappear, period." "Some ships, even much larger ones—and for argument's sake we'll forget Alex being on this one—do suddenly disappear without a trace, or with only a minor one. Not all in the North Atlantic, though the greater ratio of them do, but around the world. It's nothing mysterious. They hit something and go down fast. An iceberg, a tree. Or something explodes in them or breaks apart, the ship splitting cleanly in two sometimes." "Come on." "No, it happens. I questioned this expert with the same 'come on' when he told me. You would never think that someone you really know can be the one that something like this happens to when it only happens once or twice a year. But some ship has to be the one, and quite a number of men have to be on that ship and have it happen to them." "Well Alex's ship wasn't the one. It didn't suddenly sink, so couldn't have disappeared. It's either—something tells me this— still out there, adrift, though for some reason hasn't been located. Or has already docked or just drifted to some landing—some little uninhabited island or atoll somewhere—went aground, even, I think they call it, on a pile of rocks in the middle of nowhere—and will get in touch with whoever it's supposed to fairly soon." "I want to believe that as much as anyone. But we also shouldn't be too unrealistic. Same when you go to the hospital for a simple tonsillectomy, we'll say. There has to be some self-preparation for an accident—for the worst. Great surgeons, as well as highly precise machines—" "No mistakes. If so, they'll be corrected. Look, I really got to go. It's been a little too much," and he stood up. "Do you want me to walk you?" "I'll be all right." Kissed Iris on the cheek, patted the baby's head but was careful not to touch where they'd said the soft spot still was. Scared him. He'd imagined a few times his finger going all the way in, wondered why kids that age didn't wear helmets or something. Iris said "You don't know—Jerry would never say it— how hard it was for him to tell you this. Also, now that the folks know you know, it isn't going to be easy with them. So be—well, it's not my place—but try to be extra solicitous and patient." "She's got a point." "I will, don't worry." "Also, because I know how you can get sometimes, though this is perhaps asking you to go too much against your nature, try not to break up in front of them. They'll see you, and then who knows what?" "He'll know what to do." "Don't let off steam or tears. Got it." "You know it's only for their good I asked," she said. "Of course. I only repeated it to remember. Honestly." Jerry walked him to the door. "What else is there to say? I don't envy you at home. Mom will hold up but Dad's sure to cave in." He held out his arms, eyes seemed wet. Howard went to him, Jerry hugged him, they cried. He walked downstairs. He still had his drink. He drank it down. Ice cubes the size of small pebbles and he chewed them. He wanted to return the glass. About to ring the bell, put the glass on the doormat, then to the side of the door so they wouldn't kick it when they left in the morning. Walked downstairs. When he got home his mother was waiting up for him. She was having a drink and smoking a cigarette. She'd smoked several, probably had drunk several. "Jerry told you? Dad's a wreck. Neither of us had the heart to say anything to you ourselves. Or the courage—which one? What's the difference? I had to give him sleeping pills. The first pills like that he ever took, but I told him they were very strong aspirins. A professional man—his patients practically live on those kinds of aspirins—you'd think he'd know. He probably did but he'd never admit it. My poor boy. What a disaster for all of us. It would be so nice to fall asleep for two straight weeks.

124

But the truth is we can do more good by staying awake. Talking to the authorities. Doing what we can to see that the search planes stay up one more day. But what do you think? Will the ship ever be found? Did Jerry hear anything new? Or should we simply give up and tear all our hair out now?"

Ship's a day away from Cuba. Almost two years after the revolution there. Carries lots of medical supplies originally bound for America, guns, launchers, plane and truck parts it hadn't registered in England. Len tells Alex he'll see he gets a good job and apartment and a fine-looking wife if he stays. "If you want, of course, fly back to New York day after we dock in Havana. Or Habana. Might as well get it right from the start. But why go back? You'll live much better there than in the States and for a quarter of the money. Good food, cheap rum, great cafés, unbeatable natural scenery. Gorgeous, excitable, intelligent people, weather couldn't be better, and soon free bread. Stay put. Write up a storm for fifteen years, then let the world see it. Most of the modern writers I've read rushed, rushed, rushed and were eaten up. Or twenty years, twenty-five. You'll be the rare writer with a self-imposed postapprenticeship like that. And you'll be right smack in the heart of a historical hot time, one the whole world's noticing, but who the hell cares about that, right?" Alex likes most of the idea. Sees many women, marries, children, after awhile only speaks Spanish. His wife's a doctor, professor. He builds houses, writes mornings, nights, days off. Misses his parents, brothers, sister. Periodically he wants to write them, call. Things get worse between the two countries, invasion, blockade, harder times. He's told if he wants to leave, do it now, but without his family. He may also write to the States, but phone connections are finished. By now his parents must think he's dead. Gotten over it. His whole family. Or maybe they haven't, but he just doesn't want to have anything to do with the life he had there. Is that it? Misses them all, but no one and nothing else. He wasn't too happy there, he was also something of an adventurer, and now kind of likes it that everyone thinks the ship sank and he's dead. Years. His father's probably dead. Sick before, he couldn't have lasted that much longer. If his mother's also dead he's sure he helped her go faster than she would have. For that he's very sorry. There's more. Knows the pain he caused but didn't want to go back or let anyone know he was alive. Why? The first is easy to explain. In addition to what he's said, he'd never go back without his family. But the other thing...probably because he wanted a new life, or a much different one then, with as little past as possible, a new name, even, though doesn't quite know why. Why? Maybe it comes as close as possible to starting completely over and being someone else, with almost no past—but he's said all that— no family scrutinizing what he's doing, thinking they have the license to comment about and possibly try to change his actions, but that's all. Is that it then? No. Not quite. Maybe doesn't even come close. He just—how can he say this without repeating himself, with something that really gets it? He doesn't know why he did it, and if he does know, why he continued doing it. He's talking about not letting them know he was alive. Maybe he never really loved them that much. Never thought of that. But after about fifteen years he hardly thought of them anymore. After twenty-five years he maybe thought of two or three of them for a half-minute or so once or twice a year. They'd flash in, he'd think "I know you," "I recognize her," "That was Howard when he was a scrawny kid," "Vera before she got sick," "My father with one of his big cigars," they'd flash out. About once every five years or so he got a little heartsick thinking of them, feeling awful about what he'd done, knowing that the ones still alive must think of him more often and much longer than he does them....No, ship's going down. Alarms, sirens, gail wind sounds, maybe hurricane winds. Worse than hurricane winds if there is anything like that. Lightning, thunder, violent rain. Never been in such a storm, heard of one. Can't find a lifeboat or anyone on board. Moves around the ship best he can, holding on all the time so he won't be thrown along a passageway, down a stairway, off the ship. Everyone seems gone. All the boats either smashed by the storm or in the water, some with men in them probably, though he didn't see any of the boats go over and he can't see them now and nobody answers his shouts. He didn't understand the alarm system. It's been explained to him and they even had a quick drill, but when he heard the different bells and sirens going he couldn't tell which meant what. Asked some of the men below what the alarms meant and what he should do, where he should go, but they just shouted in Spanish at him or acted hysterically and pointed their battery lamps several different ways, one of them down, though they were on the lowest deck. Maybe the man meant the ship was going down, but he couldn't speak a word of English or was unable to then and Alex couldn't make himself understood in Spanish to him. He tried following two of them but lost them going through the ship. Couldn't find Len. Went to his cabin; empty. Ship's tipping up. He has to hold on to the railing or fall off the ship. Waves his flashlight and yells out to the water "Help, it's Alex, the American, Americano, Captain Len's friend, there's no one here, I have to get on a lifeboat right away." If he jumps he'll die almost the second he hits the water. "If you're lucky, that is," Len had said. "If you're unlucky it might take two minutes of the worst pain and dread imaginable, two to three, longer for the well-insulated or very fat guy. The shock of the frigid water and because you won't be able to keep your neck above even with a lifejacket on. Or the greatest ecstasy, maybe, but that won't last long." Ship tips up again. He keeps yelling for help, waving the flashlight. Ship points straight up. He's practically standing perpendicular to the deck, holding on tight as he can, flashlight falls to the water, when a wave smacks him, another one and another and he loses his grip and falls. Doesn't want to survive the fall. He's underwater, comes up. Water so cold he's screaming in pain, then yells "Help, hombre here, in water, *agua, agua,* save me, drowning." Sick in the stomach, throws up. Takes in a mouthful of water when he does. Goes under a little, comes up. Spikes in his head, legs feel chopped off. It's all lost, he thinks. I can't take it. Hands so numb he can't unstrap his jacket. Straps loosen enough and he slips out of it, blows out his breath and lets himself go down. For a few seconds, while he's going down, his mind whirls around, stops on a picture of his parents. It's from an old photo.

Frog Reads the News

Sits down, puts on his glasses, picks up the paper, unfolds it. Forgot the coffee. God, what a mind. Forget it. No, wants it. Paper's better with it and it with the paper. Puts the paper down, goes into the kitchen, gets the mug off the stove, goes back to the living room, sits, where's the paper? Sitting on it, sits up, paper, looks for his glasses. Can't believe it. And sometimes he has to look for them ten minutes, fifteen. Goes into the kitchen, probably left them there. Not there. Makes a sweeping look around. They should keep the kitchen neater. Put away things that can be put away. Straighten out the cabinets and shelves, clean the table and countertops, sweep and mop the floor while they're at it, wash the cabinet windows. Room's too confusing now, things open and out of place, it irritates some sense of order in him. Denise thinks he goes too far when he calls something like this disorder. She left most of these things out and drawers and cabinet doors open. Closes and puts away a cereal box, shuts all the cabinet doors, starts for the living room, feels the glasses on his face. How come now and not before? It's happened several times. Funny when it does. If Denise were here he'd tell her. Tell her before he'd tell her they should clean and keep the kitchen neater, clean the whole apartment, really. Dust, scour, sweep, vacuum, mop, tidy up. Get on their knees to clean the bathroom and kitchen baseboards—that's how he does it. If she were in another room he'd go to it to tell her about losing his glasses. "Searched I don't know how long for them." He'd exaggerate. Actually searched three to four minutes and maybe a minute of that were his thoughts about cleaning the kitchen, but to make the story better he'd say ten minutes, fifteen. "High and low, this place and that. Even looked in the breadbox and refrigerator, thinking, who knows, maybe I left them there. Maybe twenty minutes. Went through all the rooms. Got mad, even, and called myself an incredibly absent-minded jerk. I finally gave up and settled back in my reading chair with my spare pair of glasses. I searched that long for them, even though I have this extra pair, because the lost pair is the far better pair by far. Both bifocal parts are larger, less scratched, and the side supports clench my temples better. Well, and this is almost too ridiculous to tell. Unbelievable too. But when I put the spare pair on they hit up against the lost pair already on my face. For about ten seconds I had two pairs of glasses on my face, and for a few seconds I didn't know why I couldn't get the spare pair closer to my face." Maybe he wouldn't go that far. Wonders what two pairs would be like to read with or just look at things through. Try it. Too much effort. No, do. Also in case she asks what they were like to have on. Goes to his study, gets the spare pair off the worktable, goes back to his reading chair, sits, sips, puts the second pair over the first and looks at the paper. When he fits the two together he can read as well as he can with one pair on, at least for the short time he tries it. Surprises him. Distance? Looks around the room—everything seems the same; no headache or eyestrain—out the window. Man he recognizes from the neighborhood jogs by in a jogging suit, pushing a stroller. Could be dangerous if he slips or the stroller hits an uneven pavement block. Lots of them around from the tree roots underneath. Eva's flipped over in it once and he's taken a couple of spills the last few months just walking casually but not abstractedly alone. Seen him a few times when they both pushed strollers opposite ways at a normal walking pace, and they smiled or waved. Even thought of stopping him to talk about what it's like having children so late, man being around his age, and possibly sharing some child-rearing ideas, and maybe next time he will. Would like to see himself in the glasses, for he must look silly. But no mirror in the room and not the time of day to see his reflection in the window. Second pair back in its case, looks at the front page.

Hot and humid it says when it's mild and dry. Photo of the president with his hands cupped to his mouth, probably shouting to reporters. "We're off for both a working and resting weekend," he could be saying. "That's not what we asked, sir." "Kiss my ass, you snooping sonofabitch," he says very low. It's picked up by a TV news crew's long-distance microphone. "Hear what he said?" the sound man says to the crew's reporter. "No, what?" and when he finds out he yells to the president, who's holding his hair down because of the wind from the helicopter's rotors, "Kiss my what, Mr. President?" "I thought we banned those blasted spy mikes from the grounds," he says to an aide. "No, sir, do you want us to?" "What I'd really like," he whispers as they walk up the steps to the helicopter, "is to ban those leeches from coming twenty miles from me and my family." "One last shot, sir?" the aide says. The president grabs his wife's hand, fingers her palm in a way so she'll count three and turn around with him and they'll smile and wave good-bye.

"Will you play Bambi with me?" Olivia says. "I wonder if someone should expect someone else, no matter how young—I mean, within reason—to say 'excuse me' first if he or she expects to intrude on the first person's thoughts." "What?" "Nothing. I didn't say it well. Just babblebraining again." "What?" "What what? What what? Jesus, can't you let me have five freaking minutes of reading peace?" "I'm sorry. Sorry." That beaten look. No, another kind. Eyes like what? But a bit put on. "Actually, I'm sorry. First for cursing." Dog being berated, rabbit threatened with beheading; somewhere between those. "Come on, don't look at me like that any more." "But I'm still sad." "Well, all right. Maybe you should be. For dumb. I was.

For blowing up. Why can't I get it right with you the first time? Straight. You're so bloody disarming." "I'm not bloody." "Just disarming. That's to have no arms. I don't. You take my arms away. Arms for the poor?" and holds out his. "No, I'm not supposed to have any. Because you make me armless, harmless, got it? Don't worry, it's not a word you have to worry about yet." "What isn't?" "Disarming. But I was serious, even if I didn't express it clearly before, that I need a little peace here sometimes. When I need it, in other words. Which means if you have to be in this room—and why shouldn't you when you want, since it's the common room, for us all—please be quieter when you see me reading, or thinking—you know," and shuts his eyes, stoops his head a little and holds his hands open above his head and makes as if he's slowly lowering something over it. "I need peace too," she says. "So go get it. Look at a book. Read the newspaper. But not noisily, snapping the newspaper sheets and stuff. Here, take it, I'm done," and holds it out. "I don't want it. I can't read." "You can read some words. 'Stop. Go. Cold. Hot. Humdrum. Singsong, jingle-jange. Regurgitation.' Well, they all could be the same word, just about," and puts his finger under a word in the paper's maxim at the top left-hand corner of the front page: "News." "News." "Good, you got something from it. Lot more than I have lately." Puts his finger under the word again. "Snooze." "No, news." "Right. Forgot. You know, my father—that was a bad lesson, wasn't it, my news example." "Why?" "Too pushy on my part. Too obvious, which doesn't mean pushy. It means, well, too easy to see. Pushy means—well, not even pushy. Opinionated, that's what I was. Making you, or trying to, believe what I believe with my illustration about news, my example. But what I started to say was that my father loved telling me—no, none of that too." "Your father's dead." "Yes." "Were you very sad?" "It was a long series, meaning one after the other, of serious illnesses he had before he died. I was already a grown man. He wasn't like me in most ways—certainly didn't act to me much like the way I do to you. I was very sad when he died. And he had many good qualities. Lots about him that was good.

He was usually more cheerful than I am. He worked much harder too. He was a better provider, but stingier. He made more money than I, so we lived better in lots of ways—nannies, a big apartment, new cars, camps for the kids all summer. That's being a better provider. Stingy means he wasn't as free with his loot—remember *Babar's Mystery,* loot?—as I seem to be. Am. Usually. Though sometimes I can be tight—stingy, cheap. I think it's because I made very little money working till only a few years ago. I mean, at least for about ten years before those few years ago, *very* little, where I couldn't even buy myself pants. Anyway. . . actually, loot means things taken by a thief, or a soldier during war, so it isn't the right word for money. Let's just say my father wasn't as free and easy with his money as I can be, though at times I've been as tight or stingy as he ever could be and maybe much worse. No, there were some things he did—newspapers on the subway. . ." "What things he did?" "Did he do. I think that's right. 'What things did he do?' And I'll tell you, if I can still remember them then, when you're older. He was also very affectionate lots of times. You know what that means." Nods. "Always—often, rather—he touched my face—every now and then's more like it—with his hand when he'd just walk by on his way to someplace. Or at the dinner table, since for years my seat was on his right. This hand. Or my head. Touched it affectionately. And smiled when he did. A smile that showed he liked me a lot—loved me, even, I could say. What am I saying? The smile said very definitely that he loved me—I'm sure it did, when it went along with his touching my face or head. I could see that then. It still seems that way now. Meaning my opinion of it hasn't changed." "Of what?" "Of his hand on my face or head and the smile that went along with it and what it all meant. That he loved me when he did all that. He kissed me a lot too. All his children. Out of the blue. Meaning when there didn't seem to be any reason for it and so I wasn't expecting it. Just bang, he'd grab me and kiss me. I remember how. Held my face with his hands and kissed me on the cheek or top of the head. Sometimes very wet kisses. He seemed to have very moist lips—

wet, juicy. I didn't mind the wetness of them or what they left on my cheek. Sometimes I rubbed my cheek very hard to get the wet of him off. But I'm sure I did that because people thought it was cute—sweet, funny; you know." "I know what cute is. It's to be nice." "Not nice so much. Pretty. Not pretty either. It's a quality—characteristic, feature, something in somebody—that people respond to—are attracted to, react to, get affected by, like—though some don't. Some people think it's too, well—cute, I mean—cutesy, too sweet, like some candy is. Maybe nice is the best word for it, because cute's almost an impossible word to get another word for, but do you now know what I mean?" "I think so." "Sure you do. Or maybe I shouldn't insist you do if you don't or aren't sure. So: do you know?" "Know what?" "I forget too. What were we talking about?" "I forget too. But I have a story for you." "I know—my father's affectionateness. Let me just go on, sweetheart. Affection. I don't remember this but I bet he closed his eyes when he kissed me. Maybe I don't remember it because mine were closed every time he kissed me. I know for sure it made me feel as good as when he did it as I do when I kiss you, despite his wetness—even with it, that's what despite means," and takes her face between his hands and kisses her forehead. "You shut your eyes, see? Just the way I did when he kissed me, but I didn't to you, so maybe he didn't too. He also had a good sense of humor." "Who?" "My father. At least he laughed a lot and told jokes and said funny lines, though used the same ones many times. For instance 'If I had a dime'—I'd ask him for a comic book, let's say, which cost—" "What kind of book?" "Comic, though that doesn't mean they were funny. That's what comic means. Acutally, 'comical.' No, 'comic' too. One of those cheaply made books on newspaperlike paper, meaning the quality of it, the feel. Feel it." She does. "Though this newspaper, which was the one my parents read when I was a boy, never had comics, which are these little colorful drawn picture stories—colorful in the Sunday papers. That was disappointing to me because all the newspapers my friends' parents read had them. You see what comics and comic books are now?" "Cartoons." "Right. For newspapers and books. So if I asked him for a dime for anything like a comic book or ice cream cone—" "Or candy bar." "No, a candy bar cost five cents then. He'd say 'If I had a dime I'd build a fence around it.' He never seemed to say it with a nickel or quarter, just a dime. For a long time I didn't know what that fence-around-the-dime line meant. Do you?" "He'd build a fence around a dime." "But why?" "It's a special dime. Valuable one. Is a dime money?" "Sure, that littlest coin. Ten cents. So worth now about fifty cents in what it could buy. That's what a comic book must cost today. Or maybe they cost thirty to forty cents but are nowhere near as thick as the comic books I used to buy for a dime. Wait a minute. When I was teaching junior high school years ago—" "What school's that?" "It's a long story. It's difficult. A school for kids much older than you. But I saw that some of these comic books of my students cost a dollar then, so maybe they're up to two dollars now. No, can't be. But I remember when I was a kid when they went from ten to twelve cents and I thought it was too much money. I ended up buying them though and even when they went to fifteen cents. Come to think of it, there were sort of super-comic books at fifteen cents at the time when all the rest were ten, but twice the size of the dime ones." "Will you buy me a comic book?" "Not right now. They're really very silly and dumb. You like regular books, so why degenerate to comicbooks? I didn't like regular books—and not 'degenerate.' I won't even go into what it means. Just why go to comicbooks after you already started with regular books?" "I could have both." "I don't know. I know I wouldn't like reading them to you. They're all so thin and transparent. You can see through them. They're shallow, trivial, not deep, just dumb, plain dumb. Or sensational. To give you a quick charge. A bang, thrill. Garbage, that's what they are. Want me to use a bad word? Crap. And you know, to get off the point—away a little from what I was saying, which was too vituperative. I just cursed and put down and found fault with and, you know, like that, without really thinking. Anyway, I don't remember anyone reading to me, except maybe teachers to the whole class. I'm not saying this to say 'Hey, what a great dad I am.' Just saying it to say that maybe all this happened—my great liking of comicbooks—when I was twice your age and already reading. You're almost four. I was probably eight or ten or even twelve, so triple your age. What I'm saying in all this is that I probably started reading comicbooks before regular ones because the first—" "I can look at them. You don't have to read to me." "We'll talk about it. Truth is, I think I looked at comicbooks before I could read them, and maybe when I was your age. And one probably can't hurt you. Of course it can't. And you'll see how slight they are—thin, junky, good for nothing, what I said before. But maybe there's something good in them and again, I don't want to tell you—well, you know—before you read them. Anyway, my father said his dime-inside-the-fence line to all of us and just about every time we asked for one. My brothers and sister I mean. Or maybe not Vera, my sister, since that pour soul never really had a chance." "What do you mean?" "What do I mean? I shouldn't have brought it up. I meant that she was so sick so very early in her life that if she had asked for a dime from him—and by that time comicbooks probably cost fifteen to twenty-five cents—he probably gave it to her with no dime line or fuss. Maybe he gave her two dimes, two quarters, told her to buy two comicbooks or whatever she wanted the dime or quarter for. What the dime line meant though—but sure he said it to her, for it would have, if he thought this way, made her feel like a normal, regular, one of the children with no sickness, made her laugh. But what the dime line meant was that this dime was so much money, which it wasn't for him—he was just kidding us—that if he had one he'd build a fence around it to protect it. As you might with a thousand dollars." "Or a million." "Right. Which you wouldn't really. Not only—well you don't want to hear anything about bank interest." "Why?" "Because it's dollars, decimals, numbers with diagonals dividing them, separating them, making them into pieces and parts, in this case slashing two numbers, one on top of the other, in half," and makes a slashing motion with his hand, "all pretty boring and complicated. Or maybe not. Maybe you'll become fanatic about

135

fractions and mathematics. Think so?" "Sure." "Two and two. Quick. That's addition. Six?" "Four." "Close. Anyway, we still smiled or laughed every time my father said the dime line because we knew he wanted us to. It made him feel good and if he felt good he'd feel happy and then be good and happy with us. Something like that. And of course we'd be more relaxed after our—after we were first nervous about asking him for the dime, if we all were. I know I usually was, but maybe my brothers weren't. And maybe in this general all-around good mood and feeling he'd have toward us he'd even happily give us the dime without much more fuss. We were connivers, so to speak. Little phonies, fakers, saying, without saying out loud to him, meaning so he could hear, "We'll make you happy, Dad, by laughing or smiling at your old lines and jokes we wouldn't normally laugh or smile at, because we want your dime. Or maybe we laughed or smiled at the lines over and over again because he was so happy, or relatively so, meaning so-so, when he said things like that, or at least easier in feeling and mood than he usually was with us, and that made us feel good and maybe even a little happy too, do you see?" "Not quite well." "That's okay. And mood is what? Dark and what else?" She just stares. "Are you interested?" "Mood?" "Dark and light, like night and day," and frowns and says "Dark" and smiles and goes "Ha-ha" and says "Light. Two different moods, see? Not the laugh and smile but the frown expression, this one," and he frowns, "as against the other two. Forget it. And he did, listen, give us the dime when we smiled or laughed like that. Only time he didn't to me was when I asked in front of older people. Then he'd usually say, after he usually said the dime line and I'd smile or laugh, 'Don't ask for money in front of people.' But say it harshly in front of them. *'Never ask for money in front of people,'* which must have embarrassed me—made me feel bad." "That's too bad." "But I deserved it, I think, since he knew I was only asking in front of these people to better my chances of getting the dime. Since he knew I knew he didn't want to seem cheap in front of them—stingy, that word from before about money." "I know." "But I was saying something else before about what my father loved to say. Liked, loved, way before, about his family. Not the dime. I think I cut myself off," and makes the slashing motion. "That's for cutting yourself off too. Before that bit about the wet kisses." "What was that?" "You remember. My face in his hands. Before the comicbooks and comics and cartoons. Something to do with the news." "I don't remember." "Soon after you asked me to play Bambi with you." "Will you? Bambi and Faline?" "Let me try to get it first. Oh yeah. That he loved to say—" "Newspapers in the subway?" "No, that was when he fished them out of trashcans there on his way home from work when he had his dental office downtown." "What's dental?" "For dentist. His dental office. He was a dentist." "I know. Did he pull your teeth? I hear some dentists pull teeth." "Pull them out. Extract them. Never mine, but he was great at it. Wonderful strong wrists," and grips his and flexes that arm's upperarm muscles, "which he was very proud of. He wanted very much for me to be a dentist. Uncle Jerry too, and my brother Alex, who you never met." She met he, she met him. "*Whom.*" "He died too." "That he did. And maybe because of these wrists my father wanted me to become a dentist. Maybe all his sons had his strong wrists. Feel." She does. "They're bony." "But big. And forearms like his—these are forearms—big and thick too. Good for pulling tough teeth," and pretends to start pulling out one of her teeth with dental forceps, but she flinches and looks afraid and he drops his hands. "And I really shouldn't tell you about the trashcan newspapers. We all hated that habit of his because sometimes when he brought them home they had spit on them and other awful things he didn't see. I remember once opening the *World-Telegram*, a newspaper, but let's forget it. He said that his fathers and uncles all learned to read English, our first language but not theirs—the language we're speaking now, you realize; the words—by reading an English language newspaper every day." "Why not theirs?" "I'm sure they also read a newapaper in their language and probably first thing in the day." "No, not that." "Anyway, not the first thing, of course. That's just an expression. But in the morning after they got out of bed, washed, dressed, before, during or after breakfast or on the subway, trolley—ding-a-ling; trolley—or bus, if they didn't walk to work because it was near or to save on the fare." "Not their newspaper but the language. Why, Mommy?" "Why? That English wasn't their first language?" "Yes." "They came from another country which had different languages than ours, lived for the rest of their lives here. They had to work right away, even when they were ten years old almost, so couldn't go to school to learn English or not for very long. I think that's what my father said. But that's what I started out saying way before: that they learned English through the newspapers. So what, right? No great shakes, I know. And look how long it took me to get to it. Silly. But I'm almost sure it relates to my thinking before that there must be some good to newspapers, and that was one of them. Or was I speaking about comicbooks when I said that 'some good'?" "You were." "It could be newspapers too, then. But now—really, sweetheart, I just want to read this newspaper, so try playing by yourself awhile." "You read the newspaper what's happening?" "Yeah, sure. Or just lie on your bed or sit in the chair there. Or I'll turn on your recordplayer if you want, but you have to leave me be for a few minutes—maybe more—meaning no noise, talking, OK?" "I can't play Bambi and Faline by myself." "You'll have to." "I can't," and looks sad. "OK, I'll play for a minute or two, so long as I don't have to walk on all fours." "What's all fours?" "Please, no more what's-thats after this. It's hands and feet, like deer do," and gets up to demonstrate on the floor, but doesn't. "Or if there's any work entailed—involved—that I have to do—count me out. That means I don't want to play Bambi if working even a little bit hard is part of it. I'll only do it from a silent seated position," and sits and picks up the paper. "Bambi reading the Deer News, okay?" "Yes, Bambi. Bambi," looking around the room as if she can't find something, "do you know where Guri is?" "Who?" "Your daughter, Bambi. I can't find her and I'm afraid." "That's your job, Faline. You take care of the children, I look after the forest. She's not in the newspaper, I'll tell you that." "I know. Do you know where she is,

Bambi?" "I told you, Olivia, I don't." "I'm not Olivia. I'm Faline today."
"I don't know where she is, Faline. Now please, let Bambi finish the
paper. He's had a long rough day running away from wolves,
climbing out of ravines, posing for publicity shots for Disney Studios.
Let him at least get through the front page." "What's that?" "Come
on, how could you not know what it is? This, this one," slapping
it hard. "Okay? The front page? You'll let me read it or just quickly
peruse it?" "Sure," leaves the room.

Peruse. She didn't ask him. She must feel sad now, rejected, very.
Wishes he hadn't chased her out like that. Should go to her room
or wherever she is. Suggest the recordplayer again. "I'll sit and listen
with you awhile, explain what any part of the story means if you're
unsure about it. And 'peruse.' Don't you want to know what it
means?" Or read her a few pages from a story. A whole story.
"Choose the book. Take your time, I'll wait." Hug her, pick her up,
maneuver her legs so they straddle his waist and her head's just
under his chin, kiss it. Tell her while he's holding her that he's
agitated, a different word than agitated, because he doesn't know
what to do with his time right now. Not that but some excuse. That
he doesn't really want to read the paper and also doesn't want to
sit at his desk and work. Some other excuse. Just say he's sorry, he
loses control sometimes, lost it with her, shouldn't. "You know what
flying off the handle means? That's what I did. I don't quite know
where the expression comes from, but it means to suddenly get
excited. People do that and your daddy's human too, right? Don't
answer that. That was a line told by people who told jokes for a living
a long time ago when I was just a few years older than you are now.
Anyway, we talked, worked it out or almost, so it's now okay I hope."
Or suggest going outside with her, taking a ball, buying a fruit bar
at the deli, doing anything she likes outdoors or in.

Statesman dies, rand drops, drought, senate near adjournment,
car bomb, airline folds, dispute temporarily resolved on microchips,
bottom left news briefs of what's inside: high school basketball star
signs for $7 million, aftermath of terrorist synagogue attack, parking

unit aide reports corruption six years ago. Bottom right photo of the governor wearing a colonial hat. "Do I look silly? You bet I do, you big maligners, but you wanna be your party's presidential nominee in two years, you do it, true? I'll say." Seal dies in Maine. For fifteen years the mascot of the watermen in the area. One lobsterman took his boat past the seal's rocks twice a day to feed him. There'll be a funeral and the seal will be buried at sea. What's this doing on the front page? Olivia might like the story other than for the dying. Continues on page 8. Doesn't turn to it. A regional treasure, someone could say. Brought in tons of tourist money, another could say. "Sidney was almost human," someone else, "right down to his whiskers and kissing. Sometimes I thought his barking was like one of our own voices. I could make out real English words. He once told me, with the help of his flippers, the mackerel were jumping a mile from here, and was he ever right? Another time he said he saw a diamond ring in the water and I dropped a net down and got it first crack and sold it for a few hundred." He lived about ten years longer than the average seal. "Human love and care, that's what did it." Mayor will deliver eulogy. Top state officials and the head of the U.S. Fish and Wildlife Department will attend. It'll be a secular service since the seal never professed belonging to any religious faith. Several local seals will play his favorite jazz numbers at the chapel. In lieu of flowers please make all donations to the Sidney Seal Foundation, a fund set up to permanently drop fish in his nesting place in the bay.

Gets up, shoves the newspaper through the lid in the kitchen trashcan, walks around the room a few times, opens the refrigerator, grabs a slice of pastrami and eats it, drinks straight from the cranberry juice jar—Denise would object, saying it set a bad example for the kids and might even be unhealthy for anyone else who drinks the juice—gets two mop buckets and some rags out, fills the buckets with warm water, adds ammonia to one of them, gets on his knees and cleans the floor, then dries it with paper towels. Looks in the freezer compartment, sees stewing veal there, cuts up celery, carrots, onions, potatoes, puts it all in a pot with some spices and herbs and water and starts a stew going. Is cleaning the kitchen counter he did the cutting on when he remembers. "Olivia, Olivia, come help daddy in the kitchen." Doesn't know what he'll ask her to do, but something. "Olivia?" Goes to her room. She's sleeping on the covers. Recordplayer's on. *Bambi,* not the Walt Disney version she has but a woman reading from the Salten book in an English accent. He sits on the floor beside her bed, puts his hand over hers, kisses her cheek, again. Stares at her. Way her long curly hair falls over her face, rests on the pillow. So beautiful. Red in her cheeks, pacific expression. So good, interesting, clever, lively, imaginative, everything. Not pacific but beatific. Overused, but nothing short of it. Should reduce the heat under the stew, must be boiling by now. Goes to the kitchen. Not boiling yet, waits, takes the paper out of the trashcan, since Denise will want to look at it, flicks some rice kernels and an oily lettuce leaf off it, flattens it till it looks not thrown away but well read over lunch.

Frog Acts

In bed, must be late, no car traffic outside, light coming in, been asleep, up, asleep again, hears a noise in the apartment. He's on his side, front to his wife's back, both no clothes, hand on her thigh. Kids in the bedrooms down the hall. Light noise again. Could be the cat. Whispers "Denise, you hear anything? Denise?" Doesn't say anything, still asleep. He's quiet, holds his breath, listens. Nothing. Lets out his breath, holds it again. Sound of feet. Something. Moving slowly, sliding almost. Sliding, that's the sound. Could be the cat doing something unusual. Slight floorboard squeak. Cat's made that too. Should get up. Scared. Cold feeling in his stomach, on his face. Has to do something, what, scream? If it's someone then that person might get excited, frightened, start shooting, let's say, knifing. He could be in one of the kids' rooms, at one of their doors. Gets on his back, holds his breath. No sound. Lets it out, holds it. Shuffling. Sure of it. Down the hall's wood floor, just a few inches. Shuffling stops, as if he picked up Howard listening. Now he doesn't want to tell Denise. She might jump, afraid, scream, panic, man could then panic, start shooting, knifing, clubbing, something, if there is anyone there. Should get out there to see. If it's someone, face him, but with a stick, knife, something, though without saying anything

142

to Denise. For now let her sleep. Man sees her he might quickly shoot or knife him, feeling outnumbered, one to grab him, other to phone the police. Or just keep the gun or knife on her while he rapes her and Howard does nothing, stands there, saying to himself "Fuck it, I'll kill him, kill him," kids watching too. Better to surprise him, and not have Denise spoil that surprise, and try to get him out or down. If someone's there. Concentrates on his ears, holds his breath. Nothing. Holds his breath. Nothing. Holds. Something. Shuffling. Inches. Even the sound of breathing. Almost positive. Light breath, as if trying to contain it, now no more. Lets his breath out. Stomach cold, neck sweaty, face cold, feels queasy, weak. But can't be weak. Must think of something. Where could the man be if he's there? Can't tell exactly by the sounds. Somewhere in the hall. Near one of the doors? The cat? Cats don't make that shuffling sound. Wind. Doesn't seem possible. All the windows are closed. Did it when he made the rounds before he went to bed. Maybe he forgot a window, upper or lower part, or didn't close one all the way. What else could it be but that? Wind blowing a paper down the hall floor. Could be. Cats can get frisky when they're asleep. Should find out. Has to. But must be ready to come upon someone, do something, shout, kick, jump at him, hit him with something, take a wound or blow but still try to disarm him and get him down. For he's in good shape and always was strong and as a kid a fierce fighter, so might be able to knock even a fairly big man down. Could probably knock most men down if he surprises them or in a fair fight. If he gets him down or wrestles the weapon away, if there's one, then what? Then hit him hard. In the face. Kick him in the face, in the balls, pick up his head and bat it against the floor. Hit him with the gun butt if necessary. Just hit him in the head with it or anything around as hard as he can, several times, lots, but make sure the gun, if there's one, doesn't go off. Knows little about them. Just pull the trigger with the barrel aimed at him even, for what's to know? Gun's cocked, uncock it, pull the trigger, gun goes off. If it's not cocked, just shoot. No bullets in the gun, bang the butt against the man's head. Do it, if it comes to it, if the man keeps coming, if there's a man, a gun. If it's a knife and he gets it away and the man keeps coming, same thing, stick it in him. Or just hold one or the other to him and say "Don't move or I'll shoot; Don't move or I'll stick it in you, right through you if I have to." And have Denise call the police. If she's screaming, shout for her to immediately calm down. Yell out the window for help and at the top of his lungs for his neighbors to come. Break the window even to yell out of it. Noise will attract some; shouting, others. Ones right above are old, very, couldn't help, might not even hear. One below, new one with his wife, he'd come and help. He might even kick the man's face in and maybe shoot him, if they grabbed the man and told him not to move and he did. Something about him. Makes him think he even has his own gun. An accountant, moved here from a large home, kids in college, but he's a tough guy, he's talked tough and half of it against crime, what partly made them sell their house and move here: burglaries, couple of neighborhood rapes. But get out of bed now. Slowly, quietly. Find something to swing with. Best move. Be senseless not to. If the man has no weapon, he'd have the advantage. If there is a man there. Holds his breath. Nothing. Holds. Moving. Shuffling. Touching, something with his body. The wall, a door, and more creaking. That's it. Up.

Gets out of bed, his underpants off the floor and puts them on. In case he has to run into the public hallway or the street. Anyway, they're briefs and he'll be less vulnerable down there and also look stronger in them than with none on and everything hanging. A consideration. Might mean nothing. But he's big chested, narrow waisted, in the mirror he can look powerful. Looks around, room dark, little streetlight through the shade cracks is all. Denise asleep. He has nothing. Lamp? Won't do. Too big, won't swing. Then what? What's he have? VCR, TV, two of the same kind of lamps, night tables, rocking chair, Denise's typewriter on her desk, clamp lamp above it, would collapse on impact, framed photos and prints on the wall, dresser, drawers, clothes, shoes in the closet and under the bed, maybe her boots. Couldn't get a good grip on the leather tops. Night table, a foldup, on her side, probably lots of little things on it next to the lamp and books. Grab it by the legs and just rush the man. Or fold it up and wield it like a sledgehammer. Light enough to and in an open space he could really swing it. Goes around the bed, gets on the floor and unplugs the lamp, takes it off the table and sets it on the floor. Denise stirs. He stops. She lifts her head, turns it to him. He bends down to her ear, puts his hand over her mouth. "Shh," he whispers. "Don't speak. I think we're being robbed. Almost sure of it. I'll handle it, shh." She takes his hand away. "What are you doing?" she whispers. "Shh, shh. I'm going to use the table on him. Just in case. Don't worry." "Don't," she says; "wait; let me think." "The kids. No time. I have to. It'll be OK. Get up quietly and stand by the phone. Don't pick it up. Then when I say to, call the police. Shh. No other words. No questions." He puts the books on the floor. She gets off the other side of the bed. He brushes the things off the table into his hand. Earstuds, paperclip, pencil, spool of thread but no needle in it, feels around, no needle on the table, used tissues, face cream, sea shells, what feel like nail clippings, puts them on the bed. She's by the phone on the VCR. For a few seconds her hands over her face. "Shh, don't cry or let on you're here," he whispers; "important." Picks up the table by its legs, takes a deep breath but not to hear, lets it out and yells "I'm coming, you bastard—Call, call now," he whispers; "911, but quietly—You better get the hell out the way you came in and quick. Now out, get, out." Hears movement, feet going, running. "There's someone." "Police," she says low, "we need help. A burglar in our apartment." Gives the address, name, phone and apartment numbers. Both kids screaming. "Stay away, you fucker," and runs down the hall holding the table straight out in front of him. Man's not there. "You OK? It's Daddy," to Olivia. Her room's dark but she's nodding, now crying. Man's not in the bathroom. Goes into Eva's room at the end of the hall. She's standing in her crib screaming. Goes into the hall leading to the living room, feels the front door. Still locked and chained. Looks through the hall door into the kitchen. Nobody seems to be there. Walks down the hall to the living room, table in front of him. "I'm coming. I can kill you. I have a gun." "Don't say that," Denise says from somewhere in back. "You came through the kitchen, get out that way." The man runs from the living room into the dining room, then into the kitchen. Howard follows slowly. "Get out, get out." Can't see his face. Just a silhouette of him. Tall, thin, bald or hair cut close or skull shaved or wearing a stocking over his face. Running sound as if he has sneakers on. Tries to open the kitchen door to the fire escape. Why'd he shut it? Must have been the way he came in. It was locked when they went to bed. Must have shut it so the wind wouldn't wake them, wind or cold. Something. Door can get stuck. He's trying to pull it open. "Fucking-ass door. What's with it? Fuck you then," turning to Howard at the dining room door. "I'll kill you first if you come get me." "Just go and no killing," keeping the table straight out. "Fuck you, man, you haven't got nothing but that fucking board. Probably cardboard. Now back up. I've got a knife bigger than you." Howard backs up, table still in front of him. The man holds the knife out and starts to him. "Listen, just go out through the door over there on your right and we'll forget it." "Yeah, why?" "Just unlock and unchain it, that's all, and leave. You've time." "Give me all your money and I'll go. I'm not going without your money. Get your fucking wife to get it, and fast." "There's nobody else here." "You crazy?" "Just my little kid; that's who you heard." Still coming. What to do? Backs up. "Police are on the way. I set off an alarm second I heard you. I've been robbed here before. I know what to do." "Sure. And you got an alarm, you got money. Come on. Wasting my time. Fast." Anything to throw at him? Shout and he might leap at him with the knife. Fingers the table behind him for something to throw. Maybe the bottle of wine if they didn't put it away. Little silver wine holder; too light. Salt and pepper shakers, kid's boardbook, place settings, baby's spoon. Guy's too close. If he darts either way to get away the knife could reach him. Lunge at him with the table, then drop it if it doesn't knock the knife away and run into the living room. Throws the table at him, runs, knife slashes his shoulder, nicks his

146

arm. In the living room he remembers the stick to hold the window up lying on the sill. Grabs it. Blood all over the place but so what? Man's in the living room. No pain, isn't weak, cuts don't seem deep. Swings the stick back and forth, blood spattering the window and walls, and says "Fuck it, now I've had it. Get out—I'll bust your goddamn head in," and runs to the fireplace and grabs the wood Japanese statue off of it and swings both in front of him. "Bullshit, you can't do anything. Get your money—come on." "Help, police, someone, a burglar here, a killer," he shouts and then knocks things off the shelves with the statue and stick to wake Gil downstairs, get him here. Runs to the floor lamp behind the armchair and turns it on. Denise is screaming in back, kids screaming. For a few seconds he can't see anything. Man's rubbing his eyes too. Young man. Shaved skull. No stocking. Late teens, maybe twenty. Long tight upperarms, enormous hands. Black nylon undershirt. Bright celestial design—circles in circles—in the middle of it. Big teeth and awful face. Taller than he thought. Six, six-one. Knife out. Long enough to go through him. Like a hunting kinfe. A survival knife he thinks he's seen it advertised as. "You dumb prick," the man says. "Get the kids in a room, Denise, and lock the door," he shouts behind the chair. "Get it closed. Any room. The bathroom. It has a lock, you hear? Do you hear?" "Yes," she yells. "What're they doing?" the man says, looking down the front hall. "Are you locked in?" Howard shouts. "Just about," she says. Man rushes down the hall. Howard runs after him with the statue and stick. Door slams, locking sound. "Take what you want now," Howard says to his back and runs into the kitchen, drops the statue into the sink, kicks the bottom of the door, pulls the door loose, gets on the fire escape and down the ladder and drops to the ground.

Runs to the sidewalk screaming "Help, police, murderer in our apartment, 35 Ribeka, second floor." Was that good to do? Denise. Man might break the bathroom lock. Runs around the building and rings all the tenants' bells. "What?" someone says. "Yes?" "Hello?" "Who's there?" others say. "Not all at once," he says. "It's Howard

Tetch. There's a murderer in my apartment and my family's there. I just got out through the fire escape but they're in the bathroom. My wife and kids. Ring me in." Lots of buzzing. One person says "Oh Lord" over the intercom. He goes in, runs back to the door, holds it open with his foot, stretches over and rings all the bells. "Yes?" "What is it?" "Who's there?" "Does anyone have a gun? If you do, could you bring it to me at my door or just by the staircase?" No answer. "If you do have one, loaded—please." Runs upstairs, down the hall, bangs on his door. "I'm coming in with the cops, you bastard, so you better get the hell out. The door to the fire escape's open. Denise, you all right?" Doesn't hear anything. Thinks he hears something. "Yell if you're all right, Denise." "Yes, OK," she yells. "Stay there." Runs back down the hall, into the short alcove that has a door at the end of it opening onto the fire escape. Opens it, gets on the escape, man doesn't seem to have left, not a person on the sidewalk. Goes into the apartment, gets the big cutting knife out of the drawer, bottle of ammonia under the sink, fills up a water glass with it, walks into the front hall. Man's not there. Holds his breath. Can't hear him, maybe because Olivia's still crying. Maybe he did leave. "I advise you to get out now, fella. You have my permission. Go through the front door," unchaining and unlocking it and throwing it open, "or the outside kitchen door. That's open now too." The two women in the apartment across the hall look at him through their half-opened door. "What's wrong?" one of them says. "You're bleeding something awful." "Call the police. Burglar with a knife might still be inside. If he comes out—you hear this, burglar? If you come out, I'm telling my neighbors across the hall, they should let you go. Don't even try to stop him or even scream," he shouts to the women. "I'm stepping back now, burglar. I mean I'm going to the middle of the front hall but against the wall without the door. The front hall's the one by the opened front door. If you're in the living room, go out through the dining room into the kitchen or just go past me through the front door or just any way you want to go. Through the dining room into the kitchen and then out the kitchen door to the front door in the front hall. Or you want me to go into any other room but the bathroom when you leave, say so. But you better do it fast. The police have to be here soon. But if you try anything funny before you leave, I've a glass of ammonia I'm holding that I'll throw in your eyes and several knives and something to chop off your head too. Do you hear? You going or not?" "I hear," from the back hall or one of the kids' rooms. "It sounds like a trap." "It isn't. Just go. I won't stop you. You can understand why. I just want you out." "I don't know." "Through the kitchen door and down the fire escape's the best and quickest way. I did it myself just before to get out. It's easy." Listens. Nothing. No sound from the bathroom too. "I have that door wide open now. I came back through the building's hallway onto the fire escape. You can even go out that way if you want and down the stairs and out the building's front door. But you'll probably have a better chance of escaping through the kitchen door to the fire escape and down the ladder. It's still dark out there; nobody will see you. Anyway, you better be going." "OK, I'm going. Out the kitchen door. Step into the fucking living room." "Anything you say." "No tricks. You die before you pull something on me." "Don't worry, none. I just want you gone." Man runs into the kitchen and out the kitchen door. Howard goes into the kitchen, sees him hanging from the ladder about to drop, goes on the fire escape and says "I hope you break your fucking leg, you bastard. Break it. Drop, you bastard, fucker, sonofabitch," and leans over and spills the ammonia on his head. The man screams. Howard goes into the kitchen to get the rest of the ammonia but when he gets to the fire escape the man's gone. "Thief on the street, tall guy," he shouts. "Shaved skull, black T-shirt with no sleeves—an undershirt, sneakers. Thief, broke into our apartment, has a big knife." Denise comes into the kitchen carrying Eva and her arm around Olivia. "Good God, your arm." "All over. Something not to be believed, right?" and shuts and locks the door. "You have to take care of that. Is it deep?" "Two places. Not deep. Got it with his knife. One's already stopped." "Daddy's bleeding," Olivia says. "It's not so bad, sweetie," and washes the arm down with a wet dishtowel and holds a bunch of paper towels to his shoulder. Knock on the door. He starts. "Is it OK now?" one of the two women says. Beverly or Rhonda. Can never get their names straight, when he remembers their names. "There really was a burglar here?" she says, both coming into the kitchen. "Excuse me," turning away, the other going back out. "Let me get a bathrobe on," he says and kisses Denise, Olivia, top of Eva's head, says to the other woman in the front hall "Go back in there; I'll be right out," goes into the bathroom, washes the blood off the rest of his body, puts antiseptic on the cuts, gets his bathrobe on, the handkerchief out of the bathrobe pocket and holds it to the shoulder cut, goes to the kitchen. "Have you seen the cat?" he says to the three women. "She might have got out." "In our closet," Denise says. "She was as scared as the rest of us." "That sonofabitch," he says. "I thought we were done for, all of us," and closes his eyes, feels like crying but doesn't want to scare the kids more than they've been so holds back. "We called the police," Beverly or Rhonda says. "Thank you." Bell rings from downstairs. "That must be them," one of the women and Denise say at the same time. He presses the intercom's talk button and says "Yes, police?" "It's me, you fag. I know where you are. I'll get you for burning me. We had a deal. I'll get you good. Knife in your heart when you're not looking. When you're in bed or walking on the street." "Try it," he shouts, "just try it. I'll be armed from now on. No bullshit, I'm not kidding, so try it. I'll kill you first." Presses the listen button. No answer. Presses the talk button. "Did you hear me, killer? I said did you hear me? Just try your shit with me and you're dead." "Forget it," Denise says. "Really, he's probably gone. Just shut the door and I'll get the girls back in bed." He shuts the front door. "Need any help?" Beverly or Rhonda says to Denise. "No thanks, you've been very helpful as it is." "You know, this same thing happened this summer in this building." Denise shakes her head, indicates with her eyes the kids. She takes them to their rooms and the woman says to Howard "It did, almost the same thing. We didn't tell you. We forgot. When you were away. To the people who moved into F-5. But after it happened, moved out the next week. He took their money and jewelry and some other things and threatened to hurt them but didn't. I forget what they said he looked like except he was white. Do you remember, Ron?" "Not exactly. He wasn't so young, that I remember. Forty, they said, closer to fifty, and very dirty looking. They were surprised he was still hoisting himself up to fire escapes at that age." "Mine was much younger and actually pretty clean looking, and black. It's terrible, though, whenever it happens." "Fortunately, nobody got too hurt." Beverly grabs Rhonda's arm, says "That's enough chatter if we want to let Howard get back to sleep," and he sees them to the door. He goes to the back hall. Eva's already asleep. Olivia's room is dark, Denise is humming a tune to her, when he hears a siren. Siren stops, he sees flashing through the living room window, must be the light on top of the car. Then more sirens, cars, flashing, doors slamming, two-way radio and talk and static, voices in the street. He goes downstairs to meet them. Doesn't want them ringing the downstairs bell, which is loud, or even coming up, as they might wake up the kids and scare them. But he's sure they'll want to see things and make a report.

He gives a description of the man. "Most victims don't catch half as much as that," a policeman says. "But by now he's probably thrown away that shirt and has his jacket, hat and a pair of fake eyeglasses on." They look around the apartment. "He'll probably never show up again, but you never know. Usually those big revenge threats are baseless and if they don't get any of your I.D.s, they hardly remember what neighborhood you live in. But your place is very vulnerable, so I'd get a few crossbars installed over the kitchen door and possibly even a much stronger door with thick plastic windows in it instead of glass. Door you have a foot could push in with one kick." They go. He washes and dresses his cuts, cleans up the apartment, puts the kids' place mats and the rest of their little silverware and Eva's table seat on the table to get a head start in the morning, makes himself a vodka and grapefruit juice, drinks it down, makes another but after the first sip sticks it in the freezer for one of tomorrow's predinner drinks. One made him more than enough relaxed. But maybe he shouldn't get so relaxed. Maybe the guy will come back tonight, thinking it's the time he'd least expect him to. Doubts it. He'll think police will be cruising around. Goes into the bedroom with the stick. Lights are off, shades up, Denise in bed. "Are you asleep?" "How can I be? And watch out for the phone cord on the floor. I'll probably be up all night." Phone's by her side of the bed on the floor, far as the cord could go. "I'll probably be up all night myself," he says. "No, sleep, I'll stay awake and tell you if I hear anything." "No no, you sleep." He lies down on his back on top of the covers, yawns, feels sleepy, gets up, takes off his bathrobe, gets under the covers, stick by his hand at the edge of the bed. Should he get a jarful of ammonia? No, just the smell of it, even with the cap tight, might keep her up. "You still up?" "Yes; I told you. How's your arm?" "Fine. I took care of it. They won't—he won't—I don't know why I said they—come back tonight. Tomorrow I'll get a locksmith and see about getting a new lock for the kitchen door." "Call the landlord and tell him what happened. Ask him for a new door and a couple of better locks for it. No more hook and latch and skeleton key. We want real burglar-preventive locks—even an alarm on the door to go off, if someone tries. We pay enough rent." "Tomorrow I'll do that." "You don't, I will." "I will; I said so. Now you go to sleep. It's silly for both of us to stay up." "You went through enough; I'll stay up." "You didn't go through enough?" "I did, but you did more. What you did—I can't believe it. Not that you haven't done something like that before. But I don't think it ever got so bad where you were cut like that and faced the man so close." "Oh no, my head—remember?" "That's right. The intruder, at school." "And that time—hey, I just remembered something. Gil never came upstairs when I knocked everything to the floor to get him to come. Broke some very nice things too. I'm sorry. The bell jar and both figurines, did you notice?" "Too bad. It doesn't matter though. You didn't throw them away, did you?" "Yes; in the garbage. They were in pieces." "I'll get them out tomorrow. And Gil and Jane are away for a few days, that's why." "If he wasn't

I'm sure he would have come when I yelled and banged. But that time when I stood on the sidewalk and acted like a total misfit to some guy who had a gun on two men. In a vestibule. Where the mailboxes are. On my street. A gun. But I thought I knew what kind it was. A .45. You don't want to hear this again." "It's been a long time since you told me it." "It looked like a .45. At least I'd seen pictures of the gun—movies, newspapers, comics as a kid. Like a big black try square. And someone who knew, he'd been an M.P. in the army, had told me it couldn't shoot straight more than fifteen feet and the guy in the vestibule was about twenty-five feet away and down a few steps. Somehow I also didn't believe he'd shoot at me. He was a big chubby fellow, with a nice fat face. Shirt out under his jacket—a real shlub. Looked like my cousin Nat." "Still, it was something to do. You saved those men from God knows what." "He wanted them to take him up to their apartment. Rape, robbery, even worse—they didn't know and he wouldn't say. I just kept acting like an idiot out there, jumping up and down on one foot, hooting, cackling, blubbering with my finger over my lips, looking at the sky in great wonder and then down at my feet as if I were searching for something every time he turned to look at me. It worked. He came out, his back to the men facing me with their arms still raised, put the gun under his belt, looked at me as if he could squash me with that look and very casually walked down the street. I ducked behind a parked car." "And later ran up the block—" "Right. Immediately. The police call box didn't work. Nor the fire one attached to it. I wanted Fire to call the police to grab this guy whom I could still see walking down the street. And then the fellow who broke into my apartment. When we were just going together. Same thing as tonight's, just about. Two or three A.M. Maybe later. I heard him, just as I did this one—" "How long had you heard him?" "Which one?" "This one." "Minutes. I didn't know what it was. Thought it could be Kitty or the wind." "I'm glad you heard him. I was sound asleep. Who knows what he would have done if he'd surprised us." "That's what I thought. And after being up against the guy. . ." "But

what happened then—years ago?" "You don't remember?" "Just tell
me." "It'll keep you up. Go to sleep, really." "No, tell me." "You know
I don't like telling a story if I know the person heard it or knows
it fairly well." "Tell." "I didn't know what to do. I just lay in bed—sat
up, rather—thinking 'Lamp? Watch? What could I throw at him,
defend myself with?' I had nothing, just like tonight. Then—it was
pitch black but maybe my eyes were adjusting to it—he moved his
head slowly past the bedroom door frame, looking in. He had a
stocking over it, just as I thought this one might, and he must have
been six-six from where his head was behind the door. I measured
it right after and it scared the hell out of me he was so big. But I
did something that just came out of me—I actually didn't think. I
made the sound of a ghost. First very low—ohhhh—and then louder
and higher till I became a screaming ghost, but the same long oh
without break from start to finish. He ran right out through the
kitchen window he'd come in and onto the roof. And then, I suppose,
along the other roofs till he got himself down someplace, while I
yelled outside 'Thief on the roofs, close your windows; thief along
the roofs of the 200 block of West Twenty-eighth,' and maybe even
that it was the odd-numbered side of the 200 block, and then locked
my window. I slept with a bat, wish I had that bat now, but a bat
I bought the next day—slept with it for three months. Held it while
I slept sometimes. You remember—even when you were with me."
"You put it on the floor then." "I did, I didn't, I don't remember—
maybe only when we made love. I'll probably sleep with this stick
for three months. Or a bat. I should buy a bat. Or a gun. Should
I get a gun?" "What?" "Of course not, but I bet I'd be able to get
a license for one now." "What about that time, though, you grabbed
a gun from a man's hand when he pointed it at a hot dog vendor,
and he even shot him, didn't he?" "It was a fake gun—wood, painted
silver, maybe his kid's—but I didn't know it. Fact is, and this is
probably the shot I told you about, when I was struggling to keep
his arm up I could have sworn I heard the gun go off in my ear. Could
have been a car backfire or construction work explosion nearby, but

neither would have been that loud. Anyway, my ears rang for a day—it's ridiculous. The guy who did it claimed the hot dog man had put ground glass in the mustard, so he pulled out the gun. That's the story the vendor told later. I saw the gun, and again, I don't know where it came from in me, but I went up behind him—it was in broad daylight, a busy street. Or the park—I forget, but lots of people around—Grand Army Plaza, that's where, if that's what it's called—opposite the Plaza Hotel. After the police took the guy away, the hot dog man offered me free franks with everything on them and any other time when I saw him selling franks in the street. It was all so crazy." "Did you have any?" "I don't remember. Probably not. I hate those things, all pork ears and snouts, and who knows where those vendors piss outside, or wash their hands after, or with what." "What about the robbery you stopped in a supermarket?" "Come on, enough." "Just that one. I forget it completely, except for the razors." "Razorstrops. Who knows where they got them from. Five boys, none older than thirteen it seemed, and they ran and slapped those strops against the checkout counters and demanded all the money and food stamps from the checkers. I was waiting on line with my cart and yelled 'Get out of here, you brats,' and they swung the strops at me and hissed and things like that, but from ten and more feet away, and then ran out. I don't know what I would have defended myself with if they had attacked. Bread. Can of frozen concentrated grapefruit juice." "Those dividers they have on the counters. Were there other times?" "A couple. Maybe more. Let's forget them. I am tired." "The doors are all locked as well as they can be?" "Roger." "Let me check the girls again." "I'll do it."

Gets out of bed, thinks of taking the stick, leaves it. Goes into Olivia's room. Covers are on her, she's alseep, kisses her, strokes her head. Eva's room. Asleep, covers off, puts her back on her stomach, covers over her, reaches down to kiss her. Mattress position in the crib so deep his lips can't reach her, so he strokes her head, leaves his hand on her forehead. Goes through the apartment. Everything OK. Jumps when the cat walks into the living room, cat runs away.

Goes back to bed, under the covers, holds the stick. "Denise?" No sound. Holds his breath. She's breathing lightly, on her side, back to him. Lets go of the stick and snuggles up to her. She's wearing a bathrobe. Pulls it above her waist, nothing on underneath, sticks his penis between her thighs and leaves it there. Doesn't want to bother her. Really doesn't. If he gets an erection he won't do anything like press even closer to her, wiggle around a bit to show he's interested in making love if she is. Kisses her shoulder through the robe, her neck. "Do you want me to get up and put the thing in?" she says. "I'm sorry. No. I thought you were asleep. I didn't kiss you for that. Just as a good-night." "Oh?" "No, really." "It might get rid of some of your tension." "And yours, but better we just sleep. We haven't got many hours left and the kids might get up again tonight." "I don't mind if you don't. If I stop being involved in it it'll only be because I'm too sleepy or still too nervous or something of before all of a sudden came back to me and took my mind off it, but you just go ahead." "Same here then. OK." "OK I should get up?" "Sure, if you really don't mind and it's not too much trouble. But I don't want you to think I needed all that fighting and violence to incite it. I'm perfectly happy to go to sleep now holding you like this." "How about if I put it in just in case?" and she gets out of bed and goes to the dresser.

Frog Wants Out

In bed he says "I don't want to go on with what I'm doing. I have to find something else."

"Become a plumber."

"What could I do? I should have been a cop. My dad actually said 'If you can't become a doctor or dentist, become a teacher or cop. Good money and your own hours in the first group, long paid vacations and early retirement in the second.' As a cop I could have been semiretired by now or even three or four years ago."

"That's just what you needed to have become. I'd be a widow or close. You could be lying beside me now with a bullet or part of one in your spine. I'd have to feed and dress you, wipe your backside every day for years. Maybe several times a day, because you'd be incontinent."

"I would tell you to get a divorce, take other men, remarry, move out."

"I wouldn't want to."

"You would after awhile. Or I'd have divorced you by now, got myself an apartment in some special building for handicapped cops. I wouldn't let you come see me. I would probably let the kids come. But if I hadn't got shot, because I would have been extra careful to avoid it—"

"Not with your temperament and always sticking your nose and often your whole body in. You would have been shot two to three different times and the third time would have paralyzed or killed you. That's the way I see it."

"What about being a wine grower? I think I'd like to be away from people and so totally occupied like that. In the hills, probably remote dry ones, so even while I'm sweating hard from all the work it wouldn't be that humid and hot—the air wouldn't. Good smells, sights, fresh wine, and all of it except the wine good for the kids too."

"You know nothing about wine growing. Vorticulture? Vinticulture? The kids would hate it, taking a bus to school for an hour each way, and so few playmates around."

"They'd love it there. Living in a house. Family very tight. Maybe pitching in with the work. Horses, sheep maybe, rabbits bounding around, lots of dogs."

"You'd complain about the dog crap all over. The work would be too tough. It's too late to start out so late. It would take too much money."

"I could go to work for someone as an apprentice for a couple of years."

"And the money? It sounds nice, and you know I love growing things, but I'm sure it would be too rough on us all."

"Maybe I should have been a soldier. By now I'd be a major. I could even be retired by now—just takes twenty years for half or three-quarters pay. There's a fellow in my class who was an officer. I told him 'Christ, to be retired so young.' He said he isn't that young but I said 'You're around my age and that's still pretty young. No major illnesses and none foreseen for a good fifteen years. You have twenty good working years left and maybe more because you won't be working your butt off at a job for the next fifteen years.' He said the last seven years in the army were unrelievedly boring. That he never would have gone in if he'd known about them. I said 'Seven boring years for twenty to thirty years of retirement?' Or at least fifteen years of retirement before he'd normally retire? I'd go through that. I should have joined the army. Even got into ROTC when I was in college, and started as an officer. I might even have ended up a colonel."

"You would have gone off to war. You would have been shot at, booby-trapped, lost your legs. We never would have met. I wouldn't have liked most of what you thought and felt. If you had made it through the war or come out in one piece, you'd be involved with military science now, probably a little too gung-ho and rigid about most things, and you'd be deadly dull to me. Your student still talks like an officer, doesn't he?"

"Maybe talks like one but writes like a poet. Each paragraph seems scratched out by pen thirty times. Maybe he's hiding behind it, all those long descriptions, flowery language and showy emotions and words. True, I probably would have had a different kind of wife. Fluffier hair, maybe a few blond streaks in it, or just shorter or more athletic-looking hair. Maybe not as intelligent or with much interest in literature, but nice, taking care of the kids, cooking, lots of housecleaning—things like that. Same kind of sex, I suppose, though truth is I think intellectuals generally have the best sex."

"She'd have smoked. You'd have hated that. Stubbing out her cigarette when she left it for a second, emptying her ashtrays ten times a day—I could see you. Because somehow I think all army wives smoke a lot."

"You're probably right. The men too. And the hillbilly music and dumb TV shows and all that sports and pussy talk—I never could have slept in the same barracks with them. But what should I do about a different job?"

"I'm telling you, become a plumber. They do very well. Take a few courses in it while you're still teaching. Fifty dollars an hour they get."

"That's what the plumbing contractor might charge when he sends one of his men over. But I'd say twenty-five an hour when they're on their own."

159

"Thirty-five then, forty. And forty times seven or eight hours a day? You'd only have to work three weekdays a week. The other two you could do what you want."

"I should have stayed in news. But I knew after three years it wasn't for me and would only get worse. All those mindless stories, half of them publicity pieces for the person or group or institution I was writing about. Nothing in depth. The editors said 'Whataya think ya writing here, philosophy or literary crits? Cut and simplify, cut and simplify.' And also embarrasing when I asked a fireman with smoke coming out of his nose and mouth how he feels. Or people at the airport, still waiting for the plane with their loved ones to arrive, the miracle to happen—'That's the story; dig into it; more they cry, better the copy'—when it hit some mountainside a couple of hours ago. Worst kind of writing, but it was stupid of me to quit. At least so early in it."

"You probably did the right thing. I don't know what to say. Plumbing."

"Maybe I can become a cashier someplace. I'm not kidding. Something simple; nothing to interfere with thinking. Just sit behind a booth, give back change, do what cashiers do, 'Don't forget your charge card; thank you,' waiters could fetch me coffee every so often. Effortless. Days would pass. I wouldn't get dirty or exhausted. Years. Then Social Security. We'd have enough to live on from it, so long as you were working."

"In four years I'll be able to go back to teaching full time. Then, though I wouldn't be making nearly as much as you, you could quit or go part time."

"How about one of those guys who sits by office building entrances? In a uniform, usually, but no gun. Or fancy apartment house lobbies. A checker or weaponless guard. Gives out passes, sees that undesirables don't enter. One does, no trouble—he just summons the real security force or the police. It'd be easy too. Nine to five. Four to twelve. Read a book. Two books a day. Go over or even rewrite by hand the work I really want to be doing. Or driving a truck. I see ads where they teach you how to drive one in a month and then get you a job. Those guys make good money. Women too. You can come with me sometimes, share the driving load if you also take the driving course. Or I'd teach you. But better you get your permit so they can pay us as a driving team. And the beds in those trucks often have a bed in them too."

"You mean in the truck's cabin. The bed is the container part in back."

"Narrow beds but we'd be snug in them, see America, sleep under the stars or the smog. We could even take the kids sometimes, during their school breaks."

"You don't like driving much. Six hours on the road kills you. Those drivers go fourteen hours, sometimes two days running with only four hours' sleep. That's what those beds are for."

"I've got to start doing something else though."

"What I said then. Plumbers call the shots. There's always work for them. Set up your own business and collect the fifty to sixty dollars an hour for yourself. Sure, expenses and medical insurances. But four hundred a day. Say three-fifty. Only work two days a week and take three months off in the summer. You'd still earn more money and get more vacation time, or the same vacation time but no class preparation during it, than you do now and for about ten fewer work hours a week."

"What would happen if a toilet was really clogged? Needed a lot more than a snake. I've heard stories. Plumbers sticking their arms into pipes up to their shoulders. Not in the toilets so much but in the main basement pipe, with years of crap in it, leading to the sewer. Where nothing but a hand would unclog it. They have gloves on, and I guess they get used to it, but do they? Maybe that's why they charge so much: to even it all out. No, it's not for me. Why don't I just open a little store? Buy one, rather, so when I get it it's all there, goods on the shelves, the rest. At the most, work another year teaching, save up enough capital, I think it's called, and open a general store in Maine or Vermont or some country or beach town where New Yorkers and Bostoners and Hartforders and so on vacation. So, three busy summer months, probably another busy month preparing for summer, and eight slow winter, fall and spring months. Lots of fresh air and smells, but in a community—not so remote or in the hills and a school relatively easy for the girls to get to—and our food costs, because of the store, drastically reduced. In fact, everything would be. Beer, wine, motor oil, combs—all at cost. Even gas if we get a pump. We could live in back of the store, or on top of it. We could get a store with a good rear view. Of water, or whatever. Or a frame store. I don't know anything about framing but what would it take to learn? Again, apprentice myself out for nothing while doing my current job. I think I'd prefer a store like that. Better hours, nothing perishable. No problems with mice, roaches, raw garbage, credit, rats. Paints, printings, etcetera. Documents, cutting the glass, beveling the cardboard the documents or prints go inside. You know, that fastens the print—protects and supports it—to the glass but without the print touching the glass. For what would it cost to open such a store? Then turn it into an art gallery. Or a combination of the two—that's how they do it. When you're not selling art, you're framing it."

"You want to get away from the kind of people who collect art and go to openings and such, don't you? Besides, you're not a salesman and haven't the personality to become one, and to sell paintings and prints you'd have to be."

"I could become one. It's part of our people's heritage. It's American also. Everybody in this country's potentially one. All right, I'm not smooth and I don't like pushing people into anything, but that's not the salesman I'd be. I'd put the stuff on the tables and walls and would say 'Here it is, there's the price list, nothing's negotiable. It's as fair a price as I can make it without cheating the artist and breaking the gallery. Take as long as you like looking at things, come back anytime you like, have a cup of coffee or tea, herbal, decaf or regular; even some cookies.' I'd keep a box of cookies around and maybe some fruit if it were cheap. No fruit—that'd create raw garbage again. And I'd read. I'd look oblivious and remote. Nothing on my face would express 'sell.' Or I'd talk to them if they wanted, and about whatever they wanted. All right. Let's say my new kind of salesmanship didn't work. So just a frame store. I could read while I'm waiting there for customers too. Read or make frames, and cut the matting, it's called."

"Mats."

"Mats, matting, or both. But you mat them. That I know."

"The frame store's not a bad idea. Whatever makes you happy. Sleep on it."

"But you know by now I have to do something. I can't stand my work. Same thing for too many years. Little variations but not enough. I want to get away from it, from everything and all the people in it, except if they travel to our little country town and might possibly buy something in the frame store. Or just visit me in the store, because 'no hard sell.' I didn't think my job was so bad, but every day for months it seems worse. Maybe it'd take too much capital to open a store. I know I couldn't be a word processor."

"You mean a computer programmer."

"Yes, and one who also works on a word processor for someone. Don't they do both? Because lots of my students do it or have gone on to it for a living."

"Could be."

"Too boring. It'd be like prison. Maybe I could be a prison guard. Not maximum security; something lighter. Lots of different people. It would always be interesting. Till retirement age, which I'd think with guards would be early. I'd be good to the prisoners. Wouldn't wear a gun. Not even handcuffs or a club."

"Forget it. I wouldn't let you. Maybe you want something with kids."

"Did it. Secondary school and lots of junior high school teaching. No knack or authority. Couldn't get them quieted down or fired up about learning."

"Kindergarten age then. Just fun and games and the ABC's."

Frog

"It's much different now. Wordbooks. People expect big growth from kids in kindergarten."

"Nursery school. Learn to tinker on the piano. Simple stuff. 'Old MacDonald.' "

"I'd love to be a pianist. Classical. And compose. Just piano and little voice pieces. But that's another lifetime."

"Also learn a repertoire of children's songs and games. You have a nice personality for kids. You obviously like and respect them and most of the time they adore you."

"Their high voices would drive me crazy. All at once, and the running. The pay's slave wages for preschool teachers. I'm sure I wouldn't be any better at discipline for kids that age. I'd have stomach- and headaches every workday and lots of anxiety on weekends and the last summer vacation month before school begins. As I did when I taught grade school and junior high. Maybe I should become a house painter. Wouldn't take much to learn. Work alone or hire someone with me. Keep hiring, for they always quit. Worst kind of work in some ways. But I'd be able to take a radio along and I'd play good music all day. Or a tape cassette player. Nobody bothers painters playing music. They'd even welcome a different kind of music, for painters always play too loudly horrible kiddy music on awful radios with bad speakers. I suppose they're afraid the radios would be stolen if they were any better. I'd stay close to my cassette player and tapes. Palestrina. I wouldn't even know I was painting. Saint Matthew's Passion. I'd get the job over double-time with a run of Mozart flute and piano concertos. Just go in, set up and work. Apartment a week or whatever it takes. I like the idea. I really do. Bartok's quartets. Beethoven's last ones. Acoustics might be better in completely empty rooms. Four-story brownstones might take two weeks—all of Bach's cantatas or as many as are on tape. I'd do good work. They get good pay. Five hundred dollars a room. What's it take to paint a room? A day? For two coats?"

"The fumes. They'd get to you. I understand they make painters wacky after awhile and drive many of them to drink. Something in the paints and thinners acts as a catalyst for drinking."

"Maybe after twenty years of it. But I've painted. Room here and there. Did nothing like that to me. But it would get tedious, I suppose."

"So? Become a plumber. Everyone respects them. Study in a trade school at night, while you continue teaching, for half a year. However long it takes. And how long would it? I mean, if you're going to think seriously about changing professions, then this is thinking seriously. You don't want to become a master plumber right away. You can't. Then go to work for someone. Firms, I bet, always need new plumbers. The plumbers who work for the company that takes care of this building are always changing. I asked why once. The plumber who fixed that last kitchen wall leak? Is it because the contractor has so many plumbers working for him? He said no, it's because they're always quitting. Wages are okay, but they get better offers elsewhere. And you'd save on the plumbing in our own house if we ever buy one."

"That part sounds good. But maybe I should work in an office. Writing for some concern. Publicity, public relations, advertising, technical copy, company newsletters."

"I'd think you'd want to stay away from those jobs. It might not be all that close to what you're doing now but wouldn't it interfere in your own work? You also don't have the clothes."

"I'd buy a suit. And get my sport jacket mended and switch them around. Sport jacket with the pair of pants I have now and the pants from the suit. People at work would think I have four different outfits at least. Suit jacket with the pair of pants I have now. I'd buy another tie."

"You wouldn't like the schedule. Not only nine to five but work on weekends and throughout your vacations. People in those businesses are always taking work home and getting work-related phone calls at night. And windowless offices, most of them. Or little cells in honeycombs. And the new typewriters. You can't even manage an electric."

"I could try to learn. Or I'd bring my manual in."

"Someone could steal it, and what would you work on at home?"

"I'd carry it to and from work every day."

"You'd have to take the subway or bus to work or walk. Think of getting into a crowded subway or bus or walking to and from work twice a day with a typewriter. Plus the books you'd invariably take to read on the subway and during lunch and probably a sack of vegetables and fruit to supplement your lunch besides the work you had and have to do at home."

"I'd buy a used very heavy table model and leave it. Or just a standard or portable model and hide it in the office at night. But maybe a telephone answering service. To work for one. When I was in radio news people thought I had a good voice. I didn't think so. But taking calls for people. Switchboard operator for some company, even. I'd sit in a comfortable chair, read between calls. They must get ten minutes off every two hours."

"It's called a break."

"I know. I used to have them at jobs long ago and when I modeled. Maybe I could go back to artist-modeling. Twenty minutes on, five minutes off. Or was it ten off? Or twenty-five and five? That would have been awful. Didn't pay well and no doubt still doesn't. But male models are tough to get, I understand, if they're not dancers. So they might be paid more. One of my students wrote an essay on it. She still models. Very curvacious body. But that painters would rather paint anyone but a male dancer. Too stiff and muscular and they often do dance warmups during poses. But no strap on I might get an additional dollar or two an hour."

"You'd earn enough, after posing forty hours a week, to feed us but not the cat."

"Then you'll have to go back to full-time teaching sooner."

"Tell me. But say I was even able to get some adjunct work next year, who'll see to the kids, sitters? All our earnings from your modeling and my odd-jobbing would go to them, so we wouldn't even have enough to feed us. No, plumbing. If it's fifty to sixty an hour now, it'll be sixty to seventy next year. Once you have the know-how, put ads in the papers. Say you're a very literate well-spoken plumber with a good voice and who'll only play, while working, soft classical music on state-of-the-art radios and cassette players. Impeccably honest, fast-working, formerly a college teacher—people will love it; you'll be swamped with business. You work very hard at learning, so in three years you'll be a great plumber. You can then teach me. I should become a plumber too. Positions in my discipline are becoming too hard to get. We can go into business. Tetch and Spouse. Or Tetch and Teach or Teach and Teach or Spouse and Spouse. 'Spouse and Spouse will plumb your house.' Or simply: Tetch Plumbing Company. Or College Plumbing. Professor Plumbing. Or Ex-Profs or Professor and Professor Plumbing. The university jobs alone could keep us. We'll advertise in their publications. Other teachers will also jump to hire us. You know that many of them feel they can only talk to and trust other teachers. We can do it for ten years and retire. Or think what else we want to do after ten years and retire. I'd like that too. Full-time retirement first. I've other things than teaching to do. We'll train the kids in it, give them something to fall back on, since there'll always be a need for plumbers. But while we work, same ratio: two days off for both of us, five days for whatever. And summers off. We can in fact go away summers to the same places you mentioned and get our plumbing licenses there and do summer plumbing to help defray our summer costs. That way, if summer plumbing's really profitable, we might only have to work one day a week the rest of the year."

"Seriously, I have to do something else. Anything. Maybe a job in a department store. Pays minimum wage or a bit over, but right now, so what? Selling mens' bathrobes and pajamas, I once did. And boys' wear and toys, so I've experience there too. They can move me around various departments. The store troubleshooter. No, not boys. No toys. Too much shrieking, I remember. Mens' pajamas and robes. Everyone knows his size or the woman knows the size her man takes or she just holds the pajamas up to me or asks me to try the robe on and says he's a size or two smaller or around the same size. If he's a lot taller or rounder than I, he's extralarge and maybe the sleeves have to be taken in a little, but that's it, sale's completed, 'Cash or charge and will a simple bag or box do or do you want it gift-wrapped, which you get at the service desk past those doors?' They can always bring the garment back if it's the wrong color or size. Even if the man took the pins and paper out and tried the pajamas on. Why would I care, even if he lost or tore some of the paper? Pajamas were easy to pin back and I found it kind of relaxing. Lay them out on the counter; it was like folding up a dummy. Bathrobes just got belted and hung back on the racks. Hour for lunch. Or was it forty minutes? Employees' cafeteria, decent food at subsidized prices, separate dining room for execs or anybody for the day who got to wear a flower because the department was short. Only two-week summer vacations. That would hurt. But you see I have to do something else. I should have tried to become a professional baseball player. I was good but maybe not that much. The long ball. I had the wrists. It was exhilarating when I connected. But struck out too much going for the fences, which was sometimes humiliating. Could also peg it into home from the outfield without a bounce, but often too wild. Would have been retired by now, doing nicely. Gone back to school. Become a college teacher in something. Wouldn't have minded it after fifteen-twenty years in baseball. The students would love an ex-pro ballplayer teaching them. Like a war hero to some, an actor who once had a Hollywood part or the lead in a well-known TV commercial, even if I'd only played triple-A ball. With my retirement pension or whatever players get, I could tell the university just one term only, two classes max, no freshman comp or film courses. That would be ideal."

"Shoot for that then."

"I'm not needed enough."

"Become a dean if you want something different but still want to stay in the university."

"You really have to be part of the academic community. I might have a good voice but I don't speak well. They stump around the country promoting the university. My grammar's too tied to my ears. I don't have any advanced degrees and could never now sit in some classes and write a thesis to get one. They'd suspect me. What does a dean do?"

"Intermediary between students and faculty. Evaluates requests for money. Mouthpiece for the chancellor. Depends on what you'd be dean of."

"I'm not smart enough that way and could never raise money or haggle over it. I don't even know my own field well enough to talk coherently about it. I strictly dribble out what I know, while I'd think deans would have to show real expertise, or give a convincing show of it, and polish. Most chairmen and teachers are clever cookies and would read right through me. I've been lucky so far. Got the job because my own chairman thought he knew better about my deficits than I did. And since then have hidden from observation, torn up the more unfavorable student evaluations and written a few good ones for myself; things like that. One of the reasons I want out. It's too bad it's too late to be a fireman. When I lived with Lulu she urged me to become one. They had two openings in this town's one firehouse and would train you. She knew two of the men in the company and said she'd speak to them. I could have done it. For a while it sounded exciting and the possible camaraderie with the men also appealed to me. Lulu had slept with one of them and I think twice a year or so still did it with the other. She had so many things going I didn't know about. Would have been interesting though."

"Fire fighting?"

"Three men in a truck racing to put out a fire, hanging by the handstraps in back, all having slept with the same woman and maybe at that moment—wind whipping their rubber coats; well, I don't want to build it up too much—talking about it. You get very close to your fellow firemen I understand—your lives depend on one another and so on. Three days on, four days off—something like that. So you eat and sleep with them, cook for them—I see them shopping together in A&P, big fire truck waiting outside. I'd be retired now also, or almost, after twenty years. It's been that long since she suggested it."

"Why didn't she think it'd be dangerous? Little houses, probably. You stand on a stepladder and squirt out the fires. No. But you could have got a lot of reading done waiting for alarms. You could even still be with Lulu, married, children, be a grandpa, or close. You also would have become an even better cook than you are now. Or a more efficient one, just luncheonette-style cooking, which could have opened up another profession for you."

"I did that during college at a coffee shop. Opened the place up mornings. Filled the steam table with water. Made bacon and eggs and such for early customers while I set up behind the counter. Fourteenth or Twenty-third on Broadway or Eighth Avenue. I remember a subway stop was right outside on the corner. That was supposed to be good for business. Steam smoking up the windows the first hour and then dripping down them, because I opened up just when the building's heat was going on. It was also a drugstore. I wouldn't do it again. Was run ragged. My legs wouldn't hold me now. Same with waiting and bartending. You know, did it for a while till I was almost forty. Good work in that it didn't take much brains and time flew if you were busy, which I usually was. A million things to do. Keep the sugar dispensers clean and filled, etcetera. Coffee, always making coffee, even at the bar. Could never get comfortable shoes. Actually soaked my feet in epson salts most times I got home."

"I hate saying it, but plumbing. You're your own boss or could become one eventually, as you said your father always told you to be."

"I now wish I had become the dentist he wanted me to be most of all. 'We'll have a joint practice,' he said. 'Or we'll open a second office—in the Chrysler Building.' He said he had a friend there who could get us a good office. 'It's classy, not like the Garment Center. You work out of there, I'll keep the old office. When I die you inherit them or sell whichever one you want or both and retire at fifty, fifty-five.'"

"You're afraid of blood, or recoil from it every time one of the girls cuts her finger or lips."

"I'd have adapted. A psychiatrist then. Or just a plain therapist. No, I don't think like that. But they get paid fairly well, sit most of the time, hear lots of interesting stories, and you can do it in your own hours. Too much back-to-school involved. And do I really want to help people? I'm too self-interested. I'm only trying to find time for myself. But it wouldn't take that much of an effort to become a plumber, I don't think. First two years might be tough—schooling, apprenticing, adjusting to it, making mistakes. But that's why you're an apprentice. Senior plumbers work over you. But suppose he was some very dumb crude guy and twenty years younger than I? I could get through it. And customers would trust me, and I'd be patient— it might work. Because I can't teach anymore. I'm a fake. I'm not giving the kids their money's worth. I don't care if they learn or not. I'm tired of it, that's all. It's the first job I've held for more than two years and it's going on eight. I get along with just about no one there. It's too connected to what I really do, as you said."

"You're exaggerating. But look in the paper tomorrow. See what's doing. Call around. The Yellow Pages. Various plumbing schools. Maybe it's even easier than we think."

"But if the toilets are really stopped up? The floors covered with it? Not just shit but slop and gook of every kind. Tampons. A hand. Dead cats. Who knows what people throw down there."

"Everything, I'm sure. Speak to plumbers first. Maybe you don't need such a strong stomach. Maybe they draw the line about what they don't have to clean up. And for the bigger things that get stuck, they have equipment to push them all the way through to the sewer."

"But if the customer's an invalid? Dainty homes, where nobody touches anything dirty? Carpentry's out of the question. I was always bad at it, even in shop. Electricians do well but every now and then they get a terrific shock. Sometimes knocked off their feet and where their teeth chatter. They take it with the job. The anxiety of when I'd get it would stop me. I've had a couple. One when I was a boy where I couldn't speak for minutes. Literally, my tongue wouldn't function. What else is there? Typewriter repairman. One I go to charges $22.50 an hour. But so intricate, and no doubt boring, and it would ruin what's left of my eyes."

"Postman. But your feet, and you're probably too old. Stay at what you have for the time being. Something might turn up. Or become a plumber and just accept cleaning up crud once or twice a week and every so often putting your hand in something horrid."

"Garage mechanics always have oily hands and grease under their nails. Even those who wear gloves. I couldn't come home to you and the kids like that every day. Even when they wash their hands raw with heavy-duty soap. After they quit the job or go on vacation it takes a few weeks for their hands to get normal again. That's what Norton said. He did it for a year. If my hands were like that I doubt I could sleep. I'd sense them or would always be scratching the oily hand cracks. But maybe they like just about everyone else at his job gets used to those things too. Of course they do—they have to. Anyway, we should drop it for now—I should. It's getting late."

"Just one thing. What did you mean before by 'better intellectual sex'?"

" 'Intellectuals have better sex'? Slower, more sensitive and imaginative, less taken in by family and institutional proscriptions. There was something else. But I'm probably all wrong."

Frog Made Free

He suddenly seems to have lost all his marbles. Doesn't know where he is. Dark, feels movement, sounds of movement, so feels he's going someplace. A car, but no seat, just a rough wood floor he's on, so it isn't. Bed of a truck, totally enclosed, shaking back and forth, moving slowly, but not the sounds of one, outside or underneath. A train, bouncing like one. Sounding like it. How could it be? Not a real train. Sure, one with something pulling it and on tracks, but what's he, some bum tramping it in a boxcar? Smells like it, old hay, animal dung. He's sitting on a floor, still a rough wood floor, thick liquid on it where one of his hands touches, back up against someone's back, feet squashed against something like a crate or wall. Where's his family? He's no bum. Has a home, car, job, all small but as much as most, wife and kids he lives with, mother in a nearby city whom he helps support. They were with him just before, had to give away the dog, hours, a day, before he woke up. That's it: was asleep. "Denise? Denise?"

"Shh, go back to your snoring," man who's back he's against says. "It wasn't as loud."

"What's going on? What is it with this train?"

"And I'm going to tell you? Don't worry, it'll all turn out bad. Ha-ha, that's a good one. Sorry, go to sleep. Don't be afraid to, the

173

ride's for a couple more days at least. Believe me, we're all here who were here, even the ones who aren't dead yet. Sorry again. I can't help myself. I don't know what I'm saying. I don't even know if I said anything. Did I?"

"Shh, you too," someone says. "You're making more noise than him now."

"Denise?" Howard yells.

"What's with this guy?" someone else says. "Hey, pipe down."

"We're over here," she says. "Directly across the car from you. The girls are all right, sleeping now. People were kind enough to let us move near the pail so the girls could relieve themselves right into it. You were sleeping. You wouldn't budge. Rest, dear. Take care of yourself. In the morning come over."

He gets up. "Excuse me," he says, feeling bodies with his hands and feet. Stepping on someone. "Get off me," a woman says.

"I'm sorry, really. But I want to get to my wife and children."

"You'll see them in the morning like she says."

"Stay where you are. . . . Go back to where you were. . . . You're upsetting everything," other people say.

"No, now, please, I have to. This might be my last chance before the train pulls in."

"Last chance nothing. Your foot's on my hand." He lifts his foot and puts it down on someone else's or this same man's hand. "Just go back to your spot, will you? Ah, it's likely already filled by three others. Come on, someone light a candle. Let this man get to his family."

Car stays dark. "Come on," the man says, "someone break down and light a candle. This is Grisha Bischoff talking. If it's because you don't want to spare a match, I'll loan you."

A candle's lit about twenty feet away. Little he can see, car's packed full with bundles and people sleeping. Some look at him, one eye, then blink shut. "Over here," Denise says, waving at him. "Excuse me, excuse me," he says. "My wife."

"Better to crawl over rather than step," a woman below him says.

"Right, I just wanted to be quick." Gets down, crawls over people. It takes a long time. "I'm sorry, he says. "I'm very sorry." Someone punches his back as he passes. "Imbecile," a man says. "Let him be," someone else says. "He got permission. Maybe his kids need him like he says." "They need him, I need him—when you're split up you're sunk and that's final, but you have to make it hell for everybody else? OK, OK, I'll get out of his way."

He gets to Denise. "I'm here, thank you, you can put out the candle, whoever it was." Candle goes out.

"There's only room for one adult here," Denise says, on her knees. "Olivia's in a space for someone half her size. Eva's been on my chest. I'll make room somehow."

"Excuse me," he says, feeling for the person next to them and nudging his shoulder. "Could you just give us one or two inches?"

"There's no room to," the man says. "I don't have enough for my family or myself. Go back to your place. It was bad enough when she and your kids came here."

"I can't. I'll never get back. Thanks all the same." He feels for Olivia, picks her up, takes her spot, makes himself small, lays her facedown on him, feels for Denise's head, "It's me," he says, kisses her lips, for a while his lips stay on hers without moving, says "I didn't believe this just before. That we were here. I didn't know where I was, is more like it. Suddenly I was a kid, it seemed—a lost one. Parents gone; no brothers. In the dark, literally and the rest of it. I felt crazy. All I wanted was for you to be—"

"Go to sleep, my darling. Try to."

"I wish I could. We sleep most of the day; how could anyone sleep now? And the infection in my finger's killing me. When I crawled over I bumped it a dozen times and it now feels twice the size it was. It's a small inconvenience, and so what about the pain compared to all the other things, but if I can't soak and treat it it'll—"

"We'll try to do something in the morning. Maybe we can get some hot water, for your finger and to wash the girls. Sleep, though. We have a few hours to."

Frog

He kisses her, closes his eyes, head on her shoulder, one arm holding Olivia close, other on Eva's back. Very cold. Smell of shit and piss is worse here than where they were. The fucking slop pail. She had to move here? But the girls won't soil their clothes or less so than if they were over there. "If there was only something I could do for us."

"Like what?"

"Like everything."

"Right now there's nothing. Just stay close. No heroics unless it's a sure thing for us. Stay with us till the end. Wake up when I ask you. Help me keep the girls in a good mood. But now, sleep; not another word."

He doesn't sleep. Snoring of a woman close by keeps him up. Smells and cold. Weight of Olivia. Wailing every so often from people. Weeping, coughing, babies crying. Someone shouting, someone talking in his sleep. But Denise and the girls seem to sleep.

They go on like this for days. People die. No food except a little for the children. Some people share it. Olivia and Eva are always hungry and thirsty and complain and cry a lot about it. A bucket of water for the whole car is given them once a day. Bischoff distributes it in spoonfuls. Howard's finger gets so swollen that he jabs it into a nail in the wall and keeps sucking it and it starts healing. There's a slit in the door and someone during the day is usually telling the car what the weather and scenery are like. Now it's hilly, now it's flat. Lots of big clouds in the sky, but nothing threatening. More people die. Corpses are piled on top of one another in a corner and what little hay can be found is strewn over them. The bottom ones begin to smell. Now it's clear out, now it's sleeting and looks as if it'll turn into snow. Some people seem to pray all day and night now. Train stops, goes, pulls into stations, drags along mostly, stays still for hours sometimes, one time for an entire night. They pass a pretty village, an oil refinery that goes on for miles, farmers working in fields. "Potatoes they're trying to dig out that they might've missed," the slit-watcher says. "Turnips, cabbages, even a carrot or two. Sounds good, right? Look, a farmer's waving his pick at us. Hello, you lucky stiff. Look, a dog's running to the train. Do you kids hear him bark?" Nobody answers. Sunny, rainy. Denise and the girls sleep most of the time now. Olivia always seems to run a low fever and he's afraid it'll suddenly go out of control at night and she'll die. The slop pail's filled and starts running over. Some people talk of killing themselves. Bischoff gives an order. "Nobody kills himself. If you got pills or stuff that can do it, give them to me to use on someone who's really suffering or about to die. But we should be at the place soon we're going to and then let's hope it'll all be much better for us and most of us are even able to stay together as a group. Does anyone have some good stories to tell? Dreams, but interesting ones we can all appreciate? Then anything you want to make up for us or poems you remember from books or school? Does anyone have any food for the children?" Nobody answers. They haven't had a bucket of water for two days. During one stop someone asks a guard through the slit if they can get some water and also empty the slop pail. "Get rid of it through your hole there," the guard says. "You got little spoons. It can be done." "It'll probably make more of a mess than help us," Bischoff tells the car, "but what do we got to lose?" The pail's moved to the door. Denise wants to follow it, but Howard says "We got a good place together and now not such a filthy one, so let's stay." Someone's always spooning out slop through the slit, except at night. Some cardboard's turned into a funnel and they get rid of the slop faster. The pail keeps running over though, but not as much as before.

The train stops at a station. "I think this is it," the slit-watcher says. "Lots of lights, barbed wire and fences. Dogs, soldiers, marching prisoners in stripes who look like they're on their last leg. I hear lively band music from someplace, but it doesn't look good." "Don't worry, don't worry," Bischoff says. "They might be political prisoners you're seeing; we're not." They stay in the station till morning. Most of the groaning and crying's stopped. More people have died but nobody's piling them up. "It's snowing," the slit-watcher says. "Big flakes, but melting soon as they hit the ground. Plenty of activity outside, everyone being lined up, called to attention, even the dogs. Something's about to happen. A tall man in a great coat and officer's cap is pointing to the train."

The door suddenly opens and several men and women outside start shouting orders. One tells them to hurry out of the car and leave all their luggage on the platform, a second says to go to this or that truck. "What's going to happen to us?" Denise says in the car.

"I don't know," Howard says. "There's air though. Feel it coming in? Olivia, Eva—do you feel it? Already it smells better. Soon toilets, water for drinking and baths."

"Have we really got everything planned fully?" Denise whispers to him. "If they tell you to go one place, me another and the girls a third, or just split us up any other way but where we lose you or both of us lose the kids, what should we do?"

"What can we?"

"We could say no, stay with our children—that we have to, in other words. They're small, sick, need us. We don't want to lose them, we can say, lose them in both ways, and it's always taken the two of us to handle them."

"And be beaten down and the girls dragged away? I don't see it. I think we have to do what they want us to."

"We could ask graciously, civilly. Quick, we have to come to some final agreement. We can plead with them if that doesn't work—get on our knees even; anything."

"We can do that. I certainly will if it comes to that. But we'll see when our turn comes."

"It's coming; it's about to be here. I'm going to beg them first to keep us all together, and if that doesn't work, then for you to go with the girls. You'll last longer than I if it's as bad where they take us as it was in the car."

"One of us then will stay with the girls. If they don't go for it, then each of us with a child. OK, that's what we'll say and then insist on until they start getting a little tough."

There's room to move around now. Half the people have left the car. He gets down on his knees and kisses the girls, stands them up between Denise and him and he hugs her and their legs touch the children. "Should I start to worry now, Mother?" Olivia says and Denise says "No, absolutely not, sweetheart—Daddy and I will take care of you both."

"May it all be OK," he whispers in Denise's ear. "May it."

"Come on out of there," a man shouts. "All of you, out, out—yours isn't the only car on the train."

"Good-bye all you lovely people," Bischoff says. "We did our best. Now God be with you and everything else that's good and I hope to see each of you in a warm clean room with tables of food."

Howard hands Eva to Denise, picks up Olivia and their rucksacks. "This is how we'll split the kids if it has to come to it, OK? By weight," and she nods and they walk out.

"All right, you," an officer says to Howard, "bags on the platform and go to that truck, and you, lady, go to that truck with the children." "No," she says, "let us stay together. Please, the older girl—" "I said do what I say," and he grabs Olivia to take her from Howard. Howard pulls her back. "Do that—stop me, and I'll shoot you right here in the head. Just one shot. That's all it'll take." Howard lets him have Olivia. The officer puts her down beside Denise. "What will happen to them?" Howard says.

"Next, come on—out with you and down the ramp, bags over there. Richard, get them out faster. You go that way," to a man coming toward him and points past Howard, "and you two, the same truck," to two young women. "Go, you both, what are you doing?—with your children and to your trucks," he says to Denise and Howard. "No more stalling." She stares at Howard as she drags Olivia along. A soldier tugs at his sleeve and he goes to the other truck. She's helped up into hers with the girls. Some more men and young women climb into his truck. He can't see her or the girls in her truck anymore. It's almost filled and then it's filled and it drives off. "Denise," he screams. Many men are screaming women's names and the names and pet names of children, and the people in that truck, older people, mothers, children, are screaming to the people in his truck, and a few people on the platform are screaming to one or the other truck. Denise's truck disappears behind some buildings. He can hear it and then he can't. Then his truck's filled and a soldier raps the back of it with a stick and it pulls out. They'll never get our belongings to us, he thinks. What will the girls change in to? It makes no difference to him what he has. They'll give him a uniform or he'll make do. But Denise, the children. Denise, the children. "Oh no," and he starts sobbing. Someone pats his back. "Fortunately, I had no one," the man says.

Frog Takes a Swim

Olivia doesn't want to play on the beach anymore, wants to go into the water but not to swim. "Just a little more till I finish this paragraph," "No," "All right," and puts down his book, walks her into a part of the lake where the sun is, lifts her under the arms and swings her above the water. "More, more, this is fun," and he does it some more, then says he can't, too tiring, let's rest, stands her up. "Too cold," she says. Holds her arms out. "Again." "Give me a few seconds." Looks out to the lake. Sailboat way off, or something with a sail. People jumping off the ledge into the water, but so far away that even from their shrieking he can't tell if they're kids or adults and which are male and which are female. Lily pads, closer, with flowers all over. Picks her up, swings her in a circle, her feet skimming the water, then her legs cutting through it. "Whee, this is great, better than swimming. Know what it reminds me of, Daddy?" and he indicates he doesn't and she says "Twirling around and getting dizzy dancing," and he does this till his arms ache, says "No more for now, I'm all hot from it, let me take a swim," stands in place holding her till he doesn't feel he'll fall if he walks, walks to shore and sets her down. "How can we do this—for me to swim? I can't just leave you." "Yes you can. I'll stay and play here." "No, someone has to watch you," while he's drying her. "We'll ask someone here to—would you mind that?" "Do I have to stay with that person?" "No. Just that if that person says come away from the edge of the water, for some reason—a leech, maybe, or motorboat being put in—well, you do that, but that person won't have time to say much. I'll only go out for thirty strokes, kick my feet a few times while I'm on my back out there and maybe dive down once, and then swim in, a little slower than when I swam out as I'll probably do the breaststroke coming back, if that's it—you know, where the arms sort of push the water underwater. Like this—how could I be unsure what it's called?" and brings his arms to his chest, spreads them wide, brings them to his chest. "That's a stroke, like the crawl's a stroke," and demonstrates that one, even the breathing. "I think you said the first one's a breaststroke because it's your breast you're hitting." "Right. So, which person looks good to look after you?" "Her. She asked me what I was building with my mud before, and she was nice." Sitting by the beach, around twenty-five, noticed her when they walked down here and several times when he looked up from his book to see her reading hers, slim and nicely built from what he can see in the seated position she's been in since they got here, doesn't look like a local, magazine, travel and week-in-review sections of last Sunday's *Times* held down by a hairbrush and sandals. "OK, let's ask her."

They go over. "Excuse me, but I'd like to—my name's Howard Tetch and this—" "Oh sure—Olivia. We chatted before. She's so pretty and well behaved, and sharp?—oh boy." "She is, which'll make what I want to say easier. I'd like to take a quick dip—" "Go ahead, I'll watch her." "But a very quick one. Thirty strokes out, thirty back or so, maybe a little whale movement on my back out there, but that's all. And she knows—" "Really, don't worry. Even if she can't swim or hold her breath underwater, she can go in up to her waist. I'll be right here, and I'm a WSI." "I'm sorry, don't know. . ." "Water safety instructor. I've two lifesaving badges, giving me the authority to save two adults of up to three hundred pounds total at one time." "Well, couldn't be better. OK, kid. Up-to-your-knees, we'll say, but no higher and not for long. I don't want you catching a chill—getting one." "Anyhow, I don't want to go in again. I want to play here." "Fine. —By the way, your name's what?—just in case I get a cramp out there and have to shout for help. Only kidding—but what?" "Lita Reinekin." "Thanks, then, Mrs., Ms., Reinekin." "Lita," holding out her hand. "Lita," shaking it. "OK, sweetie, Daddy's going in. Be good. Do what—" "I will," and she goes to her pail and things on the beach.

He throws the towel to their place on the grass, says to the woman "Think she needs her shirt?—nah, she's OK," walks in to the water, turns around. Olivia's sitting in the muddy sand, her legs wrong, putting her two rubber adult figures into the pail. Woman's a few feet from her, book closed on a finger holding the page, he presumes, looking at Olivia. He splashes water behind his knees and on the back of his neck. Why's he doing that? He already adjusted to it when he was swinging her around. "Put your feet out, Olivia," and without looking at him, she does. He walks out some more, dives in, swims. Counts ten strokes, turns around. She's still playing on the beach. Should have told her to stay in the sun part of the beach, but he won't be out long. Swims fifteen strokes, turns around. Can't see her so well now. "Olivia...hi," he yells. "Hi, Olivia." She doesn't respond. He waves—maybe she's looking at him on the sly, which she does. The woman waves at him. Very nice, he thinks, she's very nice. And good-looking, and that long and what's probably a strong body. But WSI? Two people and three hundred pounds? How would she know what any two people weighed when they were drowning? People she didn't know, in other words. If they weighed more than that and one or both of them drowned, would she be penalized in some way for having tried to save them? Maybe he's missing the point. Ten more strokes, then thinks: give yourself ten more. Likes being this far out when nobody else is here. Ten more, looks around. People on the ledge seem to have left, sailboat's not around anymore, no motorboats today either.

Hates those things. If one came close and didn't see him, what then? Yell, scream, wave frantically, then dive deep if it kept coming. When would he start diving? Depend how fast the boat was going, but something would tell him *now*. What an awful thought though, motorboat running smack into someone and maybe slicing off an arm or leg, and he shakes his head to get rid of it. Looks to shore. Can scarcely make out anything. The woman, he thinks, where she was sitting, and possibly that speck's Olivia, but he's kidding himself. Some other movement on the grassy slope above them, really just blurs, and what looks like a light-colored blanket by a tree, but can't tell if anyone's on it. So quiet out here. Nothing as peaceful anywhere. Maybe the top of a secluded mountain where one sees nothing but trees and other mountains, and on the same kind of day: mild temperature, light breeze, mostly clear sky. Should get back. But she'll be OK. Gets on his back and looks at a bird, probably a hawk, circling way up in the sky. But time to get back. If she were calling him, would he even hear? And he's much farther out than he usually goes. There's always the chance of a sudden leg or stomach cramp, though he knows how to uncramp them. A motorboat could suddenly approach, even that sailboat, and his sense of timing in diving might not be as good as he thinks.

Starts back, using the crawl for about fifteen strokes, then the breaststroke for about ten. Can see the beach fairly well now. Woman sitting where she was. Light blanket, if there was one, seems to be gone. Doesn't see Olivia or anybody else there. Some might have left, others gone into the woods, Olivia with them for some reason, picking berries, looking for exotic mushrooms or birds; to piss, even. Or she could be behind a tree or bush, playing hide-and-seek. Stares; doesn't see her. Ten more crawl strokes, stops. Woman reading. Their towels and shirts. Olivia's toys on the beach. If they're playing hide-and-seek, why's the woman reading? Pretending not to see her perhaps. "Hello...hello," he yells, treading water. She looks up. "Where's Olivia?" Stares at him; he can't make out her expression. He swims hard the rest of the way, stands when he's able to and yells while walking fast as he can through the water "Where'd Olivia go?" "What?" she says, cupping her ear. "Olivia—my daughter— where is she?" "Who?" "The girl I left with you. Is she in the woods? Or you let her go back to the car alone?" "I'm sorry, sir," standing when he gets right up to her, "but I don't know what you're talking about. You didn't leave anybody or anything with me. You were here by yourself before—" "By myself?" "Over there, and you went in the water—" "I went in only after you agreed to look after my girl. You said you were a WSI." "A WSI?" "Look, what is this, a joke on me? You two—together—and she's hiding somewhere?" "No, nothing." "Then you want me to panic, I'm panicking. You're nuts, fine, be nuts. But—oh, fuck you. —Olivia," he yells, listens. "Olivia, it's Daddy. Come out from wherever you are, and now." Listens, looks around, runs to the woods and yells "Olivia, do you hear me?" "If there was a girl—" the woman says. "There fucking was. And be quiet. I want to hear if she yells back." Listens. "Olivia," he yells. "If you're hiding, come out. Daddy's serious. Game's over if you're playing one. If the woman I left you with told you to play a game, she doesn't want you to play it anymore either. Now come out this second." Listens.

"Stay here," he says. "If you see her, tell her to wait till I come out." Runs to their spot, slips his sneakers on, runs into the woods shouting "Olivia, Olivia." Comes on a path and runs along it shouting "Olivia, it's me, Daddy, where are you?" Path ends and he runs back along it and out into the grass and says "You see her?" and she says "No, who?" and he says "Jesus, I'd like to bop you. What the hell's wrong with you—don't you understand anything?" She says "You've threatened me enough—I have to go," and he says "Please, I'm sorry, stay while I look," and runs into the woods at a clearing closer to the beach, trips, gets up, knee's bleeding, says "Screw it, fuck it, oh shit, shit, shit," runs to the end of the clearing, shouts "Olivia, Olivia, it's Daddy, yell if you hear me; please, darling, yell," listens, squeezes his hands hard as he can, digs all his nails into his face till he's out of breath, runs into the woods a few feet, too thick, she'd never get through it and wouldn't even try, runs through the clearing to the grass, woman's putting her things in a canvas bag, he says "Don't go, whatever you do—I need someone to stay while I look up the hill for her, all right?" and she says "Really, this is crazy," and he says "Please, no more accusations from me, just give me a couple more minutes," and she nods and mouths OK, he runs up the path to the parking area, stops several times to yell for Olivia and stare into the woods on both sides, gets to his car, nothing seems changed: windows down, things where he thinks they were, shouts "Olivia, you around here? Daddy's very worried about you, so yell if you hear me," listens, runs to the other car there which must be hers if she didn't walk here from wherever she's staying or park and take the woods' path from the ledge parking area, windows up, driver's door locked, pillow in back, New England road map and several spruce cones and a sand dollar on the dashboard, microbiology textbook and magic marker on the passenger seat, memorizes the Massachusetts license plate and car color and make, is about to run back when he thinks "Why not?" and puts his ear to the car trunk, knocks on it and says "Olivia, Olivia?" runs back, woman's in shirt and shorts and is fitting her feet into sandals, place where she was sitting's cleared, he yells from about twenty feet away "One more minute; just want to check the path to the ledge; I'll run, so I'll be right back," she slumps her shoulders and an expression that says "Enough's enough already, I have to go," runs on the ledge path about a quarter-mile shouting for Olivia and looking into the woods, nobody's at the ledge, towel draped over a tree branch but it's dry and could have been there for days, runs to the parking area, no cars or people, shouts her name and runs back along the path.

"Please, I know I said no more accusations, but this is unbelievably crucial. I left my daughter with you—left her in your charge. I went for a swim." "Yes, I saw you. You went quite a way's out. I was even concerned for you somewhat." "Now listen, stop that bullshit. Those are our towels over there—Olivia's and mine. Two towels. I threw the second one over there right in front of you," and runs to the towels and holds them up. "Towels, goddamnit, towels. And beach toys—hers," and runs to the beach and holds up the pail and two shovels, pulls the two figures out of the pail and waves them in the air. "These are my daughter's. Pail, toys, everything. Who else's? Nobody else is here." "Another child could have left—" "She was playing with them when I went in to swim. You were watching her, right from this spot here. She was still playing here when I last saw her from the water about forty strokes out. You had said she could even go into the water. That you were a—did she? Is that what happened? She's in there, under there, and you don't want to admit it? God no," and he runs in, stops because he doesn't want to churn up the water, walks around looking for her in it and then walks out a few feet, dives down, swims around underwater, when he comes up he looks back to see if the woman's still there. "One-seven, forty-two, PL, baby blue, Opel," he says to himself in case she goes. If she did anything why wouldn't she go? Because she's trying to pull something off. Because he has her name. Lita something. What the hell is it? Not important now. Goes down, again and again, looking for Olivia. If he sees her he'll dive for her and swim to shore with her and pump and pump and pump till he gets the water out and breathe air into her till she's alive or ask the woman, if she really is a water safety instructor, to do it or help. Sees something in the distance underwater and dives. It's a rock with a few long pieces of waving seaweed on it. She's nowhere around. She couldn't have gone out farther. She could have drifted out there before she sank. She would have screamed. He would have heard her. She could have screamed when he was on his back and water got in his ears. Still would have heard. Maybe she's in the weeds. Comes up and shouts "Did she go down in the weeds?" and points to the area of them sticking out of the water. She throws up her hands. Treads water and shouts "Save me the trouble looking. If she drowned then say so and maybe I can still save her. People can be underwater for twenty minutes and somehow still be revived. Where'd she go down if she went down, and if she didn't, then just say where she is or what happened to her?" and she shakes her head she didn't hear or doesn't understand. He swims to the weeds and dives to the part closest to shore, but the weeds stop him. Too thick. Treads through them a few feet, puts his face underwater to look. Can't see anything past the top. He's looking in the wrong place. He doesn't know where to look. Shore would be better, if only to threaten her some way unless she tells.

Swims to shore. Woman walks to him while he walks through the water to the beach and she says "Listen, I want to explain—" "Fine, quick, that's what I want." "I mean I want to be direct with you, though God knows what good it'll do me, so I'm saying I'm leaving. I don't know what you're searching for, but it has nothing to do with me and you have to start believing that, or just thinking about it, all right?" and she turns to leave and he says "But you saw me before. If I wasn't with my girl, who was I with?" "As I said—" "But the toys. The little kid's towel with the cartoon animals on it, and her clothes in my bag up there—shirt, pants, these little Japanese beach sandals—oh, why the hell my telling you? I have to get the police. And tell my wife. Maybe you're crazy or have some instant memory-loss affliction. Maybe Olivia went through the woods and came out some other place. Or got lost somehow, but I've got to get help in searching for her before it gets dark. Look, I don't know why you're saying this, denying it—you're obviously responsible for whatever—" "If I was—" "If you were, why would you have stayed? Because I have your name. I probably have your license plate. The Opel. One-seven PL, etcetera. Because people who were on the grass when we were all here, saw me leave the girl with you. My daughter. If they noticed. So you know you're caught. So come on, will you, tell me already," and grabs her by the shoulders. "I mean it. Where the fuck is she? Tell me or I'll shake your fucking head off," and starts shaking her. "Get your hands off," and pulls his hands away. "Not till you tell me where she is." He swings her around and puts his arm around her neck and twists her arm behind her back and pushes it up till he knows it's hurting. She says "Stop that, stop," and tries to wrench free and he says "Tell me where she is or I'll break your arm off and strangle you right here. I'll do it. Now where is she?" "I don't know." "You know, you know." "I don't—please. You came alone. You have two towels but I never noticed them till you mentioned them. I was reading my book so I didn't see. I don't know anything about the beach toys and your bag of clothes. There was never a girl while I was here." "Liar, liar, liar," and pushes her arm up farther and she shouts in pain and he says "Last chance before I break it off," and waits but she's just shouting in pain and he wants to push it up more but can't. He doesn't want to break it. Wants to give her just so much pain before she tells him but he seems to have gone beyond that point and she's still not telling. "Damn your lying ass," and lets her arm go and from behind squeezes her neck with his forearm. She coughs, says "I'm having trouble breathing," and he says "That's the point. I'll cut the air in your windpipe. I'll even break your windpipe if I have to." "I don't know. . .imagining it. . .I wasn't, there isn't. . .my book. . .can't breathe," and then she's just choking and he wants to go on, he knows that at some point she has to tell him where Olivia is, but he seems to have gone too far, she's not getting any air in. He lets her go and she drops to the ground and gasps and spits and he looks at her to see if she'll say anything, then in the woods for Olivia, the lake to see if her body came up from where it sank, sees the same or different sailboat way off, a pile of stones by the beach, thinks "That's an idea." Woman's still on the ground. He runs to the pile, all too big, looks around, picks up a rock on the grass, one he can hold in one hand, runs back and gets down, she's stroking her throat, bends over her, face a few inches from hers and says "I'm going to smash this rock against your head but with such force that I'll split it open with the first crack. If you don't tell me where she is. Now tell me. You can see I mean business," and holds the rock over her face so she can see it. She says "I swear, don't know. Please, no more. I'd tell you by now if I knew. Swear." "Stay here. I'm not kidding. Don't move from this area. You can at least do that for me. If you see her, tell her to what?

To wait. I'll be back or my wife will or the police. We're at 7 Bear Road in case you have to start moving with her for some reason. That she's very sick, or you are, and we're not back. Bear as in animal. Seven. We're summer renters. Tetch, Howard and Denise. Just Howard. The Brook Isle post office knows us and we have a phone for the summer in my name. You have it?" Nods. "I mean, everything I said about what to do and our name and address?" "Yes." "Or just immediately call, or if someone comes down here get him to call, the police." "I will."

Runs to the path to the car. Maybe Olivia was in the woods, lost, and found a path and it led to the car and she's now in it. Gets to it. Everything's the same. Car's pulling in. All just in swimsuits, man with his shirt off, woman, two kids. Says to the woman as she parks the car "You see a girl around four, about this height," holding out his hand, "long blonde hair in a ponytail, very pretty, walking down that way to the main road or on the road?" She's shaking no. "In a bathing suit. Yellow. Red it was. Red-striped, one piece." "No, I'm sorry." Man beside her says "What is it, she lost?" "Lost. Or something. Too strange. I went for a swim." "You should never leave a child like that alone on a beach," the woman says. Kids have let themselves out of the car, father saying "You wait there by the door till we're finished with this man." "I didn't," Howard says. "I left her with a woman on the beach. She's still there, the woman. I almost killed her just now. She said she didn't know anything about it. It's ridiculous—she's lying—I left my daughter in her charge while I swam. I'm obviously going insane over it. With worry. Listen, I don't trust that woman. She's probably gone some other way out of the beach by now, though I'm sure that's her car. But if she's there, please, I told her to wait for my daughter. Olivia. Olivia Tetch. I'm Howard, at 7 Bear Road, for the summer. Remember that if you see the girl. Or if the woman tells you where my daughter is or what happened to her, which she wouldn't to me. We've a listed phone. T-e-t-c-h. Because I need someone to stay here in case Olivia comes out of the woods—got lost, or had been hiding—though why this woman

190

would lie I don't know. Maybe Olivia ran away from her, but something has to be wrong. But please stay there till I come back or my wife or the police. Stay with Olivia or bring her to our cottage on Bear Road. You know where that is? Very near here." Man says no. "We know Bear Road," the woman says. "Second one off 176 after the war monument." "Sure, that's right, now I see it," the man says. "Our mailbox is right across from our driveway with a big T on it in electrical tape. The Brook Isle post office knows us. I'm going for the police now to get some searchers in case she's still in the woods. But you, every now and then, even if the woman's down there, yell out her name. Olivia. Yell it out loud and for her to come to your voice—that her father told you to yell for her—or for her to shout and you'll come to hers. Please, I know I'm ruining everything for you today, but this is too important, so you'll do it?" and the woman looks at the man and he thinks it over quickly and says "Sure" and Howard runs to his car.

Drives to the cottage. Denise is feeding the baby. She looks up with a smile when he comes in, face drops when she sees his, and he says "It's very bad, couldn't be worse. Olivia's disappeared," and breaks down and she takes the baby off her breast and says "Tell me," and he quickly tells her. Phones the county police. Man there says they'll get right on it: searching party for the woods, boats to drag the lake, notify all the hospitals and trooper and police stations, someone to speak to the woman and if she's not at the lake, to find her. Lita what? He doesn't know, but her last name will come to him, he says. "One of you stay home so we can always reach you." "My wife will. I'll go back to the lake but first I'll drive around the area looking for her, in addition to your troopers and the fire department people looking. I could recognize her from a distance and, up closer, immediately. She might be in someone's car. She might be with someone who's giving her an ice cream treat at Lu-Ann's Drive-in or some such place. She might be wandering along the road looking for home or a way back to the lake and nobody's stopped her yet because they think she's a local, no sneakers or sandals and in only a swimsuit and all." "Probably little chance of that, it sounds like, but go ahead. The trooper who goes to your house will get photos of her for us to copy and pass around. You have them?" "Plenty." "Do you have that Lita's last name yet?" "No. Lita something. If I keep saying her name it could come to me, but that'll just be wasting time. Patchok comes to mind, but that's not it. Don't even know why I thought of it. If the Opel's hers, you'll be able to trace her through it, won't you?" "That or we'll try to locate her by her first name. It's unusual enough, even for around here, if she gave you the right one, that is, and if she still isn't at the lake. Nothing we can do but try."

Howard makes calls to everyone he knows in the area whose number he remembers. Help look for Olivia. Go to the lake. Search with the troopers and firemen in the woods. Tell as many people as you can to help. Don't give up till it's declared hopeless. Tells Denise to look up the numbers of other people they know in the area and say the same things. "Also ask if they know a Lita. I forgot about that. And call the police every so often just to make sure they haven't been trying to get through to us and to keep after them. But make all your calls quick so the lines aren't tied up. Of course, you know that," and runs out of the house, drives around the area, asks everyone he speaks to at the various drive-ins and shops, after he's told them about Olivia and given her description, if they know or ever heard of a young woman named Lita. Nobody has. Goes to the post office, tells his story to the postmistress and asks if she knows of a woman named Lita. She doesn't but she calls several post offices in surrounding towns and none of the other postmasters have received mail for her. "Maybe that's her nickname," she says.

Goes to the lake. Lots of cars and people, couple of fire trucks. He speaks to the police chief he spoke to on the phone. "No trace of her so far. We ordered some hounds and a helicopter in. When it gets dark we'll try best as we can with searchlights and bullhorns, but I think by nine or ten we'll have covered every foot of these woods. That woman Lita was still here. She's in her car. It's not the Opel. Hers was parked along the main road and she said she walked in, so we let her go out and bring it to the lot. Your Opel wasn't here when we got here, so it could have been anyone's—another visitor, but in his own private spot—and not seeing any commotion yet, just drove away. We put a call out on it with the plate number you gave. That Miss Reinekin—" "That's it, that's the name." "Well, she said you attacked her real bad, and showed the bruises to prove it, and that she had nothing to do either with the girl or provoking you to threatening her life. That it's all in your head, she said, which is why she stayed—to tell us. Or that you did something previously to the girl and are trying to put the blame on her. Because you came to the lake alone, swam alone and when you came out of the water you went straight up to her and asked where's your daughter. She's from near Hartford, only here for a long weekend. Friends she's staying with are with her now. They're very respectable summer prople, been coming up for years and before then the parents and grandparents of the man, and they say the woman's as truthful and right-minded as anyone they know. That she comes from a good family, well brought up and educated, never hurt anyone, and is a teacher engaged to a governor's assistant; the woman friend's known her since childhood. Just hearing all this and talking to Miss Reinekin, she doesn't seem like a child molester or kidnapper, but that's not for me to judge." "Let me speak to her." "If you don't mind someone taking down what you two say; and also no rough stuff from you, words or force." "Take down anything, and don't worry."

They go to the woman's car. She's in the back seat sitting between a man and woman, has a sweater on now, pants, glasses. "This is the man—" "She didn't wear glasses before," Howard says. "She only uses them for distance," the man says. "Let her speak. Can't she speak? Why isn't she speaking?" "She can speak but I chose then to speak for her. She's emotionally shaken. That rock over her head didn't help any." "I didn't hit her with it." "Held it over. Three inches away, if not two." "And strangling her," his wife says. "Strangling her, and nearly breaking her arm. She doesn't have to answer any more of your asinine charges or be talked threateningly to. She can even be demanding you be locked up and then suing you if she wants." "Gentlemen, let me continue," the chief says. "For the record, Miss Reinekin, this is the man you said accused you of doing something terrible to his daughter and then—" "If I hurt her, who wouldn't for his daughter? She's lucky I didn't do worse." "Anyway, I had nothing to do with it," she says. "But if this girl truly is missing—" "She's missing," the chief says. "We spoke to his wife. There's an older daughter, same description and age he gave, who's not home or anywhere to be seen. The whole county's out looking for her by now." "Then I'm sorry. It has to be the worst possible thing for the mother. But I've told everything I know of it. And Mr. Kaden here—he's not a lawyer but he knows something about it—has advised me not to talk about it further except in front of a lawyer. But a girl's missing, we all pray she's safe—" "Oh shit, just listen to her," Howard says. "—and I'll answer any more questions you have if it'll help find her. First, yes, he is the man who did all the things I said he did. I still don't know why. We hadn't said a word or even looked at the same time to one another till he came out of the water, though I did notice him go in and then swimming. Mostly the crawl but occasionally the breaststroke and once the butterfly stroke—" "I did no such stroke. I don't know how." "Well, it looked like the butterfly stroke by someone not that good at it, all that splashing and arm-flopping. But after he came out—" "He accused you and grabbed your arm and so on?" the chief says. Nods. "Nothing new to add?" Shakes her head. "Then you ought to go home, rest—we have your statement and now your identification of Mr. Tetch—and we'll go on with our search as though the girl were lost in the woods and no doubt contact you later." "You going to let her go just like that?" "It's been more than 'just that,' Mr. Tetch." "And I didn't say Olivia was lost in the woods. I said it's one of the main possibilities. I don't know where she is. She can be in that freaking water. She can be under a rock or down a well. This one knows though." "You said I may go, officer? It's been, as you can see, too much of an afternoon for me and I don't want to say now what I really think about him." "Do you have any evidence for what you don't want to say?" the chief says. "I definitely suggest you don't say anything, Lita," Kaden says. "If there's an inquest or trial or anything like that—" "You fucking liars, with your inquests and trials," Howard says. "You fucking murderer and kidnapper," he says to her. "Or you're all murderers or kidnappers. Now where is she already? Where the goddamn fuck is she?" and tries opening the door, Kaden pulls it shut and locks it while his wife rolls up the window and Lita screams and covers her eyes. Howard bangs on the window, is led away by the chief and made to sit on the grass.

Lita drives off with Mrs. Kaden, Kaden drives behind them in Lita's car. Mazda, NXH #107, dark red, Connecticut. Search goes on for hours. He calls Denise every half-hour from a police car. Last call she says friends have come and gone and been very kind but she needs to be with him. He's given his and Olivia's beach things and goes home. She puts some dinner on the table for him, weeps, checks the baby, weeps, says she has to control herself so she can think straight while there's still a chance Olivia can be found, says she doesn't understand any of it. "Now go over it, once more, maybe there's something we missed." He goes over it thoroughly. "How can anything like this happen to her?" she says. "Nothing has—I'm sure she's alive and we'll find her—but how can anyone do anything like that to her? How come they don't press that woman more? How can her friends protect her like that when they must know she's lying? The police should give her a lie detector test. They should have done it immediately. Or get a hypnotist to work on her—drugs, even, to draw out the truth—if she's crazy or has a mental or physical disorder where she can't remember things and one of those means would get her to say where Olivia is or what she did with her. What about where she's staying? Maybe the Kadens are involved. Some kind of satanic cult or just selling beautiful children or a ring for whatever kind of devious or moneymaking purpose—but in a basement there or some place. Am I thinking straight or is all this part of my own growing craziness?" He says no, it's valid, "We have to try everything that's reasonable or possible," calls the police station, hoping it would relay the call to the chief's car, is told to call him at home. "The search has been called off, the chief says. "We'll resume it early tomorrow if you want." "I want." "Not even the dogs could turn up anything. They smelled blood but nothing human. They started digging up the ruins of an old cabin. That cabin must be three hundred years old. Nobody even knew an earlier settlement had been there—" "I'm not interested. Listen, my wife and I think you should give Miss Reinekin a lie detector test, and immediately. Or just get a hypnotist to hypnotize the truth out of her, or some serums or drugs to do it." "No can do. She's got to be suspected of a crime first and then agree to the test or drugs or hypnotism, and she's not." "Then what do you say to going to the Kadens' house where she's at? Anybody think of that? Olivia could be there. A satanic cult, let's say. Maybe they sell babies or slightly older children or are into all sorts of ugly things. The respectability and old-family stuff and all that lawyer-knowledge and holier-than-thou protest shit could be some kind of cover—some ruse." "Again, it wouldn't be a bad idea if anyone in the state or county police departments believed that, but we don't. The Kadens would have to be suspects too and they're anything but that. We put out queries on them and Miss Reinekin and they're as clean as they come. Try to listen to me now, Mr. Tetch—don't make trouble. We know how you both feel and our hearts go out to you as if she were our own child, but you don't want to be jailed at a time when your wife and other girl need you so such. A state's attorney and detectives will be out to see you tomorrow morning. Please be there. Then if you want to come where we'll be searching, you'll be more than welcome." "I've complete confidence in all your and your people's abilities, so of course I'll do what you say."

He looks up the Kaden address, tells Denise to take a couple of aspirins and maybe some port and try to get some sleep. "I know what I'm doing, honestly," when she says what he's doing probably isn't such a good idea, and drives to the road the Kadens' driveway leads to, parks, walks in a few hundred feet, ample moonlight, looks around, no outbuildings about, down to the beach, boathouse with a kayak and canoe, sailboat anchored in the water, different colored sail than one he saw in the lake, wades out to it and looks inside, back up the path, looks through all the first-floor windows, sees them sitting beside a fireplace in the only lighted room in the house, Kaden reading a magazine and drinking wine or something pale in a wine glass, two women talking, fireplace going. Knocks on the door. Kaden comes to it. "You." "Listen, you've got to believe me, I'm not nuts. I had my daughter. I went for a swim. I left her with your friend. She's lying about everything. My wife and I are desperate. Right now she's going crazy from it. I'm about to too. You know what it means to lose a child like this? It's the worst feeling in the world. There is no other. Maybe if she got hit and killed by a car right in front of me. That's what it's like. Or the doctor's just told me she has cancer and only a month to live. If you have kids—" "Excuse me, but if you don't leave our property—and I mean right up to the public road—this minute, I'm phoning the police." "Hell with the police. Olivia might be here. There might even be a chance you don't know about it. Now you have to—" but he can see by his face he won't, so he pushes past him and goes inside. Kaden grabs his arm. He throws him against a wall, puts his fist under Kaden's nose and says "I'm only going to look around for my daughter. Don't stop me or I'll bust you, I'll even break you in two," and shoves him out the door, kicks but misses him, slams and latches the door, runs through the first floor turning on lights and opening doors looking for the basement, finds it, another room the women are screaming for him to go. "Scream your bloody heads off; I'm looking, I'm looking." Goes downstairs, yells "Olivia, are you down here? Are you anywhere around here, Olivia?" Turns over boxes, looks behind a huge wine rack and stacks of newspapers and magazines, only door is to a toilet, nothing else to hide someone in or behind, nothing he can see to show anything strange going on. Runs upstairs; nobody's around. Runs through the first floor opening cupboards and a bathroom and closet doors. Runs upstairs to the guest bedroom, hallway bathroom, master bedroom, unused bedroom, kids' bedroom where when he turns the lights on two boys in double-decker bunks and the women start screaming. Checks every room and closet for an attic entrance. Guest bedroom a third time. Dresser and night table drawers for anything that might lead to something, woman's valise and handbag and under the bed and once more the shower stall. Goes downstairs. "Yes, this moment, walking right past me," Kaden says on the hallway phone. "Maybe he's now going to make good on his threat to bust me in two. Well, let him, since I'm not about to fight back. That's not what I do, and you're my aural witness on that, Chief Pollard... Now he's leaving the house. Good riddance I want to say to him... No, the children and women all seem to be OK. —Sure you're all right, boys? Doris?" he yells upstairs. "We're fine, Daddy," a boy says. "Is he gone?" his wife says.

He starts up the driveway. "You should wait for them here," Kaden says from the porch. "Or they'll meet you at your place, Pollard told me to tell you. But they're on their way. You've got a number of serious complaints against you, sir. You'd better get yourself a good lawyer—one who'll be able to get you off with only a few years, for you can be certain I'll see that you're charged with everything that can be thrown at you. For slander, trespassing, verbal intimidation, assaulting Miss Reinekin, barging into a private home and tossing the occupants around like an ape. Whatever you've gone through and are going through, you can't do these things to people because of it. You have—it gives you—no moral license to, do you understand that, sir? No, you wouldn't."

Drives home, Pollard's waiting for him there, is arrested, taken to the police station, jailed overnight, state's attorney and detectives question him the next day, released on is own recognizance, search continues, he drinks himself to sleep every night, Denise is on medication for a while, search is ended, woman's exonerated, he's indicted for the disappearance of Olivia, Kaden never presses charges, Miss Reinekin drops hers, he asks for a lie detector test and passes it unqualifiedly, he asks to be hypnotized by a court-appointed hypnotist and is told his story didn't change one iota from the one he told before being hypnotized, state drops its case against him: no body or witnesses or evidence of any wrongdoing beyond parental neglect no matter how hard they looked, though the state's attorney feels sure, he tells reporters, that Howard's guilty of some heinous crime against his daughter which they'll find out about in time and charge him with and send him to prison or even execute him for. Denise doesn't know what to think through all this. She doesn't believe the woman was involved in Olivia's disappearance, but how couldn't she be if Howard says she was? That's not saying she thinks he had anything to do with it, she says, other than being irresponsible in leaving Olivia with a stranger, but how couldn't he have anything to do with it if the woman didn't? Did he lose Olivia someplace, she says once—"Quick, answer me now, no time to think of one, no or yes?" "No, absolutely not." Maybe, she says, both he and the woman are responsible in a way she hasn't figured out yet. "Are you lovers, and an accident happened with Olivia and you're covering up for each other in some way where you both assumed you'd get off?" "What am I supposed to answer to that?" "Of course; that was ridiculous of me, but I simply don't know what to think. I'm not afraid of you for Eva, but I'm also not entirely comfortable with you for her and myself. I'm just confused." Goes on like that. She won't make love with him anymore, the few times he's felt like it since Olivia disappeared, and then she won't sleep in the same bed and then the same room with him. Then she brings Olivia's bed into Eva's room and sleeps there. She puts it all down as just part of her continuing grief and confusion.

Fall's come, it's cold, cottage isn't insulated, everyone they know has left, she wants to return to their apartment in the city, he wants her to stay with him here but in a heated house. "Maybe Olivia will turn up somehow. At the very least, if we're here and badgering the police, they'll continue looking for her more than they would if we weren't here, or at least not give up looking for her completely or investigating what might have happened that day. Maybe, while Miss

199

Reinekin wasn't looking, someone came and snatched Olivia away—possibly one of the persons or a group of them sunbathing on the grass that day; or even the sailor of the sailboat I saw when I swam in the lake—and will want to turn himself in for whatever reason and also give up Olivia. Or Olivia could escape from her kidnapper—a door left unlocked a first time and she just walks out or something. I've read about such things—sometimes happening weeks later, sometimes years. That wouldn't explain why Miss Reinekin insists I was never at the lake with Olivia. Maybe she was threatened by this perscn or group not to say anything about the kidnapping or they'll kill her and maybe kill Olivia also, and that's why she's been lying all this time. Maybe Olivia was taken away at gunpoint. Lots of maybes, maybe one of then on target, or one future one. But I can't leave feeling Olivia might still be around here or in an area near here and that I might, by just sticking and looking around, think of or do something to get her back."

Denise leaves with Eva, he rents a room in town. He looks for Olivia or does something to help find her every day. Asks everyone he can about her in this county and the surrounding ones. Goes to houses and logging camps in the woods and other remote areas with photos of her. Places ads in newspapers with a photo of Olivia and him, asking if anyone was or knows anyone who was at the lake that day and saw him with Olivia or just saw anyone with her that day or any day since. Puts up her missing-child poster everywhere he can. Tries to generate news interest in her disappearance, by calling and sending letters to news editors, and when that doesn't work, in the story of the father obsessed with the search, so her picture will appear again in the papers and on local TV. Goes to the Kaden house sometimes. It's boarded up for the winter. Explores the beach and woods around the house, thinking he might have missed something the previous times; studies the house from all sides, trying to determine by the windows and dormers and roof shape and size of the walls whether he missed a room or two when he went through it. Would like to break inside, but he might get

caught and jailed or ordered out of the county or even the state for
a while. Many people in the area think he had something to do with
Olivia disappearing and that by staying on and looking for her so
hard he's just trying to establish his innocence and get their
sympathy. That's what the anonymous notes say that frequently
come through the mail or are slipped into the letter box of his building
and a couple of times under his door.

He searches through different parts of the lake woods almost
every day. Goes into them in high boots because of the snow, calls
out for her, nails her poster to trees, thinks he'll one time find a sign
of her, something hanging from a tree branch or message or article
of clothing left someplace, though maybe not till the spring thaw.
Maybe there's a habitable cave in the woods no one knows about
or a hut, same thing, but completely camouflaged. Pollard said the
searching teams covered every part of the woods, but there had to
be areas too thick for anyone to go in to, or at least not without the
cutting tools he always takes with him. He imagines coming on one
of these huts—he's come on two already not shown on the town's
survey maps he has, but with no doors or roofs—and looking inside
the window, seeing Olivia and a man talking, eating. He smashes
down the door with his foot and charges inside and knocks the man
down and beats him, continues beating him with his fists or one
of the tools till the man doesn't move. Till he's dead—the hell with
him. Two or more men, he'd charge in the same way and use his
tools on them, cutting through them, aiming for their faces and necks
and groins, and then scoop up Olivia, dress her for the cold, or not
dress her—just run with her to his car and drive to the one doctor
in town.

He goes to the lake a lot, mostly to look around it but sometimes
to think. Gone out on the ice several times to see what he could make
out on the shore from there. Crisscrossed it, walked in to every cove,
stood in various spots on it to see if any smoke was coming from
places where no houses were supposed to be. Once he thought he
saw a girl around Olivia's height on the beach not far from where

he lost her. Walked back without taking his eyes off her, yelled while he walked "Don't move, don't go away, stay there for God's sakes, it's Daddy," then imagined her on shore when he got there and putting his coat and scarf around her and picking her up and kissing her head and hands all over and carrying her back to the road where he left the car—running with her, shouting "I've found her, my little baby; everybody, I've found her, found her."

Sits in the snow in the same place he last sat with her. Tries to bring her back. Talks to where she sat. Says "Olivia, please be here. Materialize from wherever you are. Just by some miracle or something, be with me now. Or walk through those woods there, say you've been kidnapped and you just broke free or they let you go. Please, my dearest child, come back. Daddy's heartbroken. He can't live without you. He's sad all the time knowing what might have happened and might still be happening to you. If it can only be a miracle that brings you back, you never have to tell me where you were or how you got back to me or anything about it. Never, I swear."

Later he calls the police chief as he usually does once a week and says "Please bear with me again, I know I've become a terrible nuisance to you, but is there anything new regarding my daughter here or in this country or the world?" "Nothing," Pollard says; "I wish there was." "But you're still doing your best to find her, right?" "Whatever there is to be done, and there isn't anything anymore without new information or leads on her, we're doing it, sir, you can count on it. If anyone calls the special phone number we set up for her, the news would reach me in minutes. And believe me, if I couldn't get hold of you by phone right away, I'd come, or send another officer, to wherever I thought you were. As I've said I don't know how many times, I fully understand how you feel, so you call me anytime you like."

Frog Dies

He dies. How does he? He's running, collapses. Happens that quickly. Doesn't even know it, or barely. Sharp pain in the chest a few minutes before but he thought it was an upper abdominal stitch, stopped, pressed on it to move the gas bubble down, waited till the pain went, pain went, continued running. Then a sharper pain in the chest a few minutes later, and maybe just when he realizes what's happening or might be, he's unconscious, never recovers. He's in his car. He's thought for a long time he might die in a car accident. Not a heart attack in one, making him lose control of the wheel, but because of some wrong move or bad decision on his part or the driver's in another car. It's been close several times. Several times he's thought if he'd been a second slower in reacting to this or that, or if he hadn't looked to the right just then, or if the car behind him or to his side had been a foot closer, a few inches closer. . . . He just hoped neither of his children nor his wife would be with him when this accident happened. This time he pulls off the highway into a one-way street and a truck speeding his way. He tries to avert it by making a sharp right but the truck tries to avert him by making a sharp left. Three young man come up to him at a bus stop, say it's a holdup, give them everything he has, he gives them everything he has, they shoot him in the head. Stomach pains, been feeling them late at night for weeks, thinks they're because of the wine and liquor he drinks too close to bedtime while he reads, tells himself to stop drinking at least two hours before he goes to sleep, can't, one hour, never does it, treats himself with antacids, pain increases, turns out to be pancreatic cancer, he has one to two months, three to four weeks, barely has time to prepare for it, his wife and children barely have time. Then he gets so sick and weak that just about all he can do in his few waking hours a day is think about his nausea and pain. He also cries a lot, that he'll be dying and losing his children and wife, the growing up of his children, his children as adults. He's in a restaurant, fishbone gets caught in his throat, tries coughing it up, someone runs up behind him, clears a table with a sweep of his arm, throws him on the table facedown and uses a method on him to dislodge the bone, it doesn't come out, he continues to choke, can't breathe, just as another diner is about to cut into his windpipe with a steakknife, he dies. He's crossing the street, hat flies off his head, he chases it, looks both ways, no cars are coming, picks it up, gets clipped by a car. A plank is blown off a building going up and hits him on the head. A hammer falls from a building going up, a flowerbox in an apartment windowsill, part of a cornice of an old building.

His oldest daughter can't believe it at first. No, she believes it. "Daddy isn't coming home anymore," Denise tells her. "Why?" "Daddy passed away." "What's that?" "Oh Jesus, how should I explain it? It means Daddy's not coming home again ever." "But why not?" "You still don't know what I'm saying?" "No." "All right, plain and simply: he died." "I know what 'to died' is. You don't have to explain to me. I know I won't see him anymore. I feel bad, but it's OK." She can hardly sleep, is morose most of the day. When she can sleep, she twists around fitfully, has nightmares she says she'd tell what they're about if she could remember them. "All I remember is big teeth in every one of them, some with no faces, and scary dancing deer." Eats little, won't play, never laughs, avoids her baby sister, talks mostly in whispers, doesn't want to go out or to school, sits by herself all day at school looking at books or staring out the window or keeping her eyes shut. Starts to play by herself with a bear she's renamed Daddy. Dresses it in cloth napkins, toilet tissue and doll socks, feeds it her snacks, takes it for strolls around her room in her doll carriage, puts it to bed at night and covers it up to its neck and hums or tells stories to it, but she won't sleep in her bed. She sleeps with Denise for weeks, clutching a soft shark. The youngest child asks for Dada several times a day. Phone or doorbell rings: "Dada." Comes into the kitchen while Denise is cooking or cleaning and says "Dada, where?" and looks around for him there. Other times: goes into the coat closet, shuts the door and when Denise looks for her and finds her sitting in the dark there, says "Dada, looking." Says "Dada out," and turns with little quick steps in a circle, meaning she wants him to take her out. Sometimes puts her hat on, carries her coat or snowsuit around the house saying to Denise or to no one "Dada work." That could mean she wants to be in the back- or front yard where she thinks he's working or in the cold basement where he did his schoolwork and typed. But she doesn't seem sad, sleeps the same, hasn't lost her appetite, wants to play with Olivia, cries or screams when Olivia ignores her or shuts her door on her or pushes her away, goes to her toddler group once a week with no fuss. Years later when they talk about him, she gets sad. "I wish I'd known him. First I wish he were here. He wouldn't be that old. Even if he were, he'd be a big vigorous sixty-five. I've so little to almost no memory of him. Sometimes I think I've more than that, but then I suddenly know I've been leading myself on." When they're adults they sometimes look at photographs of themselves with him, with Daddy alone, of Daddy alone, Daddy as a baby and a boy, with Mother, holding both of them, cheeks against his, week after Eva was born. "This was the first time we took you out after you came home from the hospital," Olivia says. "I can't say I remember the event, but I do recall the photo." Daddy and Olivia hamming it up for the camera, Eva crying behind them.

"I'm sure he didn't hear you—I wouldn't say the same for me—or he would have stopped clowning immediately to take care of you. Mother probably just didn't see you through the viewfinder." Daddy carrying them in a garbage can, standing beside them seated on a camel, squeezed inside an igloo with them he made in the street after the city's biggest snowstorm in a decade, holding them in one arm on a beach. "He was always so lean and muscular," Eva says. "Look at that neck. No wonder Mom fell for him at his age." "He was still doing a thousand pushups a day when he turned fifty," Olivia says, "then as a birthday gift to himself dropped to nine hundred. And running three miles every morning except on the first day of a bad flu or when the streets were coated with ice. He was a little bit too musclebound and showoffy for my tastes." "Daddy a showoff? According to Mom he was self-deprecating and overly self-critical, hid himself in dark clothing, was taciturn at gatherings, wouldn't be interviewed, was invited to but never wrote articles or reviews, even in class, was unduly apologetic to his students and scarcely expressed his views." "Musclebound and vain, then. He used to flex his chest and arm muscles in front of my bedroom mirror some mornings after he thought he got me back to sleep. And I once walked in on him pulling himself off in front of the full-length bathroom mirror, though their sex life, Mother's said, except when she was just being generous with her body, was nothing but ripe and raw." Eva holds up several photos. "What beach is it?" Olivia doesn't know, calls Denise. "Chincoteague," she says, "home of wild ponies and soggy oysters. We went there for a weekend every spring and fall, before and after the tourist season. This was going to be a family tradition, your father said, even after you both got married and had children and if the oyster beds survived, but it only lasted four to five years. I remember that day well. You can always tell a great day when we have so many photographs of it, though there were some great days when we overexposed the film or quickly ran out of it. It was so windy on the beach that your father, with the emergency shovel he always kept in the car next to the emergency rope, flares, books, pads and pens, dug a hole in the sand deep enough for all of us to sit belowground and have lunch, even if Eva was still only nursing. I wouldn't go down. It just seemed too silly. I knew people would pass, hear us and take pictures of us down there. I also didn't trust the walls. I felt if they collapsed he'd only be able to get you two out and I'd be buried alive with Eva's breasts."

On his birthday every year one sister calls the other and the one who's called usually says something like "I know why you're calling; I still miss him too." "If only you could remember him better," Olivia says, "it would make these memory days more memorable. I have to do it all for us, which makes me distrust my memory somewhat, going so uncorrected and uncorroborated." "I feel I'm remembering him a little more each year. The smile, which I keep seeing: sort of soft, benign, kind of bringing me in, no artifice." "Photographs. What about his black scowling look, or the reproachful one, which could go on for hours. Nobody I've known was ever more up and down, back and forth, than Daddy. In that way, bad father. One moment he'd be all over Mother and me with praise and fondling lovingness and be thoroughly sincere about it. Then I'm off to first grade and can't find my eyeglasses and he'd rave, stamp and complain how she was the last to see them and I'm old enough to remember to take care of them and the money they cost and he'll be late again getting me to school, meaning he'll have to park the car and walk me to my classroom, and what the fuck the glasses doing for me anyway?—'You go to an eye doctor, he always prescribes—bunch of born hustlers!'—and shove his arms up to his shoulders in the kitchen trash can looking for them, thinking you might have dropped them there or Mother or me with some other garbage by mistake. And then apologize profusely when he finally drives me to school, for making me so sad and afraid and resentful and possibly a little screwy with his sudden changing moods. 'But don't worry, I'll stop doing it, my lovey-dove—I swear,' and kiss my head and hands and also my eyes, if we didn't find the glasses, and say 'So, are we friends again?' and I'm telling you, cry sometimes too because of what he'd say was his base treatment of me. I didn't know what the hell was going on, or I did but knew I didn't want to be there." "I'm glad I missed it." "You didn't; you simply don't remember it. Listen, I saw him a few times, though he never did it when Mother was around, throw you on the bed when he was changing you, angry that you peed just after he put a fresh diaper on. Or wipe your face so hard with a paper towel that I thought he'd take your skin off, all because you wouldn't eat what he thought was the minimum amount for you or you stuck your hand in the gooey food or dropped some of it on the floor. He couldn't stand a mess, books out of place, records out of their jackets, a disheveled room." "Actually, if I had the choice I'd want to remember what he did to me no matter how bad it was. Anything. But you know, a few weeks ago, when I was waking up, I suddenly saw myself falling asleep on his shoulder. Now that had to have happened, since I can't remember you telling me of it regarding either of us and I never saw a photo of it." "He had a sleeping shoulder, he used to say—but you wouldn't remember him saying that." "I certainly don't ever remember talking to him, being talked to by him, anything with talk, except in my dreams, where he's gone on about all sorts of things in speedy stream-of-c style, and more times than not that he wants me to be or why I should become one, a pianist who concentrates on Mozart and Bach and Satie and in the orchestral-piano works conducts while she plays. But I'm sure I remember the shoulder and much of the scenery surrounding it. Was the guest bed in the room with my crib a big oak double one with a headboard taller than most men?" "I told you that; my very words." "You did? Then did I have an oval mirror above my dresser that was too high to look into except when someone held me?" "We both did, which I've also spoken of, though I got to see myself in it via a chair. Mother said that whenever she couldn't walk one of us to sleep—they alternated nightly on the one being walked—she'd give us to him and we'd flake out in minutes. He used to sing songs to me when he put me to sleep like that." "My shoulder memory doesn't include that, but I'm sure he did the same for me."

"I know he did. You were in the next room and I never permitted my door being closed at night. I only found out later about him singing to me when I asked why he sang to you when he never had to me and he said that for more than two years I got the exact same special heed. They used to put me to sleep the same time as you then—eight-o-dot. I thought it unfair, considering our age difference and that I needed no sleep cajolery, but anyway, I could hear him singing to you in his high lyrical baritone gone to seed and a number of times saw him singing while walking you when I barged in to say good night to him. Love songs, mostly—how you were without doubt the weirdest, most worthless, least pleasurable—no, really, the fairest most gorgeous adorable mild-tempered redolent intelligent creature in all the galaxies, bar none, not even the ones to be discovered yet, and how sleep would only make you more squeezable, beautiful, smart and sweet. And all the words made up on the spot it seemed and I believe same went for the melodies when they weren't lifted from old show tunes and radio theme songs or from his favorite operatic arias or piano or liturgical scores. This is fun, Eva. Work on, without my help, bringing back other memories of him. It's not as if I'm talking to myself anymore."

On what would have been his sixtieth birthday Denise and the two girls go to his grave. He once said he wouldn't mind being buried, if it was no trouble, near the cottage they summered at in Maine, his mother wanted him buried in Long Island between the grave of one of her children and the cenotaph of another, Denise went along with her because she was so insistent or emotional or something about it—"Last thing for the little time I've left I'll ever ask of you," that sort of thing—that Denise couldn't resist and also because of the cost of a burial plot anywhere and maintaining it and the ticklishness of finding one in that Maine town which would admit a summer renter and one, counting the four summers Denise went there alone or with lovers, of only eleven years, who was also Jewish. They meet, without planning it, his brother there. He came with a prayer book, covers his head with his hand and reads the mourner's prayer in phonetical Hebrew and then says "Maybe, as long as we're all here, we should say something about Howard, even Eva. How we felt and have been feeling since and so on—you know, about him, theoretically reaching sixty, or just anything. Like to be first, Denise?" "You wouldn't want to?" "I don't know what to say yet, if I'm going to say anything but 'Continue to read I mean rest in peace, if you are, my brother,' and I thought I'd be polite. Please, you were the person closest to him ever, but if you don't want to and everyone thinks it's a bad idea. . ." "All I can say—" She turns to the grave. "All I can say is that—" "And about him being sixty, maybe that's ridiculous. But say what you want. Please." "All I can say is that I loved him—you, darling—very much, and still miss you and think you would have—no, *he, him, he would have,* because it's so silly. I don't believe in spirits or that he's here in any immaterial way like that. Maybe that's not the right word, or right word when employed like that, but this is where we plopped him, so fine, period. I'm sorry, sweethearts," to the girls. "I don't mean to scare you. Maybe your father's spirit is here. I'm not saying I know one way or the other, or definitively. It would be nice to think he's here in some way, or maybe not, for him—unrest. Anyway," to the grave, "I think he would have wanted me to go on the way I had and approved of most of what I did. If you're here and it's true, my old darling, or just that you agree with me for the most part, knock twice or do something earthshaking to let us know, if it's all right with the higher or lower authorities, if there are those too. —With little major disruptive mourning at first, little to none thereafter, lots of sad semisleepless nights throughout it, taking over things as well as I feel I did." "You did. Don't let anybody say anything if anyone did," Jerry says. "Nobody did that I know." "Good. They were right. You had it tough and did a great job. And sorry for interrupting. Go on, if you're not finished—please." "Taking over the householding and child rearing and moneymaking and such completely—well, not completely. When I remarried two years later and for the months I knew him before, I got plenty of help from Eric. But also that: that he would have wanted me to remarry and so quickly, just so I'd get some help and wouldn't be lonely, and also have another child, since a third's what Howard and I had wanted and begun working on, and what else? Getting rid of all his manuscripts, unpublished and pubbed. I mustn't forget that, since it seemed as important to him as almost anything for me to take care of if he suddenly died and was his written and several times his spoken wish. 'If I die but before then can't tend to this myself, after the craziness is over and everything's clearer, out all these go,' which he left in a letter envelope marked 'Incalculably urgent' and pasted on the inside manuscript cabinet door. 'And don't waste your time burning them or tearing them up. Green or black trash bags and probably the three-ply leaf kind; and all in one Wednesday or Saturday pickup and without telling anyone what's inside.' Actually, I shouldn't lie here. Olivia's giving me looks as if I'm lying, so I won't. I did, after the postfunereal craziness and in a period of clarity, send a number of those manuscripts to publishers and parts of them to magazines, saying these were the last works of my recently deceased husband, hoping that might give them a sentimental and for the publisher a promotional edge, but they were just as swiftly returned as they had been before. Only after they'd been turned down four or five times each did I get rid of them. I did keep a few to remind myself of him whenever I wanted to— manuscripts that were clearly about his life with me and his work and also the girls and us. But after a year or so I forgot about or misplaced them, though I know I didn't dispose of them, and now I haven't a clue where those remaining manuscripts are. Probably with the note he left on the cabinet door and that folder I kept with all the new rejections of his work and the list of what manuscript went where and when. Maybe, if his spirit's here and wants to tap for something it or he deems important, it can tap for that—once for whether I should try to find the manuscripts and send them out again, for maybe the promotional edge is even greater now—the widow who finds her husband's lost manuscripts after almost ten years—or two, to find them and put them in the next trash pickup.

—OK, enough, and everyone here should know that when I said I had plenty of semisenseless nights after he died, or however I put it, I meant that for a couple of weeks I felt I could have killed myself if I'd had the easy means and no kiddies and cat—that that's how, well, that that's just how, well, just end of graveside chat, and I've gone on so queerly long. Olivia?" "I miss him too much to say anything." "So say nothing," Jerry says. "Nothing's fine sometimes." "I also wouldn't know what to say. I'm too young to say anything that intelligent or right or unembarrassing. Or maybe I'm just intelligent enough not to say anything that young and innocently wrong and so not very embarrassing, or not for so long. Something, though, but you know." "So what have I been saying?" Jerry says. "Really, my little olive, probably my idea wasn't that smart a one for you kids. What do you think, Denise—should we put a closure on it for now?" "I think if they want to say something at his grave, now's a good opportunity. Nobody but you has been out here for years. And as a family we haven't been here since the stone was put up, and even then, Eva wasn't with us. But it's up to Olivia." "I'm so unhappy," Olivia says, "that if I did say anything—but I'm already crying while I'm saying this, which was what I was about to say—I'd cry." "Honestly, I don't see the point to this anymore," Jerry says. "The point," Denise says, "is that if it's simply a big quick emotional hurt that can get somewhere nothing else has been able to, all the better for her while we're here and he's there, spirit or spiritless. Tell a story then or an anecdote of you and your father, or anything." "Or nothing. Excuse me again, Denise, but as I said before," to Olivia, "nothing's OK too, and at times can be perfect." "Jell-O," Olivia says. "OK, Jell-O. What?" "Just Jell-O. Something that happened. It just popped into my head. Not a real standout memory or one that's going to do anything moving to me. But it's as good as any between us, and it was so like him, I think. It typified." "Tell it, I never heard it," Eva says. "Now I think I forgot it." "Come on!" "I was around five and it was a Sunday. It had to be a Sunday since that's what he was talking about. And I couldn't have been more than five years

212

and seven months, since that's what I was when he died. And it was about Jell-O because of what comes next. I was sick and he was going food-shopping and Mother asked him to bring back, guess. It was all I could digest, etcetera, except maybe applesauce, which I don't think we ever ran out of, even on the road, for fifteen years." "Jell-O was just about the only liquid you'd take when you were very ill," Denise says. "So. When he came back he was talking in this funny ethnic accent he always seemed to come back with from this particular market because of the people who shopped and worked there, he said." "Baltimore-Jewish," Denise says; "you can say it." "He always caught it like a cold, he said—in fact, the 'Jewish flu' he called it, and then in that accent—I can't do it, so I won't even try, or I'll sound silly. Vs for Ws and so on and lots of *ichs* and *uchs*. But that he got my favorite Jell-O flavor. 'What kind?' I probably said and he said 'Onion Jell-O.' No, this is too dumb." "You can't stop now," Eva says, "and it's new." "I said 'But this is lime,' and showed him the lime picture on the Jell-O box and he said 'No, that's a very old onion, which turns green inside like a lime. Cut any old onion in half and you'll see how green it is.' I didn't know what a real green onion was then. If I did I'm sure I would have said, just to try to be a match for him, 'But a green onion is a very young one.' And I'm sure he would have said to that 'Well this a prematurely old green onion—something happened to it in its youth. In its salad days, we could say,' and have to explain what that meant since I wouldn't have known about that too. And then given several ridiculous but sort of sensible reasons why the green onion became prematurely old. Green onion disease or fell in love with a leek who thought he was too young for her, etcetera. Anyway, I said 'Is that true, Mommy?' about the old onion turning green like a lime, and she shook her head and I said 'She says it's not true.' And he said 'No, she's shaking her head, all right, but on Sunday'—maybe I made him sound too anti-Jewishy before, and at a Jewish cemetery too. He isn't; he wasn't. I'm sure." "You didn't sweetheart," Denise says. "He sounds fine. Go on, finish." " 'But on Sundays,' he said, 'when you shake your head it means yes, and when you nod it means no. I'm surprised, you being such an intelligent girl, you didn't know that.' 'Is that true, Mommy?' I asked and you shook your head and he said 'You see? She's shaking her head. So what I said's true.' That's all. Story's over. I knew—" "No, it was fine," Denise says. "Lively, revealing; just right." "It was flat, stilted, long-winded. I didn't catch him. I never catch him. Too much made up." "Can I go now?" Eva says. "It's getting late and maybe too cold for all of you and I'm a little tired from standing," Jerry says. "Sit on the grass, Uncle Jerry." "You can't sit on the grass." "Give her a minute," Denise says. "We'll all button up our coats." "I wish I could have got to know him," Eva says. "I think I knew a little of him. I remember him playing peekaboo with me. I think I remember that and also him holding my hand. This one," showing the right. "And him feeding me. I'm in that special baby's chair attached to a table, he's sitting beside me with a book opened for me and saying 'You eat, I read,' and I think I'm saying 'Bunny, bunny' in the way you said I did," to Denise. "Maybe that's remembering more than there was. But I do remember once lying beside him on the bed in my parents' room while he was watching the news and he put his arm around me and I rested my head on his chest and I think I was holding the bottle by the nipple between my teeth and he kissed the top of my head many times. Milk in the bottle and he was propped up against pillows and maybe only kissed me once or twice. But that one I remember a lot. I can't remember anything else right now except through the photos of him with me and what other people have said about him over and over again till it's maybe become what I think I saw. Or was that Olivia's idea? She always gets there first." "Do not." "Anyway, what else, since I don't think I've said anything yet. I like the man Mom married next but I never felt he was my father. I can say that without hurting your feelings, can't I, Mom? Well, too late. Of course I'm glad you married Eric and it was nice of him to adopt us and that you love him real well, as you say. The truth is, I'm not telling the truth. I think I felt I had to say those things because we're standing here, something of him must be around in the air or underneath, and I'm superstitious and maybe a little scared. The truth is, Eric to me is my father and my real actual father, Howard, is like a ghost, a nobody, a shadow. Really, most like a shadow. A shadow holding my hand, a shadow feeding and kissing me. An apparition, I mean. See it but not feel it. That must be old stuff. I can never be original. Olivia can. Not that I don't admire her for it. I do, it's wonderful, I'm envious in the most generous way. 'My sister,' I say, 'she's great.' So what do I have to say after all my eagerness to speak? And because it is getting chilly and poor Uncle Jerry looks both bored and tired." "Just a bit tired, sweetie." "I've nothing to say. All this time, and with an all-ears audience, and nothing. If I've one thing to say it's I wish he hadn't died so soon. If I've two, and I don't see why I shouldn't combine one and two into one, it's I wish he had taken care of himself better so he wouldn't have died so soon. I don't know what that would have meant." "Entailed," Olivia says. "And you shouldn't think he was at fault. He might have ran himself too hard, but what he got ran in his family, and he did reach fifty. Maybe we'll get what he got and not reach forty." "Romantic nonsense," Olivia says. "Just get checkups and don't think it." "Then the two of you should have had me sooner, so I could have had the experiences with him Olivia did. And the photos. And you should have pushed them too, Ollie, saying 'Sister, I want a baby sister, baby baby sister,' but saying it so many times and in such a loud whiny voice that they would have started me sooner rather than listen to you anymore. Three years sooner, even two, I'll take two. I'll take one. I would have come out something the same. We look alike, Olivia and I, just as all of Uncle Jerry's kids and us look alike, so I probably would have been a slightly different looking person with the same name. An inch shorter or taller. I mean, when I'm fully grown. I'll take taller. I'll take prettier. I'll take Olivia's complexion and hair and nose and frailer legs. I'll take anything to have definite memories of me with him. Mine, I mean. A quotient— that's the right word, right?—dumber or smarter. I'll take smarter, but if dumber, then not so much so. Meaning where it'd incapacitate me. And I wouldn't take sickness either. Throwing up a dozen more times than I'd normally do over fifty years, fine, but nothing life-lasting or short-living like Howard's sister Mira." "Vera," Jerry says. "Right over here. I'm going to ask you all at the end to put a small stone on her monument just so she doesn't feel ignored. Dad's too, if we can find that many, though I doubt it would bother him, and he's probably sleeping through all this or thinking we're all such sentimental fools. Your Uncle Alex's is only a cenotaph, so we don't have to worry about his feelings unless this is where he decided to settle, and why wouldn't he? So his too, but by then we'll probably have to share a single stone. But is that all, Eva? I'm not rushing, simply asking you, but also shivering a bit, for I'd like to say something too." "All. You didn't like what I said, right?" "No no, sweetie." "Not bright, too shallow, nothing from inside." "No, it was smart, something, not shallow; felt, so very nice indeed. And what's the difference? If anybody wasn't a speaker it was your father. He'd appreciate someone trying to find the right words and failing at it. And his daughter? You can bet, not that failing's what you did, but he distrusted people who didn't hem and haw. But—Howard, on your sixtieth birthday, and are we supposed to believe that? My stringbean kid brother, the boy I ignored for his first twenty years? But you see the respect, I'd say love, you have from all those who were so very close to you. As you can also see, I'm not that hot at this either—and Mom, who's all right. Still hanging in there, drinking, smoking, coffeeing, reading without glasses and pretending to hear, a little more lined but still a beauty, was a trifle too, what was the word Eva used? frail, to undergo today. But she said to give you her love, and even confessed to me that you were her favorite after Alex of the boys, but she also said she had to admit that Alex had the advantage in that department of having a natural sweet disposition since birth, compared to us, and dying young and being the first boy to go. But—let's see. I shouldn't go on at length, for one who complained about the cold, so just may your soul rest in peace, if it hasn't been, and continue to for eternity, if it has, if that doesn't seem too deathlike a fate. That's all I can say, and I think everyone here shares those sentiments, besides joining with Mom in sending our strongest expressions of love," and breaks down. "Amen," Denise says and puts her hands on the backs of her children who are hugging Jerry, was looking at Howard's stone so didn't see if he'd beckoned to them in some way first or they came to him on their own.

Olivia calls Eva and says "I had a dream last night that Dad—Howard—returned. That he just came back, like that—knocked on the door, looked very old. Sunken cheeks, completely bald, no way we'd ever seen him in person or photos. Ugly face hairs, teeth rotted and cracked, little pits and bites around his mouth, and he said to me when I opened the door and immediately started screaming, for he was also in these awful torn clothes and smelled like piss so it really seemed as if he'd just stepped out of the grave, 'I am your father, Chutchkie.' That was his favorite nickname for me. 'I want to hug and kiss you but know what a mess I am. I want to swing around with you on a gate again but know I'll disintegrate if touched. I want to say I'm always near you, hideous as that thought must be to you, or almost always near—I stay away when it's discreet for me to. If there was only some way for me to really return. If I only could.' That's when he started digging his long fingernails into his forehead. 'If I could only be in normal clothes and health for someone my age and just talk to you on the phone, even, or whatever they have today where people communicate with one another from different places. To write a letter to you, even, if those things are still sent. I'd deliver it personally. I'd be satisfied just to slip it under your door. Leave it on your front steps. When I was alive I used to think a lot about what I'd do if you died first. I wouldn't be able to go on, I decided, and never decided against that. I loved your mother and sister but could have survived either of their deaths, though would always have been sad after that, or almost always, maybe because I would have had you to hold on to. But *you*, plop, I would have disappeared. The things you did and said that made me so happy. "I remember when

217

I was born." ' Here he's quoting me when I was around four-and-a-half, which actually happened. ' "It was dark, crowded and wet." ' For some reason he found that brilliant, Mother said. I apparently also claimed I heard music when I was in the womb, though admittedly close to term. 'That piece,' I said about some Haydn piano variation or sonata the record player was playing, 'I remember it when I was inside Mother,' and sure enough he had played it nearly every day for a month when she was pregnant. I don't trust that reminiscence, but he went for it. Then in the dream he goes on about his favorite memory of me. How he came into my room when I was sitting busily working at my little kid's table with crayons, pencils, a huge sheet of paper. After a few minutes I turned around, he said, and announced ' "I'm drawing a picture of a zoo for the kids in my class so they'll know where they're going tomorrow. Here's a cage. There's a chattering monkey. Up here's a bird with many colors. Over there's an ice cream man and balloons. The sun's shining because it's such a nice day. Way in the background it's raining, but that's over another city. There's all of us on the grass having fun. Adam, Claire, the two Ryans, Marianne. . . .Over here's a dog walking by with his master, glad to be so close to so many different kinds of animals. He's telling his master that—see the barking lines? The sky is blue, the trees are green, flowers are floating down from the branches, the girls are all wearing pretty colorful dresses, the boys are in new jeans. The hearts I put around the picture are for decoration and how we all feel. Over here's a giraffe I didn't draw very well, but I think I got the neck and spots on it OK. When it's done I'll cut it out, and after my class uses it I'll give it to you. Are you proud of me for what I'm doing, Daddy?" My Chütch,' he said to me, 'I have to come back to you, there are no two ways about it. I have to continue where I left off. I want to buy food for you, go to the zoo with you, read you a story, listen to you make up poetry, kiss you good night, dim your light, sprawl on the floor beside your bed with my head on your legs till you're asleep, maybe hold your hand while I'm doing it if you don't mind for me to, shut your light off, slowly close your door, stand outside your room with my head against the door jamb thinking of the things we did together that day or I saw you do, what we might do the next. My dearest'—this is still Howard talking—'I loved you more than I loved anyone in any way in my life. Your mother knew. We had few secrets and none about that. Eva I loved enormously also but didn't have the time with her I had with you. I'm sure, though maybe not, since she was the second and I loved my first so much, but it very well could have been the same with her or fairly close if I'd had two more years. Maybe there's something you can do to help me come back. Sounds silly, but church after church was built on miracles, or for the most part, and still keep themselves going that way somewhat or their holds over their flocks, so maybe those things do exist. Love would be able to set one off if anything could, I'd think, or one as deep and tight as mine, though so many people like me or in my position I'll say must feel and think that, so the chances if there are any must be very slight. But try to think of something to help me. And Eva. Speak to your sister and see. Maybe my big advantage over the others is that I was lucky to have such smart capable girls. Funny, but those were the exact adjectives my father used to say about his boys.' Then the dream ended. What do you make of it? I'm just following instructions. I didn't repeat any of it to hurt you." "It's a good dream," Eva says. "Maybe even a great one. I know I never had one better or near so good. Big, strong, clear, reverberatory, though with little take to the give. So much like a fine short slow artsy European movie, more Nordic than Alpine or Mediterranean, and one that most viewers wouldn't take to unless their life stories approximated yours. To be shown in four or five select theaters around the country, is the way I'd distribute it. Not much profit, in other words, and no bundle to be made through public TV either, since it wouldn't get on till 11:00 P.M. And that it sunk in so much. Improbable, if it had come from anyone else. I wish I saw him in a dream like that. All bones and stink and rot and monolog—I wouldn't care so long as I knew it was he and he spoke to me or at least showed he saw me or heard. Even in a quick daydream, just 'Hello and good bye and I love you, my little pancake,' or just some rapid eye contact, but it's never happened and by now I'm convinced it never will. Think of it: all these years and all my efforts. Staring at his photos and reading some of his manuscripts and also published stuff before I went to bed—even the most autobiographical ones and especially the few where even I'm included, albeit as a crawl-in—just to help it happen. But it's really too late at night or early in the morning for me to speak coherently about it. Tomorrow, or much later today—whichever comes first. You still at the same temp job? Say, I just had a brainstorm. Maybe if we went to church some quiet afternoon when hardly anyone but the sexton was there and prayed for him to return in one real wholesome recognizable human piece. Dad as you knew him or, more orderly, as he would have, devoid of all debilitating diseases, aged. Synagogues have never been good for that for me. I never got the impression prayer will get you anywhere there. No incense essence or votary candles for sale or come-in-and-pray-anytime policy or transformed or sorrow-torn or just trouble-free people on their knees, and they certainly don't promise to get you a step or two closer to heaven or away from hell. But tell me where you're working now." "My last week secretarying. It's no good for my brain." "Then you phone me at my studio, since you get the freebie and by leaving soon have much less to lose. Maybe I can fly in to see you in a week and we'll devise some plan like that praying-at-a-church, to bring him back if just for an hour or a day."

Olivia writes an essay about her father. "The most important person in my life," it's titled. "Actually," she writes, "he wasn't the most important person in my life. My mother was. But I didn't want to write about her. I wanted to find out what I was feeling about him. I know what I feel about her. I love and respect her tremendously. I loved my father a lot too but I had some major grievances against him. Major, by the way, was one of my father's favorite words, my mother's said, as it is one of mine, though she told me this only after I started using it a lot. Since I seem to take after him in many other ways, like my walk and ear for music and having trouble getting to the point I want to make, besides most of my physical traits, she thinks maybe my use of words was inherited from him too. And I had to look up the word 'grievance' before. I'm saying all this because I want the readers of this essay, which will probably only be my teacher Mrs. Zimkin (should I have put a comma after 'teacher'? I think so) and maybe my classmates, if she thinks it's good enough to read parts of in class or really that good to read the whole of (or bad enough to show where the unnamed student, in this case, went wrong, as an example for the entire class. I used 'entire' then because I didn't want to use 'whole' twice in one sentence. Maybe I'm wrong in doing that). But Mrs. Zimkin will probably still be the only reader, since my classmates, if they get to hear any of it, will just be listeners. (Did I really need all that space to make such a small point? And why I used 'just' when I felt like using 'only' then, I already said. But it's so unnatural that I think I'll change that policy.) Anyway, I want the reader and listeners, if there are any, to know just how honest this essay is. In both its ideas and aims and so on, as well as its conception, or just realization or execution, three more words I just looked up for their spelling. But: grievances against him. (If this essay is among the best she's ever read of a student's, Mrs. Zimkin's said, or better put, which I'm sure she'll appreciate: 'among the best student essays she's ever read,' then not only do the classmates hear all of it, if it's not too long, but she asks Mr. Zimkin, who's chairman of the English Department of a major university in the city, to read it. That would mean it would have at least two readers, but one very distinguished one. Another word I just looked up, and sorry, Mrs. Z. You're great, but he's got the prestige.) (I'm not sure the comma was necessary after 'great.' And when I looked up the rule for it, I couldn't understand it.) But: grievances. That my father wouldn't just let me eat, for starters. (I had a better example to start with but lost it in all the other stuff I put in.) That he did most of the cooking and feeding for my sister and me didn't help matters either. (Notice the proper word usage there with 'my sister and me.' Elementary ((word looked up)) for some, but I had to look up the rule for maybe the tenth time this term.) But because of that or something else—some compulsion (looked-up word, and put that way—'looked-up'—just to change things around a bit; but this time ((also notice the punctuation just then (((I mean with the semicolon))) and also now's and right after 'elementary' before, since I don't have brackets on this machine; not used by most kids my age, I'd think)) I didn't have to change the spelling I originally had, though 'originally,' also looked up, I did, since I was origginaly going to write it that way. I think that was too tricky of me. I also didn't have to look up the punctuation I so self-admiringly pointed out, though I did have to look up 'punctuation' and the adverb of admiring or admiration or 'to admire' or however one would put that ((I looked up a way to put it but couldn't find anything in the English usage book the school gives out to help me define what I meant—mean?—to say))). And now I forget what I was going to say about my father's compulsion and also where I was with all those parentheses. ('Parentheses' I definitely had to look up. I never know if it's '-is' or '-es' for the plural.) Maybe I was going to say 'just some compulsion of his.' Or 'need.' Why don't I stick with the simplest words instead of going fancy and also the simplest punctuation? But either will do. Meaning: either 'compulsion' or 'need.' Because I want to get on and done with this essay. Mrs. Zimkin said it shouldn't be longer than a thousand words. I know I'm fast approaching that. I tend to be verbose (looked up) in speaking and prolix in writing. I bet the reader and/or readers and/or listeners (I don't think that's right) think I had to look up 'prolix' but omitted (l.up for the one or two t's) saying so for some reason. I didn't have to look it up. It's a short word and easy to spell once you know what it means. And since I know what it means, I didn't have to look up the meaning either, which is the second reason for looking up a word. The third reason—but I'm really being incorrigible. Telling myself to get on with the essay and then running all over the place. (Bye-bye 1,000 words.) And 'incorrigible' is my

newest big word, I only got it yesterday from a book of the only writer
I'm reading these days, other than for those in the school books I
have to read: Dostoyevski, though some of his books have his name
with a 'y' rather than an 'i' and also nothing between the 'o' and
'e' where I have a 'y.' I prefer the way I wrote it. Looks more Russian.
But where was I? The 'third reason' for looking up a word. I know
there are a lot more than three reasons (just going through the
dictionary randomly ((LU)) to build a better vocabulary, for instance).
But the third reason I was going to write here was. . . not punctuation.
That's the word that immediately came to me though. It's probably
close in spelling or sound or length—something—to the word I
wanted. That one—tip-of-the-tongue-type stuff—means to break up
a word into syllabules so you'll know, for one thing, where to break
it off if the whole word (this usually happens when it's a long one
like syllibication) doesn't fit at the end of the line. (I didn't mean to
be tricky there. Sometimes things like that happen naturally.)
Syllibication could be the word I wanted, but it just doesn't feel right.
And I didn't look it up. (I probably should have, as I'm not sure of
its spelling—two l's or one; and if syllabule has an 'a' after its l's or
l, shouldn't 'syllibication'?) I'm obviously not sure of 'syllabule' either.
Nor which of those letters and words deserve quotes and which
sentences deserve parentheses. But I'm tired of looking up words
and rules for this essay, just as the reader and listeners, etcetera, must
be tired of reading about it. ('Etcetera' should be two words, and no
hyphen, but I like it as one. Dash? Hyphen?) That's my problem
probably, thinking I can have my way with words so early, and no
doubt one of the reasons this essay will get a bad mark and won't
be read by Mr. Zimkin or to my classmates. That's okay. I'm not proud
of the essay. Nor am I interested in that sort of thing: praise, great
grades, wider distribution. (I won't say, just as I won't with any word
or rule from now on, if that one was l.u.) But enough of all that.
I'm going to see where I left off before. I realize that this type of
honesty—telling what my every move is in writing this essay—well,
not 'every move.' I didn't tell when I got up to make weewee. Probably

because that had nothing to do in the writing of this. But when the typewriter jammed—that did, and I didn't mention it. After I unjammed it a new idea came to me about the sentence I was writing before the typewriter jammed. So I wrote it right after I unstuck the jammed keys. Then I had to wash my fingers because of the typewriter ink smudges on them. I didn't want to smudge the paper or the typewriter keys any more than I already did when I quickly typed out the new idea. Not smudge the typewriter keys that got stuck but the ones you press down on to type. The keyboard keys. And no new idea came while I was washing or until I got back to the typewriter and continued writing this thing. Anyway, all of that will be chucked now. It'll just be a straight essay, I mean. Except for finishing that line before. That I realize that this type of honesty has little to do with the honesty of what I want to say in the essay. And now I've looked back. My father and food. Not my first choice for starters but I forgot the first. As part of my grievances against him. That he forced me to eat. He didn't hold me down or shove it into my mouth. But he'd get upset if I didn t eat or not much and of course this upset me, scared me a few times too when he really got upset about it, and probably affected me after. Sure it did. It made me hate food for a long time. Made me intentionally throw up a lot of my food for about two years, I remember. And that he joked so much. That was the grievance I was going to write for starters. Funny it should come now. When after I gave up ever remembering it. And I'm not saying he joked about food. But he probably did that too, when I *was* eating well, or at least what he took for well. But just that he joked about almost everything too much. I know it got to my mother too. With me he was hardly ever serious except when I wasn't eating well. And even that wasn't seriousness; that was just plain strange. So, was he ever serious with me? Maybe when I was crossing a busy street with him and things like that. When I got a bad splinter. When I fell. All this troubled me. Bugged me, I wanted to say. Also infuriated me sometimes when I wanted to speak seriously to him about something and sometimes to someone else.

Frog Dies

If I spoke seriously to someone when he was around he usually
interrupted with jokes, or little asides, such as 'Boy, is she smart?'—in
this real put-on dummy's accent. 'I didn't know how smart she was.
Boy!' Or 'Who told you that what you just said? Too smart for it to
be me, I mean "I," I mean "him." I want to know the guy who told
you that so I can know someone who's really smart, outside of my
own daughter, of course.' And so on. That he praised me too much
too. Grievance. I wanted real honest praise, not total overwhelming
sticky silly fake praise. I wanted real honest rejection from him too.
Criticism, I mean. Something that could help. In just when I cut
something out of paper, for instance. Made designs. Drew. But I
almost never got it because of how unserious he was. But I loved
him for his affectionateness. Which he gave a lot. I must have been
kissed and hugged and said beautiful words to—'my darling
daughter, my pretty princess, my wonderful bunny'—more times in
the five years I knew him than anyone could be in, well, twenty-five
years. In a lifetime even. That he spent so much time with me too.
He could because of his job. But he also could have avoided it,
claiming work, work, important older-person things he had to do,
but he didn't. I loved him for it. Appreciated it, rather. Both. But
I didn't like it that he yelled. Major grievance. He could turn on me
in a second and this scared me too. Up and down, back and forth
he was too in his niceness and anger bursts. He probably scarred
me on that. When I hear a sudden gruff voice sometimes even today,
I shake. Also his crazy temper things and yellings not against me
this time but sometimes against everything. What I mean is— Well
I have a memory put away somewhere from when I still wore diapers,
because he was changing them then and I was on my back on the
bed he changed me on and suddenly with his fists he's banging the
bed on both sides of me and screaming not words but straight yells
as loud as he can. But he never hit me. Maybe once or twice I don't
know of. But normal for anyone, maybe even for someone who later
becomes a saint: twice, three times in five years I'll say. I'm not trying
to apologize for him. I've hit some kids and my sister for no reason

and sometimes for good reason and swung at my mother once or twice too, but of course I'm much younger. And if he hit me I'm sure it was only a slap, on the hand, probably the little top part of it, but not hard and nothing more than that. I also admired the work he did. Not admired it, since except for it just lying around on tables and shelves I never saw it, but just that he did it, never stopped, year after year, started long before my mother met him, and that he wasn't bothered or boosted by what people said of it, but that's something else and maybe not for me to talk as if I know what I'm talking about. If it had any influence on me, it'll turn up later. I like it too that he, with my mother, encouraged my reading and own creating and before that, read to me, every day and night, almost from the time I was born. So he was serious in that with me, which I forgot. Also that he dropped everything most times to get something for me. I'm talking about food, books, for my thirst, anything. He'd run into the house, he'd turn the car around and drive back five miles to the house, to get me a sweater if I was cold or my favorite stuffed animal at the time if I forgot it and was sad. So what I'm saying is he was generous most times with his time with me for a person who was really short of time, when you think that besides what he did at home he was doing two other work things. I've counted the words on two pages and multiplied that by the number of pages I've written so far and then divided it all in two and see I've gone way way over the word limit. Maybe I should just sum up now—I'm sure nobody will want to read even half this much from me and probably will just want to skip from page two to this last one—and say that I know I didn't answer the aim of the essay Mrs. Zimkin asked for, but that losing my father so early in my life was a major tragedy for me, if that isn't repeating myself after all I've said, and if this sentence isn't too complicated, with not enough commas or something or with just not breaking it up into two or three sentences, to understand. And 'the major' then, I'll say. *The.*"

Olivia sits between her mother and grandmother at the funeral. The casket's a nice wood and color, she thinks. Plain, simple, nicely shined. But she thinks her father would still say of it "Nice for somebody else, and not because I'm in it. But since it still looks too expensive and will only just rot in the ground and can't even be recycled, not for me." "Put me in a bag and dump me over the side of a boat into the ocean," he once said to her mother. "Seriously, but of course not before my time comes; I can't swim." When she said "Shh, not even for laughs in front of the children," he said "Only kidding, yak-yak, and you didn't think I was talking about someone else?" She also thinks he wouldn't like all the flowers around. He said he didn't much like buying cut flowers, even though her mother loved getting them from him. And when Olivia picked them here and there out of the ground, which she was always jumping away from him in their walks to do, he didn't much like that either. To him, even people's private gardens and front yards were public parks, to be seen and enjoyed by everyone is what she thinks he meant. She knows he explained what he meant, because she asked him to, but that part she forgot. When her mother bought flowers he often put his nose in them and said "Smells very nice, like flowers," and put them under Olivia's nose and said "Breathe deep without stopping to think and tell me if it's animal, mineral or vegetable." He also wouldn't like the electric candles by the casket. Garish would be the word he'd use. "Cheap, ugly, they even flicker," he might say. "Either wax candles or forget it. I'm not worth the real thing?" He also wouldn't like the things the rabbi's saying about him. Too flattering, lots of the facts all wrong, making him sound the way he wasn't. "Your eye is beginning to turn in," her mother whispers to her. "Put your glasses on," and she takes Olivia's glasses out of her bag, rubs the lenses with a tissue and puts them on her. Also the unnatural deep voice like a stiff actor's. Probably wouldn't like there being any kind of rabbi up there. Just friends, he probably would want to speak about him in front of all these people, or only his brother. But probably no words and nobody up front and everyone staying in his seat and no getting up and down a few times on cue and just sad piano or cello music for the time of one side of a record followed by a few seconds of silence and then everyone go home or wherever they go and his wife, mother and brother and she could go to the cemetery to do very quickly everything that's supposed to be done there. He said a few times that he never could stand anything nice said about him or his work to his face. Saying anything nice about him when he wasn't around he didn't like either, if it got back to him. "I hate compliments or giving them, except to my students if one really needs one and to my daughters and wife, but only if they don't return them." He also wouldn't like that so many people are here. Maybe the only ones he'd like seeing if he was here would be the ones who read about it in the newspaper obituary yesterday or heard about it from someone who had and whom he last saw long ago and some he even thought were dead. "I like bumping into people I haven't seen for years," he said, "better than I like making a date to meet them. Best when it's on a busy street and not muggy, overly sunny, raining heavily, unless one of us has an enormous umbrella for us both to fit comfortably under, or freezing cold. Snow's okay no matter how hard it's coming down, if you're dressed for it, since it makes the encounter more fantastic. But no commitment to stay, this way, and the conversations are usually quick, lively and full of surprises—time speeded up, then a kiss on the cheek or handshake and good-bye." He didn't like crowds, that's why he wouldn't like all these people here. Once, yes, he did, he said—Ebbetts Field, Madison Square Garden, a half-million people marching to ban the bomb or around a factory that made casements for napalm. Lots of different faces, costumes, chance to meet a young woman, a single cause or event making everyone feel together or that things can get righted through sheer numbers. But no more and not for twenty years. A big crowd leaving the same place at the same time now made him jittery. Someone might faint, others could panic, gun might drop through the hole of someone's pants pocket and go off, someone else could open fire on the crowd from a passing car or high on drugs or some political or even religious conviction drive into it, but maybe that's going too far. It's going too far. It's off the point. Large crowds made him uneasy, that's all, and there must be a couple of hundred people here. Three. Four. More people than seats. Or as many or near to it but most aren't sitting close to one another. Where'd they all come from? Which ones did he know? Did a number of them come to the wrong funeral, directed by mistake into this chapel rather than one of the two or three other chapels having services now? Is there an important or well-known Howard Tetch in this city and some of his immediate survivors have the same first names that some of her father's do and so a lot of people who read the obituary thought her father was he? "And talk about a change of mind?" he said not that long ago. "Nothing gets said to crowds or done through them, no matter how loudly a hundred thousand people yell back in unison. So now it's one to one, two on two, six people around a round table, but that's it if I can help it." He's refused just about every invite to a cocktail party or any big function like that the last few years. Particularly art gallery openings; no place to sit. He also didn't like women's perfume or men's cologne or whatever it is men put on their faces and bodies and spray in their hair, when the smell of it got this strong and there were so many different kinds of it at one time. "It's like drinking rum, vodka and scotch at the same sitting," he said. "But my nose gets offended instead of my stomach. No, that explains it too much while adding nothing and making little sense, so in the end gainsays what I want to say. And that interpretation of my explanation's trying too hard to be clever, which besides making the interpretation wrongheaded, worsens the wrongheadedness of the explanation even more. Too many fake fragrances, period. Or just 'fake smells,' since I should stay away from the sweet-sounding fake too." He also didn't much like fancy clothing on people on any occasion. Capes, floppy broad hats, big fur coats draped over women's and men's shoulders both. Ostentatious jewelry taken out of the bank vault or home safe for the day. Just overmadeup and overdressed people, hairdos that looked as if they took hours to do and cost a bundle, and so many here seem to have gone through much thought and great fuss getting ready for this. Just the shoes: so shined and new. "You didn't give half a shit about me when I was alive," he'd probably say, "hell with you now that I'm dead, or most of you. This is a show, no funeral. I'm just the ticket to be here, or whatever I am. The lure, the draw, the grease, the catch. None of those. The audience is the show, I'm just its reason for being, and a dead one at that. Did I have to explain that last remark too?" He also wouldn't like being in that suit and which people were looking at him in when the casket was open. The shirt's his: a blue button-down cotton oxford, one of two he owned and just about the only dress shirt he wore. The tie's a nice design, color and style, one he wouldn't have minded owning. But the suit he stopped wearing ten years ago but could never give away or throw out. Maybe wore it three times, at the most five. Everything else like that he'd eventually give away or throw out: shoes, shirt, pants, sports jacket, wallet or key ring or pen and pencil set he got as gifts from his mother and in-laws, but for some reason not this suit. . . . Ties, box of handkerchiefs, satin-lined bathrobe with a designer label, wicker picnic basket of different colored synthetic-fiber socks. Because it was so expensive, at least for him. Also because it was a suit, two complete articles made into one thing, each of which could possibly be used separately, and if it had come with a vest it would have been even harder to get rid of. No, the vest, if he couldn't have bought the suit without it, would have been got rid of immediately and probably by leaving it at the store. He didn't like the suit the day he bought it and left it at the store to be altered. When he was leaving the store that day, he told her mother some years later, he said to himself "Why'd I buy it? I don't like it. I'll look silly in it. Why do I almost always buy the wrong thing for myself? I came in to buy a sporty medium gray Harris Tweed suit with a vent in back and if possible with flap pockets and little domelike leather buttons. So why'd I wind up with a ventless dark brown of another kind of closer-knit tweed than I wanted, the perfect suit for a witness or guest at an execution or funeral?" He also wouldn't like the white handkerchief in his breast pocket, though at least it was

230

squared rather than triangled and sticking only a little bit out. Nor that the casket had been opened: that most of all. People he didn't know filing past. Just people filing past, most probably thinking at the time what a good or bad job the embalmer did on him and later talking about it when they got back to their seats. His mother collapsing for a few moments when she saw him. Her mother refusing to go up to see him. Olivia wanting to go up but not being allowed to till the funeral director announced that the coffin would be open only two more minutes. "I'm not scared. It won't give me bad dreams. It won't be the last impression I'll have of Daddy. I have pictures. He has books with his face on the backs of them. I'll stare at them till the picture of him in there goes away. You keep telling me how mature I am for my age, so give me a chance to prove it. He's my father, not yours. I only want to see him. I won't touch or kiss him. Someone will have to hold me up. Uncle Jerry's there now, so him. But one look for only a second, please? *Please?*" Any of it. He wouldn't have wanted to be seen. He said a while back that when he died he only wanted to be burned without any mumbo jumbo and his ashes trashed. His mother was the one who wanted it opened. After it was closed a final time she said to Olivia's mother "Why? I didn't need to be shown he was gone. Because it had been done for his father and my parents and sister and brothers, so I thought why not for him, but it was just repeating past mistakes. I should have given in to you. You shouldn't have given in to me. If I still insisted, slobbering over your knees even, you should have told me to stop instantly or leave. It's something I'll never live down for the rest of my life. Married to Howard even for a few years, you should know how much stubbornness runs on both sides of his family and how we don't mind walking over weaker wills, and that's all you needed to have told me. A reminder of what I can be. Remember that for the next time. Not for a funeral—the next one will be mine—but any time when I want to get my way. Now let's try to get through the rest of it." If her father could think, what would he be thinking now? He can think, that's all he can do now, except

231

maybe see them from someplace, and he'd be looking at them and probably crying while thinking "Oh my poor children," meaning Eva and she, "what's going to happen to you without me? I shouldn't be dead just for that. And what will I do without you? Well, it's all got to be planned. You just don't go to no place after your funeral and do nothing for a billion years. Up there no doubt has something for me to do from now on or else people like me would get tired and bored from doing nothing for so long and then make trouble for the place. Washing clouds. Cleaning air. And lots of enjoyable things to do with a lot of nice people after these chores are done. But it just isn't fair for me, that's all. Nor for them. Skip me—just for them. They know I loved them too much for me to just leave them like that. So, settled—it's all got to change. Anyone can do the things that are planned for me, and besides I'll have a billion years to do them in. But only I with their mother can take care of our little girls." He wouldn't like the chapel either. Too gloomy and uninteresting, just like the awful organ music they played. Wouldn't have liked the furniture and paintings in the other room where her mother and grandmother and uncle and she saw people before the funeral began. He didn't like being the center of attention anywhere. He would like it that he isn't expected to say anything.

Olivia's in college, dating a young man, and tells him, as she's told lots of young men, "I have or had—I never know how to word it—two fathers. So I'll say I have and had two fathers, how's that?" "Sounds good to me," he says. "One's my stepdad. He's fine. His name's Eric, short for nothing?" "What do you mean?" "They'll be a few of those. Don't worry. Just stay tuned. He's a psychiatrist. Very bright, trenchant. Biggest drawback with him is that he reads your mind right. He teaches psychiatry too, and he's very sweet to my mother. They love each other tremendously, obsoletely, and he's been as good a stepfather as anybody could want for one. Only I didn't want one. I didn't want two, get it? Some kids do, you know, something I learned by being the unofficial, meaning the self-declared president of the Association of Associated American

Associative Stepkids Club." "Is there such a one?" "Two live ones, you realize I meant. And it was good for my mother, marrying Eric, but I never wanted anyone—hold your hat, sir. Your head then, since this is where the big news break comes in. The blockbusting bombshell. 'Bombadier to archivist, let it blow.' Anyone but my real father. Did you guess that?" "From what you were leading up to, even with the animadversions. . .that's not the right word. I'm not sure of the pronunciation either. But it's a good one, yitch? Always wanted to use it in company, but intelligent company, like the opposing one, and pronounced right. But: yes, I guessed." "Smart. This kid: he's smart. Not my real dad; you, but he too. But I'm talking like this, this jerky nervous diversionary chatter, because the subject always distresses me. The subject's he. The object I can't right now turn into a pun. He died when I was six. Or five. Which is it? Definitely five. Why my kidding myself with that pretended muddlemindedment? Or trying to kid-smart you? 'Cause I know, babe, this gal knows. Some people can tell you exactly where they were and what second of the minute of the hour of the day, etcetera, it was, when they learned that World War IV began. At least those who have reached three. You didn't get that. Same with me when I learned he died. So I just subtract all those years and seconds from my present age and get the exact age I was when the big boom hit. The big broom, really, since it made such a clean paternal sweep. My own World War IV, over in a second. 'Darling, take cover; Dad died.' 'Oh no,' roar, and part of me's forever dead." "I'm not quite following you, Ol." "Follow. I can never forgive him. *Forget* him. Hoo-hoo, that was some frisbeeing flip. And unintentional. You believe me?" "Not quite." "Believe me. I can never forget him. I can get him out of my head, but the little fella always slips back in. Sometimes I think it's the same for me as it was for him with my brother. *His* brother. What's going on here? Oh, I see. He's in him who's in me." "That I don't catch." "Because the after's before the before. I'll explain. He had a brother two or so years older who died when my father was twenty-three, I think. Drowned in a ship, went down, ship-he

233

never found. They were irreversibly close and both irreversibly lost. It's all documented." "Where? When? By whom?" "Well, most. Because my father was a junior newsman and their oldest brother, Jerry, was a budding hotshot in what he did at the time, little news stories saying brother of news cub and hotshot bud among the dead at sea. My father kept them and I or my sister still have some, just as we have all of my father's later writings about it. Obviously, my father wrote, and sometimes, he told my mother, part of what he wrote came with the help of his dead brother. How so? It goes like this." "Your family's haunted." "Hauntingly. Frightfully. But don't fear. It's only a couple of gentle consanguineal ghosts in me, but that's the after before the before again. You see, his brother was a writer of the same time, long and short imaginative things, but preceded my father at it seriously by a few years. Before his brother died, my father—or 'Dad,' to shorten this a bit—only did news. In fact, he told my mother, he felt he took over where his brother had left off, though his brother had hardly begun. Dad had been piddling a bit at it, but soon after Uncle Alex died he really got with it, as if possessed, he said. I like to think I carry on the family tradition in that category, but orally, which should explain all the who's-in-me's." "It does, sort of." "Dad told my mother—or 'Mother,' to shorten this even more. It'd be even shorter using just 'Mom,' but she was never just 'Mom' to me. But he swore Alex gave him ideas for writing when he was stumped, like first lines and startling last ones and sudden plot moves, and was even responsible for some of the more usable typos he made. 'You again,' he used to say, saluting him, Mother said, and then 'Now get lost—I don't believe in collaborative prose.' In one piece, which Dad said Alex had contributed or sparked a significant part, he thought he should bill them both as its authors, but realized the tough time he'd have explaining it. Alex, the better read and educated of the two, provided him with right words, dates and historical situations and characters, besides doing some overnight editing on his punctuation and grammar and the prose's rhythm. Occasionally made the paper tear when Dad was pulling it out of the typewriter, so Dad would have to rewrite the page. Deleted words and sometimes sentences and paragraphs in the rewriting, which Dad only found out about, and approved of, much later. And also nudged him away from the typewriter to do some useful chore that didn't have to be done right away or to take his brain for a walk, when it was clear to Alex but not Dad that his work wasn't going well. Dad's wasn't. Alex, when you think of his own writing he must have missed and what he had to do to do all this, was doing great with his unasked-for stintless work. Or maybe he only wanted to keep his hand in—I just thought of that. For the day when he returns—so he won't get stale at it. Lots of experiences and people and their stories to write about where he's been, if he went or got that far or the place actually exists. A first from the real netherworld or stopping-off place, which should get plenty of critical attention and publicity and, as a consequence, sales. And if Alex could, and maybe one only can make that kind of comeback through serious or at least well-intentioned writing, why not Dad, which was always my big wish. So what am I getting at in all this?" "You tell me." "I am. I'm just stalling, waiting for his nudge or spark. It didn't come. It never does when I wait for it or try to induce it. It seems to only come, as it must have from Alex to him, in flashes, pops, minipinpricks or minor accidents when I'm least expecting it. But this: that he helps me out in similar ways. Not much but enough times to make me think it's real. Little tip on a test whispered in the air near my ear. Tiny smudge on a love letter, so I should think about writing it again or whether to mail it at all. Grabbing me—I swear I felt I felt it—when, with my head in a thought, I stepped off the curb while a car was shooting past. Maybe Alex too, but very small stuff, though I feel he's just dormant if still there. If Alex did get back, he's probably just hiding out and writing—to make up for lost time, let's say—but not seeing any of his family, unless Uncle Jerry's holding something back. But he's still my working father, Dad is, which is probably why Eric could never take that spot. For sure in my dreams too, though that's where I expect him to be, my sleeping conscious churning out images and actions of him advising me or providing me with the material to make wakeful decisions and take right-path directions. Does all this sound odd and too loose?" "Toulouse? Like the city? Or Lautrecian like zee artiste? Or just too scattered, making it hard to catch or take?" "The city? It's near the prehistoric cave area, so maybe. No, that's Bordeau or some coastal wine city or region with a B. Maybe like Lautrec. Stunted body for stunted mind? Just no focus or center, so, misconceived, half-believed, all over the place. Anyway, now you know something that's sunken in me. If you want to know something of what he conceived and probably believed, which might help you understand me and what I said better, these are some of his books." "OK, let's see. Very attractive covers, solid bindings, sort of maudlin catchy titles: dark this, catastrophic that. He was a handsome man for that period, I guess, but why the tie in most of the jacket photos? Some nice things said about each book and his body of work, but they always are, aren't they, else why put them in? But lots of suspension points in the quotes, so who knows what's missing? 'A storyteller beyond compare. . .' *if this was the nineteenth century and the world was an island with only one writer on it* . . . but you know I'm only kidding. Several different publishers, so I suppose they didn't do too well by him and he had to keep moving, or else he got a bigger and bigger deal with each new one. Maybe I should be ashamed to admit this, but I never heard of your dad or his writing. But then I haven't really kept up, or should I say 'gone back into the library stacks,' or read much since high school other than schoolwork. Neither do most of my friends or either of my moms or dads read anything but what sells or will help them sell something, so nobody would have clued me in if he was really someone to read where my life depended on it. Each of these is a fairly long-to-enormous work, with lots of dense pages, fat paragraphs, microscopic printing for the most part, and what seems at quick glance like a lot of big words. I'd be tempted to look up. You want me to read a whole book or is there a fairly short part of one or a particular not-so-long story or two that will do the trick?"

"Just start one of the books from the beginning and see if it gets ya."
"I'll take the slimmest here, if nobody objects, which also seems to
have the shortest paragraphs and most dialogue and fewest printing
shenanigans, since I have a bunch of exams coming up and papers
to do in the next weeks. And I've always, skimpy reader that I've
become—or maybe because of that, for who's got the time to waste
these days on frivolous or just no-account works—that if you don't
like one of a writer's books, you won't like any of them, no matter
how many years he bangs away at it." "You know, after all I've gone
into about myself and my relationship with him—what the hell he
continues to mean to me, for christsakes—you're taking an offensively
insensitive approach to me and him and his work." "Did he just
whisper that to you to say, to sort of start the great nudge away from
me?" "I think that remark's uncalled-for also." "Oh, you don't say?
You do tell? Well, pip pip, have a hot toddy and tip-tip-erary and
all that, old chap, and here's his herd of doorstoppers for the next
unfortunate who comes to you with fresh ears to be chewed off.
Mine, let me apprise you—" "Fuck you too, dildo, and that comes
straight from my mouth only." "So you say. So you say."

Eva writes Olivia a letter. "My dearest O. I'm at the office now
and want to get this down to you before I forget a thing about it or
more than I normally would or already have, minds being what they
are. Before the phones start ringing and intergalactic heliomagnetic
printing gadget starts binging and clients and colleagues and
corresponders and coffee-tenders start pouring into the office and
the experience gets filtered through all the events of the day and for
the most part lost. Okay: Today, just ten minutes ago imprecisely,
I saw a man on the street who looked just like Daddy did in one
of the more notable photographs with us. Same chintzy hairline,
bricky build and circus tentpole neck girth; same face, almost, with
that particularly prominent Tetch chin (some call it 'big'; thoughtfuler
callers call it 'strong'), and for the men, palisade-like cheekbones and
bosomy layrnx. I couldn't believe it and when I started gaping at him
dopey- and dewey-eyed both, I'm sure he thought I couldn't believe

how gorgeous and gamic he was and that I was in some simplehearted and -minded way trying to pick him up. Wearing the same lemon-yellow t-shirt Daddy wore in the notable, although what he was doing entering this snotty-chic office building in it is mystery utero-nummary. Maybe he had run all the way from his fancy hum in the city with his briefcase strapped to his back and only a minute before at the park exit taken his pants out of the case and put them on over his jogging shorts, knowing he could get away coming into the building in the shirt but please-not-sir the shorts. Because he had a dapper pair of pants on, sneakered feet—those are okay to change out of in your office, half the building now using brisk walking-to-work-and-back as their daily exercise (with about one a month, we learn in the health and crime reports of the building newsletter, dropping dead on the street from it or breaking an elbow or kneecap or getting robbed and/or raped)—and was carrying the unaforementioned monogrammed aforementioned briefcase that I doubt Daddy would have carried or owned, even if it had been given to him by Mom ('and,' you said she always added, to make us feel good, 'the girls'), who I'm sure wouldn't have had it monogrammed and in fact probably would have had it roughed up before she gave it and nearly imperceptibly scratched. Did what she added make us feel good? But I should move on with this before I lose it, or even more than I normally, already, minds, etc....You know the photo I mean? Daddy, with his head wrenched around neckparoxysmally, and his arms, holding us to his thighs, as thick as my thick thighs but unlike mine, looking hard as...thirty seconds went by and no better simile would come up. Daddy smiling contentedly, you laughing maniacally, me crying heartbreakingly, Mom I bet clicking what she thinks could be the pic-of-her-genetrixness jitteringly, hope filling her sleeves. But the man: looking ten years younger than his age, just as Daddy did in the pic: openhearted face, long body lean and straight, weightlifter's chest, arms and neck, so actually his build a bit bigger and bulgier so ultimately uglier than Daddy's, since Mom's said he only did situps and things and never lifted weights, gummy smile (our drawn gums, not the kind you buy), and holding, instead of two contrasting kids in just about every way but their sex, gums and chin (mood, hair, eyes, nose, clothes, size, thighs. . .) the revolving door still for me, other left-or-right holding the briefcase. CON the monogram acronymed. I continued to couldn't-believe-it and finally busted 'I swear I've no designs on your body, con sir, so disalarm yourself if that signal went on, but you look almost exactly like, which is why I've this dippy-pussed look of dumbfoundment and foundling-findment (don't I wish I said all this) on my what a look's usually on, my father.' He said 'Put that on the screen for me again?' and I said 'My father; you look just like him almost to the size of your quatriceps, and that's no lie,' and he gave me one of those 'I'm sure I don't look that young even if I'd like to think so' lines and I said 'No, petty please, don't compliment me or whomever you're complimenting. You're the spitting image of him, as my father sometimes said of other people and other times said his father liked to say, and then added a couple of times, something he said his father never did—all this, by the way, I got from my mother and my sister Hearsay—she's from the eastern branch of the tree—and that last bad add said out of a slight disquiet over meeting my father's spitting image, so flopped, though more likely never had a shot—"And that has nothing to do with spittle, drivel, drool or slaver and the likes." ' 'I assume,' he said, never beating a blink when I actually did say some of these things, 'by your tone and tense and some of the words used and your expression that went with the last few, that your father's dead.' We were through the door and inside the lobby now, had been since I first noticed his acronym, heading for the elevator bank. 'Did I? Yes I. Must've I, at least, for darn, he's gone, poor mon, for sure. No, digressive I, for plain toot is he is and I never saw him as he was and I miss him bad, real badly, Con, really. But the resemblance, you to him. Well—' An elevator opened. He said 'Hey, what're my doing here? I belong at the thirty-six-to-fifty-third-floor bank. I must have got totally absorbed talking to you. Nice meeting you, Miss,' and tipped the invisible peak over his brow.

'Wait,' I said. 'The resemblance. And there are a hundred other elevators at this bank for me to take. Or I can take the express to the seventy-eighth and walk down three flights. Or even take your elevator to the fifty-third and catch another one there to my floor. Well, it's remarkable, yours and his—the faces, in many ways your bodies—to say the least, and to say even less than that, we all must look exactly like one other person in this world, even identical twins and triplets and such, other than their looking like the other sibling or siblings in their set. And if we look exactly like a set of identical twins or triplets and so on, then like two or three or all the way up to six other people, if there are identical sextuplets who have survived. Seven, even, if there were ever, or are now, rather, since I'm talking about this happening in the same time period with some overlapping of course, surviving identical septuplets I think they're called. Eight? No, it doesn't seem possible, has ever happened, whatever a set of eight is called. And a set of identical eighttuplets, I'll call them, looking exactly like another set of eight of any time period, but without scientific tinkering I mean, or even identical septuplets looking exactly like a set of quintuplets, and so on? No, impossible, has never happened, period, though there might be a set of identical twins who look exactly like another set of twins, and almost certainly have been if we don't keep this to a single time period, or even triplets with twins or maybe even with triplets or quadruplets, though I'm no expert on these matters so don't take my word for it. I'm losing myself here, and possibly your interest, with my slapalong speculation of improbable pairings and things, and we haven't much time. So yes, he's dead, my father is, to get back to it, even if neither my sister nor I believe it. We think he's hiding out or something—perhaps a prisoner—in Cuba or some country near here like that—an island, but one we, this country, hasn't much to do with publicly but is very concerned about for political or strategical reasons or things like that, which is why there's been no word about him or efforts to get him out. It could be our country even knows something about him but isn't letting on for its own interests, though that's really farfetched, but then who can really say?' I won't go into Con's expression by now, though he obviously wanted to get away from me, if just to finish getting into his business clothes, maybe take a shower first—all in his office or one of the health clubs or cardio-fitness centers in the building—and start work, and for what should be obvious to you, I didn't want to lose him. It's a very big building, with a dozen entrances and several restaurants and cafeterias and many underground and exterior and interior aboveground shops and a double movie theater and even a post office and its own zip code, and I was afraid I'd never see him again even if I looked hard for him in it for the next few years. 'Anyway,' I said to him, 'we feel he's alive someplace—why a nearby isolated island-state I can't rightly say, or can't come up with anything right now—and that he'll eventually get back some day, if just through our dogged wills and mental exertions for him.' 'Much success with it,' he said, and then 'Talk to you again perhaps, and have a nice day,' and I said 'Yes, have a nice one, and good morning,' and that, my dear sister, for the most part, was that. When I got to the office, or really in the elevator going up, I said to myself, or aloud in the crowded car without even knowing it, 'Oh Daddy, wouldn't it be nice if it was true what I told your beefy lookalike downstairs? We've been aprayin' and ahopin' for it for so long and only wish there'd finally be some sign from you that you're on your way. By boat, by train, by magic motorbike if you wish—you name it, and for me, even come in a dream.' Sometimes I think we're a tiny bit cracked going on about him like this, don't you? Everything I said to the man. All this time spent on it in just this letter? Jeez, other surviving kids after this long a spread have virtually forgotten their pas, with maybe every so often a vivid to vague to somebody else's remembered memory returning, but fleetingly, nothing life-intrusive, his influence on them mainly hereditary. I think—you know what I think?—I think we ought to toss out every photo and letter and book and memento and so on of him, from him, about him, left by him, by him—the works. Because those are what might be keeping us back or tied in so. Seeing them, bumping into them, where we begin inventing and imagining things. And if that doesn't work, to get rid of whatever things of his Mom's kept too. Steal into her house, chuck 'em all out. She wouldn't even know, or much care if she found out, since she never goes back to them, or for his books, takes them off the shelves, while we see them every time we're there. And if that doesn't work, to get rid of every book and thing of his we know someone other than Mom owns. And then go to the major library here and with a flick of some master computer terminal switch find out on the monitor what libraries across the country, university and otherwise, his books are in. And maybe through another flick, what libraries around the world have his books, though he never sold much of anything or got any critical attention overseas, did he? And check all these books out—spend a couple of years doing it if that's what it takes—and get rid of those too. And by placing ads in the appropriate trade journals, find out where his books might be in all the used book stores and whatever remains in the remainder stores and distributor warehouses, and buy them and get rid of these too. And also, get a list of every rare book dealer and see if they have them and buy all of them no matter what the expense and destroy these too. And if that doesn't work—if he's still managing to influence our actions and so forth—he still does with you, doesn't he?—then to place an author's query in the *Times* book review section and other such places saying we're writing a book, or to make it believable, a monograph or dissertation about him and need all his letters and correspondence of any sort and anything they might have of him—magazines with his work and newspapers with reviews of his work and interviews and articles about him and first editions and autographed copies of his books and anything else of him or of his like photographs and galleys and even old hats and clothes he might have given away or left behind and someone's still using or saved, which we'll promise to reimburse them for the postage and send back special delivery express and heavily insured—and dump all these too. Go to prison for it if we have to, but first making sure we got all his books out of every prison library too. And if that doesn't work, then we should just give up thinking it's any of these things influencing our odd behavior regarding him and to form a group of two for group therapy to work his influence away or just to see why it's still there so. Or maybe we should do that first, avoiding all the expense and hassles and time put in and so forth of getting rid of everything we can of his. Anyway, what else is new with you, just to change the subject? No, because I'm deeply interested and always have been. Oops, suddenly must flit. Tingaringing and bingalinging and beginning of inter-inner office commingling besides the coffee and morning roll cart clink-clinging down the corridor, which if I don't make a move for fast will be past my door. 'Hey Jake,' I just yelled without seeing him yet and only the tip of his cart, 'a black coffee and plain danish as usual with maybe a few almond shavings which fell off some of the almond danishes on the tray—and don't tell me they didn't if you do have almond danishes today—sprinkled on top. Ah, just give me an almond danish and sugar with my coffee this time, and cream, or milk, or whatever you got that passes for them—I aim for change.' See you soon, Dachshund. At least me hopes."

Olivia sits on the steps in front of the house. "Come in," Denise says. "No, I'm not coming in. I want Daddy to ask me to come in." "Daddy can't," Denise says. "Get him then." "I can't get him and you know that, Olivia." "Yell into the backyard for him to come around front to ask me to come in." "I can't do that either, much as I'd love to." "Then up to the roof if he's on top working there or in the basement if that's where he is." "Those are two other things I can't do, sweetheart." "Call him up then if he's not around and tell him I'm waiting for for him to ask me to come in and I won't come in unless he does that." "You know that's impossible too." "No, I don't know that. Why should I know it? I'm not coming in till I hear Daddy ask me to. Or till I see him park the car and get out of it or even from the car window point for me to go in. Or till he shouts at me from way down the street to do as you say and get right in. That he'll paddle my fanny if I don't. That I won't be allowed any ices after

243

dinner if I don't. That he won't read to me or let you read to me before
I go to sleep. When he does something like one of those I'll come
in. I'll come right in. I'll zoom in. So fast neither of you will even
see me come in. You'll stand on the porch or the street or from the
car and wonder where'd she go? Did she go in or is she still around
the house or maybe hiding someplace near but not in? Because
nobody could have zoomed in that fast. Or I'll run to Daddy first
if he's in the street or walking up it or the walk or in the car or just
getting out of it, but wait first to make sure no cars are coming. Or
just run to Daddy if he's already in the house. From the back he might
have got in when we were talking here. Or from the front when we
weren't looking. Or through one of the windows upstairs. He could
have been in a tree all this time and swung down from it to the roof
and then into the window when we didn't see him because it was
a back window or we were talking or just never looked up there.
Or he could have been in some secret place below the basement we
don't know about or in a closet or some hiding space in the house
only he knows how to get into and only now came out of to show
himself in the window or on the porch or even came out of an
upstairs window to the roof to yell something like 'Hey, look-it, I'm
up here.' Then I'll be in but only then will I come in, not before."
"Oh my poor darling," Denise says and comes out and sits on the
steps with her and takes her hands and puts her forehead against
hers and a car passes and a man walking two different kinds of dogs
waves at them while he passes and Denise nods to him and says
to Olivia "We'll wait till either Eva wakes up or your father parks
the car or walks up the street and shows himself or yells to us from
the roof or the tree or any of the other things you said." "No, I don't
want to, I want to go in," and pulls her hands away and sticks them
under the bib of her overalls and gets up, goes inside the house and
slams the door. It doesn't make a bang and she slams it again and
it does. Eva wakes up crying. "Shut up, shut up, I hate you, you
little fuck, everyone just shut up for good," Olivia screams. "My poor
darlings," Denise says, walking up the steps.

Frog Dies

Eva, Olivia and Eric are on a beach trying to drag a rowboat into the water. "This thing will never budge," Eric says. "My father could make it budge," Eva says. "Here she goes again," Olivia says. "No, let her, what?" Eric says. "My father was so strong he could lift it on his back and carry it into the water. He'd need both arms and it'd be heavy but he could do it." "I'm sure he could. Or push, even, or at least drag it into the water by himself, but I can't, honey. I'm simply not as strong as your father was." "As my father is. My father's very strong." "As he is then. As you say. I've heard of his physical exploits—how strong he was, I'm saying." "She knows what exploits are," Olivia says. "You don't have to teach it to either of us. I know the word and I've told her the word." "I didn't realize that. For you see, I didn't know that word till I was twice your age, maybe three times. How old are you? I'm only kidding. I know how old. I even know how old both of you are put together. A hundred-six, right? No. But good for you—both of you for knowing so many big impressive words. Like 'impressive.' You know that word too, right?" "Right." "Sure, just as my father knows all those words and more," Eva says. "He knows words that haven't even been born yet. Like kakaba. Like oolemagoog." "He does? He knows those? Wow. Very impressive. Anyway, I'd hoped we got past that subject. I said that to myself. But if we didn't, some men are just stronger than others. That's a fact. I'd be the last to deny it. You both know what 'deny' means, I know. And some men are smarter than others. And kinder and nicer than others and have more hair and so on. But I bet no man has more than two arms. Anyone want to bet?" "My father's stronger, nicer, kinder than others," Eva says, "and much much more than that. He's taller than most others. And handsome. Much more than any others. His photos say so. Others say so." "Well that's a good thing for a man to be," Eric says. "For an older woman to be too," Olivia says. "That's what Mother says." "Good. She knows. She's smart. Me, I was never considered handsome. That should come as no surprise to you two, as it doesn't to your mother. Not handsome even when I was a young man, an older woman, a small piggy, or

245

even now as a fairly not-so-young-maybe-even-old-hog. Most of that was supposed to be funny. Why aren't you laughing?" "Because it wasn't funny and we're talking about someone else now, right, Olivia?" "I don't know." "Daddy. All that he is." "OK," Eric says, "I'll bite. Meaning, well, just that I'm all pointy ears and curly tail uncoiled and extended snout—I want to know. What else was he? *Is* he. Sorry. But tell me." "Funny," Eva says. "He's more funny than anyone alive. Sometimes people died laughing at things he said. But really, with big holes in their chests and all their bones broken and blood." "Yes, that's true," Olivia says, "the streets covered with broken laughed-out dead bodies, for funniest is what he is and always was. And liveliest too. A real live wire, our father. You're excellent, Eric— honestly, this is not to go stroke-stroke to you. And lively and smart, but not at all handsome, and kind and wonderful in some ways and we love you, we truly do, even if what Eva said and how she acted just now, but you're not livelier than our dad. No sir. Our real dad was *live*-ly! Oh boy was he. A real live wire. He was also so sad. We shouldn't leave that out if we want to be fair. A real sad wire. 'Mr. Sadwire' we should've called him, right, Eva? If you could have talked then. For you couldn't even say three words in a row that made sense. No sentence-sense I used to say about her then, Eric." "I could so say sad wire." "Hey, stop a moment, for where are we?" Eric says. "Was? Is? Which one is he?" "Is," Eva says. "Daddy's definitely an is. And sometimes when I hear from him, like I did just yesterday, I say 'Daddy Live wire, Daddy Sadwire, how dost your farting grow?' Because that's what he also does best—just ask Olivia." "That's right, she's a true bird, we have to be fair," Olivia says. "He was probably the world's greatest most productive farter for more years in a row than anybody and still is." "Is for sure. The whole world knows of him. He's been in newspapers, on TV. People have died from it everywhere, and not happy laughing deaths. In planes and parks. Hundreds of dead bodies in your way sometimes. Flat on the ground, piled ten-deep sometimes, black tongues hanging out, their own hands around their necks. Vultures in trees all around but refusing to pick at them the smell's so bad. And much worse. I won't even go into it more. Like whole cities dying, dogs and cats too—not a single breathing thing left alive. Maybe that's an exaggeration. Rats always survive. But 'Killer Dad's been at it again,' I always say to Olivia when we see this, and that time we walked through that ghost city. It doesn't hurt us because we got natural, natural...what is it again we got, Olivia?" "Impunity. Immunity. Ingenuity. That's us. We never even smell it when we're in the midst of it but we can see when we see all this that it can only be he who did it." "You girls are really funny today," Eric says. "Inherited from him, no doubt." "Oh no we didn't. He inherited it from us, didn't you know? Something strange happened in life when we were born. But everything he's best at he got from us, or almost. We're sad live wires or lively dadwires or just mad lovewires. That's because we brought up our father and are still doing it yet. Now that's a real switch, isn't it, Eva, bringing up your own dad? How'd we do it?" "I'm not sure, but that's for sure what we're doing. We didn't want to, we had our own lives to bring up, but we had no choice, right, Olivia?" "No, why?" "No, you." "He was left on our doorstep, right? Came in a shoebox with a note glued to it saying...what?" "It said 'Feeling blue? Nothing in life's true? Cat's got your goo? So do something different in your loo today. Bring up your own dad. But don't leave him in a shoebox for squirrels to build their nests in on top of him. Take him out, brush him off, give him a good cleaning. Treat him as good as you would your best pair of party shoes.' Wasn't that what it said, Olivia?" "Or was it a hatbox he came in? 'Put him on your bean against the sun, sleet and rain and your brain will seem much keener.' No, that wasn't it. 'Treat him as gently as you would your own mentally...' I forget everything it said. But we did. And I know it was some kind of box." "A suggestion box. A lunch box. 'What's inside is nutritious and suspicious. Open hungrily and with care.' And when we've brought him up all the way, Eric, I'm afraid the sad news is you'll have to move out. Because he'll be moving back in, all grown up then. Because no bigamists allowed in our family, right, Olivia?" "Right, Eva." "So?" Eva says. "So maybe in yours, Eric, it's allowed, but not in ours. Family honor. Horses' code. New York telephone directory. We're very sorry. Unbreakable rule. But let's stop, Eva. I've spun out and so have you. And we're not being nice to Eric who's been so nice to us. Renting this boat. Helping us push it into the water. Doing most of the work. Probably getting a heart attack from it. Dying for us just so we can have some summer fun." "Hey, don't worry about me, kids. Let it out. Have it out. Thrash it to me. Money and abuse are no object. Listen, I know how you're both feeling, but you have to know I also of course wish he had never died." "He never did, how can you say that?" Eva says. "Whatever. And easy as it is for me to say this after the fact and much as I would have missed if he had lived—I'll be straightforward with you—I didn't know him but have heard so many wonderful things about him that I only wish I had." "Had what?" Olivia says. "That he can't be replaced. By me. I know that. Never deluded myself otherwise. And that I wish I'd known him." "So, it can be arranged," Eva says, "can't it, Olivia?" "Let's stop—really. We're spoiling our day and being extra extra lousy to Eric." "OK, he's dead, heave-ho, hi-heave, what d'ya say, Joe, bury the problem? for what I want most now is to get out there to fish, splash and row." "Well," Eric says, "it seems we'll have to wait for a couple of strapping guys to come along and help us or come back when the tide comes in. Anyone think to bring that card with the tide times?" "Daddy will come help," Eva says. "Sometimes it only takes one and he's the one. So hey, hi, Daddy of mine, come and pull our boat into the water. You'll see. I've wished. Daddy come now," and she sits down hard in the sand, puts her thumb in her mouth and sucks it while she twiddles her hair in back and looks off distantly. "Eva, get up, get up quickly, you hear me?" Olivia says. "You're scaring the shit out of us."

Olivia's on a hilltop, alone, blue sky, warm pleasant morning, no clouds, slight breeze, strong smell of clover in the air, faint buzz of bees in the wild flowers around, perfect day, nothing but trees, hills, bay and sky in view, picks a flower, smells it, smells sweet, holds it up and says "For you, father dear. I used to love picking and giving you flowers, making you bouquets, especially out of the wild ones with a few pretty leaves on the outsides of it making it look like a bridal or more like a bridesmaid's bouquet. So here's one more, 'on the house' as you used to say," and throws it up. He shouts out "Got it. Thank you, my darling sweetheart; thousand billion thanks. I love you, my sweet münch. I take this flower and hold it to my chest. I take it and kiss it. If I wanted to be funny I'd say I take it and eat it. OK, I eat part of it, the tastiest petal and most digestible. I push it into my face. I put my nose so deep into it that some of the flower gets up my nose and tickles it and makes it tough for a moment for one nostril to breathe. I sneeze because of the tickling and maybe something in the flower. And finally I put the flower between my shoulder and chin—hold it to my shoulder with my chin—and keep it there. It's a flower from you so that's why I love it so much. It was picked with feeling. Hell, it was picked by you, meant for me, so that's enough. When this flower dies a little a little of me will die too. Nah, not as bad as that. What should I say then? When it dies completely it'll be dead completely, that's all, so what else is new? but my love for you—well, we don't want to get even hokier here, do we? No we don't. So I'll just say—I'm saying, in fact—thank you, thank you, you're so kind, good, gentle, delicate, sensitive, clever, I'm so lucky, kiss kiss kiss. And it's not my own hand I want to kiss either. Beautiful and daring too. What a kid." She closes her eyes, squeezes them tight, clenches her knuckles. "Fucking shit piss ass pus," she says.

Olivia's asleep, he's watching her from a few feet away, comes to her, gets on his knees and whispers into her ear "Can you hear me, darling? Is my voice getting in? Say no if you can't, yes if you can. Nod then. Grit your teeth, growl. Do the old blink thing, three for whatever, four for whatever. Scowl, hum, quickly lift your brow. A sign's all I want. Now I'll shut my mouth—it can be done, I promise you, just listen or watch—and hold my breath and you say or give it. The sign, I mean; something." "Yes," she says without opening her eyes. "You know I loved you, don't you? I don't have to go into a long song and dance—" "No, don't, I know," face up, eyes still closed, head in the middle of the pillow which is right in the middle of the top part of the single bed, hands clasped on her stomach under the quilt, legs tight together and straight down to the end of the bed. "You holding some flowers in your clasp?" he says. "No, why, because I look as if I'm dead?" "Just lightening things up a bit; trying to; making talk. But God forbid. Never dead. Never you. What a thing. You're just resting. I used to lie in bed like that, same way, but as a means to getting to sleep when I was having trouble sleeping, or trouble dropping off. Once asleep I slept. And you can, that way, when it's successful, almost feel different parts of your body dropping off. Not almost—feel them peeling off. 'Good night, feet,' I used to say, when they went. Toes never went first; both whole feet always went together. Then 'Good night, legs. Good night, waist. Sweet dreams, fingers. Nighty-night, neck,' chin and so on right up the body and face till it worked its way to my brain. Then, if it got that far before I fell asleep, there'd be a click and I'd be out." "I'm not lying here like this for that reason, and even unintentionally it's never been successful. I'm doing it because it makes me feel peaceful and helps me to think." "I can't sleep either," he says, "thinking how I might have hurt you sometimes." "I can sleep, but hurt me how?" "Physically a few times—shaking you so hard when you were very small that I heard your bones crack as they do with an osteopath. Slapping you once or twice or even more than that—hands, once your cheek, other places, your butt—right up till you were past five. But verbally hurting you is what I really mean by hurt. Saying stupid rotten things. Also using sneers and snubs or just standoffish silence as weapons. Saying 'Then I won't talk to you.' Or 'Then I don't like you.' Or 'You little brat: fuck you then.' Or staring at you as if you were a piece of human shit someone wanted me to pick up or just an idiot. Not often but enough. And then, not that I could have helped it, leaving you so early in your life. Relatively early in mine too, but that's not the important thing here. That hurts me the worst.

What it must have done to you. I know what it did, so why go into it?" "Sleep, Dada. It's better for both of us." "Sleep how? For a very long time? Past your own life? No, I've got to stop thinking that. But sleep for how long, my darling? You want me to go away forever then?" "No, appear, disappear, come back when you want—all that's your prerogative—but maybe not as often. I love you, don't worry, but having you here so often is just a little too much for me at times. You see that, don't you?" "I see it and I understand the problem. But you understand my problem too, don't you?" "Yes. Or I think I do, but let me make sure. What is the problem? And if there is one, how can it compare to mine?" "The problems are incomparable but mine still exists. The problem's that I can't stand being away from you for very long, nothing you don't know. From your sister too, but you a little more so since I knew you so much more. I have to see you both, in other words, is the problem. If I don't I go almost crazy. Sad with craziness, crazy with sadness. Both. Deeper, believe me, sometimes where my mind can't even reach. Sometimes I'm at the breakdown stage in my head so much do I want to see you when I know it's too soon after the last, and that's when I try to hold myself back most from coming, knowing what it does to you. So I think of seeing your sister, but I know what it does to her too. So I see you because I know you can take it, bad as it might be, better than she." "I understand it then. It's what I thought. But what can I tell you? Only that you have to think of my feelings too." "I do, I do, what do you think I've been saying here? Too many times you had that problem of not listening to what people were saying, especially me, and especially when I was making the most sense or wanted something especially done, so for you to hear. 'Olivia,' I'd say, my voice with each time getting sharper, 'that's the third time I asked you to come to the table' or 'to clean up that mess.' And a minute later: 'Olivia, Olivia, this is the fourth and bloody well better be the last time I'm going to ask you to come to the table' or 'to clean up that mess.' And you'd still sit at your little child's table, doing your cutouts, or making a book, or talking to your stuffed animals, or

251

building or drawing or just daydreaming but pretending not to hear me because if you did acknowledge hearing me you'd then have to take yourself away from whatever you were doing, and it would just tick me off. 'Olivia, goddamnit,' I'd say, 'do you want me to shout? Because I'm getting there and you how how I can shout. Then what? You'll say "You're always exploding at me" or "getting hotheaded" or "cross," and probably start crying, and I'll say, disturbed by your crying, but still "And you didn't deserve it every one of those times and this time too?" ' No, what am I saying? You've been listening. And if you haven't from time to time it'd be natural, since you're in bed with the lights out and it's late and you're probably getting sleepy or have been sleepy for a while and maybe even been nodding out." "I'm not, I haven't been." "Anyway, it's got to be me again saying things meanly and crossly and so on, but doing what I was always good at, right? But mostly trying to get you to agree with me to let me see you more than you want or can take. I'm sure I could have said that shorter. But I'm telling you, my darling, lots of times I only come to you when it starts killing me from being away from you and I can't stand it anymore or something forces me to you no matter how hard I force myself back." "Then I have to say that from now on you've got to think of my feelings even more than you have, and to try even harder to force yourself back." "I will. Much harder. Hard as I can and more, a lot more, though what's to guarantee I'll be able to, and if able to, have some to total success? No, I will be able to— I'll force myself till I am, stay at it, think of nothing else but, etcetera, resist, and resist more, and so forth, unabridged diligence and every trick in the book. And if I can only come back to you once every other month, let's say—" "Much too much." "Once every three months then—" "Still too often, I'm afraid." "Six months then, if that's what you'd prefer—but seeing you like this, speaking to you when I come back or once every two or three times speaking to you if that's what you'd prefer—" "It would be, I'm sorry. Maybe once in every four." "Then done, good, don't worry about it, because it'd be more than worth it to me. Worth it how? Worth all the effort? Worth all the killing-can't-stand-it-pains-resistance-more-resistance-going-crazy and so on, I mean. It should be, at least. And if you change your mind and want me around even less than that, or talking to you like this less than that, or talking to you any old way—mumbling, lisping, sputtering, susurrating, anything you'd want less of—than I'd have to do what you say and try even harder there to pull it off, isn't that so?" "If it's what I'd want, yes. Sorry again but that's the way it has to be." "So I'll do it; glad to. You watch, I will. But just know that when I'm not around you I'm almost always thinking of you." "Try not to do so much of that too. It's no good for you. I'm sure it usually leads to you wanting to come here and everything we've both said that goes with that. So try to sort of forget me too." "You've done that with me?" "A little. I've had to." "OK. If that's what you wish, OK. In that I'll forget you more than I have, I'm saying, which you probably know isn't saying very much."

Olivia meets a man with the same name as her father. When he phones to see her again she says no, "even though I did think you were interesting to speak to and pleasant to look at and under any other circumstances I would have enjoyed seeing you again. But you've the same forename as my father. It would be impossible. I'm trying to forget the old guy, in a way." "Then what better way than going out with a man named Howard? You'll forget him through me." "You sound a lot more overconfident than I like or noticed the other night and you also don't know what you're talking about." "Maybe I am and don't. I'm sure I am and don't. I often am and I often say things I think I mean and three hours later wonder why I said them and what did I mean. But for you I'll change—not only how I am but also my name, now how about that?" "You couldn't have known, but all those remarks—saying things you don't mean and maybe just for the sounds of them besides all those beguiling rhythmic effects, big quote unquote in there and also that name business—are exactly what my father would have said or done. He was a joker. He kidded about just about everything, besides trying to be a shocker, stunner and charmer with words, spoken and scrawled." "Then I won't change my name. I'll change yours. Or you can change yours to Howard and I'll be Olivia, though you can call me Ollie for short, or just call me Shortie, or Short for short. Or maybe I don't know what I'm saying again and three hours from now—three seconds, even—I'm thinking right now what did I say and why'd I say it?—I'll again think what did I mean, or did I already say that? I think I did. I know I did, so why my pretending thinking–oblivia? I mean oblivion, Olivia." "Even your word pranks and speech patterns are like his. Repeating, explaining, digressing, questioning, requestioning, quick-switching, going over everything he said about everything and then wondering if he might have missed an insignificant detail or two, and then three or four, and probably in the process infuriating or fatiguing or infuriating because he was fatiguing everyone he's speaking to. No, your name is Howard, my father's name was, I want to forget the name Howard for the time being, or something. This: I just don't want any man I go out with to have that name, since any man I go out with could end up being a man I'm interested in and then seriously involved with and then ultimately the man I might think of being married to, and since I for certain don't want to be married to a man named Howard, I can't go out with you." "I don't see it." "Don't you? It's not screwy or complex. It's just the way it is, despite all my efforts to make it other-is, and that's that I can't say or think of or even read or anything like that the name Howard without thinking of my father, something that's not going to change by going out with a man named Howard." "How about Howie? I'm serious. I hate the name Howie but you can call me it, but only you, remember that. You introduce me to relatives, say 'This is Howard.' Call me on the phone though, you can even say 'How.' " "He hated the name Howie too. That's what my mother said." "I don't like the name Howard either, but if I went by the name or whatever you want to call it of H.J. or something—it could only be H.J., unless I changed my middle name to one with another initial—it would seem phony and therefore worse." "He also didn't like 'Howard,' but no—not Howard, Howie, How, Ho or even H, since I'd know what that H means and other people would still refer or write to you by your given name." "I love you, want to marry you, marry me yesterday, let's have children last year and this, grandkids the next, sibilate our silver gilded annuity the supper's coming upchuck— Listen, what do I have to do other than turn myself into a full-fledged fool, which I'm ready to do for you, in duplicate, to see you for coffee? For tea then. Tea without the teabag then. Just the water, cold, in a glass, at a luncheonette counter of your choice. And just one glass, we'll share it, I'll even leave a profligate tip for the counterperson who brings it, and then I'll go. Or two glasses of cold if you wish. But I'll say good-bye right after, shake your hand and go. Or no shake or good-bye. I'll keep my hands in my pockets and my mouth closed. Or only I'll drink the water, out of one glass or two, and you can just watch. Or don't watch. Look the other way, at your shoes, the clock, tick-tock. Or watch your watch. You don't have a watch, I'll get you one. Two watches, three, one for around whatever part of the body that isn't a wrist, since I can't stand the ones with a pin or clip. Or don't even come inside. Stand outside, but at least walk a half block with me to the luncheonette, which is all I ask. And I don't even have to drink the water. I can just stare at the glass for a few seconds, maybe just ask for an empty glass but still give a huge tip, and you can be doing what you want outside, watching or not, and then either of us can go." "You're really asking too much. To see me you'd have to die, which is certainly not what I'm asking for, and be reborn to around your present age with any other name but the one you have now." "And if I die and happen to be reborn with the name Howard, what then? Coincidences like that have happened. Travesties, you can say. You can, I can—us both. Tragedies, rather, but let's not go that far, what do you say? Just give me another name this second and I'll be nothing else but that name for as long as you like. Honestly, what name would you prefer me to be? Lionel?" "If I actually wanted it, Lionel would be fine." "Not 'final'? OK, Lionel. From now on I am. Lionel, Lionel. Hey, I'm beginning to like my new name, so thank you very much." He hangs

255

up, phone rings fifteen seconds later and she picks it up. "Don't tell me," she says. "Hello, Olivia? This is Lionel, remember me? Tall, withery, walks like smoke unfolding, talks like folds unsmoking, rosy eyeballs, cozy nose holes, stovepipe legs. My voice is a trifle disguised, so maybe you don't recognize it. But it's Lionel calling, Lenny or Lionel. No, not Lenny or Len. Really, terrible names, undistinguished, somewhat lummox, and which wouldn't even suit me in a baseball game. Lionel. Good plain Lionel, but how's by you? Long time no peak." "You noodnik. All that's exactly what my father would have done and probably said." "I know what he would have done and said. I am your father, that's why I did and said it. I'm back. But I love you like a lover, not like a father. Or rather suit you like a suitor, not like a vest. For a father doesn't want to fall flip-flop for his daughter and marry and have kids by her and grandkids by their kids, if he's an upstanding man, an opprobrious father. Hey, how about that? Big words your father misuses, your suitor dissutures, like calling himself scur-a-lust and pusillan-i-must when he means foursquare and a fifth snared and six will get you a collar. In other words, where he doesn't mess around with his suit buttons, pocket flaps, lining, lapels and button holes. But God, what am I doing? Being subhuman, nonruminant, unfeeling, forgive me, for what I really should have said was I'm sorry and how long ago and only if you want to tell me, what from? And please don't say that's exactly what he would have said and with that same soft sympathetic timbre after that long silly insensitive monolo I gave." "It's true. But let's forget it. It's absolutely no use." "Did he die of happenstance? Certain circumstances? In his own arms? As my father used to say of his two younger siblings who died when he was five, of old age? Now you know where I get most of this from. And I know I'm not being funny but I have to keep you on.... No response to that?... Listen, I want to go out with you, don't you hear? Am I to suffer because my folks named me after my mother's brother who died six months before I was born? He got smacked with some shrap. Few pieces left of him are buried overseas in a soldier's grave he shares.

Is my mother to blame for forcing my father to go along with that name, and is he to blame for letting himself be forced? I could have been Abel. Nice name? The right initial? That's what they planned, Abigail or Abel, till my uncle got scrapped. I forget what H-name I was to be if I'd been a girl, but hardly matters. But would you have seen a guy for just coffee or water or an empty glass whose name was Abel?" "The name alone wouldn't have stopped me." "And my mother didn't want 'Howard.' Her mother pleaded with her to. Was still distraught, of course, over her only son's death, so said 'His loss was bad enough and almost killed me, but I'll die for sure if you don't name your boy Howard.' Is my grandmother to blame for pleading that to my mother, and before that, for naming her son 'Howard'? And is the original Howard—original as a name as far as my mother and I know, since there's no record of it ever being in the family—to blame for dying before I was born? For letting himself be drafted, let's say. For not dodging it, though who knows if in his dodging he wouldn't have been run over by a car or train, or caught, died very quickly of something in the stockade. So my grandmother got his name out of a phonebook. Opened it up, went down the columns of Smiths and came up with Howard and stopped right there. Or continued going if she didn't already have a girl's name. 'Hortense' I now think my mother settled on from the phonebook for her girl's name if she couldn't convince her mother to accept 'Abigail.' Maybe we should blame AT&T. So my mother went along with my grandmother. She was a good daughter, devoted, and didn't want to be in any way the reason for her mother's illness or death. Qualities like that should be highly prized. Even still, I should phone her right now and say 'Mom, you never did such a wrong thing in your life, so far as I know and which I'm only now realizing, as naming me what you did. Because of it, and let's not even talk about what I'll be missing out on, you'll be out a beautiful intelligent daughter-in-law and if this woman and I would have had it in us, two to three fine grandkids.' I'd love to call her up. She's dead and I only wish there was a phone for her where she is so I could call

257

her every day as I did when she was alive. I don't know why she
never called me except when I was coming over and she wanted me
at the last minute to pick up a lemon or carrot she needed for the
dinner that night, or the afternoon paper that had some lotto game
in it she didn't want to miss, or a carton, and if I wouldn't do it,
just a pack of cigarettes. But all right, no time for gripes, wouldn't
you say?. . .But whenever I did call—listen to this—every day except
when I was away in some place like Europe or Asia, where I actually
saw my namesake's grave. Taken care of very impressively. The U.S.
does a tip-top job when it wants to and puts it all together, or at
least for its military dead. But she'd always say when I said 'How
are you?' on the phone, 'All right, though, I guess.' She was never
'great.' Not even 'good' or 'not bad.' Things could always be much
better, she was telling me, maybe by my calling twice a day in the
States and coming over more and at least once a day on my short-
to-long out-of-country stays. Or maybe if she admitted things were
pretty good to OK that day she thought I might cut my calls to every
other day. I wouldn't have done that and I saw her as much as I could.
Could tolerate it, I'm saying, and also knew, even if she thought she
thought otherwise, how often and how long she could tolerate me.
Anyway, a phone call to heaven, we'll say, would make her life eternal
more enjoyable, I suppose, and also let me know by her being near
a phone that life there wasn't so strange and scary to her and if it
was she'd say." "Truthfully, Howard, and I'm sorry, but why are you
bothering me with all this?" "Because I'm trying to impress upon
you some of what I think are my more positive qualities. So far I
feel everything I've said has come out mealy-mouthed and against
me. That I was a good son, caring, responsive, and that maybe I even
have some intelligence and imagination, qualities you might think
all right. Good sons often make good husbands and fathers, it's said,
or at least the chances of it happening should be slightly higher. And
if the man's also to some extent intelligent with a little savory flair,
even better, would you agree?" "Who can say?" "Also that I looked
after people—not just my mother. And not just helping old or

infirmed people across the street and small but important things like that. But I'm interested in them, what they do and so on, how they get along without sight, and such, and though I didn't go into that before, there it is. That's going to work against me too, I just know it. But I'm not ashamed of any of this either. And she was generous with money and encouragement to me when I needed it—everyone falls into financial and emotional holes—when she didn't have to be with the money, since I was old enough to pay my own way, and she really couldn't afford it. I suppose I paid it back in attention and real filial concern, and actual helping out, like laying down rubber treads on her basement stairs and winterizing her windows each year. And by 'emotional' I don't mean disturbed in any way or bizarre. That's why I tagged the 'savory' to the 'flair' before, which you probably got, along with, because of my intentional mispronunciation of savory, the double meaning. I got sad sometimes, like any sane natural person does periodically. So I didn't change my name when I got to legal age, though wanted to. Lots of times through my youth other kids made fun of it. 'Howard Howitzer. Howard Whore.' Stupid stuff but still upsetting. I'm sure Howard was once a popular name even in this century—I know kings used to have it, or maybe that was Harold—but when I got it it was out-of-date and just too formal. I didn't change it because by that time, though my grandmother had long succumbed, my mother had got used to it of course and didn't want to be calling me something different suddenly, she said. 'Abel' I was going to change it to, simply to undo what'd been undone twenty years earlier and because to me it was a stronger-sounding and more desirable name, but let's forget it. And by desirable I'm not saying 'Oh come to me, I'm gorgeous, romantic and magnetic besides worth a fortune,' but just a better if not more appropriate name for me. Able, capable, effectual, all of which I am. Not joking. It's something lots of people scorn or feel threatened by because it represents a certain versatility and adaptability to life and even a flexibility with it, but don't let me get started why I think all of that's to the good. It is and it isn't but mostly is. But I was where?

Please—that's what I'm driving at without trying to be pushy—please try to forget your father for a minute and my personal name liability and think a little of the possibilities of a half-hour with me. One stinking little coffee's all I'm shooting for. Even rich and aromatic, but what could be the harm? And I can say that 'harm' question after all I've just said, right?. . .Come on, Olivia, right?" "You can. What do I care? And as for your rambling on too long, you're very much *right* there." "I don't remember saying that. I said 'Don't let me start' or something, and about something, but I forget what. What's good, what's bad—" "Please, already, shut up. And it's not that my father's on my mind constantly, you know, which I'm sure I've said. It's simply that I want to have him on it less." "All right. Agreed, in toto. So do I, and I'm not being facetious. That's why I said a half-hour. Maximum. Solely. Fifteen minutes could even do for me. A quick coffee, half of it milk so we can actually drink it in that time. And Monday, what do you say? I can be persistent and unrelenting but I know when a spoon's thoroughly licked, so I won't hammer away at it any longer. You say no now, it's no and no for good. And I was only joking before about marriage and children and loving you and water and empty glasses and phones ringing on my mother's bed table in heaven and so on. I'm—most people know me not like that but as a reasonable conscientious person, practical, effectual, as I said, plenty of common sense. I have to be in what I do and also conduct myself civilly. My company would lose customers by the droves otherwise. People with piles of money to play and lose have a sixth sense about detecting eccentricity in people who speculate for them. But I do want to have coffee and maybe some cake with you. Sandwich or soup if you like. Wine or beer with the sandwich, or even go to dinner with you. Take you out. Nothing fancy but nice. I'm a stocks analyst, by the way. Was your father a stocks analyst or involved with stocks in any way?" "Hated it. No." "Thank God. What'd he do?" "Never mind." "You're right. And I didn't bring up I'm a stocks analyst to say that I do all right. I don't do all right, quite truthfully, or not as well as I could with what I know, but that's not and could never be the point why I do it. I don't even like what I do that much, so it's even more a mystery why I do as well as I do, or maybe it's the answer. But just when you think you have the answer to something you don't, right? Or that's been my experience, so I'm not a very over-self-confident creature either. But I'm wholly unsuited for my work and would like to do a dozen other things, including serious pottery for a living and sitting home for the next ten years and reading every book I've ever wanted to read but never had the time to and opening my own health food restaurant, but gourmet stuff with me as chef, but you need the principal as well as the interest for that—you've heard that one. But OK, enough there too, and can I say it's all right for dinner, we'll say, Monday night? Of course 'night.' Dinner, or is it supper, is always at night. 'Dinner' 's the one that makes you think twice. But this is ridiculous, for suddenly I think it's supper that some people if not whole sections of the country use as a word for lunch and others use for dinner. But nothing else but that—dinner, supper or even lunch, if you'd prefer. And then, we see it isn't right for either of us—" "It won't be. We can see that now." "Don't say that. Put a curse on it, of course it'll turn out bad. What I'm saying is if we're both bored flat in seconds, though I know I could never be with you or anyone else, even with someone who didn't say anything. Because even saying nothing would provide me with interest why the person isn't saying anything and is it because of me or the restaurant, let's say, or what? The environs; the weather. What I might remind that person of, for instance, though there I'm only talking about look-alikes or act-alikes, not names. Anyway, that we can't even be acquaintances—and just listen to this common sense talking—we'll call it quits without any further dramatics, OK?" "Oh shoot. I feel you broke me down where I can't say no. For that's what I want to say. Maybe for the quick coffee you spoke of, just so I'll say to you 'Howard, Howie, How' till I get it out of my system for now. That's not it. What is? And why'd I even give an equivocal yes? Crazy of me. I'm afraid I'll have to radically change my mind now, Howard." "Too late. You said it. Don't take it away. It's bad to forswear. And what time? And don't worry. I'll be one-tenth the talker I was today, so you'll have to do most of the conversing while I'm doing the eating and staring. Sorry for that, I know you don't want to hear it, and where should we meet? It's yours to designate. Hey, good word again, right? Oh, sorry again for pretending to sound like a dud. Because I can use the long words with the best of them—I got a liberal arts education, as they say—or almost the best. Like my being such a long-winded prolix lexifanatic bombastic fustian pedantic euphuistic loquacious—and I swear I'm not looking at a thesaurus while I say this—garrulous nonsensical ludicrous ill-devised—I love that one, 'ill-devised'—unreflective egregious simpleminded—I'm looking for a good one now to end it—prodigiously tropological—I can't find it and don't even know what that last word means; it just came to me, snap, in my head—ignoramus onomatomaniacal-obsessed windbag buffoon fool."

Olivia writes several poems about her father. Last one goes: "Dear father, padre, in your box, with your holey socks, oh father whose heaven was art (that can't be new but was true for him), maroon muff were you formally buried in? former young lit tough's the rep you're to be stuck with? what's it mean? what it seems, curly thin-skinned hair, most in back and growing out of your shoulders like furry epaulets (boy that's bad so nix the similets), hair info according to those who know your photos, black all that for thought of you broken down and disinterred by vermin and rats worse than the thought of you dead. To be truthfully true for once, the night is night and blue and I am blue and night without the living u, I mean the loving u, no hoax or reflection intended. Mirror, scissors, rocks. Enough, this stuff's, rough. What it means, what's it seem? Further, larder, sucks." Poems like that. She's a little high. Drank half a bottle of wine at dinner before she sat down in front of the typewriter. More than a little. Before that a scotch sour while she cooked. Before that, over the newspaper, last of last night's bottle of wine, which wasn't much. Didn't know she was going to sit down. In fact, was heading for the bathroom and then bed. Didn't know why she sat down or what she was going to do there. "Well here I am," she said. "Might as well turn on the light. Might as well remove the typewriter cover. Might as well try out the keys to see if they're still stuck. Tap-a-tap. Drier air must've upstuck them. Write something? Ah, come off it, you know I can't write. Letter to the editor protesting the president. A love scene. A death vignette. A poem. You used to. First thing that comes to your head will be the first thing that gets written down, unlike all those other lackluster pieces of the past. The past: "When I was a girl of seventeen, I bit my nails till they were clean." The past: "Rose have bled, poses are you." The past: "Evanescent is deceit..." This time do it spontonasally, fontly, fabuloosely, rapsofollicly, graspberries, doodlewarts. She tears all the poems up, dumps them, most don't make the can. Shouts as she scoops together a handful "Oh frick, bloody you write them—you were the typewriter. But no blood or fugs. Just write one she pleads." Looks at the typewriter. Nothing happens. "Oh of course." Puts paper in and stares at it. Still nothing. "That's funny. The keys aren't moving, words aren't appearing, and it's originally your typewriter too, left in impeccable condition, thanks, though not since then professionally cleaned, sorry." Gets up, gets the wine, sits in front of the typewriter and drinks from the bottle, several healthy belts. "I'm going to get smashed and sick but I don't care. No work tomorrow so I can lose a day. But what about that? You want your little kid getting smashedly sick? Then type, darn ya. A poem, no time for a tome. But no threats. Jest a quest if nothing else, something you did effortlessly. Say, I should've got all that down. Could've been the start or major part or even the whole of my poem. 'Jest a fest' I could've titled it, or 'A Poem, No Tome.' " Puts paper in, machine jams. "Oh of course." Rips all the paper out, little torn pieces she has to scratch out, puts more paper in and waits. Nothing. "Spontofontly then." Types "Hair's a mess, evening's overdressed, my face a pudge, new moon needs a nudge, a loan, a tome, my drinkdome for a poem. Why must I write in rhyme all the time? Teendrone throwback. Sky's not blue anymore but I still am, blue-who. When I was a whelp and you walked me you always held my hand. 'Carry me, daddy dog,' I'd sometimes say but you said 'You'll break this old cur's back.' Some nights when I was supposed to be asleep I imagined that. You collapsed, back broken in two. I'd cry. I'd caused it. My disjoined done-for dad shot through with pain. 'Soft and small,' you said, 'my paw fits around yours like a big mitt,' and then you'd kiss it." Pulls it out, tears it up, holds the pieces over the can and drops them; most fall around it. "Screw 'em, let 'em rot." Puts paper in and types " 'Simplest said gets the best results,' you'd say, so type me, dear old cur, a poem to show you're really around." Sits back and stares at the typewriter. Keys start moving, words appear on the page. Bing. One poemlike line done, paper shifts two spaces down and over to the margin on the left. More words. All by itself. Bing. Bing. Typing much faster than she ever did, then stops. She rolls it up so she can read it. "In my box, with my hollow (more apt) sox (that's my way, shorter and stronger and then a long explanation about it), maroon muff (watch your spelling, dearest. . .oops, tupical typo ((there too)) when you're tired and out of pract), curly thinning gray hair just about bald (I forget precisely what you wrote in that last poem but I know I had qualms about the description: too opaque, thus fake), the night is black and black and I am rabble and rats and stink like cat piss and ants and worms, all cradlerobbers and all without my loving you, seeing you, drinking like a fish even (blowing it here), stinking and sinking like one too (actually blew it after the cat piss). What's it mean? Hey, I should talk, for who the heck cares? But we're in touch at last, by golly, I mean 'at least' and maybe the last, bite our tongues, and any way's a good way if we can't have it the only way, got it? I don't think I do but drat's all. Must paddle back. Life's a hoe. Got my metaballs all botched up. So what. Just over and out, babe, over and out." She waits; nothing else. She types "Come back. . . .Then tomorrow night when I'll be straight?. . .Then straighten out some of what you wrote?. . .I want clarity, you supposedly always insisted on clarity, and in my state I can't take anything hazy or vague, so maybe just

to correct what seem like a coupla misspells?. . .Then thank you, love
you, don't want to push you, goodnight?. . .Takes the page out, kisses
it, bathroom, pees, does her teeth, bedroom, undresses, puts the
paper under her pillow, head on the pillow and is reaching for the
night table light switch when she passes out.

It's his seventieth birthday. Actually, last Tuesday was but not
everybody could get off from school or work. Eva flew in from one
state, Olivia from another, they picked up their mother and drove
to the cemetery. Olivia's infant daughter is with them. They called
Jerry and he said he'd meet them. "Bring the prayer book," Olivia
said. They stand in front of the grave. Jerry says the prayer book was
in his coat pocket but must have fallen out along the way and shows
them the hole. He brought three very large black umbrellas,
"cemetery umbrellas, which I've collected from some of the fancier
funerals I've gone to recently, though I think two of those they
wanted them back," and distributed them. "I wish you all had got
to know my other brother and my sister," he says. "I know this is
an odd way to start, especially in this weather when you almost wish
you were inside your family mausoleum. But we don't meet much
and I never feel enough's been said or felt about them in front of
other people so I thought I'd give them a little due before I forget
to. Really sweet people, and talented, sensitive. Readers they both
were; advanced thinkers for their ages. Possibly I'm exaggerating for
Vera, for she was always so handicapped from such an early age that
sometimes she couldn't even turn a simple page. I forget if she even
liked to have books read to her. I know a pile of them piled up as
gifts for her. If she did like to be read to I'm afraid we were all
probably usually too busy to except my mother. I wince now when
I think of the things we gave her to entertain herself. Leather lacing,
for instance, to make scissors holders and coin purses and things
for keys. Then she gave one of them to you or you asked for one
or were asked by your mother to ask for one or for her to make you
one and you said 'Great work, great.' But what they both could've
amounted to we don't even have to say. Anybody could see that for

Frog

Vera in her preschool photographs before she first took sick. So alert, open eyed. Also in the last ones when she was around postgraduate age, though why we took them I don't know, when she was on crutches, then crutches and neck and back braces because she had so little bone back there to hold up her neck, I think it was. Then bedridden, bed sores, eighty pounds, next week it's seventy-five. She seemed like a big empty piñata whenever I picked her up so my mother could change the bed under her or get the potty out without spilling when it got too filled or stuck. I guess we took the photographs because she was smiling, and who'd want to do anything but encourage that? And also that she thought she looked, all in black and black eyeliner and much brushed and I think dampened-down hair covering her forehead and cheeks and some of her eyes and certainly the front and back neck scars—these pictures when she was on crutches—kind of chic, street-smart and exotic. In one bed photograph, which my mother I just remember kept forever on the pegboard above her own dresser, she had her hand up holding an exercise bar, was in a wrinkled hospital gown, though this was at home, and by 'wrinkled' I'm not making any criticism of my mother, but the same eyes, look, hair, big clearheaded smile. Black stockings too with the crutches to give her atrophied legs a fuller look, I suppose. And black sunglasses sometimes both in her photographs on crutches and in bed, maybe to make her look sultrier but I think just as much to hide these very dark circles around, by this time, her crossed eyes. Anybody here feel I'm talking on too long or I'm depressing you or your feet are getting soaked, though those umbrellas should be stopping that, let me know or maybe just go back to the cars. No apologies needed. I'd like to stay and finish. So, it was enough to kill you, those two. That they died, in their late, for him, to mid-twenties for her, and then when Howard went it was like being slowly tortured before you were slowly killed. Scratch that. Too literary and not even accurate as a comparison. Whenever I try those I flop. Vera had the tougher of the two lives. I'm talking about her and Alex, and I promise to be quicker and less winding. No childhood almost, while he of course had much more than that. He went to regular school, college, worked as a newsman, saw lots of the world, was starting to be a serious creative person, was once even engaged, I think. Anyway, he knew women, had jobs, got drunk, moved around. She died much too early, which I can say despite all her ordeals and such for twenty years which might've made me say 'Come and get me already.' Even cripples and people confined to hospital beds can find companionship and marry and have children if it's not with someone who's permanently bedridden too. Possibly I'm wrong there, meaning they can, though no doubt with help. I've an image of her on the floor once, or maybe this was Howard's or Alex's memory and whichever one told me it told me it a few times. Must be, since I would've been too old to have the reaction I'm now going to convey. And I suddenly remember something which did indicate she was thinking 'Come and get me already,' or at least once, but it's not what I'm going to say right now. She was on her back and banging the dining room floor hysterically with her heels and hands and shrieking that gives you temporary deafness and her hoarseness. 'Shut up,' Alex or Howard said, 'I can't think' or 'do my schoolwork' or something. I don't remember the last part, just the 'shut up.' And my mother said to him that it was only a tantrum, let her have it, she deserves it, something like that, and no doubt comforted her, but I think Vera continued to bang and cry. She did this a few times, supposedly, none, I can remember, when I was around, and one time did much worse, which is the time I meant about 'Come and get me already.' Years later, when she was thirteen or fourteen—I was away but Alex or Howard sent me the newspaper clipping—she tried to jump off our apartment building roof and a fireman swung around in a sling and grabbed her. That was the newspaper shot I got, but with the story all wrong. In it they said she was ten, up till then a cheerful neighborly girl, with no seeming meaning to kill herself, and so on. But I'm trying to illustrate something here. Bring it out. What? That the tantrum— that's right—also the suicide try, of course—was because, as my mother explained to Alex or Howard that time, she was so sick of being sick and having no life and going to the hospital every three years or so to be operated on and coming back months later sometimes looking and feeling worse than when she left and being a half-inch to an inch shorter each time and not smarter, her brains drugged duller, scars here and everywhere, a tracheotomy tube in her at home that would last like the last one lasted for months and then left with the tube hole that never seemed to close. It was so ugly. A hole, in your throat, which you always walked around with; just awful. I could barely look at it and for the most part she didn't cover it with anything like a Band-Aid, and I don't even know if she was supposed to. She was sensitive to its looks, you could see that, her eyes always following your eyes and going downcast when you took a squint at it, but maybe she was told to keep it exposed so it could heal faster. My mother, by the way, used to clean the gook out of the tube, and with hydrogen peroxide, I think, dab around the hole. She called it the worst job of her life, suctioning it, and not just because it was her daughter. Gagging work, she said. So, compared to Vera—compared to my mother, even, and that job, besides losing a few kids—we've all lived richly, even Alex. Scratch that too. Too sermony, that 'because of this we should feel that' and so on. But I should move on before you all drown while you're dying of boredom. I think I've already said that in almost the same way, today or some day close. I think I've already said almost everything a few times or at least twice. I'm not complaining, just saying, but every statement and phrase of mine, including this last one, is beginning to sound too familiar. Anyway, I suppose you know—I know Denise does—how your father felt when Alex disappeared so unexpectedly. . . . No, that's not the way to start it—so formal—and I can't even talk anymore. It's not that I'm choked up. I actually am, but it's mostly that I'm too tired. I'm in good shape for my age, even if that's not saying much. But this day's been too tough for me, driving here from who knows where, and I better remember later if I want to get home, and just getting my mind set for it. It isn't easy being the oldest child and then the only survivor and also seeing the place where I'll probably be dropped into shortly, even if it's beside them and even if I think later my wife and later still maybe one of my kids will be beside or near me, which doesn't help much to think about either. So, the end. Thank you for coming, and just 'God love you' to all our relations in the graves here—don't know how else to put it—Momma, Dad and the rest of you, which I think we can say amen to to clinch it, OK?" "Amen," they all say and he says "If you'll still excuse me, I think I'll drive home rather than to whatever you've planned to do," and folds up his umbrella, goes to his car in the rain without responding to two of them saying "I'll drive you," gets in, doesn't turn to or look back at them though they're all waving and saying good-bye, and drives off.

Olivia prays. "Dear God, please don't let my father have pain wherever he is. Any pain, in any part of him. From his toes to his head top to out to the tips of his fingers and penis and nose. Whatever part and wherever he is. Dear God, please just do that for me and I'll do anything you say and want for the rest of my life forever, I promise. Please, please, thank you." She turns over in bed and hugs Talking Bear. If she hears her mother walking or putting away dishes or turning a page, she'll cry she wants her. Wants her for what? It has to be good or she'll get mad. For water, to make peepee, or she's still having trouble sleeping, thinks she's getting a cold. She listens, hears nothing. She listens for Eva in the next room. If Eva cries or talks to herself or taps on her crib bars or wall or bangs her feet against them, she'll call for her mother and say Eva's keeping her up. She hears nothing. Why'd Eva get to get one more story read to her than she tonight? Tomorrow night it's her turn to get more. She had so many other bears she loved more than Talking Bear but right after her father died he became her favorite. Why's that? Talking Bear was brought back from some place her father had been, the only bear he gave her just by himself. She never thought of that but now she knows. When her mother said before "Just rest in bed and think, if you can't fall asleep, but no getting out of it," would that be something interesting she could tell her mother she thought? She thinks so, but it wouldn't be a good enough reason to get her here to tell her. "The other bears tell me my father isn't somewhere still alive," she says to Talking Bear. "Is that true? Should I believe them or you?" "Believe me," Talking Bear says. "It's best for you. I am closest and mostest and I always tell the truth and all I do is think of you. That's my job." "But the other bears all together, when they're together, say the same thing and know much more than you. They know more than anyone. They know almost everything there is to know when they're all together." "Then believe them. I won't be hurt. I say 'If it is good for you, it is good for me.' I say this every night before I go to sleep. Right before the last wink awake, so I haven't said it yet tonight to myself." "What about if I don't believe any of them when they're all together, or you? If I just find out for myself?" "That could be the best way. If you can find out and if you know before you start looking that you might be able to find out." "If I don't know whatever it is you said, that last thing, and if I can't find out, what should I do?" "I don't know." "The other bears all together would know, but I can't get them all together now for them to tell me. I'd have to get out of bed. That wouldn't be hard. I can inch out. I can move quietly. The door's shut. There's a rug on the floor. I could get some of my bears. But for the rest of them I'd have to leave the room. I might even have to go to Eva's room if she took some when she wasn't supposed to, but I don't think I'd have to go downstairs or outside. What I'll do, if I can't find out about my father from here, is believe what makes the most sense." "That's a good way too. If you can't find out for yourself or you're not able to, believe what makes the most sense." "Or the best sense." "Or the best sense. But if I were you I'd believe me. I tell the truth and I also know. I am for you." "But no matter what, the truth is if he is still somewhere alive but doesn't or can't let me see him anymore, I'll be very sad." "That's why I'm here. To help you in things like that. You can ask me how if you want." "How?" "You'll have to give me time to think.... You can throw me up and down and try to catch me. You can kick me and I won't say ouch. You can squeeze me while you sleep or are feeling sad. If you're away in a car someplace and I'm not with you because you forgot me or you couldn't find me, you can know I'm home waiting for you and wanting you to throw me or kick me or squeeze me while you sleep or anytime you're sad. Lots of ways. We can think of many. It's something we can also do." "How should I start to find out if he's alive or really dead or really alive or near here or what?" "You can look for him. I haven't seen him for a long time, maybe as long as you, but I hear he's around. You can ask me how I hear this." "How?" "You'll have to give me time to think. . . . I just hear it, there isn't any reason how. It's something I can do. Or we can look together for him if you want. In basements, outside behind bushes, in backs of bottom drawers. All the places you haven't looked. If we don't find him or we can't, because he's too big to be there, in a drawer, we might find a sign of him. Or you can speak to the bears. If they know everything, they might know where to look. I won't be hurt." "They said he isn't alive. When I said you said he is and I think he is and I want to find him, they said the one thing they don't know anything about is where to look. Missing bears they can help me find. People they can't. It's just something they can't do and now they don't even try." "Then we are in what your father used to call a spot. But go to sleep. Maybe in the morning you'll have your answer. Maybe I will. Maybe it will just appear. A paper we pick up that has a map showing where he is and how to get there. Something that was once a piece of scrap paper but now isn't. Or something that is and always was a map. Or we might see something written on a wall in this room. A message written in light from the outside or being written while we watch it on the wall." "I don't know how to read." "You don't know now but maybe tomorrow you will. Or maybe you'll be able to read just that. You know a few words. The message might just be in those words. 'Red, blue, dog, gray, go, he, girl, green,' and some others, and we'll figure it out. Or maybe I'll even know how to read by tomorrow. Listen to me though. What I say is true. Maybe in the morning everything you want to know or what you need to know it, like reading, will just happen or appear." "That's what bears always say. 'In the morning. Tomorrow.' They're good up to a point. After that point, they're not. It's always that way. And always when they're most sleepy." "If it's always that way, then it's always that way. Ask anyone. Though that doesn't mean it will always always be that way. And if it is always always that way, then it doesn't mean it will always always always be that way. But go to sleep. It's not because I'm sleepy. Just maybe you'll know in the morning as I say. Or maybe I'll know. Or maybe all the other bears and us together will know, something we never did once. But maybe it will probably not be so. If that's so, what?" "I don't know. What?" "Let me think. . . . I don't either."

Eva does a series of paintings called Memories of My Father. One shows her father sleeping behind her mother. Another shows him sitting on a toilet seat folding a newspaper in half. Others: squeezing lemon juice for a pitcher of scotch sours, mailing a bunch of manila envelopes in a post office, pushing the two girls in a shopping cart at a supermarket, paying for takeout food in a Chinese restaurant, haranguing her mother across the dining room table, peeling an avocado seed for planting, fork-feeding the two girls simultaneously, kissing her mother while holding on to her bottom, digging his knuckles into his temples, looking at several photos of his father, helping his mother downstairs, putting a record back into its jacket, filling a pen, cleaning a typewriter key. Eating, exercising, cooking, slicing, typing, reading, driving, raging, sneezing, aimlessly peeing, winding his watch, brushing his teeth, grating a carrot, unpinning her diapers, filling her baby's bottle with milk, in a hospital dying. Brown tweed suit, button-down blue shirt, light gray tie. The family stands above it staring inside, Eva on a box, Olivia on tiptoes, his mother crying. He looks healthier there than in any of the others. The paintings are exhibited and get lots of attention and reviews. The gallery sells the lot. Two are bought by European museums, one by a prominent Japanese art collector. Most of the drawings for the paintings sell too. Newspaper article, long critiques in art publications, two-page spread with reproductions of some of the works in a popular newsweekly, interviews. "I feel awful," she writes Olivia. "First, that I didn't keep even one for myself. That's because I couldn't make up my mind. 'Daddy in the Tub'? 'Daddy Showering'? 'Daddy Shaving the Back of His Neck After Giving Himself a Haircut'? When I finally chose the tub one, it was just being bought for the most money, even if it was one of the smallest and no better framed than the others. The gallery owner said to me 'My dear, we must pay expenses and keep peachy relations with this particular buyer, who's already begun to sock away funds for the most expensive work in your next show. Choose another,' but by then admissible bids were being made for the other two, and the few remaining I didn't feel merited keeping. Secondly, that I didn't offer you whichever one you wanted for nothing. Especially the one of you and Daddy holding hands and he with your backpack over his shoulder as he walked you down the hill to school. I got you both from behind. You seem to be looking at a squirrel in a tree running. I think it's a good one. Now I'll probably never see it again, though I've some like slides of it. Also, that I should be on my way, or already made, as one idiot critic put it, and partly because of Daddy. What about all the paintings I did before? The Laughing Mom series. Bombed quietly. One-dimensional, that gallery owner kept being told. They didn't get the joke—'Say "Cheese"', even though I know you can't float a whole show on one pun—or see, as we say, the new nuances in them, among other delusions. No reviews, one sale, and I think that one to Uncle Jerry and Aunt Iris, who still haven't unpacked it because they want me to believe someone I didn't know and possibly a hotshot influential art collector bought it. It wasn't you, I hope, since half the sale went to the gallery, another ten percent to the gallery for announcements, hangings and cheap opening night crackers and wine in paper dentist cups, and the rest she's still promising me. Besides, I'd have given you any two Moms you wanted. Best thing about that gallery is that it dropped me flat. That's what I need most to get into and go on with the next series. As it is, I'll probably have to start debasing my present success and maybe give away half my earnings to old age homes for artists to start anything new. But what'll more likely happen is that the Moms will now sell. They had some good things in them, but everyone seems to think the Father ones were more lived than the Moms, though technically as virtuous. But all the scenes in the Mom paintings I experienced and all the ones in Father I made up. I had nothing to paint from because I had no memories of him. Just photos of different sorts and groupings, and I wasn't going to reproduce blown-up versions of those. They'd be so cold, except perhaps my reaction to them, and it's also been done to death before. You should have painted the Father series. You showed lots of talent once. It's all I can remember of you for years. Drawing, painting, tracing, coloring, cutting out and pasting things together to play with and for collages and mobiles, designing and illustrating your own books. Or we could have done Father together. You giving me your head snaps and telling me if I'm getting them on the canvas right. And dabbing here and there and even splashing all over the place if you wanted, for I'm sure you're a better artist dormant than I am active and that it'd all come back to you in a flash and with an intelligence and feeling my works lack. And then with paintings, if it's really bad or there's a serious mistake, there's little you can't cover over and change. Now it's too late. They're done, bought, hung, insured, guarded by guards and alarms and maybe even attack dogs in some places. And many probably can't be located and, if I wanted to, destroyed, since some collectors think announcing they've a collection is like asking for a major break-in. And somehow I don't see myself doing alone Olivia's Memories of Our Father. Though who knows? Since after I do a series on you and a shorter one on Grandma and an even shorter one called Other Relatives, a Bad Marriage, a Number of Lovers and Some Friends, I won't have any place to go. Maybe sculpture. That'd get me doing something new. Though suddenly I see myself sculpting bigger-than-life-size bas-reliefs of all of us, starting with Mom just giving birth to you, and Daddy, in this same scene, in hospital gown and mask and holding you in his arms and weeping voluminously, a moment, Mom's said Daddy called, the happiest in his life."

Olivia's in the city to give a paper. Her husband and two children come with her to see some sights, go to a few art museums and a recital and play. On the last day of the conference she says "I'm going to skip the rest of it. How many seminars can you go to? I've learned all I'm about to learn before what I've learned starts depercolating. And I've made enough new contacts and seen more than enough old colleagues and friends, and I need to relax and enjoy myself a little before we head home. This might seem an odd way of doing that, but I'd like to drive out to the cemetery to pay respects to my folks and Grandma and Uncle Jerry, as I haven't been there for years." She doesn't know exactly where it is or even the name of it. "It's in Suffolk County, I know that. I remember we'd drive through Nassau County on the expressway and then see an entering-Suffolk-County sign. Or maybe it's the other way around, but we'll know which counties we're leaving and entering when we see that sign. And that the cemetery's about ten exits past that sign and called something like Brookside or Breitenbrush or Baron Birch or Beth something—but I'm sure it starts with a B. If we drive out on the Long Island Expressway—the road you get from the Midtown Tunnel, or off Vandam Street, I think it is, after you cross the Fifty-ninth Street Bridge—I'm sure I'll recognize the exit sign for the road or route number to the cemetery in whatever county it is that had that you-are-entering sign, or it could even have been a you-are-leaving. One thing I remember distinctly is that there was a service road alongside the expressway going east just before the turnoff and then a couple of sod farms along the two-lane road to the cemetery and a number of cemeteries down that road, though I'm sure the farms are gone now. Anyway," she says to the children, "you'll see some of Long Island for the first time, and of course where your closest relatives on my side are buried, if we get there. And we can stop for lunch at a fish place on the Island and maybe even go to the ocean later. I don't think you've seen the Atlantic, except from a plane, have you?" They start out, half an hour later pass the entering-Suffolk-County sign—she says it looks like the same one from years ago and seems to be in the exact same place—but for the next fifteen exits, no service road or familiar landmark or road name or route number on an exit sign that she'd follow to the cemetery. "Is it possible they've done away with the service road? It was about a mile long. I remember there was a famous-make—I can't think of the name now—cosmetics corporate headquarters on it, or maybe only the plant, but that seems to be gone from around here too. I thought the route to the cemetery would all come back. That I'd just go from A to B to C, once we left the city, but there's nothing left out here to bring it back, or else I've completely forgotten everything but the entering sign in ten years, or however long it's been. I should just look it up." They stop for lunch at a diner off the expressway, she looks in the phone directory under Cemeteries but doesn't recognize any name, and after several calls to different places she locates Eva. Eva can't remember the name of the cemetery or what exit it's off of or the town it's in or even if the name begins with a B. "To tell you the truth, I think D. David something. Or Dav, Duv, Darien—no, that's a town in Connecticut. One of Uncle Jerry's children might know. If only the other uncle and aunt hadn't died so young. There'd be a bigger pool of cousins to draw information like that from. But I'm terrible. Most times I can't even remember either of our grandfathers' names." Olivia calls one of Uncle Jerry's children and he doesn't know the name or where the cemetery is, except for it being on Long Island and somewhere off an expressway—"I remember you went right for a long ways once you left the off-ramp of the expressway"—and says he's ashamed to admit that he hasn't been out to it since his mother died. "I doubt my sisters would know either. They're even less interested." "Who keeps it up, if it is kept up?" and he says "Our grandfather bought the plot long ago for practically nothing, I remember my dad saying. Then he sold off a few parcels of it, it was so big, making back twice what he put out for the entire thing, and paid the cemetery enough money to keep the plot mowed and clean for about seventy-five years. Dad told me I'd only be called—or one of us, meaning you and Eva too—if one of the monuments fell over or the plot was vandalized in some way or the town wanted to move the graves to some other place in the cemetery to make room for more town road or something. Maybe one of those things already happened and the cemetery has changed hands and the new owners don't bother with that kind of notification anymore. Or the old owners don't or they tried to reach us but we've all moved around so much that they're now waiting for us to notify them where we are. But with vandals and such is the only time we'd have to pay something, till after the seventy-five years when we're supposed to take over the maintenance costs. But by then, which of us will care, right? We'll all probably be buried elsewhere—I know I'm going to, and not just because there'll probably be no room at the family gravesite—so I'm sure our kids won't be interested in it either." "As for caring about it," she says, "I suppose that depends when those seventy-five years are coming up. And as for my kids' interest, maybe that's one of the things I'm trying to stimulate today by coming out here with them, though I think I just thought of that. But you sort of hope, no matter where you'll be buried or they'll be living, that they and even their children take care of this site so it doesn't become a little forest, don't you? Because some places in very old cemeteries, and I'm talking mostly about European ones now, just look so sad and ugly." "I've seen them on my trips there but never felt anything bad about it. They even looked kind of interesting, all packed in very tight and overgrown. Listen, if that's the outcome, because of whatever it is, historical or indifference, you face it." She goes back to the table. "Maybe we passed the cemetery exit, she says. "Anyone mind if we drive back to that entering-Suffolk sign and then come back this say again till we reach, say, the turnoff to the Fire Island state park? Deal is, if we don't see any roads to the cemetery, we'll go right to the ocean." She asks her husband to drive this time so she can watch the exit signs and service roads more carefully and anything else that might help them get to the cemetery. They drive back, turn around, about five miles past the Suffolk sign she sees a little sign on a road off the expressway that says "Wellingham National Cemetery" and has an arrow on it. "That could be it," she says. "Not the national cemetery but the road with maybe a few other cemeteries on it, including ours." They exit, drive along that road— "No service road near it, sod farms on it, but it could still be the right road—just widened threefold because of the increased traffic on it or just crooked politics we'll say"—and see a cemetery. "It doesn't look familiar, nor start with a B. But it's the right religion, not a national cemetery, and on the same side of the road ours was and the approximate distance I figured the road to it would be from the expressway exit and the expressway would be from the Suffolk County sign." They drive in, her husband goes into the office, comes out shaking his head. "Nothing even close to a Tetch here," he says. "But there are two more nonnational cemeteries on this road, and three or four exits farther on the expressway is a Meldana Boulevard with about five cemeteries on it and two that start with a B, one of which is called Beth-El. Does it sound familiar—cemetery or boulevard?" "The Beth part of it does, but let's try the two on this road first." Both are the wrong religion. They go to Meldana Boulevard, pass the first cemetery—"Starts with a B, all right, but the wrong religion, so why even bother with it?" The second cemetery's an annex to the national one before. The third cemetery's on the other side of the road than the one she remembers was on. "Let's check it anyway. Right religion, no B, but my memory could be wrong on that account and also which side of the road it was on. And they could have changed where the main gate was, making the back part of the cemetery the front part now, simply to make it easier entering or they wanted it off a much wider and even grander road like this one." They drive in, no Tetches here, though there is a Titch, the office worker says. He looks up the name in a book: Randolph and Evelyn, parents; Carolyn and baby Arthur, children. They drive past the next cemetery to Beth-El. "I'm almost positive this is it. Right side of the road, religion, the Beth—even the 'El' is coming back to me now, I don't know why—and the main gate looks familiar and it's not that farther away from the Suffolk sign than where I thought the cemetery would be. Let me see if I can find the plot on my own. I'd prefer that, just coming on it, and even just to see how good my once-great memory still is, rather than going to the office and given directions to road L, lane six, row double-A, plot 117, and so on." She directs her husband to where she thinks the plot is. They get out. No Tetch tombstones or benches there. "I think it's over there, actually," pointing to a place several rows away. "To the left of that tall pointy stone. . . . The breeze," as they're walking to the plot, "is just about what I remember it was like from the times I used to come here with my mother and Eva and a couple of times with my first husband. He didn't want to but knew how important it was to me for him to come. Also how shaky I'd be driving back alone. It must be the flatness of the place and the openness that creates it, this breeze all the time. Really, almost everything looks the same, but with a lot more graves around—all that over there was just empty grass. And that grove of trees along the boulevard there was a lot shorter." They reach where she thinks the plot is. No Tetch there. "Let's go to the office," her husband says. "Even if the gravesite's somewhere around here, we can look and look like this for hours and I don't think we'd ever find it." "I have to go to the ladies' room anyway," she says, "and I'm sure the kids do too." She doesn't recognize the office but doesn't think she was ever in it. The office worker looks up the name Tetch in a book and says it isn't there. "Titch, Tutch, any name like that?" Olivia says. "What I'm suggesting is that in the last few years or so—if this book was entirely reorganized, for instance, which I think it would have had to have been, at least worked on a little—there might have been a typographical mistake." The woman looks. "No name even near it. 'Tisch,' in fact, is as close as it gets." "Could you give me their first names please?" The woman later tells them that seven exits farther on the expressway, "almost to where the island forks, or perhaps a bit after it, is Cranberry Road. Just count off the expressway exits

279

from the Meldana entrance. I don't know the exact expressway exit number, but at seven get off, go right on the overpass and then straight for half a mile or a mile—I wish I could remember what route number it is—and you'll hit Cranberry. If you get lost, ask around for Cemetery Road. That's what it's more commonly called, though not officially on the maps, it has so many cemeteries on it. Eight, maybe nine. After that, the cemeteries are mostly isolated. An eighteenth-century cemetery here, an old slave cemetery there, one for Chinese fieldhands someplace from a long time ago, one even just for artists, and lots of modern ones of every religion and denomination, but all by themselves." "Tell me, is there a directory for all the cemeteries on the island of the people buried in them?" Olivia says. "No such thing." "For the county then or a directory only by religion?" "Nothing like that." "Cranberry Road doesn't sound familiar," Olivia says in the car. "But let's try it. If it is near where the island forks, then we'll be fairly close to Fire Island State Park, I think, or even the Hamptons. Or Montauk, which can't be an hour's drive from that exit. If you're going to see the Atlantic for the first time, that's the place to see it from. Giant cliffs, hidden inlets, all very dramatic and, if they haven't done their best to ruin it, quite beautiful. Heck, I could even be tempted to stay over. Off-season rates now, so it shouldn't set us back too much. Even if it does, what do we care?—we're sort of vacationing." "Stay over how?" her husband says. "Our luggage is in the hotel. We've paid dear for that suite." "So we'll buy a few toothbrushes and clothes. Things we've needed and can use after today. And if we don't, it'll be like camping in. But it's one night I'm talking about, and it's just lousy money." "Listen, Cranberry Road can't be the one your cemetery is on. It's got to be a good twenty to thirty miles past where you thought it was. It's impossible, it's unrealistic, it's lots of things." "OK, no Montauk overnight. But what more do we have to lose—half an hour at the most—by driving down Cranberry Road? If no cemetery looks right—we don't even have to get out of the car—I'll quit." They get on the expressway, count off the exits, follow the woman's directions, can't find Cranberry Road. They stop at a service station. "I never heard of it," the attendant says. "And you live in the area, or know for sure there's no Cranberry Road nearby?" her husband says. "I've been here almost all my life." "Cemetery Road's what it's also known as, we were told," Olivia says. "I never heard of that one either. There's a cemetery on Deepdell and another on Indian Fort and that's it for miles around here, except for some backyard family grounds and under-the-tree things and a pet cemetery that costs more, I heard, than for a person." "I give up then," she says to her husband. "This never would have happened, you realize, if my grandfather hadn't been such a perfectionist in seeing to the maintenance costs so long beforehand. We should appreciate what he did, I guess—saving us the time and expense—but what did he think, that my father and Uncle Jerry wouldn't have taken care of it? And his two other children, if he did all this before they died? From what I know, all of them were every bit as conscientious and meticulous about things as he, but maybe not as wily with the buck. Maybe that's it. It was too good a financial arrangement to pass up then. Or the maintenance contract also covered the plots he apparently sold off because his own was so large, giving them even added value, but I'm being unfair to the man. I'll find the cemetery though. Not today, of course. Information about it should be among my mother's papers, though I don't even know where most of those are now. Or my cousins might turn up something, or Eva, but I doubt it. She's always made sure I kept the important documents—that she'd lose them. But something has to be around somewhere—on the burial certificates for my parents, if there are such things. There have to be and officially recorded; you can't just put a body into the ground. Or the rabbis for their funerals, if they're still alive and I can remember their names or where we got them from. Dad's I'll never remember. Too far back. Mother's I got from a friend of mine—Liselotte—who married her, so she'll know or have it on her marriage license. Or Uncle Jerry's kids could give me the names of the minister and rabbi who did the services for their parents' funerals. Then I'll fly back alone—make a special trip for it and rent a car at the airport and drive straight out here and leave stones, enough for all of us since we've all in a way been out to see them, and on all their graves, aunts and uncles also. I think I owe them that. I don't owe them anything—I simply want to do it. I also want to see how the plot's been kept up after so long. And if it's deteriorating in any way or not kept up in the way I think it should be, to give the cemetery additional money to maintain it better." They drive to the ocean, park, take off their shoes, roll up their pants and hike up their skirts and wade in the water and sit in the sand. Then it gets too cold for them and they return to the car and drive back to the city. As they're approaching the Midtown Tunnel Olivia shouts "Mount Zion—it just came to me; but the next time."

One memory keeps coming back. They're on a bench. It's summer, Maine, they're eating fruit bars. He isn't. He's drinking coffee out of a styrofoam cup, the cap on with a triangular hole he tore out of it so he could drink without spilling. Black coffee. Some sugar in it. One pack, which he emptied into the cup, twirled the coffee with a wooden mixing stick—this isn't part of the memory but from other times when they were on the same bench, doing almost the same thing—which he then licked the coffee off of and put into his pocket to later put into the cook stove for kindling. "It's pure wood, why waste it?" he said that time or another. He didn't do it with their ice cream or fruit bar sticks because they were too messy. "Something new," he said earlier that summer in the store where they got the fruit bars and coffee. "I take sugar in my coffee sometimes. I never liked it that way before, but I do now in the afternoons. Maybe I don't eat enough during the day and my stomach's hungering for food, so the sugar. Anyway, the coffee wouldn't taste good now without it." But in the memory they're only on the bench. The bench runs the length of the red windowless left wall of the general store. The wall faces the road that leads to the private road they live on. Their house is about two miles from the store. A little more than two, her mother used to say. " 'Two point one miles on your odometer to the private road on your left,' we used to tell first-time visitors and UPS drivers, 'and then between .3 and .4 mile to our house on the private road. If you come to Alleluia Farm on the public road,' we also used to say, 'you've passed our road, so turn around and .6 mile from the farm's sheep shed you'll see our road on the right. If you don't know what a sheep shed looks like or missed it, then just about .3 mile from the ninety-degree arrow will be our road. If you end up at the public docking area, that's as far as you can go and it's 1.7 miles from the commemoration plaque of some 1812 War British ship shelling down there back to our road.' " They'd rented that house for a number of summers, at least five before she was born. They rented it the following summer also, so this memory doesn't keep coming back because it's one of the last good ones of him. There were lots of good ones, that summer and others. Bad memories too, plenty of them. But no memory of him comes back nearly as much as this one. Her mother didn't want to rent the house the summer after the following summer. And the next summer, when she felt she could go back to it without being reminded so much of him and affected incapacitatingly by those memories, it was already rented to the people who had it the previous summer. Those people continued renting it for several summers and then bought it, something her parents and then her mother had wanted to do for years and the owner always said they'd and then she would get first crack at. He didn't give it nor even tell her it was up for sale, but by then land prices there had boomed and she wouldn't have had the money. But the bench. They'd just come out of the store. The last thing he did inside was pour his coffee from a pot in the automatic coffeemaker-water boiler on a table to the right of the door. That's what he always did when he was with them and had coffee. The table, with a linoleum cloth, also had a serve-yourself hotdog apparatus, which they used a few times that summer but not that day, the cooked franks in the hot water compartment at the top of the apparatus and the New England-style rolls in the compartment at the bottom. Mustard, relish, ketchup, minced onions, teabags, sugar and sugar-substitute packs, plastic utensils, styrofoam cups in two sizes, were also on the table. Also a microwave oven for cooking hamburgers and barbecued-beef buns and grilled-cheese sandwiches kept in a refrigerated case to the right of the table. And mixing sticks, pepper and salt shakers and packs, probably paper plates, but she doesn't remember that. He always got the small-sized cup. Napkins and a little sign about the possible health hazards of microwave ovens when they're on. "I drink too much coffee as it is," he said a few times. Before he got the coffee he got them their fruit bars. When he was also buying groceries there, which her mother said they kept to a minimum because the store was so expensive, he got those first, then the fruit bars, then paid for it all including the coffee and had it bagged, or bagged it himself if he was in a rush and the kids were under control or he just felt like doing something energetic or helping out, then got his coffee. "There can be a system to almost everything," he once said or said in different ways a number of times. Sometimes Eva disappeared and he'd say "Eva, Eva" and glance around and then shout "Eva, Eva" and run to the door and open it, look outside, run through the aisles till he usually found her sitting on the floor with some items she took off the shelves in her lap or around her. "The coffee I like to get last," he once said, "because I like it very hot so I can drink it for about as long as it takes you to eat your fruit bars. If you noticed, we almost always finish at the same time. Also because," or something like this, "I don't like carrying it around the store while getting you fruit bars and while I also might have groceries and sometimes even Eva to carry. Ice-cold things like fruit bars I don't like to have start melting before we leave the store, but you also have to make some kind of compromise in almost everything too. So better they start melting a little than one of us gets burned from my coffee." The fruit bars never melted that much before they got out of the store because they didn't melt quickly, for one thing, and for another, it rarely got that hot inside or outside the store, and there was also never that long a checkout wait in the store, possibly because he always bagged his groceries whenever they got both groceries and fruit bars, but she doesn't remember that. He slid open the freezer case that had the bars, ice cream pops and bulk ice cream and things like that. This is how it just about always happened. She raised herself to look in. Eva tried to raise herself, then held her arms up and he usually picked her up for a few seconds so she could look in. Sometimes Olivia tried to pick Eva up to look in. When he slid open the freezer case he always first told them, if they had their hands on the lid which they usually did, to take them off so they wouldn't get pinched. He once said he got pinched by one of these lids when he was a boy and it hurt terribly and gave him a blood blister. He had to explain to her what a blood blister was. She probably screwed up her face. It sounded very ugly. She probably thought of the blister for days, imagined it several times bigger than it was. "How did you get rid of it?" she probably asked him. If he said he broke it with a needle or by squeezing it hard, she probably screwed up her face even tighter and said something like "That's disgusting, I don't want to hear any more about it," and for days probably thought of him trying to break the blister with a needle and by squeezing it and the blister breaking and blood all over his hand. If he told her he left the blister alone, which is what she should do if she ever got one, and that it went away by itself that way, which is probably what he did say if she asked him how'd he get rid of it, she probably said something like "That's what I'd do anyway but where does the blood go if you just leave the blister alone?" "What flavors are there again?" she usually said after he slid the lid open and she looked inside. "I always forget some of them and some of them look alike—red ones especially—and there are always new ones or they change." "Today they have strawberry, raspberry, banana, coconut, lime, no lemon today, cantaloupe, watermelon and something called mixed berries, which is a new one to me but I suppose we can both guess what it is." "What?" "Mixed. Everything. All the berries." "Any other flavors?" she usually said. "There are others from other brands, but they have artificial everything and

285

natural nothing besides too many of the numbered colors, so choose only from the ones I gave." "I like coconut a lot but I think I'll have strawberry today." "Me too," Eva always said. He got the bars out, handed them each one and told them not to start opening them till they got outside on the bench, paid for the bars and coffee, got the coffee, sugar, several napkins, mixing stick, and they went outside. He always held the door open for them and helped Eva down the step. If someone else was going in or coming out, he kept the door open, for up to a minute sometimes if that person was lame or carrying a baby or that far away but it was obvious he was coming to the store. "Don't hurry," he'd say if that person was hurrying to the door now because he was keeping it open for him. "I'd hate for you to trip or something worse as a result of my saving you this slight physical effort." Actually, he charged everything at the store, she now remembers, except for something like the local weekly if that was all he was buying, or if he was alone and only buying coffee for himself, for instance. She doesn't know when that would have been since when he went to the store he either went for groceries or for a few dollars' worth of gas when the tank was very low or to get them a treat after a trip to the town library or a swim at the lake or he made a special trip from home with them to get them fruit bars or ice cream pops and himself coffee, and usually those times to give her mother an hour or more alone to work or rest. They went outside, sat on the bench. This is where the part that keeps coming back begins. Not the part about buying fruit bars and coffee. Nor sitting on the bench and tearing the tops of the fruit bar wrappings with his teeth to open them. First she and Eva would usually try but they were never successful at biting a hole in the wrappings or just pulling the wrappings off. Nor pulling the wrappings off after he bit through the top parts nor handing the bars back to them. Nor going around to the front of the store to put the wrappings and empty sugar pack into the trash can there, but before going saying "Don't get off the bench while I'm gone." Saying it sternly. "Olivia, make sure Eva stays seated and you stay seated close beside her." For cars were parked near the bench, some of them pulled almost right up to it, a few times the front fender was over it, so he didn't want them standing up or even stretching their legs out when he wasn't there. Now that she thinks of it she doesn't know why he left them there like that. If Eva had wanted to get off the bench, she either wouldn't have cared that much or wouldn't have been able to stop her. Sometimes she hated Eva then and wouldn't have minded if she was in a situation where she could get hurt or even killed, she remembers thinking. She also didn't like to physically stop anyone from doing anything and also didn't feel she had the strength to. And Eva, though she wasn't even two then, when she really wanted to do something was very stubborn and strong. He was taking chances, not being careful. She doesn't remember anything bad happening from it, and he always ran around to the trash can and back, so it was only a matter of seconds, twenty, thirty. Why did he think he had to get rid of the trash so fast? Fast like that, yes, once he got up to go, but why get rid of the trash and so little of it so soon after they made it? Anyway: from the time he came back and sat. The coffee, when he ran to the trash can, she thinks he always left on the bench but a few feet from them, if nobody else was sitting that close. If somebody was, or rather two people on either side of them, then she doesn't know what he did with the coffee when he ran to the can. He couldn't have run with it. But this part. Eva was on his left—he'd sat down between them—she on his right. He once said, sitting down between them this place or another, "I like sitting between you two because then I can hold you both at the same time," and squeezed them into him. But starting with this. They're both licking their fruit bars. He's picked Eva up and set her on his lap. He's pulled Olivia so close to him that her ear's pressed against his rib cage. His right arm's around her. His chin's resting on Eva's head. His other arm's supporting Eva mostly from his elbow up while his hand brings the cup to his mouth to sip from. It's a fair day, they're all in shorts and short-sleeved shirts and probably sandals. They're looking straight out. No cars are parked in front of them so they have an open view of the road, house across it, trees in front and around the house, blue sky, little white clouds. Occasionally a car passes, stops at the main road if it's coming from the point, directional signals flashing either way, but it doesn't seem to distract them. Eva's leaned back against his chest. He kisses her head. Olivia's nestled into his body, top of her head wedged into his armpit, his hand stroking her head. He takes his chin off Eva a few times to kiss Olivia's head. But mostly his chin on Eva's head, Olivia nestled into him, the girls licking, he occasionally sipping and kissing, all three of them not saying anything and just looking straight out. That's all there is to it. It went on for minutes. She doesn't know why it stayed.

Frog Restarts

It all happens so quickly. She wakes up, complains of pains. He says "We all have them now and then and mostly early morning or late evening. Just take a couple of aspirins," which she does. The pains continue. Then trouble walking. First she almost trips, then she trips. She calls it an accident. Then she almost trips and trips again and the pains get worse and in more places. He tells her it's the body getting used to its age. "Growing pains when you're a kid? Growing-old pains when you're approaching middle age. I had them; I'm sure that's what they were. You remember my back and shoulder pains and the one that made my right arm, every three months or so, and all the way down to the fingertips, feel as if it were being ripped off. And those lasted two to three weeks sometimes and this went on for years. I didn't trip or anything like that, or not that I can remember, but I think the pain was equal to even being a little worse than yours. Only thing that helped then was lots of aspirins spaced out during the day. And a visit to the osteopath when the pain really got bad. They know the body like no one else and their prices are fair. I could probably do a little of that manipulation myself," and he gives her a massage in bed. She says it makes her body feel much better. Then, because he's still behind her and her rear end's raised and she's nude, he starts playing with her down there and they make love. In the morning she says she hasn't felt so good in weeks. "Maybe the combination of those two in the order we did them is exactly what I needed." "I will be glad to cooperate," he says. "Fully, frequently, probably not repeatedly, but to the best of my agility or something—in the future, I'm saying—if all that doesn't sound too juvenile and silly."

A few weeks later he's in the car pulling up to the house. She's coming down the front steps, has to hold on to the railing, is dragging her leg. Pain on her face, her free hand's shaking and she grabs the railing with it or else it seems she'll fall. It hits him. How could I have been so dismissive? What a jerk, what a jerk. He yells "Stay there," runs to her, walks her back to the house, calls their doctor. On the day of the appointment she says "I'm sure it's something simple." "I'm sure too," he says, "but let's find out." Their oldest daughter says "What's wrong, Mommy?" She says she's going for a regular checkup, just as they do with Dr. Miriam once a year.

The doctor thinks it might be nothing worse than a pinched nerve as her osteopath says, and tells her to take two very strong aspirins three times a day for two weeks and then see if her condition improves. Also to stop seeing the osteopath. "It might be the workout he gives you plus Howard's massages that are exacerbating a muscle injury or making some other relatively minor ailment worse." She does what he says. The pains continue. She trips periodically. Sometimes when she sits or lies down she doesn't think she can get up by herself. Twice Howard has to help her downstairs and walk her to the car. The doctor thinks she should see a neurologist. The neurologist examines her and suspects a serious neurological disease. He puts her through several tests: brain scan, spinal tap, others. She's nervous about them. Howard tells her "Listen, better we go on as usual and not worry so much before we hear the results. It might be nothing. The old pinched nerve, even, that Dr. Aman once begrudingly said it could be, since all doctors hate any diagnosis or suggested cure that comes from an osteopath. The neurologist is more likely just ruling out possibilities rather than looking for them. Probably the worse that'll happen is you'll have to take prescription painkillers or muscle relaxants for a while and you might feel funny from them and your face puff up a little."

The neurologist calls. It's what he thought. "At her age," he tells them in his office, "drugs and treatments should be able to arrest it. There are variations of the disease and hers isn't the most serious." She takes the drugs, goes through the treatments. She gets weaker, starts using a cane to walk, braces on her right arm and leg, then has to walk with a metal walker or Howard's help, collapses several times, has trouble keeping food down, loses sight in one eye, several other things go wrong or change, is put on an experimental drug, treatments discontinued, she can't get out of bed and sometimes not even out of a chair by herself, becomes blind, partially paralyzed, is hospitalized, released, gets worse, hospitalized, dies.

He thinks of how they first met. It's a funny story. He was going to a wedding reception in an apartment building. The bride and he had once been lovers. He thought it odd being invited to the wedding, but she explained it in a note with the invitation. Amy, this woman, was separated from her first husband when Howard started seeing her. He was bartending then and she and a man friend, just back from a week on St. Thomas, came in for banana daiquiris. He talked with them, when the man was in the men's room he asked her for her phone number. One day her husband came by her apartment for something when Howard was there. His complete set of Conrad, which was still in her bookcase. It was late morning, Amy was making them breakfast. There was a quarrel. She doesn't remember what it was over or if she was involved in it. She thinks it started because her husband, who'd come without telling her and tried to get in with his old apartment keys, then complained that she'd changed the locks. So she had to have been involved in it. But Howard stood up to him and even stuck his finger into her husband's chest and made him back off. She thinks her husband said "How do you know I'm not carrying a gun?" which he did sometimes, and that Howard said "What the hell do I care? If you did remember to put bullets in, and the right ones, you'll probably shoot your bloody balls off pulling the gun out." Anyway, the incident seemed to do something to her and her husband, because from then on she was never afraid of speaking up to him or thought him intimidating in any way and he never again treated her abusively or not for long, and in fact a few weeks later he very calmly consented to the divorce she'd been asking for for a year. She thinks she might have even told him she was thinking of marrying Howard, which was never true and could never have been true, but she used it as part of her argument. She continued with Howard for about a month after that, realized they'd never work out, then met Hank, fell in love as hard as she ever had, now they were getting married, so Howard was invited, to the rather rudimentary small church wedding if he wanted to go but more to the reception after, since if it hadn't been for him she might still be fighting that psycho sonofabitch ex-husband of hers for a divorce and by now might even have been killed by him.

So he went into the building, made a left at the end of foyer when the doorman must have told him to go right, a woman was waiting at the elevator. Pretty, he thought. The door opened, they got in, he waited for her to press a floor button, she didn't, he pressed seven and kept his finger by the button plate and asked what floor she was going to, she said "I'll attend to it when the time comes, thank you," he said "Please, no need to worry. I'm going to a wedding reception on the seventh floor—the doorman let me through—so I only asked because I was closer to the buttons." "Thank you for your explanation," and she looked at the door. Hair, face, voice, expression, clothes, words she used, self-possession, that she didn't smile fakely at him to conceal what she really might feel. He tried not to look at her too much; didn't want to disconcert or irritate her or make her more nervous if that's what it was. But he could hardly stop looking at her. She was beautiful, in ways his dream woman: high cheekbones, long light soft hair, bright eyes, large breasts, slim waist, what seemed like solid legs, big full forehead, other things, her height, books in her bag, obvious intelligence, shape of her lips, no trace of makeup, white teeth. At seven he said "Good day," she nodded, he got off, she immediately pressed her floor or the "close" button, door closed, and he saw that the apartments here were A to D with the service steps directly across the elevator but no door or passageway leading to anything further and he was going to G. "Oh Christ," he said, when the elevator opened a couple of floors, or maybe one or two more than that, above him. Must be she. He quickly thought of something. "Excuse me, miss, it's me. Or mrs. or ms., but it's I, the fellow who got off the elevator on the seventh floor?" "Yes?" "Well, the wedding reception isn't here. No loud partying, voices, glasses tinkling, music the bride said they were going to have nonstop. Maybe I've the wrong floor or apartment number or even the wrong building or street number. The tenant who's giving the party is Rukovsky." "Rergovsky? If it's that, which I don't see how it can't be, since they're on the seventh floor, then you'll want to go downstairs and through the lobby to the east wing of the building. 7G." "There's a second elevator then?" he said, walking upstairs. "Two wings, two elevators, yes." "Is there another wing other than those two? Just so I don't end up in it." He was on the eighth floor, started for the ninth. "Only two." "So I must have gone left instead of right downstairs. Funny, for the doorman said the wedding reception, when I told him I was going to one, though I never got around to giving the tenant's name, was to the left, seventh floor. That I' d know which apartment it was by the noise. I doubt there'd be two afternoon wedding receptions going on in this building today." "Sunday, June, a fairly large building in a very active city—who can say? But somewhat improbable there'd be two receptions like that given on the same day by people with names as close to the ones we mentioned, and both on the same floor even if in different wings. Besides, there is no Rukovsky on the seventh floor in this wing. You must have misunderstood Nicolo's—the doorman's—directions. And I know the Rerkovskys. Not well, but at tenant meetings—they're big in that—and two of those meetings in their apartment. Darlene and Sid. They must be hosting the party for your relative or friend." "Friend," he said, reaching the tenth floor where she was. "Listen, excuse me, and again don't be alarmed, and I didn't mean to climb up, but I just thought of something. You probably won't go for it, but I'd love to take someone to this reception. And by now you must know"—she's already waving her hand in front of her—". . . no, please, just hear me out, that there really is a reception and you know the Rerkovskys, even if not well. And maybe even the bride for all I know." "Believe me I don't." "So—wait a minute," for she'd turned to the door, "abrupt as this must seem—and never never turn your back on a stranger when you're in a situation like this, woman alone, in front of her door—anyone alone, not that I should be considered one in that respect—dangerous, at all threatening, I mean"—she turned back to him, angry, hand with her keys behind her—"and even loony sounding as my suggestion could also be thought as, though it isn't so much and I'm not—would you come to it with me? Which you probably knew I was going to say. That hand-waving before. Or just meet me there?" "What are you talking about. Absolutely not." "Why? I've been invited and I'm inviting you. If it's—" "It is, whatever you're about to say. Because I don't know you and don't want to know you and definitely don't want to go to a reception of any kind today. It'd seem peculiar too. The Rerkovskys would ask and I'd have to say I just met you in the elevator and then spoke to you for a minute on my floor, and why am I speaking to you hypothetically about this or even speaking to you about anything on my floor? You could be something you're not saying you are. This could all be a pretense. Look, be smart and take the elevator and go to your party," and she unlocked the door while staring at him, went in, shut and locked it and threw the bolt hard. They talked through the door for about fifteen minutes. To get her to come to the door he rang the bell several times and said between ringings "Please, don't call the doorman. I'm nothing like what you might think I am. Truth is I'm incorrigibly harmless, never been in any adult trouble. I only want to speak to you through the door for a few

294

seconds to a minute but no more to explain some things and then I'll go." The first time she came to the door she said something like "Get away from here now or I'll not only call the doorman and the super but the police," and then went away from the door. He could hear her footsteps on the wood floor. The second time she came she said "I'm not playing around with you, sir. If you continue to ring and don't get off this floor, I will call the police. I've the phone in my hand now. Dot dot dot with the numbers on the buttons and you're done. If you run away from here I'll have them look for you at the Rerkovskys. If you're also not there, then they'll have my description of you. And if it's true what you said about the bride being your friend, they'll speak to her, find out who you are and go to your home. If there is no bride or wedding and you had no plans to go to the Rerkovskys, then I'll ask them to knock on every door in this building to ask if anyone was expecting you. And if nothing comes of that, then for them to drive around the neighborhood looking for you, and then keep watch over this building in case you plan to return."

He forgets exactly what he said to make her continue listening and not call the police, if she was really going to. Days later she said she didn't have the phone in her hand then but was thinking of going to the living room to call. He knows he said he wanted to give her a quick rundown of who he was and what he did and where he lived and so on, just so she'd have some idea of him and know or at least think there was a greater chance of it that he was rational and respectable and no criminal or kook. That way maybe she'd look differently on him. And maybe, though without opening her door if that was the way she wanted it, and preposterous as this outcome probably was, give him her name and phone number so he could call her some later time. And "later time" not meaning tonight but in a few days to a week or as far off as she wanted, but he would hope relatively soon. Or if she preferred to call him, he could give her his name and phone number. Certainly his name. He gave it. Waited for her to give hers. She didn't. He could even give her the names and phone numbers of people he knew whom she might know and she could call them about him. Would she prefer that? If she did, he'd wait till she got paper and pen or he could even write the names and numbers out for her or slip a paper and pen under the door so she could write them down. She didn't answer. Really, he said: intelligent, decent people. Educators, writers, a translator, a magazine editor; even a publisher of a small trade house here in New York. He listened. She didn't ask who they were or if that was what he did: write, possibly teach. He was going too far, wasn't he? he said. But, quite truthfully, though he also knew he wasn't telling her anything she didn't already know, he was attracted to her and didn't want this to be a lost opportunity where he'd never see her again. Which was why, of course, he was making such a terrible fool of himself and putting her through all this and risking being grabbed by the super or the police. And don't worry, he said. None of her neighbors had opened their doors to look, nor had he heard any of them come to their doors or open their peepholes. They must all be out. She didn't say anything. Or just very circumspect, or apathetic, inattentive, uninquisitive, reclusive to a fault or for any number of reasons didn't want to involve themselves in possible trouble. Tenants were tenants whatever New York City building you were in. Would she agree with any of that? Then what did she think about anything he'd said so far? Still no response. He asked if she was still there. Yes, she said, from right behind the door. And if she had called the super or the police? No. Then could he also tell her, and then he'd go, how he usually felt at parties when he went alone and essentially didn't know anyone there: uncomfortable, a party imposter, which was another reason he'd asked her to come with him. That had nothing to do with her, she said. He could go, he didn't have to go, all that was his business solely. He knew, he knew, he said, but was just saying, maybe for lack of anything else to say. No, that wasn't so. He also told her what the bride was to him. That they had once been very good friends, mates for a while, and he wasn't saying this to do anything but state a fact, though why he felt he had to state that fact was perhaps another matter and one he should look into. . . . But the bride and he didn't work out, and also why she'd invited him. It was a strange story. He started laughing. He didn't know if he could tell it through a door or keep it to thirty seconds, for that was how long she said she'd give him before she probably would call the super. He told it in a minute. One minute-ten to be exact, he said, looking at his watch before and after. She thought the story bizarre and funny. The part about the gun especially. Did he think her husband was serious? Just a big windbag, he said, or seemed. If she were he she wouldn't go to the reception. He really shouldn't have been invited, for it'll probably make the groom uncomfortable seeing him there. He believed another ex-lover of hers would be there too, he said; the one who'd come in to the bar with her for the daiquiris. Even worse, she said. Something was slightly off about this woman. But he was right not to have gone to the wedding ceremony, though she didn't know if he hadn't gone for what she'd consider the right reason. But now to think about taking someone to the reception whom he'd just met in an elevator in the same building the reception was? It'd seem his motives were questionable now and that he wanted to take her to make it an even better story to tell or to get back at the bride some way. No, positively not, he said. He wanted to take her for the reasons he gave before, which he was sure she didn't want to hear again: his unease at going alone, but much more so because he was attracted to her, that lost opportunity he mentioned, and thought if she came with him it'd be a pleasant enough place to get to know her a little and perhaps other way around for her too. Festive atmosphere, lots of convivial people, familiar building, two elevator rides and a short lobby walk to her own apartment, if it were cold out he'd say she wouldn't even have to put on a sweater, etcetera. But if she wanted he could skip the reception and they could go out for coffee or any kind of snack, all on him, not that he didn't think she could pay for it. But better yet why didn't she just come to the reception for half an hour? She didn't say anything. Even less time than that if she wanted. That way he could fulfill his obligation to go to the reception, since he had told the bride he'd be there and that seemed to mean something to her. And he supposed they could get coffee there as well as at any coffee shop and certainly far better snacks, maybe a glass of champagne if she wanted, and they could talk for part or most of that time, and that would be that unless she wanted to stay longer. If she didn't, then he could stay and she could go home, or they could take a long or short walk after that half an hour to less, and then she could go home and he'd return to the party or just go home himself. Probably that. But what does she say? She didn't know, she said. He was a most convincing arguer or fabricator. Not so, he said. He was usually inarticulate, garble-mouthed, preternaturally slow to think of the right things to say to win any argument or just thought of them too late. There was an expression for that in Yiddish, another in French, perhaps most languages—what you thought after the door had been slammed on you and you walked downstairs. Steps-in-mouth. Tongue-unfurled-only-on-the-dark-stairs. For arguing, convincing, more than simple conversing, even explaining, just weren't for him, except now and then, like maybe now. And as for lying? She'd said fabricating and she was sorry she'd said it, she said. No no, he said. He didn't, why would he? since in addition to other reasons, probably the most flagrant was that he was such a poor speaker he'd be seen through too easily. Though with the door shut it was true he might be more adept at it, since the person being lied to wouldn't see his giveaway face. No, what he did do well was run on unintelligibly about relatively nothing and make it seem no more than that. But really, what does she say? She still didn't know, she said. He swore there'd be no problems. Not on his knees, for he had his only good dress pants on and he was going to a party— No, no more bad jokes, for the time being. And ten minutes at the most?

She invited him in for coffee. Maybe that'd be the best idea, she'd said, though she wasn't sure why. They talked, drank tea and ate toast. Her expression when she'd opened the door was reserved, observing. He'd said then honestly, he had no gun and then that

that was a stupid remark. After awhile she said there didn't seem to be anything menacing about him but she still felt he'd acted very strangely, pursuing her when everything she'd said and did was against it and he could have been locked up. He said maybe once, twice in his life had he acted that way but never so inexorably. She said he was either lying to her, again or for the first time, or had forgot. Their respective families, educations, what each did professionally, where he lived and they'd been brought up, how'd she got the apartment, something about a print on her wall above the piano: naked woman riding a big furious bull, and not about what each thought it meant. Was that, he thinks he said, what playing the piano was to her? She laughed—not then, and he forgets what it was over or even if it was something he'd said that did it. Soon after she said maybe going to the party for half an hour—he'd asked again when she was still smiling—would be all right. Even if she wouldn't know anyone there but the Rerkovskys, she liked champagne almost more than anything and at wedding receptions you usually got the best. She was kidding of course, and maybe it wasn't such a good idea—it'd seem she'd come only for the party. Those questions she spoke about before would probably be asked: how'd they know each other, and so on. So they'd lie, he said. Oh, what should she do?—give her five minutes to dress. She shut the bedroom door. He sat on the couch not believing his luck and hoping she wouldn't change her mind. They went. She said once that she was having a good time, smiled warmly at him several times, spoke at length with Sid Rerkovsky about a neighborhood park problem and that she thought she could be of some help, told Howard after about an hour that she was leaving and he needn't walk her to her door. He stayed another hour, went home, couldn't stop thinking of her, wanted to call her, told himself not to for a couple of days, drank himself to sleep while reading several days of papers. They saw each other a few afternoons later. For almost every other night for months. Had an argument: she said he'd been repeatedly rude and hostile to her mother and to a lesser extent to other people and that was something she couldn't take in the man she was seeing. He said her mother had been hostile to him from day one, which would make him rude to her he supposed but didn't know, and as for the other people, he didn't know what the fuck she was talking about. They broke up, got back together a month later: he'd phoned, asked if he'd left a very important book to him at her apartment, knew she'd see through the pretext but thought he had to use something like it than saying straight off how much he missed her, dreamt of her, could hardly work because of her, that he'd been writing one a night these idiotic gushy poems about her, did she think they could meet to talk over some of their differences and so on? She said she didn't remember seeing the book but would look, but before she hung up, was that really why he'd called? He said it was a pretext, knew she'd see through it and was glad she had, and how much he missed her. . . . They met, talked, started seeing each other again, he moved in with her, they had dinner at the Rerkovskys a number of times and had them over once, got married, the Rerkovskys wanted to give the reception in their apartment but she wanted to have a small wedding in her apartment and didn't want the Rerkovskys to be at the even smaller ceremony there. Had their first child less than a year later, moved to where a good job was for him, another child, she resumed teaching but evenings, lots else, then what happened to her happened.

Now he's back with the woman whose wedding reception it was. Gail. She's divorced, has a child. He got a Christmas card from her nine years after her wedding reception and wrote back saying what had happened to him since then. "You might remember the woman I came with, but I doubt you'd remember much on such an exciting day. Much that wasn't connected to you, I mean." She'd sent him a Christmas card the two Christmases after she got married. He sent her a card back for the first one but doesn't think he got around to answering the second. Must have been just after Olivia was born, so too busy to, or just didn't see the point. Then he stopped hearing from her. From the Rerkovskys he'd learned she moved to Rome with her husband, and soon after that he and Denise left New York and lost touch with the Rerkovskys. It was the Rerkovskys, she said, who told her what school he got a job at years ago, which is where she sent the card, hoping he was still there or it'd be forwarded. She called him a few months later saying she'd be attending a conference in his city and would he care to come by her hotel for a drink. Did. They met downstairs, drank in the bar. He called the sitter to see if she'd stay another two hours, they had a quick dinner in the hotel cafe, went to her room for beers, made love. They corresponded and called after that, visited each other, she wondered why she hadn't found him this attractive back then. "I think I would have asked you to marry if I had. Maybe fatherhood and having been married and holding a responsible job and security and all you went through with your wife's illness have toned you down a ways. You were often a lot too argumentative and unsociable and crazy to me then. Even your sex was a bit too flaky, picking me up with you stuck in me and pinning me against the wall and sometimes banging me against it till you came. That hurt. Who cared if you got lost in it—I used to get bruises on my ass and back. It used to piss me off, if you remember, since you continued trying to do it even after I told you how I felt." "I'd probably still be doing it if I wasn't ten years older and no doubt somewhat weaker. Last time I tried it with Denise was a couple of years ago—she was a little heftier than you, and she never complained when I did it—and I could barely pick her up. I think I even fell. Anyway, something for you to thank the aging process for." "Even your foreplay action has changed. You used to rub my cunt too softly and kiss it too hard and I could never get you to switch those two." "That was your and Denise's doing. I figured that after the two of you had said it, and also some vague remembrances of other women saying something like it in the past, I had to be doing something wrong. Didn't make me feel that good either, realizing my technique there had been off some thirty years, even if some women might not have been aware it was, but I'm probably wrong there too."

He told her he found her much more attractive now too. He'd always found her attractive, face and body, with legs and a rear end that gave him a hard-on almost every time he looked at them, but he could never love her. As he did Denise. And other women before Denise. Certain things about her. She annoyed him at times, though he didn't say so. Things she did and said. She was educated but not in areas he found interesting. She read stupid books, wanted to see what he knew would be banal movies and plays. She too frequently watched moronic TV. She was too showy in appearance. She barely tolerated the music he liked and hated it when he had it on in the car. "It's depressing, funereal, old." Her voice was often fake. There was something unnatural about her in lots of ways. Too much time in front of the mirror, inspecting herself, clothes, trying out faces, poses. Sometimes he caught her. And that it didn't embarrass her when he did. Hair, which she seemed to change the style of every other month, and nose, which she was seriously thinking of getting bobbed and pugged. He'd never touch it, he told her, if she did get it fixed. But he was lonely for close adult company and inherently horny it seemed and depressed when he did it to himself. There'd been two women for short periods before her and both he showed minimal interest in and they dropped him abruptly. Their sex was good. She got him started even when he thought he wouldn't feel like it, and let him do it whichever way and whenever he wanted to, even when she was sleeping, except for picking her up. She was smart and well respected in her field, perceptive about other people, had a few bright congenial friends. She was a good mother and daughter and warm and attentive to his girls. And generous with money—and made lots of it and stood to inherit a bundle, which didn't influence him and he'd in fact always got along better with much poorer women. Thought of interesting things to do with the girls and them, got him away from his work, was lively, sometimes funny, energetic. Great cook, kept a clean house, did his taxes better than he, went out of her way to aid disabled people across the street, and other things. So one day he says "Hey listen, what're we fooling around for—why don't we get married?" She says "Only if you're absolutely sure you want to. Occasionally I don't feel you really love me." "I do. I want to marry you. Both very much. Only, promise not to get a nose job. We'll write it into our marriage contract. I don't know what I can agree to to meet it. Certainly nothing about money, since whatever I save has to go to my girls first, and it'll be chicken feed compared to what you'll be able to put away. That I'll keep my sperm count high in case you want another child." "I won't. And I can't promise. I've an awful nose. It's long, droops, and has bumps. Some women look sweet with a drop dripping out of a nostril or hanging off it, but I look gargoylish. What I think of myself is important, so I probably will go through with it in addition to surgery with the chin and around the eyes if I think I need it later on." "At least, before you let them break your nose and hack away at the cartilage, give me a day to try to talk you out of it." He wonders if he'll ever end up loving her, be glad he's married to her, be able to continue to make love with her, can keep up the pretense for years? He thinks with the sex he can, since he's able to separate it when he wants to, but doubts he can with the others. So what then? They'll stay married for a number of years, with luck till around the time his girls might not need her as much or need him, to restrain him sometimes and for his self-control and composure, to have a companion anymore, and also when he might be too indifferent or lost something somehow to care about having a woman around for just company and sex.

They get married. No honeymoon. He doesn't want to leave his girls so soon after the marriage. Desertion. Gail and her daughter move into his little semi-detached house, she gets a high-paying job in his city, in a few months has the roof reshingled, basement finished, most of the furniture replaced, kitchen recabineted, tiny backyard and front and side grass areas sodded and planted with bulbs and fruit trees, and knows more places to buy things and go to and has made more friends than he and Denise had in years. He tells her he loves her whenever he feels she needs to hear it, but he never means it. Wishes he did though. That he could think about her wistfully during the day, late afternoons long for her to come home, want to jump her before they get into bed, cuddle with her through sleep, dream of making love to her, kiss her lips when he gets out of bed early morning to exercise and run. He still thinks about Denise a lot, as much as he did before he met Gail. Doing day-to-day things. Typing, driving, fluffing a pillow. But also, if he can't get an erection with Gail and wants to, he'll think about making love with Denise, especially with him on his knees behind her and one time in particular when the lights were on or it was daylight and she had her rear raised and vulva opened, and usually gets one. Also, if he's about to come with Gail and she's close to it or he feels if she does he'll sleep better because she will or else he wants her to come before he does so he can then, once she's done, enter her from behind, he'll think of Denise just after she died or when he opened the coffin the night before the funeral to have a last private look at her and kissed her forehead and wedding band or when she was bedridden and unable to move even a finger or toe. Then his penis will shrink, ejaculation be stalled, and he'll press their pelvises together and go through the motions and rub her where she likes if he can get his hand there and she'll usually come and then he'll urge or turn her over on her hands and knees if she isn't on them and maybe think of making love with Denise or just Denise nude or just of her vulva if he has to to get an erection and do it in the position, if she moves back and forth at the right time, he likes best.

He also continues to read letters Denise sent him before they were married, look at her photos. Two especially. Nude Polaroids of her seven to eight months pregnant with Olivia. Maine, secluded rented cabin, tips of trees and ideal summer sky behind her, standing on the top porch step, he must have been sitting or lying on the porch when he took them, looking down at him skeptically and saying to herself, she later told him when he asked, "Why am I doing this for you and what if someone gets ahold of it? I'm so bloated and deformed, it'll come out pornographic." He promised to only take one but then lied and said his finger was over the slot when the photo came out and took a second with her consent before the first was developed. She wanted to destroy both but he swore he'd never let anyone see them or leave them in a place where they could be found accidentally. They were the only nude shots he had of her. Huge belly, enormous breasts, it seemed twice as much pubic and armpit hair but that was probably just the shadows, ankles swollen, thighs wider, face chubbier, big dark aureoles, and so on. Same position and look in both, so he doesn't know which one he had to lie to get. He cut the borders off them and then some of the porch and sky till they fit into one of the plastic sleeves of his wallet's photo section under another photo. Doesn't remember what photo they were under then— maybe the same one as now, which is of his mother, standing between his uncle and aunt, their arms interlocked, posing merrily at Denise's and his wedding reception. Meantime he's gone through three or four almost identical wallets. He wishes he'd taken nude photos of her when she wasn't pregnant. Soon after he met her, for instance, when he said if *Playboy* had a pictorial essay planned on nude assistant profs, she'd be a great choice (she wasn't flattered, said his remark was dumb and young), or about six months after she had Eva, when she'd slimmed down to her lowest adult weight, done lots of muscle-toning exercises and swimming and jumping rope. Even her buttocks were getting hard. Taken pornographic photos, even. Front, back, lying down, legs spread apart, fingering herself, shots of them making love taken with the aid of a timer, from behind with her rear raised, vulva opened, head turned around to him. He once asked her to pose nude when she wasn't pregnant—a simple shot, standing and smiling— when she was stepping out of the shower and he held up the unopened Polaroid camera. But she said the only reason she let him keep the nude ones he had of her was because they didn't resemble her except for the skeptical expression somewhat when she's doing something she doesn't really want to but oh what the fuck, and her hair when it had been dried by the sun after a shampoo, brushed hard and pinned up.

Frog

If Gail knew about the photos and letters and little tricks he used to get or lose an erection and how he felt about her, she never let on. Years. Then she tells him their marriage is a sham and she wants a separation. Springs it on him. First she asks him to sit. He'd come back from work, hung up his jacket, put his briefcase and books on the living room chair he always puts them on, the three girls were playing somewhere, he went over to kiss her, she put her hands up to back him off, asked him to sit, get a drink if he wanted—a hard one preferably, even if that seemed, she said, like something someone might say in a bad movie or lousy book, but it might be useful to have, though she hoped not to throw at her. "What do you mean? What is it? You're making me nervous. Are you ill? Can't be if you're talking about throwing drinks at someone." That's when she says their marriage is a sham, she's known it for a year, she doesn't believe a kind or polite word he says to her except when it's about what she cooks or when she in any way makes life easier for him, and she's been faking for months, as she suspects he has, her sex and most of her orgasms with him, what there were of them. "I'm surprised about the sex part," he says. "Your orgasms particularly seemed every bit authentic. I for sure have been involved in it almost every second. As for the other stuff, I'm surprised but not as much, since I'm not very convincing when I say just about anything I want very much to get across and especially affectionate and complimentary things, and I also have a way of saying things that come out sounding opposite of what they mean." "Horsecrap. Anyway, what I'm getting to is we should separate. For half a year, let's say, so the girls will begin getting used to it while still holding some hope we'll get together again, which I guarantee you there's no hope of since my ultimate aim is to get an unacrimonious divorce." "Absolutely not. I mean, sure, unacrimoniously, if it ever came to that, which I don't want it to, for one reason because it'll hurt the kids too much—my two and Susan. And why the hell a divorce? I love you and feel very strongly we can work out whatever it is you think's fouling up things and also that I can convince you, despite

306

my speaking problems, that you're dead wrong about what you think I feel and don't feel about you. First off, let's talk about what brought all this up. You think, for instance, I've had a lover or two? One-shot flings even?" "No, though maybe you have. When you bring it up like that, it's usually true. Not that I'd care, now, unless she was carrying something communicable. Because I now have one, you know. But why would you know? You mainly think of yourself and would probably be glad he was taking some of the sexual pressure off you. He's clean though. If you'll permit me: bags first till I had him medically checked out. I'm smart enough not to get temporary or terminal anything because I suddenly got the hots for someone. An untemperamental mature man whom I've little emotional feeling for but I adore sleeping with and being with sometimes too. He can be a gas. Are you upset?" "Sure, yes, very, what do you think? Screw it. You want to take lovers and don't believe we can work things out—" "Never, even if I wanted to." "Then better you do leave. Though I'm sorry about Susan. In my own way I love her, so I'll miss her. I can continue—we all can—to see her, can't we?" "Certainly your girls. And you too, if she wants. She probably will, for a while, when we move to a new neighborhood and her social life sags, but then she'll consider having to see you a stiff pain in the ass. She's practical and unsentimental and you pretend to be the reverse. Can you ever stop being a fake?"

He says some words to her, she to him, then: "Fuck you," "Eat shit," "Same here," "Stick it up your skinny hole," "Oh, very fine words," he says, "You miserable shriveled-up prig should talk?," he pushes her, she takes a swing at him and he twists her arm till it hurts, all three girls have come downstairs and been watching, she leaves the next week, the two never saying a word to each other and trying to be in different rooms till then, his girls see Susan regularly but she won't see him no matter how many times he apologizes on the phone for having hurt her mother. They divorce, she moves in with her lover, meets someone on a business trip and settles in the city he works in. His daughters thought of Susan as their sister, they tell Howard. "We'll take a trip West this summer," he says, "drive through where she lives and you can spend a day or two with her. More if she has time and you want. I'll stay in the motel and read and do some work." "Marrying someone with a child can be a disaster for us," Olivia says. "Next time fall for someone without one. Then if you want to have another, do it with her so the baby will have to stay or later on be shared." "I'm too old for another child and I don't want another wife. I've never loved any woman since your mother and I seriously doubt I could. I didn't even tell Gail that. That was mean of me. From now on I only want to be with you kids till you're all grown up. After that you can visit or stay but it'll be best if things go bad for you with someone else that you try to hack it out on your own. Do you understand?" "No." " 'Hack.' It's too dated a word. Work it out with him, or if you're without him, then by yourself, in other words. Clearer?" "It's not that. Just most times you seem a lot healthier and not so strange when you're with someone. That last thing with Gail we won't count. Eva and I are going to try and find a nice lady for you."

Years. He doesn't go out with any women. Wrong. One he took to a movie, shook hands good-bye at her door and didn't call again. She did and he said he was sorry. Another for dinner at her apartment. He thought maybe he should try something, just to take the big plunge again and she seemed responsive, and he made a move and she said she had nothing like that in mind when she invited him over, and showed him the door. It's not that he's lost his sex drive, he thinks. Sex drive; funny term. Or not that much, but how can he tell? He does it to himself much less often than he did after Denise died and before he met Gail; that should be an indicator. Even those are mostly motivated by health reasons to avoid something with the prostate. Doctor's suggestion. But then he still stares after women's behinds and legs as much, fantasizes having sex with women he sees and meets, gets plenty of spontaneous erections and they seem to be as hard most of the times and stay up as long. He's sure it's mainly because his kids are older now and he's afraid of getting caught by them or leaving some sign of it around. When he does do it it's usually afternoon when they're in school though he'd prefer it late at night when he's in bed. It's also not as exciting anymore, no matter what drugstore and picture aids he might use, which could be another indicator. And though it doesn't take any longer than it used to he often thinks while doing it that he should be doing the whole thing with someone, not just this by himself, and that takes away something.

A couple of friends want to hook him up with this woman or that but he never wants to. He usually says he likes the way things are, not so hot as they might be at times, and also doesn't want to hurt his daughters again, and other excuses: couldn't for the life of himself call up a woman for a blind date, wouldn't want a woman calling up him for one, would never go to a dinner arranged just so the host could make a match. Uncomfortable. A large party partly for that or just to go to has been OK but so far all the available women he's met at them didn't interest him. Only other way would be to meet a woman accidentally. In an elevator even. Times he has and was interested he didn't know what to say quick enough before they got away, and then wouldn't call them, when he knew who they were or how to reach them, because he didn't feel he knew them well enough to call to arrange something. Then Olivia talks about her Russian teacher in high school. "She's divorced, no children, very intellectual, unstrange and nice. She carries these enormous nontextbooks with her everywhere and you can always see her reading them when she's not teaching, and scribbling down notes about what's inside them I suppose, even when she walks to the parking lot. And she's pretty as anything, with this big athletic body, and she used to be a beauty contest winner too." "I never liked the type. Not the athletics. That can be all right if it's not where she gets carried away. Goes pro or runs three times as much as she needs to keep her weight down or build up her lungs. Or is afraid, missed one run, 'Oh my goodness, I'll decay in a day' or 'I'll become a balloon.' But the kind of mind, I mean, that would enter such a contest, much less to win. 'Tuck in your tum, Hon, and grin for the pubic'—excuse me, but that sort of thing." "She knows, but that was around ten years ago and she pooh-poohs it too." "Ten? Then she's much too young for me. It wasn't a thirty-and-over contest? No? Then the age gap could never be jumped." "I heard she goes for older guys and you're still relatively good-looking, youthfullike and crazy-excessive sometimes and so on." "For your sake then or just to prove something, I'll have a look at her next time I visit the school. More. I'll do what I've done since you started kindergarten and that's to check out your teacher while checking up on how you're doing from her point of view."

Olivia points her out at the next parent-teacher meeting. Already admired her at the last one without knowing who she was. Attractive, intelligent face, nice body from what he can remember and now see of it in a seated position from about twenty rows back, neat, nicely simply dressed, hair becomingly done, smiles when something's bonafidally funny, frowns same time he does at several of the speakers' shortsighted or long-winded or just simpleminded remarks. After the auditorium meeting he goes to her classroom. Large library of great Russian books for the students. Travel posters of Russian cathedrals and long Leningrad buildings. Poster-sized blowups of modern Russian novelists and poets. Corner table with a samovar on it where Olivia's said the teacher and students occasionally have pechenie and Georgian tea. Listens to her conversations with parents before him. Soft voice, clear speech, common sense, good choice of words, a few he doesn't know or has forgot and jots them down. Exomorph, vertiginous, chimerical, philippic, quid pro quo. Olivia's doing exceptional work; he says she always has. He's done a heck of a job with her alone; her mother laid it down year by year for him in a notebook, even how to braid the girls' hair. Then what else can she tell him about Olivia except more praise? Pasternak, Chekhov, Babel, Leskov, Mandelstam, Ahkmatova, Nabokov, "Tsvettava . . . I can never pronounce it, less ever spell it." She does both, says he came close, quotes some lines in English from poems he's never read. "Beautiful. Naturally I didn't altogether get them. Oops, there are daddies behind me, so I'll go. Maybe another time we can go on with our non-Olivia talk if she continues to do as well." "I'd be delighted; you know where I am." She'll never be interested in him, and tells Olivia that on the way home. "I'll speak to her and find out." "No, please, forget it. I don't want to start again and I certainly don't want to get you involved. She might lower your mark to an A-plus." "Grade. And she's way above that." "Mark, grade. I don't know why I always make that mistake. It's from before I taught. You make the mark, you mark the grade. But 'Oakujava' I think is how you pronounce his name. As for the spelling—as with Tsvetaeva before Ms. Munder told me—I could only guess. I should've mentioned him, is what I'm saying, rather than just poets and fiction writers. Wouldn't have narrowed me." "She's played him for us. Also for his perfect diction. O-k-u-d-shav-a." "Really, you got to swear you won't. If I later think differently about myself in relation to her, I'll call her or just arrange to bump into her by chance as she leaves school. Like 'Oh, I was on my way to pick up Olivia. She's not expecting me, and just between the two of us I'd rather talk lit and troubadours with you.' But she needs someone younger, stronger, smarter, singler, handsomer, head hairier, clothes clothier, in every way still shiny and on the way up, and not some seemingly semicontentedly cloistered dumpy grump who prizes just good wine, a few soups, a number of records and books, that hard-crusted bread we get delivered from Canada, and you girls."

Olivia comes home next day and says "Amby wouldn't mind your calling her. She said 'Your dad seemed intelligent, cultured, obviously serious at what he does, and we have some of the same interests, including you, meaning me, which was the one part of what she said I didn't like. Too trying-to-please-me and maybe through me, you, something I never saw in her before. 'So,' she continued to say, which you can tell from my voice change, 'I don't see why we couldn't spend half an hour over coffee, unless it would disturb you,' meaning

311

me again, which was OK this time, since she was showing she was aware of the possible conflict, she being my teacher and me so often still talking of my mother, and things." "You do? Me too, my sweetheart." He calls her. They have coffee after her school lets out. Olivia waves to them and then points them out to her friends as they walk down the hill to the coffee shop. Start seeing each other, marry. She wants a child. He says he doesn't think he has the energy to help bring up another one but if she wants it, fine, all right, "Three was what we originally planned...Denise and I. Excuse me. Nothing there meant that wasn't there, but you know what I mean." They have a girl. He's never really in love with Amby. She's nice, all that, but something keeps interfering. He just doesn't feel what he'd love to for her. It'd so simplify things. This way's unrealistic, bordering on the crazy, can only make him unhappy, also Amby and the girls. She's still very pretty, good figure, nothing she does or says puts him off, but he hardly even ever wants to put his arms around her or kiss her. No long deep ones when he does as he sometimes even did with...he can't believe it, forgot her name, Susan was her daughter; Gail. Rarely gets erections. When he does they're rarely full. A few times she's said "What's wrong? Something I've done? Anything I can do?" and he said "It's nothing, maybe my bloodless age, I'll see a doctor if it doesn't get better." They usually have to work hard before anything happens with him. He looks at Denise's photos when she's not around. Especially the pregnant ones, nude and clothed. Remembers how he felt then. Sex just about every day till she went to the hospital three weeks overdue. They were warned not to. Hates looking at the photos he's in with her. Not because he looks so much younger. Hell, he was much younger, so no problem there. It's that he was much happier then and in them. He can't think of life without Denise. Exaggeration. Sometimes he thinks he can't live without her. Another way. The three girls, they're wonderful, he loves them, always wants to be with them, if something happened to one of them he doesn't know what he'd do. Forget it. What he said about life and living without Denise expresses a lot about how he feels. He prays she'll come back. "Dear God," he says in his head, Amby asleep beside him, "I don't believe in you but will in every possible way if you bring her back and in the condition she was in before she got sick plus whatever natural aging and minor-illness effects that would have taken place. I'll make everything good for this hurt. Which will probably only have to be to Amby, but whatever you want, I will." This is silly, he right away thinks, praying and this prayer. If there's a God, He can see straight through it; if there isn't, then what's the sense? He writes poems to her, most going something like this: "My love, my dove, it's what I feel, awfully unpoetical as these lines must be to your trained ears, but it's tearing at my entrails and is that any better than gripping my gizzards or quickening my doom? Come back, I'm on a rack, the birds have stopped singing for me and now I don't even see them when they pass close overhead on a clement day or beg for attention or crumbs at my feet. What do I mean? I'm a bird. I'm going cuckoo for you. Cuckoo, cuckoo, I miss and worship you, my fellow indivisible cuckoo."

"It's just not working," he says to Amby one morning, she's feeding the baby by spoon, he's in the next room putting in toast. "What isn't? The toaster?" "Listen, hell with this goddamn toast and eating," and he pushes the toast up and throws it into the sink. "What's wrong with you?" "What's wrong? What's wrong?" he says coming into the livingroom. "Listen, I still—hours every day. No, that's a little too farfetched, but I know it's a short to moderately long time and just about every day. Please, stop feeding her for a second. This is very important. You have to have my complete attention. I have to have yours, I of course mean, for I might not be able to say this again. I was saying 'long' for something like this—a long time, almost every other day, and year after year, even when you wouldn't think I would...the general you and maybe you-Amby too—think of Denise. There we are. Denise, that's who." "You're a liar or a bastard. You just want to get out," and she drops the spoon and runs upstairs. The baby cries in her highchair. Food runs out of her mouth. He sits, wipes her, says "There, there," finishes feeding her, takes

313

her out for a stroll. He speaks to Amby again later. "I'm sorry. Listen, just sit. I'll try to stop thinking of her. I know we should stay together—you and I. I want to. Olivia and Eva also shouldn't lose you as they did their mother and then Gail. And lose their baby sister too, whom I'm sure you'd want to have total custody of if we separated or divorced, weekends this and that, which wouldn't be enough for them—would be a great loss." "You speak of her as if she isn't yours." "I do? Where? Because I'm sure she is. Who else's could she be? Meaning: sure she is. I know you haven't had lovers. Neither have I. I'd never do that to you. Meaning, that's not what I'd do to you. The other thing—it's all in my head—I'm guilty. Listen, I'm a confused man; very. Denise's death must have turned off some important lights in me. And they just don't make, or they're too tough to find anymore, the same kind of bulbs—but enough of that crap. I should get a new lamp though, right? Or see a lamp fixer, even if he charges ninety-five an hour per. So what? What's money in something like this, and I'm covered. We are, and I want us to continue to be. Listen, don't pay any attention to what I'm saying. But I loved her deeply. I told you that when we met. But I also told you it was all over, except sad moments that come back now and then. That was natural. We agreed. But she got sick. She deteriorated badly and too quickly. Bam, I looked around, she was gone. The girls and I were heartbroken for a year. They could have got out of it sooner if I hadn't been such a mess. Well, natural, natural, guilty as I still am about that too. Though they turned out all right, are turning out all right, and what else could I have done about it much as I wanted to and tried? Most of the time tried—I milked a little of it too. But it takes a year—it took a year—I thought, but some of it obviously stayed. Obviously. I still can't quite get her out of my clunky head. Not 'quite'—more. I'm a schmuck, a fool, something's still got to be wrong with me and maybe I've gotten progressively worse. It's ruined all my relationships with women since. The ones I wanted to be close. We've talked about that. Till you came. You were supposed to be different. Your patience with me, my feelings for you.

Mutual, the other way around, though not my patience. And you were. You are. There isn't anyone like you. But that woman keeps coming back. I can't get hard-ons? Most of the time. Fine, now you know why. I'm almost sure that's it. And I've pictures. I look at them of her. Nude ones even. I used to jerk off to them, now I don't, maybe because I no longer can. Physiological, psychological—something, or the two combined. And her old letters. Me, with my bad memory, I've memorized whole passages. I sit and sit and stare at them, as if I expect the script to disappear and then her hand to write the same letter again or a new message to me. One time I actually thought I saw her hand doing this. I was ecstatic, though I couldn't read it. First the hand, then the arm, then the whole body, I said to myself then—I won't be able to sit still when it gets to the breasts and face—when the image of the hand faded. It's crazy, I know. The entire thing. Or very bizarre, terrible, out of kilter, but it's something and probably much worse than I've said. In those adjectives. But I don't know what to say about it to you anymore. Thanks for continuing to listen to me. I shouldn't have married you. Neither Gail—no one but my first wife. Denise. Meaning—but you can see what I mean. I'll see a doctor. A head one. For the head. It was unfair to marry you, was what I meant, if I had any idea I was going to act like this—and I did—or even to have started with you. Well, we got a nice baby out of it. And I still love you—that's no lie—that's the truth—and need and want you—all that—and certainly for you and Gwynne to stay. I think it'll get better. Don't ask me why I do— something just tells me all of a sudden. Maybe all I needed was this—to let it out. I almost know it will, in fact—get better—so trust me, please. I'll get down on my knees. A bible. Anything. Swear on my beloved mother's head. Actually not that, since it's too much name-in-vain business and also too much like part of an act. But whatever, if you want, to convince you I truly believe all of it will get better to the point of being vastly to completely improved. I mean by that: you and I and also my body and mind. OK, I'm done, thanks again, listening and so on, and now you." "I don't see it, really. Let's

315

say I'm skeptical, based on what you've said. If it's gone on for so long and with so many women and has only gotten worse, why should I think it will get better because of one voluminous and somewhat confusing airing-out? That said, we can still try. There are the children. I don't love you anymore, but we'll see about that too. But enough. The baby's waking up."

They try. He tears up the pregnant photos. Doesn't want to throw away all the pieces—sees himself tucking away two or three in some corner pocket of his wallet—but feels he has to. Also the poems and most of the letters. Two, and innocent ones, he puts in a file folder marked "keepsakes for the kids"—she's talking about taking her summer vacation in one of them, her grandmother's illness in the other and what it was like visiting her in a nursing home the first time. Goes to a therapist with Amby and to the same one alone and at each session says he's thinking less and less of Denise, more of her, feels their recent efforts at saving the marriage are working, but not much of that's true. Though it will be, he thinks, and for now she feels a lot better toward him. They have sex more often than they've had in a year, but it mostly doesn't work for him. When it does he's usually only hard for a short time and only twice did it end up for him in even a little thrill. She says a couple of times "Don't worry, you'll be the same bellowing bear as always, down on me, under me, in me, all around me, if just a bit less of that perhaps, modifications for age factors and all, but certainly this more than anything takes time. The essential thing is we both feel infinitely better about each other, true?" "Without question." He still has a tough time holding her hand or putting his arms around her or pressing up close to her, except in bed, and there mostly to keep warm. He kisses her without feeling but seems to do a good job not showing it, the way she kisses back. Maybe she's thinking of someone else or is kissing him like that to goad him on. If so, hasn't worked. Sometimes she whispers in his ear, something she never did before like this, "Go, bear, go, bear, do it, any way you like." He usually apologizes after, says he wishes it was better for her no matter what it is for him, and she says once "No real problem; I'm getting a few kicks out of it." He starts sneaking looks at Denise's photos in the kids' keepsake folder. Some with the girls, others of just her, one of her in a bathing suit when they were on a beach building a sand whale with Olivia. It's the only one where even a little of her bare legs and a lot of her bare arms show and more of the top of one breast than in any other photo, but she's mostly hidden behind their beach equipment. He stares at the photo sometimes, trying to imagine from the way the breast's shaped in the suit and on top what it would look like uncovered. In a book of hers—the valorium edition of Yeat's poems that had been her first husband's—a photo drops out when he's reading it of Denise and Eva in a bath. Eva's first bath in a real tub, he remembers. Denise yelled from the bathroom "Howard, come quick with the camera—we have to catch this; she's an absolute scream. She wants to swim first time in and I think she's almost doing it." The print's not a good one and he can just about make out, because she's helping Eva stand in the tub, which body's which. He gets out the two letters and reads them almost every day, trying to find something in them he might have missed. A sexual or amorous reference or suggestion to him or anything hidden or not initially obvious of any kind. He also starts praying again for her return, things like "Please, if it can be done, let it be done, for me, for our girls, I'll give a finger, a hand, an arm if You want, anything to get her back in one healthy piece and if the cutting off of it doesn't give me too much pain," and finally in another confessional burst tells Amby all this. She says "Perhaps you should go to the therapist twice a week in addition to the once-a-week with me," and he does for a couple of months, no change, maybe even gets worse, searches the house frantically a few times for something of Denise's he doesn't know is there, curses out loud to himself when he can't find anything, tears up an entire room's carpet because he thinks he remembers she for some reason hid something under it, digs up a plant she planted thinking maybe when she dug the hole she intentionally or inadvertently dropped something of hers in it, and then says to

Frog

Amby "Look, to avoid any discomfort or whatever you want to call it—call it 'hell' for all I can do about it now: hell, hell, I've become a freako wacked-out maniaco the last few months—I think I should start sleeping in the bed in the basement and maybe even start cooking and ka-kaing and living my whole fucking horrible life there."

She leaves with Gwynne. He sees Gwynne every Sunday, a month every summer, promises himself no more women ever. For what's the use? He might get excited by one a few times, for weeks, a month, then it would happen again: Denise, letters, searches, praying and ranting like a madman, screwing up another woman's life and maybe even another kid's, confusing his other children's lives even further. Or maybe he wouldn't get excited by any woman but he'd try doing it with them from time to time to prove something— that he could still attract them, was still attracted by them—and how could he fake it now if he can hardly even get it up to do it to himself anymore? Olivia and Eva go to college, Gwynne to kindergarten. He likes living alone and getting older and gradually weaker; fewer chances; he can go crazy when he wants, so long as his daughters are away; drink till he passes out if he feels like it. He puts up photos of Denise all over the house. On walls, up against things: every photo he can find of her. Then has negatives made of his favorites and gets these made into positives and lots of them enlarged and puts them around too. He writes poems about her again, stories, one-act plays but they're all terrible, bring back nothing to him, don't make him cry or laugh or excited or anything and the writing stinks too, and throws them away. Does drawings and then portraits and whole-body paintings of her from memory. Several of them nude, but the only resemblance he thinks he gets is the shape and color of her vulva pubic hair. He puts one of the nudes on the floor, jerks off to it, when he's about to come he falls flat on the canvas but miscalculates where he is on it and does it on her belly. Then he thinks this is disgusting, he's gone from bad to almost hopeless, not only seeming nuts and becoming a dumb drunk and slob but doing

318

something sickening and sick to her memory, and jumps on the painting, kicks a hole in it, rips it and all the other canvases off their stretchers, dumps the drawings and canvases and burns the brushes and stretchers. What now? No art form left to express himself about her. Music, but he can't read a note and his extemporaneous piano playing is just banging. Singing, but his voice is flat. Dance, and he takes off his shoes and runs across the room in a dancing motion, eyes closed, arms out as if he's going to embrace someone, and slams into a chair.

He throws away most of the photos. Leaves up a few of her with their daughters. Cleans the house, fixes up the yard, paints the girls' rooms, gets some new furniture. Olivia goes to medical school, Eva joins a theater company, Gwynne enters the third grade. He retires, tries to drink moderately, exercises every day, wants to make himself look presentable and the house comfortable for his daughters when they visit him. He resumes reading a lot, mostly religion and philosophy now. He tries to find writers who can explain some things about his life. Who might have gone through what he did or some of it or just be better able to express it. His depressions and obsessions and other things: past mistakes and repeating them, Denise dying and his almost twenty-year reaction to it, how to lead the right life with his particular personality, whether the right life is a realistic or suitable goal for anyone, sex and love, sexuality and creativity, his heavy drinking sometimes. Who will make him want to turn to them when he needs to or thinks something terrible in him might be coming on. He can't find any. A line here, there, a passage, a paragraph, sometimes the words click for pages or a chapter and he thinks this is the writer for him or the book he's been looking for, he just knows, and goes through the whole book and gets increasingly disappointed, and maybe then through some of the other books of this writer, or at least one or part of one more.

He starts going to art museums and galleries, trying to find in the work there something that might apply to his life or be deep or hidden inside him or just give him pleasure in some way, maybe stimulate him to do creative work of his own again or what? Just to be at a big safe cultural place with other people he doesn't know ambling by. One nude in a museum painting looks very much like Denise: body, face, hair when it hung loose. This isn't what he came here for, he thinks, to find a figure in an artwork that looks like her, but he forgot that occasionally what gives him pleasure or makes him think about his life or sets off an action or idea leading to some kind of work comes unexpectedly like this. It isn't the painting's subject that interests him much, which is of a woman sitting on the edge of an unmade bed, drinking from a simple cup, holding a matching saucer in her other hand, seems to have slept nude and just woken up, clothes hanging out of a drawer and on the floor all seem to be hers, memo pad and uncapped pen by her leg, book, radio, eyeglasses, nailclippers and lamp on the night table, semiabstract seascape in a broken frame above the dresser, walls and furniture quite shabby, rowhouses through the completely opened window rundown and some of them torched, sun coming up over the tall building at the end of her block, clock between her feet says ten to twelve so it must be winter and some very northern country she's in or the clock's stopped. Painting's called "Mourning Woman Rising," though her face doesn't show it—she just seems to be enjoying her day's first coffee or tea—and if a double meaning's meant, and it isn't that she's mourning for her poor circumstances or the stopped clock or neighborhood in some way, it gets by him. The painting was finished last year and bought for the museum by an anonymous donor. He goes back to this "New Acquisitions" room for weeks, stays in it for an hour or two daily, usually leaning against a wall, finally asks the guard, one of a few who float around this wing of the museum and he's come to greet or say good-bye to, if a couch, as the museum used to have in almost every room years ago, couldn't be put in this one so he and other people could look at the paintings and such without getting tired. The guard says something about crowd control, new museum rules, also the insurance company wouldn't permit it, can't. He wants to cut the woman out of the painting, take it home, hang it up but not to masturbate to it. He rarely tries that anymore to even a nude magazine photograph he might come upon or what to him is a provocative lingerie or swimsuit ad. Few days later he goes to the museum with a single edge razor blade to cut the figure or the whole painting out, whichever he can do fastest, but walking up the museum's great interior stairway he says to himself "No, trouble again, and big trouble this time too if you're caught, which you'll be of course, so go back, don't look at it today, maybe even stay away from it from now on."

He goes straight home, has a thought which he quickly writes on a piece of paper as he walks into the house: "Sometimes things you can never understand destroy you." Not a bad thought, he thinks, complete and pungent, or one to come out of nowhere like that, if that's what it did—at least the apparent nowhere—and tries to write another line but nothing follows it. Tries again several times that day, takes a pen and pad to bed with him in case something comes, tries to write a follow-up line the next morning, hoping it'll lead to many lines, pages, even a book-length manuscript one day, then types the original line, scissors it out of the paper and tapes it on the wall above his typewriter. Then he writes it in inch-high letters and tapes it over the typewritten line. Then writes it in even larger letters using Gwynne's crayons and tapes it on the refrigerator door. Then writes it in various sizes using different writing implements and tapes them around the house. Then buys a poster board and poster paint set and starts painting the thought in two-feet-high letters, which he plans to nail to a living room wall, but stops a couple of words through and says "What am I doing now, that's enough, don't let it get the better of you as so much of the same thing did before and before and before." He throws out the poster board and paints, tears up all the papers around the house he had the thought on except the original handwritten one which he puts in his night table drawer, and goes back to reading novels, poetry, going to concerts, museums and plays, listens to a lot of recorded music while he cooks and eats and reads and rests or just contemplates, most of it for solo voice or all-male or all-female chorus but with no musical instruments and several centuries old, visits his oldest daughters in the cities they're in, takes long walks, goes for a swim each day, has a coffee and torte now and then at a neighborhood coffeehouse, men and women become companions again, lots of interesting things to do and discuss and go to with them, but he always falls asleep holding his own penis.

Frog's Interview

I wrote a letter suggesting an interview with him. He wrote back "I've been interviewed twice in the last three years and the day after each interview I told the interviewers to erase the tapes and tear up their notes. I'm not articulate or glib or confident enough for one. I also ramble on too much and have little to say about my life and work and the practice of fiction writing. So, wouldn't want to waste your time, but thanks."

I wrote back saying I'd still like interviewing him and gave him several pages of possible questions. "Just write your responses to them. Say anything you want. Let loose and be provocative if need be. It probably was the tape recorder and presence of the interviewer that ruined your last interviews. Since you have been a writer for so long, maybe this is the most natural way for you to be interviewed."

He wrote back "I don't like to be interviewed any old way and I don't like to read these interviews either. I'm not interested in why writers write or what they have to say other than what I get from their fiction. I'm not interested in just about any nonfiction other than some major poetry and a few readable plays, and also an occasional newspaper article, and that mostly to read with my coffee

323

to start the day and maybe to sit on the toilet with. Listen, I don't want people knowing where I came from, who my parents are, the effects of being the youngest of seventeen children and the only boy in the family, my wives and kids, my dogs and cats, the two gorillas I had as pets till they tore the mail satchel off our postman's shoulder, the various jobs I've had and continents I've lived on, my prison terms, why one leg's a foot and a half shorter than the other, all the hand-me-down girls' clothes...but you've got it. How my life leaks into my fiction and vice versa and what comes from the real and what from the imagination and what kind of instrument I use to sharpen my typewriters every morning, and so on. I also can't answer your questions in writing because I'm a writer who only writes fiction. Whose only nonfiction, in fact, since I was a pimp maybe 25 years ago, was an article called 'Why a Pimp Can't Write Nonfiction.' And I only wrote that out of spite because the university quarterly that was devoting half an issue to my work plus a complete bibliography, wouldn't pay me a cent for the stories it was also publishing in the issue but would give me $200 for a 500-word article. Besides, no understanding of me or my...but enough. I'm easily confused, distracted and tormented and almost nothing does this quicker to me than an interview or prospect of one. So, thanks again for asking."

I wrote back saying "I tried, it didn't work, I respect your reasons for not wanting an interview. But now I've something different to ask of you. The letter with all those interview questions was written on a word processor, and before I could save the letter an electric storm wiped it out. I didn't mention it before because I thought you might think I'd be too incompetent to interview you. If you still have the letter, could you please make a copy of it and send it to me? It took two days to compose those questions—it was, quite frankly, one of the most tedious chores I've done and I'd hate to repeat it—and I'd like to use them on another writer I've lined up to interview."

He wrote back "Listen, I'm a lousy interviewee—how many times must I say it? Interviews make my head ache, stomach sick, nose bleed, and later I'm mean to my family, I knock down clothes in closets, I put washed dishes in the cupboard before they're dry, I punch walls and then can't type for days, I begin seeing myself as an imposter as a teacher and an impersonator as a thinker and a masquerader as a writer. I believe that fiction writers..."

I wrote back "OK, the truth, which I was too embarrassed to tell before. Maybe you didn't notice—my embarrassment was that you'd think I sent them intentionally, so I could squeeze a comment out of you, which isn't it at all—but what was also on the last page of that letter of interview questions I sent you were two first drafts of poems I wrote. I composed them on a word processor, forgot to tear them off the bottom of the letter, and only after the storm wiped out the letter and I had canvassed the house for my poems did I realize what must have happened to them and where they might be. I've tried recalling them from memory but all I can remember is that they were two of the best first drafts I've ever written. Please, if you have that letter, send the poems to me? Tear off and throw away the interview questions, even if that is the only copy there is of them—compared to the poems, I don't care about them anymore."

I called him from Paris several weeks later—heck with the expense. Those poems had definite possibilities and it was killing me that they were lost. His wife answered, I told her why I was calling, and she said it would be futile to try and get him to the phone. "Tell him it's not for the interview anymore," I said. "If he's an artist—a serious writer—whatever he is—just a decent person— excuse me, but you know what I mean—surely he'll understand why I want my poems back." "He's in his room working on the first draft of a new story. It's the only time he gives me express orders not to disturb him for anything, except if one of the children suddenly gets violently sick or hurt or there's a fire or something, and even that depends on the size of the blaze. If I think I can put it out without him, he's said, then leave him be till I hear him stop typing. For you see, two to three hours of agonizing first-draft work gives him two to three months of pleasurable rewriting till the story's completed,

325

and as a result of it, general well-being for the house and all its occupants during that time." "Tell him I'll be in the States and passing through Baltimore in two weeks. If he's found my letter by then, would he save it for me? And if he hasn't, would he let me look for it where he might have left it?" "I'm sure he would," she said, "so long as you don't touch anything on his desk without his permission."

I was in Baltimore two weeks later and called. He answered the phone and I said "Please, I don't want to waste your time further, but did you find my letter?" "I found, I found," he said, "so what's the big fuss?" "The big fuss, sir, are those two poems of mine. As for the questions in the letter, I could still use some of them for an interview I'm doing in Washington tomorrow with Rodney Stein." "Oh, big man, Stein—you're interviewing the right guy, and you'll get nothing but cooperation from him. He has a big book coming out, from a big publisher and with big publicity money behind it, so an interview or two will get his name around and help the book sell and maybe jack up the paperback sale price and get it to one of the big clubs, which should eventually interest all the chains to stock it. Believe me, if you want to be a serious writer today who makes a decent living from his books and also get lots of awards, you have to be interviewed in the right places from time to time, if you can't capitalize on your reclusiveness and indifference to interviews. So what am I saying? Nothing. I'm rambling. Be glad I didn't grant you that interview."

"My letter, sir. Could I come by now? I'll only be a minute." "Sure, come, pick it up, make my desk just a little less cluttered, but leave your tape recorder in the train station locker or wherever you are." "I wouldn't think of interviewing you, sir. I know how you feel."

I cabbed over. He was waiting outside for me, waving my letter. He gave me it, introduced his family, invited me in for coffee and cake. It was a small, modest house. Outside: a tiny yard, one tall tree, lots of dead patches of grass, some flowers, bushes, redwood table and cheap chairs, a swing set. Inside: not much furniture and most of it damaged and old, lots of kid stuff on the tables and floors, in the dining room a large cardboard playhouse with piles of children's books and two small rocking chairs in it, long high bookcases running the entire length, except for the windows, of three living room walls.

"All those are my wife's," he said. "I own about twenty books and they're all under or beside my side of the bed. I'll keep it a secret what they are: modern poetry and fiction classics and a volume of one writer's letters, plus *The Odyssey, The Idiot, The Aeneid* and Aurelius's *Meditations*. I buy a lot of books, and after I'm done with them and if my wife doesn't want to read them or doesn't think she can in a couple of years, I give them away or, if they're awful, throw them out. I don't like accumulating things. For instance, when I've completed a fiction I dump all the drafts of it but the finished one. When the manuscript's put into book form, out it goes too. Some writers have told me to save the manuscripts for a university library one day, but they haven't provided me with the storage space for this old junk, nor the confidence that any library would take my work. Besides, it'd be like having my unwashed underpants there for people to study, with all the holes, stains and stretched crotch area and elastic bands. Anyway, all this shows why I don't like being interviewed."

"I'm sorry, I don't catch that," I said.

"I'm not a bright guy. Fact is, I'm dense and intellectually dumb. You can see that by what I say and how I say it. I might know my way around a typewriter keyboard when I'm alone with it, and that for sure is arguable, but just about nowhere else. Many times my five-year-old daughter can understand what I'm reading to her—a children's book—better than I. Probably sometimes because she's only listening when I read, while I'm speaking, so also concentrating on the delivery. I like to act out all the roles, just as I do when I write, though she prefers I read it straight with no vocal interpretations. Other times my wife and I read the same book and I have to ask her what lots of parts mean. She never does that to me and not

327

because she's reluctant to. Listen, in my classes I often miss the easiest things. It's become a joke with my students. We'll all read a student's story, though I'll read it three times to make sure I got it so I don't embarrass myself. But I'll still often misconstrue a character or scene or the entire meaning of the piece while few of them will. After I find out where I went wrong I have to slap my head and say 'God, did it again. Stupid, stupid.' It always gets a laugh. So why's the school keep me on?"

"That'd seem like a good question, no offense meant, of course."

"My front gold tooth, full head of ungraying hair that's always parted on the left side and trimmed, neat appropriate clothing for a teacher my age, ankle bracelet I occasionally wear, my pat-on-the-back personality, mostly, plus my giddy acceptance of more work than two or three men could endure. Don't ask me. I don't know. So what am I saying in all this?"

"Please, I've no intention to interview you. As I said—"

"For instance, what could I say about those questions you sent me—can I have them back a moment?" and I gave him the letter. "They make sense, but for another writer. Stein. He and just about every writer worth his word processor can answer anything and sensibly, intelligibly, cleverly, profoundly, even if they didn't understand or hear the question. Me? Well I'll give you an example. 'What's going on in American fiction from your point of view?' Writing, lots of writing. Short stories and novels. Some novellas. Short shorts are in. Cuffs are out again and pleats are back. 'Is there any significant dialogue going on between writers or schools of thought that will make a significant difference?' Sure. Yak-yak-yak. It never stops. As for the significant difference, I wouldn't know, since the minute I hear the yakking. . . See? Nothing. Let's take another."

"Really, sir, you've made your point. May I have my poems back before you smudge them?"

" 'Is the American novel keeping up with the social, economical, political, religious and technological changes in American life?' You bet it has. If it doesn't sell it's shredded up faster than it ever was.

Truth is, I don't give a shit about any intellectual drip or ideological current or economical river or social ocean or political or technological cesspool."

His wife came in and said "You don't have to get crude."

"So I'll say it daintier. I keep up with nothing, not even contemporary writing. No time. I father, son, husband, teacher, writer, semidetached homeowner. The little time I get for myself, I go to my cellar, shut the door. I blank everyone and everything out. I do my pages. One to two to three. They add up, spill over, get in my way, when I leave I sometimes have to kick piles of them aside. Eventually they amount to a manuscript. Small to large. When it's done I quickly start another. My life down there's a concatenation of fabulations. Sound good? I can't stand those things, whatever they're called."

"You're only interested in amounts?" his wife said.

"I'm interested solely in going to the cellar and shutting the door, if only for a few minutes. The messages—reasons—cause—explanations—I blow my nose on. 'How do I fit in?' it says here. I don't. There's no room. The house is overcrowded with writers and the furniture's painted on the walls. If rooms were added to it, I'd only be told after they were filled. Not that I didn't once try to get in, but they said I was being pushy, "Wait your turn. . . .You're stepping on my toe. . . .I'm holding this place for someone. . . .You're too noisy and preventing people from sleeping standing up.' I got out—I'd only made it to the foyer. 'Ether, ether,' I cried. But another. 'Fabulist,minimalist, where are you?' I'll take the Crispy Chef's Shrimp, not too spicy, and start off with cold Szechuan noodles. Look, I belong to no movement. If I did, I'd hold it till it was still, turn it around from me and say 'See the pretty birdy?' and run in the opposite direction."

His wife said "Come on, people are interested in backdrops. Why not be slightly gracious and even informative for once, and not a hypocrite. For you yourself read the Joyce biography, was involved in the Beckett one till you lost it, and carried Kafka's when we went to Prague."

"Only for the maps,"

"Try. I might even learn something about what you do. She took the letter from him and read " 'In what traditions do you think your work follows?' "

"My dad's. He said 'Every day is labor day.' "

" 'Do you feel like an American writer?' "

He started waving an imaginary flag, dropped it, picked it up, kissed it, said "Pheu!" and pretended to spit. "What're they making these things out of lately? Tastes so artificial."

" 'A New York writer?' "

"Turdy-Gurdy and Merde Avenue. I says, what, what?"

" 'Explain the phenomenon of being so widely published and yet still kind of struggling for recognition.' "

"Keeps my weight down, muscles toned, body in fighting condition, so is among the best things to have happened to me."

" 'What's your relation to the New York publishing scene?' "

"I walk past their buildings sometimes when I'm in New York. They dwarf me."

" 'Why do you publish with the small presses and small mags?' "

"Unlike the biggies, they haven't learned yet how to avoid me."

" 'Where and how did you begin publishing?' "

"OK, a serious question, so rates a serious response. Hold your pantyhose, folks. Someone sent one of my early stories to a fancy quarterly. They took it and wanted to see me immediately about a few minor changes before they sent the issue to the printer's. I went to their office. It overlooked the East River, tugboats going past, hamper factory standing still, sunken living room, framed photos of contemptuous lit lights on the grand piano, an opened bar. 'No thanks,' I said. I was on my lunch hour from a news job I had and still never touch the stuff till sundown. It ended up where they wanted a total rewrite. I rewrote the story totally and they said they wanted a total rewrite of the rewrite. I rewrote the rewrite totally and they said they wanted a total rewrite of the rewrite of the rewrite. I decided they'd never publish this poor five-page story of a New York merry-go-round and sent them the original draft. Never heard from them again and six months later that draft was published. I learned almost all I needed to know about editors and publishing from it."

" 'What about commercialism?' "

"Never had the chance. But let's change the subject." He took the letter from her and read 'How do you teach?' I say 'Hi, my name is, nice to meet ya, now start with those lines or similar introductory or valedictory ones and write a short story of any length.' Say, that gives me an idea for one, and just when I've been looking for it," and he went downstairs. "My letter," I said, but he'd already shut the door.

I looked at his wife, she raised her shoulders, so I tiptoed down the steps after him. He was typing away at a long table. It was a dark room, a small window over the table but not much light coming through it, even on this sunny day, probably because the window was almost at ground level. A reproduction of a Giacometti drawing of a face was right below the window, or maybe it was an original— I'd ask him. A painting by a child was next to it. The painting was signed by his oldest daughter and said at the bottom of it "Daddy writing again," and showed a man at a table with his hands over his ears and his mouth open as if shouting. There was no other furniture in the room except a file cabinet to the left of the table with a huge dictionary on it. On the table, besides the manual typewriter and at one end of it the typewriter's plastic cover, was a thesaurus, writing reference manual, ream of erasable paper (sixteen-pound weight), box of second-sheet paper, two fountain pens, bottle of black ink, postage stamps of several denominations coiling out of a mug, lots of eraser pencils, all needing sharpening, letter and manuscript envelopes, mucilage, stapler, nailclipper, paperweights (sea-smoothed stones), architect's lamp, wood box built to look like a little foot locker with probably lots of writing aids inside, pencil sharpener shaped like a duck. "Excuse me, I know I shouldn't be disturbing you now, but may I have my letter back please?"

"No no, I'm through. It was very short—three pages—which could end up being thirty, but who knows? So thanks for indirectly helping me fill that void. I'd do almost anything for you now, except of course give that interview."

"I wouldn't think of it, sir. But if you are having so such fun at it, or think it can still be useful in some creative way—could you tear off my poems and give them to me?"

He started to, read something from the letter that seemed to interest him, said "Hey this is good—I could never write or say anything like this, so lucid but literary. 'Your style, then. It sounds so undecorated, conversational, unstylized, spoken, even reads at times like quote unquote bad writing or neglected conventional writing. Yet the reader is aware of your deliberately ignoring standard sentence structure, syntax, punctuation, etcetera. Can you comment further on how you compose or what this style says about the people, places and situations that you write about?' I could if I was another writer. 'Were'? And you don't want it 'situations you write about' instead of with the 'that'? But I'm done down here for now—got my first draft in. It must be an uncomfortable place also, with only one chair, for the person not writing," and he covered the typewriter and went upstairs.

I followed him, out to the backyard, he reading the letter as he walked. After we sat he read " 'Your work seems to be influenced by European writing, the French writers of the sixties in particular. Is this true?' Is the sun too hot for you? I always stay in the shade, but there's room for both of us here." I shook my head. " 'Can you talk about how the family or everyday life motivates your life, work, message?' I wonder where everyone is. Usually you hear one of them. With the baby, you have to make sure she doesn't wander through the gate to the street. Sweetheart?" he yelled.

"They're with me," his wife said from the second-floor back window. "I thought you'd want to talk undisturbed."

" 'What writers should we be watching? Who have we overrated or ignored? Who are the characters you feel closest to, real or fictional? You seem drawn in your books to people with frenetic, almost neurotic tendencies, certain individuals with overactive imaginations, no?' You know what I think?"

"Certainly, if you want to answer."

"That you'd be much better off, if you don't mind my saying so—
and my wife will agree with you that I've got too big a mouth
sometimes. But to give up this notion that interviews with artists
of any kind are useful or important whatsoever. The best thing is
just to do your work, put out the magazine with the most exciting
stuff you can find for it, and also tend to your own poetry, if that's
what you do. So what I'm going to do now will be a service to you
in the long run, believe me."

"What's that?" I said.

He tore up the letter and threw the pieces behind him, "Now
let's have some fresh coffee, or even a glass of wine. What the hell,
it's Sunday, isn't it?"

"My poems," I screamed.

"Oops—I forgot. That was thoughtless of me."

"You did it deliberately."

"No, I told you—I don't think lots of times," and he got on the
ground and gathered all the pieces the wind hadn't blown away. "We
can tape it back together," he said, picking some pieces out of the
bushes. "I know how you feel. It's happened to me. Just losing a
page or two, though nobody ripping them up in front of me." He
spread the pieces out on the table, but he'd torn them too finely.
He saw I was sad and said "Look, I can drive you someplace—the
train station or wherever you're going. Washington, to see Stein—
right? I'll drive you there—leave you in front of his house; that's how
lousy I feel about this."

I didn't want to be in a car with him that long, but I did want
to get away from him and I had nothing to lose if he drove me to
the station. I got all the pieces together, asked him for a plastic bag
and put them inside. His daughters came with us. He said they love
seeing the trains pulling in and out and to run around the big
renovated station, and it'll give his wife a little time to do her own
work.

We drove to the station. I said good-bye on the platform but
refused to shake his hand. I took a seat, and while the train waited

to go, he and his daughters waved at me. I opened a book and tried to concentrate on it, but I could still see this multiple flapping going on outside. The hell with him, I thought as the train left. He's a complete fop, fake and fool and I don't mind telling the world about it, not that anyone will be interested.

Frog's Mom

Weak, weak, it's all so weak, and he rips it out and throws it into the trash pail. Done this before. Out it comes, into that or if bad aim onto the floor, tearing first, sometimes tearing up what's been torn and throwing it back in, grabbing out pieces sometimes and tearing some more, often banging the table with his fist after, maybe stomping upstairs and pouring coffee from the thermos, or making fresh coffee even if there's fairly fresh coffee in the thermos, yelling out to no one in particular "I'm going out for a few minutes," taking a circular walk around the neighborhood, not looking at much because there isn't much—bird in a tree, squirrel nibbling or digging up a nut, cat or dog in a window looking as if it wants to go out, someone jogging or opening a house or car door or walking a dog, letter carrier delivering mail, only occasionally something like a gardener transplanting pacysandra or a treeman fifty to a hundred feet up sawing off a limb or even some kids playing out front or swinging on a porch—drinking a half glass of wine, quarter glass, just a sip of sherry and maybe straight from the bottle, munching a celery stalk or carrot, peeling, without washing or peeling, even eating its thin tail string or the inch or so of the top, tearing off the skin of a navel, biting down hard on an apple, picking up a newspaper section and usually without reading or anything but a headline or caption putting it down. Now he just sits. Weak. That's what it was. Piss, shit, fit for the trash. Bangs the table top. Just did it for fun. "What's that?" Eva asks upstairs. "Daddy must have dropped something," Denise says. "That's Daddy mad," Olivia says. "Daddy gets mad a lot."

Writes: "There once was a man. Was once. He was a big man. Thick neck, puffed-up pecks, six-feet-sex, puissant-plus." Weak. Pulls it out. Turns it over to stick back in to type on. Something's on the other side from another work he stopped. " 'Mrs. Simchik stinks,' a boy said, and got whacked. 'Don't ever say the word—' " That was it. Doesn't know what he planned to follow it. Couldn't come up with anything, probably, besides the prose. Doesn't know when he wrote it: last month, year; just ended up in the scrap pile. Weak. Weak. Throws it into the pail. New scrap paper in. "There was a woman. She was my mother. She's, is. My old mother, mother of young. He went upstairs. Phoned her. I did. Went, up, phone, reached, dialed. 'Mom, how are you?' 'Not feeling that great today, thank you for calling.' 'Why, what's wrong?' he said, 'What's the matter? What's up?' for he heard it almost every time before, similar words, same tone, minor complaining, nothing good. 'Well actually, now that you asked me, I'm dying. That's what the report came back from with my doctor.' How was he reacting when she said this? Shock, that's all: 'What! What!' 'I'm saying, that's what Dr. Gladman said the report confirmed that came back from the cab. I'm not saying it well because it so upsets me. I took extensive tests. I didn't tell you because I didn't want to bother you. Your children, job, home, you've your own troubles. I had to work it out of him. Worm it out. I had to ask and ask and finally I said "What is it, it isn't good, we both know that, I can feel it and you can see it and the tests and reports all prove it, isn't that right? So tell me, I'm a good listener." ' 'You said this?' I said. 'Surely he said "No, you're all wrong, Mrs. T." ' 'Surely he said yes, I was right. "Listen, Mrs. T.," he said—he called me Rachel, actually, just as I sometimes call him Bill. Though he always calls me Rachel now. He's very nice, very friendly. He said "If you want the truth, it doesn't look good." ' 'This is terrible, I said; 'what does one say? For one thing, that you go to someone else for another opinion, of course,' and she said 'I have,' and we talked some more, I said I was coming right up to see her, called my older brother, he also hadn't known, we'd meet at my mother's, I took the train, three hours, cabbed to it, subway to her place from it, total of four hours, when I got there my brother answered the door and said he'd found her dead."

Weak, weak, but suggests what's on his mind. Mother then. When? Long time ago, try; when he was a boy, start. "He throws something—a hammer—was aiming for the closet with the tool chest on the floor next to it, the closet next to the breakfront with the opened tool chest on the floor, the tool chest on the floor of the closet next to the breakfront, I threw a hammer at the tool chest on the floor of the opened foyer closet but it went through the breakfront next to it. My folks were away for the weekend in Old Saybrook. Gil Dobb's the resort was called. Gil, they said, served two-pound lobsters for lunch, inch-and-a-half thick veal chops for dinner, grew and cut flowers which he put in vases on the dining room tables every meal, ironed the tablecloth himself sometimes so it was done right, sold antiques in his antique barn, was a *fagele* whose longtime companion was rarely seen on the grounds and never ate at Gil's table in the dining room. They went there every fall for their anniversary and my mother always came back with some of Gil's antiques (hand-painted plates to hang, converted kerosene lamps, chamber pots, soup tureens, creamers, something else she liked to collect whose name he forgets—Toby mugs), his father with a big basket each of apples and pears and a few dozen freshly laid eggs. I was scared they'd punish me, my mother especially (my father would probably just call me a stupid kid and say what I'd done was only to be expected), since the breakfront was originally her mother's and had some prized objects in it, none broken and many bought from Gil. But when they got home around dinnertime Sunday night—" No, weak, but just see what comes out by finishing it. Shouldn't take long. "They came home the next night. He was worried the whole day. He was told by his brothers to go straight up to her and say he broke it. He did. She still had her coat on, his father had just set down a basket of fruit and asked the boys to help him with the rest of the things in the car. But he quickly told her. 'Mom, the breakfront, look at it, I broke it.' She looked, got on one knee, put her hand through the place where the glass had been—a quarter-section of the breakfront, he doesn't know who took the broken glass out before his parents got home—and waved and said 'Yo-hoo, here I am, how's my baby boy?' "

Weak, uninteresting, ends up well for her though, but what else from then? She once took him and his sister Vera to see Santa Claus. This one's stayed around; see where it leads. "Carla and George walked through a dimly lit corridor with their mother to get to the elevator to see Santa. Elves greeted them from behind reindeer and trees, some littler than he but with high grownup voices, one handed them each a wrapped present. An elf ran the elevator. It went straight up to Santaland, he thinks it was called. Christmasland. Toyland, it had to be." The present was handed them right after they saw Santa. "They were the only ones in the elevator. It was decorated like a snowed-in log cabin. The elf hummed a tune to himself as the car rose. Was he instructed to or maybe even not to? This wasn't in George's mind then. A carol was being sung from somewhere in the car, but a different tune than the elf's. He remembers his mother said this wasn't just any old Santa they were going to but one they had to pay for. Hence the present. The corridor upstairs was also dimly lit and ended with a long line of waiting kids and their parents. They'd passed two other Santas in their rooms but were directed by an elf to this one. He doesn't remember sitting on Santa's lap. Santa wasn't old, seemed if he stood up he'd be as tall as a circus giant, had no belly. An elf wanted to take a photo of him with Santa and then Clara and him with Santa but both times his mother said too expensive. The exit door from Santa's room opened onto the toy department. He remembers being surprised by that. A guard stood on the toy department side to keep people from sneaking in." So what? Has little to do with anything. One time in the same store though . . .

"One time in the Thirty-fourth street Macy's his mother told him to wait over here. What she did was buy a box of sanitary napkins. How's he know? Because she had a shopping bag with something shaped like a box in it when she came back and he thought it was a surprise for him, just by the way she said 'Wait for me here and don't move from this spot no matter how long I'm away,' as if she didn't want him to see what she was buying for him, even if it wasn't around Christmastime or his birthday and she said she was going to another counter on the first floor and there was nothing for children on that floor that he knew of or could see in that store. She was away a long time. He had nothing to do. He wanted to move to another spot, at least a few feet away—the perfume smells from the counter she put him next to were bothering him—but didn't. A couple of times he thought maybe she forgot where she left him. It was the world's biggest store he'd been told a few times, so she could have made a mistake in directions herself or come back to where she thought she'd left him and decided he was lost. Should he try to find her? Or maybe just yell out 'Mommy' till she came. She wouldn't like that if she heard it and one of the guards they seemed to have all around on this floor might just grab him and throw him out of the store. Or just try to get home by himself? How would he do it? He didn't have the fare for the subway or bus. He wouldn't know how to get to his subway station or bus stop even if he did have the fare. But he knew the name of his station and it was in this borough, so maybe if he told someone it and was able to borrow the fare, he'd get there. Once out of the station he thinks he could find his way home, since it was only three blocks away along the avenue you come up into and then just a short walk down the street. Better to stay put though. If his mother thought he was lost she'd get the whole store to find him or call up his dad to have it done. But how he found out what was inside the box was that night he looked in the bag. It was still in the foyer coat closet. He couldn't see any pictures or words on it that would make it seem like a present for him, so he asked his brother Alex what the box said. Alex looked at it, said 'Kotex' and that he thinks it's something women use for their behinds or someplace but he doesn't know what for. 'Cleaning, probably.'" Nothing there either.

"She was born on the lower East Side. Her father from her descriptions of him was a benevolent tyrant." Weak, weak. "A dictatorial benevolist." Forget it, besides wrong. "A disapproving wretch, egotist, let's face it: a mean bastard who spent more time trimming and waxing his Franz Josef mustache than with his kids." She'd never. How does she describe him? "Everyone feared him." "My mother sipped her drink, took a deep drag on her cigarette, said 'Could you pour some more in it? I've been a good girl by nursing it for an hour, but now it's all melted ice.' Then 'When my sisters and I saw him on the street we'd cross to the other side to avoid greeting him. Because whenever we did happen to meet him on the stairs coming up or turning a corner, he always criticized us. "Your hair's uncombed, your button's undone, retie your shoelaces and pull up your socks—you look like a slut." He owned a liquor store-restaurant. Let's face it—a gin mill. The Polish girls who worked for us—they all had names like Sophie and Anna and Christina— also cooked for the bar's free-food counter. One time one of those big pots the food was cooking in.... One time a very big pot of stew, which when they were scoured and we were a little younger we also took baths in, fell off the stove on top of Aunt Rose. It scalded her whole body almost, till this day she won't eat any hot meat dish like that or really any liquid that's hot except tea. She had to be rushed to the hospital. What am I talking about?—the doctor came. I was the fastest one home at the time—I used to win all the athletic contests in grammar school, besides all the musical and intellectual ones too for girls—so I ran to get him.' " Weak, weak.

"His mother did very well in school. When she graduated high school she told her father she wanted to be a doctor. He said 'One doctor in the family's enough.' Her eldest brother was an intern then. 'Women worked as secretaries or assistants or nurses or stayed home.' She then wanted to be a lawyer. Her father said 'One lawyer in the family's enough.' Her next eldest brother was in law school. 'How many ambulances you think there are to chase? Besides, women don't become lawyers unless they don't want to have children and want to live only with women and smoke cigars and be like that.' Then an architect. 'I don't want any architects in the family, not for my sons or my girls. For one thing, it's no profession for a Jew. It's all run by Gentiles and they'll keep you standing there for years before they give you even a tent to design. For another reason, because I won't let you try to do something stupid and useless like that where as a woman you'll have double no chance. Maybe you got the brains for it—that I can't say. But get a job that can carry you till you make a good marriage—that's all you need. You want to continue reading— to improve yourself or because you like books—do it while nursing your children or watching them in the playground.' She got an office job; evenings and on matinee days she danced in a big Broadway review. Some man she knew, and without telling her, had sent her photo to a beauty contest sponsored by a newspaper. 'I think it was the whole city I represented,' she said about it recently, 'or maybe just Manhattan. In fact, first I was Miss Rockaway, then from that I became Miss Brooklyn, though I'd never stepped in that borough except to go to its beaches sometimes, and then Miss New York, so it had to be for the whole city and maybe even for the state. It was so long ago. I can't look in the mirror most times when I think what a pretty face and shape I had then.' 'You're still quite beautiful and you've kept your weight down,' he said. 'For my age, perhaps, but that counts for next to nothing. Maybe less than that, for people look at me, when I've done my face and hair right and I don't have these rags on and what I'm wearing is basically black, and think "She must have been very beautiful once—a hundred years ago." Anyway, I kept lots of photos but never clippings of those contests and shows, since I didn't want my dad finding them and learning about me. He thought all beauty contestants and show people were goats and tramps. In a way he was right, besides too much liquor and taking whatever drugs we had then and some of the men playing with boys. But I was nothing but a good girl right to the time I married your father." Weak, weak.

"As a boy I loved looking at the albums and manila envelopes of photos from when my mother was a showgirl and beauty contest winner. None of the bathing beauty photos show her with a ribbon across her chest saying what Miss she was. 'Because of my dad I only kept the ones that had nothing like that on them. Ones he might find, let him think I was girlishly posing for a boyfriend or a roving photographer on a boardwalk or beach.' 'But it was in the papers, wasn't it?' I said. 'Good point; I didn't think of that then. No, now I remember. It was in them but nowhere near as much then, and he only read the Yiddish and Polish dailies, which had nothing about it.' 'Then his customers could have told him.' 'That's true. If they did, he never said. My feeling is none ever said anything because they knew he'd get so mad they'd be banned from his bar for life.' She said she was Miss New York. Her sister Rose said it was Miss Coney Island. 'I was her chaperon at it—Mama wouldn't let her go otherwise—so I remember.' 'Then how'd she get to the Miss America contest?' I said. 'She became Miss Brooklyn or something—Coney Island being in that borough—but that part I know less of. It was your Aunt Bitty who chaperoned her to that one, though she wasn't your aunt then because you weren't alive yet, and she died a few years after that.' My father said that whatever Miss my mother said she was is true. 'She's got a memory like a machine that never stops. And all that was a little before I met her. Only thing my mother and I were interested in was that she came to me a whole woman. You think that's funny—go on, laugh, wise guy—but it should still be important to you, if you were smart. Of course, if she hadn't been what we thought she was, I wouldn't have tossed her back, though I might have asked her father for a larger dowry.' 'You would have told him?' 'Probably not, since he was already very generous. Gave me a gold watch, a big wedding—Cantor Rosenblatt sang, considered the best cantor in the world then—plus some cash to start the apartment with. I probably would have just lied to my mother and then done a lot of *davening* in *shul* because of it.' 'Because of what—lying to your mother, or the other?' 'What are you, a cop? Because of everything and nothing, you satisfied?' " Doesn't work. Concentrate.

"His mother was almost Miss America. First or second runner-up—she was never sure, she said, even when it happened. One photo he especially liked of her then had her in a one-piece bathing suit, barefoot, holding a ball over her head. A beauty. He should borrow it to show his daughters, or just pull it out of the breakfront drawer next time they're there. 'This is Grandma, can you believe it? When she was younger than your mother is now by almost twenty years, and thirty years younger than I.' Short black hair, big dark eyes, radiant smile—" Not radiant. Beaming smile, bouncy smile, just a big beautiful mesmerizing smile. Checks the thesaurus. "Short dark hair, big black eyes, bright smile, brainy face, bathing beauty figure—for then. She was curvy but slim, with small breasts. 'I wouldn't win with those breasts today,' she said. 'But they were good enough to nurse four normal-sized babies and each for more than a year. Doing it so long probably kept you kids from getting fat like your father in later age, if you have his genes for that.' Long perfect legs. Near perfect. Almost perfect. Athletic. 'The woman who became Miss America—' "

"My mother was first runner-up in the Miss America pageant of 1922 or '23. Maybe even '24, since she later danced on the stage for two years till her father pulled her off it, got engaged to my father soon after, married in '27 and had my oldest brother at the end of that year. Or was he born in '28? He's eight or nine years older than I almost to the day. 'The woman who won the contest,' she said, 'was a Miss Sunshine. That was her last name. We all called her Sunny, though she was a real bitch. I don't remember her first name or what state she was from. Pennsylvania, I think. Ohio. She looked typically Polish and most of the Poles came from Pennsylvania and Ohio then. She was a striking bleached blonde with that little upturned nose the real Poles have—much more so than mine, and squinched. I would have won the title—everyone said so—if they had counted talent and intelligence as qualifications then. Sunny couldn't do anything but smile brightly and strut her behind, which were really no better than mine. While I danced, sang, knew something about manipulating marionettes, and played Bach and popular music on the violin. I also had graduated a good public high school with an academic diploma and very near the top of my class, and I don't think Sunny or very many of the other contestants ever got past primary school.' George White was one of the judges and all the runners-up were invited to dance in his Scandals that year. This famous woman mimic was a *shikker*. This famous male singer slept with boys. This one had twenty stray mutts in his dressing room and once a month one would be found dead in the alley outside. Several of the dancers ended up living off sugar daddies and one she especially got friendly with married a cattle baron in Argentina who beat her to death. 'I avoided the stage-door Johnnies like the plague. Mr. White knew I was repulsed by them and gave me special permission to leave through the lobby.' She was one of the six women to introduce the Charleston and one of the twelve to introduce the black bottom, 'or maybe it was the other way. I know that for one of those dances six girls were on one side of the stage and six on the other. Some of the outfits we had to wear barely covered our bosoms and pubic areas. But I made sure, with skillful pinning or these pink beads I glued on, that my nipples were never exposed, though they were awfully painful to take off.' She danced in two or three movies made in a studio in Long Island City. *The Song and Dance Man* one was called, 'though it was also known as *The George White Scandal Movie*—maybe that was its title.' Helen Morgan and Don Petricola were in it, she thinks. 'There still wasn't sound yet, but when I saw it I seem to remember songs sung and shoes tapping and brief applause. What I remember most is the work I put into it, after spending nine hours at the hospital every day, and the rotten pay.' "

"His mother, after graduating high school, got a job as a medical secretary in the x-ray department at Bellevue. 'I worked personally for Dr. Katzburger, perhaps the foremost roentgenologist of his day. He wrote books and books on it and the governor and high officials of different states and presidents of countries and wealthy and important people like that came to him. I wanted to be a doctor and thought my father, who was totally against it, would change his mind when he saw how well I did at the hospital and was told by professionals there like Dr. Katzburger what a fine doctor I'd make. But he always said "Marry one, don't become one, and you're in the perfect place to meet one. It'll be cheaper and faster, you won't have to work so hard studying and later practicing, and you'll wind up getting just as good medical treatment being married to a doctor as being one, and what would you do with your practice once your babies start to come?" ' "

"His mother's mother was a saint. Mine was. My mother's mother was a saint. The whole lower East Side thought so, my mother said, 'or let me say "the Jewish part of it." Crowded as our apartment was, with nine surviving children, two live-in Polish maids, my parents and an uncle who always lived with us but wasn't really my uncle but my father's boyhood friend from Dembitzer near Lemburg. Bei Lemburg, in German. Or maybe that's where your dad's folks came from and mine were from Christapolia bu Schmetz. I don't know what the 'bu' means, even if I was very good in German in school. Maybe it's Polish. But really, we slept two and three to a bed then, though Uncle Leibush always had his own room. Still, she put total strangers up if she heard they had no place to sleep. And for days to weeks, whole families of landsmen who just came over on the boat with no place to stay, and on holidays she often took poor people off the street to feed, no matter what their origins or religion. Stern as my dad was about most things, he never said boo to this. Maybe because we had all kinds of food cooking nonstop anyway, what with the needs of his bar right downstairs, and the guests never slept anywhere but in the hallway on the floor.' Photos of her mother were always on her dresser. Same with my father's parents on his. She had blue hair in them—'Gray turned blue because of some photographic tinting process,' my mother said. And a big gawdy broach she said had been painted on the photos by the photographer because he thought she looked too plain. 'She had her hair dyed blue for thirty years,' my Aunt Rose said. 'Then it wouldn't go back to its natural color when she wanted it to, which by that time she couldn't find out what it was. The broach was my father's wedding gift, but was missing from her jewelry box after she died. We think my sister Bertha took it when the rest of us were in the funeral home. It was worth thousands even then.' My mother's mother worked full-time in her uncle's bakery as a little girl, became a model for Milgrin's when she was thirteen, 'which even that time,' my mother said, 'was one of the fanciest women's stores though not on Fifty-seventh yet,' married at fifteen and had a dozen children. 'Nine out of twelve was considered a pretty good ratio then, even for someone with a little money and local influence like my dad. So besides being generous to a fault, perhaps, she was also a great beauty—' "

"His grandmother worked as a fashion model for a fancy New York women's store when she was fourteen. She told them she was older. His mother apparently inherited these looks, or maybe she got them from her father who was quite handsome, for she became a beauty contest winner and then a dancer in the Ziegfield Follies. 'I was strictly a dancer, I want you to know—not a showgirl. They had to prance around stark naked at times, while we had enough covering our pubic area where we didn't have to keep it shaved as they did. We also had at least one breast unexposed, if maybe just the nipple part of it with a single black or red or violet bead, depending on the costume color. My nipples were sore because of it for the two full years I was in the show. Your father, once he met me, went to it practically every night. He got front- or second-row seats and a lot of those times he went with his friends—The Filthy Four they were known on the lower East Side as, because of their carousing and womanizing and so forth. He kept doing one terrible thing to me then. He'd wink and wave at me to get my attention whenever I danced on his side of the audience. I got Flo—Mr. Ziegfield—to let me dance as much as possible on the other side of the stage whenever I saw your father there.' 'What happened when he sat in the center, if he ever did?' 'Then I'd keep my regular position and take the abuse. The other girls adjusted to my position switches easily, since we were a great crew, always looking out for one another, which we had to, for the men thought we were all whores. After the show he'd wait for me with the other stage-door Johnnies, but I avoided them like the plague. I got Mr. Flo—he knew I came from a strict family and was a good girl—to give me special permission to leave through the lobby.' 'So when did you really start going with Dad? Or why did you even continue to see him if he acted this way?' 'You should ask first how we met. It's a good story, full of intrigues and laughs. Not romantic, though. Your father was never like that unless he was terribly guilty about something that he had no intention of telling me what. Then he'd just hand them to me— flowers, but a real big bouquet—and turn around and go straight to the dinner table or wash up.' "

"My folks met this way. My father's aunt had a photo of my mother on her mantel. She was in a bathing suit and high-heeled shoes and holding a parasol. The aunt had cut it out of a newspaper, framed it, and when anyone asked who the woman was she said she had it there to show that a beautiful girl with a terrific figure and what was obviously a sparkling personality and great intelligence on her face, could also be Jewish. My father saw it and said he'd love to meet a woman like that, and she told him a neighbor who saw the picture said the girl's father owned a bar and grill on the corner of Delancey and Essex and that when business was really booming the girl worked as the cashier."

"My father's aunt had a photo of him on her mantel. He was on a horse, wore jodhpurs, dark shirt and tie, and held up a riding switch. A cousin of my mother's mother, delivering a dress she made for my father's aunt, asked who the man was and if he was single. There was an eligible young woman in her family and maybe a meeting could be arranged. If it ended in marriage, did she think the young man's father would pay her a matchmaker's fee? 'He's to give you for his boy? It's the girl's father who's supposed to give.' 'But this girl is something out of the ordinary. She's already a great beauty, and her face hasn't even fully formed yet. She's built like a Broadway showgirl, and in fact is one, but only as a lark—she's thinking of becoming a doctor or something in science or law. And she has the intelligence of a genius and personality and liveliness that make you adore her in a flash, besides coming from such fine people that her father spends two months every summer in the most expensive German spas, but only to rest from his investments and business.' 'My nephew is also considered to be a good-looker, as this photo shows, though losing his hair and maybe getting too big a pot too early. He's also the perfect brother and son, giving them anything they want, and is already a dentist with one of the best practices on the lower East Side.' 'If he's that good a catch and something works out between them, perhaps the girl's father will want to give a matchmaker's fee and we'll split it, but without anybody knowing we did.' "

"My father rammed into my mother's brother's parked car outside the Masonic meeting hall they were both going to. He went into the hall, waited till the speaker finished, went to the podium, clinked on a water glass to get the audience's attention and announced he'd banged into such and such car outside and wanted its owner to know he was ready to take care of all the damages and related expenses and even to drive the owner home, since that's how bad a condition the car was in. My mother's brother was so impressed by this, and also the commanding way my father had gone to the podium and spoken and joked in front of so many people, that during the drive home he said he wanted my father to meet his sister."

"My father saw a beauty contest picture of my mother in a newspaper, said to himself 'That's the girl for me, and if I've got as much to offer as people tell me, no reason not to shoot for the best,' thought her last name was familiar, asked around about her, found out who her father was and where she lived and worked. She was a medical secretary in the x-ray department of a big New York hospital. He went there, asked for her, said 'Listen, Miss, I could've done this through a friend—Benny Gernhart, the prizefighter, who says he grew up with you on Rivington and not a nicer girl did he ever know—but I decided to come here myself and say that I fell off my seat when I saw your news picture, am already falling off my feet talking to you for a minute, and if you'll do me the pleasure of coming out to dinner with me any one of these nights, but preferably this one, I'd be extremely honored, and that's no bull, excuse me,' and from behind his back he produced a bouquet of flowers, gave it to her, kissed her other hand, said 'That's something I've never done before, so it must show something, even to me, how I feel about you,' said he'd phone in an hour to see what her decision was, and left."

"My father saw a photo of my mother in a newspaper. She was in a sedate suit and hat, legs crossed, sea and beach behind her. The article said she was the first Jewish girl to win an important New York beauty contest—perhaps the first American Jewess ever to win such a contest—was from the lower East Side, lived with her family, was one of a dozen children, worked as an x-ray technician in a large New York hospital and hoped to win the Miss America contest 'less for myself than for the City.' 'I can't say how beautiful I am—that's for others to judge. But if performing talent is a consideration in the contest, I might have a chance.' He thought 'That's the girl for me if there ever was one,' asked around about her, no one knew who she was, called the x-ray departments of several New York hospitals, one person who answered said he'd get her to the phone. She got on, he said 'Hello, Miss Cole?,' then got cold feet, as he put it, and hung up. Later he said to himself 'Listen, if I've got as much to offer as a lot of people have told me—shrewd mind, decent looks, a good nature, a great practice—no reason why she shouldn't be interested, but not over the phone. I don't speak well over it and my voice comes out sounding too rough. I'm better at face-to-face meetings.' Next day he went to the hospital's x-ray department and was told it was her day off. He went back the next day and said 'Listen, Miss Cole, I hear you're a great x-ray technician—tops in the city, a good friend said. Benny Genhart, he's a ranking lightweight and I think had his hand photographed by you after his last fight.' 'It had to be x-rayed by someone else, since that's not my job.' 'Then maybe he only thought you were a great technician or even the doctor by the way you handled things, but he said you're the person to see. For I've got a foot bone I think's broke and since I'm a dentist who's on his feet all day—my office is in the same neighborhood you're from, Benny said.' 'I don't know this Benny you're speaking of.' 'Then maybe he only said he knows someone who knows you or what you do here, but I'm on Clinton, not far from where I think he said you live.' 'If your foot is broken or needs an x-ray you should see a doctor about it first. Just as someone with a bad tooth would go to you first before thinking of having it x-rayed. Though you do your own x-raying, so the comparison doesn't apply.' 'Look-it, why should I lie? Why start off on the wrong foot with you—and not the broken one— and I don't even have a broken one or even a bad one? How's that for not lying? So I'll start off right. No feet. I saw your newspaper photo last week, went jitters over it, kept it under my pillow for several days—OK. That's a fib too. I just folded it up and stuck it in my jacket pocket here. It says you live on the lower East Side, which is where I'm from and now have my dental practice. I showed the photo to some friends—I do know Benny Genhart. We went to grammar school together and I fix his teeth for free. He always needs plenty of work on them too, in his line, but he wasn't one of the ones I spoke to about you. I asked if anyone knew you or how I could arrange to personally meet you. This is the truth now, but cut my tongue out for the harm it's going to do me with you for admitting it, and someone—Tommy Rosenblatt. No, no Tommy anything. No such name. Another fib. I just checked around. Called to different hospitals' x-ray departments, is about it, and this one said you worked here. So I came over yesterday—maybe you heard. Came back today, obviously, and, to sum it up, I'm not at all disappointed in what I'm finding and I'd like very much to go out with you. This afternoon for lunch, even, which I'll cancel all my appointments for, or anytime you like.' She said 'I don't go out with strangers, especially ones who learned of me through a news article, and now I've got to return to work, so good-bye.' He followed her down a hall, saying 'Look-it, I know my approach was all wrong with you.' . . . It's not my usual way. . . I'm usually so quiet and polite. . . .Well, that's not entirely the case. . . . But I was just so taken with you and now I want to do anything I can to make things right again, OK?' She said 'First of all, not that this is any of your business, but I've been seeing someone quite exclusively for the last few months. And secondly, do I have to ask the resident on this floor to get you to stop following me?' He said he was sorry for disturbing her, even sorrier to hear there was already a man in her life, bowed and left. He wrote her several apologies that week. She didn't answer. He phoned her at work and home and when he told her who it was she hung up. One time he gave a fake name to her mother who answered, and when she got on the phone and found out it was he, she hung up. He sent her flowers at work every day for a week. She sent a note to his office thanking him for the flowers and saying they cheered up a lot of patients in the men's and women's wards where she had taken them without ever unwrapping them, but would he now please not send any more? She couldn't go out with him, she didn't see any reason why there should ever be further contact between them, but if he persists then the next people she speaks to about him will be the police. He went to her father's café for dinner every weekday night for a week, hoping to catch a glimpse of her. If he did and she saw him, and he'd try to make sure she did, he'd stand up, bow, pay the check—if she was the cashier and he'd managed to avoid looking at her till the end of the meal, he'd just bow and put the money on the table—and leave. He thought this might do something to make her a little curious about him. She came in the last night he thought he'd go there. The moment she saw him, and before he could stand up, she turned around, went over to her father, still with her back to him pointed in his direction and said something angrily, and left. Her father and several waiters gave him dirty looks for the rest of the dinner but never spoke to him about it and her father went into the kitchen when he got up to pay and leave. He wrote her a letter next day apologizing for his actions the past weeks, said they wouldn't be repeated and offered to give free dental checkups and treatments to her and her family for as long as they liked. He didn't hear from her, didn't expect to, and started seeing other women. About a year later he parked his car the same time her brother parked his in front of the men's social club they were both going to. Her brother's license plate had MD on it, his had DDS, as they went into the club they talked about where their offices were and what kind of practices they had and later exchanged cards in case the patients of one might need the services of the other. My father asked if he was related to what must be a former Miss New York by now. The brother said the title wasn't anything the family was proud of and his father still didn't know and would probably throw her out of the house if he did. Worse, she was now dancing almost nude in the Scandals, which if his father knew he'd drag her by her hair off the stage he wouldn't care in front of how many people. The brother had tried talking her out of it. Then tried keeping her from making some performances by locking her in the bedroom and bathroom. But she got out through the fire escape once and the other times banged the door so hard—their father worked in his bar and cafe downstairs and they were afraid he might hear—that their mother told him to let her go. My father told him what a fool he'd made of himself with her a year ago. The brother recalled it, was sure she never thought of it anymore, said she'd dropped the boyfriend she was so serious with then. They became friends— 'Because I liked him,' my father said, 'not to get to her; that I gave up on forever.' The brother told her about him, said what a likable

clever fellow he was, that he had a big booming practice, how
ashamed he was of the way he'd acted toward her then, and advised
her to go out with him if he asked, though he hadn't mentioned her
name or even alluded to her since that first time at the club. She
said 'Keep it that way. Don't so much as suggest he contact me. For
certain never invite him home.' My father introduced the brother to
a woman friend and they got engaged in a few months. My father
was invited to the wedding. My mother said she wouldn't go. But
this was her favorite brother, the one she always looked up to. 'People
used to think,' she's said to me, 'that we were girlfriend and
boyfriend, we went to so many places together and were so close.'
My father nodded to her when she came down the aisle as one of
the bridesmaids. 'I ignored it.' He asked her to dance at the reception.
'I knew he would and had rehearsed what I'd say: a definitive and
perhaps also a vociferous no. But I was sitting at the wedding table,
everyone was laughing and very happy and I didn't want to dampen
things in any way, so I accepted. As I walked to the dance floor with
him I told myself I'd let him know how I felt regarding any other
dances or conversation or nodding of heads between us. But I'd also
had a bit of champagne by that time and I wasn't used to it. I rarely
touched alcohol till I was around forty, when your father got into
trouble. So maybe I was a little tipsy, but I don't think that's what
made me change my mind about him so quickly. He danced very
well and I had always loved to dance. His hands were very soft. They
were always that way till he gave up dentistry. That came from the
many washings of them with a special pink soap solution before he
treated each patient. I don't think he ever used any other. After he
died I gave the last three gallons of it to a relief agency that was
collecting old dental equipment for hospitals in Africa. He smelled
nice too and his cheeks were very smooth. From a barber-shaving,
I guess, but I never asked him, or if I did, I forgot what he said.
He also looked very handsome in a tuxedo. His hair was cut perfectly,
what he had of it. His skin was tanned from a weekend in Lakewood
the previous week when he did nothing but ride horses and swim

and sun. He was also extremely polite. Not at all pushy and brash as he was in the hospital and from that time on. Everyone there seemed to like him. 'Hi Simon, Hiya Doc,' other couples on the floor kept saying, and several people slapped his back as we danced past. We went to the bar for more champagne after our second or third dance and I could see right away, just in how he joked with the bartender and the people around us, that he got along with everyone and would be lots of fun. Maybe that was just the professional pose he'd developed—making the patient feel comfortable under stressful conditions and also to get new patients. But it was still nice, that night, to be with so popular a guy. Also what I liked, which came from what he said and Uncle Leonard had told me about him, was that he was a wonderful brother and son: generous and attentive. And someone, like me, who wanted a half-dozen children at least, so it turned out there were things and thoughts we had in common. After—during our first date, when he was wearing normal clothes again and maybe hadn't just come from the barber's. Even before that, when I opened the door of our apartment to let him in that first time—he seemed much too fat and bald and plain looking for me. And the thought of seeing a man who has his hands in people's mouths all day was a little sickening, but I got over that after he told me how often he washed them. But there was still something powerful and warm about him that first night. Though we never had any experiences together before we got married, I always had the feeling he was a real man. Also, my brother getting married must have contributed to my change of mind that wedding night and for my quickly changing it again on our first date. So you can say it was a number of things that did it. Even that he had a flashy new car. He and Uncle Leonard were two of the few men on the lower East Side to have one then. No, I've got it wrong. I'm talking of around 1917, when your father became a dentist and said he bought his first car.' "

"My father and my mother's brother parked in the same lot near their offices. My father was a dentist, Uncle Leonard a doctor. This was in 1923 or '24. They got to know each other during their walks from the lot to their offices. They kept their cars in a private lot because they were often vandalized or stolen off the street in the neighborhood their offices were in. My father always had the matchmaker in him. Nothing gave him greater pleasure than bringing people together, he said, except making a bundle of money in one killing. 'Through my practice I knew or knew of lots of single people, and because I felt I was a good judge of character, it was easy for me to hook them up. If it worked out and they happened to throw a new suit my way or a weekend in Lakewood for me because they were so happy, I didn't refuse it.' He introduced Uncle Leonard and Aunt Teddy. She was the daughter of a diamond dealer whose teeth he took care of and who'd told him he was looking for a professional man as a husband for his daughter and was prepared to give a huge cash dowry. 'I knew he meant me. But when I saw her picture I knew she wasn't my type, so I thought of Uncle Leonard, whose practice wasn't doing too hot. He was a good G.P. but like the rest of your mother's family, had no personality.' My uncle was urging my mother to go out with my father who was attracted to her. She was a beauty contest winner, had been top of her class at Washington Irving, worked as a medical secretary days and danced in a Forty-second Street review nights and matinees, and wanted to be an architect or lawyer. Uncle Leonard brought my father over the house several times but she never took to him. 'He was bald and fat and though he had a nice small nose he wasn't that good looking, I told my brother. And he'll only get balder and fatter and like everybody's nose, it was sure to grow. I had an image of a slim elegant handsome man for a husband, with a head of hair. And because I wasn't looking for one then and was considered quite pretty and intelligent and my father was reasonably well off, I didn't say boo to him, though practically speaking I knew he was a good catch.' My uncle continued to press her. ' "Just for lunch once," he said, "and if there's no spark, I won't nag you again." There wasn't for me. He was entertaining and personable enough but I felt he'd never be someone I'd be deeply interested in. His mother was everything to him, for one thing, so I knew his wife would always come up short. But he pushed and pushed. Phoned every day. Sent my mother and me expensive presents and flowers. Wined and dined me, few times I consented to go. And he made my dad laugh hysterically whenever he was around him, while no one else had ever got a ride out of him. And my brother, whom I worshiped—he used to say your father was a diamond in the rough who only needed a touch of polishing from me. But he kept insisting he was the most dependable good-natured well-heeled man any girl of my background and education and now "age," since I was falling on twenty-two, could hope to find and that my Dad would never let me go back to school. So, one thing led to another. I never did find him that attractive in all our years of marriage, except when we were dressing formal. He really put time and money on himself then, no handkerchiefs hanging out of his pants pockets, and the shiny black clothes hid his fatness and made him sort of more graceful. There was another beau though whom I was attracted to then. Henry Morton, who was as distinguished and proper as his name, which I think was something else shortly before I met him. Messer or Moscowitz. Maybe if he'd been a little more of a rough-and-tumble guy your father was I would have tried harder to land him. But he acted like a neuter and wanted to amass a fortune before be settled down, and he was only starting out then. He cried uncontrollably when I told him I was marrying your father, but made no counteroffer. If he had I think I would have run off with him, despite what it might have done to my family. He later had children, I understand, so it wasn't as if he couldn't do anything. After I'd had my first two and was very pregnant with you—no matter how hard I dieted you grew and grew and coming out nearly killed me—he came to Prospect Park right across where we lived to ask me to leave your father. As a joke I said "The kids?" and he said "We'll have our own soon after you have that one." I remember the afternoon clearly. It was bright, sunny and warm. The girl had her midweekly half day off, so it had to be Wednesday. Your brothers were in a sandbox. He popped out of nowhere, I was on a bench knitting, and said he was going to the zoo or just dawdling around taking in the meadows. Later he said he'd been coming out to spy on me for two weeks and had even peeked through the blinds to see me resting in bed. We lived on the first floor of an apartment house: Vera Court it was called, which is how I got the name for your sister. He said he hadn't made his fortune yet but was getting there, and had never stopped loving me, and so on. Seeing how I saw myself as a big block of blubber then it was a nice feeling to be thought of so desirously, even if I didn't like him asking me to give up my children for him. I wondered what he would have asked me to do with you once you were weaned. When I said I couldn't go away with him, even if he agreed to taking along my two-and-a-half children, he cried like a faucet again and that was the last I saw of him, running screaming out of the park and across the avenue, with cars stopping and dodging all around him, or at least by the sounds of their tires and horns I thought they were. For a few days I read the obituary pages thinking he might have killed himself. Anyway, that night I told your father. He said the man must be crazy or was drunk but he'll come out of it. Sometime after he pointed out a wedding announcement of Henry with a girl from high society. Her family—known anti-Semites—couldn't have known he was Jewish. Even the last name of his deceased parents had been changed to his for the announcement. Your father wanted to send an anonymous note to the girl's parents that Henry's real first name was probably Chaime or Herschel—he didn't like anyone but himself getting away with anything. In the end he spoke appreciatively of him as a swindler but not as a man who made it on his own as he had.' "

"My mother had a sweetheart when she got engaged to my father: Howard Morton. I was around forty when she told me this and I said 'Howard, the same as mine? What was that all about?' 'Maybe it was Herbert, or Henry. No, it was Howard. I never thought of that before.' 'You mean you didn't name me after him?' 'Of course not. Maybe deep down I remembered what a distinguished-sounding name it was. In fact, I can almost bet it helped get him where he got. For I'm sure without it or an equally distinguished first name, and a plain enough last one to go with it, he wouldn't have passed as a gentile and got into society and rich because of it. He ended up owning trains. I suppose I thought the same thing, in different ways, would happen to you. At the least that people would look up to you a bit more. Little did I know we were coming into an age where people got ridiculed for lofty first names or if they didn't have one that could be shortened to a single syllable and that Jews with the most Jewish names and faces could get into gentile society without passing.' "

"My mother liked to recall going to the silent movies as a kid. The tickets for anyone under ten were two for five cents. 'I'd stand outside the theater holding up my two cents and say "I got two, anybody got three?" Then some girl or boy would say "I got three," and we'd buy the double ticket and go in together.' " No, that was his father.

"His father kept calling, visiting, sent flowers, jewelry, offered to straighten or cap her and her sisters' teeth free, took her to the best shows, restaurants and nightclubs, professed his love every way and any time he could, in taxis, on the street, during intermissions and over food, said he'd make an adoring idolizing husband, she said she'd rather have her spouse ignore or even take a swing at her than that, said 'OK, no down-on-my-knees like a big jerk and painting your toenails: just solid soulmate loving and lionlike lovemaking or some tumultuous unbridled jungle or forest beast,' she said 'Please, where do you get these ideas?—not from me,' said he wanted to have five children by her, girls and boys, and when she said she'd always wanted ten and the major majority of them boys but was definitely not thinking of them from him, said 'Ten then—I can afford to. You won't have to lift a finger. The best hospitals and docs and after-they're-born care. The world? You got it. On a silver platter.' She said that was an awful figure of speech. That heads belonged on silver platters. Cooked turkeys. Aspic molds. 'No, you're nice and bright and I admire what you've done with your life. From no-shoes-in-the-summer-to-save-on-the-shoe-leather to sending yourself through dental school while working at the post office ten hours a day and ending up with one of the biggest practices on the lower East Side as you say, but we can only go so far at being good companions and friends. I know lots of pretty girls. I'll introduce you.' 'Maybe I set my sights too high, but only you.' Her father wouldn't let her go to college to get a profession so she got work for little pay as a secretary. 'You're beautiful and you're built well and you're not as stupid as most girls your age,' her father said, 'but your looks won't last forever and you haven't got enough upstairs to only get along on your brains after. Marry him. He's a smart guy and makes everybody laugh. All in all he's the best of the fifty or so beaus you've had. And that he's crazy for you means you'll never have to do a stitch of laundering or sewing and looking after your children if you don't want. You like to read books and go to shows? You'll have all the time you want now, and stuff you buy from bookshops and not have to get from the library, plus two-month summer vacations in the mountains with your kids. Nannies. The boats these days are packed with them, most just wanting a few dollars a week plus room and board. Clean Irish and German girls who'll bring up your children like princesses and chairmen of the board, but with an iron fist so they're not crawling all over you when they're sick or should be asleep.' Finally she said yes. 'I'm not sure why. He wasn't that bad looking. He had very strong but at the same time delicate hands. He bathed a lot, never smelled. He was humorous and shrewd with money and had a certain animal something that I think as much as any man's matched mine. Nine years older than I but he thought young and seemed in relative good health and didn't drink that much. Deeply drawn to him? Everybody knew me. No man was ever good enough, but I have to admit some excited me a lot more. Maybe because nobody pursued me harder, so I just gave up. If that was it, I must have been nuts.' They got engaged, broke up. He didn't want her to return the ring but his mother sent his aunt to her house to get it. 'I knew I could do better. And with someone who wasn't as fat and bald and hadn't such a sure-to-ruin-your-life mother. And who still didn't have this thing about his poor past where he had to wipe his nose with coarse paper towels he took in big chunks from restaurants and public toilets and day after day refolded and used the same brown bag he packed his lunch in till it was practically in shreds. Her father said 'You marry him or I'm throwing you into the street and never letting you back. I was never this dumb since I was a boy but I already gave his mother half the dowry money and now she's calling it earnest gelt and won't give any of it back.' Engaged again. 'I'm not sure why. My father and brother and that he came to where I worked and said he still wanted my hand and kept sniffling and drooling till I had to say yes so he'd stop. If I had learned later it was all a ruse, just to get a beautiful woman for a wife and as he said to up the odds that he'd have beautiful children, I would have killed him.' Before she met him she'd won several beauty contests, almost became Miss America, danced in the Scandals and then the Follies on Broadway and in a few movies. Turned down a dinner invitation from the Prince of Wales. 'The type I liked least: a rich roué and lush. He was very gracious when Flo introduced us, and I was told he'd singled me out of the line and then got even more excited when he heard I was well read, but his face was already so depraved that just shaking his hand I didn't know what I'd catch from him. Now I wish I had accepted. Not for any ideas about being the First Wallis Simpson—he wasn't ready for that for years and it'd be too far-fetched to think he'd choose Jewish—but to have had the story.' Wealthy women and men sent her flowers and expensive presents backstage but she returned all the presents and devised ways not to even bump into them after the show, for she said they were hungry wolves out after just one thing. 'Who wanted to be another pearl on an already lengthy strand? That's what my mother told me she used to think when she modeled for Milgrin's when she was fourteen and every man who came in with his mistress or wife tried to paw her behind. Creeps then, creeps in my time, no doubt creeps now and forever. As for women with women, lots of the other dancers did it and sometimes just for fun they said, but to me nothing could be more repulsive.' His father sat in the front rows or overhanging front loges of the theater almost every night during the last weeks of her stage dancing which was around when he met her. 'He came in with his cronies—all of them dentists—and said they waved and winked and occasionally whistled and clapped at me whenever I danced near. It never distracted me since I couldn't see them because of the footlights. And I was deaf on my left side where they usually sat—their right—from when a grade-school teacher smacked me when I talked back. Oh, I was always a devil. I don't know what happened to me.' Her brother-in-law stole their car during the wedding reception. His father had bought it new that week, morning of the wedding parked it in front of the wedding hall, planned to drive it to Atlantic City with her after the reception, then back to Manhattan next day to board a ship for a two-week cruise to Cuba. 'We had it at the Academy of Music, with their orchestra. My mother-in-law wanted Klezmer. That's what her daughter had at hers and I guess it also brought back her blissful old village life filled with ignorance, beatings and poverty, but my father wouldn't hear of it. He wanted couples to dance, maybe a tango or turkey trot or two but mostly civil waltzes. To him there was nobody in the world like Emperor Franz Josef. He had a neighbor do a needlepoint of him in parade dress on a horse, which hung in our living room, and wore his Franz Josef mustache and had many of his mannerisms for fifty years. So he said to her "If you insist they be there, have them come out without their instruments. Just to drink and eat and dance and throw up in the lavatories," which they did. He was a great sport with money and minced no words. The Academy was the swankiest place we could have had it at then, not being old-time Yankee Doodle Jews, and it was done completely kosher. That was against my father's eating tastes and his beliefs and jacked up the price of the reception by more than half, but my mother-in-law, who loved pork and brains at our house, wouldn't come to it if it was any other way. Your father even had to buy his brother a tux for the wedding, and the most expensive there was or he wouldn't show, plus buy his mother a diamond watch exactly like mine and diamond earrings in place of my engagement ring. They had him under their palm, that family, except for his father who was a sweet schnook.' Or his uncle got someone to steal the car, but to use it to transport bootleg whiskey. 'He slipped out of the party and was gone for hours. Nobody missed him since we had more than two hundred people there, with Cantor Rosenblatt, perhaps the finest cantor of his day and still at the top of his voice, singing during the ceremony. It would be like having Jan Peerce and Richard Tucker both during their heyday. They were brothers-in-law, you know, but I forget which one married whose sister. This was all during Prohibition. In fact Uncle Lewis got my father all the liquor for the party—Dad had folded his bar long ago when he couldn't get liquor legally—but weeks before. My sister was in on that car. Two connivers. She proably said "Go now, I'll cover for you, it's the fuchsia one right outside, anybody ask for you I'll say you ran off with the bride." She's OK today, too blind and weak to joke or cheat at anything but getting a second shower at her nursing home, but he never stopped being in the rackets till he died. The Syndicate, then Murder Incorporated. For all we know he carried out the contracts or did the body disposing—one of those, or maybe you graduate. I forget what Brooklyn bay most of those bodies ended up in, but it was famous for a while. New York Jewish boys were very big in that then. My brother Robert used to say half his childhood friends ended up in prison and the other half in law school. Whenever he went to Sing Sing to see a client, ten other men in the halls there would yell out "Hiya Bobby, remember me from Rivington or Cannon Street or P.S. 62?" Lewis once showed us his gun, trying to impress us—he was a little guy so it made him feel strong. But your father told him Lepke himself was a patient of his and that whenever he treated him he demanded he leave his guns in a locked cabinet just for them in his laboratory. Gurah's teeth he'd never treat as he heard he stabbed his dentist from the chair once for no other reason but that the novocaine didn't completely take. They found the car while we were in Cuba. It stunk so such from whiskey that we had to almost give it away. That was pre-vinyl and before fabric treatment, so the cloth just soaked it in. There was even blood on the seats, but probably from one of the many broken bottles in it. The homemade Prohibition whiskey was bottled in the cheapest glass. So we took the train to Atlantic City—Lewis and Ellie in front of the Academy throwing rice at us as we left—or borrowed someone's car. Or someone drove us there that night and we took the train back to the ship the next day. Something about cars and trains sticks in my mind though.' "

" 'You won't believe this,' my mother told me. 'No one would if I swore on a stack of bibles and had motion pictures with sound on them plus six of the most reputable witnesses. Your father called his mother on our wedding night to say I was a virgin. Right from the hotel room. It must have been 2:00 A. M., or maybe it was seven or eight, so the next day. He thought I was still asleep. He just sat at the edge of the bed, placed the call through the lobby desk and whispered in Yiddish to her "She's all right, one piece." Then I heard her say back in Yiddish "Good, for tragedy for you and me and everyone connected with your marriage if she was anything but." Your father taught me Yiddish just so I could speak to her. I'd taken German in high school and did well at it so I had a head start. Every other day for an hour he sat down with me for conversation in it. First the curses: *Gehn bud* and so on. Then a few weeks before the marriage he asked me to have my father get me tutors for several hours a day because I wasn't learning fast enough to be fluent by the time of the wedding. She was an ignorant woman. Let's face it: a tough shrewd illiterate peasant who loved what she was and never wanted to be anything else. Who wouldn't even learn our yes or please or thank you. His father, who got out in the world more as a darner and weaver, at least spoke some broken English and apologized for not knowing more. You of course know you're named after her: Hinda—Howard. It was the last thing I wanted to do, but she died three months before you were born. I always hated to say this, but that was the happiest pregnancy I had. With Vera, which should have been the best since I had nine months free of my mother-in-law, your father was already in trouble.' "

"My mother talking: 'My mother and mother-in-law were sitting at the main wedding table with me. "Let me see the nice jewelry Simon gave you," my mother-in-law said. So I held my hands out to show her the diamond watch and engagement ring, both of which she'd seen ten times before, but never in front of my mother. I say "my mother," since if my father was at the table at the time she never would have asked it. She knew he'd see right through her immediately and tell her off. Oh, my father was on to her from the start. He was born of peasants but moved himself to the city quickly and became a man of the world. Anyway, all this was in Yiddish, you understand. Not my mother. Besides English she spoke Polish and German, but never in front of us. That they only did when they got into fierce arguments. Then my mother-in-law said "Why don't you take them off so I can really have a look at them?" So I took the ring and watch off and held them out. She took them and turned them over and over and said things like "Very nice, very expensive, my son has very good tastes and knows how to take care of a lady. Listen, my darling," she said, "let me hold them for you while you're on your honeymoon. I heard those Spanish islands can be very unsafe places for Americans," and she started putting them in her bag. Did I let her? You must think I was crazy. She wanted to keep them to see if I was going to be a virgin that night. If your father told her I wasn't, and he'd never lie to her on anything, she would make him leave me and she'd keep the jewelry. And if she was told I was a virgin, which I was but she never believed him because of my good looks and dancing in all those Broadway shows and with almost nothing on sometimes, she would have kept the jewelry anyway because she would have said he was lying to protect me.

So I told her no, if I feel unsafe before we go I'll let my mother hold them for me. And if I don't feel unsafe till we're on the cruise, I'll leave them in a safe they must have on the ship. That way I kept my jewelry. And when he told her the next morning I was a virgin—called her just for that purpose, right from the hotel lobby phone before we went in for breakfast—she had no reason to argue with him about it. As it was, I had to sell all my good jewelry months after your father went on trial, as the lawyer costs and your father not working had made us almost dead broke. Good thing she was gone by then or she would have died during the trial or when he went to prison. What am I saying?—she'd never let anything hurt herself. She would have just pretended she got some kind of heart attack, and then he would have got very sick over it in prison and perhaps died. Maybe I'm being too hard on her, but for the first ten years of my marriage that woman ruined my life. If ever there was a real witch in this world....Well, I could tell you stories.' "

"A story his mother liked to tell. 'Make what you want of this. I suppose it shows what a devil I was. I was playing hooky. First time too, and I walked around the neighborhood, feeling free but not really finding anything interesting to do—I always had to be stimulated—so I walked around my school a few times. Dumb of me when you think of it, but I was probably trying to make some point. I was pigheaded and a tomboy too. So I yelled up to Miss Brody's window—the assistant principal and a real doll. She'd say "Your principal is your pal; that's also how to spell it." I loved her. Always very kind to me. I yelled "Miss Brody, Miss Brody, here I am"—she wasn't Irish, you know. Brody could be a Jewish name. From a town in Poland where they congregated. They came over here. The immigration official would try to pronounce their names—Dyzik, Pytzik—and say "I can't say it, how am I supposed to spell it?" So he'd look at their cards which had where they were from and what shots they got and say "Brody, you're from Brody so your name's now Brody, a good American one." You didn't fight it, if you could in English, since you were afraid of being detained another week or sent back. She was the first Jewish assistant principal in the system, it was said. The public schools were dominated by the Irish then. They probably thought she was one with that name, but it's surprising it first went to a woman. Maybe because there were so few Jewish men teachers because the pay was so bad. Worse than anyone's. But if they didn't know she was Jewish, then really no surprise, because they probably had about a dozen Irish women assistant principals by then, so what was one more? But I yelled "You can't see me, Miss Brody, but I can see you." I couldn't, but that's what I kept yelling to get her attention. "I'm playing hooky, Miss Brody, what do you think of that? I'm not going to school today or any other day, or if I do, only for a day a week and only the day I want." I'm telling you, I was something. She finally came to the window and said "You come straight upstairs, dear, or you'll be in deep trouble, I hate to say." I said something like "Why should I? I'm having too much fun walking around free as a bird." Just then she said "Watch out, dear, someone's coming," and slammed the window. Everyone knew my father and was afraid of him. He was out for his daily hour stroll from his café. Cane he didn't need, for show, always the freshly blocked homburg. I thought it was the truant officer she meant and started to run. But he had already come up behind me and put the hook part of the cane around my neck, grabbed me by the scruff of it and marched me into the school right up to Miss Brody's office. Then he threw me on the floor there and said "You're too easy on her. She yells like that from the street at you or stays out of school without our permission, this is what you do," and he lifted me up by my hair and slapped me hard on my left ear. Oh, I heard ringing and buzzing, besides all the pain, and when the noises stopped I heard him saying "And maybe even harder to her, maybe much harder. She'll learn, and her parents will only thank you if you smack her like that. That's a promise." I was deaf in that ear for weeks, but he wouldn't let my mother take me to a doctor for it. I still only have about ten to twenty percent of my hearing there. Maybe it was because of his slap. But maybe it was bad before that and his slap made it worse. I don't want to apologize for him but I do want to be fair. Or maybe it was always that bad, from birth, or even before, and we only became aware of it after he slapped me and I started complaining I couldn't hear in that ear, to take some of the blame of playing hooky off me. And then who knows? Maybe I was a hundred percent deaf in that ear before he hit me and his hitting me improved it by ten to twenty percent, but still made us realize my hearing problem. I don't remember any hearing problems before, but that's not saying there wasn't. Probably not. But Miss Brody. She was a lovely person. The first to urge me to be a doctor or lawyer or something substantial. But she never so much as touched me after that when before she used to hug me whenever she saw me in the halls or so. And other times shove or nudge me gently when she thought I wasn't doing things just right when she knew I had it in me to.' "

"His mother: 'Something very eventful early in my life? Let me think. Anything—right?—but which stuck and not just remembered now. This one I've thought of a hundred times since. I was no more than thirteen. My mother sent me to Fourteenth Street to buy dresses for my sisters, both the older and younger ones. I took the trolley and went to Rothenburg's and Hearn's, the two big stores there. Off Broadway. They had a walkway a number of floors up connecting across the street two of the buildings of one of those stores. A very new thing for its time and I liked looking at it and imagining things.' 'Like what?' 'People walking across, looking down at me, wondering what I was looking up at. I think the walkway is still there. I went to both stores to comparison shop. Then after seeing what they had in dresses, I bought them, maybe stopped at some outside stand-up place for a tea and cake, for she also gave me money for that, and went home.' 'Yes. So?' 'That's all. It was a pleasant day that I took the trolley and did all this. I don't remember that but she wouldn't have sent me in the snow or rain. I would have got wet, then a cold because I was so prone, and the trolley stop was three blocks from our building, so the boxes would have also got soaked.' 'You had to carry all this. Wasn't it too much?' 'I was always very strong, and at thirteen, maybe near my strongest.' 'Did you resent doing all this while your sisters weren't?' 'Why? It was probably only two or three boxes with the five dresses in them—four for my sisters and one for me. So with twine holding them both or two and one for each hand or all three together, it couldn't have been too hard. Besides, the trip was interesting—the building bridge, the trolley rides—so something I'd say they missed out on.' 'Well did anything happen on the trolley? It break down? Something you saw from it like a horse from a horsecar bolting or breaking loose and you got scared?' 'Not that I remember.' 'Did you get lost or anything like that?' 'Depends which time you meant. I did this every spring for about five years till I was eighteen.' 'Then the first time. For instance, maybe you forgot this but did a man make a pass at you on the trolley or streets or in a store because you were already so beautiful and filled out, according to your photos? Or someone molest you, even, let's say, or just winked at you and you didn't know what it meant and got scared?' 'No.' 'Then someone try to cheat you out of your money in or out of the stores?' 'I'm sure people didn't do that as much then, at least to young and old people. I told you what happened on the street and then with the bank last month with my checkbook and a Ginnie Mae?' 'Unbelievable. I don't know how it could have happened.' 'What don't you know or believe?' 'I mean I know it happened and how. But that someone would try to take out, or whatever one does with a Ginnie Mae, though I'm not quite sure what a Ginnie Mae is, and not get caught when he was standing next to the banker at the time she called you to see if you had authorized that check? That's what happened, right?' 'First he ripped the handbag off my arm. So fast I didn't even see his face. I've no idea even how old he is, and nobody else did who saw him, or they wouldn't say so. My shoulder ached from that wrenching for a week. Then the same day, maybe four hours later when I'm still shaking over it, he or one of his pals tries to open a Ginnie Mae with a check that was in my bag. The banker only called me because there's a state or federal law—

something—maybe that particular bank's policy after seeing so many people like me swindled like this—saying any check five thousand and over has to be cleared with the account's owner. Suppose he'd just made the checkout for four thousand nine-hundred and nine-nine?' 'Maybe there's a five thousand minimum on a Ginnie Mae.' 'Anyway, I said no, that I'd never written a cheek that high in my life and for her not to accept it,' and hung up and only then realized it had to be from the checkbook in my stolen bag. And also that I hadn't only not asked what her name was but what bank she was with, though she did give me all that when she first got on and say it was way out on Long Island. You know, me and memory, which with new things only get further apart. Maybe, because she said she'd get back to me in a day or so, I didn't ask her name and bank again, but she never did. I've a strong feeling she was in on the whole thing.' 'Why?' 'That she never called back. That I never heard from the police. Five thousand. That's major fraud. You read where the FBI comes in on things that high. Besides, as a banker she has ways of checking if I have five thousand and over in my account, which I do but shouldn't. People say I should put most of it in Money Market or CDs.' 'Well, if you do have more in it than you need for your checks, sure. But if she was involved, why would she have first called you? And why would the check have been made out for five thousand instead of four thousand five-hundred, for instance?' 'What do you mean?' 'If banks only make these authorization calls for five-thousand-and-over checks, then she wouldn't have had to call you if this one was for forty-five hundred.' 'That I haven't figured out yet. Maybe she doesn't have a bank way of finding out how much I have in my account and was only finding out this way.' 'How?' 'By saying "Did you make out a check for five thousand?" And if I had said "Five thousand? I'm lucky to have five hundred in my account," she wouldn't have bothered. No? Wrong? Anyway, that's not what I said. And I never got back the check she mentioned or heard anything more about it from anyone. If they caught him, this check swindler, or even if he ran away when she was making that call to me, she still would have had the check he left, if he left it, and I should have got it back by now, right?' 'I'd think so but I don't know.' 'So where is it then? She's in on it, I'm telling you, and I'm worried for my money. For myself too, because just by talking to me she knows I'm an old muddleheaded cow and therefore vulnerable, and she also knows a lot about how much money I have. Not just the checking account but probably the savings, stocks, how much Social Security I have coming in. She could use her expertise and all those computer machines banks have and pull the wool over my eyes.' 'Really, I'm sure it's nothing like that. But maybe I should phone all the banks on Long Island till I get one that knows what happened to your check.' 'Sure, call, run up a two hundred dollar phone bill for yourself. Suffolk and Nassau counties are long distance and unreasonably high compared to phone rates for places of much greater distances. And what'll it get you? Even if you get the right bank, think you'll get the right person? And if you do and it's our Miss Possibility Bank Fraud, think she'll give you the right information? You won't even know you got her, is what I'm saying, and she'll steer you around till you're dizzy and lost and give up hope. The truth is, so you won't be worried about me, I'm not that worried, as I closed the account right after her call and opened another one. So she couldn't touch my money with the old check if she tried, and with the new checks I'm never going to carry the checkbook around. Just one or two checks from it in my wallet, which will be one less load to carry in my bag.' 'But if they get your bag they'll get your wallet. Did you have your wallet in the bag that guy stole?' 'Sure, with everything—money, laundry tickets, library card, card to get me on the subways and buses for half price—but no credit cards. Those I keep in their own pouch that I'd forgotten at home.' 'I was wondering, since you never spoke of it. But I just thought of something. Did you have your checkbook balanced on its transactions' page?' 'Yes, always. I do it after I write each check. You know me: meticulous.' 'Then that's how the thief knew how much you had in it. Believe me, take out three-month CDs with most of your money in it. Keep two thousand at the most in your check account. Then if you need cash suddenly, other than what your Social Security brings, use one of the CDs after it matures. And if it's two months away from maturing and you don't want to be penalized for cashing it in early, borrow from me till it matures. Or I'll give you whatever you need when you need it—no borrowing. You were plenty generous with me when I was short to broke, so why not, when Denise and I can afford it? But you won't go for that idea, so the best thing is to have several three-month CDs running in a way where one matures every month or semimonthly. That way you'll always have cash available. And it won't get complicated, as the bank lets you know a week or so before the CD matures and then rolls it over automatically if you don't cash it in.' 'I'll think about it.' 'Please. Or do something, if not that, with most of your checking money so it earns a good interest. But listen—about the other thing. I'm still not clear why the shopping-on-Fourteenth-Street story stands out in your mind so much.' 'When?' 'The one you gave me when I asked you to tell me something memorable—eventful—from your childhood. Your mother—the dresses and trolleys.' 'Maybe because she trusted me and liked my tastes. She always did.' 'That's fine, and it must have made you feel very good that she did and not the others, your sisters, but is that really the only reason you remember so well the first time she asked you to do it?' 'That's all. I think it's enough.''OK, but I'm not going to use it. No disrespect to what you remember and how you value it and such, but nothing there or just not enough.' "

"She's coming home from shopping. Two shopping bags—too much to carry—but it was a nice day so instead of ordering by phone and getting perhaps not their best produce and paying a five dollar service charge, she went to the supermarket and of course bought too much. A man comes up behind her as she starts down the steps to her brownstone. She turns around quickly, says 'Yes?' He says 'Nothing, lady, what's with you? I'm only going inside.' 'May I ask what your business is in this building? You don't live here.' 'No, I'm visiting a friend.' 'Who?' 'A man—a guy I know.' 'What's his name? I know all the tenants here.' 'This one just moved in,' and he goes past her, into the vestibule and rings several bells. She puts down her bags, opens the vestibule door and keeps it open with one foot and says from the outside 'You rang more than one bell. That doesn't seem as if you're ringing your friend.' 'He told me his bell's not working so to ring a few others to get in.' Someone on the intercom says 'Hello?' 'I'm looking for Bob,' the man says. 'No Bob here,' and the person cuts off. 'I know he's there,' the man says to her. 'Maybe he's in the bathroom. I'll go in with you and knock on his door.' 'What floor is he on?' 'I know what floor. The one above this one or the next. It has a little peephole in it, I think.' He thinks a moment. 'That's right, it has.' 'There's a law in this city that every apartment's front door has to have a peephole in it, not that every landlord complies with it. This one has though. And there isn't any Bob in the building. No Robert, Rob, Bobby—no name like that. I even know the men who live with the single women in the building, and the names of the two sons of the married couple. No Bobs. I'm sorry but I'm afraid if you don't leave I'll have to summon the police.' He punches her in the face, pulls her into the vestibule by her blouse and grabs her pocketbook as she's going down. She goes down and holds on to her pocketbook and tries to pull it back while she's screaming. He gets over her and punches her in the head and face and then kicks her in the stomach. She lets go of the pocketbook and he runs outside with it. She said she tried to scream again but started blacking out. She said she was afraid of blacking out for she thought the man, thinking she could identify him, might come running back and kick and punch her till she was dead. She said she knew, even while she was saying it, that she shouldn't have said she'd summon the police. She also regretted mentioning there were single women in the building and that she had spoken sarcastically to him about the city law on peepholes. A delivery boy passing the building sees her in the vestibule, comes downstairs and opens the vestibule door and asks if anything's wrong or maybe she's just a homeless lady resting.

She can't answer, tries to lift a finger, just stares at him. 'Are these your bags out here? That's what made me see you. I knew no one would just leave them there like that. Something you want me to do for you like bring them in? Are you hurt? Now that I see you close, you look it. But I don't have much time.' She said he kept looking up to the sidewalk as if to make sure nobody was taking his shopping cart filled with orders. Her mouth's full of blood and a tooth or two is broken and a temporary bottom bridge also broke loose and is in her mouth somewhere and she's afraid of choking on it. She starts swallowing blood, spits it out and the boy runs upstairs and quickly pushes the cart past the building. She said he probably got repulsed by the sight of such an ugly old woman spitting like that and what she was spitting and must now look like. She lies there. People pass on the sidewalk but none look her way. No sound comes out when she tries screaming. A tenant leaving the building opens the door into the vestibule. 'Mrs. T?' he says. He sits her up. She points to her mouth and starts choking. He says 'Something inside your mouth?' She nods. 'Is it the blood,' he says, wiping her mouth, 'or you want me to take whatever it is out?' She nods. 'You can't spit it out?' She tries to, shakes her head. She said she felt the bridge was getting more lodged in her throat and she was starting to panic over it. She starts gagging. The man didn't want to stick his hand in her mouth, he later told her. Not because he was squeamish but that he was afraid she might lose control of her reflexes and chomp down hard and bite off his fingers. He'd heard where that had happened. Or read it in a newspaper. " 'Good Samaritan Gets Fingers Chewed off by Person He Saved" or something,' he joked about the headline saying, 'if it was a paper where I'd learned of it.' She later told her son the man probably gave that excuse to spare her feelings and that he really didn't want his hand in her ugly broken mouth. He lies her flat on her front, slaps her back, raises her to her knees and forearms and slaps her back, when that doesn't work he grabs her ankles and holds her upside down and keeps bouncing her on her head or in the air till the bridge and two teeth come out.

'Is that it?' he says, still holding her upside down. 'Yes.' 'All there is? The isolated little teeth and the connected ones?' moving them with his foot below her face so she could see them. 'Please. I feel vomit coming.' When she's being wheeled on a stretcher to the ambulance she overhears him say to one of the medical crew 'I still can't believe I actually did it. I just took a chance, thought I might even be making things worse, but it worked. I've been in a position to but never helped anyone that way before or ever had such physical strength. I felt I could have held her up and bounced her up and down for hours, and it was such fucking ecstasy after her teeth came out.' Later in the hospital one of her sons says she should think about moving. 'The neighborhood's getting too rough.' 'The neighborhood's never been better,' she says. 'The best boutiques, good restaurants, fancy bars and bookshops. Landlords are getting two thousand a month for one-bedroom apartments, fifteen hundred for studios. People are doubling and tripling up in studios just to afford living in them. It's all fair-market value now, once a rent-stabilized or rent-controlled apartment becomes vacant and the landlord puts in an air conditioner and splashes on a little paint, and those are the going fair market rents. It's crazy to pay it, but the whole area's been vastly upgraded with all these young hardworking people moving in and brownstones being converted almost everywhere you look.' 'But with all this so-called nicer clientele more and more druggies and ripoff artists are coming in to rob them. You're elderly. They think you have money because you live around there. Or else they jump you for the few dollars they think you might have on you, if you happen to be wearing your knockaround clothes on the street, because you're an easy target. There's got to be some solution. No old age home or moving in with Jerry or me, since you're much too independent for that and for your age still pretty healthy. Maybe a building with a doorman or guard always downstairs and elevators and that's monitored in the laundry room and places and everything's safe and well run and clean. If you want, in the same neighborhood but not in a small unprotected walkup where a thief can just lean on the front door to open it.' 'I've lived in that building—what are you, fifty-three?' 'Two.' 'Then for fifty-one years and I'll never get the same space I need and like anywhere else for the rent I can pay. It happened once, this beating, and mostly because I had a big mouth, but it won't happen again. I'll get my locks changed at my own expense, walk the other way, as your dad used to say, from possible muggers, and only go out when I'm next to sure the streets are more crowded than yesterday.' 'And if, despite all these precautions of yours—an alarm system on your windows, for instance. That's a must anywhere in New York on the ground and second floor. But if some nice-looking, well-dressed mugger or two, for that's what I read how they often appear these days, to fool you, besides being well-spoken and with a couple of books under their arms too. But if one does come up behind you as you're going into your building, what'll you do?' 'If I don't recognize him, male or female, and there's even an inkling he's suspicious, I'll say "Oop's, wrong building—not you, me, and walk back to the sidewalk and call the police from the callbox at the corner, not that it'll work and if it does, that they'll come in time to catch him. But please don't think you're going to keep me locked inside all day and turn me into a hermit only reading books and baking cookies and breads. My life's empty enough.' "

"She's on her way to shop when she sees, two buildings down from hers, something funny going on inside the vestibule. The door's all glass, little iron grillwork on the front but no curtains or anything to stop her view, and a man's on the floor with his pants half off and the top of his backside showing and going through what seems to be the sex motions. She doesn't want to look hard, since in this neighborhood sometimes it can be anything you think it is and often much worse. But his hands are hidden so maybe he's just doing it to himself, bad enough but not something threatening to her. Or maybe he's having heart seizures on the floor or whatever they are like that. But then she sees another pair of hands—different, a woman's or older girl's—shoot up around him and one of them tears at his shirt and the other reaches for his hair as if to grab and pull it but never gets there, his head always backing away when her hand gets close. Maybe they're both doing it together, high on drugs or something, not tenants there of course but from the outside, permanently or temporarily out of their right minds. No matter what it is someone should go to the door to see and possibly help, and she looks around but nobody is on the street up or down or if they're far away she can't see them, and if they're in the windows looking at her she also can't see them because of her bad long-distance eyes. She wants better to just get away. But then if the woman's unwilling in all this, and that those hands aren't part of the sex act but her fighting against it, she has to do something immediately like scream to attract attention or just to let the man know someone's watching and maybe he'll stop and get off her and go away. She walks down a step. He turns around—maybe he saw her shadow, because she thinks she walked too lightly for him to hear her—and sees her and pushes the door open a little with his foot and says 'Mind your own business, lady, or you'll get the same thing to you.' Then he turns back to the woman he's on and starts pumping harder as if to get the thing over with right away. The woman yells 'Please, don't go, stop him,' and tears at his clothes. He punches her and she's quiet and then he looks around again while he's pumping on her and says 'See this?' and balancing himself on the door with one hand, picks up and holds out a knife. 'I'll cut your head off if you don't get out of here. Go to your fucking place where you live and lock yourself inside it for the next ten hours and shut up forever about everything you saw.' 'But you're on the street. . .doing it.' 'You heard me?' and he swishes the knife in the air. She walks back to the sidewalk. The woman screams. The man's still on top of her, doing it harder and holding her face down with his hand it seems. She hurries down the steps, bangs on the glass with her keys while she yells to the street 'Help, someone, fire, fire,' she heard she's supposed to yell if she wants people to really take notice and come. 'Help, please, fire, a woman's getting raped, mauled, burned and raped. Fire, fire.' He gets up, turns to her, penis erect, grabs it and jerks it back and

forth a few times and then points to her and laughs, zips up, opens
the door as she reaches the top step, woman's on the ground pulling
down her skirt and crying and clutching her neck, runs up the steps
and grabs her from behind when she's gone maybe five feet, hits
her head and she goes down. Then he grabs her head by the hair
and smashes it on the ground. All she remembers. He must have
done it several times by the injuries she got but she only remembers
it that once. Later in the hospital her son says 'From what the police
suggested the man had finished raping the woman and took her
wallet. Then after he knocked you out he took your handbag and
must have spit on your head because there was saliva all over it, or
maybe you got it from the sidewalk when he knocked you down
and beat your head against it. No one from any of the buildings
around called the police.' 'That doesn't mean they saw and didn't
call. It could mean nobody might have seen or heard anything.'
'Really doubtful, but OK. The woman who was raped was the first
person to come to you. She sat you up so you wouldn't choke from
your bleeding and busted teeth and stopped a car to get the driver
to call an ambulance and the police, both for you and her. Look,
from now on no stepping in when you see something suspicious
looking or terrible happening. Don't even call the police from a street
callbox or from your home or anywhere. The attacker might know
where you live or go to great lengths to find out to get even with
you. You did enough of that in your life. Let others take over. Now
do you understand me? Just no more, and Jerry tells me to tell you
the same thing.' 'I can get a whistle, she says. 'One that's on a chain
and looks like a nice pendant, so when I go out I can wear it around
my neck without anybody much thinking about what it is. I've seen
them advertised in the better jewelry stores—Fortunoff's and Tiffany's.
If I don't blow it immediately when I see something wrong going
on, I'll go down the street fifty feet to blow it. Every tenant on the
block and maybe in the immediate neighborhood should have one
or just carry a regular police whistle, but that I shouldn't expect. But
just think of it. Suppose I blew my whistle, someone heard it and

blew hers. Then someone else heard that whistle and blew hers, till on and on this whistling went till the sound of it, altogether or just a few of them or one or two last ones, reached a policeman walking his beat or in a car. It might for now be one of the best ways to beat these crime things. And the rapist or mugger, or just a car thief, by hearing the whistles will have to know he's a caught man if he stays. I'm going to bring it up at the next block association meeting. Or even contact the association's president to call a meeting to talk about the growing crime on the block and my whistling idea.' "

"I open the door and immediately feel a breeze in their apartment. Something's wrong. It's winter and this wind and my mother always keeps the windows shut in weather like this and all the downstairs rooms are lit. From the foyer I see what seem like little pieces of paper floating to the kitchen floor. A burglar, must have been going through something, her handbag, and scattered them, tissues and loose things, when he heard me and ran off. I yell 'You're in fucking trouble with me, mugger,' and run to the kitchen, not there and no sound of him, look around for something to hit him with, nothing really good in sight and I open a kitchen drawer. The candlesticks in the dining room! And I run to it. They're on the table, I grab them, bang them on the table edge and yell 'I'm going to pound the living shit out of you with these clubs I got so get the hell out, mugger, you better get the fuck out right away,' and with a candlestick raised to clip him I walk into the next room. No one there. Window's open, bars pried apart, so that's how he got in. He go out? Probably has a crowbar himself unless he left it outside. He go upstairs? Should I shut the window and lock it to keep him from coming back or make it a few seconds tougher for him to leave? I shut but don't lock it since nothing I do with the window will be better than anything else. I check the bathroom. Empty, same with the shower stall. Stairway and upstairs hallway lights are on. He can do something to me from the top of the stairs when I walk up, so I keep the candlesticks pointed out in front of me. If he has a gun I'm sunk. If there's more than one of them I'm probably sunk too but I have to take a quick look around to see that my folks are OK. Ceiling light's on and all the dresser drawers are out and one's on the floor and closet door's open in the girls' room. I look inside the empty closet, toilet, under the bed. I go down the hall to the boys' room my father now sleeps in. Door's shut, room's dark, closet's open, drawers all out, but he seems to be sleeping peacefully. I get close and he's snoring softly. I kick around under the bed, poke inside the closet with a candlestick, other in my right hand always raised. He stirs, tries to turn over; I tiptoe out. Living room's unlit. I go through it, then back to whack the almost ceiling-to-floor drapes with the candlesticks, circle the easy chair and card table and feel under the couch to see no one's there, go to my mother's room at the end of the front hall. Hallway light's off, also the ones in her room. I stand by her door, don't hear anything. Behind me's the baby's room. It's always locked, when there's no guest occupying it, an added protection for them she thinks in case someone climbs in from the street. I turn the knob, doesn't open. I say 'Mom, Mom.' No sound, can't hear her breathing. I've done this lots before, listened at her room after my nightly check of my father, and when I didn't hear her breathing I often thought she might have died in her sleep. 'Mom, Mom, you OK?' I go in, come closer to her, listen but always looking around in case the thief springs out at me. Her bathroom. I go in it, shut the door, turn on the light, candlestick ready to clip him, open the shower door. I go back into her room, both closets are open, poke around inside them, kick under both beds, bend closer to her, still don't hear anything, put my ear near her mouth. She's breathing and from the little light on her face coming through the venetian blind slats seems to be all right. I check the rest of the closets in the apartment, curtains, under the piano, anyplace he could hide. I unlock the backyard door and go outside, see no crowbar or anything like that, must have been a very thin small man to get through those bars or a kid, or maybe the bars were pried apart by a man and a kid went through them into the apartment. They had to have come over one of the fences of the neighboring backyards. Two have barbed wire on them and another has what looks like razor blades on wire but nothing it seems someone with thick gardening gloves couldn't push aside to get over or through. I shout 'Hello, hello. Tenants on West Seventy-fifth on the north side of the street and West Seventy-sixth on the sorth, or just the odd-numbered buildings on Seventy-fifth and the even-numbered ones on Seventy-sixth. This is Howard Tetch, son of the Tetches in number 37 on Seventy-fifth Street. A thief's been in my parents' apartment. Broke into it. Pried apart the bars of a backyard window and ransacked the place. Nobody's been hurt but the thief's out in one of these backyards now or on a roof, if he hasn't gotten away from the area by now or God knows into somebody else's place, so make sure all your windows and backyard doors are locked.' I start giving it again. Someone opens his window and says 'Stop shouting.' I see the window but not the man. I say 'Didn't you hear what I was saying? Thief in the neighborhood. Broke into my parents' apartment just ten minutes ago. The Tetches. He's the former dentist in number 37—his shingle was outside for more than forty years till a few years ago—and she you always see around. You must have seen her from your window there if you can see me. When it's nice out she has coffee and a cigarette out here a few times a day and in the summer waters these bushes and her plants. My father too— reading his newspaper and even in the cold weather when it's not too cold, sitting here with a blanket around him.' 'Stop shouting, people are sleeping,' and closes his window. Some lights have gone on or are going on in other apartments, a few windows open, but all behind shades or in the dark. I go back in, bolt and lock the door, go to my father's room. Though I yelled almost right under his window, he's still sleeping peacefully, or maybe he woke up and went back. I check his bag. Full. I empty it in the toilet and attach it back to the tube. I check his diapers. Empty. I hate doing it but when he's shit I change them. Those two jobs are mostly what I come here for around this time every night and to see if there are any messages my mother's left me in the kitchen about what I could do for her or Dad the next day or phone messages I might have got here because I have no phone. I go to her room. She's sleeping. I get down on my knees by her bed and say 'Mom, Mom, it's me, wake up. It's OK, Dad's all right, but wake up, I have to tell you something.' She stirs. 'Can I turn on the light?' I say. 'Turn it on. Everything's all right?' 'Fine, considering. Listen, don't panic but a thief's been in the apartment,' 'I know. He was in this room. I first thought it was you. But to make sure because of what's been happening in the neighborhood lately I kept my mouth shut. In fact it happened to Aunt Bertha and Irv where they live a year ago, so I knew what to do. You remember: Bertha slept through it but Irv kept quiet when some burglar lifted his wallet off the night table and slid his hand under their pillows and got Irv's watch. So, when I heard this man opening drawers and going through them and closets, I knew it wasn't you. I figured if he thought I was asleep he wouldn't bother me. At least the chances of it would be better than if he thought I was awake and could later identify him. Of course if he wanted more than he got then wake or asleep he'd beat me up till he got it out of me. But I must have fallen asleep after he left the room. Don't ask me how. I was scared to hell and planned to just lie there for fifteen minutes and then go to your father. It's probably because I didn't sleep all last night your father got me up so much with his bad dreams and making ishy. But you say he's OK?' 'Still sleeping; I emptied his bag. And the man only got into your pocketbook, it seems; presumably took all your cash and credit cards.' 'The cards I keep hidden elsewhere. But the money, good, let him. I always keep some in there and the pocketbook in a conspicuous spot on top of the kitchen radio, just in case for things like this. Thirty-one— three crisp tens and an old single—as if that's all I have, plus change, which might be enough to satisfy a thief to think his break-in was worth it. He break anything?' 'Just this,' and I show her a candlestick. 'I got those from my Uncle Leibush as a wedding present. Dad and I did.' 'The other one's just as dented. I did it, I'm afraid. I was going to hit him with it. I bashed the table with them—I'd come in on him while he was going through your pocketbook—so he'd be afraid I was serious and had something really lethal to get him with and race the hell out of here.' 'Which table?' 'The dinning room one.' 'My good table? I bought it when we moved in here. You can't get anyone to fix those anymore or get any silver candlestick like these without paying for an expensive antique. And it's a soft silver; won't go back. But you got excited for a good cause. Do I have to get dressed now? Police say they're coming right over? Usually, if the thief's gone, they take their time.' 'You know, I forgot to call them. I'll do it right away.' 'Maybe my insurance covers the table and candlesticks. By all rights it should. But probably they'll say the damage could have been avoided.' 'So say the thief did the bashing. That he saw me come in, grabbed the candlesticks and banged them on the table and said to me "One step, sucker, and I'll smash your head in." I'll tell the police that's what he did and said.' 'You'd be lying. And please don't tell Dad what you said you'd say, for that's just what he'd want you to do too, get the insurance. And listen. If he's not up and doesn't get up again tonight, we should let him sleep and not even disturb him with it later.' 'The police will probably want to see his room.' 'If we can't stop them—for what are they really going to find?—let's let him sleep till they come.' "

"Part of a police report my mother gave. 'I was in my bank, doing my normal weekly depositing and wanting to withdraw a little cash. Suddenly behind me I hear "Nobody move, everybody get down, this is a robbery." Really, in that order—"Don't move, get down." What did they think we should do? Because if you can get down without moving, you're really doing something. It was stupid. Unfair too, for someone could get killed not doing the right thing because of these confusing orders. And if you didn't speak English which a lot of people in this city don't, or not well enough to understand that hurried garbled gibberish, what then? But that fits my theories about bank robbers. That they're all stupid. If they were the least bit smarter they wouldn't be robbing banks, for one thing. For I'm sure, what with bank guards and plainclothesmen and just armed storeowners bringing in their own money, they have more of a chance of getting shot in one than we do with so many of them robbing banks. But you don't want my theories, so I'll stick to as close an account as I can give. This man said "Don't move, get down, robbery. Pull your coats over your heads or just keep your eyes shut and your face flat against the floor." Finally we knew. We should get down—for how else can you put your face to the floor?—and not keep our coats over our heads standing up. It sometimes takes cunning to be an innocent bystander. And right after that he confirmed our hunches about what to do by shouting "Now down, down, nobody make a move. First one to pick his head up gets it blown off with a shotgun." By this time I was already getting down to the floor. I didn't fly to it. I couldn't. I got down slowly, one knee, then the other, then spread myself flat on my stomach and chest. If I had tried to get down quicker I might have broken a hip. I knew that and hoped the robbers would know why I was getting down so slowly. They must have. For though I was, from what I saw, the last one to get down by almost a minute, they didn't complain. And since I had no sweater or coat for my head, though they didn't say sweater, they just said coat, but I'm sure a sweater would have been all right, I put my arms over it and kept my eyes shut tight for the rest of the time till they left. From what the tellers said later, there must have been six to seven of them. For each line had a man or woman with a handgun, they said, and one who could have been either. And there were five lines operating. I remember that, quickly observing which one was the shortest to get on, when I came in. And behind us were two different men's voices ordering the customers on line and all around to get down and stay there. Though maybe it was just one man with a couple of different voices: high and low, excited and controlled. Anyway, that was all there was to it for me. They told us to stay put on the floor where we were for ten minutes after they left, but most of us got up the second a teller shouted they were gone. All this a bit hard to believe, wouldn't you say? Happening in the middle of the city, fifty customers or so in the bank and maybe fifteen bank employees, two of them armed guards in uniforms, plus another five thousand people strolling and pushing strollers and selling umbrellas and things in the street right outside and going in and out of the subway entrance in front of the bank. And to top it off, two policemen from a double-parked police car right across Broadway having a snack in a café. They didn't go through my pocket book or anybody else's, the robbers. One man, after everybody got up, did stay on the floor weeping, and a whole bunch of us went over to comfort him. It seemed he'd been robbed something like this—guns, get to the floor!—just a few months before, but in that one he also was kicked when he didn't unzip his jacket pocket fast enough to turn over his wallet. He was afraid they were the same gang and they'd rough him up and maybe even kill him because he recognized them, besides crying because it happened twice in so short a time. We told him not to worry. That this can't be the only gang in the city robbing banks. And since this one did it differently than his last one—didn't take our wallets and watches and things, and waved pistols instead of shotguns behind us—it almost had to be a different gang. He said that suppose it happens again? What's he to think every time he goes to a bank? I told him that if I've been going to a bank about once a week for more than sixty years and this was the first time it happened to me, chances of it happening to him a third time in the next year were slight. Someone else said that the first fifty of those sixty years weren't such violent ones in the city and so shouldn't count, but anyway what I said seemed to calm the man. Only other thing I can remember now is how one customer started complaining, about ten minutes after the robbers left, if this meant there wasn't going to be any bank service here for a few hours. No one else of us did. In fact a group of us said that once the police finished questioning us we'll share a cab to the nearest Chase branch on Broadway and Sixty-third and maybe even have lunch together after to talk about all this.' "

"A photo of his mother. Mother's photo. Mother photo. Photo of mother. Photo, just 'Photo': She's on a boardwalk, is young, late teens, very early twenties, leaning against a railing, beach and water behind her, in a swimsuit, could be any beach, no cliffs to the side or boulders in the water, flat and endless sea and sky, holding an American flag on her shoulder, doesn't seem to be cold, big patriotic smile as if it was a nice bright day to be saying 'I'm proud to hail from the good old USA,' while the strollers on either side of her have heavy coats and furry hats and caps on and seem to be shivering. He found it in a drawer of photographs in her apartment. Had gone through the drawer to find snapshots of her and his dad and one of them both, small enough to put in his wallet. Wanted to open the picturefold to show people his gorgeous mother and handsome rugged-looking dad, the two lovey-dovey or kittenish together, the era. Showed the photo to her and she couldn't place it. 'Maybe it was from my bathing-beauty days, but they were always in August or July. I did a little modeling then too and of course those chorus parts in dancing movies. But I can't think of a movie or ad where I wasn't in flapper clothing or skimpy or lavish costumes, some weighing a ton with a ten-foot train picking up spit and stuff from the floor, and I never did a bathing suit ad, if they even had them then. Maybe the models in the photo are the people in warm clothing. You know: being photographed in the summer for the fall or winter lines and they just happened to be walking on the boardwalk to their shoot when my photographer snapped me. But that wouldn't account for their frozen appearances. But look at me there. I'm a hideous old hag now but I think you can say then, despite my funny plastered-down hair and overluxurious lipstick and rouge and the unflattering bathing costume that also fattens my thighs, that I might be considered beautiful. Men clamored after me, photographers were always stopping me on the street or at the beach asking me to pose, and I was forever getting pinched, propositioned and whistled at. And though I was only a chorus dancer I still got more love letters and hot poems and flowers and candies and cheap jewelry and other junk than the stars did and I had to devise all kinds of ways to avoid those lechers after the show. Most of them thought

I was an ignorant city kid turned promiscuous hoofer and just wanted to butter me up before taking me to bed. But I was impossible to get as your father liked to attest. The hardest he ever met, which I think is why he married me. He could have had as a wife a number of well-to-do fairly good-looking women with not half bad bodies and from much finer families. But he invested so much money and effort into our courtship that he wanted to get some returns. I think he got the best of the deal. I'm sure he continued to play around now and then. He practically ruined us with his reckless investments and avoidable run-ins with the law. For the first dozen years of our marriage he saw a lot more of his mother and sister and cronies than he did me. And he was hardly there for you kids ever and with his indifferent to painful dental care to you all and refusal to let me send any of you to another dentist, helped deplete most of your teeth. While I was a virgin when I married him. Always stayed faithful and available. Never argued with his tyrannical momma or demanded more than the most necessary domestic things. Did what I could to clean up the messes he left and quarrels he started over money with shopkeepers and such and never got a nod of thanks for it. Threatened to leave him I don't know how often. And even though he never said a word or slipped up a sign to suggest he'd mind much if I went, I never even stayed away a day. And then, while I was also playing nurse and nurse's aide to your sister till she died, I took care of him as if he were an infant for the last ten years of his sick old age.' "

"Her father barges into the apartment, pushes her husband aside, tells her he's going to pack all her things and take her and the kids to stay with him till he finds her her own place. She says she can't leave him. It'll be just what he wants. He's at least an adequate provider though so niggardly at times, even if he's always the big spender with his friends, that she has to steal from his wallet when he's sleeping or showering or forge his signature on savings withdrawl slips. It isn't that she still has a lot of feeling for him left. He's too thoughtless and avaricious and there's never any real

386

lovingness or anything much there but self-centeredness and she expects he'll one day give her syphilis if she ever gets back in his bed. He treats the children like distant relatives or better yet as if they're the next-door neighbor's or even better yet as if he's their avuncular bachelor uncle who once every two years comes to visit them for a few days. He simply isn't cut out to be a husband or father, but as a devoted brother and son he's the best. They weren't kidding, whoever told her, that they broke the mold when they made him. But it's no joke. He's going to be in serious trouble one day, not just some petty night-in-the-clink stuff, and that's when she'll pack up the kids and leave here. She'll have to. He'll wind up in prison and she won't be able to afford this place. But to give him that pleasure now? He won't moon for her or beat out his brains as to what he did wrong that she left and he'll even be relieved to be on the loose again. Even? He'll call it a red-letter day, whatever that is. Besides all that she's sick of him needing her just to have someone handy to shut-up, keep the kids out of his hair, cook and serve him elaborate just-like-momma-made breakfasts and dinners every day when he wasn't taking other people out to eat or mooching a meal, and to throw her weekly allowances across the dinner table at her as if she weren't a low-priced chippy but a clean whore. None of these are really good-enough reasons and it isn't that she feels the kids need at least a shadow of a father around till they've reached whatever's that certain age, but for no known reason to herself she's going to stay, and she takes out the few clothes he put into the valise, closes it, puts the clothes back in the drawers and asks him to put the valise back up in the closet."

"For a few years he thought of himself as a serious painter and painted nothing for most of those years but large canvases based on photographs of his parents with his two older brothers. They were six and two then, seven and three, five and one, four and a few months, and in a few of them and especially in the ones he liked to paint most, she was pregnant with him. You couldn't tell from the photographs but she told him she was when he showed her them. 'That's you,' she said, pointing to her flat belly. 'I carried small. People when they saw me in my eighth month would often say I never looked slimmer, am I on a special diet? My diet was that I didn't eat much when I was pregnant because almost everything I ate I threw up. That meant you kids came out frail and diminutive, and two of the three boys were so unnourished they almost died from it, but I forget which ones. Anyway, the third was almost no better off. I was nauseous with all my boys from the day after conception till a minute before they put me out to deliver them. In fact with you that's how I knew I was pregnant. But with Vera, don't ask me why, I didn't have a single sick minute with. And she came out twice the size of any of you, and rosy, exuberant, almost a movielike version of a lively newborn, and howling inside the birth canal during the last few seconds of travel before she shot out. People have always said that was impossible, but I heard her. All ironic, of course, since by the time she was three she was sick with the disease that would gradually ravage her till she became half her natural weight and greatly shrunken, all feathers and empty bones. But the sickest I ever got was with you. I often couldn't leave my bed for days. If I look happy in this photo with you it was because I was a good poser, having had a little experience as a dancer and model, since at no time did I feel any cause to smile. I literally cursed you daily for being inside me and I think a few times I consciously tried to abort you and swore over and over never another. But while I was so sick, tossing around all night and not permitted any more complex medicine than a spoonful or two of simple pink antacid for fear it'd harm the baby—doctors knew so little about it then—your father slept like a log and groused when I didn't, since in bed I sometimes kicked him in the belly for being so healthy and sleeping so well. But for all those nine miserable months, I had nine wonderful ones nursing each of you. It was a pleasure in every way. Your father loved the way I'd filled out and, let's face it, got all hepped up when he saw my breasts spread and the baby being fed, and became for the only time sort of solicitous and very affectionate to me and I also never felt hungrier or physically better. But nothing was worth so much nausea and I cursed you boys so much when I was carrying you that I'm surprised none of you came out with the plague. Maybe Vera's illness came from all those accumulated curses against her brothers finally heard. A backlog of them and really only one higher being to answer them, so it took a while and because of the delay got misdirected. Odd how it turned out, with you the worst to me ending up the healthiest child. But who knows what Alex's health would have been if he hadn't drowned when he was twenty-six—maybe a lot better than yours. But if there's one thing I really know it's that I would have, if given half the chance, died right then and there or just a slow death but with her pain and disfiguring illness, simply to give her a completely-free-of-it healthy or just normal few years. But who's to say what I'm saying has any sincerity behind it when I know even when I'm saying it that wishes aren't granted and prayers are never answered nor curses ever heard.' 'Well, I think we should at least leave a little of it open,' he said and she said 'If you want. ' "

"She visits her husband in prison. It's a long train ride up, or seemed that way, but now looking back she sees it couldn't have been more than an hour and a half, maybe two. The trains were very old, the windows were still open in the hot weather then; the passenger cars were more like very long subway cars going aboveground, but between stations not as fast. All that, plus stopping at every stop, probably had something to do with making the trip seem longer. Also that she had to take the subway to Times Square and then the Forty-second Street shuttle to Grand Central to get the train. If it had had a shiny high-speed look to it she might have remembered it as going faster. It also could have been her mood. She never felt good going, always felt worse returning, so she was never able to sleep or read on the train, even a newspaper. He was awful then: cranky, angry, bitter, inconsiderate, unfeeling. Tough as it was for him to be there, it wasn't so easy for her either. But he never said things to her like 'How you holding up? It must be rough, not just this back-and-forth trip, but taking care of the kids and being so short of cash and going along on your own day to day. I'm miserable without you too and for what I've done to you, but please don't let that add to your upset; I'll get through it OK.' She left the children in the care of someone. All of them except the youngest go to the same elementary school three blocks from their home, so it shouldn't be too tough on the woman. She's allowed to see him once a month for up to two hours, and every week if she wants, except the one she comes up for the long visit, for ten minutes. Documentary trips they call those. Sign this, that's it, out. She's never gone up for just those ten minutes. Wants no part of them: so cold. If there's business between them she saves it for the long visit when they can also talk about other things. The business stuff can be brutal and it's also a long trip and so many preparations and expensive for just ten minutes. They're not allowed to touch. Signs say it everywhere, unless the couple is given written permission by the chief guard. 'They might give it if I'm a perfect boy for a year,' her husband once said. 'But fingers through the hole only, so expect no kiss.' Glass is between them where they sit. A screened hole the size of a silver dollar in it to talk through and a hole the size of his fist at the bottom of it to eventually touch fingertips she hopes and to put things through for him to sign if she has to. When that happens a guard unlocks the hole on her side, another guard stands beside her husband, and the paper and pen, having been inspected by the chief guard in the anteroom before she comes into this meeting room, are put through by the guards. Then the hole's locked, and after he signs, hole's unlocked and the pen and paper's passed through to her guard who reads it to see her husband didn't write anything he wasn't supposed to, like, she supposes, 'Put a hand grenade in a cake to help me escape,' or even 'I love you dearly and want to screw you madly,' and given to her. Today she wants him to sign a change-of-name form for the kids. 'Where does that leave me?' he says. She says 'What do you mean?' 'It means no one will ever know me through my kids.' 'It doesn't have to mean that. It could mean we just wanted to make their lives simpler by anglicizing their names.

Frog's Mom

But all right, I warned you not to do it, you kept doing it. I warned you some more, you kept doing it some more and a whole slew of other stupid things which thank God—don't worry, nobody can hear me—you were never caught at. I warned and warned you even more—' 'Stop harping on me. Don't be a bitch. You know I don't like bitches. I never did and you're acting like a total worthless foul-mouthed nagging bitch of all time. It makes you look ugly when by all rights you could be pretty.' 'Insults won't change my mind or the conversation's direction.' 'Sticks and stones, go on and tear me to pieces and chew up my bones, think I care? Think I'd dare? blah-bah-bah, you rotten bag. Just lay off.' 'Stop being a jackass and trying to avoid this. Please sign. That's all I ask. Please please sign.' 'Why?' 'We've gone over it.' 'Why?' 'It's best for the kids.' 'How?' 'You're like a broken record.' 'How?' 'Because they're being hounded, as I've already told you, hounded by their schoolmates and people because their father's in prison and lost his dental license and was involved in a smelly citywide scandal and newspaper stories and photos of you and the whole world and his brother knows of it and other things. Because you're famous in the most terrible low way. And through you, guess.' 'So it'll be better by the time I come out.' 'The news stories. Think, why don't you. Just don't sit there pigheaded, unconcerned for anyone but you. People will never forget or not for thirty years. The *Mirror's* centerfold photo of you on the courthouse steps, for one thing.' 'What was so wrong with it? I was dressed well, looked good, big smile, wasn't in cuffs.' 'The lousy change, nickels and dimes, falling through your pants pocket and rolling down the steps and you chasing after it like a snorting hog.' 'What's the snorting? What's with these pigs?' 'Panting. You were out of shape. But for the money, is what I mean. The same kind of man running after petty change where he could break his neck or get a stroke, would try to save a few dollars in fines by bribing a building inspector. Whatever it was, that's why they took it and used it and it was ugly.' 'I told you to sew those holes.' 'That's hardly my point. Besides, you cram so much change and keys in them, your pockets are always going to have holes.' 'I need the change for the bus and subway. And newspapers.' 'Since when do you buy your own newspaper?' 'I buy it.' 'Maybe the Sundays. The rest you take out of garbage cans.' 'Sometimes if it's a clean one and just laying there on top, but obviously clean and looking almost unread, why not? Why waste? So many people waste. I was brought up poor and taught not to.' 'Sometimes some of the ones you brought home had spit on them, and once, dog doody.' 'I didn't see. The subway station was poorly lit or something. But one out of a hundred. So what?' 'Let's drop the subject and concentrate on the other one.' 'What other one? If it's what I think it is, there isn't any other one.' 'Three peoele have already sent that photo to me through the mail. All anonymously. What did you do to make so many enemies? Anyway, it's an example of how many people know about it regarding the children.' 'I didn't make enemies. If I made a lot more money than most other dentists, maybe that's why. Jealousy, and this is how they get even with me, but behind my back. Or there are thousands of crazy people in the city who do nothing all day but read the papers. And when they see a man down, someone they've never even laid eyes on but through the papers think they know, they get their kicks pushing him further. But believe me, people will forget. In a year, two at the most. I'll be old news, or their minds don't remember that far. The few who don't forget, the hell with them. I'll tell all those nutjobs and sickies that I did it standing on one foot.' 'What do you mean?' 'That it was easy—this is—and in some ways, even good for me. I've met lots of decent people here. Gentlemen. Men of means. Big successes in all kinds of fields. Future clients, some of them. They have me working in the prison clinic.' 'I know.' 'So, for one thing, I'm able to stay in touch with the latest dental gadgets and machines. It's very well equipped. But best yet, I see twenty patients a day, all men from the prison. No thieves or killers but tax evaders, embezzlers, extortionists, but not strong-armed ones, plus some draft dodgers. Those I don't especialy like, in what they're doing, but that's their business. And then the conscientious ones who won't go into the army for their own more personal reasons. Moral, religious, none of which I go along with or else don't understand, but at least they're better types. And they all got teeth. Most, I just look in their mouths, pick around a little and take an x-ray or two to satisfy them, since they usually have nothing wrong with them a quick prison release wouldn't cure or else need major bridgework, some of them complete upper and lower plates, which the prison's not going to put out for. They let me extract and fill and even do root canal to as many teeth as I want, since they don't want their immates walking around in pain and maybe kicking someone over it. But they feel the more expensive work, which means sending it out to a dental lab, the prisoner should pay for himself on the outside. All of which is to the good, since when a lot of these men get out they'll come to me.' 'How? You won't have a license to work when you get out.' 'I'll get it in a year, maybe two.' 'You might get it in ten years if you're lucky. That's what I've been told.' 'By who?' 'The license people and Democratic club leaders you sent me to speak to for you.' 'Don't worry, I'll get it much sooner. But till I do I'll get different kind of work and do very well in it. I did in dentistry—started with borrowed money and no more skills than the next dentist—I can do well in other things. And by working at it long and hard and mixing in the right places a lot. I bought a house for us from it, didn't I? A building, Five stories of it and you decorated it to your heart's content.' 'Fine. One where it cost more to keep up than the rents we get plus all the problems that go along with it.' 'What problems? Be like me. Tenant complains, tell him to move out if he doesn't like it. And we also got our apartment from it. Two floors. And my office, so those were supposed to make up the difference. And it was an investment if the neighborhood ever turned good. Not only that, we had other things. A full-time maid. One left, another came the next day. And a car whenever we needed one. And summer vacations for all of us but especially all summer for you and the kids. So stop complaining. I can do all that again no matter what I go in to. And maybe a little dentistry—the hell with them—you know,' and he makes jabbing motions with his thumb over his shoulder, indicating he'll do it on the side or behind their backs. 'Till everything comes through.' 'That's exactly what you shouldn't do. They'll find out— one of your good friends who's an enemy will squeal—and you'll land right back here getting acquainted with all the latest dental instruments.' 'Anyway, no job is that complicated unless it's a real profession like dentistry and medicine and law. But I'm sure I won't have to do anything else for very long. The people you spoke to were being extra cautious. You're my wife? How do they know you also weren't working for the state, in return for helping to reduce my sentence or getting my license back, by letting them say "Well now, you want him to get his license back sooner than ten years you'll have to pay for it." They're no dopes. I never should have sent you to them, but thanks for trying. Because of course they built up the time to you till I get my license back and pretended to be saints. But when I see them I'll talk to them like a boy from the boys. And on a park bench—no one in fifty feet of us or where the air can be bugged—and not in a restaurant or room. I know what to do.' 'What? Bribing them?' 'Shut your mouth. That one they heard. Say something quick and silly as if you were joking.' 'They didn't hear. And like how,' she whispers, 'by bribing them?' 'Shut up with that word. I'm serious. Smile. Make believe you're laughing, the whole thing a joke.' She smiles, throws her head back, closes her eyes, opens her mouth wide and goes 'huh-huh-huh' through it. 'OK,' her face serious again, 'what'll you do? The same stupid thing?' 'That time was a mistake. I did it to the wrong inspector.' 'He was a city investigator, not a building inspector.' 'I thought different. He was an impersonator, that's what he was—a lowlife *mockie* bastard in it for a promotion or raise. Or maybe he does both—inspects, investigates—when there's cause for alarm or just that things are getting too hot in the department that other inspectors are taking graft. So one true-blue one in there. But they all take, so they wouldn't use an inspector to investigate.' 'You did it to all the inspectors. Fire, water, boiler, sewage—whatever they were, that was your philosophy in owning a building. Even if I'd seen to every inch of the building and complied to the last decimal to every city rule and law, matter of course you handed out fives and tens to them.' 'To keep them happy. They expect it. They don't get it they feel unhappy and can write out ten violations at a single inspection, some that'll cost hundreds to correct. Or my office. I got water and electricity and intricate machine equipment I depend on and I don't want them closing me down even for a day. Every landlord knows that and every professional man who owns and works in his own building.' 'It's a bad way to run a brownstone, and dishonest.' 'But it's the practical way, or was. Did we ever get a violation before? Why do you think why not? They're all on the take or were till the investigation, and probably now are again. There's a lull, then it's hot; it never stops. Cities are run on it, the mayor on down. What happened then was they were using me. They wanted to get a professional man bribing an investigator inpersonating an inspector so they could say "See, even doctors and dentists give bribes, so how bad is it that our building inspectors take them? Dentists earn five times as much as our inspectors and get from the public ten times the respect, but the briber is as serious a criminal as the bribee," or whatever they call them, the bribed guy who takes. And that's why they trapped me and that doctor in Staten Island and the CPA who owns a much bigger building—an apartment one, twelve stories—in the Bronx. I met them both, since they're both here for around the same-length terms as mine. Nice family men and they shouldn't be in prison. For what good does it? You want to make them pay, have them work in city clinics or helping the poor with their taxes for twenty hours a week for the next few years. Ten hours, but where it adds up to about what they'd put in nonsleeping time here.' 'Please sign the name change.' 'I can't. I know you think it's best for them, that it's going to help their future. But today's big graft and news story will be tomorrow's trash, or something—yesterday's news. Last year's. Last two. That's what I wanted to say. No one will ever have heard of the case or remembered my name from it by then. "Doc who? Nah, what graft story's in the paper today?" And I'll be out and practicing again with an even bigger clientele. And if I'm not? If they're so stupid to deprive my family of a good livelihood and the country of a lot more income taxes because of some dumb bribe I gave a dumb building inspector or investigator or actor, then I'll do something else. The Garment Center. I'll sell dresses or sweaters or materials. One fine gentleman in here on some illegal immigration or something offense owns a large suit and cloak house on Thirty-fifth Street and says he' ll take me in as a salesman the minute I get out. If he's still in here, he'll tell his partner to put me on. Not road selling but the showroom. He thinks I'm sharp and palsy-walsy, so just the right type, besides knowing my way around and eager for money. And it'll give the house a little extra class, having a doctor working for them. They all wanted to be doctors or dentists or their parents wanted them to. Or some other house if that one doesn't work out. Most of the men here bullshit, so you can't really count on them. But I know lots of people in the Garment Center, and also one of the ones from here might come through. And in it for a couple of years, working very hard, I'll learn enough to start my own business. I can do all that, why not? and then we'll be rolling again. But to have my kids walking around with the name Teller when I'm Tetch? How am I to explain it?' 'You don't have to.' 'No, I do.' "Meet my son Gerald Teller?" "Was your wife married before and the boy kept his real father's name?" "No, I'm his real father. Same blood and nose." "Then why the different names?" "Because all the kids want to be bank tellers when they grow up and my wife thought it'd give them a head start." ' 'That's just stupid,' she says. 'Why, you got a better explanation? OK. "Because I was in prison for being too honest and my wife thought to really jab the knife in me to get even she'd change the kids' name so no one would know they were mine." Because you don't think that's what people will ask? Over and over they will. For what father has a different name than his kids'?' 'People we know are always shortening or anglicizing their names. But if you don't like that one, I was thinking of another. Tibbert. It sounded good.' 'It sounds awful. It has no meaning. It sounds like a bird or frog or some little barnyard animal singing by a brook or up a tree. "Tib-bert! Tib-bert!" Anyway, something silly sitting on a lily pad in a pond. Look, don't give me that paper. You do, don't give me the pen, because I won't take both at the same time. I won't be pressured. Just because I'm here, I haven't become a jelly fish.' 'I'll tell you what you've become.' 'Sure, and you're my wife. But what about Tibbs as a name? We'll start shortening the anglicized. Or Tubbs? Or Terbert? We can change Howard's name to Herbert and he'll be Herbert Terbert. Or forget the T. Who says in a name change it has to start with the same letter as Tetch? Sherbet. Gerald, Alex, Howard and Vera Sherbet. The Sherbet kids. They can go on stage. Tell jokes, take off their clothes, do little two-steps. I don't know why, but it all sounds right. Or the Shining Sherbets. Up on the high wire. You can change your name to Sherbet too and go back on the stage or up there in the air with them. You still got the face and figure for it. Or just divorce me if you want.' 'Oh please.' 'I'm not kidding. You want it, you got it.' 'What are you talking about? Though don't think for a few moments I haven't thought of it.' 'So think of it some more, think of it plenty. What the hell do I care anymore? You're so ashamed of me—' 'It's not that—' 'You're ashamed!' 'Well I told you not to do—' 'You told me and you told me you told me and I did it and admit it and they had me and now I'm here doing it on one foot and soon I'll be out on both, or not so soon but a lot sooner than any of my kids' lifetimes so far and later everything will be forgotten and the same. Except I probably won't be doing those things again, that's for sure, but you'll still be hocking me about it till I'm dead. In fact your hocking will make me dead. Look, you want a divorce, it's yours, on a platter. Take the house, the kids, the platter and whatever you find in the mattresses. You find another kid there, take that one along too.' 'Don't give me what I don't want. When you get out and if you still want it, we'll talk. The children will be a little older then and maybe more able to adjust to it. But not now.' 'Why not now? Why not? Why not?' The guard on her side comes over. 'Anything

the matter?' 'Nothings the matter, thank you.' 'She says nothing but
let me tell you what she wants me to do,' tapping the glass to the
paper on the table in front of her. 'He knows,' she says, 'they all have
to know. It had to be screened before it got to you.' 'So good, everyone
knows. But did you know,' he says to the guard, 'she wants to force
me to do it? She thinks I'll bend, because prison somehow has
weakened me, but not me, sir, not me.' 'Please, Simon, let it ride,'
she says. 'OK, it'll ride, to please you. Everything to please you,
except that goddamn name change.' 'Let that ride too.' 'I'm afraid
to say your time's about up,' the guard says to them. 'That's what
I really came over to say.' 'OK, OK, thanks, but just a few seconds
more. —How's the new dentist doing in the office?' he says to her.
'Better than the last. He seems to be busy, mostly older people—
plates, extractions, primarily, from talking to a few of them going
in and out.' 'Just like me then. I pull out about ten teeth a day here
and does it ever feel good. And some of these guys are bullvons,
with teeth like dinosaurs'. —I'll pull out yours too, Mr. Carey, if you
want me to—no charge.' 'Thanks but no. Ones I don't need I let fall
out.' 'Smart guy. And I know you're Carey because you got it stitched
on your jacket. Don't let me fool you.' 'You didn't.' 'But no plates
here,' he says to her. 'They won't shoot for it for the prisoners. But
I already said that. I'm repeating myself when I've only seconds left.
I'd like to be making them. Keep my hands in so I don't get rusty.
Does he pay the rent on time?' 'First of the month. And for the
summer, when he was going to a dental convention in Chicago and
then on to a vacation somewhere—Denver, he said; the Grand
Canyon to hike and ride horses—' 'Lucky guy. Not the hiking, but
I used to ride horses. Once in army training, then in Prospect Park
a couple of times. I've pictures. You've seen them.' '—he gave me
two months in advance. I think he'll be there for as long as we like.'
'Tell him not to get too tied to the place. Or why not? I'll open an
office someplace else. It doesn't always have to be in my own home.'
'Time's really up,' Carey says. 'Now we're all breaking rules and can
be penalized. Your wife, with shortening her visits. You, because of

that. Me, in that they don't like me being this lenient at the end of a visit and I get a talking-to—' 'Can I kiss her hand through the bottom hole here?' 'Afraid not.' 'Right now she wouldn't go for it anyway.' He stands. 'Good-bye, dear,' she says. 'I mean it: please call and write as often as you can. And try to forget most of what we went over today—what might disturb you.' 'The kids. Give them each a big kiss on the head from me.' Carey signals a guard behind the glass, who goes over to her husband. 'Tell them I love them like nobody does but don't tell them where I am.' Carey shuts the speaking hole. 'Gerald knows.' Her husband cups his hand to his ear and his expression says 'What?' 'I don't want to get you in trouble here,' she says louder, 'but Gerald knows.' 'Yeah, I know, I know,' he shouts, 'but not the others and tell Gerald not to tell.' Carey opens the hole and says 'Everything all right, Yitzik?' Yitzik waves that everything's fine, puts his hand on her husband's shoulder and says 'Please don't make a fuss.' 'Me? A fuss? You hear that, Pauline? This nice guard here thinks I'm going to make a fuss. —Not goodtime Simon, sir. Not a chance,' and without looking at her or back at her he goes with the guard through a door. She puts the paper back into a manila envelope, winds the string around the tab in back to close it, goes through her door, is asked if anything was slipped to her by the prisoner and is given her pocketbook back, calls for a cab, leaves the prison, takes the cab to town, goes to a bar near the train station and has two strong drinks, something she only started doing every day once he went to prison and which she has one or two more of and never has supper or lunch the day she visits him."

"Each of his parents lived with their parents till they were married, then moved to Brooklyn when they came back from their honeymoon. They'd already furnished the place: a large ground-floor apartment opposite Prospect Park and with a woman working full time for them from around the second month after they got there. 'I had a difficult pregnancy from almost day two of my marriage, so the woman always had plenty to do, since half that time I could barely get out of bed.' She was a virgin when she married. His mother was. A story she told a lot was that when she was pregnant the first or second woman to work for them complained of ' "serious female ailments." ' His mother took her to her own gynecologist and he said she was pregant and had syphilis and rectal tissue damage and if he were her he'd get rid of the woman right away. 'Lax morals like that and not too careful, you don't want her taking care of your baby. For one thing, you won't know what she'll drag into the house while you're out. For another, she might develop a fantasy about taking your husband away when you're big and bloated and so not as attractive.' 'I discharged her on the spot though with two weeks' severance pay and the address of a good a.b. man if she wanted. I felt sorry for her for she said her boyfriend had deserted her and her entire family was in Ireland. I should have known better, having been a medical secretary though for a roentgenologist, but I thought syphilis could spread sometimes just by touching the syphilitic or sitting on things she'd put her bare bottom on or touched. I'd also seen photos of people, though mostly newborns, who had it in the mouth and I winced when I pictured her kissing my baby. Also the "lax morals." But I knew your father would never fool with her. She was too pimply and pudgy for him and she didn't seem to bathe or brush her teeth enough and she wore a cross. I didn't want to tell him my real reason for discharging her. He wouldn't have given her the severance pay and might have even docked her a week's wages for jeopardizing the health of our unborn baby, or some insincere excuse like that. Anything to save money. For he never expressed any interest in the baby's or my health during the pregnancy. I'd come home from my monthly examination and near the end, from my weekly, and he wouldn't ask a word about it or how things were going or even once think of accompanying me.' But every good woman then was a virgin, she told him. 'Oh, I played around. Did what we called harmless petting—squeezing fingers, a bit of kissing with our mouths closed, rubbing each other's backs very hard—but no more than that. Now I regret it. To only have experienced one man in your life isn't enough. I should have had

Frog's Mom

more adventures before I married. Gotten madly involved with a couple of men, had an affair that nearly broke my heart before it dissolved, even gotten pregnant by some rotter who didn't want to help me and had an abortion all on my own and at my expense. Maybe not that far, and no venereal diseases. Traveled more. Then I could have drifted into marriage a little more easily. But your father persuaded me. He had a way with words, a wonderful smile and a great sense of humor.' 'I remember. And you've told me most of this.' 'So I've told you. So what? It only indicates how true it was. But whenever things turned sour for him he could be as disagreeable as they come.' 'I know. I saw that too. Over the dinner table. Christ, the battles you had, and all over money, He'd throw your weekly allowance across the table at you and you'd yell you won't be treated like that and throw it back and all of us kids around and he'd yell and you'd scream—' 'I don't remember that.' 'It's true. I've mentioned it several times.' 'I don't remember that too. And Gerald has no recollection of those arguments.' 'He was out of the house by that time. But let's forget it. Maybe it was wrong of me to bring it up, or at least now.' 'We argued, and over money sometimes, because he could be tight, as I know I've told you, but not at the table. That's one place it stopped. I didn't want to ruin your meals, send you to bed with bellyaches because of it. But I felt—your father—if I massaged his scalp enough I could bring some of his hair back and make him handsomer. And I put him on a diet and a regimen of exercises from the day we came back from our honeymoon, hoping to make his body less flabby, so more attractive to me, but it never worked. He went, with or without me, to his mother's for dinner two to three times a week. Think of it—they lived off Delancey, we lived in the middle of Brooklyn, but that often. Took the car. All right, traffic wasn't as bad then and you could park where you pleased, and for our first ten years his office was either in her building or right near her, so he could just close it and walk over. And most Sundays and Friday nights some of you children went with him— she loved feeding all of you and her cooking for that kind of food

401

was pretty good—so it gave me some relief. I know I've told you he worshiped her. The very ground, even if it had gook on it sometimes, and worse. One of my greatest fears was that my father-in-law would die and she'd come live with us, even though she had a daughter to go to. But your aunt was poor, living in a space half the size of ours with your cousins running all around and her husband a schlemiel and your father doing most of the supporting for them, so I knew she'd come to us, where we had a maid and he'd let her boss me. As it was, she died first and your grandfather wanted to live alone. I would have taken him in but I doubt your father would have let me—his silence and nebbishness made your father uncomfortable. You know your father phoned her at least once every day when she was married.' 'You mean *he*. Or possibly *we*.' 'He. But by all rights he should have been married to her, so maybe that's what I really meant. I don't know that much about psychology. I in fact think it's a science, if that's what it is, started by crazy people and kept alive by them—the people who run it—but that part about some mother son relationships they speak of I believe. If it was possible to marry and have a family by her, he would have. I'm kidding, of course, when it comes to your father. Both of them, though she hated her husband. Dirtied all over him. And phoning her that much as your father did would have been a nice thing to do if she'd been a nicer person. I know I'd appreciate it if you did it every day, or certainly wouldn't mind it—even every other day—if we usually had something interesting or useful to say. Because they spoke—they really spoke. Oh, just hearing from you that often would be nice, forget that it has to be interesting. But you're so silent on the phone most times you'd make me wonder in those calls what I'd done wrong with you the previous times. I know you don't mean it, but that's what it provokes. Anyway, she wasn't a nice person at all. She was a mean wicked bitch who made life hell on earth for me those first ten years. I know I've said this also, but I've never gotten over how much she ruined my life then and how he let her. Your father was a pansy only regarding his mother. Did I ever tell you what my cousin Elsa said about her?' 'The bit about her being a prostitute on the lower East Side? Malicious bullshit, only because she thought you wanted to hear it.' 'No. She was a very hard woman, so I could believe it. Besides, Elsa, who I knew for a long time and trusted—she didn't tell stories or cater to anyone—said friends her parents knew in your grandnother's building swore she was. That they saw men enter her apartment when her husband was out, and heard the goings-on through the walls. The whole neighborhood knew. But she wasn't the kind who walked the streets. She took in a couple of steady men a week—three or four—to make ends meet. When your father, who was the oldest, was very small and your grandfather wasn't doing well, which was mostly always. He drank too much; was a good darner and weaver but couldn't hold a job. Maybe this—her giving it for money and her husband soused in a bar several days a week—was why your father gave so much of his income to her and your Aunt Ida and her family. Because he knew— had seen it—might have been locked in the bathroom when it was going on, or told not to leave it. No, he'd probably be in school, if he got to be that old while she was still doing it, and they had no bathroom—only a public toilet in the building's hallway. Maybe he was put in a closet each time. But anyway, he was ashamed of it— what she did—though we never, Dad and I, talked about it once, so I don't know for sure how he felt. And once he had the money he wanted to make up for what she'd gone through for him and his brothers and sisters and also wanted to prevent Ida from doing what her mother did. That's a possibility, since Ida had few scruples too. Or maybe his mother did it because she enjoyed it, and thought what the hell, she'll make some money out of it. And your grandfather was not only a poor provider but too drunk, or had some other problem, to fulfill her, or after awhile to do it even once. He seemed like it. Nice but a weakling. But doesn't it make sense?' 'What' 'That your father was scarred by it and that's what made him look down on women so. He felt sorry for her in one way, hated her for having done it, in another way. It's all very complicated—beyond me.

Though maybe I should have been a psychologist after all, fake as the field is. But she was so ugly and fat that I think what could a man have seen in her to want to pay for it again and again? She was even ugly and fat in the photograph of her as a child bride. She was always, even at fourteen, an old lady and a sourpuss, which is sad. Though maybe she was extra special in the bed department, knew tricks nobody did, or just extra cheap and every so often tossed one in for free, but I don't want to think of it.' He died two months to the day before his grandmother was born. He means— They were still living in Brooklyn then. Said that. Three boys, Vera on the way. His father kept his office on Stanton and Cannon, he thinks it was, till his mother died. His father's mother, and maybe he should check a map. His own mother got pregnant the first time she had sex with his father. People thought, she said, they'd slept together before their marriage because his oldest brother, Gerald, was born three months premature and was conceived the first night. 'I let everyone who wanted to, believe it. It made me into a more interesting person and it's what I, or maybe I'm only thinking this in retrospect, wanted to do, but not so much with your father. Let's face it: almost not at all. Gerald had croup because of his undeveloped digestive tract. Life was misery for us because of it. I'm sure for him too, but they say babies that age don't really suffer that much pain. At his briss— a mangled job, but not a peep. Maybe it was the wine smeared on his lips and the moyl's spit as an anesthetic around his prepuce just before he was clipped. But he cried day and night for half a year from his croup. Your father was hardly home then. His mother, cronies, and he worked all the time, even on Sundays. Not Saturdays though. He was still orthodox on Shabbas except for carrying money and driving a car. He stopped right after his mother died and we moved to Manhattan. I still have his tefillin, bag and boxes and straps, if you ever want it. Just as a keepsake, and it's very old and in good condition so may be worth something one day. Gerald thinks it's the ugliest thing existing and won't have it in his house. It does at times look like some dark crouched-up creature ready to pounce out of the drawer at me. Your father's father lived for about six years after his wife died. You remember him.' Doesn't. 'You should. Because you were named after her, he played with you more than with anyone when he was here.' Her mother died a few years after he was born. 'You remember her?' No recollection. 'It was horrible. She could have lived another twenty years. The doctors operated on the wrong problem and killed her on the table. I don't know why I wanted to become one when I distrusted them so much. But that happened years after I gave up my goal of becoming a doctor. My dad lived several years after that. Of any of your grandparents, I'm sure you remember him.' Nothing. 'But he read you stories, fed you dinner, took you to the park and to your first movie and merry-go-round, taught you whole sentences in German and was the first adult to understand what you were saying in English. He used to love telling all you kids about when he was in the Polish calvary and his white horses. No, that was my Uncle Leibush; my father fled the country because they wanted to put him in the army. And Leibush wasn't really my uncle. We called him that because he was so close to us. I know you remember him, since he lived till you were around ten and visited us once a week.' 'He's the only one of those people I remember, and even something about the calvary. Full white hair, bushy gray mustache, lanky and statuesque, always in a suit and vest even in warm weather, and he walked with a walking stick or cane. A cane.' 'That's nothing like him. He was short and stocky, had no walking problem nor affected one, and didn't have a single hair on his skin. He had some condition. You've seen people with it. That's another reason I thought you might remember him, though he almost always wore a sea captain's cap, which was supposed to resemble his Polish calvary cap, outdoors and in. He came to America after my father, was only going to stay with us till he got on his feet. Landsmen of my father—whole families of them—were always doing that with him. He was that kindhearted—he even paid the way over for some of them—but Leibush ended up living with us most of his adult life. He was in love with my mother—that's why he never left.

Gentle and outgoing, compared to my father's gruffness and reserve—you could see why she'd be attracted to him too. Go ask my father why he put up with it. Probably financial. Leibush opened the bar and grill for him at five or six every morning while my father slept till noon. Then he finished his work at the bar around midafternoon and my father, except for coming up for dinner most nights, never got home till two or three A. M. They even say Aunt Rose was Leibush's daughter through my mother. Look at her next time and then at one of the photographs I have of Leibush and see whom she resembles.' 'Mom, Mom—' 'I'm not joking. Everybody's said Rose looks like no one in the family. Taller than all the girls by about four inches, those googly eyes and thick lips, she even got sicknesses none of us did and escaped some that all of us got at the same time. Don't mention anything about it around Rose. The secret's been kept from her all this time, even if by now she must suspect. But Rose is dead—last year, or the one before—so what am I talking about?' 'I'm sorry.' 'Still, don't ever tell Uncle Gil. During her first few years of marriage she probably thought she could be disinherited; after my father died, I don't know what. But I'm sure she thought for something like these reasons or others he might leave her if he found out she was momma's love child, so she never said.' "

"My mother threw out or gave away or loaned, without there being a good chance of getting it back, anything of mine when she felt like it. My electric train set. The one thing, I told her months after I graduated college and went to Washington to work, I wanted kept in my closet or the basement. 'I might want to give it to my own kids one day. When I have them. It'll certainly be valuable twenty to thirty years from now, if one has to look at it that way.' She gave it to my youngest cousins a year after their father died. 'Aunt Gussie was broke. Ben left her with no insurance, an overdrawn checking account and nothing but big waddings in all their mattresses. She pleaded with me for some of my boys' old toys. She knew I gave you kids everything of the very best you wanted, and with a basement to store things in, she guessed I still had some of them. So I gave her what I thought you'd never use again and which they'd love most—a twenty-year-old train set—and they appreciated it tremendously; really.' 'The set was around forty years old. I found it in its original box on top of some garbage cans down the block. Someone must have thrown it out because it wasn't working, or maybe it was put on the street by mistake. Or someone had several sets—you know how some rich people are—and got rid of the oldest to make space. Alex fixed the wiring or something in the engine— that's all it needed, plus a new transformer, which it took me months to pay him back for—and for years it was my favorite thing to play with on earth.' 'So there was little money lost in it, realistically speaking. And if it was that old when you found it, it was ancient and no doubt in ruins when I gave it to them, so what great value could it have had?' 'Personal. I'd put little clay figures I made into the engine and on top of the coal car and at the back of the caboose, get down real close with my eyes right up to the passenger car windows when I made it pass very slow, and it looked like a real train. And just that I dragged that box home all by myself—none of my friends would help me, jealous, probably, that I found it first. And with Alex's help made the best thing I ever had out of it, except for maybe that used tricycle that could be converted into a bicycle, someone gave you for me, and which was stolen in a week. Because you never would have bought me a new set of trains.' 'Something like that—like even that tricycle-bike—with so many kids, was just too expensive for us, fairly well-off as we were for a while. Anyway, to me it was a piece of junk. The tracks scratched your floor. And when you played real rough with the trains, crashing then intentionally or using them as dive bombers or something, the engine made holes in the floor. I was also always afraid you'd electrocute yourself. That thing was forever shorting and blowing the fuses, wasn't it?' 'No. Maybe once. That's nothing and I don't even think you were home. I replaced the fuse myself and later told you about it.' 'Anyway, what can I do now? I'll try to remember not to repeat anything like that when your heart's so set against it.' 'You can ask

Gussie for it back.' 'After so many months and when her boys are practically taking the trains to bed with them at night? Please, put yourself in their position. These kids have gone through enough. Their father dying so young. And their being so young when he died. And he was a good father—attentive—just wonderful to them. And his debts and their mother practically begging for them and their being forced out of their house into a cheap apartment and her working at the worst kinds of menial jobs the first year to get them back on their feet. I helped by giving what I could—money, when your father wasn't looking, and everything else, like your trains— and still do, though don't mention a word to him about it. But now for them to lose these trains? Forget it and just feel good they're being distracted by them for an hour or two a day. I know Gussie's very grateful to you.' 'I never got a card or anything saying so.' 'She's got other things on her mind. Don't be hard.' A year later, after I continued to be upset about the trains being gone, I wrote Gussie asking if she'd mind giving them back or anything she and her sons might want to part with of them. 'Though old and not really worth anything, they had a certain sentimental value, which my mother didn't realize when she gave them to you.' I was even willing, I said, to buy her boys a new set if it didn't come up to too much. She wrote back that her sons had busted the transformer and engine and cars where she was almost sure they couldn't be fixed, so she gave the whole thing to a junkman, tracks too. My plants. I went to Europe for a month, left two grapefruit trees with her I'd started from seeds some ten years before and which were about five feet tall, one starting to produce grapefruits the size of tiny mothballs. I'd heard that was impossible. That the seeds had come from ordinary store grapefruits that had grown on grafted trees, and so had no sex. There's a better word for it. When I came back she said ants had got on the trees— I'd put them in her backyard—and she threw them out. 'Ants?' I said. 'What are they? You brush them away. They don't hurt people or trees.' 'These were the biting kind—red ants. I was afraid they'd not only nip me when I had my coffee outside but get into the house and all through the cupboards, and that you'd understand why I did it. You know, when you leave something with someone, who's doing it as a favor and which could possibly be inconvenient, although this wasn't. Just a little watering every other day as you told me to do, which I liked—it kept me cool and gave me something to do—though getting rid of them, they were so heavy and spread out, was no easy chore. But anyway, you're doing it with a little risk involved, that's what I'm saying. I could take sick and be unable to water them for a week or remember to tell anyone to. Or something worse happening to me, which could leave them unwatered in a drought, let's say, for the entire month.' 'But none of that happened. And you could have told me what you were going to do with the ant-infested trees and I would have told you not to. I called from Europe every ten days or so, so what was the rush? I would have asked you to phone a few friends of mine and one of them would have come over and put them in a cab and kept them in his or her apartment till I got back. I only chose you because I thought they'd be cheerful and colorful—some more greenery—and also because they could use a month outdoors.' 'I didn't think I had the time to wait. They were swarming, seemed to be multiplying every day, and once I had the super put the trees out front, the ants disappeared from the backyard, except for a black ant or two, which I'm used to. So I was right. There had to be something in those trees that was attracting the red ants. The little grapefruits perhaps, or the smell of the leaves. If it's any compensation to you, the trees were gone before the garbage truck came, so I'm sure they got a good home.' He put signs up on her block's lampposts and parking-sign poles and the bulletin board in the corner candy store, saying that two grapefruit trees, approximately five feet tall and one bearing miniature green fruit, were placed by mistake in front of such and such building on around a certain date and he was willing to give a modest reward for their return or replace the trees with two good plants, but no one called him about it and his mother said most of the signs were down in a day. His manuscripts. He got a teaching job in California for a year and left clothes and two dresser drawerfuls of manuscripts in what they called the boys' room in her apartment. He told her he had sublet his apartment to two men who needed both closets for their clothes and more shelf space for their knickknacks and books. Besides, they found his manuscripts on the shelves an eyesore. She said 'Don't worry, I've got nothing but room in that closet and dresser, so they'll be nice and safe here and I promise never to read what's on the papers.' 'Read them, I don't mind. About half are type-scripts—you know, the original manuscripts, if that's what typescripts are. And the rest I just wait to keep and maybe use some day or at least give a last hard look at before throwing them away.' He returned and stayed with her at Christmas for a couple of weeks, looked in the dresser for his manuscripts and later asked her where they were. 'Oh, gone, did you need them? I thought they were all published, and since you had them in magazines and books as you said, you had no use for them anymore.' 'Half of them were published, but even most of those I could have used if I ever wanted to rewrite the magazine stuff for a book. And there were tons of unpublished work that some of I have copies, most I don't, and which I might have wanted to rewrite or take parts out of or use in some way. Why didn't you phone me when you were thinking of throwing them out? I wasn't in Europe or Australia but just a dollar-a-minute call away.' 'It wasn't the money. You know I'm not like that. Money, for all the good it's done me, I piss on, as your father used to say. But the pages were getting brittle and yellow or maybe most of them were old like that when you put them in the dresser. But every time I opened one of those drawers—' 'Why would you so much?' 'The first time out of curiosity. To see how they were and if I could rearrange them or stack them better. Then when I saw them all crumbling apart, I looked more and more often, and each time I looked they were worse off than the last. I thought of you, but didn't know how to preserve them. I tried mothball flakes—just sprinkling them on, which I read in the *Times* would help—but then my friend Marion down the block said they might make the paper crumble faster. But it was like walking into a sawdust mill, every time I opened the drawers and so many little pieces had fallen away. I'd also heard that roaches and mice love the ink and glue in paper—' 'What glue? These were all typewritten or photocopied pages.' 'That waxy coat you had on what you said was erasable paper. If these pests like glue, I was sure they'd like that or would smell it, and you know I'm scared to death of those things.' 'If you were really afraid you could have put them in an airtight trunk.' 'Where do I have one?' 'You could have told me, about the whole thing and your mothball flakes, and I would have phoned a luggage store around here and had them deliver one to you. It would have been a little extra work for you, transferring it all to a trunk, but probably no more so than sticking them in the garbage cans outside. But I also would have paid some worker—the woman who comes to clean for you once a week—to do it and to bring the trunk down to the basement, or the super for that. Because those things—the unpublished stuff—were practically priceless to me.' 'Then you should have taken them with you if they were so much to you that way and in the very trunk you say you would have bought for me.' 'I told you when I left. I couldn't be shlepping them from city to city like that. I thought they had a safe place here till I got back. I also wanted to be away from them for a while, thinking—who knows?—that some new idea might come to me about them if they weren't by my side. That's how it works sometimes.' 'Well I'm sorry. Doubly so for thinking I could do something good for someone by letting him keep his things here. But people think my place, because of the basement and that I have so many spare bedrooms now, can be a warehouse for them, but OK. I'm also sorry, for when the pages were discomposing to nothing, to think I was doing the right thing by getting rid of them. But my worst fears—roaches and mice, and even rats, possibly, though we've never had one in the house but I have seen one on the street—got the best of me. There's nothing I can do about it now but grieve along with you. But just for my sake, since this is beginning to kill me too, think if all you said was so valuable to you, really is.'

Books. She once gave half the books he had in his old bedroom to Salvation Army or some organization like that. 'They knocked on the door. I have a bell that works, but they knocked. They were very polite, though, when they told me what they wanted my old books and furniture for. The poor, handicapped, and so forth. I was affected by it, thought I could do some good for them and also clean out my place a little, which I'm always promising myself to do but never really get around to it. So I gave them a couple of broken chairs and an old card table and lots of odds and ends in the basement and then some of the books in the bookcases in the boys' room that looked the oldest and also in the credenza in the back hallway.' 'My books were the oldest. A few were more than a hundred years old, and precious to me in other ways. Novels, poetry, critical works, essays.' 'Some were so old they were coming apart.' 'I would have had them rebound.' 'But you didn't. And these people were so needy. And they said they'd box them and carry them out, giving me a lot more shelf space for my own books, besides cleaning up whatever mess they made. They did. Your room and the basement were cleaner than when they came. They also gave me a tax-writeoff slip. Asked me what amount I thought everything was worth—I said three hundred dollars though didn't think it was half that—and they wrote the figure in. I'll never use the slip—I don't earn enough—but you can have it if I can find it. Besides all that, you haven't looked at those books in years, so I thought you lost interest in them and wouldn't mind what I did. If you hadn't gone to your room for something else, you never would have noticed they were gone. Be honest with me: you weren't interested in those books anymore.' 'Not true. You don't follow my every move. When I come here I often go to my old room, take a book out and sit on the bed and read it for a few minutes, or even longer, and if my interest's sparked or renewed, I take it home with me. But I never told you or showed you the book and said "May I borrow it?" because the book was mine. Just lucky for me I took what I did those times.' Candlesticks. When he was going to Hebrew school to learn his Haphtarah and such to get bar mitzvahed, he got involved for about a month selling raffle tickets for the synagogue. The boys who sold the most, he was told, would get a big prize, one they'd treasure for life. Besides, the synagogue would always be proud of them. So he went around his neighborhood selling raffle tickets, and tried to sell them at whatever function his parents gave, and cornered strangers who came to the house, like the furnace man, delivery people. He sold the most for anyone in the pre-bar mitzvah group and was invited to the synagogue's auditorium to get his prize. Rows of chairs had been set up, a cookie and juice table was at the side, his name was announced, there was a little applause, and he walked to the podium and the rabbi shook his hand and presented him a box of two wooden candlesticks 'made in our new state of Israel.' He had his mother use them at dinner that might. His father complained they made the room so hot he was sweating, and they were snuffed out before the meal was over. After dinner she scraped the wax off them and put them in the curio cabinet in the foyer. When he got his own apartment about ten years later and didn't have much to put in it, he thought of taking the candlesticks, but didn't like the looks of them. They were drab, old-fashioned, reminded him of Hebrew school, which he'd hated, and if someone at dinner turned either of them over and saw the 'Made in Israel' sign stamped into it, he might be thought religious, or zealotic, or even Jewish, when he sometimes didn't want to be. He began to admire the candlesticks about ten years after that, wanted to take them home and use them, but felt they'd been in her cabinet too long to remove. If she ever asks him if he wants them back, he thought, he'll take them, but not till then. About a month ago he was at his brother's for dinner and saw them in his breakfront. 'Where'd you get those?' he said. 'Mom. She said "Aren't these yours?" and I said "I don't know, are they? From when?" and she said "Hebrew school, when you were a bar-mitzvah boy and won first or second prize for selling an enormous number of something—rafffle tickets or candies." So I thought well, it could have happened. I was always doing things like that for the synagogue when I wasn't playing hooky from it, and Iris liked them a lot, so I took them. Mom also said she never cared for them much and only kept them in her foyer cabinet all these years so as not to hurt my feelings. So I didn't think I was really taking anything from her, even if she occasionally says things like that just to give us things because she knows we won't take them otherwise. But what do you think? To me they're kind of graceful and pretty, and they're obviously fairly old, but I'd never put candles in them. If they burned all the way down the wood might catch fire.' Howard said 'They're nice, but I think Mom got her boys mixed up. I was the one who won them by selling the most raffle tickets for my group at the synagogue a few months or so before I was bar mitzvahed. I even remember the ceremony when the rabbi gave them to me.' 'No really, I think Mom was right and I did win them. Once I began talking about them in the car ride home with Iris, I started remembering how I acquired them. I recalled canvassing the neighborhood and all the local Columbus Avenue stores to sell raffle tickes for prizes the synagogue was giving—tickets to the opera at the old Met, for instance. Box seats, in fact, I just remembered, with Lily Pons and I think Richard Tucker in it. He was a member of the congregation at the time. And by selling the first or second greatest amount of raffle tickets, though I don't remember being in any age category or anything, these candlesticks are what I got.' 'Then I must have been the winner of a different kind of raffle contest. Or the same kind—the West Side Synagogue was always big on benefits at the Met if they had Jewish stars in them—but about seven years later. But OK, let's forget it. You might be right. And what good are they if I can't use them? I've accumulated so much stuff in my apartment that I can't stand owning anything anymore that has no purpose if it isn't at least extremely aesthetic.' His old van. She once gave a tenant in their building the extra keys to it and said she was sure her son wouldn't mind him borrowing it for a couple of hours if the man could find a parking space for it good for tomorrow. 'He came downstairs and asked if you'd help him move something heavy from Brooklyn to his new apartment here. He'd seen your brightly colored van and thought you might also be doing private moving on the side. You weren't here and for some reason I volunteered giving him the keys. Maybe because he's so nice, pays the biggest rent in the building by about double, and has a very dependable job. He was willing to pay fifteen dollars for the two hours, twenty if it came to three, which he said was the going rate for a van with no driver or mover with it, but I told him to work all that out with you when you got home.' The van stalled on Manhattan Bridge. The man couldn't get it started, walked to a garage on the Brooklyn side, drove back with a mechanic and found the battery, wheels and windshield wipers gone. He had the car towed to the garage and called Howard's mom. Howard answered and the man said 'A valve's shot and needs replacing, plus of course the wheels and battery now and the wipers, for when you need them.' 'I'd like to get another estimate on the valve job and check around on the wheels,' and the man said 'Listen, sorry as I am that it happened, it's really your problem coming from years of use on the van, and I also haven't the time to hang around here bargaining with this guy. From what I know about cars, and as a kid I tinkered with them and worked in gas stations for years, what this guy's charging can't be more than twenty to thirty bucks higher than what another mechanic would charge, and to get it to another garage for an estimate you'll have to pay an additional tow charge. What I suggest is you junk it. It's only good now for its parts.' Howard asked the mechanic to make an offer, which came to the amount of the tow charge. She was always doing things like that. A while ago at dinner he asked her why. She said she thought she explained it well enough at the time each of those things happened. 'My train set then. It was an old Lionel and has to be worth a thousand dollars today. The only answer I'm looking for is what could have possessed you to give it away when I'd pleaded with you to keep it?' 'You didn't plead. You said try to keep it around, which I did but then years passed and you were away and I assumed you lost interest in it. Besides all that, are you going to go that far back to get something against me, for some reason? Your poor cousins needed diversion, nice toys. And *poor* because of what they'd gone through emotionally and also because Aunt Gussie could hardly pay her rent at the time and was still suffering tremendously over Ben. You remember: he just tipped over on the golf course and that was that. I was the first one she called.' He said she never did things like that with her other children and she said 'Sure I did, except to them, and now only Gerald, it was just plain common human error on my part or a misunderstanding because I didn't hear right or they didn't explain it well or compassion or good neighborliness from me, and they never made a big stink out of it. You seem to hold some sort of deep grudge against me, which I was unaware of till now.' 'Joe,' he said. 'I almost forgot it. I'm off to camp for the summer when I'm eight or nine—Miss Humphries's—and when I come back he's suddenly gone. "Where's Joe, where's Joe?" I remember screaming, hunting through the house for him, surprised he didn't greet me at the door as he always did, and after this long, even more so.' 'He was all your kids' pet, not just yours, and I think you're exaggerating your alarm at the time. You came home, you didn't know he wasn't there till I told you, and then you looked a little sad but said you were hungry and asked for a snack or lunch.' 'That's not so. I remember it the way I said it. Because it was such a terrible thing to me, the picture was put there that day and stayed. For weeks I'd been looking forward to him jumping all over me when I got back, and he didn't. I remember even telling my bunkmates at camp what he'd do. And Joe was my dog almost exclusively, since I was just about the only one to feed and walk him and give him Christmas gifts and things and he always slept under my bed when he could which meant the day or two a month you let him. But everyone knew whose dog he really was. "My dog," people called him, meaning "His...the kid's...Howard's." ' 'He was tearing up the apartment.' 'Probably because I was gone. So you should have loaned him out for the summer or put him in a kennel.' 'Not only when you were away. He caused what would

416

be today hundreds of dollars a year in furniture damage and this went on for all the time we had him. Your father never wanted him in the first place. But because he came free and you kids begged on your knees, even if we knew none of you would ever take care of him, though you say you did, he gave in, which talking of surprises, was a lulu for me. I never minded the damage that much—I could live with a scratched chair leg or couch cushion thrown up on—but your father couldn't or just used it as an excuse to get rid of Joe. Also the succession of girls, after Frieda, working for us. Very prim, some from good working class families. While you kids were in school or away they had to walk him and none of them liked it when he did it in the street or sniffed another dog's feces. Besides, Joe could be an angry dog, and they said he occasionally snapped and bit.' 'Never. He licked, he kissed, or only showed his teeth when someone provoked him.' 'If you say. But you remember I did go all the way out to Long Island by train with you to look for him and had convinced your father that if we found Joe we'd have to take him back.' 'Maybe you only did it to make me feel good at the time, but I appreciated it then and still do.' 'No, I don't waste time like that; we were really looking for him. Place where they last saw him, pound where some dogcatcher might have brought him. The man your father had given Joe away to was taking him to his summer bungalow out there, and Joe had jumped out of the car window when the man was getting gas.' 'That's one story I never fell for. I remember Dad saying the man had left the car window open only about eight to ten inches. I don't see how a big dog like Joe could have squeezed through it and especially at the top.' 'That's what your father told me. If he was lying he was doing it to us both, which means I did go on a wild goose chase. Anyway, what are we quibbling over, since we'll never know.' "

"Memory of it starts with them stepping off the train, then standing alongside it, conductor near them, same uniform it seems train conductors have always worn, gray cold day, cold gray day, but that's the way he always pictured it, contrast of the dark train and gray backdrop, his mother looking this way and that with an expression what's she supposed to do now? She told him to sit on the bench inside the station while she looked for a cab. Next thing he remembers they're sitting at a luncheonette counter in town, which they must have walked to for through the window he can see the train station across the street. While he ate she called a few taxi services in town but no cabs were available. It was wartime, gas shortage, gas rationed, scarcity of cars, cabs were considered a luxury out here, she was told, two of the three taxi services listed in the phone book weren't even in business anymore. Most of that he got from talking about it with her years later though never telling her the main reason he was interested in the trip so much. There was about an hour, a half-hour, during it when he can't remember ever having felt so close to her. The counterman said the one operating taxi service would take her if she were a local or a regular customer off the train, but since she just spoke to them it was too late for that. Two men seated at the end of the counter near the wall phone asked if they could help her. She told them what she'd come out for. First a trip to a gas station several miles out of town to show the people there a photo of a dog and ask if they've seen it around since he jumped out of a car there a month ago. Then to the local dog pound to look for the dog. They said they'd take her and her boy, no charge except for the cost of the gas and maybe if they could bum a few cigarettes off her. She said no really, that was too kind, but they could certainly have the cigarettes. They said it's OK, they've nothing doing at the moment, just so long as she doesn't spend all day at the garage and knows they're going to leave her at the pound; it'll only be a mile walk back along the boulevard to the train station if she can't get a cab or another hitch. Next thing he knows he's walking beside his mother, his hand in hers, across the street to the corner where the car's parked. Next thing after that he's in the back seat and the men in front. When the car was pulling away from the curb the driver quickly rolled down his window and spoke to a man running up to him, either a policeman or someone in the army or marines. Their conversation was jovial, seemed to go on for minutes, then the man outside waved goodbye to the men in the car and bent down to where his face almost touched the back side window and smiled and waved to Howard who was right behind the driver. By this time there was lots of cigarette smoke in the car, from his mother and the two men, but it didn't seem to bother him. Maybe because of the fresh air from the opened windows, maybe something else. He wondered how the two men were able to fit in front. Only because his mother and he were so crowded in back. Was the front wider than the back? He didn't see how, still doesn't, at least not by that much, for the men were big and there seemed to be plenty of space between them and between each man and his door. When they started driving he thought the men might be bad men who were going to do something awful to them. Kiss his mother, steal her pocketbook, kill them both. She must have sensed what he was feeling for soon after she patted his hand and said don't worry, it's going to be a nice trip and I hope we find Joe. But sitting in back with his mother. This part of the trip has come back to him many times, maybe even a hundred, when no other part of it has. In fact, to get to think of any other part of it, it almost always comes after he thinks of this. Pressed close to her, the scratchiness of her wool jacket or coat, her arm around him, other hand stroking his hair, part of the way his head on her lap, cool silk or rayon dress or skirt, her hard leg his head rested on, hand stroking his cheek and the back of his neck, he even thinks he remembers her leaning over and kissing the top of his head, but most of all his eyes closed and his head and torso squeezed against her side and her arm around his shoulder or back and other hand smoothing his forehead and running through and curlicuing his hair. They'd been alone outside lots of times in different places. She once took him to a movie at night. They sat in the mezzanine and he was allowed to find the men's room by himself and then to choose any one candy he liked from the two candy machines. All the times she took him to Indian Walk for shoes and after that to Schrafft's where she'd let him pocket a few sugar packets and he'd have a vanilla ice cream soda and have to sit on a phone book to reach the straws. Cabs to several places, usually the doctor's. But they've never, he believes, been alone together in so enclosed and cramped a space. He's saying maybe that's the reason, helped it happen, or maybe it was also something she was feeling toward him or something else at the time that made her act to him the way she did. Maybe even the cigarette smoke had something to do with it, for them both; he just doesn't know. They must have gotten out of the car at the gas station, but he's never remembered it. When he's talked about it with her she's said she doesn't remember any gas station, just the train and dog pound and quite possibly the luncheonette, which does strike a bell, maybe from all the times he's mentioned it—'Though if that was the case,' she's said, 'I don't see why not the gas station too'—but she can't say they were there for sure. So maybe she changed her mind about going to the gas station or the men suddenly didn't have enough time for both the gas station and pound or else convinced her not to go: that it was silly, for example, to think the dog would go back there once it escaped. During the drive the men turned around every so often to ask her questions and she answered them gaily. He remembers smoke pouring out of her mouth and nose when she laughed and spoke. Actually, he doesn't know how accurate that memory is. It could have come from lots of other times, for she always smoked and spoke a lot and at the time laughed a lot too. She was having a good time though. That he definitely recalls. She smiled and laughed like the times when his father put his hand around her waist and planted a kiss on her cheek or grabbed her around the shoulder and with his eyes open kissed her lips hard or when he grabbed her waist and hand when there was some radio or Victrola music on and did a couple of dance steps or twirls with her or when he teased her in front of the children, all this was in front of the children, or said something about how beautiful their mother was or what a great figure she still had, though he usually jokingly called it 'figger.' He felt cold in the car—probably because of the opened windows for the smoke—and putting her arm around him and their bodies so close made him warm and probably made her warmer too. He doesn't know why they waited a month before going out there to look for Joe. Phone calls to the gas station and pound and the man who lost Joe were made but that was all. His guess is that he badgered her till she gave in or she thought that after a month of him being depressed about it, only going out there to look for Joe would make him feel better. She's said 'I suppose we went out there when we did because it was the earliest I could find time for it.' 'I know we got a cab to the pound,' she's said, 'and I'm almost positive it was from the train station. Though I might have gone to the luncheonette just to call for it, but there were certainly no men.' 'Well I definitely remember them,' he's said. 'Two of them in the car, that they were young, the car old and leather-smelling till you all started up with smoking. Big bushy hair on one of the men. I forget the other's hair and I can't say whether the driver or guy beside him had the bushy hair—I think the driver. Maybe the car was actually a cab and the driver was a cabby and the guy beside him a friend going along for the ride or a passenger going in the same direction as us but getting off last. And this passenger or friend was the one with the bushy hair and the driver's I never remembered because I couldn't see it under the cabby's cap. And the uniformed man hurrying over could have been a fellow cabby and the uniform I saw might have only been his cabby's cap. Or else he wore it to complete what I think was sort of the standard cabby's uniform then and that was with a waist-length yellow jacket, leather or cloth, though maybe I got the color wrong and even the material and design. But what's it matter really? And it also wouldn't account for the luncheonette I swear we met those two men in. Maybe the driver and his friend were having lunch at the time and one of the cab companies you called from the train station, you say—the only one you said was still in business because of gas rationing and no new cars being made—or even from the luncheonette, if let's say the phones at the station were tied up and we crossed the street to call from there—said if you want a cab you'll find their one available driver having lunch this very moment at the luncheonette across from the train station, or the same one you're in. Or maybe we went in there to call for a cab or have a bite before we did and met the cabby by accident. But all of us sitting at the counter for at least a few minutes—so maybe you and I didn't have lunch there or even a snack, though I could almost swear the man had plates and coffee cups in saucers in front of them. Then walking to the corner where the cab or private car was parked. And the pudgy uniformed cabby or policeman or soldier hurrying over to the driver's window right after the car pulled out, and the man waving good-bye to me good-naturedly, though that might be an embellishment, his smile and bending down to me to wave; still, it stays. But without question the cab or car ride, long or short, to the dog pound, which I might have slept part of the way through, so comfortable and close was I in the back with you, even if my head was lying on or up against what I remember as your itchy jacket or coat, which normally would have kept me awake.' They went to the pound. Neither recalls how they got back to the train station, though she thinks she told the cabby that took them there to wait. 'That's what I'd usually do in a situation like that and in an area I wasn't familiar with. And cabs were cheap then and the waiting period particularly, or else I just called for another cab from the pound. For sure we didn't walk.' The man at the pound said it was unlikely their dog was there, she said, after so long and especially since the last time she called him about it, but he'd show them around. They went into a large airy room with about forty cages with dogs in them and a few cats. They walked down one aisle and back along the other. None of the dogs looked at all like Joe. Then he heard a dog barking from behind a wall. 'Listen,' he said, and listened. 'That's Joe.' 'Don't be silly,' his mother said. 'This gentleman will tell you: if he's not in this room, he's not here.' 'That's Joe, I'm saying—coming from through there. I know how he barks. He knows I'm here—must have smelled and heard me—and wants me to come get him.' The man said the next room was where they kept animals that had recently been brought in. 'If they don't show any signs of illness or anything, we let them in here. I know not one of them even remotely resembles an airedale.' 'It's him, don't tell me,' Howard yelled and started for the door to the room. 'Just to amuse him could you let him in there?' she must have said something like. She doesn't remember saying it, neither does he, but it's what he thinks she would have said from the picture in his head of her at that moment. They went in. It was a small room with no windows and only a little artificial light. Four or five dogs in cages on tables and they all started barking when they came in. 'At least we looked,' she said outside the pound. He wanted to go to another. Said something like 'Joe was a great runner and could have run twenty, even fifty miles in one day from where he jumped out of the car.' She said they've done enough to find Joe today, that she's already called every pound on Long Island twice but would call each of them a last time this week, but that they now have to catch a train so she can get home in time to do some other important things, and so as far as she's concerned the matter's closed for the day. If she said that in those words he probably said what does she mean when she says a matter's closed? He probably also cried but stopped in a minute or two or just quietly sobbed but went along with whatever she said. He doesn't remember any part of the trip back or anything more about that day or ever thinking of doing anything to find Joe again. Memory of it ends with them in front of the pound, wide gray sky behind her. He assumes the whole trip took about six hours and that it was dark when they got home."

" 'When I was a little girl,' his mother said, 'till I got to around ten, we slept two to three to a bed. Girls with girls, of course, boys altogether. Under lots of thick quilts when it was cold, one pillow per bed, and four of the girls in two beds in one tiny room and three boys and my two older sisters in two beds in another small room. My mother or one of the Polish girls would have to wake us up because we slept so heavily. She'd bang two pots together most times to do it or tinkle a spoon against a glass if we were already stirring. Strange we all slept the same, for in the next room the others had to be gotten up that way too. And also that we were all sent to bed the same time, even though there was twelve years between the oldest and youngest. I suppose my mother wanted to make sure she got an hour to herself. Or if there was any hanky-panky between her and Uncle Leibush, who lived with us, that would be a good time, with my Dad still at work.' For years after she got married she woke up around eleven or even noon. The children would be in school or in the nursery or bedroom with the live-in maid. His father would have left for work at seven. 'Some people like to have their teeth fixed before they go to work,' he said, 'because it's their only free time to or they think if they're still half asleep they won't feel as much pain. And lots of my patients I don't give novocaine to when they need it because they want to keep the bill down.' Then she'd come into the kitchen in her bathrobe, make fresh coffee (his father had his breakfast made by the maid), read the paper, smoke some cigarettes, have a second or third coffee, then bathe and dress. 'It was a little bit too hedonistic,' she said, 'but I loved it while it lasted. It made me feel like a real lady and late at night I got lots of good reading done.' She changed this routine when his father went to prison and she had to get a full-time job. Then she'd be up before seven, shower and dress, get the children up and ready for school, let the nanny in for the youngest child, make herself a quick breakfast, leave the house with her two youngest sons but in front of the building go left to the subway station while they went the other way to school. 'A kiss, a kiss, a kiss,' he remembers her saying on the sidewalk, after his brother and he started off, and she'd get down almost on one knee so they could one at a time or together come into her arms easier and kiss her. A few months after his father got out of prison she started getting up around nine, after the children had left for school. They had a housekeeper who'd make breakfast for his father, wake the children up and help then off to school, take the youngest to kindergarten and pick her up and take care of her the rest of the day. His father had a number of jobs for about ten years before he got his dental license back. Factory worker, shoestore salesman, department store floorwalker, then for eight years selling materials in the Garment Center. He always left early to get to work before anyone else. 'No matter how menial a job it is, the boss appreciates it,' he said, 'and the extra hour gives you a jump on everyone else. So you do it for show and possible advancement and the little time alone everybody needs and to make more money.' She was an interior decorator by then—she'd taken an interior design program at night while he was in prison—and once her business got going she'd usually begin seeing clients around 11:00 A. M. His parents came home around the same time at night and there was lots of take-out Chinese-American food and dishes like lasagna and roast turkey and flanken soup she'd cook to last three to four days. She started sleeping poorly twenty-five years ago, she said, when his sister's disease got much worse and the first symptoms of his father's showed. 'I got up five to six times a night, just as I do now, but then to help them, running from one room to the other sometimes.' He said a few times it could be the black coffee now she drinks late at night and, after his sister died, the hard liquor she seems to start drinking around noon. 'I don't drink coffee after dinner and I only nurse a drink or two a day, and when you're here for dinner or a chat and the way you pour, maybe a bit more.' He once checked her bourbon bottle and in three days it was two-thirds gone. 'You have anyone over for drinks since I was here last?' and she said 'No, why?' 'This bottle. You couldn't have consumed that much since then. The woman who cleans up for you, maybe?' 'You mean to sneak? No, and what about how much is gone? I bought that bottle almost two weeks ago. They say twenty-two shots to a bottle, so it's right on time.' 'I think I opened it for you when I was here last,' and she said 'Couldn't be, since you were here about six days ago and I never could have drank so much in that time.' 'That's not the way I remember it, but I could be wrong.' 'You're wrong, believe me, dead wrong. I'd be puking every night instead of just tired if I put so much away. As I've told you, I nurse my drinks, put lots of water in them, and ice, which becomes even more water the way I drink them, and lots of times after that ice melts I put in some more. Sometimes I think it's the taste of the bourbon-tinted water I like rather than the bourbon.' Almost every time he speaks to her on the phone she complains she didn't sleep well the previous night. 'Last night I was up almost the entire time. I put on the TV at four in the morning and watched it—the cable weather station, for nothing more interesting was on—till six, while I read and did my needlepoint, and then lay in bed for an hour trying to keep my eyes closed till it took away too much energy from me and I got up for the day. I know old people don't need that much sleep, but a few hours wouldn't kill me.' From what he's seen and she's said over the years her day runs something like this: bed by eight or nine, sleep till ten or eleven, read a book or watch TV in the sitting room while she sews or does needlepoint, back in bed listening to radio call-in shows and reading and sometimes sleeping for an hour, in the kitchen around three or four, a drink, some coffee, watch TV or read or both, back in bed, sleep for an hour or so, up, coffee, bathe, fresh coffee, half a toasted bagel or slice of dry toast, read the *Times* delivered to her building's vestibule, maybe make cookies or bread, preparing them now, baking them later, every other day a short walk around the neighborhood or block but sometimes, even when the weather's nice and she's feeling well, not leaving the house for three straight days, shopping for food, about every other week stopping to sit for an hour on a bench on one of the Broadway islands and listening to other elderly people talk, a phone call or two, her sister, her sister-in-law, a real estate agent calling to see if she's interested in selling her building, slice of bread or the other half of that bagel with cottage cheese for lunch, maybe a tomato or green pepper slice and a couple of radishes or celery stalks, drink before, drink after, sip it, forget where the drink is, pour a new one, drink from it, the other, thinking they're both the same glass, bourbon, little water, lemon slice or twist if one's been left over from the last time he was there or if he cut a number of them for her later and put them in wax paper and told her where they were in the refrigerator, since she likes twists better than slices, every five days or so opening her mailbox, every other day for an an hour working on the books for the building which she hates, every Friday telling the cleaning woman what work needs to be done and pitching in with some of the lighter chores, once or twice a week letting a building inspector in or oil burner man downstairs or accepting a package for a tenant or telling the delivery boy to leave her groceries on her doormat and then dragging the box or bags into the foyer and almost item by item carrying the groceries to the kitchen, once or twice a month depositing the rent checks in the bank and getting a few weeks' cash, seeing her doctor and dentist twice a year, week every summer staying with him and Denise in Maine, drink before dinner, dinner around six, slice of Gruyère or Brie or tallegio cheese on bread, maybe a baked potato with a pad of butter or butterless sweet potato or yam and piece of fish or half a can of white tuna or piece of chicken from a breast she baked and which'll last three days and a salad or a carrot and a few of her cookies but never her own bread, those loaves she gives away to neighbors or freezes for her sons or grandchildren who once every week or two stop by or come for dinner which they usually bring cooked and prepared or make there with their own food, about two out of every three Sundays lunch at home with her sister-in-law and then a walk along Columbus or Broadway to look at the shop windows and perhaps have an ice cream or in Central Park if it's not crowded or rowdy or the music too loud and then sitting, before her sister-in-law takes the bus home, along the wall outside the park opposite the bus stop, drink after dinner which she nurses till she puts the glass with whatever's left in it into the refrigerator for the next day or carries it to bed. 'If you are going to drink,' he's said to her in various ways, 'and I'm sure a little of it's OK—blood vessels, and to relax or for the lift it gives and just to have something in your hand other than another coffee or cigarette—why not wine or beer? The hard stuff isn't good for your stomach after a certain age, at least not more than a shot a day. Fifty, I'd think, if you've drank your share for a while, is when one should call it quits with it, and you've gone more than thirty years past that. Fine, means great constitution, ability to withstand liver and kidney corrosion or wherever it is. And your mind's still sharp, which I hope, if I inherited it right, means good news for me. But from my own experiences, it gives you a gnawing often aching feeling in your gut that keeps you up nights or a good slice of them. Or a glass of sherry or port, if you want to drink something late at night to help you sleep, another of its pluses, but not the cheap stuff but the better Californian or Iberian kind. And no coffee after three or four in the afternoon, and if you can keep it down to just one in the morning and then tea after and preferably herbal or vegetable teas or substitute coffees bought in health food stores, even better.' 'When I was a girl,' she answered him once, 'I thought I'd never take a drop of alcohol in my life. I was surrounded by it, that's why. My dad owned a saloon downstairs and the fumes from it rose to where it got in our bedroom window three flights up or through the floorboards some way, passing through the ceilings between us. I wasn't crazy. My sisters smelled it too and we always woke up with the stench in our hair and on our freshly laid-out clothes. His clothes also stunk from it and from cigarette and cigar smoke, something I also thought I'd never touch or marry a man who did, because he was in that place fourteen hours a day. I blamed alcohol for my not seeing him except an hour at dinner when he came up and if I bumped into him on the street during one of his brisk walks when he said he had to get out or not breathe, which is another reason I hated alcohol so much, though he never drank anything but a little schnapps every now and then and several glasses of religious wine on the holidays.' She often looks exhausted when he visits her and says she hasn't slept well the previous nights. She quickly uses up bathrobes and he's been buying her one every other Christmas. He once said 'Maybe it's your mattress that's keeping you from sleep,' and went to her room and felt it and said 'It's lumpy, slumps sharply to the side, I'm surprised you don't roll off it and end up sleeping on the floor. Let me get you a new one—a whole new bed, even. This year's Christmas gift instead of another plaid robe.' 'What for? It's still a good bed. Aunt Terry gave it to me when I had my double one taken out.' 'That's my point. It was probably her son's first bed. Even if the frame's still OK, the mattress must be sixty years old. Get rid of it. Get a double one so you can turn over in it without falling out, have a place to put your books and newspapers on when you read in bed and then fall asleep while reading without being poked or rattled by them.' 'Why a double for a single woman? And then I'll have to buy several changes of sheets to replace the ones I gave you when I sold the double bed.' 'I'll give you them back. Or buy you some all-cotton ones for the ones you gave me. As a birthday gift if you won't take so much for Christmas. But a single bed's for kids just out of the crib and convicts; it's too confining, part of some punishment.' 'I'll think about it, maybe it's not a bad idea,' but she'll never let him buy it for her nor get one herself. It'd have to collapse first and be declared unrepairable by both his brother and he and the super. Then she'd say she doesn't care what size bed she gets, queen, double or single: she won't sleep well on it anyway. When he moved out of town and came in for a weekend on some business or just to see her and slept in the old boys' room in her apartment, he'd hear her late at night or very early morning flushing the toilet, chopping or slicing vegetables on a cutting board, prowling about the house with her slippers flopping and sometimes past his door with a glass tinkling, could smell cigarette smoke, sometimes hear the TV going, hear her hacking loudly or trying to cough up phlegm or blowing a clot out of her nose, smell bread or cookies baking, coffee brewing, a stew starting which she'd jar and give him to take home because she doesn't eat red meat, twice heard her typing, forgot to ask what but he thinks a letter because after one of those times she asked him to mail one for her when he goes out. Later those mornings he'd say she seemed to have slept badly last night and she'd usually say 'I slept better than I have since the last time you stayed over. I don't know why, since I'm no longer afraid of a break-in after all those locks and bars and alarms and steel doors I had installed, but my mind feels much easier with you here.' Sometimes he's said 'I hate to bring this up again but maybe you'd always sleep well if you didn't drink and smoke and have coffee so late at night.' 'What drinking?' and one time he mentioned the glass tinkling and she said 'That tinkling was from an inch of drink I put back in the refrigerator yesterday and added some ice to this morning and which will probably be, because you're staying another night, the first of the only two I'll have all day.' One time she said 'Leave me alone, stop hounding me about it, for what other pleasures do I get? If I lived this long with them in pretty good health, I'm not about to die because of them, and if I suddenly did, what of it? I'm already eight years older than your father was when he died at a respectable age and some twenty years older than my parents ever got and which I never thought I'd be.' 'When I was a girl,' she said recently, 'I was spilling over with self-respect. I dressed beautifully, did my nails, we had a girl for this but to get it done the way I liked I ironed my own clothes, bathed with a special rough soap to clean out my pores, washed my hair every night even though I had to boil water to do it, combed and brushed my hair till it shone, held it with tortoiseshell barrettes I saved up months for to get, was always chipper and alert in the morning, sharpest one at home and in class, would often run to school just to get out of breath because it felt so good, could beat up some of the bigger boys when they got too cheeky with me, played ball so well and ran so fast that I was called, in spite of my good looks and feminine clothes, a tomboy, ran errands for money after school till around dusk and between each of them studied my schoolbooks. Later on I found I wasn't a day person anymore though I certainly kept up my appearance and wardrobe. Now with old age everything's gone to pot. I could care less what I look like. I forget to eat and don't bother with makeup or wear nice clothes and do little with my hair, though the beauty parlor I went to for forty years is still right around the corner. I'm a mess and I should do something to correct it. Maybe now that you're here for the weekend I will. You've always let me know when I've let myself go and I'm grateful for it.' 'You haven't, and when have I let you know that much? You still look good—your skin and the way you carry yourself and the texture and nice gray color of your hair, and unlike most old people your nose hasn't grown too long and in fact has stayed thin. What I wonder about is why you wear torn stained housecoats around the house and slippers and socks that are falling apart when you must have new ones or the money to buy them.' 'Because I can't sleep and so always wear the easiest clothes to slip off just in case I suddenly feel like getting into bed, and also that I've become a slob. But you keep harping on me about this and also what you're not saying about my hair and face and I'll change.' When he lived in the city and she invited him for dinner, he'd sometimes ring her bell, get no answer, let himself in with keys, call out for her, go to her bedroom door to see if she was asleep or sick. Sometimes he'd leave a note that he was here and left and other times he'd sit in the kitchen for an hour or two sipping scotch and listening to a classical music station if it had good music while reading one of her newspapers or the book he always carried with him when he went out, then would leave a note saying he waited for her, she must have slept badly last night so he was glad she was able to nap for so long, hope it isn't that she's coming down with something, he took some salad and cheese and bread so don't worry—he ate plenty and had a drink too and he'll call her tomorrow around noon. A few times he'd hear her clopping in her slippers from her bedroom, then she'd come into the kitchen in her bathrobe, say she was sorry but she'd only put her head down to rest a few minutes, she wasn't hungry but he should go ahead and have something, and she'd turn on the ovens and burners to warm up the food. He'd eat just enough to satisfy her and eventually convince her to have a slice of toast and cheese and glass of milk or some cottage cheese or yogurt before she had a drink. 'When I was young I talked and talked and talked,' she once said. 'Some people thought it a problem. When I got older I just talked and talked. By your age I was listening more than talking, and now I have nothing to say.' When he sat with her at one of these dinners or took her out to eat, after they talked about the food or the restaurant table and her health and she asked and he briefly told her how his work and other things were going, they didn't talk much unless he thought up things to ask her, a lot of which he'd asked before and so often knew the answers: what she did the last couple of weeks, whom she's seen and spoken to recently, anything interesting or unusual that might have happened to her lately, what's the book she's reading about? she go to any recent movies or see anything she liked on TV? anything particularly excite or disturb her in the papers? what about that woman with the strange Indian name who eagerly testified against her mother who's a judge? what about that beast who beat his child into a coma and then instead of helping her smoked cocaine after? how'd she get along when Dad was in prison? was it tough going back to full-time work after so long? any friends or relatives cut her off once that mess started? any of the women she danced with on stage or in movies become celebrated actresses or dancers or known in any way? who were some of the more famous headliners in the show? she have anything to do with them offstage? ever see Gershwin? she remember her first impression when she heard Stravinsky or Bartok or even Mahler? she ever try to return to the stage after her father pulled her off? did he actually drag her off during a performance or rehearsal or just told her not to go to the theater again? she have any interest in the election? she ever have any interest in politics? who was the president she admired most? what's she think of this new information that Roosevelt didn't do enough to save the European Jews? other than the fellow she's mentioned a lot were there other men she was in love or infatuated with or could possibly have married before she met Dad? he fool around a lot or was that all just gossip? how would they have split up the kids or time with them if they had divorced? how close did it get and how often? what was it like living for a while with someone she didn't like? either of them take it out on the kids? did she ever think of living with a man when she was unmarried? what stopped her and would it stop her if she were a young woman today? did her father fool around? what was it like living by gaslight? her eyes get tired reading or playing the violin or was the light as bright as in the average-lit room today? how'd firemen reach the top floors of six-story and seven-story walkups then? were the lower East Side streets as teeming as it's been said? she feel safe alone on them at night? can she recall a woman or girl getting raped on the street or in a park or anywhere then by a stranger? what kind of violence did she witness then outside her apartment? were there still many horses on the streets? she get interested in the book he gave her last week? if she has a choice does she prefer what's been called a good biography or a great fiction? her parents have a radio or telephone when she was a girl? did radios play classical music then or just what did they have on them? she go to concerts or poetry readings or art galleries and museums when she was in her early twenties or even in her teens? what she think then of Picasso and Braque and Matisse and artists like that? she read or see or was aware of any of the literary magazines? Pound, Eliot, Stevens? when she first hear of *Ulysses* the book? anyone she know bring it in as contraband or buy it when it came out here? how's her sister doing? she hear from any of her favorite nieces and nephews? doctors think Uncle Lewis will pull through? when and where did she learn to drive and in what kind of car? what was the farthest she ever drove west? what's she remember of World War I? outside of lighting candles on Friday nights once Vera got very sick was she ever religious? what was the thinnest she ever saw Dad? does she remember him ever having more hair? what did they discuss then? was it ever a problem for her that he rarely read books and perhaps outside of grade school never a line of poetry? were there sex manuals at the time? her brother Leonard and older sisters prepare her in any way for sex? were there blacks in her elementary and high schools? what did she do the day of the Crash? she remember the day Roosevelt died when they were all in the same room crying? what forms of contraception were used in the teens, twenties and thirties other than condoms, the rhythm method or where the man pulls out or woman moves aside? any

433

one teacher make a difference? what were some of the beers sold in her father's saloon? Thomas Wolfe, Thomas Mann, Kafka or Babel? what can she remember about the bohemian art scene in Greenwich Village then? the village life of her parents and what they said about their parents' before her parents boated over here? what meals she like best that her mother or her mother's Polish girls or Dad's mother cooked? they lock the doors at night then? when he was a boy they really keep the lobby and front doors unlocked when school was out or just over for the day? any relatives of hers and Dad's still over there when the Nazis came? when she go up in her first plane? she have any gentile friends she could take home when she was a schoolgirl or from her jobs later on? she ever go out with a non-Jew? what was Cuba like on their honeymoon? she get drunk on rum there? what did bathtub gin taste like? she ever take a drug in the twenties just to get high? she read Gertrude Stein or just about her in the papers during her famous trip here? Hemingway when he was starting out? is he right that she never liked Faulkner and why? what did she and Dad do in Europe that time they went other than drinking beer at Heidelberg Castle and champagne at the Folies Bergère? what was it again Dad said to Jimmy Durante and Durante then said to him at that Coney Island nightclub or beerhall where he entertained? she ever go to Luna Park and what was it like? did a proper young woman ever go into a subway washroom? she ever get along well with anyone from Dad's family? what made her call Dad's father such a schnook and schmo? What were the Polish towns again her parents and Dad's came from? when she was pregnant with him and before she had to change his name to one with an H when Dad's mother died where'd she come up with Peter Anthony? what was it like being in the opening-night audience of a new O'Neill play? they ever go to the ballet? would she like to one of these days? what was the greatest single thing including mind-reading acts and trained elephants that she's seen on a stage? the day Lindbergh landed? has she changed her mind about Israel and the Palestinians in any way? she read the paper today? how about that cult leader on the West

Coast who as a disciplinary example to the rest had his little daughter beaten to death and then hung out a window by a rope? outside of lynchings were there things like that then? she really come in second or third in a Miss America contest or did it have a different name then or was all that just to enthrall the kids? did Fitzgerald's antics and works make an impression on her early on? was the Charleston difficult to learn? has life sort of measured up to what she thought? she often talks about death but if she stayed healthy would she like to live another twenty-thirty years? is there any philosophy she's followed or thinks she should have? if she had one or two pieces of general life advice for him what would it or they be? what were conditions like giving birth in a hospital then? did he really start to come out in a taxi? was she allowed to watch or assist her brothers and sisters being born on the kitchen table? does she know how either of her parents were born? what's she think of him as a father? are there any similarities he has to Dad other than physical? what did Dad truly think of him? what were some of the nicest and worst things he used to say about him? would she be honest for once and say what she thinks are her greatest disappointments regarding him? does he measure up in any way to what she thought he'd be like or be? she think he has any regrets how things have turned out for him and his present prospects? any writer she thought great whom she hasn't heard anything about or much for fifty to sixty years? Dad ever take him for a solitary stroll in his pram? did Sophie Tucker really sit with them at the nightclub she was singing at and try to drink Dad under the table? he really do his term standing on one foot or was all that just a big boast? how was it Edward G. Robinson sat for a few hours in their sitting room one afternoon? she remember the time he was small and fell down a coal chute up the block and she had to pay the coal man a dollar to climb in after him? the time a popsicle got stuck to his tongue and she thought the best thing to stop him from crying hysterically and possibly choking on it was to pull it off? wasn't that earthquake something with the ratio of killed to injured ten to one? what was the worst personal and worldly

435

catastrophe she's heard of or had? the worst worldly or personal catastrophe she's ever known? how well can she still speak Yiddish and French? would she like to go to a kosher restaurant one of these days? would she make gefilte fish for him and his family if he brought over all the ingredients and the three kinds of fishes he thinks it is already ground? what were the first words he said? she recall his first steps or were there just too many kids? who of her brood showed the most intelligence and coordination and creative abilities and sensitivity and things like that from the start? does she still have that synagogue say memorial prayers every year for Vera and Alex and Dad? what's she think of people spending more than they earn or can pay back in good time? did she or Dad instill ideas of frugality or penuriousness in him or she think they came on their own? Not that he's really that interested in it but does she think the federal deficit's going to cause another depression or runaway inflation or will ever be improved? does she still think of Vera and Alex every day as she said some years back? she mind him asking questions like that? she think Gorbachev will carry it off or summarily get poisoned by the Kremlin kitchen like perhaps the last two or three guys? was she one who thought Stalin a louse from the start? is there anything she wants to ask him? is there any one woman he's known she's intensely disliked? does he ask too many questions? is there anything she's been curious about him for years but never said? is there anything she thinks he wouldn't answer or face himself? how does she think things are going between him and Denise? as husbands come and go where would she rate him? if she can't really hear him then doesn't she think she should get her hearing aid checked or just go for another ear exam after so many years? is there anything to this that he can't remember her or Dad ever reading to him? did Dad like to put him on his shoulders or when he was very small carry him in one arm? how did she take him along when she wasn't using a nanny or stroller or older brother or pram? she still get her teeth checked twice a year? did she ever get a response or even a thank-you from any of the people she sent his last work to?

which of the desserts looks good to her even though he knows she won't touch it? does she think he drinks too much wine with his food? what is it about this place that they always go to it when there are ten other restaurants within a ten-block range of her house? Sometimes he's suggested she go to her general man and get a prescription for a mild sleeping pill or tranquilizer to help her sleep. She's said 'I never took one of those things in my life, never wanted to though sometimes I probably needed to, and it's not because I think I'll get addicted, but I'm not about to start taking them now.' 'Why?' 'Because I want to fall asleep when it's natural to and not through stimulants.' 'They're not stimulants. They're relaxants or whatever the technical term is.' 'They stimulate you to relax or sleep. They do something or they wouldn't have to be prescribed.' 'You take coffee; that's a stimulant.' 'Not for that. I take it to relax and pass the time away and because I like the taste of it, something you could never say about a tranquilizer or sleeping pill. And it does relax me, the two or three cups I have, but not enough for sleep.' 'Then alcohol. You take that and technically it's a depressant, isn't it, which I think would be worse than a relaxant or sleeping pill to get you to sleep.' 'It doesn't get me to sleep, even though you've told me to take a glass of sherry or port at night for that, and it doesn't depress me. If anything, it picks me up and keeps me going gently, the one or two drinks I have in a day.' 'Then go to a drugstore and buy a bottle of Nytol or one of those.' 'Sometimes the over-the-counter drugs are more dangerous than the prescribed ones. You know that when they suddenly jump to have to being prescribed.' 'But it's been years of you not sleeping well—ten, maybe fifteen.' 'That's OK; I'm still healthy for my age. If it slows me down at times, it's better than dropping me dead. And when all my worries go, good sleep will come.' Whenever she says something like this he doesn't want to say 'What worries?' He knows she'll say 'Bills to pay, checkbooks to balance, getting over to the bank, filling out complicated city forms, the building, waiting all day for oil burner men and inspectors and delivery boys to come.' He calls and says 'Hi, Mom, it's me, Howard,

how are you?' and she says 'All right, I guess. I was up all night.'
Usually he says 'I'm sorry, what's wrong?' but this time he says 'Sorry
to hear that.' Sometimes he thinks 'I've heard all this so much and
in the same exact delivery and the same lines' while she's saying
something like 'I should sleep better tonight though, now that I've
spoken to you.' The conversations are always short. He doesn't like
talking on the phone to anyone or not for long and if he's particularly
brief that call she says 'Is anything the matter with you? You don't
sound well.' 'No no, I'm fine.' 'Really?' 'Yeah, sure, in the pink.' She
always ends the call with 'Thanks for calling, and I love you,' unless
she's very tired or sick, and he usually says 'Same here with me,
much love' or 'Me too.' 'When will I see you?' she says this time and
he says 'I'll try to come in soon.' 'Good. How are the children—
Denise, the whole family, of course?' 'Fine, fine.' 'Nobody with
colds—nothing like that? With the weather so changeable as it's been,
that's when they come.' 'No.' 'Good. And how are you?' 'Fine, you
know me—almost always healthy. But how you doing? Everything's
OK?' 'I don't sleep. I just can't these days. Maybe an hour, two. I
seem to worry about everything—the bills, paperwork for the city
I don't have to have in for weeks to some of it for three months. It's
stupid, but I do.' 'I've said this before, and I'm not saying it now to
make you upset or that I expect you to change your mind or anything,
but you really should go to your doctor and have him prescribe
something very mild to help you sleep. Or just talk to him over the
phone and have him do it. I'm even surprised, when he last saw
you, he didn't suggest it on his own.' 'He did, but I told him what
I'm telling you now. I never took them and I'm not about to start.
I don't know what's the matter with me. I know that at my age I
should relax about life a little, so why do I worry about these things
so much? When I figure it out, I just might relax. Because I'm not
sick for someone so old, knock wood. None of the ailments. And
I have enough savings and income from the building to live without
struggling, and a roof nobody's going to take away from me. It must
be my nature to worry over nothing, I suppose. But the children,

Denise—they're all okay?' 'Yes,' 'Good. You?' 'Fine, thanks.' 'I'm glad. Any of them around so I can speak to them?' 'I'm calling from school and am actually on a ten-minute break from class.' 'Then I won't keep you. And nothing's really happened in my life since I last spoke to you, so I don't—except one thing. Did I tell you about Cousin Nathaniel?' 'No.' 'I didn't tell you? You know who I'm talking about?' 'Nat, Ida's son. What's wrong? He's OK, isn't he?' 'He's finished. Beyond life. I read this little newspaper article about it days before I heard it. It's a real story. You have another minute? Or call me back when you do or I'll call you if I don't hear from you.' 'No, tell me, what?' 'He was stabbed to death. In his apartment. I read this little article in the *Times* last week—' 'Stabbed to death?' 'First hit on the head all over. Then stabbed as if the person went completely crazy when doing it. Cut to pieces, hacked. But this article I read— At the bottom corner of the page, could easily be missed, so I don't know what attracted me to it, said an unidentified man was found stabbed to death with multiple wounds in his apartment on Avenue J. Neighbors had complained of the smell for four days, so they called the police. Or he'd been there for four days and they only started smelling it for three or two. When it said Avenue J, I wondered if it could be him. He'd taken over Ida's apartment when she died, which was their whole family's once—you remember, when you were all young. How much older would he be than you?' 'Seven years, eight. But because I think he's a few years older than Jerry, maybe even more. But good God. Dinners all the time there. Fridays. I can't believe it. In the same apartment.' 'That's what I thought when I first read the article. When it said unidentified man I almost knew it was him.' 'But Avenue J's a long avenue. Thousands of people must live on it, so I don't see how you could have thought it was him.' 'It just entered my mind. Because he was such a loner, maybe. And he was so strange, I heard, these last few years—worse than he ever was— that who knows what kind of people he might have hung around with or let in for what. His sister didn't. And he's the only person I know who lives on Avenue J since his mother died. But that's just half the story, what I told you. Hanna—I'm not going to get you in trouble with your school?' 'No, what?' 'What?' 'His sister Hanna.' 'She called me a few days after he was found and told me it all. The funeral was only last Sunday. I don't know why it slipped my mind not to call you when I found out. I guess I didn't think you'd be that interested or just that you're so occupied with all the work you do and just the problems with small children—sickness and things.' 'But I don't understand you. He was my favorite cousin when I was a boy. So really the only one I ever got close to, since I hardly knew the others. He and Hanna, but he would also come over to the house, take Alex and me places.' 'That I didn't know. But it was at Pinelawn or something. A veteran's cemetery on Long Island. Funeral and burial both. Hanna was hysterical most of the call. But she said that's where he always wanted to be buried, to save on the cost for them, since he'd been almost penniless for years. Taps and everything, she said they had at it; beautiful chapel and immaculate grounds, so as nice a place to be as anywhere. And everything except the rabbi, since she wanted her own, and half the casket paid by the government. I didn't go because I didn't know of it and I couldn't have got out anyway and I don't think Jerry would have driven me.' 'Sure he would have if he wasn't supposed to be out of town that day. He's told me Nat was his favorite cousin too.' 'I wish I had known that. But how they couldn't identify him immediately when they knew he lived in that apartment I don't understand. Maybe he just never went out much lately or only when neighbors and the super couldn't see him. He had that kind of peculiarity in him. What I'm saying is his appearance might have changed so much recently—starving himself, if he was so penniless, though I'm sure he could have eaten anytime he wanted at Hanna's or her girls' or borrowed if he needed from her—that they didn't recognize him. Or else— 'Come on, don't go off like that.' 'Why? Since he lost his shoe store, or walked away from it—the story's never been straight—he's been peddling toys up and down Broadway and not making a dime from it. He was sloppy, dirty, half the time unshaven for days, Hanna said. Nothing like his father, who was always perfectly groomed and spotless—so nobody wanted to buy from him and he was stuck with what he wanted to sell. Hanna said the police were letting her into his apartment for the first time this week and I bet she finds nothing but toys and thousands of his old jazz records.' 'About his appearance change, I bumped into him last year at around 116th and Broadway and he didn't look much different than he did at Dad's funeral, only paunchier. We had a nice chat on the street. I wanted to take him in for coffee, but he said he had to deliver the boxes he was carrying.' 'Those were the toys. He was too ashamed to tell you he'd become a peddler. But I didn't know you saw him.' 'I told you then. I was staying with you that weekend. I even brought up the records with him—that when we were kids he used to bring us into his room to play them for us—but he said he got rid of them twenty years ago.' 'Anyway, the story is that he went to the veteran's office in Brooklyn to collect his pension check— no one gets them mailed, or social security checks, in his neighborhood, Hanna said. Afraid they'll be stolen from their mailboxes, if the boxes still even have locks on them. And then he cashed it at another desk and left with a man he seemed to only have just met there, people said. It was obviously this man who went home with him and killed him for the money he saw he had. The door wasn't broken in or fiddled with. The police said it looked exactly like something somebody would do who walked in with him—a friend, or someone later let in. Nathaniel couldn't have had much money if it was a veteran's pension he was on. He was nothing but a buck private, if I remember, and had no disability from the war. Though who knows what Dad might have arranged for him years ago and even what that man might have thought he had. He saw two hundred dollars in Nathaniel's hands, he imagined two thousand in his home. But Dad did that for Nathaniel's father when he fell off a stepladder through a window at work. Workmen's Compensation and his insurance company wanted to give him the bare minimum—said it was his fault plus something about the store not having him properly on the payroll. Dad spoke to some people and maybe even fixed things with some schmears and got him full disability pay for life and also for Ida after Jack died. Your father was very smart about things like that when people didn't work for it or deserve it and my guess is that Ida asked Dad to do that for Nathaniel too when she saw the kind of character he was going to end up as. He'd do anything for that family—there was no better brother and son. And then Nathaniel, as the way I see it, with a temper sometimes like his mother's and Grandma Tetch. You remember all the stories I've told you about her. She used to beat her children with broomsticks, Ida included. That whole family, except your father, were either weaklings or violently nuts. Anyway, when the man wanted the money, Nathaniel must have fought and talked back like I think he would because of his temper, and that's when he got beaten on the head several times and stabbed when he kept on fighting. You have to admire him if that's what happened, though I don't know how many times your father told him, when he had his shoestore and there was a chance he might get robbed—you know, they all worshiped Dad and usually took his advice—to just give the money up and anything else they wanted.' 'What a way to go though. Just awful, awful.' 'Terrible, I know. And they don't think they'll ever get the guy. Somebody nobody ever saw before in the veteran's office, if it was him. And if it wasn't him who did it, then the police are really stumped, according to Hanna. Not that she wants him caught. She's afraid if he is, then his friends or the killer out on bail will come after her for no better reason then that he'll think she pressed the police to catch him or she knows something more about him than she does. She knows nothing, she says, and wants to keep it that way, so she's not pressing. That's what she told me. You ever hear anything like that? But look at me. Before all this about Nathaniel I was going to say nothing happened in my life since I last spoke to you, and in a way that's still true. But what's the best time to call you so I get you and can speak to everyone else?' 'Six.' 'Then that's when I'll call. Not tomorrow, since I just spoke to you, but the next day or the weekend. I'm tired now but I'm sure I'll be in much better shape to talk next time.' 'Stay well, then.' 'Thank you and thanks for calling, and I love you.' 'Same here with me, Mom.' 'What?' 'I said much love to you too and I hope you're feeling better—have had enough sleep, aren't so tired—you know, the next time.' 'Something must be wrong with our connection all of a sudden, or this hearing aid. It works and it doesn't. I think it's even made my hearing worse, for it was never that bad where I didn't hear anything. Let me adjust it. . . .There, now say something.' 'Hello, hello, I'm speaking, can you hear me, Mom'?' 'No, nothing, just faintly, as if you're a million miles away. What time did you say was the best to call, and loudly.' 'Six, six.' 'What?' 'Six! Six!' 'Oh, I'll just take my chances and call some time this Saturday, but only after I get this rotten thing fixed. I'm sorry, dear. Bye.' "

"He's in his mother's neighborhood and decides to drop in. Though he has the keys to her apartment, he'll ring the vestibule bell. If she doesn't answer, he won't let himself in. She could be napping, resting, taking a bath, just wanting her privacy. She's walking up the steps of her building's areaway when he's coming down the block. 'Mom?' he yells from across the street. She doesn't look his way. 'Mom, Mom?' he yells, crossing the street. She reaches the sidewalk, holding on to the wall and then the short iron fence on top of it to get there, stops, takes a deep breath, and starts down to Columbus Avenue. Probably has her hearing aid turned off or else not in. He starts to run after her, then thinks follow her, see what she does for a while, he's always been interested and has never done it before, maybe because this is the first chance he's had. So he follows from about fifty feet behind. If she sees him he'll say he just rang her apartment bell, she didn't answer, he didn't want to disturb her by letting himself in if she was home, and was heading now to Broadway to catch the subway or bus. She walks slowly. Every three buildings she stops to rest. She looks at the sky or the tops of buildings while she's standing still, to the sides, a couple of times behind. He doesn't wave and she doesn't seem to notice him or not as her son. One time he pretends to tie his shoe when she looks at him, another time when she turns his way he actually has to tie that same shoe. She's carrying a small canvas shopping bag and she probably has her handbag in it. She has on the black sneakers he convinced her to buy a few years ago to make walking easier, or they could be a second pair. Black slacks, shirt and jacket and with her hair handsomely combed and pinned back, so she could be dressed for going to just about anywhere: a movie, stores, a stroll. Near the end of the block she stops and looks at the second-story window of the building she's in front of. She smiles and waves to it. The window opens, a woman's head sticks out. 'How are you, Kathleen?' his mother says. 'Fine, thanks; nice day for getting out, I'd say. How is everything?' 'All right, considering. I thought I'd do a little shopping.' 'What I should do with the weather this nice. And the family?' 'You know—you hear from them and you don't. And yours?' 'As well as can be expected.' 'The same thing?' his mother says. 'But worse.' They chat for a few more minutes. He sits on a stoop, takes a book from his jacket pocket and pretends to read while listening to them. His mother tells her to try to come for lunch tomorrow or the next day. 'Nothing elaborate; we'll talk.' 'The next day I can make it.' 'Then I'll see you there at noon if I don't see you on the street before then, dear.' She waves, Kathleen waves, and she goes to the corner. She looks left and right, then across the avenue as if she's only now deciding which way to go. Left, crosses the street, stops at the third store along Columbus, goes inside, comes out with an ice cream cone, strawberry it seems, sits on the bench in front of the store and eats it. He looks in the window of a children's toy and clothing store next to the ice cream shop. If she sees him and calls out his name he'll say 'Mom, oh hi, I was in the neighborhood, stopped to look at all the nice things in that store for Olivia and Eva, not that I'd ever buy anything—way too expensive—but I was on my way to see you. In fact I was going to call you at the corner phone there in about ten seconds. I guess I would have got nobody home.' A young woman and her daughter sit beside her, filling up the bench, the girl right next to her. 'Hello,' she says to the girl. 'You know, I once had a little girl—you're around what, seven, eight?' 'Six.' 'Six? My, how much more grown up you look. And what am I talking about? I've a granddaughter your age and had two your age before they grew up and became big. But my daughter when she was six had long dark hair like yours and was slim and pretty like you too and she also loved ice cream cones. What's your favorite flavor? I bet I can guess.' 'Flavor?' 'What ice cream cone do you like best?' her mother says to her. 'Vanilla.' 'Say it to the lady, and in a loud clear voice; don't be shy or intimidated.' 'Vanilla!' 'I've told her a hundred times: If there's anything I can do to prepare her for the adult world, it's that. I won't have her—you know, mealy.' 'My granddaughter too. But that was my favorite flavor when I was six,' his mother says to the girl. 'Till I switched to strawberry—I don't know why I did—and it was my daughter's favorite flavor all her life. Vanilla was.' The two women talk while the girl eats her ice cream and looks at the traffic and people passing. The talk quickly gets into large families—the woman came from one, so did his mother— 'The Jews years ago and the Irish forever,' his mother says, 'nothing insulting intended'—and then their voices gradually get lower and he hears the words 'breasts...breast-feeding...warm compresses on them to draw the milk up, and also drinking dark beer and stout.' His mother's giving advice—'I nursed all mine for more than a year and nobody thought I had the equipment for more than two months'—but it must be for someone the woman knows, for her breasts don't seem like a nursing mother's and her stomach's flat, and where's the baby if she has one? Maybe at home with a nanny or someone, and he could be all wrong about her breasts. A woman he knew who he thought was almost flat chested, and when she took off her blouse the first time, 'Oh my goodness, gosh, I had no idea, not that it should mean that much or I'd feel any different to you if they weren't so large, but still...' and went up to her from behind and put his hands around her on them. She still had her bra on and when she unhooked it and slid off the shoulder straps and twisted her head around to kiss him, breasts and bra fell into his hands. Palo Alto, back of a house by the train tracks, twenty-three years ago. The woman and daughter stand up; the two women shake hands. His mother finishes the ice cream in the cone, bites off a piece of the cone, looks around before spitting it into the paper napkin he didn't know she was holding, drops the napkin and cone into a trash can beside the bench and continues down Columbus. She still stops every forty feet or so, sometimes a deep breath. A young woman passing her looks at her standing still, stops a few feet away to look back at her, goes back and says 'Is everything OK?' 'Yes, thank you. Just resting, but I can make it fine to where I'm going, dear.' 'You're sure you're OK?' 'Positively. You're a sweetheart for asking.' Sidewalk's now crowded because of a row of vendors near the curb and the enclosed restaurant patios jutting out from the buildings. Her eyesight's not good and she refuses to wear her glasses outdoors, so there's even less chance she'll recognize him now. She does, he'll say 'Mom, why hi, I was just over your place, rang the outside bell, no response, so I let myself in—I hope you don't mind—and when I saw you weren't home, thought you might be on Columbus or in one of the stores here and came to look for you. If you weren't, or I couldn't find you, I was even going to walk to Broadway to D'Agostino's and Fairway, the two other places I thought you might be. Like to stop in for a coffee or snack someplace, on me?' She crosses the next street and goes into the supermarket at the corner. He follows her, picks up a basket by the door, puts a few beers in it from the cases stacked at the front of the store, too good a buy, loses her, looks up the nearest aisle, goes to the entrance and looks up the first aisle and sees her at a meat counter looking at what's there. She takes out a chicken—whole, parts, he can't tell—puts it in her cart, some beef—cubes for stew, looks like—at the dairy section gets cottage cheese, yogurt, two or three different foreign cheeses, goes down an aisle and gets scouring powder, big box of laundry detergent—how's she going to carry it all? Probably will have it delivered—Brillo, silver polish, floor wax, then several cans of tuna, seltzer, marmalade, English muffins, lettuce, carrots, radishes, scallions, bananas, kiwi, a cantaloupe. 'You think this is ready?' she says to the woman who weighs the produce. The woman taps and smells the cantaloupe and presses its ends, says 'Think I know what I'm doing? I see the regular man doing it, I do it. But he's off today, so don't go by me.' 'Let's say if you were thinking of buying it—would you?' 'You're asking me that, customer to customer, I would, 'cause it's a great buy, and I'd keep it in a warm spot for a few days, but not the stove, you know? Now the bananas,' weighing them—his mother puts the cantaloupe back—'yours are good, you could eat them while you're walking home. But the ones over there—too green, so I wouldn't touch them.' 'I think those are Spanish bananas—plantanos, I think they're called—and are supposed to be green. You cook them.' 'Do you? They look like green bananas to me that'll take weeks to ripen.' 'That reminds me,' and she squeezes a number of avocados, puts two of them in her cart. 'Nice talking to you, dear' she says. 'Same here. Have a good one.' Package each of figs and dates, jar of apple sauce, several jars of baby food pear sauce, two six-packs of Dutch beer from the cases in front, and goes to the checkout counter, writes out two delivery forms, pays by check, says 'I wrote on it to leave the packages by the door,' gives a dollar tip for the delivery boy and leaves. He quickly pays for his beers on the express line, goes outside and sees her crossing the avenue at the corner. She buys a used book at a vendor's table on the sidewalk, goes into a card and party goods store at the corner and through the window he sees her smiling and another time laughing as she reads some cards. She takes one to the counter up front, he goes to the open door to listen. She sees him she'll say 'Mom, hi, I happened to be in the neighborhood for something (he'll think of what), passed this store and saw you in it, but for some reason I could never stand these kinds of shops. Too what? Schlocky, meretricious, if I've got the word right for what I mean, and that cloying incense smell from the candles or something—soap, I don't know—though maybe that's all unfair of me and I don't really catch their value and worth—the stores', not of course the candles'. Anyway,

I decided to wait out here till you came out or saw me from inside.' But the beers. 'Mom, hi, I was looking for you on Columbus, saw a good buy for Dutch beer advertised on Pioneer's window, so went in and bought a few and coming out of the store saw you crossing the avenue. . . .You were in Pioneer at the same time? Amazing, but I just shot in and out. Anyway, saw you were having such a good time browsing through the cards—they can be very funny, I know—that I thought I wouldn't spoil your fun so would just wait outside. What do you say? Like to have a bite or drink someplace?' She tells the salesman behind the counter how different cards are from what she remembers them ten, fifteen years ago. 'I'm almost sure I told you this before, but I can't believe how risqué some of them are. I'm no prude, but do they really permit it? Can someone be arrested for sending one of the dirtier cards through the mail? I'm not joking. Monkeys doing it with people in one. Grotesque statues having orgies with figures in paintings. I'm sure it isn't only that my attitude can be a little out of date.' 'Oh no, we get complaints about them from every age. But plenty of people, and I'm not justifying the cards, find them funny and cute, and they cost more than the others, so the owner's happy. But you got a good traditional one—one of my favorites, both universal and clever. Whoever's getting it will get a big lift.' He wonders who that is. Nobody's birthday or wedding anniversary's coming up that he knows, and from what the man said he doubts it's for a religious holiday. Friend of hers he doesn't know of? Better yet. He turns to the window as she leaves, looks at the party material while watching her reflection cross the avenue. How would he have explained his window-looking? 'I was thinking of the kids—their birthdays—I know that's three and four months from now, but you have to plan ahead. . . . But what crap. And the prices!' She sits at a table in front of a Mexican restaurant. He sits at an outside table of the adjoining restaurant—Indian; he didn't even look—and when the waiter comes up, 'No food, please; just a European or Japanese beer, or Indian if you got.' She orders nachos and cheese and a draft beer. Draft he should have asked for. She leafs through the book she bought while she eats and drinks. She sees him he'll say 'Mom, I don't believe it, patio-to-patio restaurants—what a fantastic surprise. I called you just ten minutes ago—was in the neighborhood so thought "Why not?" But wanting to know if you'd like to go out for exactly what you're having now, a snack and beer. I didn't know you liked those nacho things. I can't—the cholesterol; my doctor would have a heart attack—but you're incredible, arteries like a child's, and if I had known I would have suggested taking you to a Mexican restaurant long ago. There must be some things there I could eat. But think my patio will mind if I move my beer to yours? I'll just drink up and pay up and get a beer at your table.' She reads several pages in the middle, the last page, closes the book and has a look as if she doesn't know by what she's read if she wants to read the whole book, looks at the people passing, lights one of those he supposes he could call them cheroots. A young man at a table on one side of her asks if he could bum one from her. 'Of course—take two; less I smoke of these, the better.' He takes one, asks what book she's reading, she lights his cheroot with her lighter. Asks if she reads a lot. Was she a teacher at one time? Has she always loved good literature? He wishes he read more. He wanted to read that very same book for years, but in college was too busy with studies, in graduate school too busy with his thesis and teaching, and now at his job too busy working. 'Carry it with you,' she says. 'On the subway or whatever you take. Long elevator waits. That's what my son says he does and he gets an extra ten-fifteen pages a day in that way. Here; it only cost me a measly two dollars and I know after a few minutes with it I'll never finish it. At my age—well, anyway.' He wants to give her the two dollars; she won't think of it. 'Then let me treat you to another beer.' 'No, one's my limit in the afternoon.' Thanks her and says he's going to do as she says: 'Read between the cracks.' She doesn't understand. 'It's an expression: whenever I find a few minutes free.' 'That's it,' smiles, pulls a newspaper out of her bag and reads. He sits back and opens the book and looks at her. 'Excuse me, I don't mean to bother you again, but I just noticed you read without glasses. You've never worn them and you've read so much? What's your secret?' 'I wear a pair for distance sometimes but don't really need them. Neither of my parents needed glasses either, though my father wore them because he thought they made him look more like Emperor Franz Josef.' 'Which emperor was he?' 'Of Austria and Hungary before the first World War. He idolized him; emulated many of his mannerisms and dress; so much so there was a framed photograph of him—this big—over my parents' bed. Strange now when I mention it.' The man thinks about it: one eyebrow up, couple of forehead furls. She reads the front page for a few minutes, pays, wishes the man a good day—he's startled away from the book, waves it at her and says 'So far, great; thanks'—and heads back up Columbus. On the next block someone shouts 'Mrs. Tetch? Pauline?' and runs over to her. Woman he knew from the neighborhood when he moved back to it fifteen years ago and introduced his mother to. They kiss, woman asks how she is, his mother says 'All right, I suppose, for an old dust bag like me.' If either sees him—he's looking at one of the sidewalk tables: unisex jewelry: rings, earrings, nose rings, clips and things for the hair—he'll say he was on the subway uptown, got off to see his mother—'But how are you, how are you, a great double surprise,' and kiss them. The woman's talking about diet, health, alternative medicine, good food, lots of organically grown fruit juices and greens and grains, a mail order house in Pennsylvania where you can get health foods sent to you—she'll bring her the catalog; 'A lot more expensive than store-bought health food—you can even get fresh apples and carrots and bread and nondairy cheese—but it comes right to your door, so why not try it? It can give you a few extra years.' 'I'm too old to start into that,' his mother says. 'Where were you thirty years ago?' They talk for around ten minutes in the middle of the sidewalk. People have to walk around them; one man passing him says to his companion 'What's with those two? Don't they know they're holding up traffic? People can be so unaware.' He wants to say to him 'Come on, give them a break; she's an old lady.' He crosses the sidewalk to a store window; men's clothes, too fancy and expensive for him; but what would they say if they saw him? 'You, the original cheap jeans and T-shirt guy, thinking of buying those clothes?' 'Oh my God—hi. I was just on my way to see my mother. Truth is, I saw you two there but was curious, long as I was in the neighborhood and you were still busy talking, as to what these stores think men wear these days? Obviously plenty of men do wear what's in there, since half of them on the street have on a lot of the same stuff in the window along with some of the self-mutilating jewelry there on the sidewalk. But what a surprise. How are you both? I don't know which of you I should kiss first.' The women are kissing goodbye. His mother holds and pats the woman's hand and says 'You know I always had a special place in my heart for you the moment I first met you and was devastated for you when Barry died.' 'I know; thanks, Pauline; no one could have been kinder after.' He forgot about Barry, doesn't think he's thought of him for years, even though he has two of his huge paintings hanging in his home, which the woman had given him, and had wheeled him in the park every day for an hour or so for a few weeks before he died. His mother continues up Columbus, stops, rests, looks in store windows—women's shoes, women's handbags and gloves—goes into a gourmet shop and has some things weighed; about a quarter-pound of sliced turkey breast, he sees through the window; salads scooped into half-pint and pint containers; a pickle and two onion rolls. She makes onion rolls better than he's bought anywhere, even when they're a couple of days old, but they're usually to give away; she hardly eats what she bakes. She puts the grocery bag into her shopping bag, stops in front of the ice cream store—she's not going to get another cone, is she?— sits on the bench. She tells the young man eating ice cream beside her that her heart suddenly started palpitating rapidly; she felt faint, that's why she's sitting without buying an ice cream. 'Though I bought one from here just before.' Should he go to her, say he overheard, is she all right, does she want him to hail a cab to get her home or to a doctor or hospital? The man says 'Do you want

me to do anything?' 'Excuse me, what? My hearing aid is going on
and off again.' 'I said do you want me to do anything for you—your
heart?' 'No, thank you, it's just about passed. It always does after
I sit or lie down for a few minutes. It wasn't serious, so don't worry.
And my hearing aid's working again.' What would he say if she had
died right in front of him? He wouldn't say anything. He'd get down
on his knees, hold her to his face till the police or ambulance came,
cry and cry, and only if somebody thought he was crazy and wanted
to get him away from her, say 'I'm her son.' She asks where the man's
bicycle is. He's in bicycling gear—backwards cap, shirt, special pants
and shoes, fingerless gloves. He points to a bike fastened to a parking
sign pole. 'When you were buying your ice cream, weren't you afraid
it would get stolen?' 'Even the best bike thief couldn't break that lock
in less than two minutes. It's made of the highest-tension steel—
you'd need the kind of clippers that not even police cars carry—and
I never keep my eyes off it for more than a minute.' He's looking
in the window of the children's toy and clothing store of before,
would give the same excuse to her he thought up then. 'From what
I've read,' she says, 'these city thieves are always one step ahead of
the police in the latest gadgets in everything—guns, bulletproof vests,
picks for locks, even knockout darts. And maybe they'll just want
to take the wheels and leave the lock and frame part behind. You
always have to be more careful than you think.' 'If they're that
desperate,' but he can't hear the rest of what the man says because
of a truck with a defective muffler and bouncing-around cargo driving
past. She pretends to have heard, nodding while he talked, or maybe
she's become adept at reading lips. She says she's completely better
now, thanks him for his concern and walks to the corner and goes
up her street. A landlord on the block stops her to talk. He turns
around, opens his book and takes out a pen and uncaps it and holds
it over a page. If either of them sees him he'll say he saw them just
now but suddenly got an idea about this book, which he'll be
teaching next term, and wanted to write it down before he forgot
it. 'Hi, how are you though? Nice to see you both. Funny, but I was

just on my way to see you, Mom.' The landlord says 'You can't walk along Columbus—but every nice day, not only weekends—without getting bumped into or pushed into the street or asked or even threatened for money by beggars, though most of them look as if they live better than you or me. The clothes they got. And why aren't they working at a real job when they're so strong looking and young? I'm not talking about the skinny women with the children, who are pitiful.' 'No one panhandled me this time,' his mother says, 'but I know what you mean. Maybe they're just—the healthier looking ones—not in their right minds.' 'Oh they're in their right minds, all right. To work like that for your money? Your hand out—sometimes two hands out for two people at once—and a few of the same words each time: "Money for food?" "Money to get back to Trenton?" One actually told me that, and next day he told me the same thing. "Money for my babies?"—but you don't see the babies; it's just a line. And no physical effort in it either, and I hear some of the better ones pull in four to five hundred a week tax free and probably with Monday-Tuesday off. I'd take the job if it was offered me.' 'There must be more to it than that for most of them. Like I said: troubled heads; drugs. But I can never refuse anybody begging. It doesn't happen that often, and what's a dime?' 'A dime? You give them a dime and they'll throw it back if not poke you. It's a dollar for coffee. It's two dollars for subway fare for him and his friend. It's five dollars to help get him a hotel suite so he doesn't die homeless in the street.' 'No they wouldn't. Still, I like Columbus better now. It's prettier, more exciting. You have a greater choice of places to eat.' 'But to shop? For the essentials?' 'There are still some stores for that, or you go to Seventy-second or Amsterdam. But because of all the people walking and hanging around on it, the neighborhood's safer than it ever was.' 'This one's getting robbed, that one's being raped, and you say it's safer. Not the sidestreets. And the worst elements are coming here for a day, while before because they lived here you at least knew their face.' 'So it's the same. Or worse in ways. I forgot. I'd have to ask the police what they have to say.' She then asks about a new form the city sent landlords regarding property taxes. 'I don't understand it,' the woman says. 'As usual it's too complicated for the average nonlegal mind.' 'That's why I brought it up. Neither did I or Mr. Benjamin up the block, but I thought maybe you or your husband might.' 'No, but we're seeing our accountant early next week about lots of things and he's very good at those. If we find how to fill it out, want me or Lloyd to drop by and help you?' 'Please or else I'll have to travel downtown to the city rent office for it. And of course you'll take home some fresh cookies I'm baking this weekend and a couple of frozen zucchini breads.' She continues up the block, stops, deep breath, steps off the curb carefully, crosses the street and carefully steps onto the sidewalk in front of her building. She takes out her handbag, reaches into it, probably for keys, though he's told her to have her keys ready for use in her pocket before she even starts up the street, and if outside her pocket, then concealed in her hand. She takes out the card she bought, slips it most of the way out of the envelope and looks at it and smiles. Puts the card back into her bag and pulls out her keys. She looks around. He's told her to do this before she goes downstairs to her building, in case anyone's around who looks as if he might follow her into the vestibule. Anyone is, she's to walk to Columbus, where there are always more people than on her street, and if the person follows her, to go to a store marked Safe Haven on the window or door and tell someone there to call the police. She turns around, still looking for suspicious strangers, he supposes, and sees him across the street waving at her. She waves back and he crosses the street and says 'Mom, how are you? I was in the neighborhood,' and kisses her on the cheek."

"He takes his mother out to dinner, drinks too much at her apartment first and then at the bar while they're waiting, because she wants one, for a window table, and gets sentimental and sad to himself about how old she looks and fragile she is and weak her voice has become, though doesn't want to reveal what he's feeling. But for the first time, he believes, he sees her as—"

Frog's Mom

"I asked my mother to tell me a thing or two about her mother she remembers the most. She asked me what I meant. I said 'A memory, some incident, something she did to you or around you or to anyone—anything, a trait, habit or ritual she went through, religious, dress, food, or otherwise. But just something that keeps coming back and back to you—a quirk, even, or some physical gesture or a pretension—and you do or you don't know why it does come back or why you can't forget it or even what it means to you or just in itself, but something that possibly, well you know, exemplifies her, but it doesn't have to be as sweeping as all that.' She looked at me as if she still didn't understand. I shrugged as if saying 'What's wrong?' 'Really, sweetheart, you're not making yourself very clear, and I don't think it should be blamed entirely on my hearing.' " Enough, give up.

19

Frog's Sister

She was a very pretty child. People thought she'd be the best-looking one in the family, possibly a beauty like his mother. Complexion, nose, eyes, hair, smile, face shape, long neck, fine features. It's difficult describing looks. There's a photo. There's always a photo. In a large plastic bag of photos he keeps in a file cabinet drawer in his office at school. Has no room for it in the house and his mother lives too far away to keep it there. But that's the one he thinks of when he thinks how pretty she was and beautiful she might have become. A posed photo, as much as a child can pose, by a professional photographer his parents had hired when she was around three. Since it was summer and he knows what year it was and when she was born, she was six to seven months past three. They had rented a bungalow for the summer in a bungalow colony near Peekskill, New York. So his father could drive up weekends. Morning Glory Park, it was called. No significance. Later photos: when she was very ill, dressed in black, couldn't get around except with a walker or on crutches and not for long on either of them. Thin, gaunt, twenty to thirty pounds lighter than what should have been the normal weight for a woman her age and size. But that's another thing. She was supposed to become the tallest member of

456

the family: six feet or six-one. Based on the growth chart compiled by her pediatrician. In the top two percentile in height and something close in weight when she was born and then when she was a month old, half-year old, every annual checkup till she was five. That's when she showed the first sign—cross-eye—of the disease that would kill her twenty years later. First operation when she was six. Another when she was nine or ten. Several in her teens, one in her twenties, all crippling her more but done, doctors said, to stop the disease from spreading. If there was a family motto: "Doctors Like to Cut." Years later his mother would say "Was any of it necessary? What we put her through so early. If I had it to do over I wouldn't let them cut into her so soon and maybe not at all. Those operations just replaced big ugly growths on her neck and back with long ugly scars, and I'm sure they metastasized the disease faster." And a few years ago: "Today, of course, she would have been cured or at least not died from it." He was with her that morning in the hospital. Where most of this will probably take place. It's been on his mind. They knew she was dying. Her medical man used an expression when she was brought in. "There aren't any nails left to bang into her coffin." Or "nails left in her coffin to bang in." He said that to them because of the more well-known line about nails and coffin he used the previous time she was brought in. Tubes all over her body and under her bed. But what? Last time she was measured—it was nearly impossible; for years she couldn't stand or lie down straight—she was four-eleven to five-two. And weight, couple of months before the last time she went into the hospital, was sixty-eight pounds. He was curious. She'd become so light. So he put a scale by her bed, weighed himself on it, picked her up while his mother was changing the bed under her or pulling away the potty, and stepped on the scale with her and told his mother to see what it read. Later his mother said they shouldn't have done it, what was to be gained by it? and he could have slipped on the scale "and that's all we need is for her to break her hip." She's brought home several days after she was born. He's waiting at the door with his next oldest brother.

A nurse he's never seen before is carrying her in a blanket. His parents are behind her, all bundled up, laughing, and waving at them. A big to-do in the building's hallway before they even get in. Someone, while she's being passed around, asks how he likes her. He says he just met her, so doesn't know but thinks he likes her fine. How do you know if you don't know her yet? He's supposed to have said, one of his remarks often quoted by his father, "For now she's too small to do anything wrong to me." She's on her back kicking the floor and screaming. He doesn't like her. She looks so ugly. She makes so much noise. She cries and whines too much. She's no fun to play or be with. She never says anything smart or nice or think up new things to do. She's always cranky and complains. Her face is red and twisted and wet too much. She's allowed not to eat what he has to eat and doesn't like. Can't they see? She's only screaming for attention. Or she's trying to get him in trouble by making believe he hurt her or wanting people to think that. Someone get her to stop. Her screaming's busting his eardrums. Plug up her mouth or he's going to do it for them or start screaming at the top of his lungs too. His mother says his sister can't help it. She's frustrated, she says. He doesn't know what that means and every definition his mother gives doesn't help. It's not being able to deal with her sickness, that's all, his mother says. So what's she so sick with? She's just sick, but something worse than a headache or a cold. An earache? he says. If it's an earache, he can understand. Then she should be in bed with that heating pad under her bad ear, which for him doesn't do anything but give him an upset stomach, it's so sickening and warm, but for everybody else it seems to work. Something much worse than that, she says. He's too young to understand what. But he has to begin tolerating her tantrums—sympathizing with her, even—helping to calm her down, if he can. In other words, putting up with her the best way he knows how, or at least a lot better than he's been doing. She's just faking, he says. He'd grab her up and twist her wrist and start spanking her hard till she stopped crying. She tells him to go to his room and stay there till he can come out and say he understands. He says he can't understand, he'll never understand. She's just a brat and everybody should know it. He's slapped and pulled to his room by his hand. She's got a hole in her throat. He learns a new word, tracheotomy. He learns another new word, trachea, but this one he forgets fast. He learns other new words: windpipe and bronchial tubes and larynx, but the last two he quickly forgets what they mean too and how to say them. Bronchee, monkey, long key. It's an ugly hole in her neck, pink and full of wet flesh like a fingertip gash, with a little dribbling like spit coming out of it sometines. He doesn't know when the hole's uglier, with the tube in or out. She has it in her when she comes home after each operation. It makes his mother sick when she has to clean it or use it to suction the gook out of her neck right past the hole. He can't wait for the tube to come out for good and the hole to close. It never does all the way but gets smaller and smaller till after a while it's about as big as a little asshole when it's closed and he can look at it for a short time without turning away. Sometimes, though, and he doesn't know why now and not then, he has to excuse himself quick and run to the bathroom because his stomach's getting sick. He begins feeling sorry for her. No more yelling at her, she wasn't a brat and he can see it was something else doing it to her. She's in a hospital bed at home and doesn't look like the same girl that left. Skin's yellow and black marks under her eyes, checks are deep and lips are chapped and cracked, and something about her hair and eyeballs. Came home on a stretcher carried by two men. Ambulance outside with its roof light turning and a few people on the sidewalk bending down to look past the building's vestibule all the way back to the apartment's foyer. "It's my sister. She had a bad operation at the hospital that almost killed her, but she'll be getting better at home." "I'm glad," someone says. "You be a good brother and take good care of her." "That's what I'm doing. I'm trying to keep the street quiet for her, because she's right in that front room. Anyone beeps a horn too much, I'm running over to say something." He tells his mother how he feels and she says it's about time. Then she says she's sorry for saying that and pats his head and says it's wonderful he feels that way and she hopes he means it deeply because it's much better for Vera that he does. "If she thought you didn't want to look at her or hated her the way she is or just didn't like her, you never know what could happen. She could just give up and die." Later she says it could never come to what she said it could. It would just mean a lot to Vera and no doubt help her get well faster if he showed her the kind of nice attention they all know he's capable of. She's in bed in the hospital after her second operation. That would make him around eleven. Bar above her bed to hold on to or pull herself up with when she gets stronger. Flowers and cards all over the room. Toys, fruits, boxes and tins of candy. Lots of tubes and hanging bottles near her. A new radio she doesn't want played and dolls and stuffed animals she wants taken home or turned away from her. That same sick face again, arms black and blue, scrawny. She hardly says a word to anyone but his mother and usually so quietly his mother has to put her ear to Vera's lips. "What? What? Don't repeat if it's too hard to." Her head never leaves the pillow and mostly faces up. Something's been drilled into the top of her skull. Someone calls it a sinker and he thinks of fish. Another new word, traction, which he almost never understood but could see what it was doing. Each time she moves her head even a little he thinks her scalp's going to be pulled off. The weight attached to the cable seems heavy enough to give him some trouble lifting. She doesn't seem to be in pain but he doesn't see how unless she's being drugged. He wonders how the sinker will come out without another operation. He asks and someone says don't worry, it's like a tooth. He thinks of his own teeth, which fell out while he was eating or came out with a little jiggling, and thinks that might not be it but he's satisfied with it. He hopes she doesn't come home with it in and the pulley and weight and his mother says she's going to be in the hospital that long just so she won't. A visiting nurse comes for two hours a day at home to relieve his mother and do the harder chores. Vera won't let anyone do the suctioning but his mother. She says it hurts too much when anyone else does it. His mother pleads with her that she doesn't do a good job sometimes and maybe just this once it should be done properly, but Vera squinches her eyes and pounds her thighs with her fists and shakes her head violently. He has trouble looking at her in the hospital bed from one side because of the urine bag hanging off it. Sometimes it's so full and the tube to it is still dripping that he thinks it's going to burst all over the floor or else go back inside her without bursting and kill her. He sees her body filling up with urine till it leaks out of the neck tube and he has to shake the thought off. But he's also drawn to the bag, often checking how high the urine is, and occasionally tells people it's filled or that the bag's very dirty and she needs a new one, but they always say it has a little ways to go yet or that the bag can be used a couple of more days. There's a big party for her sixth birthday. Friends of his parents, cousins and uncles and aunts, kids from the block who don't even know her and a few who seem too old to be there. The room's decorated with streamers, flowers and balloons, all the kids have party hats and noisemakers, folding chairs and a special long table have been rented, lights have ben set up around the table for a movie a man's been hired to make of the party. There's mixed drinks and catered canapés and things for the adults, hamburgers and hotdogs and potato salad and different sodas for the kids, a huge ice cream cake is brought in by two waitresses, three musicians play the kind of music he once heard at a wedding, a clown pulls rings and bracelets and money and a baby rabbit out of Vera's ears and mouth and gives her the jewelry. She's very shy through it all and won't look at the camera whenever she's asked to. She blows out the candles after several tries and with some help from his parents and everyone cheers and claps and sings "Stand up and show us your beautiful face," and his father lifts her to his shoulder and walks around the apartment with her and lots of the older people kiss her fingers and knees and shoes. He asks his mother why such a large party for her and she says it was so much fun and everyone had such a good time and it was so wonderful seeing so many of her family and friends together for once that maybe she'll give them like this for all her children from now on. His mother wants him to read to Vera a half-hour a day. It'll take her mind off things, she says, and her eyesight's gone bad and she refuses to be examined for glasses. Whatever he chooses to read she doesn't like and she can't think of a book she wants him to read. She doesn't like any books, she says. There's nothing in them that ever means anything to her and someone reading one to her would make what's bad even longer. He says he'll read fast, she'll see, so pick a subject she's interested in and he'll go to the library and get a bunch of books on it. If they don't have it, their mother's said he can buy any book she wants at a bookstore and as many as two a week. She says "Nothing," then she says "Pottery." He says all right, he'll get them, even if they won't be very interesting reading for him. What is pottery? she says. She's heard the word and liked the sound of it. He says at her age she doesn't know what pottery is? Maybe that's why she should be reading books more. But she must be kidding him, and she says she is but he can see she's not. He ends up reading her *Robinson Crusoe* because he has to read it for a book report at school. Most of the times she falls asleep about ten minutes after he starts reading. Or stares up at the ceiling and when he calls her name and asks if she's listening, she doesn't answer or look at him. It's the drugs, his mother says. Maybe in a few months she won't have to take them anymore. His reading is making it much easier for her to rest and fall asleep naturally though, which she also needs to do, so look at it that way. His brothers and he always know about her next operation a week or so beforehand. His mother usually announces it to them at the dinner table about an hour after she's told Vera. "I'm very sad to have to say this, though it is, what I'm about to say, going to take place for a very good purpose..." "I know what you're going to say," Vera said once, "and I don't want to. The doctors hurt me. They come at me with sharp blades and big clubs and cut and beat me to ribbons and I feel most of it when it's going on but I'm too doped-up to keep them away or say anything. And then it hurts for such a long time after and none of the painkillers do anything to make it stop and I get uglier and smaller and worse each time. I know I'm going to die because of the operation this time, either when they're doing it or soon after." "No you're not. It's a simple operation, the simplest of any of them. More for correcting a little thing from the last one than doing anything new this time. Probably not even an IV after it or any intensive care. You'll be up and around maybe an hour or two after you come out of the anesthesia, if they even have to put you out for it." "That's what you said before the last one and it was the worst and most painful one I had. This one will be even worse. And the one after it, if I don't die this time, even worser." "What are you saying? This one should be the last." "That's what you said before the last one. I remember and you do too and everyone else here does also but you'll all pretend you don't. You think I'm dumb and have lost my memory because that's what my sickness is supposed to do to me too. And why does it always have to be me? Why doesn't someone else here get sick like me and have to go in for one and I can have a rest from them for once?" "I'm sure if one of us could—" "I won't go to the hospital for it. I'll run away first. I'll kill myself first, even. It's better than having a lot of doctors with half faces cut me up and hit me with hammers to help me die." "Believe me, darling, this one should be the very last. I was mistaken the last time. I understood wrong what the doctor told me. This one you'll be on the operating table a short time and home in a day or two. And you'll have dinner at the table with us that night if your stomach can take it and you'll go to sleep in your own bed when you get home. If I'm wrong again— If there are sudden complications while they're operating, and they don't expect that to happen. Or something they just discovered because they have you opened up— then it won't be because I was mistaken or didn't understand what the doctor told me. These things sometimes happen. But I truly believe and hope and pray and everything like that, my sweet darling—we all do—that it won't happen this time around with you." She's always dressed as if for a party and has her little valise packed with bedclothes and bathroom things and a few of her smaller bubbled-glass and alabaster animals when she goes to the hospital. She's always at the door with the valise and with her coat and hat on and once holding a child's umbrella, waiting for her mother to finish her coffee and maybe have another cup and brush her hair and put lipstick on and get her coat and handbag out of the foyer closet and make sure she has all the documents the hospital needs and enough cash in her wallet and her checkbook and a paperback to read and her keys. His father always goes to work about a half-hour before. Vera's already waiting at the door. Kisses her and says if he's not too tied up with last-minute patients he'll see her at the hospital tonight. His mother and she always go alone together. Vera won't let anyone carry her valise outside or put it in the cab. A couple of times he ran up the block with one of his brothers to get a cab for them, then had to run down the block while his brother rode in the cab to their building. He should have been in school by then but his mother wanted Vera's brothers there to say good-bye. He kisses her and his mother and waves to them and the cab drives off. His mother always looks through the rear window and then waves back at them till the cab slows down for a red light or is about to turn the corner. Maybe she was holding on to Vera when the cab came to a stop or turned, afraid she might fall forward or hard to the side. Vera never says a word these mornings. Head always faced down and she never looks straight at anyone or responds to any question or remark, even his mother's. When his father crouched down and hugged her and said something in her ear, she stared at the door. His own last words to her on the sidewalk are always "Good luck," and then he wishes he hadn't said them. She might think the operation's going to be much worse than she's been told. That she might need luck after all. For why have her brothers stayed home for her, why's everyone being extra nice to her? Two of these mornings he tells himself, when Vera's about to get into the cab, not to say good luck as he's done the last times, but it always comes out. Say "See ya," he tells himself one of those times, "See ya, Vera" or

"I'll see ya," which is what he almost always says when he leaves one of his friends or brothers, but something stops it—he forgets while he's telling himself to say it and instead says "Good luck." His mother always later says Vera was the same way in the hospital: silent and resigned and acting like a phantom when she was checked in. "I had to do all the answering for her—how old, date of birth and so forth, any cold or sore throat the last few days?" And then when she went upstairs to her room, had lunch and dinner—"I had to check off what I thought she wanted to eat and drink; she wouldn't give me a clue." And when she went for some tests or aides and doctors came in to prepare her for the operation if it was to be the next day. His father never gets to the hospital those nights but always leaves the house early the next day to be there in time for her breakfast. If the operation is for the next morning, he skips going there that early and comes after work much later that day. Once he went away for a couple of days when she was being operated on. A patient of his had invited him to a Catskill resort he had a big interest in or owned. His father said he took the man up on it only because the operation would be too much for him—it was to be the most serious she'd had—and he'd be more problem than help if he hung around the city during the operation and went to the hospital right after. But his mother used to say he just didn't want to pass up a free vacation. Years later Vera told him, when she got into an argument with him about something else, that she still held it against him, but other times she said she'd never given it much thought. "You did right. You wouldn't have been any help. You only would've cried when you saw me with those stupid tubes up my nose and pester the hospital workers with all sorts of questions anybody could answer or nobody could, making it embarrassing and even more painful for me. Because the staff sometimes takes it out on the patient if the visitor makes scenes or insults them or even asks questions that can seem as if he's criticizing them a little. Only Mommy knew how to handle things there and could help me and only Mommy did." "Glad she was there then," his father said, "for I'm too much of a softie when it comes to the sicknesses of my kids. But just remember who insisted on the best doctors and hospital rooms and postoperative care for you and who paid all the bills." He visits her in the hospital the day before an operation. She's in her room waiting for him in a wheelchair. He says "What would you like to do?" and she says "I don't care—anything," and he says "Mind if I wheel you around and explore the place a little?" and she hunches her shoulders or gives him a face and he wheels her around the halls into the waiting rooms and the solarium and to the little closet that's a library and then toward the children's playroom. "Did you have lunch yet?" he says while they wheel and she says "Look at your watch; use your brains." "Is the food good here—better than at the last hospital?" and she says "That's one of the dumbest questions I've ever heard, even from you." "Is the girl you share the room with nice?" and she says "Your questions are getting so dumb I'm not even going to let you know I've heard them anymore." "What do you want me to ask or say then?" and she stares straight ahead, and he says "Come on, you're not being fair, I came here to see you, so answer what I asked," and she says "Don't ask, don't say, use the time to think what you've been saying for a change—and you're supposed to be one of the smarter ones in the family?" "Listen, I know what you're going through and I feel lousy about it, the whole world does, so what am I asking or doing or anything that's so wrong?" and she says "Now I'm serious about ignoring you, you dumb dope, so you'll only be talking to yourself from now on." Lots of things in the room to play with, a volunteer lady who gives out juice and cookies and pieces of fruit to the children who can drink and eat them, another volunteer walking around holding up cups and cookies to several childrens' lips. Some are completely bald. He's never seen that except during the ringworm epidemic at school this year when lots of boys and girls came with their heads shaved, but they kept hats and scarves on all day except when someone knocked or pulled them off. He tries not to look at them, doesn't want to make them feel bad. Same with the ones who sit and groan or who drag the upside-down bottles and tubes attached to them on what look like wheeled coat stands. Some are sleeping and a few are so skinny and sick looking they seem dead or close to it, while others you wouldn't know were sick except for their hospital gowns. His mother told him to be cheerful. "You have a tendency to get depressed over things like this, but for Vera's sake make believe everything's hunky-dory. Otherwise, do me the favor and don't go." "So this is the playroom," he says. "Mom told me about it. It's beautiful, very nice. Like a snack? Any of the games interest you? I'll gladly play." "It's ugly here. The games and toys are for morons, which most of us here are going to become if we're not already are." "You said you weren't going to answer me anymore, but I'm glad you did. It's nice talking. Better than just staring or standing or sitting still. But tell me, why do you say it's ugly? Look at the walls. My favorite shade of blue. Bright but not blinding. Peaceful, cheerful, and it seems recently painted. And the pictures hanging up seem interesting and nice. Not just your regular kids' stuff. What do you think that one's of? Maybe just a design." "It's of nothing. And the blue's awful on the walls. If vomit was blue that's what shade it'd be. The whole room's awful. It stinks from medicine and disinfectant and diaper rash and shit and pee. That's because most of them can't control themselves anymore. You must have a nose cold." "I don't and I don't smell anything funny. Maybe only soap." "Then get the holes in your nose unclogged. But yesterday a boy younger than me, even, died right in this room." "Oh come on, nobody dies in a playroom. Unless he falls off something and breaks his skull. But they don't have anything that high here—I'm sure just to prevent that. And probably because we're in a hospital, and the part of it just for children, the dying from the fall couldn't happen anyway even if someone climbed to the top of the curtain there and dived off and landed flat on his head. Too many nurses and doctors to help right away." "He died in his wheelchair fast asleep. I was here but not near him. He was dying anyway. Anyone could see it when they wheeled him in. Mouth open, stuff running out, and more tubes than the usual. But his mother thought his being around not-as-bad-off kids would help him. All of a sudden they shooed us out or wheeled the ones in chairs like me and later we found he died, though the nurses and aides won't say so. But is he around? Because he was way too sick to be sent home. I know what room he was in and that bed was empty today and the card with his name's off the door. Sometimes, I heard, they put kids in the very last room down the hall when they're dying or only have a few days left to live. But that one's taken by someone else we've never seen, since the door's always closed and the window on it's got paper over it." "I don't believe it. If this boy who you say died was that bad off, then as you said he wouldn't have been in a regular room like yours for everyone to see." "You're wrong. Sometimes they die here all of a sudden. That's happened in almost all my hospital stays. A nurse even got in big trouble this time because of it. She's not supposed to listen to what mothers want on things like that. If you're dying you're supposed to do it in that last room or your own room if that's all they have, with the door closed and the curtains around you and no other patients or your family in it. You do some asking around here about it and you'll find out. But that's why I don't like it when the nurses pull the curtains around me." "No, I didn't know you didn't." "You've seen my face when they do. I'm afraid I won't come out. That they can do something, decide my time is up and the bed's needed for someone else—I've heard that too—and put their hands over my nose and mouth or use a pillow or something or just stick a death dose in my veins and good-bye. But they curtain me all the time when I have to go kaka and pee and can't get to the bathroom myself, which now is always." "Let's try talking about something else, Vera. This has to be disturbing you." "Like what? There's nothing else. My operation tomorrow? That I'm feeling 'oh great I'm going to get sliced up again'? Can you get me out of this thing into a normal chair? I've got cramps shooting up my back that are starting to make me scream." He gets a nurse and aide who lift her into a soft chair. He should try changing the subject again. He's not doing a good job here. His mother will come and

Vera will say he made her feel even worse. He should be taking her mind off things, cheering her up. "By the way, your friend Kitty sends her regards." "So what?" "She's your old friend. I'm just saying I bumped into her on the street." "She's lost." "Maybe you'd like her to call you. She could still do it today." "I don't want to speak to anyone." "Almost all our relatives have called and want to see you, but we say you'd rather not till you're feeling better." "Till they learn I'm not dead." "No, till a couple of days after the operation, or whenever you want. We're doing the right thing by saying that for you and keeping them away, right?" "What are you talking about? When could they come? Today? Yesterday when I'm in tests all day? Tomorrow when I'm operated on? Make sense." "I meant the day after you came in, for instance." "What do I care? Have them sleep under my bed here, for all it means to me." He says maybe she'd like him to read to her. He could get something from that library closet. He thinks he knows what she'd like, unless she wants to be wheeled there to choose one. Or maybe she just wants to read something herself. If she did, he'd sit beside her, read a book he brought with him. It's OK by him. "What you can do is turn my chair around and pull it up to the window so I can look out. That way I won't have to see anybody but their reflections. And you're strong. You lift weights and do millions of push-ups a day. So pulling the chair's what you can use it for, and then let me look in peace." "You're saying you want me to go home?" "You want to go home, do it." "I don't. I'll stay as long as you like, and certainly till Mom comes." "If you change your mind and go before then, make sure you tell someone at the nurses' station so they know you're not coming back to wheel me to my room." "I told you, nobody's going." He pulls her chair to the window, takes the bed pillow off the wheelchair seat and fixes it behind her, sits beside her, takes her hand because he thinks maybe that'll comfort her a little, she looks at their hands together and then stares out the window at the river, boats and barges passing, Long Island or Brooklyn across it, maybe the reflections of people in the room, and falls asleep. He looks out the window a while. He'd like to go to her room and get the book he brought with him, but taking his hand away may wake her. After about a half-hour he signals one of the volunteers to come over and asks if it's possible for her to go to his sister's room and look in his left- or right-side coat pocket for a book and bring it to him. "She's sleeping so peacefully and needs to, I don't want to disturb her." The woman says there's been a number of petty thefts and one major one in the patients' rooms the last few weeks, night and day, but probably not on the children's floor, so she'd rather not be seen going through anyone's pockets. He says if she can get the pen and pad or just the pad out of his right back pants pocket, since he's sure she has a pencil or pen, he'll write a note with his left hand giving her permission. She says "I'm really not supposed to leave the children unless for something like going to the ladies' room or when someone relieves me, but I'll get a nurse's aide if you think it's that important and perhaps he'll do it." He says "Don't bother, she should be up pretty soon." He stays like that for another hour till his mother comes. He's slept the night in the visitor's lounge, washes his face and brushes his teeth with his finger in the men's room, goes to her room and knocks in case a nurse or doctor's inside. No answer, so he lets himself in saying "Vera, it's me, I'm coming in, okay?" She's in the same position he last saw her in late last night, on her back, tubes for this and that, monitors on, blip-blip sounds from one of them, face sweaty or glazed, one side of her mouth dropped and agape, eyes half open if that. She could be asleep or awake or maybe she's gone into a coma. He says from the foot of the bed, while moving a few inches from side to side to see if he can catch her eye, "Vera? Hi. Good morning." Her eyes go to him and he stays still. "How are you? It's still very early. I slept the night in the lounge. On a chair. Someone was already asleep on the couch when I decided to turn in but not when I woke up, and the other lounge was locked. My back aches," stretching, "but nothing bad. I should have asked a nurse to open the other lounge—the one at the end of the other hall—but I didn't think of it. Maybe that's where a doctor or two sleep, if they've been on duty all night, and they wanted it locked. But minor stuff, right, so why am I bothering you with it?" She just looks at him, lids still half-closed. Drugged look, but she seems to be hearing him. Part of one side of her head's shaved, he just notices, but he doesn't know what for, since there are no plans to operate on her this time. "This will very likely be the last time you'll be taking her here or to any hospital," the doctor said. "Why?" They hadn't asked why but he said it anyway. "Because I don't see how she can pull through this time, plain and simple. She's been a lucky girl to have gone home the last two times. So to speak, lucky." "Vera? Can you hear me? It's Howard. Your brother. That was some sleep I had. I couldn't find a place to stretch out, so I had to sleep mostly sitting up. Remember I spoke about it? The other man on the couch? And it was cold. A nurse offered me a blanket but I said no thanks, I'll use my coat, but it wasn't enough. I was freezing. What do they do in those lounges after ten o'clock, shut the heat off? Yet it's plenty warm in here. Just as it was the times late last night I came in to see how you were doing, and you only slept with a single or double sheet. Though good sheets," rubbing the top one between his fingers, "—thick, but smooth, but not thick enough if the temperature here was the same as in the lounge. To keep you warm, I mean—the sheets. I just thought of something. If I was going to buy cotton sheets, which is the only kind I like—the synthetic kind is so itchy— and which can be very expensive in the department stores, I'd buy them at a hospital linen supply place if they'd sell them to me, right? Because it might be they'd only sell to hospitals and places like that. Probably a reasonable price, and good quality, because they have to go though so many washings. Every day, and I guess certain high standards that hospitals insist the manufacturer keep. But you feeling OK? Should I come closer so I don't have to talk too loud—maybe that's disturbing you, my voice—and where you can still hear?" Her breath will be bad. She can also stink of urine and shit and other things, but that he can take. "I'll come closer." Does. Her eyes move with him. "Good. You're on to me. Your eyes. So you can hear me if you can see me, I'd think. Can you? —Is there anything you want? A nurse? Water? Have they been in to see you yet? This morning, I mean. Want me to mop your brow? Are you hearing me, Vera? I hate to harp on it, and if it's any effort to answer, please don't. But can you nod? Can you shake your head? Remember—nodding is to say yes? Shaking your head is for no? —I guess even if you were trying to nod and shake, you couldn't tell me with a nod or shake. Let me put it simpler. Even I didn't quite get what I just said. Nah, let's forget it. I'll give you a break for once with my trying to explain things. I don't know why, but I sure can get tongue-tied. And then sometimes, bam, I'm articulate, but very articulate, talking the way I always want to. But how about blinking your eyes? Can you blink them when you want to? Like now, for instance. No? Want to try? Two blinks for yes and one for no—that sort of business? You know, so we can set up some sort of system where you can tell me what you want or need, including the end of my stupid chatter, right? Let me take care of your brow first. I'll be right back. I'm going to your bathroom to get some wet paper. OK? OK?" He gets paper towels in her bathroom, wets several sheets, dabs her forehead and cheeks with them. "Does this hurt or in any way feel uncomfortable? I hope not. Does it feel better? What about this?" and he pats her lips with the wet paper. "Your lips are getting dry. We don't want them cracked. Then we'll have to take care of them, sores, discomfort—you know. It's this tube with the air in it, I think. And the hair hanging over your head's wet. From sweat, probably. I'm going to tamp it dry." Pats her hair and face with a dry paper towel, sits beside her. There's a smell, doesn't know what of, but not bad. Doesn't want to sniff deeper, if she is watching him. "Let's forget all the questions from now on. It's getting so where even I can't stand the sound of my voice anymore." He smiles. "Can't get a laugh out of you, right? Well, you've always been a serious type. Dad always said that about me, but it was really you. I wish I could be like that. A thinker. Deep," and he jabs his temple. "It's good, maybe the best way. You think about things. You just don't let everything pass, as I tend to do. But mind if I take your hand? If you mind, try tapping my hand with your finger or rubbing it or pull your hand away. I swear, I won't mind. Even pinch me. I could use some waking up, and not just from sleep." He takes her hand. It's cold and the palm's wet. He dries it with a paper towel, gets up and dries the other palm, her eyes always on his, and sits and bends his head down and shuts his eyes. He's about to cry. Tries not to, biting the insides of his cheeks, but he cries. He says with his eyes shut and head down "I hope you're not watching this. I'm sorry, if you are, but you know I don't like seeing you like this, so that's why. How I wish you were all better. I'd give anything to help you get well in a flash, and you will get well, though in time." She pulls her hand away. "Well look at that. You see your hand? You pulled it. That proves you're getting well. Tugged it right out of mine. Were you able to all this time? And blinking and tapping too, I bet. I'm sure you were, but you were just holding back. Stubborn, aren't you, or something." She closes her eyes, her lips move. "No no, don't try to speak. Not with those tubes in you. The nose." Her lips continue to move. Spit comes out. "Oh, gee." He wipes it with a paper towel. "No, too rough, the paper." Wipes it with his handkerchief. "I swear, no germs. It's clean, I haven't even used it. This handkerchief, I'm talking about." Her eyes open and he dangles the handkerchief in front of her. "Wait. Those lemon-flavored swabs. I just remembered. There's a drawer full of them." He pulls out the drawer by her bed. They're there, a whole box full. "None here. I'll go to the nurse's station to get them. For your lips. They're still too dry. I'll be right back." He leaves the room and cries outside. Goes to the station and says "I know there are lip swabs in her drawer, but to get out of the room I told her—" "Who is 'her'?" the nurse says. "My sister, Vera Tetch, 4–26, down this hall." He gets swabs and goes back. The door's shut while he'd left it partly open. He knocks. A nurse comes to the door and says "Give me five minutes." "Is she all right?" "Sure, just cleaning up. Make it ten." His parents are out. His oldest brother's in the army, the other's working as a movie usher. At seven o'clock he says to her "Don't forget. Mom said for you to be in bed by eight and lights out by eight-thirty and asleep by nine." She says she doesn't have to. "You're not the boss." "Yes I am, at least for now. You heard them tell me to give you the order if you don't do it by yourself." "That still doesn't make you the boss. I'm staying up for as long as I want to till Mommy comes home." "That's what you think." At eight he yells down the hall to her room "It's eight, Vera. Start getting into your pajamas and don't forget to wash up and brush your teeth. I forgot that's what Mom said for me to see you do too. Your hands and your face. And both sides of your hands and don't forget your neck." She doesn't answer him. At eight-thirty he yells down the hall "I hope you're in bed and all washed and your teeth brushed and in pajamas because your lights have to go out." Ten minutes later he yells "Your lights aren't out yet, Vera. Come on, they have to." At nine he goes into her room. She's in regular clothes, sitting on her bed, talking to a doll in each hand. "Would you like to have breakfast?" she says to them. "Yes we would," one says, and the other says in a different voice "No we wouldn't," and they both bow several times. He says "Now I asked you." She turns to him as if she just noticed him there and screams for him to get out of her room. "It's private. You're not supposed to be here if I don't want you to." "Listen, I promised Mom and Dad. They're paying me. They'll come home and find you playing and think I didn't do my job. We'll forget the washing and teeth. Now where are your pajamas? Don't worry, with your look—I'll leave before you start putting them on." "I'm not telling you. Just get out." He gets a pair out of the dresser, holds them out to her, one doll says to the other "What's your favorite dessert for supper?" He grabs that doll and puts the pajamas in Vera's free hand. She throws them and the other doll at his face. "That's it. You could have taken my eye out with that. The shirt has buttons on it and I even think it scratched my cheek." "Good." He unbuckles his belt—just as his oldest brother did, slowly—takes if off and says "If you don't do what I say I'm going to beat you with this. Now pick up the pajamas and go to the bathroom and put them on." She suddenly looks scared, he doesn't know if it's an act, jumps on her bed, curls up and starts crying. "Then put them on, goddammit, put them on." She's now shrieking. He holds the belt over his head. Same thing Jerry used to do with Alex and him. Sometimes beat them with it and sometimes pulling their pants down and beating their behinds with it and sometimes leaving welts, pants down or up. When their dad wasn't home and their mother complained to him about something they did. They'd be in their room, sent there by their mother, and they'd hear Jerry in some other part of the apartment yell something like "What! Again!" and then charge to their room in these heavy army boots he always seemed to wear then, and if their door was closed, throw it open so hard it banged against the bookcase behind it and knocked things off the top. Usually by this time they were both huddled together on the bottom bunk of their double-decker bed. And it worked. They did whatever he said, after. Or when he came through the door they'd start pleading they'll do whatever he wants or never again do whatever it was they'd done and apologize to their mother any number of times he wants them to, but usually it was too late. They could see it in his face. After the beating and they were crying, Jerry would rethread his belt and say something like "Tough shit if it hurts. Just be good and not filthy mouths and I won't have to do it. Because you think I like to, you two dumb schmucks?" "Now will you, will you?" he shouts and beats the buckle end of the belt on the other side of the bed from her. She's shrieking. Then he thinks what am I doing? Who do I think I am? I couldn't hit her with this if I was paid to. "Just go to sleep. Even in your clothes if you want. Or don't go to sleep or do anything, but I'm out of it. And tell tell tell all you want and what I did, for all I give a crap," and leaves the room and rethreads his belt. If she told, neither of his parents or anyone else ever said a word to him about it or looked at him in a different way the next few days. They go to the same summer camp together. "Why's your sister so scarred up?" some kids would ask. One time he overhears a boy say "Last prize is a dance with Vampire Vera at the next social." He tries to defend her: she's gone through serious operations; it's been tough on her since she was a little girl; she's been tested to have a high IQ but has never had a real chance to use it; the scars are suppose to get smaller and smaller and in a few years almost go away; if they saw pictures of her when she was small they'd know how beautiful she could have been. But he still hears the comments and cracks. Her coordination and eyesight's bad and she loses her energy fast and she can't play most of the sports or be part of a lot of the camp activities, or just does them poorly and clumsily. The other kids mostly ignore her. She's probably made fun of in front of her. Her bunkmates and the girls who swim in the lake with her probably even have trouble looking at her undressed or in a swimsuit or in the shower house and he's sure she picks this up. He sees some of it in the mess hall. His bunk's table is on the boy's side but he sometimes stands up to look over a lot of the other tables to see what she's doing. Most of the other five or six girls at her table are usually talking excitedly among themselves. She's usually just eating slowly, or staring at the spoon or fork in her hand or food on her plate or playing with the salt-and-pepper shakers or looking at the roof rafters or the huge wooden scrolls on the support posts with the names of all-around campers and best athletes and such from previous years. She always lags behind her bunkmates when they're going to this place or that. He'll often yell "Vera," and wave and point that he has to go with his bunk and she'll wave and stop to look at him. In the rec hall during a movie or show, she's usually at the end of the bench, a foot or so from one of the other girls in her bunk, not talking to anyone, staring at the stage curtains or empty movie screen. A couple of times he sits beside her and says "So how you doing?" and she says "All right," and he says "Hear from the folks or Alex or anybody recently?" and she says "No, you?" and he says "I'm not allowed to sit on the girl's side but just thought I'd come over a second," and she nods and smiles and he says "Well, got to go— why don't you talk to your bunkmates next to you?" and she says "I do," and seems sad when he goes and turns around to look back at him now and then before the lights go out and show begins. "This place isn't for her," his counselor says. "Nobody will tell you because the directors don't want to lose the second month's fee when there's no guarantee they'll get a girl to take her place. But I see it. I'm going in after med school for psychotherapy—the mind, the brain, the whole emotional mishmash—so I can pick up your concerns and anxiousness over it and a lot of what she's going through too. You should tell your folks. She'll go home at the end of the summer much worse off in the head than she must have been when she came. Why? Because she's taking a beating. Call them, I'll pay, and if the camp kicks me out for squealing, OK." He calls home. "Let her stay," his father says. "Tell that guy to keep his nose out of it; she'll make friends soon." "Listen to what Howard's saying," his mother says. "She's unhappy. It's doing her worse than good. It was a mistake thinking she'd get along well there. Let's cut our losses for her sake." They say they'll discuss it further together and then with the camp directors and her counselor, and that weekend they drive up to take her home. He helps them carry her luggage to the car. It's rest period and her bunkmates lie and sit on their beds reading comic books and playing card games and checkers and then look up and say goodbye to her, when Howard says she's going, as if she were only leaving for a couple of hours. He thinks, walking with her to the car, What's she thinking? He tries to make it out. She's glad to see her mother but seems sad to be going. Some kind of defeat's on her face and in the way her body slumps. All her smiles today have been fake, her voice so low to those girls they could hardly hear her. "What? What? None of us can understand you," one of them said. He was hoping one or two of them would come over to her, help him with her things, say "We'll miss you," and kiss her, even say "Write and I'll write back." He thinks he can sense what's inside her: stomach hurting, chest crying or just feeling full, tears held back. Standing by the car she tells her mother "I tried to do whatever they asked me. Made my bed good; ate when I was asked to, even things I hated; went out for things I could do. I think I was having a good time and was liked. Maybe it's best going home though. We'll go to the beach sometimes when it gets too hot, won't we? That's what I liked best about camp, the nice nights. You're lucky," she says to him. "Listen, none of it was your fault, so don't think so," he says. "Some places aren't right for people. I've had delivery-boy jobs for stores when I shouldn't have the owners were so mean. And this camp concentrates too much on competition and sports. I'll be glad to get home also." "Why? Everybody's been nice. I had no problems that way." He wants to make sure not to say the wrong things, so he says nothing else. She's lying, she knows he knows it, and maybe she knows he is too, but so what? He kisses her good-bye, careful not to press her back where there might be some new lumps there, kisses his folks, and the car drives off. Waves till he can't see it anymore. Just as it disappears his father honks twice. Walking back to his bunk he thinks maybe if he had defended her more. Made her laugh more, spent more time with her somehow, spoken to her counselor about her, tried to get her bunkmates to include her more, and so on; punched a couple of noses. Later he's in a way relieved she's gone but thinks sadly of her a lot and writes her almost every other day. Short letters, but so many in three weeks that he has to borrow a stamp to write his parents for more stamps and envelopes. "Dear Vera," one letter goes. "It's muggy and awful here. A real heat spell where even the nights are hot and the lake water is like a steambath and the cesspool, which opened up again, stinks everything to heaven. I envy you away where there are fans to blow on you and also to be the only one alone with Mom and Dad this summer. As for me, I'm not having too good a time. Last year my bunkmates were friendly and smart, but this year they are always fighting and acting stupid. Like throwing things in the messhall and saying silly things to girls and making fun of the head counselor behind his back and Rabbi Berman and Aunt Lois, who aren't so bad. I'll be glad when camp's over. Not only to get out of here and see my friends on the block, but to see you and Mom and Dad again. Love to all, Howard." She never writes back but when he calls she thanks him for his letters. "Nice as the weather's been since I've been back, I'd still exchange places with you today if I could." It's June and she tells him her room's much too hot and she doesn't know how she's going to stand it this summer. He's working as a permanent sub in a junior high school and offers to buy her an air conditioner if their parents won't. His mother says they would have bought her one long ago but they've been told the building's wiring won't take it. He goes to a discount store to price them, finds one that uses the least amount of power of any of them and which the salesman says will only be priced this low for one more day, and buys it. If it only blows the building's fuses but not the air conditioner, the store says it'll take it back. It's a simple one and to save money he carries it home and installs it himself. He tells his parents if the building's wiring gets destroyed when he turns the air conditoiner on, he'll pay for an electrician to fix it. "Look at you," his father says. "Just four months on the job, now no money saved, and soon in debt if the electricity conks out. Nobody knows how to blow money like you." The air conditioner works fine and in the morning she says it made her room so cold she couldn't even get out of bed to get blankets. "You have to adjust the dials before you go to bed," and he shows her how again. He complains to his mother that Vera never even thanked him for it. "That was two weeks' salary, and if I have to pay taxes this year because I made over the minimum, nearly three." "She's thanking you, don't worry, but in her own way. She told me, but not to tell you, she's praying for you, though for what particularly she wouldn't say." He's alone in the apartment with her. It's night, around ten, and he was told by his folks to check to see she has her covers over her before he goes to bed. He goes into her room. It's lit by a little night table light plugged into the wall. The covers are on the floor and her nightdress is above her waist. She has a little pubic hair around that area. He's never seen any before. She's sleeping. He picks up the covers, covers her and leaves the room. He gets halfway down the hall and is excited. He wishes he hadn't covered her up. He'd go back and from the doorway take another look. Her hair wasn't the big black bush in the magazine but like a little light brown Hitler mustache, if that's what color it was. Red, even, and right above the crack and none of it around. He should have got closer and looked some more. Done it on tiptoes, held in his breath. He goes into his room and takes off his clothes to put on his pajamas, turns sideways in front of the dresser mirror to see his hard-on in it and begins playing with himself. It gets bigger and straighter and he puts his pants back on but not the undershorts, tries to press the hard-on down but it won't go so has to hold it to his stomach while he zips up so it doesn't get caught. He goes into her room. Knows he shouldn't. Whispers "Vera, you up?" If she says yes—moans, even; blinks; anything—he'll say "Sorry, just wanted to make sure; good night." She doesn't move, eyes stay shut. "Vera, you up?" he says louder. Again, if she is, good night, and out he goes. But nothing of her moves. That enough? Should he say it once more? Pulls the covers down to her knees slowly. She's in the same position as before. Flat on her back, arms down her sides, legs a little parted, nightdress way it was. He gets closer to that area and looks at it. "Vera, you asleep?" Watches her eyes and mouth for just the slightest movement. If she wakes, well, he doesn't know what he'll do. He feels around her crack for a hole, finds it and sticks his finger in. After a few seconds he moves it around. It's what he thought and heard. Wet, soft, deep as his finger goes, which is just a little ways in, not even a joint. He takes it out, pulls the covers up. He goes to his room, unzips his fly, can't get his hard-on through it it's so stiff so unbuttons the pants and pulls them down and plays with himself facing the mirror. The door, and he shuts it, turns the key and resumes playing with himself. He's done it before but nothing's ever come out. He heard when it does he could almost fall. He does it harder and faster, from one end to the other, and it begins to hurt. He zips up, and holding his penis inside his pants, starts for her room. "That's enough," he says to himself, "you've seen and done plenty, if anyone finds out you'll be killed," takes his hand out of his pants at her door and goes in. She's in the same position asleep. He hopes asleep.

"Vera, are you up?. . . I'm just checking on you, seeing you're all right, the covers are on you. Mom and Dad told me to." She doesn't move. If she did, said anything, he'd say "Well, everything seems all right, so good night." He pulls the covers down slowly. Same position, hands cupped up rather than palms down, maybe her legs a bit closer together. He stares at the crack, finds the hole again with his finger, sticks it in, little deeper than before and moves it around. Still wet and soft and some little bumps now. Then he thinks "Enough, she'll wake up," takes his finger out and covers her up. Starts to go, then says "Vera, you awake?" She says nothing, nothing on her face moves, hands and legs stay the same. "If you are up and say anything about this to anyone, I'll kill you. I'll kill you when nobody's around. I mean it, I'm serious as I ever was about anything, don't say a word about what I did, to me or anyone, or I'll kill you dead." He watches her face; nothing. Should he say it again? Goes to his room, puts on his pajamas, shuts the light and gets into bed. What have I done? I shouldn't have gone back after I did it to her the first time. Just should have taken a look, covered her up, and if I had to, gone into the bathroom or my room and tried to jerk off. I'm dead; she'll tell; nothing will ever be the same again. He squeezes his eyes tight as he can, grinds his teeth, digs his nails into his knuckles, smells his finger. Smells as if he stuck it up his behind when it's clean. Smells the others on that hand; they don't smell at all. He goes into the bathroom, washes his hands and with a washrag and soap scrubs that finger where it went in, brushes his teeth and gets back in bed. He lies there a long time, thinking he'll never get to sleep and in the morning his brother and parents will drag him out of bed and yell and scream at him and do he doesn't know what. His brother's asleep in his bed next to his when he wakes up in the morning. He washes, dresses, goes into the kitchen. Vera's having breakfast, doesn't smile or say good morning as she usually doesn't, his mother's making coffee, smiles at him and says "Good morning, darling, sleep well?" He watches their reactions to him the next few days. No change it seems. Wonders if Vera was awake either of those last two times and if she was, if she told his mother, and if his mother thinks not talking about it to anyone is the best thing to do. He knows if his mother told his father but said don't let Howard know we know, his father would still let him have it, and maybe even with his hand. But insult him terribly; call him a disgusting pig who from now on has to be watched and maybe should be caged. But no change in anyone. Brother goes about his business; Vera looks and talks to him normally. After a while he feels she was up just the second time he touched her, because nobody could stay asleep so long through it, and he did stick it in deeper and move it around more than the first time. If someone played with his penis when he was asleep, he thinks he'd get awake after a while. And if a finger was stuck inside him, he'd definitely get awake. He knows he'll never do anything like that again. If he ever sees her sleeping naked, he'll just turn around and walk away. Not even cover her up. Or maybe just cover her, if it's cold and it seems the covers had fallen accidentally to the floor and not just been kicked off or down the bed, but not look at her crack. He thinks about the incident on and off the next few years. Shudders every time. Sometimes it comes when he's just looking at her face, and not even when she's looking back at him. He doesn't know why, but it comes back to him, putting his finger in, and he has to shut his eyes and shake his head to get rid of it. A few times it's when she's got a hospital gown on, at home or in a hospital, and which always seems to fall a little over her left shoulder. Maybe that's the side she was operated on most and lost more bone than the other and so has less shoulder to support the gown. After a few years he thinks she never told anyone in the family about it but had been awake both times he fingered her. He'd be duping himself or just a fool to think something like a finger in her wouldn't have wakened her the first time. And if that's not it—let's say she went sound asleep immediately—then also because he didn't know what he was doing then with his finger and so had to be a little rough. He's also beginning to recall a slight smile on her when he threatened her. Why's he see it now when he didn't think he saw it then? Maybe he didn't recognize it as such then or just didn't want to. If he'd seen it then it would have meant to him she was awake and he'd then feel for sure he was in the worst trouble he'd ever been in. But that's the face he's starting to see whenever he remembers threatening her. More than that: it's the face he sees, though the face through the rest of it—when he was probing and fingering her and so on—was of one asleep. Years later he tells a woman he's been going with for months about it and says she's the first person he's told. He's around thirty. She says "What took you so long to tell anyone? It's common stuff. I hear it all the time from women friends. My own brother did it to me lots of times and much worse. Occasionally he'd wait for my mom to leave and then go straight to my room, tear off my blankets if I was in bed and even asleep and say 'Pull down your bottoms so I can take a peek.' He also had me whack him off a few times and one time I had to wipe him clean and then wash his tip over the sink. I drew the line when he once wanted to stick his prick in. Only an inch, he said, and I told him I'd tell the police if he so much as tried, and maybe even say he's been trying to rape me for years. So what did he say? 'What about your rear end then? That way you can stay a virgin and not get babies and I heard if it hurts anyone, it's the guy.' He was really wild." "Why'd you let him do anything to you?" "Why'd your sister?" "It was only once, or twice in about ten minutes, and for all I know she actually might have been asleep." "She was up; don't go kidding yourself again. Only reason she pretended being asleep was she was curious, or possibly scared. As for me, I thought it'd get him to treat me better. You see, he fancied himself as, and my mother encouraged him to be, the man of the house, what with our dad dead, but he took advantage of it and became a real mean louse. I also never thought she'd believe me if I told her what he was doing. To her, that schmuck was God. But everything turned out OK. We got it all out at a shrink—a family counselor we went to as a family for a year. And now we don't even think about it or as anything more than sadistic growing-up experimental kid stuff on his part, and on mine, that I should have said 'Lay off or I'll call the cops or kick in your nuts' from the start. And on my mother's: birdbrain neglect that she was lucky didn't turn into catastrophic life-changing big brother inseminating little sis." "I know you said he made you masturbate him and maybe worse, but did he ever stick his finger in you too?" "Finger. Toe. Once a pencil. That's why I say, he was a sadist then. But he turned out fine and I've no fears he won't be anything but a terrific father to his girls." "I'm not even sure I can look at the sonofabitch now after what you told me." "Oh, lay off the guy. He was just a jerk who since then's done a complete reverse. At least he talked about it openly by the time he was twenty-five. While you, you've kept it in and have most likely whipped yourself to death over it several times, even if what you did wasn't one-fiftieth as bad." His mother says "What can we get her to amuse herself? She stares at the walls half the day, doesn't have a clue what to do with herself once her teacher leaves." They get her paints, pastels, an easel and smock, modeling clay. She tries a few times and then says: "I'm not the artist type. My stuff is so amateurish and hopeless it makes me feel ugly and dumb just to look at it. I think I'm more the type that likes making things people can use." His mother has him get Vera craft materials at a hobby shop and she makes leather scissor holders and book covers, beaded necklaces and cloth trivets and wraps them and at the dinner table gives them as gifts. "It's not my birthday or graduation, or not that I know of it," he says, "but thanks. It's very pretty and handy." "I'll make something else for you then with leather," and he says "Nah, one's enough. Not that I don't really like it, but spread the good work around," but the next night she gives him another wrapped gift. "Look Mom, Dad," he says "it's to hold my keys." Feels and smells the leather. "Smooth, and very nicely cured. Smells almost like the actual cow's hide, but nice, though, and now my keys won't scratch my thighs or cut through my pants pockets and make all my change spill out." Later he says to his mother "She should be doing something, if it has to be crafts, that I can say 'That's fantastic, that truly shows talent.' Something I can honestly admire if not use—

we, all of us—and give her real credit for and which she can get better and better at over the years till she even becomes an artisan at it, why not? and even sells some of it. But work stupid but well-meaning institutions give brain-damaged people to do? It's humiliating. Or demoralizing. Whatever it is, I hate it for her." His mother says "She hasn't a storehouse of talent and imagination and any pushing her to be more artistic will make her feel ugly and dumb again and maybe even make her head hurt. Let her do what she enjoys doing and feel it's adequate and you continue faking your admiration whenever she gives one to you." She next gives him a lanyard with a whistle on it and he says thanks, blows it, says "Nice tone, not too tweet-tweet. Maybe I'll wear it at the next square dance I'll do-si-do to," and she says "Where's that?" and he says "You know, when you call the calls or whatever the caller does," and she says "When did you ever do one of those?" and he says "At camp, when I used to dance, not call. But I'm really only kidding. But it's nice, this, though what I can use it for. . .? Maybe my keys if I'm wearing pants without pockets or something—like athletic shorts for the outside but when I also have no shirt on with pockets in it," and she says "Really, if you don't like it, or can't use it, I know someone who might," and he says "Well, then you should probably give it to him or her, for it is, to tell you the truth, kind of wasted on me. It's not quite for the city and I'm always in the city, not that I want to be, and I suppose also I'm just not a lanyard man," and he gives it to her and she looks hurt and he says "Excuse me, but what did I say? Honestly, Vera, it's good work. The colors are lovely and so's the design and it's just about perfectly constructed—'fabricated,' is the new word. And if I had to make something like that—if I so much as tried—it'd be all over the joint, a perfect mess. But what if—but maybe I shouldn't say this, though if I don't I'm sure I'll regret it even more, so here goes. What if you started doing something that would thoroughly take you over and make you want to do it every chance you got and which, let's say in a year or so or just whenever it happens, could eventually become something like art or just great or truly excellent crafts? Because you show talent here with this lanyard—with the bracelets and leather works and that cloth hot pot thing—I always forget the name of it—you truly do. The colors and way you make them and such and the quick way you picked it all up, besides the variety of different crafts you've done." "I'm not interested in making things like that, but thanks for what you said about my work," and she doesn't show him any of it after that. A few weeks later he asks his mother what Vera's been up to with her crafts, "since she hasn't given me anything in a while, and come to think of it, even shown me it or spoken about it," and his mother says "She seems to have lost interest in it and I'm afraid is back twiddling her thumbs most of the day, when she isn't staring out the window at the sun and burning her eyes," but gives no hint she knows what took place between Vera and him. His parents buy her a special television set she can control from her bed. She gets to like a couple of the afternoon soap operas and follows them every day. Just to get her talking about something, he asks her "So what is it about these shows that you watch them so much?" He tells himself that whatever she says he's going to answer "That's nice, that's fine, makes sense, very interesting, now I can understand." She gives the story line of one of the shows for the last two weeks and says "Maybe not to you, but to me it's kind of fascinating. Also the acting is very good and the whole thing feels like real life but not any that many of us live. All that plus looking forward to it and probably guessing what's going to happen next has hooked me and a few million other people, like a good novel would to you that takes place over a few centuries. You know, very long and involved and with family after family and lots of living and dying." "Actually, some of the things you described do make me think it could be good, like a long-term infection that doesn't make you sick or anything and even makes you feel chipper." She invites him to watch it with her one day after he gets back from teaching junior high school. He says "Usually I'm too bushed to do anything but nap for an hour before I have to start correcting papers and things, but one day I might." "You'll see you could get hooked too. I've even read where big-time college professors changed their class schedules when one of the soaps moved to a different time, just so they wouldn't miss a single minute of it." "Well, if they can watch and appreciate it, why not I? I could even use a daily rather simple distraction like that, which could be why they do it, to clear the head a bit, or maybe it is that engrossing and good. Tomorrow then, if I don't fall asleep on my feet second I get home." He tells himself "Remember, if you don't like it, which you know you won't, don't say so. Just nod and say it's pretty good and you could see why someone of any kind of intelligence could get hooked on it, but you only wish you had the free time most college professors have, but you have a ton of paperwork and lesson plans to do each weekday if you want to keep your weekends relatively clear. During the first commercial break she says "What do you think so far?" and he says "Not bad, not bad," and during the next break she says "Did it get any better for you?" and he says "Why, don't you think I'm enjoying it?" and she says "You're obviously not. Fidgeting around; chewing your cuticles; that sourpuss look you always have when you're bored with something and feel you can't get out of it—that one goes back to when you were a boy," and he says "Oh, that's my stomach acting up which it's been doing all day—teaching often works on my muscles there in addition to giving me cramps," and she says "Listen, if the show's junk, say so. Because what are you holding back for, my feelings?" and he says "Well they mean something," and she says "Believe me, whatever you say's not going to hurt me or change my watching it," and he says "OK then; all right. To me—mind if I talk while it's on?" and she presses the remote control and the show goes off. "To me the whole thing feels made by admen for idiots." "That sounds rehearsed." "No. If it's good, then it's a mistake. And you're no idiot by a long shot, so I don't know what you see in it; though maybe those professors are, experts in one line but dumb and young in most everything else. Or maybe today's segment is an isolated bad case and all the other days are five times as good," and she says "This one's fairly typical, in story and the rest." "Then I don't know what to say. But when the commercials are more gripping than the story and better acted and directed, then we better watch out." "What's wrong with the acting? You saying it's bad?" "I'm saying it's quacking, not acting. I'm saying any schnook off the street could do better. You hear about casting couches? This one must have had a dormitory hall of them, one side for men and the other for the young beauties." "What are casting couches?" "You know. Couches where actors are cast on, like in bronze and stone. Forget that; didn't turn out. And the bad acting's probably not the actors' fault either, for what do they have to work with? 'Good-bye.' 'Good-bye?' 'That's right, good-bye.' 'You're really saying good-bye?' 'You got it. I'm truly and absolutely saying good-bye.' 'You can't mean it.' 'I mean it, my darling, I mean it.' 'Then why'd you call me now your darling?' " "OK, I get the point," she says. "Wait, I'm getting to the heart of it and having fun. 'Force of habit.' 'Force of habit?' 'Yes, force of habit. Now good-bye.' 'Shall I see you to the door at least?' 'See me if you wish but it won't change my leaving.' 'I'll see you to it then.' 'Then see me, for no more protests I hope on either of our sides.' " "What do you mean by that last thing?" "It's nothing; another flub. Then, after six commercials and several station breaks with minicommercials, back to where we left him seeing her to the door. The camera zooms in on his hand on the doorknob. Maestro, doorknob music. Then closer to the pinky ring she once gave him. "This is painful," she says. "Painful, but not close?" "Nowhere near. They don't repeat talking like that. They almost never follow the same couple scene after scene. And how would we know she gave him the ring? Was it yesterday's show? Was it today's? You're being silly." "He says so at the door. 'Want the pinky ring back you gave me when I was your darling?' 'No.' 'No?' 'No.' Actually, what they have there might not be so bad. Modern drama. I've always thought someone should write a play or book where the whole two acts or two hundred pages of it takes place between the time the guy gets out of his chair to go to the window a few feet away till he reaches the window and looks out. Or gal. And maybe at the end all he or she does is look out of it a second and raise a hand to wave or say hi or tries to raise the window and gives up after one try. So I'm saying this soap maybe has something going for it that I didn't know. Maybe all soaps if they're all as slow. But I'm tired, as I told you I'd be, so my judgment of them could also be very bad. School teaching knocks the living stuffing out of you. The kids today—" "You really didn't give it a chance. You came in with lousy opinions of it and then did everything you could to back them up." "I gave it enough, didn't I? Ten minutes, around—what more's it need?" "If it was a book how many pages would you give it? Twenty pages, you'd have to. That'd be about thirty minutes for a fast reader, maybe forty for a slow. "If it was a lousy book I could tell in five minutes. Just three pages—the first two and the last and maybe an extra thirty seconds to zip through the middle. Because crap is crap and doesn't need anymore time than that. Just as that stupid soap was, which you're too smart not to know. So what am I saying? I'm saying if you have to watch anything on TV when the sun's still out and we're not on daylight saving time, maybe an educational program on another station at the same hour?" "What about if I don't watch anything because I can't?" and she looks around for something and he says "What do you mean?" and then "What are you looking for?" and she grabs the glass off the night table and throws it at the screen, doesn't break it but the glass breaks when it hits the floor. "Oh, smart, smart," he says. "You want to kill us all if the tube explodes and sets fire to the room? Brilliant," and he leaves. "Hell with you, bastard," she yells. "And the tube couldn't have exploded because the television was off," and he says "Maybe, maybe," gets to the end of the hall, then back to her room to pick up the glass. "Martyr, back, wonderful, don't cut your hands I'm supposed to say," and after he's got all the glass but the tiniest pieces he leaves the room, They don't talk to each other at dinner. After, his mother talks to him and he says he would have gone in anyway to apologize and goes into her room where she's on her bed reading a magazine and says "Look, I'm sorry, the whole thing was dumb of me, please accept my apology and I came in not because anyone told me to but on my own." "I don't want to talk about it. You're so freaking stuffed with yourself you stink." "Fine, good, get it out on me; you should." "I'm not *getting it out*. I've thought about it and you're a mess." "Look, my standards, if that's what they are, are stupidly and most likely falsely and just all-out-of-proportion high. And to me I have this misguided, don't ask me where it came from, idea that art-art-art is God, so what can I say? I'm probably a fake." "Oh, when you get right down to it a lot of what you say's true, even if the way you say it is horrible. I do watch these dumb shows to stop from being bored to death, when I should be doing something else with my time. Like what, though's, the problem." "No no. Watch the good stuff, that's all, and maybe some of the bad stuff too when you're totally bored; it's only human." "Really, much as I hate admitting it and still think your a swollen-headed mess, you changed my mind. You want the set in your room from now on? Because I don't." "No, keep it and never listen to me again on this, or just think some more before giving it away." "If you don't want it can you wheel it to Mom and Dad's room? They said they wouldn't mind having one like mine they can regulate from bed." That's where he puts it. In a closet, which is where his parents want it, and from time to time someone wheels it out for her, but not out of the room, for something she especially wants or thinks she ought to watch. He takes her to the movies. "Take her to a movie; she hasn't been in years," his mother said. "You want to go to a movie?" he said. "Sure, I love them," she said, "but who's going to take me and how we going to get there? It'll take me a year to walk to Broadway to get the bus." She's begun to smoke so wants to sit in the balcony. He can't stand tobacco smoke but will take it for her. He asks if they have an elevator here, "you can see my sister can't take the stairs too well," and the usher says "No elevator; if it's that she wants to smoke, she can do it in the ladies' room, but that's one flight downstairs." "If you have to go," he tells her, "do it now; I don't think there's a bathroom upstairs." "No worry; I always go twice before I leave." She hands him her metal braces, grabs the stair railing with both hands and climbs the two flights to the balcony. She has a lot more trouble with the steps in the balcony because there are no railings along the aisles. He says "Maybe I should have got the loge seats. They seemed so much more expensive, but what the hell. Want me to run down and quickly change them?" "I'll just be in people's way while you're gone. And by the time you get down and back we can be up there, and who's to say they'll have any? C'mon." The theater's jammed. It's a popular movie, won a few Academy Awards in the leading categories the newspaper ad said, and the people around them all seem to be laughing. "If I see a single seat, want me to grab it for you?" "I don't like sitting alone; nobody to tell what I think about it. Don't worry, we're almost there or thereabouts." When he finally got around to asking her if she wanted to go to a movie and they looked in the paper for one, this one had already begun. But it was the one she wanted to see most and she didn't want to wait for the next show, she said, as he might lose interest in going by then or say it was getting too late, he has to work tomorrow and so on. So he ran outside, up the avenue and got a cab and picked her up in front of the building. "Only front two rows audience seats or last three rows balcony," an usher was announcing by the ticket booth and he looked at her and she said "OK with me; I want to see it and might not get another chance till it comes around again in a year. When the movie ends we'll come down." She seems to be struggling so he grabs her arm to help her walk up the last few steps and she says ouch. "That hurts; too much pressure on my arm goes straight to my brain or spine or something, but it's like a bullet shot in me where you touched." It takes twenty minutes to walk from the lobby to their balcony seats. People around them are still laughing and even howling hysterically. She gets in first and he turns around to look and doesn't yet see what's so funny. Jack Lemmon. He can be a funny guy. And something about an apartment key he heard on the way up and some pretty actress he's never seen before who seems to be overdoing the New York accent. He bought her what she wanted

491

at the candy stand. "Anything?" "Pick it, the kid's flush." "What's 'flush'? "Cash, on me, more than enough." Popcorn, soda, ice cream bonbons that seemed pretty expensive for the size of the box. He didn't say anything, but his look when he got his change back. "Well, since I see my being here as kind of an occasion, " she said, "I might as well treat myself big or let you do it." "That a way to go." He carried it all up for her with the braces. Some of the popcorn spills when he quickly turns from the screen to her when she says "C'mon, sit down, you'll see it better from here," and he hands her the soda, popcorn and box and starts picking it up. "What're you doing?. . . Leave it, we've already caused too much fuss." It's the last row, nothing behind them but wall, so he can bob around and sit as tall as he wants. He sits, drops under the seat what popcorn he picked up, lays her braces quietly on the floor, helps her off with her coat, she gives him back the bonbons and says "For some reason I can't open it; the fingers; they feel stuck," and he rips the plastic off with his teeth and opens the box. "Help yourself," she says but he says he hasn't been able to stand any kind of ice cream since he was a soda jerk at a summer resort and saw—, but she shushes him, points to the screen and they watch. She smokes six cigarettes during the forty minutes till the movie ends. At one point she put her head close to his and said "Liking it?" and he said "You know, it isn't for me to say this but—," and she said "Please don't talk about my smoking," and he said "But your clothes are going to stink from it— mine too—not to say your health," and she said "Let me have what little fun I can get, will you? and you're also killing the movie for me," and sat up straight again. Most of the balcony gets up to leave when the movie's over and he says "Should we move down?" and she says "Who wants to get trampled in the rush," and he says "Fine by me, so long as my eyes hold out—yours doing OK?" and she nods, "and nobody behind me to complain of my big head." When the movie gets to the part where they came in he says "Think we can go now?" and she says "Why, did we see this? Can't we see it to the end though? I'm having a ball." He hates seeing a movie he's just seen. Even as a kid, hated it, for even a few minutes, and doesn't think he's ever seen the same movie through twice in his life. He looks at his watch. It's a dark part of the movie and he can't see the numbers and hands on the dial, but he says "It's getting late," tapping his watch; "I have to be at school tomorrow half past eight at the latest," but she pretends not to hear him or she really doesn't, everyone around them laughing so hard. She's laughing now too, harder than she's done since they got there, maybe for his benefit, but then she also might understand the story better now. A combination of things perhaps, one contributing to or taking away from the other, but too difficult and not important enough to try to figure out. He shuts his eyes, slumps down till he's lower than the seat top, tries to sleep, but her laughing and everyone else's and the loud sound track keep him up. Who can sleep in a theater? he thinks. His father, even at operas. "Only comedies," she says when they're putting their coats on and waiting for almost everyone in the balcony to leave. "No serious stuff, which I'm sure you'd like better. That is, if you ever want to take me again. And if it's the balcony that made you so irritable, next time you can stick me up here and then sit downstairs and come back for me after. I can get used to sitting alone if it's a picture I can laugh hard enough at. Though this one was both serious and funny, don't you think? A very tricky plot, with some serious actors in it, and suicide's nothing to laugh about, if I got what happened right. I know she didn't kill herself, but they did have to walk her around." "Irritable? Me? No, it's just—well, cigarette smoke might make me that way a little, but I'll get accustomed to it. Hold my nose through most of the show, or something. And twice a month if you want, but from now on let's try to get here from the beginning." "I don't know. Sort of makes it easier for me getting here when everyone else is already in. And coming in the middle of the picture and trying to make out what's happening is sort of a challenge." He takes her to a movie a few weeks later and then a couple more times in the next few years. He dreams about her recovering, for several years before she died and lots of times after. In one he says "Good morning," and she says "Good morning to you, sir," and gets off her crutches, throws them behind her, he jumps at her to stop her from falling but she steps back, shows how she can walk without crutches and says "I can even fly now," and puts out her arms, closes her eyes and starts humming, rises about ten feet, flies in a circle around him and then into the clouds. "Come back," he shouts. "Don't get carried away. There are planes up there. Spacecraft, lunar junk, wild birds, no air." In another he's hurrying to junior high school to teach when a car pulls up, she's at the wheel and leans across the front seat and says "Hi, like a lift?" "Sure, but since when do you drive?" "Oh, I've been practicing in my hospital bed and wheelchair, and stick shift too." He gets in beside her and says "What is it, some special handicapped car?" and she says "Oh no, I'm all better now, I've just come from the hospital," and lifts her legs above the seat and shakes them. "Watch out for the cars," he yells and though her car hasn't moved, her feet go back and forth on about eight floor pedals, so fast he can hardly see them. "I can walk too but why walk when you have a car?" "And your crutches?" "First thing I did when I got out was put them under the tires and run over them." "You should have given them to the hospital or Goodwill," and she says "Symbolism over reality any day. You never went through what I did, so how could you know?" Another one she's in a wheelchair, slumped over asleep and held in by a waist strap, tubes in her nose and coming out from under the blanket on her lap, when she suddenly crows, rips the strap off and tubes out of her, stands and kicks the chair back so hard it bangs against the wall and falls over, and starts walking around in circles, sniffing the air like a dog. "Look at you, you're walking," he says. "Mom, Dad, look at Vera. It's a miracle." "That's right," she says, "and this is the way I'm gonna be from now on. I can't stand the position I was put in," and walks out of the apartment, building, down the block, walking so fast he can't catch up with her even though he's sprinting. "The world's fastest walker," he thinks. "I'll enter her in the Olympics if they have such a race. She'll win medals and fame for the family and write a book about it and make millions and not have to worry about anything again in her life." He stops when he's out of breath; she turns south on Columbus and next thing he knows she's just a dot at the tip of Manhattan and then he can't see her. His father hands him binoculars and he looks through them and sees her walking as fast over a huge suspension bridge. Cars are speeding toward her but she zips around them. "Vera," he yells, "Vera," and then loses her. In another she's in a hospital sitting against the side of her bed. Frail, gaunt, hair a mess, skin yellow, sores on her legs, feet twisted in. "I've been thinking," she says, "—do I smell bad?" "No, you don't smell bad," he says. "Well I've been thinking. I don't want to live another minute and you have to help me do it." "Do what, live?" "No not live." "No, do, live. You smell good. Maybe there'll be a cure for you some day. Sure there will. I've read articles, people have sent you them." "You think so?" "I'd almost stake my life on it." Suddenly she's four or five, same ugly hospital clothes on though, and then quickly becomes around fifteen and her body starts blossoming, little bumps, then big breasts, hips develop, legs lengthen, thighs harden, and she's wearing a thin summer dress and Greek sandals, they used to call them, with the straps wrapped halfway up her calves, hole in her neck and shoulder slump gone, bed becomes a chaise longue on a patio somewhere, flowering trees behind her and behind them a lake. "I told you," he says. "You did, didn't you, Mr. Knows-it-all and always so good to me, so prophetically correct and sweet, does anyone in the world deserve more than you?" and she gets up, comes over, puts his arms around her and her hands in his side pants pockets and kisses him on the mouth. "Oh boy, she's a hot number," he thinks. "What am I going to do with her now?" In another she's stepping off a train onto an empty outdoor platform. Tall, meticulously dressed, hair done up, no sign of her illness. And must have been a long journey, he thinks, what with all the luggage that's now beside her. She seems to be looking around for someone as the train pulls away. He says "Hey, I'm here, over here," and keeps shouting and waving as he approaches her, but she doesn't turn to him or seem to hear him. "Vera," he says, standing next to her, "the trip's done wonders for you. What was it, some kind of tour of various spas?" She keeps looking around but never at him. Then she shakes her head, is disgusted, picks up two valises and what looks like a makeup case and walks to the small train station. He lifts her one trunk onto his back, almost collapses from it, holds it by an end strap with his hands over his shoulders, and follows her. "Right behind you," he says, "if this thing doesn't kill me first. And hold the door, please, hold that door," but she lets it swing back into his head. In another she's sitting at a table in the staff cafeteria of a junior high school he taught at for years, arguing with another teacher about a book they've all read. "The author portrays her as a whore. She's no whore. No woman's a whore. The whore's the author who portrays women as whores so every man and lez can stick his finger in while he reads. Because when she sticks her finger in it's for her pleasure, pure and simple, and perhaps as a mnemonic device, but not for whores who think all women are whores, lezies and fingers." "You make no sense and are also downright offensive in your references to lesbians," the teacher says. "And what do you make, you big bag of haggard figs? Fart on me, fart on me, why don't you?" and she stands up—"Your crutches, watch out, you'll fall," Howard says—and she says "Hell with my crutches, who needs them?" and grabs them off the floor and breaks them over her thigh, says to the teacher, who's never stopped eating, "You're lucky I didn't wrap them around your little onanist's neck," and slaps the sandwich out of his mouth and stomps out of the room. "Crude, rude and wasteful, is the way I'd characterize your sister," he says, "and you're fired." In another he's sleeping in bed in his old room, little light from the streetlights coming in through the venetian blind slits, when the covers are slowly pulled off him, he starts shivering and says "Please, whoever it is, I'm cold," and looks up and sees she's naked and has the body and body hair of his wife. She says "Mind if I come in—I'm frightened," and he says "I'm not allowed to—I promised the folks," and she says "Why, because I'm supposed to be sick and sad person? Well, you don't see me crying or on crutches or canes or in a wheelchair or anything, so I must've recovered or else always been well," and she slips in beside him—"Please, it's a narrow single bed, go back to your own"—kisses him on the chest, tickles his nipples, grabs his penis and jerks it till it's hard—"That's reflex, not feeling; it's even happened when I've sat with a plain empty box on my lap"—gets on top of him; he tries to buck her off and she says "Don't be a rotten bastard; I might, like everyone else in life, be frightfully to moribundly sick tomorrow or even later tonight, so let me have my kicks while I can"—sticks his penis in, arches back to sort of lock it in and bounces up and down on him, while he's looking at the door, waiting for his parents to burst in and thinking of an excuse to give them—"I couldn't help it; she forced me to; she's become so strong and big that she simply overpowered me; I also thought that for all the permanent harm it'll do me, maybe it'll do some short-term good for her in some particular way, and I also didn't want to wake the two of you up. . ." His mother, Vera and he are at the airport; he's leaving for a year on a fellowship at a California school. Vera says "Wait, nobody go away," and on crutches goes into a shop, comes out and waves her hands no and goes down a passageway and disappears, comes back just around the time they're thinking of looking for her, with a newsweekly and cheap paperback copy of Edna St. Vincent Millay poems. "I thought you'd like them for the plane. I won't pretend I've read the poems or even know how to say her name, but it was the only poetry book they had and from what it says on the back cover it seems very good." He kisses her cheek, she lowers her head and blushes, he wants to tell her that if she has another operation he'll fly home immediately and stay as long as she likes. That he can't thank her enough for the book, which he'll start reading right away on the plane, even before the magazine, which he also thanks her for. That right now she seems balanced on the outstretched crutches like some winged statue of victory on top of an institutional dome. That he'll come home for Christmas for a month and maybe Thanksgiving if the fare isn't too steep and they'll go to restaurants and movies and just spend lots of time talking at home. That he'd trade places with her if he could. He's had twenty-eight good healthy years, so he'd be willing to take her place from now on if she could be healthy again. That if she ever needs some of his skin for grafting, which the doctors said she might need, and of course any amount of his blood, whose type they share, she can definitely count on him. That she should think about coming to California with Mom to see him for a week or two, but when the weather's nice so they can see the pretty hills and big smelly trees and exotic flowers and flowering citrus trees, with eventually real fruit on them, he hears the area's known for. That he's going to buy a used car there and they'll drive all the way to Santa Barbara or the Hearst Castle if she wants, even if it turns out to be farther than Santa Barbara, and back along the ocean route through Big Sur where they can even camp out for the night. That he'll try to write her almost every day but certainly a couple of times a week and of course call. That he loves her very very much and she's in his thoughts daily and she'll be in them even more a day when he gets out there and he'll miss her she can't know how much and he really thinks, though he doesn't know why he feels so sure about this—maybe it's the way she's been looking and acting lately—but that she's going to get much better the next year, off the crutches, no more of those urinary and eye problems to add to it and headaches and such, gaining weight and maybe even height and walking and doing just about everything normally again. And that there's always the chance he'll get the disease too, as the doctors said, and that she's set the standard how to deal with it year after year. The departure's announced, he kisses his mother and her good-bye, thanks her for the book and magazine and tells her to take care and he'll call them soon after he gets there, the plane goes, he sits in his seat crying for a while, reads the magazine cover to cover, opens the book when lunch comes but the pages start falling out while he's turning them. One of the first things he's going to do after he finds an apartment and gets set up in

California is stick the loose pages and rest of the book into a postal bag and send it to the publisher with a note complaining of the lousy binding and asking for a new copy plus reimbursement for the cost of the bag and mailing the book to them. He and the woman he's living with like going to a different restaurant every other week. They take Vera with them every third or fourth time. One time she says the Indian food's too hot. "If you take me again, please not too spicy a place?" She doesn't like the Mexican food. "Too heavy and any food that has chocolate in its main course has to be in deep trouble to come up with something original." Philippine food's too peanutty, Chinese food too gooey, Japanese food's pretty but has no taste and the small portions make you feel gypped, German food seems as if it's been left on the stove for days by mistake, Cuban and Ukranian food seem unclean. "I appreciate being invited—it's nice just to get out—but I wish I liked tasting different foreign foods or saw the point to it as much as you. Have you ever eaten French—I'm sure you have," and they tell her if it's any good it has to be too expensive for them, and American food, which she wouldn't mind having—"Since summer camp I've loved things like succotash and chicken à la king"—they feel they've had too much of it at home and they also like drinking different foreign wines and beers. The woman's very attentive to her, holds her arm when they walk, makes sure she gets the best taxi and restaurant seat, provides her with magazine articles she thinks she might be interested in, always compliments her clothes, often comments about her soft sultry voice and long straight well-groomed hair, that she has a perfect little model's nose and beautiful small fingers and ears and how smart she is not to use rouge and nail polish and hair spray and how well she takes care of her cuticles and nails. Once when he goes to the men's room she says "I wish I could be like you. Beautiful, a natural height, breasts, hips that don't look like a six-year-old's, your posture, educated, engaged to an all-right guy, the chance to drive a car and go to work and have kids. I hate my life but don't tell my brother any of this. Say I'm satisfied, to a degree, if he asks what we talked about and you say 'life.' But sometimes I wish I could suddenly die and nothing really helps that feeling. Religion sometimes, psychiatrists no time, I never took to booze or food as a release. And because my insides are so bad in various places after so many operations and the wear and tear on them from the disease, I'm not supposed to smoke, but screw that I say, since it's my only peace except sleep." The woman tells him all this later and he says "Why doesn't she have more incentive to do something with her life? Sure, death, that's a good one to scare the shit out of you and which she's talked a lot about and years ago actually tried, because she hasn't the fucking imagination or spunk to do anything harder, like possibly doing something. For she has the use of her hands, her brains have the potential, she gets around on those crutches OK or can always take taxis, and she certainly has the time. She doesn't have to go out and hack it, everything's given her, the libraries are stacked with the best anyone could read, the state and federal government will pay for any education she wants for as long as she likes right up to a Ph.D., and Social Security or some other big agency guarantees her a decent income for life and even more—if the rest of the family dies—should she suddenly fall flat on her face or can only meet things halfway," and the woman says "Why do you take her out and spend the time with her you do and talk and say you think about her so much if after all of it you still can't put yourself in her place?" "Wait a minute—what did I say? Maybe you're right. I can be a little too hard on people. Let me go to sleep on it, but Christ I'm being straight-out honest when I say I wish she was a more interesting and better-read person and had some intelligent things and few other experiences than her repetitive nonevent bland ones to talk about when we go out," and next morning, mostly so the woman wouldn't think him a bastard, he says "You were right on the mark about Vera last night. Maybe I'd had too much to drink or something at dinner and it got me mean and angry, but I was being totally insensitive and unfair." She tries killing herself with aspirins when she's around ten. His mother sees her acting giddy, thinks she drank some liquor from the liquor cabinet, sees the empty aspirin bottle, throws her down, sticks her fingers down her mouth till she throws some of it up, gets her in a cab to a hospital to have her stomach pumped. Later Vera tells her she's never going to try anything like that again. For a day or so she felt sick of her condition and didn't think anyone liked her but her mother and that her father even hated her and that's why she did it. "But getting that tube down my neck was worse than any killing myself could be. They must've thought I wasn't awake, but I never felt anything so painful and disgusting in my life." A couple of years later she cuts her wrist with a razor blade she got out of her father's razor. Howard's in his room when he hears his mother scream. His brother and father run through the apartment to the upstairs bathroom. He runs too but they tell him to go back to his room and stay there. The cut isn't much and his mother bandages it up. A few weeks later, though his mother told him not to mention any of it around the house and never to Vera, he says to her "Please don't let the folks know I'm talking about this, and if the question bothers you don't answer it, but what did it feel like when you did it to your wrist and what in hell made you do it?" "First of all," she says, "don't curse. Second of all, doing it hurt very much. When the blood started shooting out I suddenly got scared and couldn't go any deeper. I didn't want to live, that's all the reason was, because I'm sick of the ugly way I look and my body all crooked and that I know it's all only going to get much worse. But all I got from it was a lot of gushy attention I didn't want and a big bawling-out from Dad. I felt so dumb. I'll never try anything like that again. Mom's also said if I kill myself she'll kill herself right after and then haunt me in heaven forever or just crack up in real life and never again be the same." She's fourteen when she goes to the roof of their building and sits on the edge of it looking down to the street. A man in a window across the street yells "Hey miss, hey miss, what are you doing up there, get down," and when she turns away from him and just stays there, he calls the police. A policeman comes to the roof and says "Don't worry, I'm not going to get too near you, but what are your parents' names and where do they live?" and she says "They're away for the weekend, my only brother at home's at work, and the woman who's supposed to look in on me went shopping downtown and won't be back till much later today." He moves nearer and says "Good, that's a nice clear sensible answer, you sound great. Now come on off of there, kid, really, it's no good for you and I don't want to work hours past my duty," and she says "Step a step closer and I'm sliding myself off. I don't want to live but I don't want to jump right away." "Why don't you want to live?—go on, tell me, I'll listen," and she says "Not to you." "I can understand that; I've got a uniform; you're afraid of it maybe. But will you speak to a minister or rabbi or someone from the clergy like that?" and she says "A priest. I like them best out of all those because they have time only for regular people and give everything they earn extra to the church and poor." The street's now blocked, lots of police cars and vans and fire trucks down there, lots of people looking up. Occasionally she hears her name called and a couple of times she thinks she recognizes the voices, but she stops looking down or at the windows across the street, almost all of them with people in them looking at her, and only looks at her hands or the people on her roof or a plane passing or just the plain sky. A priest from a local church comes to the roof and tries urging her down. "You have everything to live for. No matter what our state of mind or physical health, we all do. Think of your dear mother. Your brothers and father I've heard. There is never a good reason to take your own life." She says "There's no way I'm getting off here except head first to the street, so thanks but no thanks. It's a long climb and you seem to have trouble with your legs like me, so I'm sorry for making you come up." "Would you instead show your appreciation for what I did and your respect for my age and weak legs by accompanying me to my church where we can talk without being surrounded by all of this?" ' No, but if you want to talk, do, so long as it's from safe distance away," and he says "Fine, I for one don't like heights so if I have to be up here I'm happy where I am," sits on a parapet separating adjoining roofs, takes a beret out of his jacket pocket and puts it on, "To protect me from the sun; I'm fair-skinned, so subject to its strokes," and says "Now tell me, my dear, what brought all this on? And take your time and speak loudly, my ears from this far away aren't good and I want to hear every word," and she talks about her illness and childhood and operations and scars and that she has no friends, only people who feel sorry for her or are paid to do things or be with her, and some people the last two years have almost gagged at their first sight of her and nobody but nobody but her mother truly loves her, but that's all right, why should they? she loves nobody but her in return, and don't tell her God loves her too because she's heard all that, she's visited a priest to speak, maybe from his own church—is his the one a few blocks down between Columbus and Broadway?—and he says no, that's a cathedral, his is farther uptown but he knows the one she means and its very fine head priest—and she says anyway, if he says something about how everyone isn't perfect in life but is in the eyes of the Lord and so on, she'll say everyone but her it seems to be like, and she forgot to say she of course doesn't want to hurt her mother but she more than that doesn't want to go on anymore like this which is worse than hurting ten mothers if they were all like hers, and she only wishes, so she could be sure to die and not just get a broken neck or leg, that this building was fifteen stories high instead of five or whatever it is when you count that open areaway her mother calls it you go four steps down into from the street. He listens, tries to reason with her at several points, finally says what looks beyond bearing today can suddenly be thought thoroughly bearable tomorrow and even a gift of sorts because it forced her to reconsider her existence which in the end will give her the essential spiritual subsistence to live, and then they are always devising new cures for everything, medicine is like that these days, the good news about her cure might even be in the mail now to her mother or doctor or being printed this moment on sheets at the newspaper plant so they can all read it later today, so he's sure if she comes downstairs with him she'll look upon this as one of the more capricious events of her junior years but not one to be ashamed of one bit, for she is only questioning deeply and acting fervently and being profoundly human and all that's to be respected and even revered by all well-meaning intelligent men, death is tied to life as she must now see, she has made the connection that most people never make in their entire lives so why rush things, does she understand what he means? gives up after an hour, says it's become too hot for him and he'd feel ridiculous sitting here under an umbrella when there's no rain and besides that he's not well himself, he doesn't want to say with what but part of it is something very personal that most older folk get which now forces him to go downstairs, but if she wants to talk to him some more to have the police phone him, he'll be by his phone the next few hours and will immediately cab over, and if she only wants to talk about other things on this or any other day, simply phone him and he'll come directly to her home just as she is always invited to his. Her brother Alex comes, tells her he called the resort their folks are at but they've gone sightseeing for the day and can't be reached. She doesn't look at him, watches two pigeons nestled under a roof eave across the street, follows the path of a contrail and then stares at it till it disintegrates, every now and then stands on crutches and stretches, ignoring the oohs, ohhs and noes from below. During one of these stretches, when she's watching an enormous orange sun set into the river, a policeman swings to her on a sling hooked up from the next roof behind her, grabs her around the waist and swings back with her to his roof. She cries and kicks, is given an injection, is unconcious by the time she's put into the ambulance, Alex all this time never letting go of her hand. Howard doesn't know how the sling worked. It would have had to be somewhat large and complicated, for safety reasons and because the police knew they only had one shot at it and there couldn't be any mistakes. Wouldn't she have seen it being set up and been wary of it? Maybe she wanted to be saved that way, risky as it was, rather than just giving in and going downstairs on her own. He never asked her. In fact nothing about it was ever mentioned between them. People from the street yelled "yay" and applauded, some shouted "Tarzan and Jane." He was working as a guest waiter in a summer camp upstate. There was a front-page photograph of her sitting on the roof, legs hanging off it, in both morning tabloids. He learned of the incident when Alex sent him a letter a week later talking about lots of other things but which included about ten lines typed out with *x*'s and *n*'s and *m*'s and then scratched out with a pen. It took him a while to decipher it; held it up to the light; held a lit match behind it; tried erasing and then dissolving the ink. "She's okay now, out of the hospital first on some stupefying and now a tranquilizing drug. Roof door's been padlocked, violating all F. D. laws. Just hope she doesn't incinerate the place to kill herself next time and the ground floor exit's blocked. I know what your impulse is but don't waste your hard-earned dough and scant day-off time coming in to see her. We've been told to put the whole thing away for good. Poor kid. Who could blame her? Newspaper articles and photos enclosed. They don't even come close. Don't let on I wrote." He calls home, Alex answers and says—Vera or the folks must have been near—"Hi, everything's jim-dandy here, the folks fine, Vera's just great, you're lucky to be away. City's been sticky with humidity and temperatures in the upper nineties for a week, so even with the fans blasting at high we can't sleep." By the time he gets home at the end of August all the newspapers about it have been thrown out. He tries talking about it once but Alex says "Shh, shut your trap, someone might hear; anyway, it's old news." There's a brownstone on the block for Christian missionaries passing through on their way to Africa or on their way back to wherever they live in the States. She becomes friendly with the woman who runs it, is invited in for chats, then prayer meetings, bible classes, dinners in the refectory, Sunday teas. She makes friends with the young violinist son of a couple who work there. They stayed in New York rather than go back to Africa or wherever they came from in the States because their son got a full scholarship at Juilliard when he was fifteen. Howard finds this out only years later at a chamber music concert near the summer cottage he and his wife rent, when his mother's up visiting. "That man playing," she whispers, "—the one sweating so. I'm sure he's the same violinist Clintwell Vera was friends with at the Heatherwhite House." "Come on," he says, and she says "Seriously. He's heavier and older, but the same sweet soulful face, and he used to sweat a lot then too." After the first piece he says "I never knew about him. I mean, he's a fantastic violinist and all that. I even have a couple of his recordings—one a Bartok violin-piano duo and the other a Bach partita, I think, with a sonata or another partita on the other side— but with Vera?" "You were away. California. Should we speak to him after, though he probably won't want to know she didn't survive." "It was so long ago; he won't remember her." "Of course he will. They were close friends. She used to bring him home for lunch, play checkers and cards with him in her room, do all sorts of things together: sit out in the backyard and tell funny stories and laugh. For a while I even thought if there was anyone who'd marry her, it'd be he. Simply because he'd overlook her illness, being so involved with his violin, or out of some Christian act, do it because of that. They weren't in love, I don't think, and she was a few years older; but he was very religious and withdrawn and shy and had no other real friends, she said, so I don't think there was any young person closer to him at the time. Then he graduated and moved away." They see him talking to a couple on the veranda during intermission. He's holding his violin and bow, though he didn't play in the second piece, and is mopping his hair with a hand towel. Probably he was in a studio in back practicing, for it isn't that hot. "I have to know—you coming with me?" and she goes over, excuses and introduces herself, says how much she enjoyed his performance even if she isn't the greatest connoisseur of classical music—she likes it, though, make no mistake about it—but she wonders, mainly because her son thinks she's imagining it—she points to Howard who shakes his hand, says "Howard Tetch, her son; enjoyed your playing very much, very very much"—if he could be the same Clintwell who lived with his parents in the Heatherwhite House in New York City many years ago and knew her daughter Vera. "Sure, Vera; Vera Tetch. She helped me," and turns to the couple and says "Her daughter helped me with my writing and math when I was a young man or I would have flunked," and asks her and doesn't seem surprised to hear Vera died twenty years ago. "I'm sorry. Thank you for stopping by," and resumes talking to the couple, something about an excellent inn nearby with an unbeatable breakfast. After about two years of being around the mission house, borrowing their pamphlets and books, going with some of them to a religious retreat for a week, she announces at dinner "I hope this won't be taken badly by any of you, but I plan to convert." "Over my dead body," his father says. "If she really wants to," his mother says, "and she feels it will help her in ways, there's nothing we can do." "You're going to tell me? Over my dead body." Vera says "I'll do what I have to; I'm old enough; there's no law to stop me," and leaves the table. "You're old enough to be confused," his father shouts after her. "There might be no law but I'll stop you by locking you in your room. By burning down that Christian house. By getting the police after them and running them out of town." A few months later she says "I've an announcement to make. I don't know if any of you will like it, but I'm now a Christian. I didn't go through any ceremony, but I feel I am and for now that's enough for me. So from now on, please don't consider me a Jew." "You didn't go through a ceremony, you're no Christian," his father says. "And even if you did go through one, I wouldn't accept it. You were born a Jew, your mother and father are Jews, your whole family is from your brothers on down, so you're stuck with it. It's the best religion, so feel good it's still yours. But tell the world you're a Christian and I'll tell them right back you're crazy." She says nothing, leaves the table crying. The next day she leaves a note by the phone saying "Please keep this here till everyone has read it. Dear family, don't include me in any of your Jewish religious observances from now on, except if you only want to invite me as an outsider. Thank you. I love you all always and I will pray for you all always too, no matter what you might think of that. Vera." That's the last she brings it up at home. She talks about it privately with his mother, his father never mentions it again to her. She goes to church with some mission people on Sundays and religious holidays, spends lots of time in the mission house setting up tables for dinner, cleaning up rooms as best she can, doing little chores. She says she does all this because she wants to and that they've offered her money for her work but she's refused. When she dies several mission house people come to the chapel that night to pay their respects. Vera's in a closed casket in the room, the funeral's the next day. The woman who runs the mission house kisses his mother's cheek, shakes everyone else's hand, asks if she can speak to the family outside the room. His father says "I know what you're about to say and it's no." The woman says "Perhaps you do know but my conscience compels me to tell you, to find out. May I speak?" "Speak, speak." "Vera told me a few months ago, long before she went into the hospital, that if she died—" "That she wants to be buried a Gentile with a Gentile ceremony and so forth. I know; I told you I did." "But she wouldn't mind what kind of cemetery she was buried in, Jewish or Christian, but would prefer, if it was the former, to be near her parents." "She wants to be this; she wants to have that; she can't have both and everything. I hope you told her that. Because where we have our plots is a place for Jewish burials and monuments only. Maybe on one side of us and along the road to it are other cemeteries for Gentiles, but that's nothing to talk about since she's going in the ground tomorrow." "I told her there was a problem and also to tell everything she told me to her parents. She said she tried, but wouldn't explain further. I said if what she wants does happen, and that I don't think it'll happen at a time when I can be of any help—I meant by that to try to tell her I was much older than she and so would die long before her—I'd do what I could. But that she should still try to work it out with her family." "Did Vera ever say anything about it to you?" his father says to his mother. "She said she was undecided about everything," she says, "but leaned to being a Christian." "There, case closed. A Jew's buried a Jew, otherwise he can never be at rest. His soul. I think that's Jewish law. If it isn't, it's still what I want for her." "I only wanted to get it off my chest," the woman says. "As far as I know she was never baptized. Even if she was, and I don't see how I couldn't have known of it, you've gone through too much with her these last few years and we'd never think to interfere." "Can't we make some sort of compromise?" Howard says to his parents. "Mind your business," his father says. "It's too late for anyone to stick his nose in." When she's in the hospital the last time, Howard says to her "Want me to read anything to you? Or tell you a story, or reminisce?" She shakes her head. "I've brought an anthology of poems. The Oxford, look at it; enormous. It could be from any century you want." Shakes her head. "From the Bible then?" There's one on the side table, with several ribbons and envelopes sticking out of it as bookmarks. "No," she says, "nothing feels right. For a while I liked it. Maybe the next day." "I could start at the beginning. It'll give me something to do, so for me. And I've never read any of it except in Hebrew school when I had to for my bar mitzvah, so it'd be a good chance for me to get in to it again. I'll skip all the lists, just concentrate on the beautiful parts and good stories." Shakes her head, seems to lose consciousness. "People call her the mayor of the block," his mother says in a letter. "Almost everyone who lives on it, or at least gets out onto it, knows her, and same with lots of people from other blocks who walk through ours to get to the subway or bus and back or who work around here. She sits against the railing out front and people stop to talk to her. Every now and then one of them asks if she wants to go to the store with them or a museum or have lunch at the luncheonette down the street or one of the restaurants around. I think for the first time since she was three she's really happy. She's opened up. She wishes strollers, some of whom she doesn't even know, a 'good day' or expressions like that. She watches over babies in carriages sometimes in front of a building, if someone asks her to, or a double-parked car if the driver's not going to be too long. And of course the people at Heatherwhite House have been a godsend. Not only welcoming her in but twice rushing up the block soon as I phoned them, when Dad and Vera fell at the same time in different rooms and I couldn't pick either up. And when the weather's not so nice, she goes there, sometimes for all day, or friends she knows from the neighborhood come to see her here. She's reading; she's busy; she's taken an interest in ancient choral music and stained glass, all from going to church. She never seems to have enough time to do everything she wants to, which is terrific. She's deteriorating physically, though. Her face looks wonderful—bright and cheerful, that gorgeous smile—but her body has more of those café au lait spots than ever and a couple of new spongy fibromas on it. The neurologist wants to see her, but I don't see how we can put her through more surgery if he asks for it. Suppose she says no—that she doesn't even want to be examined by him—what am I to do? I think I can convince her, but do I want to? Everything will change for her—her mood, on and off the street, so no more big smiles and spontaneous yoo-hoos—and there isn't a fresh place on her neck or back to cut through anymore and I don't want them going through old scars. . ." His brother Alex saves money for a trip around the world. Bus to San Francisco, tramp steamer to Japan, teaching English there for several months to earn some more money, then Hong Kong, Taiwan, Thailand and so on. Two days before he's to leave she takes the bus ticket and several hundred in cash from his drawer, flushes the ticket down the toilet, spends all the money on gifts for relatives, anonymous donations by mail to charities, a lavish lunch at an expensive restaurant for friends and acquaintances, a hundred dollar bill to a scavenger going through garbage cans on the street. That's what she tells his mother. Alex postpones the trip. Doesn't want to take money from his folks or borrow it from anyone. "I want to go free and clear," he writes Howard. "I also don't want to speak to Vera yet why she did it. She's not ready, it might hurt her too much, she's got her own problems, and I already know why. She's jealous of my being able to clear out when I want for as long as I like, and we've gotten tight since I moved back home, so she also doesn't want me to go. By staying a few more months I can earn back the bus ticket and what she stole and also do what I can to get her used to my going more and to what she did to me..." He rents an apartment on the East Side, borrows his brother Jerry's convertible to move his books and typewriter and some furniture and boxes of different things. It takes several trips. She drives with him, holds onto the mattress handle to keep it from falling out while they go across town, stays in the front seat while he carries his things to the top floor. Every time he comes downstairs she smiles and waves at him. One time she has her straw sun hat off and is brushing her hair. Another time her head's back and she's smoking without removing the cigarette from her mouth and her arms are stretched out on top of the seats. Another time she's singing along with the radio. Another time she starts up the car—he left her the key to show a policeman in case one says the car's illegally parked and has to move—and honks, pats the passenger seat next to her and says "Hop in." Another time her sweater's off and the sleeves are tied around her neck and she's behind the steering wheel and pretending to drive. "I'm doing something useful for you by coming along, aren't I?" she says once. "Without you I couldn't leave my stuff here or go upstairs. It would have all had to be done by professional movers I can't afford." He goes up, comes down. She's put two lamps and a box of clothes on the sidewalk. "I feel as though I'm your girlfriend, doing good things for you. Not helping you carry your stuff up because it's too many flights and too heavy things for a girl to climb up that far with them who's even in the best shape." "I wish you could see the place, help me arrange the furniture and suggest what colors I should paint it—both rooms. Just give me advice; the woman's touch." "I'll fly. Or carry me. I'm pretty light." He laughs and she says "I mean it. On your back, not in your arms, and once I'm up, I'll get down the stairs myself." He thinks it'll be memorable for her, exciting, she'll talk about it a lot, think he took one of her suggestions seriously, and later he'll tell her he's going to take every bit of advice she gave him upstairs. He parks the car in a good spot, bends down, she gets on him piggyback, and he starts upstairs. The flights are long and steep and he's exhausted by the time they reach the fourth floor. He puts her down, says "I don't think I can make it. All that moving before did me in. Maybe another time when I'm not so wiped out." "No, now. We won't think of it another time. Either of us won't be in the mood. Or you'll feel silly doing it or you'll know your neighbors by then so you won't want to be seen with me on your back, and by that time you'll have painted the rooms and settled on where all the furniture should go. If you feel too weak carrying me, sit me anywhere till you feel strong again." He does it that way next flight: stops every five or six steps and sits her down. His shirt's so soaked that her skirt and blouse get wet. She says "No problem. When we get home I'll put them in the laundry bag and take a bath." She does half the next flight by sitting on the bottom step and pushing herself up step at a time. Then she says she hasn't the energy to do it that way anymore and he says he doesn't see how he can carry her up any farther. A door opens one floor below, no head sticks out and she says "New neighbors, don't worry; heavy luggage, just moving in." "Hi," he says, "how do you do; Howard Tetch. I'll be in 6D." Door closes and he gets her on his back and lugs her to the top, sets her down, gives her her crutches and they go into the apartment. She looks around, checks into everything including the shower stall and oven and broiling compartment and refrigerator's vegetable bin and butter chamber and little freezer and every drawer in the dresser left behind, suggests paint colors and furniture arrangement and where all the pictures should go on the walls and that he should get shades and a new toilet seat, cleans the inside of his windows and the bathroom mirror, takes some hangers out of a box and hangs them in the bedroom closet, puts a cake of soap in the soap dish above the bathroom sink, gets out two mugs and a pot and a box of teabags his mother gave him before they left and makes them tea. "One real piece of advice, though it'll cost you," she says. "Get window grates in the living room or they'll be climbing down the fire escape into your apartment every other week. When I was waiting for you downstairs some very suspicious-looking characters were looking at me on the street. If I hadn't been sitting in the car I'm almost sure they would have stolen it or at least felt around inside for dope and change." His mother asks him to come along with them to Washington. "We'll train down, you'll have your own hotel room, we'll try to be in an adjoining double. She always wanted to see the Capital. You worked there, it's nothing new for you, but if she gets sick or falls down and I have to pick her up on the street, I'm going to need someone and you can also show us things ordinary tourists never see. That little subway in the Congress building you spoke about. We'd both be interested, and maybe we'll go visit our congressman and stand in that place under the dome there where you said someone can hear you whispering from the other end of the room. And her operation's in less than a month, so I said I'd take her anywhere she wants that's within a few hours by train from New York, and no expense spared for either of you. It could be her last trip anyplace, for who knows what condition she'll be in when they discharge her or, God forbid, if she'll even survive it sufficiently to ever get out of bed." "The White House," he says. "The Capitol, the Smithsonian, or the Phillips Gallery—you can't believe the little masterpieces they have there," and she says "Suddenly none of those places seems very interesting." "The zoo. It's outside, where we should be on such a beautiful day, and if it's too tough walking around we'll borrow a wheelchair if they have them. Smokey the Bear's there, or one of his descendants with his name, and she says "That's stupid, that dumb bear in trousers." When they finally get her to leave the hotel she only wants to sit on the Mall writing picture postcards to relatives and friends and snacking on hot dogs and sodas from vendors. She also wants to be photographed with whatever famous building or monument that can be seen behind her while she sits on one of the benches or pool walls on the Mall, bangs combed down to her eyes, hands folded on her lap, serious face, shirt buttoned to the top and pulled up to cover half her neck, crutches always out of camera range. He goes into the National Gallery while they stay outside, hurries through a few of what were

513

his favorite rooms, from a pay phone there calls some old girlfriends in Washington. One's married with two kids, two aren't listed anymore, one agrees to meet him at the hotel bar around nine the next night. At dinner in the hotel his mother says to her "If you're not enjoying yourself here or are disappointed in anything, say so and we'll do whatever you want," and she says "There's too much to see that needs walking or bumping along in some dumb tour bus. And I don't want to be shoved around in a wheelchair and be stared at, and besides that I miss my own room," and they go home right after breakfast the next day. On the train he says to them "Damn, should've mentioned the Washington Cathedral and the Arab mosque," and she says "That would have been nice. I thought of it, saw them on the map, but didn't think you'd want to go." Large group photo he has of all twenty children or so and the owner and two counselors at the summer camp they went to for two months. Most of the campers standing or sitting on the dock, feet in the water or dangling above it. Few, like him—the older boys—standing in front of the dock in water up around their waists and chests. It's obvious he's freezing, teeth chattering, so probably the professional photographer had them stand in the water too long. Or maybe they'd been swimming awhile, photographer came down and told them to stay in the water longer till he took the photos. She's standing on the dock, only in her underpants, hands, which she's squeezing together, hiding most of her face. Little part of her face he sees is smiling sweetly. Her body looks healthy: legs straight, solid lean torso. She's the prettiest girl there her age, even if her hair's been clipped badly by the camp owner. He thinks she used a bowl to do it, or maybe that's what his parents said when they saw the photo or when he and Vera got home, and he took them literally. His mother thought she should spend the summer in the country, being with other kids and him, good air, cool nights, eating food straight from the farms and lots of activities, before she was operated on for the first time that fall. Years later she told him the doctors had said there was a fifty-fifty chance Vera would survive the operation and that when she was wheeled into the intensive care unit they never thought she'd pull through. "My one regret is that I let them go ahead with it." "What could you have done? Tiger in one door, lion in the other, both mean and hungry." "There might have been other ways. Diet, for instance, but nothing I explored. The surgeon was very prominent and convincing and quite striking looking and also a former classmate of our pediatrician, so I needed more will power than I had and your father said to do what I thought best, he was staying out of it. But if she had died unscathed and with only a little pain in three years, which is all they gave her without the operation, wouldn't it have been better than living horribly for twenty?" He's in her hospital room and she's pointing to her mouth with her arm that's attached to the IV. She can't speak because of the tube in her throat. "You're thirsty?" She nods. "I can't give you anything with that thing in you," pointing to her throat. "I'll have to ask the nurse." He's in her hospital room and she's sleeping. Tubes in her, but she looks calm, sleeping without making a sound. He sits beside her, takes her hand in his and kisses it. She opens one eye and looks at him. He says "I'm sorry, did I disturb you? I'm sorry," and kisses her hand and puts it back on the bed. Her eye closes and she seems to be sleeping again.

Frog Fragments

How to start? Have a drink. How to start. Paper in and think. How-to start. Sit and type. Coffee and write. Kid and man. Fart and art. When I was a teen. Breakfast, dinner and dread. What's he mean? What's it seem? Done before. Start again.

Takes his daughter to school, goes home. Wife's on the phone. "Yes, no, OK, maybe," hangs up. "Oh, it's you. I'm afraid I have bad news for you. I'm afraid I have sad news for you. I'm afraid I have mad dad news for you. Are you ready? Get set." How about one about growing sick and old? Over again.

Takes his daughter home, goes to school. Student's waiting at his office. "You said you'd be here by three-fifteen—that's what the sign on your door says too—but I've never in my three years here known a teacher to keep his posted office hours." "Not true. I was late for a good reason. Are you ready? Well get set. My daughter took seriously ill. Do you feel better now? We had to rush her to the doctor—I did. My wife's also seriously ill. Besides that, my mother broke her hip yesterday and had to have a pin put in it today and my other daughter's recovering from chicken pox. Add all that up plus my continuing inability to adjust to my brother's drowning close to thirty years ago and my sister's slow disease and death more than

516

twenty years ago and taking care of my invalided dad the last six years of his life and probably also the loss of my one and only dog when I was around eight and the only tricycle or bike I ever owned stolen from in front of the candy store when I was inside buying a vanilla cone and what you got is hard knocks." Over.

At home, daughters in school, in the basement typing, wife in their bedroom writing, hears a sound behind him, jumps, yells "Whoosh," just his wife halfway downstairs barefoot, smile, untied bathrobe, towel over her shoulder, hair hung loose and in her hand shampoo, "I was about to shower when I thought. . ." "Why not, though you scared the hell out of me, as I was deep into doing a new scene, but I can always go back to it, and I usually gain more than I lose when I do—material, distance, be right there," pushes the chair back, hands on the chair arms to stand up, she says "You don't have to get up if you don't have to. Just pull your pants down and we can do it in the chair, and it's the right time of the month so though I might need some fiddling around with I don't have to prepare."

At home, daughter's in school, wife away for the weekend with her folks, baby with her, cats in the attic, dog's in the manger, horses in the stalls, pigs building brick shithouses, cows coming home. "Mumma, Dooda, plead bleed to me, you neber read to me, or I want you with me to clay." Continue to read a book (she), dental journal (he). Goes to his room, lies on his bed, stares at the side wall of the brownstone right outside. City noises: garbage truck, street being dug up, when suddenly a plane, gets louder, seems lower than just overhead, runs to the window, sees it crashing through all the backyards before nosediving into their living room.

Home, he is, everybody's left, school, work, cats are dead, no dog, farm animals, he's trying to work, phone rings, rushes upstairs. "Yes," he says. Picks up the receiver. "Yes," says into it. " 'Ello, George?" man says. "No George here I'm afraid." "You afraid? What for?" "Done that one. Say something else." "George, George, that you there?" "Yes, George, everything's George, I'm alone at home, for the next three hours completely free, so I can do what I want. But remember that expression from about twenty years back? Thirty perhaps? Are you as old as you sound, meaning my age? Everything's George, meaning all's OK." "What're you, coming apart, man?" "What number did you say you want? George did you want did you say?" New page.

Basement typing. Cats somewhere around the house biting. Children, wife, have none. Little fat dog jumped over the big bovine's balls. Fiddle moon man leaped over the lilywhite dam. What's that, dream? You believe in free thinking or free-associating or free living or love? Answer one or column four. Waiter, I'd like a Peking duck made in Beijing. Or the Beijing muck made sing-a-ling-ching. What're yuh, green? But what a news day. Old evil eyes flies, Polish star dies, tangled tykes in mangled bikes, tanks over tents—rhythm and rhyme over reason—all that fall, break. Can you get all that in less than twelve hours' notice? Picks up the typewriter and drops it. Read the other day that typewriter repairmen can fix anything but the carnage. The carriage. Once the carnage breaks, throw the machine away. Goes upstairs, stops halfway and stares at the wall.

At school, class comes in. They're quiet, some smile, few shuffle their papers on the long oblong table. "Well, how are you all today?" "Just fine thanks, I guess," young man says. "Don't guess, say straight out." "OK, just fine thanks. . . I guess." Several laugh. "That's the spirit. Well, now down to business, shall we say?" "Sure, what's the first order?" young woman says. "Yes. Order. Give me three in column A and the rest of you get F's." All laugh. Lifts the table at his end. "Hey, my books, Doctor," someone says. "Call me Howard, or Mr. Tetch, if you can't call me by my first name. Or even Teach, or Mr. Teach, but I've told you—in my family my father was the doctor, though a dentist. 'Open, open wide, wider, it won't hurt but for an hour.' I won't even tell you how he took care of my teeth. Now that's a story. No x-rays or novocaine, but he scrub-brushed his hands before—they always smelled of soap—and lots of pain." Lifts it higher till it stands on its end. Everything on it slides off. "What the fuck he think he's doing?" someone says. "What's this, we're supposed to write an exercise about it?" someone says. "One on professorial craziness," someone says. "Pedagogical patheticness," someone says. "Doctorial, if that's what the word is, dottiness," someone says. "No, just a man coming apart, or do one on teeth. Bring it in next week, three to five pages, class dismissed," and he sits, hands over his face till he thinks they've all left, says to himself out loud "If this is what's called having a fit, I'm having it." "I'll stay with you," only student who stayed says, prettiest he's ever had in a class, Lucy, Lisa, Lois, something, long blond this, strong lean that, tall, small, broad, flat. Another he's stared at in the hallway from behind till she disappeared, then looked around to see if anyone caught him. "I'm certain you were only trying to tell us something by what you did, like our lack of basic writing skills and interest in serious culture, and our poor critical sense, and I love your work." "Always?" "Hard to say, since I don't know if it'll always be as good." "Heck with my work. I meant will you stay with me always, at least the way you and your contemporaries might understand that word." "Line-by-line edit me if you like, sir, but isn't that what I just said?" "I don't know. I can't think. I've never been good at following conversations. People speak, I'm dreaming or wondering about something else. It even happens at movies—what's being said on the screen—so imagine me in lecture halls. You can see now what I meant when I said in class I was such a lousy student. And to top it off, my folks argued bitterly when I was a boy, for years I thought they were going to divorce and all the kids would be split up, a brother died when he'd been my best pal for more than twenty years, my sister went through hell dying before she managed to pull it off while I was sitting there right by her bed, and my wife's recently flown and I always have to be at home by the phone for my kids. Please," his arms and lips out to kiss, but she shakes her head, "Nothing like an old fool," she says and leaves the room. "That's what my mother also used to say. Not about me, of course, since when she said it I was a kid, and her exact words were 'No fool like an old fool,' but

OK. Though old fools can be good. Ones I'm thinking of know what to do, don't ask for much, are thankful for whatever you give, have a little income, sense of humor, and nobody appreciates a young mind and body better, I'll tell ya. But I can see it your way too."

On the street, walking the dog. Has no dog but imagines he's one. Has one. Woman passes. "Nice dog you have there," he says. "Nice dog you have too. What's its name?" "Airedale," he says. "But he's no Airedale." "I always wanted one, my father would never let me have one, now that I'm old enough and on my own to have one I have no money to buy one, so decided to call him that. Actually, I did have an Airedale once. Part. Do you have time to listen? We lost him when I was a boy. It's a sad bad mad dad story. Actually, he lost him. Wanted to get rid of him so gave him to a friend to get rid of but told us he'd run away. The dog did. I shared him with my two brothers and sister, you see, but he was really me. Mine. Since I took care of him for the most part. The hind part. What's your daddy's name?" "My doggy's? Scott." "For Scottie? But he's no Scottie. Course he is. Only kissing. Kidding. Excuse me." Puts his lips and arms out. "You wouldn't want to, would you?" "Won't your doggy run away?" she says. "Right. So what happens? Happened? Just that for a moment he looked big for a Scottie, that's what I meant when I said he wasn't one. I have a Scottie too, so to speak. A nephew named one. Scott. He's not a Scot though. He's a Litvak, or would be one if he'd been born where all his great-grandparents were born, or is that the other thing?" "What other thing?" "Litvaks always go with something else. One steals horses, the other owns them. That's what my dad used to say and sometimes used to say his dad used to say it. People who have heard it would know what I mean and which one does what and possibly what's the other's name. I was also never very good in school at explaining what I mean. What's your name?" "Scott." "Come on." "Sarah." "With two *t*'s or one?" "Sarah. Two *t*'s." "I did have a dog. We all shared my dad. But you can't say—I know you're not saying—that losing a dog at the time you lose it would have to take second place to losing a dad, that is, if you're a kid. But I had to do the dirty work the last six years with him. Not had to. Did. Holding his prick inside the urinal for his piss, cleaning up his shit, taking his anger because he hated being so helpless and sick. Those things can scare. Scar. But you're going. Gone. I've probably nothing more to say anyway and if you do I'm sure it's not to me. Story of my life? And how could we, since you're already down the street. Say, nice dog you have there, lady. What's its breed? Is it on special formula diet? Has it been spayed or fixed? Does it get enough exercise a day and at least fifteen minutes of it free run? Is there a Scottie newsletter as there is for Airedales? Quite the society we live in, right? More news than noses. Everything you never wanted and then some and not only what money can't buy. And I didn't even get to ask its name. His."

He's walking his cat. Cat walks beside him. He stops, cat does. His wife used to do that when they had four cats. Before she was his wife. When she could still walk like that. Long walks with the four cats, all originally hers. They'd take them to Maine for the summer in two pet carriers, mother and son in one, sisters of these triplets in the other. They'd meow the whole way if a window was open or the side vents were opened wide or vent blower was on high or when a big truck or bus passed. Then they'd howl. "Can't you shut them up?" he'd periodically say. "It's disturbing my driving." And under his breath, sometimes she heard or some of it and would say "What?" or "Speak up," he'd say "Gas them, for Christsakes," or "If it was up to me I'd throw the dumb assholes out the window." They had to stop every two hours or so so the cats could use the litter box. Siamese. She walked them to the beach and along it and back. Up there, shore. They walked single file. Wife first, before she was his wife, when she was able to walk like that. Son second, sisters after him, mother last. He'd watch them go and come back from his workroom window. Sometimes when she saw him she held up the mother cat and waved her paw at him. He waved back once, another time stood up and made a sweeping bow to the cat, but usually he just sat there looking at them, no expression change. He wonders what she thought of that then. If any of the cats lagged behind, she'd whistle and they'd run, mother not so fast, and if the son stopped short and quickly turned around in a crouch to hiss at the others, one of the sisters—one who wasn't going blind and was always second in line—would race straight toward him and at the last instant leap over him, sending him scurrying. She also walked to the top of their road, they'd follow, single file, and sometimes along the town road a short while. When a car came they dashed into the bushes, only came out when she called them by name and they'd resume walking, same single file. Then she walked three of them, when the son died. Two, when the mother died. But much slower now, not so far, not down to the water, up to the road, but just around the grounds. Sometimes she fell or couldn't go any farther or was too tired to and she'd call him and he'd run out and help her back to the house, cats behind or beside them, no particular order. A few times he heard her but didn't want to lose what he was working on so didn't respond. She later said she fell before, couldn't get up for a while, or couldn't move another inch—her legs suddenly stiffened or collapsed on her or there were these terrific spasms—and called him, several times, she supposed he didn't hear because he was in the toilet or showering or out back or down by the water, managed to get herself up, but it was a struggle, and back to the house, which took all the energy she had left and so much time. He'd say he was at one of those places she mentioned, or would make up another one—the heat, so without even knowing it he fell asleep at his desk, or stomach cramps, he heard her but was flat on his back in bed and couldn't for the life of him get up or even yell—and was sorry he hadn't been there to help. There's only one cat now. One walking beside him. She's blind, walks into things a lot, they step on her tail or push the chair back on it more often than they used to, so maybe her hearing's also bad, uses its whiskers and bumping head to tell where it is and what's in front of it when it wants to get around. His wife doesn't walk with it much anymore and when she does it's with two canes or a walker. "The lame leading the blind," she's said, "or the crippled or impotent or useless or whatever you want to call it. The washout." But she's glad he walks with the cat, since it's getting some exercise and fresh air and she doesn't like it outside unless someone's with her. There are coyotes, bears, hawks.

He walks his horse. Once rode a horse. Or the horse rode him. In summer camp. His folks gave the camp extra money to teach him to ride. It's what he'd wanted to do for years. Saw himself as a future Canadian Mountie or a cowboy shooting a rifle in the air while leading the last great cattle drives, but both where he ends up marrying a beautiful pinchwaisted lady who knows how to ride. Horse was big but he wasn't afraid to get on it. When he was told to mount, he said to the riding instructor, a young wily-looking guy, tight Levis, no shirt, tatoos, huge arm muscles, bandanna around his neck, no fat, "Left side you get on it, right? Or right side, maybe I forgot." He either had it right or he didn't, right now he couldn't say which side the rider's supposed to get on or why, but he needed no assistance. Foot in the stirrup, grabbed the part that sticks out of the Western saddle, hoisted himself on. It was so high up. Why'd it seem so high? Or why didn't he think it'd be so high? Already knew the horse was big and he was a little guy. He supposes, for some reason, he saw himself sitting at the horse's eye level—and maybe when its head was bent over a little—rather than his own. It was scary up there but he didn't show it. "Try not to fall," the instructor said. "You can break your neck and be paralyzed for life. It's happened but was never my fault. If you do fall, try sliding down the horse's side but away from the hooves, as one kick from that mother and he can squash your head for good. That's what happened with a few of my people learning too. I didn't feel too bad because I told them not to and they thought they knew more than me, so they got what they deserved." Now he didn't want to ride. Afraid of the horse and being up so high and didn't trust this guy. But the money was paid, couldn't be returned, his father would give his mother hell over it, since he felt they were paying too much for this camp as it was, and word would get back to his bunk he's a sissy, so he stayed. Was also afraid to get off and be hit by a hoof and this guy seemed so tough and mean he didn't want to ask him how to. "Giddyup," the instructor said. "What?" "Best way to learn is to start galloping right away, I say. Same like tossing you into a pool. That's what I'd do if I was teaching you how to swim. Hold your head down under water, even, so you know what it is to hold your breath. You learn riding instincts right away, how to hold yourself in the saddle, use the reins right and where the horse knows you're not scared and the boss, so he tells the other horses in the stable—I'm not kidding you; they speak. You might get thrown but you'll at least have that out of the way and if you don't give your horse some fun like that he's going to get angry at you. But if you want—" "I do, thank you." "Sounds pretty chickenshit to me, but OK, we'll go at a walking pace first. I'll follow you. Give him a couple of heel kicks to get him started." Howard kicked it gently. "Harder, harder, what do you think it's got horse hide for?—like this," and kicked the horse's rear. Horse sort of snorted and grunted and then bolted off, galloping or cantering. Just going very fast. He pulled the reins and horse went faster. Yelled "Grab him, call him, I can't stop him." Horse went off the path, down between some trees, branch slapping Howard's face, up onto another path, instructor behind him somewhere yelling "Pull the fucking reins, you stupid shit; the straps—pull them with all your might and then hold on tight." "Did." "Hard." Pulled them very hard and horse stopped, stood almost straight up, his front legs sort of making a boxer's jabbing motions at that bag they practice timing and maybe punching with, a punching bag, then came down hard on his front hoofs twice and Howard fell off, immediately scooting away on his hands and knees, but the horse was already some thirty feet away, eating grass. "You stupid idiot, you OK?" the instructor said from his horse right above him, slapping at some bugs on his chest. "Why'd you run off like that?" "Me? Why'd you swat my horse?" "What I swat?" "Swat, kick, like it was a football you were booting." "What are you, fucking nuts? It was you. But go around lying like that to anyone and I'll come take your dumb face and stick it in the freshest horseshit." "All right; I kicked, you didn't." "You still saying I did?" and he threw one leg over the horse as if he was getting off. "No, I'm saying that's what I did and you didn't; kicked. But too hard—not the way you told me to—I mean." "That's because you don't belong on a horse. You could've broken its leg, run him into a tree or rock and your pop would have paid plenty for it, enough for ten pansy campers at your camp for a month. I'm taking your horse in before you kill him. You get to the stable any way you find and tell them you don't want lessons anymore, if I was you. I know I'm through teaching you." "Truth is, I don't want to ride anymore. Just not for me." Instructor rode off pulling Howard's horse. Look at those stupid muscles, he thought. I hope the mosquitoes kill him, no shirt. He sat in the grass, ripped out a blade and chewed on it, ripped out handfuls and yelled "Fucking pig. I'd like to tear your head off. I would. Give me a fucking chance. Give me a gun. I'd sneak up on you at night, even if you were sleeping like a baby in bed, and blow your fucking dumb head off."

A whore rode him. A friend came over, waited till his mother was out of the kitchen, said "I had a great lay yesterday; best in my life. Biggest tits you ever saw; nipples as fat as your thumbs. Great body. Almost no bush. Nice lady too. Young; pretty good looks. Small nose and nice breath and so clean the whole place smelled of soap. When I was on top of her I got my nose in her armpit and not a whiff. She made it so nice it was like screwing your own girl friend. And she told me to bring my best friends. If I get her five guys, she'll give me a lay free. Ten, and she'll throw in the works, anything but up the ass. Make sure you tell her I said to call." He phoned from the corner candy store, she said "Yeah, sweetheart, I know Fred; a funny guy," and he should come by tonight seven sharp. Fred sat on the stoop outside. She wasn't that young, sort of plump, plain looking, through her bathrobe she looked like she might have big breasts, told him to take off his clothes, but if he wants leave on the socks, and let her wash his dick, he stripped, put his penis over the bathroom sink while she sat on the toilet seat lid, he got hard in her hand while she washed him with soap and she said "Jesus, I don't know how I'm going to stuff this thing in me, big as I am down there. I just feel a little tight today, but we'll give it a try." She patted him dry, led him into the bedroom, opened her bathrobe, let him feel her breasts—"You like them, huh? You younger guys go ape over big ones but to me they're a pain in the ass"—took off her robe, got on the bed, said "You too, come here," he sat on it, squeezed her her nipples, tried kissing her, she said "Come on, I don't want to seem grouchy but I only got so much time, just stick it in," she did, pulled him down almost flat on her, they went up and down awhile, she said "Hold it, pull out, will you? That thing of yours is killing me—it's too farther in than feels good. Maybe I am a little tight like I said or you're too big. How old are you? Usually I can take anyone your age—even dicks bigger and fatter than yours—for as long as it takes them to make it. Here, let's try something different," and slapped his behind, he said "What is it?" she said "That's the signal to get off, sweetheart; haven't you ever been laid before?" he got off her, she motioned with her hand for him to get on his back, he said "I'm sorry again but what are we doing?" she said "I'm getting on top of you, dummy, something I don't do for everyone and for sure not for what I charged you," got on top, put it in, leaned over him and began moving up and down, he tried moving with her and she said "You don't have to; leave it all to me this time, OK?" sat straight up and went up and down on him, he closed his eyes, she said "You like it like this, right? I can see by your expression," it felt so good he couldn't speak, "Like ride-em-cowboy, right?" he kept his eyes shut, nodded, also didn't want to look up at her because last time he did she had this ugly grin, maybe it was the light and shadows doing it, but which might take something out of it, felt himself coming, still had some time, saw himself as a boy on a horse bareback, nude with no pubic hair, lots of curly head hair waving behind him, riding in a field and then into the sky and the horse, with him sitting straight up on it, jumping right into the flaming sun, came, "Felt good for me too," she said when she stopped bouncing on him. "Didn't hurt and where I finally got slipperier. So, worth the switch all around, right? Now let's get off and cleaned up." Went to her once after that but she said that last time was special because she wasn't feeling good but wanted him to get what he paid for. If he wants her on top again it'll cost double because the guy usually holds in twice as long and sometimes goes dead limp on her and she's doing all the work. For the next few years with whores he'd ask them to do it that way and they'd always ask for more and he'd think it too much or would never have enough. He'd argue, saying it usually took him half the time that way, but not one ever gave in.

He walks the car. Got the keys out of his brother's dish on the boys room dresser. It was their dad's car but mostly Alex who drove it. Afternoon, Saturday, he supposes, because at that age, sixteen or seventeen, he was always working after school weekdays till around six. Stick shift, he feels good behind the wheel and would like to start reading the book in his back pocket so people who see him will think it's his car, starts it up, knows he's not supposed to, his dad's at his office downtown, Alex off somewhere so not likely to catch him and if he does but he sees him in time he'll just say he's sitting in the car, car's parked down the street from their brownstone, so his mother and sister won't see him from the front bedroom windows if they happen to look, hopes no neighbors or tenants of his parents will see him and if they do, don't tell, releases the handbrake, knows how to do that all right—with his foot on the foot brake—shifts to first, feet now on what he thinks are the right pedals, starts raising both feet, car stalls. Let's see: clutch for this foot, gas and brake for that one—makes sense—but if the pedal's no longer being used, how long's the foot supposed to stay on it and how quick should it move to the other pedal if it has to get there? Pulls up the handbrake, practices on the pedals a few times, opens the window, spits out of it as his father's done a lot, though nothing much had collected in his mouth, releases the handbrake, starts it up, car jumps forward, stalls, forgot from before to put the clutch into neutral. Does, starts it up, go reverse first so they'll be plenty of room coming out, but how to shift to reverse? It's a tricky movement, Alex said when he taught him how to park for about five minutes, where you have to go down from third but with a little detour, tries where he thinks reverse is, car stalls. Spits, starts, stalls, starts, stalls, gets it to creep in first, feet very light on the clutch and gas pedals, then in jerky back-and-forth movements, out into the street, quickly shifts to neutral and pulls up the handbrake. What he'll do is drive around the block, and if he gets the hang of it, then a couple of times around, in first and maybe second and if nothing's in front of him when he comes down this block, in third and park here and if the space is filled by then, in one of the other spots on this side but as close to this one as he can get so Alex won't think the car's been moved. Shifts to first, gases it, car won't move, releases the handbrake, car stalls. Starts it up, shifts to first, honks from an oil truck a few feet up the street, it can't get past the way his car's sticking out, he doesn't know if he should creep and jerk farther and pull up alongside one of the cars across the street, or go back. Turns the key to start it, buzz-saw-through-steel sound, pulls key out, won't come, shifts to neutral, car stalls. Truck honks, starts the car, shifts to what he thinks is reverse, car stalls. Spits, starts, stalls. Maybe he should go around the block only in first and come into the spot frontways, seems to be enough room and if not then a larger one a few spots down, lock up, put the keys back in Alex's dish and forget about doing anything like this till Alex is in the car with him teaching him to drive. If Alex notices the car's been driven or moved, he'll just say he was trying out parking but will never do it alone again. Truck honks, so do about five cars and truck behind it, he gets out, "Something seems to have conked out in the car," yells to the truckdriver, "maybe the battery; I'll have to push it in," tries steering it with his hand through the driver's window while pushing the car back, it doesn't budge, leans in and releases the handbrake, car starts inching back on its own, he tries stopping it by pulling on the window frame, then runs around the back to stop it, its back wheels bump against the curb, car's now jutting out at a right angle to the street. Honks, beeps, air horn from the truck, scaring him, someone yells "Hey, move it or I'll pick up the fucking thing myself and put it on the sidewalk," gets in, starts it up, wonders if he should try reverse again to go over the curb enough so the trucks and cars can pass, or go forward and down the street and around the block. Maybe he should ask one of these drivers to help him park it, saying it's a friend's car he borrowed, he knows how to drive automatic shift but not manual. "You crazy dickhead!" Alex, running up to his window. "What the hell? Get out of there, turn the ignition off. Leave the key in. Just give them to me. What are you doing with them anyway? They mine? Where're the brains you're born with? Just move over." Does, Alex gets in, truck horn, car beeps, "Hold your horses, why don't you?" Alex yells out the window. "Don't you see I'm taking care of it? —Ass schmucks. And you, you putz. Boy, if I told Dad would yours be in a sling." Drives the car out, stops parallel to the next car, smoothly parks it in two moves.

In a car with Dora. Hers, she's driving, they're arguing. They argued on and off for their five years. The first few weeks were great, maybe a couple of months, love, when they walked they stopped to kiss on almost every block, after that, intermittently nice, now-and-then passion, but lots of fights, always reconciling. Lived with her for two years, wanted to marry her and have a child, she didn't want to have another baby but he thought if she married him he'd eventually convince her to, she got pregnant, wanted an abortion, he didn't want her to, reasoned with her, begged her, threatened to hole her up in their apartment for months, tether her to the bed when he went out, keep her tied up and gagged in a closet if he had to, releasing her only when it was too late for her to abort and too dangerous for her to induce a miscarriage. He wanted a child, he wanted their child—all this was taking place in the car on the Taconic Parkway to her parents' home upstate—and he'd do anything for her if she had it and married him, or she didn't have to marry him (when she gave him a look), just have it but continue living with him, or not even that, have it but also have her own apartment if she wants, one they have now or a smaller one, don't ask where he'll come up with the money for two flats but he'll get it, he'll work doubly hard, doing any kind of job, more bartending, waiting on tables when he wasn't bartending, cleaning up the restaurant's kitchen after closing for more pay, plus living like a slob to keep his own expenses down, so long as she'd let him see his kid whenever he wanted, or just weekends, month in the summer, during the week a little, he'd never leave the city while his kid was in it and if she moved away he'd follow her just to be near it though he'd never be a nuisance to her, he'd even babysit it while she went out with men, here or in any other city, while she even stayed out all night with them, that is if she was absolutely adamant about not marrying him or continuing to live with him or even seeing and sleeping with him after she had the baby. She said "Really, that's nice of you, and all that might be a great deal for someone else, but it's simply not the right time for me to have a baby." "It's never the right time for you with anything," he said. "That could be true, and try to hold your voice down; you know it distracts my driving. Anyway, unlike you, I already have a child, so there's no urgency for me to have this one, and now that she's in school I can finally find some time for myself. I want to get a good-paying profession, not these pimply demeaning jobs all my life where I can't save a dollar." "You can have all the time you want if you have the baby. I'll keep us just fine, in one place or two, for a couple of years. Then, go out, study, work, anything—I'll help cover whatever education or babysitting you think you need. Or start studying while you're still at home, taking breaks from baby work. Or stay with the baby for just a year after it's born—half a year if that's all you want. It's not what I'd choose for it but I'll spring for the day care too. I'll borrow from my mother, even, or my brother— they'll give for something I want or think as important as this. Or I'll both work and take care of the kid whenever you need me to so you can study and work and get jobs and go out with men and do whatever you feel like. I'll even keep the baby myself—I'd love to. Bring it up from day one if I have to—all alone; you can be anywhere you want. Visit it or be with it whenever you like too. Weekends, month in the summer; two months—I won't need long stretches in the summer with it since I'll have been with it the rest of the year." "Stop talking crazy. My decision's final. Abortion's on Tuesday. I'm not putting if off for anything. I can't put it off—it can only be done the first trimester and I'm coming to the end of mine." "I want the baby. It's mine as much as yours. Just because it's in you doesn't mean you own it. I love you and I'll love it and I want our baby. Please," crying, "please," banging his lap, the car seat, she said "No tantrums, talk calmly, you'll knock us off the road." "Listen, I'll be a good father—" "I know, I know, you've been wonderful to Gretchen. We both love you for it but I don't personally love you enough to marry you now and I'd only have another baby if I were married and I'll probably never marry you. We should in fact probably end this thing of ours for good, because it won't work out. It's not. We knew it almost from the start so why were we so stupid to carry it this far? It simply wasn't the right time for it, no matter how much you hate that word, and with marriage and babies timing and right moves based on rational and right decisions are everything, and you got me two weeks after I left my husband." "Two months." "A month then. But on the rebound. Not the first man I slept with after him but first I got serious with. But now we've got to believe all that's finished. That's almost a must. Better you get your own place and move out and I'll take care of myself." "Please, I'll change. Whatever you might think wrong with me and us—a total transformation. I know I've said that before, but being parents this time will do it." "Oh shit, shut up about that already." "But it will. Your attitude and feelings to one another—your mate, your wife, everything's strengthened." "Or weakened. Or they kill each other." "Not us. And you'll never see a father like me. You think all men will be fathers like Lewis was to Gretchen." "Not true. I've met lots of wonderful ones, and he wasn't that bad. Maybe I painted him unfairly; I was wrong if I did." "Then I'll be different. I'll cook and clean up for us, I'll change all its diapers, do everything—please don't laugh, I'm not being silly; I'm giving examples. I'm saying I'll do everything there is or you want me to or just make if fifty-fifty if that's what you want, and not because you want it but because that's fair. You deserve to finish school and get a job you like and which pays well and do what you want outside the home for a change. And I've the energy for it all, work outside and in the home and work on my own work—" "No and that's final." "Please reconsider." "No and that's final, the end, finished, we, the matter, talking about it, whatever we're talking about, everything, done, finito." "Then let me out. I don't want to ride with you anymore. I don't want to see your face anymore." "Hey, if that's how you feel, ditto, but I can't let you out on the highway." "You can. Just pull over and leave me on the shoulder. I'll walk to the next town or to a gas station on the highway and get a hitch to a town from there. I can use the time to walk—to think, I mean. I need to think a lot about it all and walking to the town or gas station if they're far enough will do it. And then I'll take the bus back to the city and you can explain to your folks why I'm not with you when I started out with you and you'll be glad to be rid of me, so let me out, now. Now. I want to get out," and he opened his door, she said "Stop it, don't be insane, close it, put your seat belt on, close the door, you stupid idiot, and lock it," and he said "Then stop the car and let me out," and she slowed down, he closed the door, she picked up speed, he opened the door, she slowed down and signaled right, he closed the door, she pulled over and stopped along the highway. He got out, was crying again, sat down on the embankment with his back to the highway, "Go, don't worry about me, if that's what you're doing, which I'm sure you're not. I've got good shoes on. It could even turn into an experience—it's a nice day—I used to do a lot of this, walking, hitching, here, Europe, years ago, before I knew you, so just go," and she said "Fine, you were a daredevil those carefree days, but at least let me drive you to a town with a bus station. The one you walk to might not have one," but he waved her away, under his breath said "Eat shit, you fucking witch," she said, his back always facing her, "You have enough money on you?" and he said yes, though he didn't know, and she said "OK, then I'm going," dropped his book beside him, draped his sweater over his shoulder and drove off. He sat awhile, heard a bird but didn't feel like looking for it, saw an ant and smashed it with his fist, ripped grass out around him, tore some of it up and flung it around him shouting "Bitch, bitch, bitch, and I don't care who the fuck hears me," looked around, cars and trucks passing, all the drivers looking at him, got up, wondered which way to go—back? should he cross the highway?—he didn't remember the last time he saw a sign for a town or an exit though that didn't mean there hadn't been one a minute or two back, he just hadn't been looking, go forward, something tells him an exit's coming up, so maybe he did see something and if he gets tired he'll stick his thumb out. But then he should cross the highway, for if he does get a ride maybe it'll be going all the way to the city. Crossed it, didn't get the equivalent of two city blocks when a car honked behind him, recognized it as hers. She pulled over. "I was coming back to go around for you. Really, come with me, my parents will be disappointed. And maybe while we drive we can talk some more about it if you promise not to make any more demands." "Then you haven't changed your mind about the abortion?" "Please not again—promise not to—literally—or I'll drive off and this time not come back nor be home whenever you get there, or anything." "At least kiss me." "I can't now. It's the last thing on my mind. Please get in so we can go. My mother worries." He opened his door. "But you'll promise before you get in?" "I'll try not to talk about it." "Not enough." "I won't talk, no demands." He sat with her in the hospital, holding her hand while she was in bed waiting to be wheeled in, not saying anything, book opened on his lap but not reading it. If only she'd say "I'm making a mistake, let's get out of here before it's too late." Then the nurse came in and said "You're next," and he said "Last chance to change your mind. I still want it very much and I'll do everything in the world for you and the baby and you wouldn't be, I'm sure of it, the first one to change her mind here like that." "I'll see you later, sweetheart. You'll be here?" He drove her home after, she fell asleep against his shoulder as they were crossing the George Washington Bridge and he was about to point out the huge spotlit American flag spanning the two main supports on the New Jersey side.

Drives his daughter to school, parks, holds her backpack, walks her into class, does this all year. Last week of school he says "Want to go in on your own today?" She says no. Next day he asks the same. She says "I think so." "Do if you want to, don't if you don't want to; it's all up to you. I think you're ready." "Yes, I do." "Good, because someday this is how I'll leave you off every time. I'll pull up, kiss you good-bye, open the door for you from the inside or if it's raining, from the out, you'll leave and wave to me and I'll wave back and probably blow you a kiss and if you're real nice to me you'll blow me back one and then run into school. If it's raining I'll get you inside with an umbrella unless you're dressed for it." "OK, I'll go by myself." Comes around her side, opens the door, takes her backpack out, puts it on her shoulders, kisses her head, her hands, she says "Bye, Dada," he says "Bye, my sweetheart," she starts for school, up the steps, waves to him from the landing railing, looks sad, he says "What is it?" she says "I want you to come in with me." Drives his daughter to school. "Bye, darling," "Bye, Daddy." Opens her door from the inside, she gets out, he hands her her backpack, kisses her cheek, says "Be careful of your fingers closing the door, or want me to do it?" she says "You always tell me that and I'm always careful," shuts the door carefully, starts for the steps, turns to wave at him, he's waiting for her to turn, smiles, waves, blows a kiss, leans out her window, "Have a great day, sweetheart, good-bye," and she goes up the steps. Drives his daughter to school, glances at her, something's different about her, looks at the road, glances back, missing or changed, "Your glasses, they're not on you. Damn, what the hell, can't you remember any bloody thing?" she says "They're not bloody," "I know they're not bloody, I'm just saying, goddamnit," makes a turn at the next street, backs up, goes back up the hill to their house, "Fucking stupid kid," he mumbles low, looks at her, she's about to cry, did she hear? why'd he do that again? now she'll be sad for hours unless he apologizes, parks in front of the house, runs in, "What's wrong?" his wife says, "Glasses," "They're on your face," "Hers; where the hell are they? that fucking dimwit kid," "On the dining room table, but don't make it awful for her, don't scold her," "I won't; it's what I feel like doing but I know what it does to her too," runs out, she's still sad he sees through her window, gives them to her, she puts them on, he drives down the hill, says "I'm sorry, very sorry, I was wrong, not you. Because what am I expecting from you? You're only six and you already do more intelligent and helpful things than kids twice your age." "No I don't." "You do, take it from me. I should have made sure you had your glasses just as I do your backpack and lunch and quarter for milk and so on." "No, I should." "Then both of us, but I was all wrong and am sorry. Forgive me?" "It was only a mistake," looking straight ahead, never at him. "What, my yelling, mumbling those awful things under my breath with the stupid hope you'd hear them?" "I didn't hear them. What did you say?" "Just stupid things. Your daddy's an ass. But what did you mean a mistake?" "Leaving my glasses home. But everybody makes mistakes." "That's right. That's why I'm saying I'm so sorry." Pulls up in front of her school. "We're late. Want me to write a note to Mrs. Barish saying why?" "No, it's only a few minutes." "I wouldn't say I yelled at you or about the glasses, just that I lost track of time or something." "You'd be lying." "A little lie, what's that? So she doesn't have to know everything that goes on with us. And look at me, sweetheart." "She says you don't have to every time. I'll get in trouble if you do," and doesn't look at him. "Please say you're sorry then. I mean that you know I am and you forgive me." "You always get so angry. You scare me when you do. I think it's something I've done." "You're right. I'm sorry. You're right." Puts his hand out to turn her face to his so she'll look at him and he can kiss her. She opens her door. He barely pecks the back of her head as she's getting out. "Your backpack." She comes back for it and he hands her it through her window. "And your glasses. I must've smudged them when I got them for you because I know I cleaned them this morning." Takes them off her, wipes them with the front of his shirt, gives them back. She puts them on, blinks a few times through them as if testing them out, turns without looking at him and goes up the steps. "Sweetheart," he yells out her window. She doesn't come to the railing. He waits for about a minute. What he deserves, he thinks. What's he doing to the poor kid?

Thought several times what he'd do if a policeman stopped his car when he was on his way to pick up his oldest daughter at school. He'd explain he was picking her up, he'd meet him at any spot he wanted right after he gets her but he didn't want her waiting alone too long in front of her school. The policeman probably wouldn't go for it, would think it another excuse, one he might not have heard but another one, would make him wait while he looked at his car registration and driver's license and perhaps put both through to some central police checkup. What would he do then? He'd say "Listen, I'm sorry, but I really have to go, my daughter, I'm frightened for her, please, I've never asked a thing from an officer before, but this is too important," and if the policeman said he couldn't go, he'd say "Fine, I'll wait it out then, but please don't take too long," and when the policeman looked back at his registration and license or was doing something else like that, he'd drive away, no doubt the policeman chasing after him, but speed to the school, through red lights if there were any and it was safe—he wouldn't care by now, he'd be in about as much trouble as he could get into with the police—and after he picked up his daughter he'd take the consequences. Or he'd ask the policeman to call the school from his car if he could or have his precinct house call the school to have someone there bring his daughter to the school office where he'd pick her up. He's told her what to do in a situation like this but he doesn't know if she'd remember what he told her. She's five—smart but only five—or maybe the policeman would let him off almost immediately, say he understands, admonish him briefly for driving over the speed limit or whatever offense he might have made to have the policeman go after him. He's thought about this a lot when he's driven from his job to her school to pick her up. He's driving from his job to her school to pick her up, not thinking about what he'd do if a police car stopped him, when he sees through the rear view mirror lights flashing behind him. Police car, wants him to pull over. Or maybe it wants to get past, and he pulls into the right lane and slows down, but the police car stays behind him, lights flashing. What was he going, five, maybe eight miles over the limit at the most? He'll already be five minutes late picking up his daugher. Should he speed up? What did he decide to do if this happened? Oh, dope, dope. He's told himself he doesn't know how often not to speed along this stretch, and not just when he's picking her up but anytime he's on it. It's a speed trap—he's seen police cars hiding in side lanes, cars being ticketed on the road, sometimes two and three at a time. Pulls over, gets out of the car as the policeman's getting out of his. "Why didn't you stop sooner?" the policeman says, approaching him. "I'm sorry, officer, I didn't see you." "You saw me enough to pull into the slow lane." "When I finally saw you I thought you wanted to get past me, since I didn't think it was me you were after. If I was doing anything over the speed limit, it was three, maybe five—" "I clocked you at twelve over it." "Twelve? I don't see how, but I'll take your word. I'm sure your speedometer's in much better shape than mine." "My radar." "Your radar. But I'm very sorry. I know no excuse makes it right, but I was in a hurry to get my daughter at school. Number 122, on Endicott, in Mt. Bradley." "What's she, sick?" "No, I'm just picking her up. Maybe I should have said she was sick, but I'm not like that, and they get out at 2:45 on the dot. I don't like her standing there waiting for me." "Then you shouldn't have been speeding." Sticks his hand out. "Driver's license and car registration please." "I can't give them now. I mean I'll give them, of course, and you check them, but please let me get back in my car to pick her up. I'll do it and drive right back here with her—it shouldn't take ten minutes. Because you see, sometimes there have been strange guys hanging around the playground there—the schoolyard after school so maybe in front of the school too. There have been complaints—a couple of the girls touched—and you know, in this city or around, every now and then a kid gets picked up by a stranger and is never seen again. And I consciously made an effort not to speed, but I suppose I was so eager to get there so she wouldn't wait that I went over the limit. And I'm already," looking at his watch, "almost five minutes late." "No can do. And five minutes or so will be all right. Lots of kids coming out, school buses taking their time, lots of parents picking up their kids." "But it takes a minimum of five minutes from here. So that'll make me ten minutes late at least if I even leave right now. And around ten minutes after she's let out, the place is almost cleared." "I'm sure your little girl knows what to do. She goes to the office. You must have told her." "I have, but she's in kindergarten, is only five. A young five. She's the second youngest in her class. I mean she's smart but she forgets my instructions." "Kids often do. Your license and registration? This shouldn't take long if you don't force me to send a check through on you and your car." "Don't send a check through. I teach at Wilma. I live in Bradley. When I get a ticket, and I can't remember the last time I did, I send a check for it the same day. All my papers are in order. There's nothing wrong with my life. Be a nice guy, really. Whatever fine I'm supposed to pay for speeding, I'll pay. I'll meet you—at your police station, my house, this same spot—in ten minutes: five to get there, five to get back—or any place and at any time you want." Hand's still out, fingers motioning for his papers. "Here," and he gets out the license and registration, car insurance form, gives them to him, "but please let me leave now. By the time you go through these, check me through your precinct, write up a ticket and so forth, I'll be back." "I can't let you go without your license and registration, and I don't need this," giving him back the insurance form. "Look, it's already been eight minutes—more. Theoretically—on paper, let's say—she's been there thirteen minutes—maybe fifteen to sixteen minutes, if there's traffic at the Kealy Avenue bridge and an unusually long light from here to her school—and how do I know my watch is right? I could be slow." Policeman looks at his watch. "I've got 2:43." "That's about what I have. But by that time—fifteen minutes after her school breaks—all the buses have gone, the principal and teachers have gone back in or got in their cars and are driving home." "I'm sure her principal or teacher, seeing her out there waiting, will take her back to the office or your daughter's homeroom." "The principal doesn't come out every day—maybe every other or every third day—and her teacher just brings the class to the exit door, goes back to her room a few minutes later and then out the back way to the staff parking lot to get her car to go home. Nobody will be there. Strangers might. If I'm lucky a mother or two in the schoolyard with their kids. But they won't be watching my daughter, and if they happen to and see a man they'll think he was her father. Or maybe one of the fourth or fifth graders will be there. They sometimes hang around outside because nobody picks them up and they can walk home when they want and if they normally take the bus, today they might decide to stay. Some of those kids can be tough. At least too tough for my daughter, who's shy, easily cowed and afraid. Some of them don't live in the neighborhood so think they can get away doing anything in it once school's over." "Then those kids wouldn't walk home. It'd be too far, for you have to live a minimum of a mile from school to take the bus. As for the others you mentioned—looking at the driver's license and then staring at him—"chances are slim they'd hang around, and who's to say they might not be nice kids. You've no glasses in the photo." "I didn't need them when I got the license." "But you wear them when you drive, so you should have them on in the photo and noted on the license that you use them when driving. The photo and what you look like driving have to match. Wait here. Let me put in a quick check on you," and heads back to his car. "For what," following him, "my no-glasses? I'll get a new license. But everything else is OK. The car's mine. The insurance is paid up. We haven't had a ticket in years. Please," through the car window now, "can't you see the importance I'm talking of? Call my wife then. Not my wife—my kid's school. I don't have the phone number but it's P.S. 122 on Endicott Street, and my daughter's Olivia." "I can't reach anything on this but my base unit and other patrol cars." "Then have your unit call. I don't know why I didn't say this before. But immediately, because it's getting late. Eighteen, nineteen minutes. To bring her to the school office and have her wait for me there." "They don't like me making arrangements like that for anyone, and she'll be OK; I know it. I'll put the check through, and if everything's all right, give you a warning and let you go." "But she'll also be scared something's happened to me. Or she might start walking home herself, if nobody comes out for her and I don't come and she's all alone for so long. I've told her not to but she could. It's up a long hill. A car could stop and say 'Give you a lift, kid?' and she might fall for it. Adults can convince kids. Or the guy might stop at her school and say her mommy or daddy told him to pick her up—that he's someone who works with me and my car got a flat or I'm very sick and her mommy wants him to take her to the hospital where I am—and she wouldn't question that. What kid would? I've warned her but not gone into details so as not to frighten her. Or she could be dragged into the car. It happens all the time. You know that. Come on, don't you have kids?" "Two, in first grade—twins, and my wife picks them up." "But if she didn't? If she was stopped by a cop—" "Then the teacher stays with them. And if it's for too long, then they'd stick them with the after-school-program kids till one of us showed up. But nothing will happen. Like your kid, they know to go inside the school." "Well, they're at least a year older than mine, and there's two of them, so they think better together. But one kid—" "Stay with me, will you? I don't want you scooting away," and calls in, says "Reardon, yes," gives some lettered code, reads off the license plate and driver's license numbers. Howard runs for his car, gets in, policeman yells "Hey, what the —," drives off, policeman after him, siren on, red light up ahead, what the hell, too late now, goes through it, is doing seventy-five in a forty-five zone, he'll explain all that later, policeman right behind him, his hat on now, another light at the bridge but this one cars in both forward lanes waiting for it to change and cars pulling off the bridge into the lanes next to his, policeman pulls up behind him, gets out, gun in his hand, points it at him, says "That's enough, I'm taking you in. Get out and keep your hands up and spread." Gets out, runs, doesn't look back, the policeman won't shoot him for trying to get his kid, across the bridge, up the hill, cuts through some houses' yards, gets to school, she's sitting against the wall in front of the school, looking at a book. "Suppose I ran for my car now, drove to her school, what would you do?" "Put a report in on you." "Please tell them to phone her school." "You're making me take longer than I should, and I can't hear both them and what you say. If you want to get away from here sooner, you're ruining it for yourself." Howard stands there, looks around him, the road. Cab's passing, empty. Signals it, cab stops, he gets in, cop yells "Hey, don't go," he says to the cabby "Pretend you didn't hear. I'm picking my kid up at school. I'll give you fifty bucks up front and take all the blame for your driving away, saying I threatened your life if you wouldn't drive. That I even pretended to have a gun," and shows him the inside of his wallet with the bills in it. Cabby grabs for it; he pulls it back. "Go first, and you don't want him seeing you take the money." Cab goes, he drops the money on the front seat, policeman's in his car now and following them. No red lights, tie-ups, cab's there in less than five minutes, she's standing out front, crying. He jumps out and hugs her. Looks at his watch. Twenty-three minutes late, theoretically. She probably went back into school. Though she could have started up the hill and even be home by now. Or a stranger might have picked her up in front of the school or while she was going up the hill or even a few steps from their house. She could be in some room, park, basement, abandoned building, being beaten, fondled, raped. She could be in a car, on the floor, driver's free foot pressed down on her neck, going to Washington, Delaware, some other neighborhood here. She could be frightened out of her head, screaming, fighting back, dead. What if she isn't at school when he gets there? Or walking up the hill, at home or at any of her friends' homes? If she were at one, friend's parent would have phoned his wife saying she was there and also probably told the school office she was going to be taken there. Her teacher would have told the office to call or called herself if she took her back to her homeroom. Or maybe a friend's parent saw her waiting in front—friend of theirs or parent of one of her friends—and said she'd wait with her out front or in the office till her mother or father came. Or this parent could have driven her to her home or his daughter's home without telling the office but got a flat on the way in an area without a nearby phone. "OK," policeman says, handing him his license and registration, "everything checks out fine. I'm not going to ticket you this time but if I catch you driving as much as two miles over the limit I'll stop and ticket you for that time and this. So you've been warned." "I can go?" "Yeah, sure, go." Runs to his car, drives the maximum speed limit to her school, she's not outside. Runs inside. She's sitting in front of the office, books on her lap. "Where were you? They called home for me and Mommy didn't answer too." "You came in here by yourself?" "Yes. That's what I was to do; you and Mommy said." "Boy, that's a relief, knowing you knew. You're so smart. Ooh, what a darling," and kisses her hands, puts the books on the floor and picks her up. "I was so worried. I got held up in traffic. Long lines of cars. Couldn't get past them and couldn't call here because I couldn't get to a phone. And where'd Mommy go if she didn't answer the school calling? They call a lot?" "Lots. Five, ten times." "Then she can't be in the garden. At first, maybe, but then she would have heard the phone the second or third time they called and knew someone was trying to reach her badly, especially that we weren't home yet, and come in just to be there for the next time they called. It worries me. It could be something with her or maybe Sister. Let's get home quickly and see."

542

Frog Fragments

He's on the toilet. Lulu yells from the living room where they sleep "I smell gas. I mean the kitchen kind—no joke—you?" "Yeah, I smelled it too. It's probably one of the oven's pilot lights. I meant to light it but had to rush in here to crap." He hears her go into the kitchen, light a match, an explosion. He's quickly wiping himself when she rushes into the bathroom, nightgown and hair on fire. "Howard," she yells and he gets up quickly and wipes himself with the toilet paper he had in his hand and she rushes into the bathroom, hair and nightgown on fire. "No, I understand you meant the stove's gas. I smelled it too but had to come in here to crap. Probably just the oven or stove's pilot light. Wait a second and I'll do it." Half minute later an explosion. He's still shitting but jumps up, sits down a couple of seconds to finish, is wiping himself quickly with the paper he had bunched in his hand when she yells "Howard" and runs into the bathroom, hair and nightgown on fire. Explosion, "Howard!" he jumps up, sits down to finish shitting, "Wait," he yells, jumps up, wipes himself quickly with the paper he already had in his hand when she runs in, nightgown and hair on fire. What to do? Fire in the hair seems out. Drops the paper into the toilet, rips at the nightgown till it's off, stamps on the pieces on the floor till the fire's out. "My hair's still on fire." "No it's not." Pats it, she screams, he feels around for fire, feels warm but not hot, pushes her head into the shower curtain and smothers her head with it till he's sure the fire's out. She's screaming, her son from his bedroom's screaming— "Stop it, Carl," he yells; "it's all right; your mommy's going to be all right"—opens the shower curtain so he can see her, fire's definitely out. "What should we do?" he says. Looking at him but not looking at him, mouth open wide trying to scream now it seems but nothing coming out. Wraps her head gently in a towel, more to soothe her that he knows what he's doing than for any known purpose, says "Let's go in the other room," to get out of the smells of this one and change the scenery for her. Holds her elbow tip and the fingers of her other hand and starts to walk with her; she falls to the floor. Carl's crying from the bathroom door now. "I said go to your room, for christsakes; don't watch this," but Carl stays there. He tries to pick her up and she yells "No, it's killing me where you touch." "Well you can't stay on the floor." "Sit her on the potty," Carl says. He flushes the toilet, flushes it several times thinking maybe lots of rushing water sounds will make her feel cooler, puts the seat cover down, "I'm going to sit you here for the time being," pulls a towel off the shower curtain rod and spreads it over the seat cover. "Got to be careful of infections. Now, I'm going to help you up very gently, very very gently. You're all right. You're just a little burned and it was terrible what you went through but you'll be all right." She opens her eyes on him, still doesn't seem to see him, smiles at Carl. He lifts her up by two places that don't seem burned, some of the burned nightgown's stuck to her and he'd like to pull it off but thinks some skin would come with it, her head hair stinks, underarm hair where it's been burned, little blisters in some places already forming, she's peeing now but he lets her do it on the floor though he moves his feet and tells Carl to step out of the way, sits her on the seat cover when she's done, says "Does it hurt much?" "Everywhere." "I don't know what to do for burns," bending down and wiping up the pee with the towel he used for her head. "Just sit here. Carl, try not to let her fall over. Your son will stay with you, Lu, but don't fall because I doubt he'll be able to stop you. I'll call the police," and in the kitchen shuts the oven off, dumps the towel in the trash, opens the window all the way, calls, woman gives him the number for an emergency ambulance, calls, man says "Want me to send one right over? Usually gas-oven-fire people don't need us by the time we get there." "Just a second. —Lu, do we want the ambulance to come over or if we have to, should we go to the hospital in a cab?" No answer and he says "Hold it" and runs into the bathroom and repeats the question and she says "I want the hospital, I want the ambulance, what do you think!" Goes back and says "She says she wants to go to the hospital in an ambulance. She's badly burned, acting irrationally. I think she could also go into shock." "Just if we come we'll have to take her to the hospital or charge you for it if you decide not to go.

It's just that sometimes all you need, if you need anything more than over-the-counter remedies by the time we get there, is your own doctor, which we don't drive people to." "He says are we sure we need to go to the hospital, Lu? He's saying—ambulance man on the phone now is—we could go straight to a doctor by cab." No answer. "Lulu? —Listen, she's badly hurt, not responding. Only doctor we know of is some pediatrician's name someone gave us in case her son gets sick. And I'm sure we have enough money around or can borrow it to cover the ambulance if that's what it is, so come quick." They come. He's put a clean sheet around her and his heavy bathrobe over her, got a neighbor to take Carl to nursery school. She stays the night at the hospital. They cut most of her head hair off. He says he likes it, makes her look younger and athletic, that she has a pretty forehead that should have been exposed like this long ago. She says it's the first time since she was four or five that she didn't have long hair and bangs down to her eyes. "What was left of my pubic and underarm hair I shaved off myself since some of the aides here who do it look like your typical New York creeps. I was always too hairy. Now I'll even be hairier when it grows in." "Won't bother me. Blacker and bushier the better." They talk about how the accident could have happened. They had a couple over for dinner, smoked some drugs and drank a lot of wine, must have left the oven on, she says. Or one of them turned the oven on when the pilot was out but never used the oven—is that possible? He doesn't see how. "We cooked a meatloaf, baked potatoes and heated the bread in the oven too, if I remember. Also a strudel. To warm." "Then I don't know how it happened," she says. "For how could the oven go out if it had been turned on for the meatloaf and the other stuff? And how could the pilot light go out too, since if the oven was turned on and the pilot light was on at the time, the oven would have lit and stayed lit and so the gas wouldn't have accumulated for the explosion. Was the window open?" "No. That was one of the first things I did after the accident—opened it. Even if it had been open, the wind from it wouldn't have blown out the oven flame since the oven door was

545

also closed." "Maybe there's a draft coming into the oven we don't
know of. It's an ancient one, and this is New York—capital of the
world—so nothing works." "Then how?" he says. "How?" "How!
Maybe before I went to bed I was so, let's admit it, stoned, that instead
of turning the oven off, since it might have already been off, I turned
it on thinking I was turning it off, but while the oven pilot light was
out. But I was high, not stoned, but stupid and tired as I also was
I still could have made that mistake." "That's it with drugs and booze
for me," she says, "since if I hadn't been so groggy from sleep and
all that shit we took, I would have opened the window before I lit
the match. I would have in fact shut the gas off and opened the oven
door and the window before I lit it, since the way things were the
oven was bound to explode." When she gets home she won't let him
raise the blinds during the day or even open them more than a crack.
She stays in bed or in an easy chair most of the day, not saying or
doing much, mostly just thinking about things, she says, and wanting
the room as quiet and dark as he can tolerate it. Whenever he wants
to talk about what's disturbing her she says she doesn't want to go
into it yet. "If you think it was all my fault what happened, tell me,"
and she says best thing now is for him to just shut up. Week after
she comes home she says she wants to go back to California. They
came to New York so she could take an accelerated course in interior
design and get a diploma from it. He says they spent almost all their
money getting here, paying the first month's rent and giving a
month's security with it, winter clothes for her and Carl, things they
couldn't borrow for the apartment, so they can't leave yet. If she's
that depressed, which she obviously is—not reading or wanting to
see anybody and barely eating and the silent treatment and no sex
she's been giving him—well, they can't afford a regular psychiatrist
but maybe there's a free or very cheap one, subsidized by the city
or some religious organization or something. He was subbing every
day in local junior high schools and doing a little art school modeling
at night, not making much but keeping them going. No, she wants
to go back right away; tomorrow if they can. Impossible, he says.

"And you sublet your house for six months." "I'll tell them it's an emergency—there must be a legal loophole for situations like this—and get them out. Fuck them; they're nice people but I'm sick and a mess and need my house back now and the warmth and good smells and companionship of California. I'll camp out on my front yard if I have to; they'll just have to understand." She leaves the next day with Carl, will stay with friends till she gets her tenants out. They speak on the phone and write letters and she always says she's eager to see him, Carl misses him so much he's begun to wet his bed again, she doesn't know why he can't pick up and leave right now. Money, he says. He's living cheap, stashing a lot of cash away, replenishing what they lost moving to New York, still looking for someone to take over their apartment lease so they can get back their security. He stays till the end of the school year. When he gets to California she says she's been with someone the last three months, "a beautiful new dude in the area who, maybe because he never saw the originals, doesn't mind my butch cut and hairy cunt"—"I don't either; let me see it; because I told you I'd probably prefer it to the way it was"—"and who I thought I'd stop seeing when you got here but now know I can't and that I'm more than likely more involved with this guy than I am with you. Though if you want, long as you're here and came so far, we can ball one last time." "Oh why did I waste my fucking time with you? But I'm horny as hell after four months," so he stays the night, tells Carl the next morning he wishes it wasn't this way and he'll write and call him and send him things and hopes to see him in a few months, flies back to New York, moves in with his folks and stays for two years, helping his mother take care of his father, and driving cabs and posing nude and subbing in junior high schools.

His father comes home from the army. Years later his brother tells him it wasn't the army but prison. But for now it's the army. He's sure there's going to be a celebration tonight though nobody's said there'd be. Maybe they're keeping it from him because it's a surprise one and they're afraid he'll tell it. He wakes up early, thinking his father might have got home late last night, goes to his parents' room, nobody's in it and bed's made, in the kitchen his mother says he should be here by the time Howard comes home for lunch. He leaves the house, tells the boys he walks to school with and his teacher and best friends in class that his father's coming home from the army today, can't wait, he's a major in the dental corps and was stationed in New Mexico, that's way out west, and lies that he was supposed to go to France to fix soldiers' teeth, but then the war started to end there and they pulled him off the troopship. He runs home for lunch, hears them arguing through the front door, arguing as he goes into the apartment, "Dad, Dad, it's me, Howard," he says from the foyer, they're arguing in the kitchen. "Eat shit then," his father says. "You should talk. And really, just wonderful words to wait so long for." They see him. "Howard, my darling little child, how are you?" and he gets down in a crouch and Howard runs into his arms and is picked up and kissed. "Whew, you've become such a load." His mother's been crying, he sees from up there, looks angry, fists clenched. He says "How was the army?" and his father says "The army was fine, just what I needed for a year and a half, much as I missed you all. How have you been—a good boy?" "Did you ever get overseas?" "No, they kept me in Albuquerque the whole time. That's in New Mexico, near the real Mexico but still America." "I know; I saw it on the map. Mom showed me it around all the mountains. Were there Indians and wild horses there? That's what some people said there might be. And how come you have no uniform on? Did you hang it up? You don't have to wear it when you're home?" "Wait, hold it," putting him down. "One question at a time. No uniform because I've been discharged. That means I'm out of the army, home for good. And it was always on loan—not yours—so I had to give it back. If I didn't I'd be arrested. And Indians and horses? Not so many Indians; plenty of horses." "Did you bring me any army patches?" "Was I supposed to? Don't worry, I know who to send to and I'll try and get some." "Did you ride the horses?" "Never had time. Work work work, teeth and more teeth, and they were short dentists. But lots of mountains, lots of deserts, lots of springs." "What are they?" "Springs. Water coming out of them, gushing or bubbling. They were lucky to have so many for New Mexico needs all the water it can get. So does the whole West, I think." "Did you bring me anything from there? An Indian bracelet like I wrote you?" "All that's still in my luggage. When it gets here I'll have lots of gifts for you and all my darling kids. Now eat your lunch. I think that's what your mother put on the table." He eats. They leave the kitchen, shut the door and start arguing in the foyer. She tells him to go back where he came from and stay there, for all she cares. His father says any place would be better than here. "But what I want to know is why you have to act like that?" "Like what?" "Like a filthy rotten conniving bitch." "You pig, you swine. . ." If his father left would he want to go with him or stay with his mother? Depends who Alex would go with. But if his father went back to New Mexico and took him he could learn to ride all those horses, there'd be all that country, he could shoot guns and climb mountains and slide down parts of them, maybe make friends with an Indian his age. His father was only in the army there though, so he wouldn't move back now that he's discharged. But suppose his parents broke up and his father only moved to another part of the city and wanted him to come along, what would he do? He doesn't know. Then suppose a judge, like in some movie he saw, said choose who you want to live with, your mother or your dad, what would he do? He couldn't live without his mother. He'd hate not living with his father, and without Alex and Vera if they chose to go with his father, but he'd just have to settle for seeing them all as much as he could. Does that mean he loves his mother more than his father? He can't answer. He doesn't want to think about it. If he got that far as to say he knows who he loves better, he knows he'd be struck down dead by something or for his whole life after that seriously cursed.

In the park with his mother and sister. Nice day, very few people around. "Let's go look at the ducks," he says. "You go down, be careful, I'll sit and watch you from here." "No, I want to stay with you," he says. "I do too," Vera says. They continue walking. A vendor. "Can I have something?" he says. "May." "May I have something too?" Vera says. She nods, opens her pocketbook. He gets an ice cream. Vera wants a popsicle and pretzel. "Don't be a hog," he says. She gets a big warm pretzel. "Sit down on the bench so you don't sully your clothes while you're eating." They sit on either side of her and eat what they got. "Can I have some of yours?" Vera says. "May," he says, "and no." "It'd be nice if you both could share what you have, if only a single bite and lick." He gives Vera a lick, she breaks off a small piece of pretzel and gives him it, they eat that and then continue to eat what they got. "You know, you're both doing something that I can say doesn't quite please me but which I'm sure you're both unaware of, do you know what that can be?" "What?" he says. Vera says to her "I don't know, what?" I'm sure if you did know you'd correct it immediately. It's OK though. You'll learn on your own while you're doing it—or not doing it. That's a hint. Do you know what I mean now?" "No," they say, "what?" "Or you'll find out after from me. Go ahead, eat your snacks." They eat. Little while later she says "You know, you're both still doing something that displeases me, and now even a little more so than before, have you thought about what it could be?" "What?" he says. "What," Vera says, "because I haven't found out yet." "You'll find out sooner or later, I'm sure. Though I wish you could find out on your own and correct it on your own too." "Is it something I said?" he says. "If it is, I'm sorry." "No." "Something I said?" Vera says. "Nothing either of you said though it does have something to do with words." "Then I don't know what it is," Vera says and gets up and skips off a few feet, points at a squirrel circling the trunk of a tree till it's in its branches, skips back and says "Did you see that? It was like a skip rope." "How like a skip rope? A skip rope's straight. You're seeing things," and eats his ice cream. "You both still don't know what it is you're doing wrong? Because you only have a little time left to correct it." "No," he says. "Is my shoelaces untied?" Looks. "No, they're tied. Did I get ice cream on my clothes? I don't see any. What did Vera do?" "Same thing you're doing and which is still displeasing me." "Can you give us one more hint?" "No more. If you can't think of it, you can't, so let's forget about it for now." "Can I go and skip like Vera?" "Of course, do what you wish, I'm not saying no. But finish your cone first if you're about to skip or run." He finishes the ice cream, chews on the cone, skips off, Vera skipping after him. They stop to watch a couple of squirrels jumping from the branch of one tree to another. His mother catches up with them. "Are you finished eating your cone?" "Finished. Where should I put the napkin?" "Hold it till we get to a trash can." "I didn't have a napkin," Vera says. "I'm lucky, you're not." "Now that you both enjoyed your treats, want to know what you did that was so wrong and which made me practically ashamed of you?" No, he thinks. "What?" Vera says. "You didn't offer any to the one person who didn't have any." He laughs. Vera looks at him and then laughs. "I'm serious, what's so funny? If you get something, you offer the person who doesn't have any some of it. If there are several people who don't have it or anything like it and you're the only person who does, you offer them all some of it. If there's a crowd, then you eat it without offering." "Why?" Vera says. "You could have had an ice cream or pretzel," he says. "You have money." "You're missing the point. You were both being selfish. I wouldn't have taken any if you had offered, since I don't like ice cream or popsicles much and can't stand pretzels, but that's not the point either. The point is to offer even if you know the other person doesn't want any. Always remember what I'm telling you here. I don't want what you did repeated. Otherwise I won't know what kind of children I've raised and you can count on what I'll say if you ask me for a treat after the next time." He felt so good, feels so bad now. Vera doesn't seem to feel bad though. She's still smiling and says "Why not pretzels? Too salty?" "That and other reasons." "Oh. Can I go now?" and his mother nods and Vera runs off. "And you? Any response?" He can't speak, his throat's choking him, and she says "OK, I think I can guess what you'll do next time," and sits on a bench and watches Vera circling a tree looking for a squirrel that just ran up it.

Frog

Poor grades and too much homework and what else?—couldn't take the regimentation and strictness in the specialized school like the hallway order (no whistling, no talking, keep walking), so first day as a transfer student at a high school way up in the Bronx. Had to give a relative's address to get in there, as the two regular high schools in his own borough were said to be too tough. Gets off the elevated train, from the station platform high above the street sees the school and a bell tower on top of it like a real school and all the grass and trees around it, down the steps, starts running to school when a block from it a hamburger and hotdog truck's being turned over. "Heave-ho!" When the truck's on its side he sees it was some boys who turned it over. A man climbs out of the serving window waving a long fork and shouting "You motherfuckers. You goddamn thugs. You'll get nothing from me now, nothing. You could've killed me." "Eat shit," "Cheap prick," "Dago pimp," and a couple of them scoop up pebbles and stones and pretend to throw it at him. He ducks, kneels behind his truck. They laugh, bang on the truck with their fists and sticks, run past Howard and some other boys. "What happened?" Howard asks the boys watching it. "A dumb old fuck," one says and they head for school. "What was that all about for?" he asks the man. "Protection, the bastards. But who they think they're kidding I need it from? I know who they are. I'm not selling around your school anymore. Thieves and thugs and future murderers in it." "But what kind of protection you mean?" "What're you asking me when I got other things?" Police sirens. "Better beat it like the others or they'll think you're in on it too. Or maybe you are. Come to gloat." "No, really." The man tries lifting up the truck. Actually gets it a little way off the ground. Howard helps him but together they get it no higher than the man did alone. "Maybe the cops will pitch in," the man says. Howard thinks to stay to help them lift it, maybe the man will give him a tip, think him a nice kid and tell the school people what he did, but it's getting late for school and he doesn't even know what room he's in, so when the police come he goes.

Frog Fragments

Walking out of school to the train to get to work when some boy says "Hey, look at the fruity white bucks on the fag." Turns to him, thinking maybe it's one of his friends or someone to take the train downtown with. "Oh, want to make something of it, faggot?" "Just leave me alone." "You're going to do something if I don't?" Other boys pouring out of school surround them. "Dump him, Cal. Clobber the fucker." He pushes past some boys and heads for the train station, hoping a teacher or one of the football players on the student patrol will break it up if anything more happens. He's shoved hard from behind. "C'mon, prick!" He's done this before. Loses control. Years later he says it saved his neck lots of times. Now he doesn't know if it would have been better all those times to keep walking away. No broken nose. No kid lying on the sidewalk with his head cracked and eyes closed. Another with his white turtleneck sweater all bloody and looking at Howard as if saying why'd you jump me so fast and have to go for the face? And just to have had that control. Drops his books and jumps him and gets him in a headlock and squeezes and punches his face while whirling them both around and takes some stomach blows and the guy scratching his neck and cheek but squeezes and punches his face some more and throws him to the ground and pins his shoulders with his knees and sticks his fist under his chin and says "Had enough, schmuck, had enough? 'cause I'll bust your fucking ears in, I'll pick your head up and bust it on the fucking concrete," and he says "Yeah, lay off, enough, you're OK. Your shoes are nice. I'm going to buy a pair." "Bullshit you are," and gets up. While they were fighting, boys yelled "Kill him, C. C. Poke the twit's eyes out. Kick his nuts off for me." When he walks away someone says "Fucking faggot won." "All right, come on, that'll be it, boys, everyone go home," a teacher says.

He's in college, walking to his waiter's job, it's around eight. Someone says "Look at the fruitball." They seem drunk, guys his age. He stops. "What're you stopping for, fruitball?" another of them says. "Because I don't like being called a fruit." "My friend said you're a fruitball, not a fruit. But maybe you are a fruit. A fucking fruitball

553

fruit. You suck old men's dicks in caves." Jumps the guy, gets him in a headlock, takes some body blows but squeezes his head tight while punching the back of his neck and his face. The friends try pulling him off. The guy falls to the ground. Face a mess, busted nose seems like, lips split, blood all over him and Howard, eyes looking up at them sleepily, he's trying to talk. "Shit, you really did a job on him," one says. "A fair fight, I declare it a fair fight," the biggest of them says, "and a fucking good one. But if he hadn't had so much beer in him I bet he would have creamed you." "Want me to help him up?" "Nah, you better get the fuck out of here. You don't look too good yourself." Knuckles cut, that's about all, and his face maybe, and his sweater's torn. It's not his. His brother Alex's who says next day when Howard shows him it "My goddamn sweater. Look what you've done to it. Cashmere. Not even a month old. Even if we got all the blood out, which we won't, and the best darner for the rips, to me it's absolutely ruined. Next time use your stupid head and show some control by passing by whoever calls you a fag or Jew kike or whatever they throw at you. You're paying for it out of your wages. Cough up. I know you have a cigar box in your drawer stuffed with tips." "That's for Europe." "Forty-five bucks, and the sweater's now yours."

They hear about her in a bowling alley. Chippy, for five dollars, bright red hair, very white body, not too old—thirty, maybe thirty-five, but she keeps herself in great shape. They say he should call her. "You know how to speak to older women." "Me?" "Yes. You got brains, use big words, have a smooth voice almost and not such a New York accent, so you sound older. Call her." Calls. She says "Who gave you my number?" "Ellis." "I know Ellis. He's a good guy, everybody he's mentioned to me so far has been very refined, so come on over at eight tonight, and tell Ellis thanks." "There might be a problem, since there's a few of us. Is that all right?" "How few?" "Three or four, though there also might be another." "Four is the most I'll go for. More and you have a commotion, since my place isn't as big as a palace. So now with four, when you do come up, do it one by one, first door off the lobby marked stairway. I'm on the second floor, 207. The rest of you, when one client's up, stay outside and away from the hotel and don't gang together." "Ellis said it was five dollars each, OK?" "I don't know what you're talking about, sir. Five for what? For the six cigars you're interested in buying, fine. But you should know that like a doctor I hate talking price over the phone. It's undignified, so remember that or don't bother dealing with me." "Good," Ellis tells them after his call. "With four she'll give me a freebie. But watch out. She has a small white poodle named Snowball who'll steal your scumbags right out of your wallet if you leave your pants pockets hanging open." It's his first time. One of them says that even if they each plan on using a scumbag, they should drink lots of water before so when they get off her they can pee all the syphilis germs out if she has it and some managed to get inside the bag. They meet later at this guy's apartment, drink a canteen of water each, draw straws as to who goes first—all of them wanted to and he gets to be second—and go to her hotel and up to her floor together. They thought that all of them should get caught together rather than one getting caught while some of the others had already gotten laid. They don't know what to do when they get to her floor, but one of them finds a laundry closet and three of them stay in it while the fourth goes to her door. The closet's dark. "Any of you got a hard-on?" he says. "Because I sure do. Biggest I think I ever had. I can't wait." "Me too," one says. "It's poking a hole through my pants." "I'm jerking myself off now," the third says. "It'll last longer that way when I'm in her, since I know it'd take me two seconds if I didn't." He makes some noises. "Jesus," Howard says, "don't do it over here; you'll ruin my clothes." "It's all right. I'm facing away from you, I think, and I did every spurt into my hanky. Now I'm going to be in her forever, since I'm the last." The first guy comes back in about ten minutes. "How was it, how was it?" they all ask. "She was much older than Ellis said. Forty, maybe, like one of my aunts. He just said it so we'd go to her and he'd get a free lay. Still, nice tits that didn't hang and no wrinkly stomach, and she didn't stink. I came all the way in her I thought I'd go out the other side, but she just laid there like she didn't feel me at all, and I didn't see no dog. Since I've already been laid once, I'd call it just average, while for you guys for the first time you'll love it." "Come on, Howie, get it over with," one of the other two says, shoving him to the door. He leaves, knocks on her door, she looks at him through the peephole, lets him in, is smiling, her almost orange hair held down by a band on top like a girl's, skin so white as if if she went on the beach for a minute when the sun's out she'd get blisters, soapy smell all round her, in a belted bathrobe and bare feet but one of her breasts he can see where it's open. He's so hot for her he almost can't stand up his head and chest's so woozy. She says "You're a pretty cute-looking kid. You the one who called? You sounded much older than your age. That why they had you call me, so I wouldn't be frightened off by all your ages?" "No, I volunteered." "This your first time too? OK, but I hope not, because I hate showing the ropes each time. Takes too long." "Why, the other guy was his first? He told us he's been laid before." "Him? He was a good guy all right but had to be told everything. And not 'laid,' will you? You 'make love.' Or you 'go to bed.' At best, you 'have sex.' Be refined. That's what I like in all my men, young or old. Otherwise, we all feel messy. OK. Five dollars first. You can put it in there," and he puts it in an empty cigar box on a table. "Now you're entitled to undress." He takes off his clothes, folds them neatly on a chair, trouser legs over its pockets, tries not to show he knows he has a full hard-on. "Ellis said—" "Oh boy, you're ready to go. A real broom handle. The wonderful young." "Yes, well. But Ellis said you had a dog Snowball. Do you?" "He's shy of people, almost never emerges from under the bed. But you might see him if you don't talk loud or gruff. Here, give me that thing." She grabs it, squeezes it hard while staring at the head. "Just want to see if anything wrong comes out of it. Nothing. You're clean. Now I'd like you to put a condom on even if that's not what you bargained for. I've got them if you don't." "No, I don't mind and I brought one," and gets it out of his wallet. "Let me see it," and she turns it over in her hand. "It's a good one, not in your pocket for a hundred years." "No, I bought it just the other day. And Ellis said also that Snowball steals these things out of your wallet if you're not looking. He had to be kidding though." "Steals them? The little yipper? What do you think I have, a circus dog? Just put it on. You got your pals downstairs." Tries to. Practiced with one once but not over a hard-on. She says "You roll it on, oafy, like a sock in the morning," and does it for him. When she's doing it he thinks he's going to shoot into it. She gets on the bed, takes her robe off and hangs it on the bedpost behind her, opens her legs and says "Well come along, darling, climb on." "You mean the bed?" "I mean everything, darling," and points to her cunt. He gets on the bed, squats in front of her but doesn't know where to put his knees, inside her legs or outside of them, or quite where to stick his prick in. In the hole he knows but where exactly is it? He got a quick look when he got on the bed; she's got a little square orange bush but he didn't see the crack where he thinks he should. "What's the wait for? Just say it's your initial time and you know from nothing and I'll show you how it goes. It'll take longer but probably not as long if you start experimenting on me." "No, honestly, not like the other guy. This is my third time but last two were in the dark and the girl I was with was more experienced and she put it in for me." The legs have to be inside hers he now sees and moves closer, gets on top of her and takes his penis and without looking pokes it around where he thinks the crack should be but doesn't find a hole. "Ouch, what're you doing? That's my ass and I don't want any of that stuff. You want to do it, find a man, but don't come back to me after. You want me to do something else to you, with my mouth, that's in addition and will cost you another five, but never the rectum. Never." "No no, all I want's the regular." "Then tell me you never done it before and stop wasting my time." She grabs his penis, jerks it a few times— "Don't, I'll shoot"—"Then let's get going," and sticks him in, brings him down on top of her and bounces her bottom a few times. He bounces the way he thinks he should and they're bouncing together when the phone rings. "Hold it a second," she says. She pushes him up and reaches for it. He starts to get out and she says, her hand over the receiver, "Stay in. If you come you come, and this'll only take a second and you've already used up your five dollars' worth. Yes," she says into the phone. "Yeah, I know you. Yeah, I remember you. Yeah, I said so already, the guy with the Persian lamb collar and hat, and what? Sure, when? Fine, got it, I'll remember. I don't have to put in down, I've got a fine memory. Johnson, that's your first name, I know, see ya." All this while he tried not to think of his penis or feel it, looked around the room, painting over the dresser, window blinds with a droop of a few slats in it and lights from buildings across the street through it, listened for the dog under the bed but heard nothing. She hangs up and says "You didn't come? I thought I heard something. I don't care if you didn't make a sound or still have an erection. The wonderful young can usually keep it up after, so don't tell me that. Pull out, let's see." He does and she looks at it. "OK, let's finish." He says "I've suddenly got to pee bad, is it all right?" and she points and he runs to the bathroom, pees for about a minute, comes back, she's reading a fashion magazine in bed and says "Boy, you sounded like a horse in there. OK, now what do we do?—always something with you, more effort than you're starting to be worth," and gets a condom out of the night table drawer, puts it on him, lays back, he gets on the bed, looks at her crack, sees the hole and puts his penis in and comes down on her and starts bouncing. "Could you go up and down too? I'll finish faster." "Oh sure," and she bounces up and down, he's pressed tight to her, smells the cold cream, it smells like it must be fresh on her face and neck it's so strong, comes. She slaps his buttocks when he's done jerking. He just lies there. "That little tap means to get off, darling. A signal." "Oh, I didn't know." Gets up and off the bed. She says "That was good, right? Call me again anytime if you want, alone or with only one other friend, and don't be passing my phone number around like it was a cigarette. Keep it special, it'll be better." "I will call, and I won't be passing it around. What do I do about this now?" holding his penis up, tip of the bag with the come in it hanging over his hand. "What'd you do with your girlie?" "I didn't use one. She was on a period she said." "Well, don't take it off here. In the bathroom, flush it down. And only use the tissues from the box to clean yourself, not the towel if there's one." He goes in it, rolls the condom off and lets it drop into the toilet, flushes, cleans his penis with soap and water and dries it with tissues, little pieces stick to it so he sticks it under the faucet to get them off and pats it dry with the hand towel, comes out, she's in her bathrobe reading the same magazine, he gets dressed, she goes to the door, unlocks it, puts her face forward and lips out, he kisses them, grabs her breast from inside the robe, she says "Don't start unless you want to pay another five and think you can do it extra quickly." "I don't. I haven't the money." "Till the next time then. Now tell your friend who's next to be discreet coming up here. No noise. To act like a gentleman. And no elevator. That's the rule. Now you know what 'discreet' is?" "It means don't make a big deal coming upstairs." "To do it as if you're reserved and a quiet person and live in the hotel. They won't bother him if he acts like that. OK." Opens the door, looks out both ways, signals for him to go, he goes, heads for the stairway but turns around moment her door closes and ducks past it to the linen closet, knocks, they open and he goes inside and says "It was only so-so, her face kind of greasy though her body OK, but at least now I can say I've been laid."

It was about a year after. Working at a catering place delivering orders when the man who sends him out on them holds up a wrapped tray of canapés and says "This customer a relative of yours?" "Why, Tetch? Could be, as it's an unusual one," and the man says "A Mrs. Howard," and he says "That's my first name." "I know, only making a joke; where's your sense of humor?" and gives him the tray and another order and exact change for both out of a ten and he goes, few blocks away rings the bell downstairs which has the apartment number he wants but the name Chandler on it. "Yes?" a woman says. "Delivery, ma'am, for Mrs. Howard, do I have the

right place?" and she says "Sure, you got it darling," and he's rung
in, goes upstairs, apartment door's opening right across from the
elevator when he's getting out of it, woman in a bathrobe belted tight,
Chippy, has to be, doesn't seem to recognize him or show she does,
same style bright red hair, same soap smell or something coming
toward him as he goes to her, very white skin, freckles around her
nose, he doesn't know if the bathrobe's the same one as before, what
the hell's she doing in a regular apartment in a nice apartment
building twenty blocks from her hotel? "How much they sticking
me for?" she says, taking the canapés, looks at the bill taped to it,
he's already excited, gives him a five, he gives her change, puts a
quarter into his hand and says "Here, go and buy yourself a cigar."
"Thank you," and just as she's shutting the door he says "Chippy?"
and she looks at him and says "What'd you say?—forget it," and
continues closing the door and he sticks his foot in it, though he
had no thought to, it just got there, and says "I know you, Chippy,
I went to you about a year ago," and she says "You got to have the
wrong party for whatever you mean, little mister. The name's
Howard, like on the order slip, and if you're saying you don't like
the tip I gave you, though I don't know anyone else who wouldn't
think it generous, give it here," and holds her hand out and he says
"Yeah, the order slip, but not like on the bell downstairs." "That's
my friend's name downstairs, but what's it to you? Now I'm telling
you, he isn't home now but the super is, and if that doesn't get you
moving, I'll call the cops and have you run in. Now get your foot
away," and he says "Listen, I don't mean trouble and will go when
you want to, so you don't have to call anyone, but I remember
everything about you, even the robe but maybe a different color. Can
I come in since nobody's there. I can pay," and she says "Shut up,"
looks around, "Get in, you stupid kid," and he does, she shuts and
locks the door. "You got ten bucks? And you better be quick about
it too, since I got someone coming here soon for these canapés," and
puts them on the table by the door. "If not, then you got to scoot."
"It used to be five," and she says "Ten now. Five, if it was five then,

was maybe the last time I used that price," and she touches his erection through the pants and says "Look at you, ready to roll. Come on, hand it over or go," and he says "Can't we do it for nothing?" and she says "You crazy? Get out of here if that's what you're thinking," and starts pushing him to the door, and he says "Then just a hand-job for nothing? I won't take long and then I'll leave right after. For the truth is I have no money but the quarter you gave me, as I just came on at work and yours was the first tip of the day," and she says "Oh brother, you really pulled a fast one on me. And everybody who says it won't take long, even you kids, takes forever. What the hell my going to do with you now?" and he says "Please, I'll bring customers like Ellis did," and she says "I don't need customers; I've enough, even by charging ten," and he says "Please, I'm really ready as I said; it'll take ten seconds," and she says "Oh, to get rid of you, come in here," and he follows her into the bathroom, "Pull your stupid pants down," he does, she grabs his penis and pulls him to the toilet by it, lifts the seat and starts jerking him over the bowl. He's still holding the other order by the string and drops it to the floor, gets so excited he falls to his knees, she says "Get up, I don't want it on the floor," he grabs her legs under the robe to hold on to, moves his hands up, nothing on, feels hair, the hole, sticks his fingers from both hands in, "What're you doing? I didn't say any of that, and get up. Hell with you, finish it off yourself," and she lets go of him and leaves the bathroom, he gets up and finishes it off in a few seconds and washes up and comes out with the order and she says "I'm really pissed at you. I should even ask for my quarter back, you little brat. Now get the hell out, and I hope you didn't mess up my fucking bathroom," and he says "I didn't; I did it into the bowl and cleaned up without a trace. A kiss?" and puts out his face and she says "I'll kiss you one, with my fist—you probably messed up all my linens in there; just get going and don't bother ever coming back, you're off my list for good," and opens the door and shoves him out. He calls some of his friends from work, says what happened, she jerked him off while he had his fingers in her, she was all excited and he would've screwed her but she wanted too much and he thought this for nothing is better than screwing for ten bucks, and when they meet that night, five of them, one says "Hey, let's go visit her. We'll get ourselves in somehow and ask her to screw us all for free or just jerk us all off. She doesn't want to, we'll threaten her, bring knives but keep them under our coats till we have to show them. Shit, hand-jobs she can do two at a time and then we'll be out of there fast as Howard, we'll tell her. She doesn't want to do anything, we'll also say we'll tell the cops about her, and the knives only as a last resort and just to scare her, of course. He says "Not me, she could have cops there as customers when we try to push ourselves in, or just a customer with a gun or something or just something like acid to throw at our faces herself," and this guy says "If cops are there, which isn't too likely, we'll say 'Sorry, we had our appointments with her mixed up,' or we thought we could come by without calling her, and as for the other things, hardly." "I can get in trouble, she knows where I work," and another of them says "A whore's going to make trouble for you? She'll never show her face. That's the point, I guess. That once we get in she's got to do what we say, since there's five of us and it's not like we want to be future customers of hers. We only want this once and she's a sitting duck for us since we know where she is and what she does." He still says no but doesn't want to miss out on the excitement and maybe getting laid and another hand-job but this one finished by her and even a blow-job as someone else says they might also be able to make her do while she's giving two others handjobs, so he says "OK, yeah, sure, but do we have to take knives?" and they go to one of their apartments first, say hello to their friend's mother and that they only came up for some cold water and soda and go to the kitchen, get kitchen knives there and put them under their coats or in their belts, Howard and another guy don't want to but one of the others say "Everybody, we're in on this together, all for one and do or die and that sort of shit," say good-bye to their friend's mother, go to Chippy's building, decide while they walk what to say and who's to say it, ring her vestibule bell, "Yes?" she says, "Flowers from Mr. Tibbs, the florist, ma'am," guy who was chosen to speak says, "Bullshit, flowers, beat it or I'll call the police," and they ring several bells in the building, has about twenty apartments, four to five to a floor, a few people say "What? Hello? Who is it? Who's there?" but nobody rings back, ring some other bells and more people ask questions which they don't answer but one rings them in, they stay quiet downstairs, a man yells down "Is that you, Thomas?" the spokesman yells up "Sorry, sir, wrong building, made a mistake," and points to the front door and makes hand motions and another of them opens it and lets it slam. They wait, door upstairs closes, five minutes, then go up, spokesman knocks on her door, others stay to the sides or crouched on the floor but out of view of the peephole, "Yes?" she says, "Flowers from Mr. Tibbs, ma'am, and has to be signed," "I'm not expecting flowers or anyone, so good-bye," "No, it's true, ma'am, just doing my job— open up and you'll see," and she says "Even if you put a basket of bouquets in front of the hole here I wouldn't open up, so you better get moving or I'm calling the police right now," and one of them from the floor says "Whore's gonna call the cops?" "Fuck you, dopos, you've been warned," and goes away from the door, comes back a few minutes later while they're figuring out what to do next, stay here, leave, ring again and say there's just two of them and they're friends of Ellis and will give her ten bucks each to get laid and then when she lets them in to grab her and make her do whatever they want for free, and says "They're coming, have fun, boys, for if you don't think they do favors for me and that I also wouldn't press charges, you're crazy." "Let's go," Howard says, and the spokesman says "She's full of it," and he says "What if she is? She's not opening up, we're never getting in there, and I'm going before something I don't like happens," and starts downstairs, they follow him, outside he says "Let me ask you. What if she had her pimp with her and it was his apartment she was working out of or if she had called him instead of the cops to deal with us and he had come up from downstairs while we were there? Those guys got real weapons and can be very mean and rough," and one of them says "Why didn't we think of that? I know I sure wouldn't have tried what we did if someone had brought it up."

They're hanging out on Broadway, sitting against a parked car, night, when a car pulls up, "Hey," the passenger yells, a friend, the driver another friend beside him, new Olds 98, "Want a ride? Hop in." They get in, "Where'd you get it?. . .Whose is it?" and the driver says "A cousin's," and Howard says "Nice car. . .feel the leather," and the driver's friend next to him says "Actually, we shouldn't lie," and they laugh together, "We saw it doubleparked in front of Tip Toe, motor running, vent window open, keys inside, so pinched it," and he says "This is a stolen car?" and the driver says "That's it, babe, now where you want to go?" and he says "Out of it—stop the fucking thing," and the front passenger says "*See*, I told you not to pick them up—let the fraidy-cat out," when they sideswipe a cab, tear of metal, "Holy shit," the driver says and puts on speed down Broadway, cab following them honking his horn, "What the hell we gonna do now?" front passenger says, through a red light, almost hitting some people crossing, cabby still behind them honking and now flashing his headlights on and off, right on Seventy-seventh Street, "Pull up so we can make a run for it," guy next to Howard yells, car brakes, stops, halfway up the street, driver runs out his side, front passenger out his, Howard's door on the left won't open though it's unlocked, guy on right has trouble opening his door, Howard looks back, cab's stopped and driver jumps out of it and runs to their car, right door opens and friend falls out, gets up and runs, Howard's door still stuck, goes out the other back door, starts running to West End Avenue, hand on his shoulder, "You!" a man says, but he gets out from under the hand, runs to West End, crosses it, Riverside Drive, into the park, through it north, couple blocks away hides behind bushes, everything seems quiet, birds, far-off traffic, that's all, waits, coast seems clear, goes back to Eighty-third Street but on the other side of Broadway looking for his friends, nobody's there, walks around the block and comes back, still nobody's there, walks home, sees a commotion on Seventy-fifth where their car was, figures the cabby never recognized him from the back, goes up Seventy-seventh, cab still there, stolen car, police around, a crowd, he asks a man what happened, "Some kids shot someone on Ninety-sixth, stole a car, crashed into a few of them and wound up here, that cabby over there following them because he was the last one to get clipped, but they got away." "Jesus," he says, "anybody hurt?" "I told you, someone shot." "Oh God, that's awful. Dead?" "Don't know. Ask the cop, not that he'll tell you anything," and the man leaves and he watches for a while, it's just a lot of talking between the cabby and the police and some people around him who say they saw most of it, and goes home.

They pick up a Volkswagon and put it into the lobby of an apartment building and wait for the elevator man to come down, open the elevator door and see it. He looks around, through the lobby doors to the street but doesn't seem to see them. "Hey hey, over here," they yell, and he shakes his fist at them. They're all laughing and run away. There's an old lady in the neighborhood, they call her the Black Widow, always wears black, carries a black umbrella, black hat with a veil over her face, and whenever she sees them she says "Stinking filthy kids, you'll never be anything, go away, leave this street in peace," and shakes the closed umbrella at them and sometimes raises it as if she's going to hit them. They always laugh at her and sometimes dodge around her swinging umbrella and say "Black Widow, Black Widow's going to bite," but one day when she's doing that to them, just shouting and shaking the umbrella, one of his friends comes up behind her and dumps a street can of garbage over her head. Some of it's dribbling down her and she screams savagely at them, in another language they never heard from her before and can't understand, and most of them laugh as if they never saw anything so funny and they all run away. When they get together right after at a candy store they go to he says "Really, it's got to be wrong, she's just nuts and didn't deserve that." They say "Sure she

565

did. She's a crazy old bag who doesn't know if she got garbage on her or rain or what." Next time he's with them and sees her walking their way he says "Come on, let's not do anything; let her yell and scream and wave her screwy umbrella all she wants." "What are you talking about, if she comes after us, and we got to have every day our fun," and he crosses Broadway and watches the lady walk around them, not shouting or waving her umbrella and looking a little scared, and they chant "Black Widow, Black Widow, Black Widow's lost her bite." A gang comes up to them one afternoon after school, they're from the West Fifties and Sixties, he can tell by the gang name on their jackets, and one of them steps out from the others and says "The Saxons challenge whatever your gang's name is to a fight." They say they're not a fighting gang and have no gripes against them and if they want them to move on, they will. The gang's about four times larger than their group and some of the members in it older and bigger, though there are a whole bunch of small young kids with them too. The gang calls them chickens and pansies and when they start walking away the gang follows them and then chases them till they see a cop; then they run back downtown. A week later on Broadway again the gang suddenly rounds the corner and runs at them and jumps them. Two are on him and a little one is trying to pull off his shoe and he swings wildly at the bigger ones, rips at their hair, kicks their balls, pulls at and bites one's ear, shoves the little one into the street, knocks one of the older ones down and picks up the other one in a bearhug from behind while kicking at the one down and doesn't know what to do with him but the guy's punching his head so he throws him against a store window they're up against. The guy goes through it and glass breaks around them. All the fighting stops, the gang members rush to their friend in the window who's screaming he's been stabbed, he got it in the face, and Howard, who's bleeding from a lot of little glass cuts, and his friends run away. Day later they hear from someone who knows a member of the gang that the guy got glass in his neck and almost bled to death and has to stay in the hospital, and the gang's looking for Howard. They all stay away from the neighborhood for things like hanging around it and going to parties, go to parties in the Bronx and Queens, and a few are escorted by their older brothers and fathers to and from home. Then they're at a party in the neighborhood, maybe two months later when their contact with the Saxons says they've dropped the matter and aren't interested in them anymore, lights are out, soft music on, each of them has a girl to neck with, drinking the father's liquor of the girl who's giving the party, when they hear from the street "Hey mama boys in there, come on out." There are about thirty of them, big and little, all in their gang jackets it seems, across the street, in it and on the sidewalk right outside. "Hey, we see ☐ ☐ ☐king through the windows," they yell. "Look, don't be ☐ on out, all we want to do is powwow." They stay put, ☐hat to do, maybe call the police but that'll get the girl ☐h her folks she says. Then the phone rings. "Someone ☐ funny voice wants to talk to you," the girl says, giving Howard ☐ phone. "This is Crazy Louie. We'll let you all alone if I can have ☐ack at you on the street this minute, no matter even if you beat ☐ants off me." "I'm sorry," he says. "I've nothing against you and ☐ fight if my life's at stake and I don't see why anything should be like that now. Anyway, you got to think I'm nuts going into the street alone with you and with all your friends, not that I want to any time." "So I'll tell you what. I'll have them all get away. It'll only be me out here and if you want I'll even have one of my arms tied behind my back. If you don't want to come out because you think I'm a better fighter than you, that should give you the odds." "Listen, I'm sorry for your friend through the glass, but he was picking on me, three to one, so I had to do something. And I heard you use your feet more than your hands, so I'm sure you'll still kick the shit out of me." "Hey, baby, I'm going to dust you up bad, very bad, so why not have it done today?" "No thanks," and he hangs up, tells them what Louie said. One of his friends says "He could be drunk and you might be able to beat him up and then we'll all be off." "You out of your head? Where you think he got his name from? There's no stopping him. He fights like a maniac, butts his head, kicks you everywhere, vomits on you if he has to, pounds your face against concrete till you're half dead. That's what I heard. And those guys use zip guns. Beat up Crazy Louie and they could use it on me." One friend calls his father who he knows has some pretty tough friends over for cards and the men come over in top coats with the collars up to their necks, six of them, mostly big guys except for his friend's father, and each of them keeps his hand in his side coat pocket as if packing a gun, and they say "All right, you kids, we're cops, so you better beat it or we're running the bunch of you in," and the gang takes off. Howard and his friends stay away from the neighborhood for parties and movies and things like that for another month. Then they hear from their contact that Crazy Louie got busted for stomping someone almost to death, some of the older Saxons got drafted into the army, and the rest of them have a gang war goin′ with a gang south of their territory and have sort of lost interes′ them.

Time he shot a man in the heart but always said it was in s′ defense. Came out again when he said to his wife "Is there anyth′ you ever held back from me?" and she said "Plenty of things, wh′ "What were they?" and she said "I don't know—things. Little. Big. All forgotten or unimportant by now and probably not so important or potentially memorable then." "Anything big that you can remember?" and she said "What is it, you want to tell me something big you've kept back from me? Go ahead then." "No, I don't have anything, I'm just making conversation. Because of that movie on the VCR the other night and you fell asleep to—what was it called? Anyway, the woman asks her husband that and I thought it was a good question for conversation starters so thought I'd ask you. Actually, though, now that I think of it there is something I never told you." "So just say so." "It's not so easy. You tell me something first that you've kept back." "I don't want to, or I can't think of anything." "Then I'll keep to myself what I thought of telling you." "As you wish," and she continued eating her salad, sipped some wine, smiled at him over her glass, he didn't know what for. Nor could he make out what the smile could mean by the kind it was, for it was a small tender smile, nothing he right now deserved. "You ever say anything to anyone you particularly regretted saying and which had grave consequences but which you never told me about?" and she said "Maybe once, twice, but it's all gone. Probably with my first husband, maybe a couple of times with you." "Ever steal something as an adult or do something against the law—worse than running a light—you never told me about?" "No." "Something really terrible to the kids, but same thing—where I didn't know?" "No, I don't think so. Screaming, yelling, humiliating them a few times, but I never once even spanked them or smacked their hands." "An affair with someone while we've been married—even a one-night stand or quick afternoon thing?" "Not since we met and I would have told you." "Anyone kiss you at a party or dinner or someplace?" Shook her head. "Then one from the past—not a kiss but a fuck or an affair that you never told me about, all the way back to when you were a kid. Because I think you said you must have told me, as I've done with you with I think all my women and girls or all I could remember up till the last time I told you, about all your guys starting when you were fifteen with number one." "Seventeen. Listen, this is getting to be too much like a grilling. You don't want to tell me what you seem to be aching to, save it for when you do. Some little chickadee you're doing it with now or some time back?— sure, I'd like to know. I think we should always get those things out. But you never tell me and don't give any suspicions that's happened, I won't be curious." "It's not a woman. There's been nobody since we met." "As I've said, same here." "Good, but you've got to be a little curious what's on my mind." "A little but not enough to try and squeeze it out of you or where I'll remember tonight's curiosity tomorrow and want to follow up on it." "You know that fellow I killed just maybe a year before I met you?" "What of him? It's not exactly something I'd forget." "I didn't kill him in self-defense as I said." "You murdered him?" "Not that far, or I don't know what you'd call it.

I was afraid, that after I turned him in, he'd come and kill me when he got out of prison. I didn't know what to do—I had the gun on him—so I thought—the gun I took from him—" "I remember; wrestled it." "I didn't even know if it'd work or there were bullets in it but thought the best thing to keep him from—well you know, because he could surprise me sometime in the future and next time I wouldn't be so lucky—was to kill him." "Wait wait." "Because I didn't think much of his life. I was almost sure he would kill me if I ran when he had the gun on me. He was a freak; I could see it in the way he stood and spoke and his face." "Wait, I mean it, wait. This is hard to take in such a fast lump. Go slower." "All right, from the start. He said he'd kill me if I didn't give him all my money. After he grabbed me from behind, stuck the gun to my head. Kept it there. Right on the street. Then on my neck. Kept it there. Then when he marched me into the park, close in the small of my back so nobody in a car passing would see it I suppose. I gave him all the money I had in the park. He looked at it, ripped the wallet apart for more— all this is nothing new to you but I'm getting to where what happened differently happened—and said there's almost nothing here, 'give me what you're hiding.' I said I'm hiding nothing. He said 'Bullshit you're not.' That's when I thought he's going to kill me for nothing and I better do something quick or I'm dead. So I said—this came to me to say and do it—'Holy shit!' and looked up at the big park wall behind him on the drive and he sort of turned, sort of thought I was faking and turned back to me but by this time I had shifted a bit out of his gun aim and jumped his gun arm to hold the gun up and started wrestling with him for it. But the gun didn't go off accidentally into him when I was wrestling for it. By the way, I saw some people looking over the park wall at us but they just kept looking and then left even though I yelled for help. But I wrestled it away from him, got it, backed up and pointed it and said 'One step and you're dead. I'm gonna kill ya, you fucking bastard, just as you would've killed me, if you come a step closer.' That's when I noticed those people and asked for help and when I thought does it have bullets in it and suppose it doesn't go off? He probably has a knife and he'll kill me with it while I'm trying to bang him over the head with the gun butt. I also thought this because he seemed so casual when I said that about killing him—and you notice those people never came forward to say they saw me pointing the gun at him—and he said 'What're you talking about, man?' and started walking toward me. I yelled 'One step, just one step,' as a threat, but I now see it could have been misinterpreted by him as meaning he's allowed to take only one step toward me. But the gun was no doubt jiggling in my hand but still pointed at him and I wasn't backing up and he suddenly looked scared as a man who thinks he might be shot would and that's when I knew it could go off. Then I didn't know what to do. Something hit me. A thought. Suppose I let him go or turn him in, what then? Turning him in's what he probably thought I would do, and by the way, he'd stopped, meaning stood still, second he looked scared of getting shot, if that's what it was. 'Let me go,' he said, 'you got the gun,' and threw the little money he took from me at me. I let it fall, blow away, didn't take any chances looking at it or to stop it. Maybe that was his plan—I didn't think that then—throw something innocent at me to distract me, and people are always jumping for money, and then he'd grab and kill me on the spot. But I couldn't let him go, first thing. He's a murderer and a thief. Surely he's killed before. Maybe lots before. That's what came out in the police report and newspapers. I thought it then but the papers said he'd been in prison when he was sixteen for killing someone during a robbery and then killing a friend he robbed with in that robbery to guarantee him shutting up. So, two at least that we know of. But he was a kid, did good behavior, model prisoner—graduated high school in prison, the Bible also—so they let him out in about seven years. All in the papers; I didn't know a thing. He was in fact still on parole when he robbed me. You remember, or you don't. And if I turned him in, I thought—even when he was asking me to let him go—he could come out and kill me for putting him in. For what'll he get? This was really all in my

571

head then. One, two years, he'll get—since I didn't know of his murders and being on parole—but short enough time to remember me when he gets out. He was also such a mean tough-looking guy. He looked like a savage. His hair, expression, grin he had when he was robbing me. He smelled and his speech was awful and vulgar and his clothes were so sharp I just knew almost everything about him and his attitudes and such and he pushed me into the park and treated me before I got the gun as if he'd slit my throat as much as he'd tie his shoelaces when it was over. Meaning they meant the same thing to him. He could care less. Maybe shoelaces more because he could trip if they were untied, hampering his escape a little, while me dead on the ground wasn't a worry unless he got caught, and he looked for a while till I got the gun from him like someone who didn't think he could ever get caught. Another reason for hating him, his fucking smugness. He told me 'Don't call the cops, man, don't.' Now we're dealing with only what's new to you, never been said to anyone. 'Just let me go, you keep the gun,' etcetera. And I said 'No, I'm holding you for the cops'—that's what I suddenly decided to do, though how to get them I didn't know or think about just then—and he said 'Come on, they get me for this I could do a long turn. I'm scared of jail. I won't be the same when I get out. I've never been in, this is the first thing I've pulled like this and only because I was desperate, and all my friends tell me prison's hell. For you see, this whole thing with my voice and threats and that gun was an act, man, a big fat act. So please, let's forget it and that will be it between us, you'll be rid of me forever.' When he said that I thought if I turn him in I won't be rid of him forever. I mean, I didn't believe what he was saying now about this the first time, because earlier on he'd convinced me when he talked about killing me. He actually had said—something I must have told you—'You don't turn up more dough than you got here,' meaning my wallet, 'you're going to get killed in your fucking head with this,' waving the gun. 'Bullets, though,' he said, 'in the mouth.' And put it right up to my mouth and then shoved the barrel through my lips and I had to pull up my teeth or he would have broken them with it shoving it in. I remember I gagged it went in so fast and far. And that was the exact moment when I thought he means it, or close to that moment—somewhere around when the gun was going in or was in—and that I've got to get the gun away from him or run. And run, he'll shoot me in the back, then stand over me and shoot me in the head. That's also when—I'm talking now about when I had the gun on him and he tried to con-talk me about being rid of him forever—that I thought his life is nothing to me, nothing. That I hate his guts and face. That I should even kill him because he's such a horror and threat. That then I'll be rid of him forever. That his life is worthless, useless, by anybody's standards. More than that, he'll kill others when he gets out and probably look for me to kill and besides that he still might be able to trick me now, so sooner I kill him the better. For these guys are full of tricks, I thought. And he's fast and clever, and I was strong but no kid, and he'll do something very soon to get the gun from me before I can yell for people up on the drive, if anybody who hears even answers me, to get the cops down or before I can get him up the park steps to the drive and then hold him there for the police. And then with the gun back on him he'll kill me sure as I was standing there, nothing I'd say making a bit of difference to him. So, a little jumbled up these thoughts—then, and the way I'm now trying to convey them—but around then when I thought I had to kill him to save my life. One way or the other—I'm repeating myself a lot now, but I want to make sure I get you to understand what was going on in me then—one way or the other, now or a year or two from now, he was going to trick me and kill me, for that at that moment was what I was absolutely sure of. That the chances of him doing that there before I could get him to the cops were probably a lot better than the chances of my getting him to the cops, so I shot him. Put the gun right up to his chest where I thought his heart was—he made no move for it but looked no more frightened, as if he didn't sense what I was going to do—and pulled the trigger twice. I was glad when I heard it go off. Relieved because it went off and had to have hit him badly and probably killed him. Pulled it twice just to make sure he wouldn't get just slightly wounded. He flew away with the first shot but the second got him too. But you don't want to hear the details. I didn't want to do it into his brains where I knew I could kill him or seriously disable him because the whole head up there is just about brains so it's not as if I would have missed them, but I didn't want brains shooting out. I thought that then. Later I was glad where I'd shot him because the other way would have been difficult explaining to the police. Anyway, I wanted to tell you, to get it out." Pause, she drank, he drank, she kept looking at him, then said "That it?" "That's it. I'm sure there's more, but that's it." "Whew, that's some story," pouring them both more wine. "I don't mean to sound light or trifling about it, or look it, even, pouring this wine, but I don't know what to say. Maybe what I don't understand is why you chose to tell me it now. It's almost as if it can't be true. You've told me everything about your life, or essentially so, so something of it would have come out by now." "No, it's for real. Maybe none of it came out because when I want to I'm good at being a great fake. And I never told you before because, well, when I met you, first years of our marriage and so forth—I thought you'd be afraid of me if I told you. That if I had this in me, what else like that could he possibly do? That sort of thing. I mean, you've seen my anger before. Rages sometimes, throwing things, screaming at the kids, kicking doors—and that you'd remember the killing story and think maybe he's capable of something much worse than rage. That the rage could lead to something not like a killing but a beating. That I could start smacking out at people—you, the kids. Anyway, some instinct in me you'd be scared of. Impulse, I mean. Then I forgot about it for years or a couple of times thought of it but it was the wrong moment to tell such a thing and then I saw this stupid movie you fell asleep to and the question thing came up and then from that to this and that I'd never told you, never told anyone, never wrote about it, never did anything with it except maybe hid it in some things and works I did, and that a long enough time had passed where I could tell you. So that's my big secret. It's all true. The whole thing stuck to me clearly and you can well understand why it would. Maybe talking and writing about it gets rid of it, and since I never did either, but there it is." "I've nothing comparable to it," she said. "You don't have to. That was just a lead-in on my part, that movie question thing; or something that led to my disclosing it, anyway." "Nothing. I slept with an old boyfriend—the architect—a few weeks after I first met you, and that's my big secret. I've never told you, right?" "No." "That's all I've ever held back to you of that magnitude, small as it is. I didn't think it'd do any good telling you so early in our relationship, since I didn't know you that well and so didn't know how you'd take it—jealousy, for instance. Just telling me to get lost forever, which I didn't want you to do but thought you were capable of saying. And then I never thought it worth mentioning after awhile or what would be the use of telling it? or just forgot it, mostly." "Where was I when you were sleeping with him?" "It was once, and you mean literally? I don't know. Home, maybe. Yours. But he called up—I forget his name..." "Bill. Bill Williams. I remember the name because of the double Bill and that there was a popular deejay by that name when I was a young man. And when I was a boy, also an actor whom I liked—curly blond hair, nice face, the sailor look at the time, and that your Bill used to call you up for the first few years I knew you. 'Who is it?' 'Bill.' 'Who is it?' 'Bill.' And of course also the poet though he, like the deejay, but not the actor, used a middle initial and kept to William." "Anyway, this Bill was the only time and the only one once I started seeing you. In fact—OK, this just came—you and I had broken up for a few weeks and it was a number of months, I believe, after we'd first met. I thought we were completely through. And he called, wanted to go out for dinner; I thought why not? After, he wanted to come home with me for a coffee or drink; I thought why not? though most likely had some idea what would happen. Then I thought why not when he wanted to go to bed with me after we'd had some brandy, maybe too much brandy, though that wasn't the fault. He'd always been a good lover and you weren't part of my life any longer, but that was it; once, done. The next day or that night he left and he called again—you and I were still through for good—and I told him I was sick—I was, I think. And then you and I got together again, I forget how but we did—" "One of us called. Something about a book. You had one of mine or I had one of yours—" "Something though. And so the next time he called after that, and the next and the next and so on, as you said, I had to tell him we were together again and then deeply involved and then that I was marrying you and I couldn't see him for dinner. For tea, perhaps, if he wanted, and I think he said he'd think about it but didn't call back. And then even when I was pregnant the first time, while he probably thought that by then our marriage had busted up or was giving that idea a chance." "Tell me, are you making all this up to have something—a big secret—to tell me to sort of take some of the awfulness off what I said? In other words, for me?" "No. And that was the end of him. But are you making up about killing that man the way you say you did to have something interesting to say to me?" "No, swear it." "Or to get a big secret out of me, which if it was so I must have disappointed you with." "No again; what a thing to say." "Then are you sure you didn't simply imagine it happening that way but after all these years have come to believe it? That the gun really did go off accidentally while you were tussling for it?" "No. I shot him in the heart intentionally or intentionally where I thought it was. I knew I was close to it and I happened to have been right." "What'd the police say about shooting him twice? For once would have been enough, it seems." "The police? Nothing. They seemed to immediately believe me. Patted my shoulder consolingly till they saw I didn't need it, but mostly dealt with the body. Then some routine questioning at the police station—paperwork, formality, they even told me so, though maybe that was a ploy, though I don't think so—and I was out in an hour and even offered a car escort home. And later at this inquest the city set up, it wasn't a big deal either. They believed I squeezed the trigger twice because my finger was on it. In other words, that

I did it that way instead of once for no other reason than that I did it. Impulse, instinct. That it wasn't unfair or unusual or unjustified force or whatever the legal term is when you have a district attorney's inquiry into it. 'Improper defense'? A man's scared to death, his life's at stake, so in that state—and of course I made them convinced that was the case and said nothing about knowing where his heart was. I told them I didn't know how many times I pulled the trigger. I think I could have emptied the clip into him, if there were more bullets in it—I didn't check and never found out but at the time I was aware if I pulled it three times I might be in serious trouble—and they still would have bought it. In other words, they knew the guy was a killer and they wanted me to get off." "Let me ask you this. You think the man, when he got out of prison, would have tried to kill you, if let's say you had got him to the police and the city had been able to send him to prison for holding you up?" "At the time, yes. Now, I don't think so. I doubt he would have remembered my face after so long. Because he would have had to be there, with his record, a couple of years, maybe a few. Though it was in the newspapers, my address and although no photos, though some were snapped of me when I left the inquest, so maybe he could have found me out that way. Sure he could have. But I doubt, judging by his speech and looks, he would have been smart enough to know how to go about it or remembered where he'd put the news articles when he went in. Then again, a relative or friend of his might have kept the articles—for some reason, such as thinking he was a celebrity because he was in the papers, cut them out and he got hold of them when he got out and there it was, my name and address. But it wouldn't have made the papers if I hadn't killed him. But if it had—after all, ordinary man stops killer from killing him and holds him for the police with the killer's gun, they could have said. That doesn't happen too often and especially in a fairly nice Manhattan neighborhood and everybody loves it when the good guy, we'll call me for this supposition, wins. But by then, if it had made the papers and he hadn't died and he'd got a copy of it or saved it himself, I had met you and moved into your place about two years after the incident, so he might not have been able to trace me. The post office doesn't forward mail after a year, and to tell you the truth I wouldn't have asked them to for even a day and also would have kept my name out of the phone book forever." "What's the mail got to do with it?" "He could have come looking for me and not finding me at my old address, asked the mailman where I moved to. They're not supposed to, of course, but the killer could have conned him into giving it. 'I owe him a hundred bucks.' 'He said he wants to sublet my girlfriend's apartment.' " "So the mailman would say 'Write him, it'll be forwarded.' " "And he could say 'It has to be done today. By tomorrow I'll have blown the cash,' or 'The apartment will have been rented.' Anyway, if he had come for me, then without knowing it I might have been protecting you too by killing him. He might have only been out for me but you were with me so he killed us both. Witnesses; get rid of them. And let's face it, he was a killer, so in one more time, they could throw away the key, and what was one more life to him? Ah, maybe I shot him because I wanted to shoot someone or even kill someone most of my life and knew I could get away doing it to him. Perfect opportunity; gun, which I never had, and easiest way to kill someone, right? And ideal victim, someone just about everyone wants killed. No, that's not it. Anybody I wanted to kill I've done it same way most people do, in my head." "What'd it feel like after you shot him? I mean, were you disgusted, horrified? I've never asked you, and as long as we're on it." "I just looked at him and thought 'Good, he's dead, he won't bother me anymore, the sonofabitch, but now I've got to start concocting a good case for myself. Also, there was some ecstasy to it. I stopped some filthy creep from threatening me and probably killing me when he had the jump on me and here I am to say it—'Unbelievable!' I screamed. One word, and twirled around once with my hands in the air like this, like some Hasidic nut dancing, and then yelled 'Help, police,' but by this time some people were already looking over the park wall and said 'Hey, what's going on?' And then I thought 'Holy shit, they saw me spinning around, I'll have to give some excuse for that too.' So I brought it up first to the police and said I was dizzy after I shot the man, didn't know where I was, in some crazy mental state from what happened, and they bought that too. But that's enough, right?" "You don't want to go on? I could understand that." "There's nothing more really to say. I've brought you up to where you know the rest." "Most of what you told me in the past, if I could be honest, I forget, but all right. The police came, I remember that, and then the questions there and at the precinct, which you mentioned before—all right." "So what do you think?" "About you in all this? It was so long ago. What's there to say? You might have been justified. Maybe there's no justification in killing someone cold-bloodedly like that. But you might have been in such fear and panic for your life after being so menaced by him that you didn't know what you were doing so you shot him, maybe to stop him from attacking you with what you thought might be another gun or a knife he had hidden. Did you think of that?" "Sure. I'm almost sure I said so. That he'd trick me somehow. But no, I was perfectly rational, or just rational about it, all the time. I thought I might get killed during the robbery but once I got the gun away from him—" "It's amazing how you were able to do that. Just having done it successfully must have put you—or could have—into some strange state of mind. Power. The superhumanness of it. I mean, people are often having fantasies about it, but who actually does it? The adrenalin must have been overflowing. So much so—" "I suppose. That I don't remember so I can't say. Anyway, where was I?" "I don't know—where, do you mean on the street?" "And it's getting a little tiresome as a subject, don't you think?" "It is a bit much, of course, but if you feel you want to go on with it . . ." "Nah, let's forget it for now and maybe forever. I've told it all. Now maybe it can start dropping away from me; I wouldn't mind. Finished?" and he pointed to her plate. "I'll take them in." "No, I'm getting up," and stacked their plates, put the silver and wine glasses on them and brought them into the kitchen and put them in the sink. He finished her wine and his, though didn't know whose glass was which, and went back into the dining room. She was still at the table, looking at him as if she didn't know what to think. "Did I take your wine too soon?" he said. "No, I was done with it; you finish it." "Yeah, I might." "As long as you're up and dealing with the dishes, mind if I just sit? The whole thing—what you did, went through that night, all that stuff—is really coming to me. It's horrible. People shouldn't have to go through such things but they do, right?" "For sure," and took the bowls and platter and bottle of wine, brought them into the kitchen, poured another glass. "If you want to know what I'm doing—did you hear that pouring sound?" "No, what?" she said. "I was in some other thought." "Well if you want to know what I'm doing now—I'm drinking some more wine, after finishing both of ours, to sort of obliterate—help make disappear faster and maybe for the rest of the night if I'm lucky—the memory of what I did." "Do. It's what I would. You deserve it."

In California, at a party, lots of pot's smoked and wine drank, he gets tired and says he'd like to go, Lulu says she'd like to stay, "All right, stay if you can get a ride back but if not, I really have to go; I can barely stand up." "Will you be able to drive?" and he says "Fine, if I go in the next ten minutes," so she asks around, gets a ride back with Rust, "Oh that guy, Mr. Horns. He'll probably want to jump you two minutes into the ride," and she says "Don't be a dopey; be thankful he's giving me a lift or I'd bug you all evening for taking me away," and they kiss good-bye and he drives home, pays the babysitter. He's asleep, wakes up, pats her side of the bed, maybe she's in the bathroom, falls asleep, wakes up an hour later, walks through the house thinking maybe she started reading on the couch and fell asleep, goes into her son's room to see he's OK, "Mommy," Carl says without waking up when Howard lifts his foot off the floor and puts it under the covers, goes back to sleep, is jostled out of it sometime later and she says "Howard? Listen, Rust and I are in the living room," and he says "What time is it?" and she says "Late, getting to morning, and you were right, we are sort of making it—do you mind my telling you this?" and he says "I predicted it, right? You shared one of his fat joints, got hot when he started talking about his money and deals, so nothing's stopping you two. That fucking guy; someone ought to do it to his wife and see how he feels. Anyway, what do you want from me? I'm tired. You want to do it?— you always did with him—do it, the hell with you," and he turns his back to her, thinks what is he doing here? she's in her bathrobe? she probably already fucked him; there's nothing to them anymore and it's only her kid keeping him here which is silly, fucking stupid, and she says "Don't go to sleep, and don't get so angry. All we've been doing is kissing, feeling each other a little and now he wants to ball me and I said I wouldn't while you were in the next room but would if you joined in with us. So would you want to? Rust said he'd go for it if it's the only way he can ball me, so long as he doesn't have to stick his pecker in your ass—that's the way he put it—or do anything with his mouth to you. For I'd love to make it with both of you in the same bed, and I sure don't want it with him on that clunky couch or floor out there. And you mentioned it with me and another woman if we found one we both agreed to, so why not the other way with me?" "Carl," and she says "He's dead to the world, and we'll lock our door just in case he gets up." "No lock," and she says "A chair up against it," and he says "That never works. One push and it falls over." "Up tight under the knob, which I'm sure Rust can do if you can't. And if Carl asks why we locked it, we'll say we were having an all night bull session, something he's used to and the chair was where one of us was sitting. Or at worst, not that I like carrying it this far, we were all getting high and didn't want him to get any of the smoke. But he's not getting up so long as we don't rant and scream during it." "All right, all right, but no homosexual stuff whatsoever—not even handholding. It's you and me and you and him and that's it, even if I think I might puke halfway through it." "Hey listen, I thought I was nice including you in. But if you don't want, I can always go to a motel with him if you have no crucial objections and don't mind looking after Carl," and he says "It's OK, you want it and I'd like to get laid too." "Great," and she goes, comes back with Rust. He's only in his briefs and is holding the rest of his clothes. "Hi," Howard says, "Hi," Rust says; "where should I put these?" and she says "On the floor or the chair, or even in the closet—we've plenty of hangers," and he says "No, I'm not that fussy," and puts the clothes in a neat pile on the chair, shoes on the floor underneath it. "Wait, we need the chair for the door, don't we?" and puts his clothes on the dresser, shoes underneath it, wedges the chair under the doorknob several times till the door won't budge. "Now what?" and she says "Get in bed, you funny guy, ladies in the middle," and takes off her bathrobe, Rust his briefs, and they get on the bed, Howard still under the covers. They all lie back, look at one another, smile, Rust says "Anyone care for a quick toke?—it's in my pants," and she says "Too much of a fuss." "So why don't you two start?" Howard says, "since you were doing it," and she says "You're such a joke," and kisses his mouth and turns over and kisses Rust and strokes his penis and he puts his hand between her legs. After a minute Howard says "So am I supposed to be doing anything while this is happening?" and without looking she reaches her other arm over, feels around the sheet till she grabs his penis through it. "Jesus, you're stiff," and Rust says "Is he? I feel plenty sexy too but can't get my bloody rutter up yet." "It's probably the situation," Howard says. "This room and our bed and that I'm used to her, but I'd think if it was the first time with her you'd get something going. Don't worry, it'll come." "If it doesn't I'm going to feel awfully stupid," and she says "I think I can fix it," and shakes it, jerks it, flutters it, rolls it between two hands, blows on it and says "Up, funny fellow, up—because when I squeeze it, you know, it looks like it's got a helmet on," but nothing happens. "Maybe if you sucked it," and she says "I don't want to, not with Howard in the same bed. Either of you wants to give me head, that'd be okay." "I'll do that," Rust says, "I love your bush, though I won't guarantee it'll help me. It should though, right? Or what if you did it to Howard and I'll watch? It'll be nothing strange for you and then I'll go down on you and we'll see where to take it from there," and Howard says "I'm sick of this shit, let's just get it over with," and pulls her down on her back, she says "Whacha doing, sweetie?" gets on top and she says "We're not doing that yet—hey, hey, man, too fast," but he holds her down while she tries to get up, forces her legs open, sticks it in and in a few seconds comes. "You rat, that wasn't nice," pushing him off her and he turns his back to them, stiffens his body for expects her to hit him with her fists or kick him, says "Go on, go on, do it any way you like with him now, I'm turning in," and Rust says "I better split, he's mad as hell, next thing he'll be beating on me," and gets off the bed—"I'm not beating on anybody, you schmuck"—and starts dressing. "Hey wait, Rust," she says, "—hey Howard! Apologize, say something to him or he'll think you're creepier than you showed. —Screw him, I'll see you to the door," and they leave the room, Rust going out in his socks or bare feet so he's probably carrying his shoes. Howard shuts the light, faces the wall, hears the front door open, then close in a few minutes and she comes back and turns on the overhead light. "He wanted me to take a drive with him—do it on the beach if we have to—and I would have but didn't want to come back for my clothes and have to explain things to you. You're really something. A bastard. You had to show off your dick and your overquick comes. You'll be lucky if he looks you in the eye again. Anyone could have done what you did. Squirt squirt, you're finished—not a hint of finesse or sensibility or any originality to it. I'll never do it with another woman and you, for I know you'll only use it to get your kicks watching us screwing and then lay her and humiliate me. Hey, come on, you hear me— you're not sleeping. Well jerk yourself off for the next week, for I'm sure not getting in bed with you," and she leaves the room, probably for the top of Carl's bunkbed. He tells himself even if what she said might have something to it, he's got to get out of here; it's no stinking good and will never improve.

In California, doctor friend calls and says would he like being one of the subjects in a series of medical experiments of various psychoactive drugs at the hospital he works at? Twenty dollars a session, once a month for four months and each time a different drug. Sure, he says. "Maybe you want to talk it over with Lu first?" "Nah, sounds interesting and I can use the extra money and it fits in perfectly with my day-off schedule at the store." He tells Lulu what he'll be doing the next four first Mondays of the month and she says don't. "It could mess up your head." "What're you talking? It should be fun, the money's good, and I've for a long time wanted to see the inner doings of a medical research situation. And all they'll be testing is my breathing, blood, motor control and anesthetic use of the drugs too with a few pinpricks to my toes, and one other thing, but all safe and clear and at the V.A. hospital on the ridge, so not that far." Gets up early for it, has half a bagel and coffee though was told not to even rinse his mouth after twelve last night, drives there. His friend comes into the room while he's having blood taken out of his arm and says "I won't be around for it but you're in very capable hands. If there's any trouble, which nobody's expecting, they'll know how to bring you right down, and results here will be in a paper read by scientists of several disciplines around the world." They prick his buttocks and feet, have him squeeze some instruments with his hands, run in place, breathe through an oxygen mask for a few minutes, give him a cardiogram and put him on some other monitoring machines. Then they give him the drug in liquid form in a water glass. He asks what it is and is told it's synthetically made, this one from a lab in France, but that's all they're allowed to tell him except that it's never been used in research on humans before or available on the street. "How'd the animals take it?" and the aide says "No adverse reactions in any kind of way." He gets high in a very short time. The aide says "Feeling different yet?" and he says "You bet, I'm flying," and the aide says "Try to hold down the images and reports of them while we take more blood out of you," and he says "I doubt I can take a needle of that size this moment." "It isn't that long," and shows it to him. "Three inches, and not all of it goes in you, and then only in the fleshier less sensitive part of the arm," and he says "It looks about a foot long and a circumference of a hotdog and I can see all its barbs. One, two...five of them. That thing will rip through my vein and cause a bloodbath." "Howard, you're hallucinating a little. Could a hand be more than nine inches long? and look at the needle in comparison to mine. But we're not so naive where we don't expect some overreactiveness of the mind too, so let's put you through a few of the less anxiety-causing tests and then go back to the blood one when you calm down." The aide puts his hand behind Howard's foot and says "Did you feel that?" and he says "No, what?" and the aide says "That's because I didn't do anything. You're alert, not fooling around with us, good. Some subjects though—it's all high, getting stoned, nothing else, as if they're only here to enjoy themselves and the staff are their pushers." Then the aide jabs Howard's foot with something sharp, holds up a pin while Howard's screaming and says "Took it out of my new shirt this morning, though sterilized it of course. Wasn't that bad, admit it," and he says "It was like you poked me with a knife. I don't want anything like that again either." "Howard, please don't be difficult, *please*. You didn't strike me as a fake when you came in and I still don't think you are. But there are tests to be done, you contracted to do them, so begin accepting that. Better they be done without warning you again, correct? because then you'll even get more anxious." "No no, you're right, I'll try. But just go easy on me for a while." "Will do," and he shakes Howard's hand. Another cardiogram, some things for his hands to squeeze and feet to push, couple of reflex tests and then the aide puts the oxygen mask on him and tells him to relax and breathe normally. After a minute he feels he's running out of air and points to the mask and the aide nods and looks away and Howard takes it off. "You sure there's anything in there?" and the aide says "I'm sure; now on, I'm afraid; we spoke about this," and looks tough and puts it back on Howard roughly. He wants to do what he's being paid to and he doesn't want to do anything that will look bad for his friend, but after about thirty seconds he feels he's being smothered and takes the mask off. "I'm sorry; even if your saying the mask's doing the opposite of suffocating me, the point is I feel like I am, so you should be satisfied with that part of your research." "It's not part of it. We don't care what's in your head. What the machine's monitoring of your breathing is part of the research, but it's not monitoring you're short of breath. But OK, you're uncomfortable, we don't want you to be that, so we'll put this off. But not forever, Howard. We have a well-populated lab ready and waiting for your samples and if we don't give them more readings and blood and urine—" "Urine I'll give you plenty of. In fact I have to pee." "I don't want your urine now. But they'll be getting paid a whole day for nothing. You know what that costs? And do you know we only have so much government funding for this research? And do you know the government's been penny-pinching on this kind of research for the last three years because they think guys like you will only want to take advantage of the free drugs? So what are we going to do now, Howard, what in goddamn's name are we going to do?" "I don't know." "One thing we're not going to do is get tough with you. But also don't give us any further troubles with these goddamn tests." "You just did get tough. You threatened me." "I threatened you?" "You did, in words, mannerisms and voice." "I threatened him?" and he turns around to his assistant. "I didn't see you did," the assistant says. "I didn't, that's why you didn't see. Howard's off on a hallucinatory bender and we're tired of hallucinations. They're boring, they're stupid, they're of no use." "You're still threatening me with your voice and words and I'll have to take my ass out of here if you do it again. I didn't volunteer here to get roughed up by you." "I'll tell you why you volunteered, Howard—want it straight? It wasn't for the twenty bucks every month. No, I won't tell you, I'll keep my big trap shut, because you shouldn't be getting more anxious by what I say. So I apologize to you, Howard, sincerely and without equivocation, and Miss Doris, our research assistant today, is my witness I did. Now please now, go along with us on these tests. Trust me that your fears are all in your head, both of me and the pain and suffocating and such, and what's in your head can be easily removed by not thinking of it, OK?" "I'm sorry but I can't, except for the push-pull stuff with the hands and urine if you want and cardiograms and easier things like that." "Perhaps to reassure you more let me get the doctor whose research this is, busy as he is and disturbing as this interruption might be to him, but let me get him, Howard," and he goes, comes back with the doctor. "What is it, Mr. Tetch, something bothering you about all this?" the doctor says. "That's natural; so go along with it," and he pats Howard's leg and turns to go. "Wait. I was saying to him— Kennedy—that I can't go along with any of the tests but the stress and reflex and maybe a little jab or two with the pin on my feet, but the blood and oxygen are too much for me. If it's the drug that's doing it, what can I say? But you're a scientist involved in these things, so you should know that if it feels that real to me—" "Do you know who you are telling his business to?" the aide says. "One of the foremost psychopharmacologists in the country and probably the premier researcher of psychoactive drugs on this continent." "Shut up, you," the doctor says and elbows the aide in the ribs so hard he grabs the part hit, winces, bites his teeth. "That's it, I'm done here—not even push-pulling the squeeze things," Howard says. "You guys are going crazy over this. Where are my shoes? Where's the locker I put my things in?" "I can get them for him," Doris says. "Don't you get anything for him," the aide says. "If you think you're leaving, Howard—" "I'm leaving, all right. Next thing who knows what the two of you will cook up for me." "Listen, my friend," the doctor says, "I will have none of this childish nonsense. Never has an experimentee acted like this with me. Do what you agreed to and don't make us think you signed on only for the drugs." "That's exactly what I told him before, Doctor," the aide says. "I am talking. Do I need you to comment? You got us into this by letting him renege on this and that so much till he thought he was conducting the experiment, so be quiet and let me speak. —Now, my friend, if you won't do all the tests we've scheduled you for, we can't leave you this way, can we?" "Get me Dr. Meyer. I want him down here on this." "Dr. Meyer is an anesthesiologist, not in this wing, and busy in other things all morning. I believe he told you, but you are high, so perhaps you can't remember. But I was saying I'll suspend all your tests, close down my lab for the day and cause us a thousand dollars in wasted expenditures and wages, but we will have to bring you back to earth from what to you is only a big trip. The fastest way, since I don't want to endanger your life with more drugs for that, is to have my associates wrap you in plastic and stick you in a tub of ice. It's that or your consent to continue the tests after, let's say, a ten-minute break—no more." "Let me think. Way you put it, probably best thing is to go along with you, but let me think," while he's thinking he's got to get out of here, right now and in his hospital gown and bare feet if he has to. "Just leave me alone for those ten minutes till I can try to cool myself down." "I can agree to that," the doctor says, and they all go. He waits a minute, looks out the room, no one's around, very quietly gets his clothes and book out of the locker and puts the clothes on in the room, then on all fours crawls down the corridor, past the room they're sitting in talking, stands and goes upstairs. The guard at the door says "Your pass to get out." Gave it to the aide when he came in. "Yes, my pass. It's. . .let me see," patting his pants pockets, then jumps the turnstile and runs out the door. The guard yells; Howard doesn't know if he's chasing him. His car's parked in a hospital lot about a quarter mile away, up a hill, but he thinks he can make it never letting up speed. He's fast, guard's heavy, probably slow. "Hey, Howard, come on back," someone shouts. He looks back on the run. Two men in white doctor or lab coats, neither looks like the aide or doctor from this distance, running after him, but they'll never get to him by the time he reaches the car but might by the time he starts the car and drives off. He gets to the car. Didn't lock it because he can't and he jumps in, keys in this pocket, no this pocket, oh Christ the keys and wallet and pen are in a bag in a safe in the hospital, has a spare ignition key taped in the coils somewhere in the driver's seat, fingers around from underneath, pulls it out, tears the tape off, puts the key in, won't start. "Don't do this to me," he says, "don't. Please God, get it moving." Men getting closer. Forty feet. Other about ten feet behind the first. Never saw them before. Not lab coats but one in a white sweater, other in a pink shirt. Car starts up. Pink Shirt jumps on the hood, rolls off it when the car moves. "Fuck you, you stupid putz," Howard yells, not stopping. "Wanna get killed for this, get killed." White Sweater stands to the side of the road, shouts "My friend's hurt bad, sir. Help me get him back to the hospital in your car, he seems unconscious," and Howard shouts "Bullshit, and tough shit," and keeps driving. In the rear-view he sees Pink Shirt standing up, brushing himself off, White Sweater going to him. "Yiippee-hoo-ha!" he says when he's out of the hospital grounds, "you ain't gonna ice no super city kid, you hicks," and slaps the dashboard and punches his palm and then grabs the wheel again when the car suddenly swerves. Steady, drive carefully, watch out for cops, he tells himself, you're still zonked. Gets home. Lulu's outside, says "The hospital called just before, wanted to know if you were back. I said 'So soon?' —Boy, are you ever high; I can see by your eyes." "You can? I escaped from them. They wanted to dunk me upside down in ice water when I wouldn't go along with their smothering and bleeding me to death." Tells what happened. She says "They want you to come back right away. They'll even come and drive you if I can't, as they don't want you behind a wheel and they can't have you running around loose." "Never going back, except maybe for my wallet and keys and pen in a few weeks," and falls to the ground, sticks his nose in the flower bed she was weeding. "Ah, flowers, how I missed them." "You, the original brick and block man? Their shit's nothing new." He grabs a couple of loquats off the tree in the front yard, rips off the outer layer of one and says "How come we never eat these?" and bites into it. "Fyeh, it's sour," and she says "People only snitch them off the lawn for jellies and jams, stupid." Carl comes out. "What's he doing? He's supposed to be in school. I'm feeling so good I thought we could have a little morning sex." "He only goes afternoons, don't you remember? You should take a shower and just go to sleep. You might think everything's beautiful and lovey-smoothy, but you look and smell disgusting and are in terrible shape."

Frog

Phone rings. "If it's the hospital," he yells to Carl who's running inside to get it, "tell them to stick it." "Shush," she says. "Don't teach him ugly manners and words." Carl yells out "It's Alan." Alan says "Let me get you and bring you back. I promise I'll stay with you and they say no more tests. All they want is you to be here till the drug wears off, as they don't want you doing anything irrational in your condition and losing them their Public Health funds." "Tell those sadists if they don't let me stay here till I come down I'm going to rob a bank and blame it on the drug they gave me." "I'll tell. But I should have known better with you. You guys will do anything to have another dramatic experience recorded or just a great anecdote to tell about your endless battles with the establishment. Just, when you get it all in writing or pour forth about it over some beers, make sure you change my name or at least don't say I'm still your good doctor friend."

They make love the night before and in the morning, while he's looking at her from behind dressing, he gets excited and starts kissing her and she says "Why not?" and they do it. Then they dress, have breakfast, he says he'll call her, and that afternoon someone knocks on the door. It's Chantal, a French au pair girl for friends across the street. "How'd you get in downstairs?" and she says "The door was not locked. I thought it the best way since I heard you tell your lobby bell never works." "Phone, that's how people get me if they want me to come downstairs to unlock the door for them or just for me to come down to go outside. But fine, glad to see you, how are you, what's new, like a cup of coffee?" "Wine if you have; it's my afternoon off from Timothy. It's a very nice place you have here, very poor, very artistic, but I bet you hate when people tell you that." She sits on the bed, which is also his couch, reaches over to the night table or side table for a magazine or book, thumbs through the magazine, "This one we don't have in French—no fun for no advertisements," drinks her wine, eats the crackers and cheese and apple slices he puts on a plate for her, yawns, puts the glass down, her arms up, he thinks for him because of the way she smiles at him now and he says "Tell me, and if I'm being off-base, tell me that too—" "What

590

is this 'off-base'? I love your expressions; all of New York's." "Off-base, is off-base. I'm very bad at definitions, I just know words. 'Improper'? 'Not good behavior'? So I hope I'm not being that way, but did you come here to make love?" "I never did it with you, isn't that right? I know I kissed you once, but I could be wrong in that too." "In the Jankwitz's kitchen. I went to the fridge for a beer and you were there and we talked about wine, I think, and I don't know, I kissed you or we just kissed." "And we didn't make love? Why do I think we could have made that? Sometimes I get so wiped I don't know what I before that did." "No, we didn't. I know I thought of asking you out but didn't know how to go about it, since you worked for my friends." "You telephone me there and say would I mind to go to a museum. Do you want to start making love now? Thing is, I only have an hour more and I could use it to take off pressure from work with Timothy all day, and because I would want to with you." While they're making love she says "You smell like you have another woman on you or else you wear perfume. But a woman's, not a man's. I know those things." "I don't have either on me. I don't know what it could be, since I don't use aftershave lotion either and I'm afraid I haven't even shaved yet today." "That's OK. But you should always wash if you make love with one woman and then another." "All right; a woman slept the night here. Then you came by, I'm glad you did but didn't know you would, so I didn't have time to wash." "You could have done so in the bathroom while I took off my clothes here. Or in the kitchen when I went to the bathroom to put in my disc." "What's the difference. We're doing it already. But if it makes you happy. . ." "I'm happy with you, yes, very, but I'd be more happy if you would wash. Else, it would interfere in my mind and I don't want that now. I want all the pressure off. I will say that the perfume's nice but not the smell, so this woman must have good taste." "*Touché*," he says. She doesn't smile. "Hey, that's French. Maybe that's not a language you understand." "That's silly. It doesn't make you attractive. Go." He goes, washes his whole body with a washrag, the genitals and face a second time, comes back and they finish making love. "I still have most of an hour and I can be fifteen minutes late," she says. "Want to go to the park to walk, or have a demitasse on the street?" "Next time. I have to get some work done now." She leaves and he goes back to work. At around six he thinks he'd like to make love to three women in one day. He's never done that. Two's the most, which he's done a couple of times. He calls some women he's slept with. One says "You're horny, right?" "No, honestly, why do you say that?" "You only call when you're horny. I don't mind when I feel that way also, with you or anyone else I've had sex with, or even when the call suddenly springs that feeling on me, but not tonight." "I only want to go to a movie. What happens after, if anything else like that does—" but she says she's in a hurry and hangs up. Another woman says she'd love to meet him but she's busy with something. "Tomorrow?" "Tomorrow I'm tied up; make it tonight." "I'm free the day after tomorrow," she says. "I'm not sure what I'll be doing then. I know I wrote something down about it, an appointment of some kind but I forget what time. Let me get back to you." "That's not nice. Why'd you call if you really don't want to make plans?" One doesn't answer; another has an answering machine. He says "If you get in before nine or ten and want to meet, call me. I could cab down or you could cab here and I'll reimburse you for the fare. Or we can meet at a bar near you. But call. It's Thursday, October 16th, by the way." Then he remembers someone he met at a book party a few weeks ago. He wasn't attracted to her but she was to him. Started a conversation with him, gave him her number though he didn't ask for it. "In case you want to phone me. I'd be interested." "Thanks, I will," but didn't think he would. He forgets where he put the number, remembers her last name, looks up several spellings of it in the phone book and calls and she says she's busy tonight. He says "What about after if it's not too late?" "I might be able to get free. It's only dinner, and he's not someone I'm especially involved with; more like just a good friend who'd probably even understand." "Can you meet me by nine-thirty, ten?" "I think I can," and gives him the name and location of a bar in her neighborhood. She calls when he's getting ready to go and says "I'm glad I caught you. I won't be free till around twelve or so, will that be too late for you?" "Too late. If I wait around I'll probably feel like going to sleep by then. Sure you can't make it sooner? I was already showered and dressed and set to leave." "That's almost the earliest. We only had a snack instead of dinner and then went to a play. That's where I'm calling from. And after it he says we have a little dinner party to go to and then there's the getting rid of him, since I think he now thinks he's more than just a friend." "Skip the party. Get a headache or say you've work to do tomorrow. I don't know what kind since I don't know what you do, but it's got to be something." "I told you at that party. I'm a book designer. The one in fact you went to the party for." "Great. There's plenty of work to be done there. And then let's say we meet at your place at eleven." "That's cutting it pretty tight, since I might not get a taxi so fast, but I'll try to make it. I'll say the play's longer than I expected, even if I'm not sure how long it'll be. There's another act but it has twice as many scenes. Maybe we should meet this weekend. I actually do have to be at work around ten tomorrow." "No, we started it for tonight, let's keep it. Eleven-fifteen, we'll say. And I don't have to stay long. We're just meeting." He's at her building at eleven, thinking maybe she got home earlier than she thought she could. Rings her bell, no answer. Then stands in front of her building, feels conspicuous waiting there so walks around the block and rings her bell again. No answer. Waits outside, thinks maybe she came back when he was walking around the block but was in the shower just before and didn't hear him ringing. Rings her bell, no answer. Walks around her block, a cab's pulling up just as he steps down into her vestibule to ring again. She and a man are in it. It's almost 11:40. She gets out. What if the man does? He'll leave the building and continue walking and then look from a little distance away to see if the man goes in with her or the cab's still there, and if she stops him stepping out or on the street he could say "Elizabeth, what a surprise. I was seeing a friend of mine—thought this was his building but it must be the next—but is this where you live?" Not that but something. Man doesn't get out. She blows him a kiss from the sidewalk, cab speeds off and she runs into the vestibule. "Hi," he says and she jumps; "You scared the hell out of me." "Sorry, I didn't mean to alarm you, but didn't know how to alert you," and puts his hands on her shoulders and kisses her. "Gee, boy, what is with you?—I don't even know you," and laughs. "Let's go up quick," he says. "Sure, you're in a hurry for something?" "You." "Oh my, what passion. What is this, a race for the fastest conquest?" "Nothing like that. Just that I'm also eager to get into your apartment. I got here early; it's cold down here and waiting on the street." They go upstairs. Once in she says "Like a drink, anything to eat?" and he says "No, let's just go to bed, do you mind?" "Wait, we got time, and I'd like a glass of wine and something to nibble on—I'm hungry, what with only an early snack." "No, really, later, bed now, do what the doctor says, please?" and she says "That could be funny; what do you mean? Oh, all right, give me a moment," and he says "Only a moment, if it's to put something in or to pee." "Those are it, but kiss me again, will you?" and he does, hard, tongue squishing around in her mouth and she says "Mm, mm, I like," holds up a finger to mean one minute, he supposes, and ducks into the bathroom. He looks at his watch. 11:53. Her clock. 11:51. He gets undressed, down to his undershorts, rubs his penis through the shorts till it's hard, sticks his hand down and starts jerking it, stops when he hears the bathroom door open, she comes out, "That clock right?" and she says "It's electric, I set it by some radio program time, why?" and he says "Nothing, just that my watch is all off," takes her hand, she says "Bedroom's down there," he says "Let's do it right now on the couch," and takes off her blouse, "Help me out with this," he says, trying to unhook her bra from behind and she says "You know, I don't know if I like this. It might be getting late but you're making me miffed with your rush, whatever-your-name-is," and he fakes a laugh, says "Sorry," starts kissing her, she him, gets her bra off, skirt up, panties down, his shorts off, both of them on the couch, rubs her down there for about thirty seconds and then sticks it in, looks at the clock when her eyes are closed and head's the other way, 11:55, then the last numeral changes to six, pumps harder, she says "Hold it, I'm not even halfway into it yet," comes. "Oh, that was bundles of fun," she says, "bundles—for you. Next time don't forget someone might be doing it with you, maybe even a human being." "I was overexcited, what can I say?" Looks at his watch. "I should have taken this off. I could have scratched you with it and it somehow shouldn't be on someone when he or she's making love." 11:59. Minus the two from her clock and it's 11:57, at the most fifty-eight. Later in bed with the lights out she tucks up behind him and rubs his penis but he knows he won't be able to do it so says "Huh, wha?" and pretends to be asleep. When he wakes up early the next morning he thinks maybe he should tell her why he was in such a rush last night. She's got a good sense of humor, a nice disposition, so she might even look at it as a big laugh. Anyway, he doesn't feel good about the deception and she might even suspect something, so out in the open like that she'd be hurt less. If she gets mad, hell with her then. Won't be any great loss if he doesn't see her again, and he was being honest with her, so what does she want? He could be a fool, he could say, no less than just about anyone, and if she can't accept that, he's sorry but OK. Then his hand, pulling it out from under his leg, lands on her thigh and he strokes it and then glides it along the curve of her behind, starts to get excited and thinks he's never done it four times in twenty-four hours with any one or two women, at least as far as he can remember. Tries to remember. No, never, three times at the most, which he's done with two or three women individually and probably with a couple of women too, one in the morning, another the same evening, but not for a few years. If he'd done it four times in twenty-four hours he'd know—it'd stand out. So he starts fondling her breasts, she seems asleep but then seems to awake, plays with her down there, she grabs his penis, turns over to him, says "Let's just go slowly this time, OK with you?" and he says "Fine," since he has almost two hours before the twenty-four are up, "any way and as much time as you want."

Frog

He's in the cottage typing in their bedroom upstairs, wife out for a run, daughter's downstairs with the new farm set they got her the other day, when a screen door slams, sounds like the one to the porch and he yells "Olivia, what are you doing?" no response, "Olivia, Olivia, you hear me?" nothing, runs downstairs, she's not in the living room, looks out the back windows, not on the porch or the path going down to the water, runs out the other living room door to the front of the house, not there or on the road going up to the town road, runs around the side of the house and looks underneath it, runs around the other side, yells "Olivia, where are you, answer Daddy now," runs up to the porch, looks around from it, runs into the house, upstairs, not there, looks out the windows, yells out one of the bedroom windows "Olivia, Olivia, do you hear Daddy? come right back to the house," listens, runs downstairs, kitchen, out the back way and down the path to the water, stops in front of the boathouse and yells "Olivia, where are you? it's Daddy, yell you're OK," waits, no response, no sounds, runs through the boathouse, looks on the beach, nobody on it, no boats in the water, shouts "Olivia, it's Daddy, are you on the beach somewhere? answer me," runs up the path along the creek to the house, shouts for her, then yells "Denise, where are you? stop your run, come back quick, Olivia's missing, Olivia's lost; Denise, it's Howard, I need you to help me find Olivia," runs back into the house the back way, upstairs, under the bed, behind the clothes on the clothes line, looks out the windows, under her bed in their room, downstairs, bathroom, shower stall, guest room off the porch, back inside the house, behind the couch, where else hasn't he looked? outside the front way, up to the woodshed on the left, around it, in the woods all around the house, calling for her, runs up their road to the town road a quarter mile away, from the town road shouts for Denise and then her, runs back, stops to stare at all the trees past the field, the big boulders and uprooted trees in the field, runs the rest of the way to the house, upstairs to look around and out the windows, downstairs, guest room, under the house, down to the water, runs a little way along the beach both ways, back to the house shouting for her and Denise as he runs, inside, outside, woodshed, cups his hands and yells loud as he can "Olivia, Olivia, yell for Daddy, yell the word *Daddy*, yell for me, sweetheart, yell, yell, yell everything's OK," listens, "Denise, come quick, Olivia's not here, I can't find her, help me to, help me," bangs his head with his fists, screams "O-liv-i-a," runs to the back of the house, that's where he's almost sure he first heard her go out, wonders where to look next, what to do next, it'll start to get dark in a couple of hours, maybe hour and a half, he should call the town clerk, the sheriff's office, the town fire department, they'll know what to do, in minutes they could have dozens of searchers here, but one more run, down to the water, stands in front of the boathouse and looks up and down the beach, runs right up to the water and looks back at the beach and bushes and trees, runs up the main path, around the house and little way up the road, stops, shouts her name, yells for her to yell she's here, if she's in trouble yell *help*, "Yell anything you want, Olivia, anything, but yell, yell," listens, bird sounds, wind in the trees, car from somewhere far off, chain saw even farther away, crickets or some insects, runs farther up the road, sees her walking toward the town road about ten feet from her, he's about a hundred feet away, should he shout? will she know to stop if he doesn't shout? should he run up without shouting and grab her? she might step onto the town road before he gets there, shout and he might scare her onto the road when she was going to stop at the edge of it, he shouts "Olivia, stop. Olivia, stop. Don't move another step." She stops about a foot from the road, turns around and leans her head and body forward as if trying to make out who it is. "It's Daddy, my sweetheart, stay right there. Don't move. Don't do anything, just stand still. Wait till Daddy gets there. In fact, come to me, my darling. Come to me now." She stays there, still looking at him. What the hell's wrong? Why's she doing that? Car shoots past. She turns to it, watches it heading to the point. "Olivia," he yells, walking to her. Don't run or she might get scared she did something wrong and run onto the road. "Olivia, look at Daddy."

She turns to him. "Don't move, sweetheart, stay right there. Just stay there on that spot and don't move." Continues walking to her. Van goes past the other way heading to town. She looks at it, turns to him. He continues walking at a normal pace. "Come to me, sweetheart, Daddy wants to give you something." She doesn't move. He's close enough now to see her face seems scared of him or he doesn't know what. "Anything wrong, sweetheart? Come to Daddy and tell him," holding his arms out as he walks. Gets about twenty feet from her, smiling so she thinks he's in a good mood. She just stares. Rattling sounds coming from the point, which she turns to. Car shoots past pulling an empty boat trailer. He walks fast while she's looking at it, grabs her hand and pulls her down their road a few feet, puts his arms around her and hugs her, then backs up, holds out her hand with one hand and slaps it hard with the other. She starts bawling. He continues holding her with one hand and says "You scared the hell out of me. I slapped you that hard so you'll remember never to run away like that again. Do you hear me?" She's crying. "Do you hear what I'm saying?" Still crying, eyes shut tight. "You hear me. I don't like hitting you but I did it for your own sake. I thought you were lost, that I'd never find you, do you know what that means?" but she's still crying and he says "OK, but I'm not going to pamper you, it's too important that you remember the bad you did," and starts pulling her down the road by her hand, she falls to the ground, intentionally or because she stumbled, and he says "Come on, get up, get up," and drags her a couple of feet and then picks her up, she's still crying and puts her head on his shoulder and he lifts it up so she won't think she can be comforted now, but has to keep holding it up and then says "Oh screw it, you're smart, you heard and understood everything I said, just please, sweetheart, never run away like that again," and lets her rest her head, kisses her cheek several times while she's sobbing, and walks back to the house.

Summer camp. Her name's Valerie. She's going with someone for about six weeks, breaks up, smiles at him a couple of times while they're in a group and other kids are talking, so he thinks he has a chance. She's short, blond, pretty, a great all-around athlete, doesn't talk much, he's pretty shy himself. He and his bunkmates sneak out of their cabin after taps and go to her cabin. He sits at the end of her bed and looks away to his friends mostly, most sitting on other girls' beds, she mostly looking at her friends lying in their beds, then when his bunkmates think it's time to sneak back, he moves a little closer, bends over and kisses her. "Would you like to sit together at the movie tomorrow night?" he says. "If they let us." Next night when the lights in the social hall go out for the movie, he sneaks over to her, she makes room on the bench and they hold hands and for a while he has his arm around her and she leans her head on his shoulder. They dance at the next social almost only with each other, at the lake when all the seniors have an evening cookout they toast marshmallows and roast franks and potatoes and snuggle under a blanket he brought down and kiss a few times under it, kiss at the farewell social when someone shuts all the lights off for about fifteen seconds and yells "All the couples on the dance floor, kiss," and last day at camp he goes to her cabin, she's dressed for the city, has stockings and flat shoes on, the stockings are too big or she's not wearing them right, so her legs look funny, her dress is heavy and looks as if it's for the winter, they walk a little ways while holding hands, he looks around, no one's looking, and he kisses her and asks if he can have her phone number in the city, he'll call in the next few weeks and come out to Williamsburg where she lives. She says "I'd love for you to, but don't call on the sabbath; that's when we don't answer the phone." He sees her at the bus station in New York a few hours later; she's with her parents, he's with his mother and brother, and he waves to her. "Who's that?" his mother says. "His girlfriend," his brother says. "Last two weeks of camp they were always together. His first girlfriend and he's already getting married." "That true?" his mother says. "You're too young. Wait a couple more years." He worries about calling her. What will they do in Williamsburg? What will they talk about a whole afternoon with none of their friends around? Will he have enough money for a date? Suppose she wants to go to a movie in one of the fancier downtown Brooklyn theaters and maybe take a cab there or back and then sandwiches and sodas after in a place he can't afford? The cab he'll say no to because he likes going by subway or trolley or whatever they have out there, but he doubts he can say no to the rest. Was she as pretty as he remembers? She looked silly in her city clothes that last day and she might even be in dressier clothes and high heels when he sees her. And he doesn't have any good clothes. His brother's are too big unless he rolls up the sleeves of the shirt and doesn't button the top button and makes the tie with a fat knot, but the rest he doesn't have any of his own, not even shoes where the leather isn't cracked. He gets an after-school job, saves up enough in a month to buy a sports jacket and for a date, tries his brother's pants on and finds he can wear them if he pulls them up very high and belts it tight but also uses suspenders, calls her, she says she thought he'd call sooner, he says he wanted to but was very busy with school and work. "Oh, I suppose I could have called you, but I was told by everyone not to. If he wants to call, he will, and if he doesn't, he won't, they all said." "Who told you that?" and she says "Friends, one who's been dating someone for a long time, and my mother." "You spoke to your mother about me?" "Only that I met this nice Jewish boy at camp, one who wasn't religious or anything but was smart and polite and he may come see me." He says that's what he called about, if it's still all right, and she says she'd love to and gets her father to give him subway directions. The father gets on and says "So where you live, kid? If it's all the way out in the Bronx, it's too far to come here, no matter how wonderful my wonderful daughter is." When she gets back on he says "I don't think your father likes me," and she says "Don't be silly, he has no opinion of you, see you Sunday." He worries about it all week. She's too sweet. She'll say sweet things all the time and how happy she is he came to see her and like that and it'll be the dullest afternoon of his life. It might get very warm that day and the clothes he has to wear are flannel and heavy wool and he'll be burning up all the time. He'll be too shy to say anything, and she could be too shy also, and he doesn't want to meet her folks, have to sit with them awhile before he and Valerie can go out. She lives too far away. Maybe that most of all. Suppose he gets to like her, what then? He'll have to go to Williamsburg every time. In the spring it won't be so bad, since they can go to Coney Island and Rockaway from there, but now he'll be missing seeing his friends in the city one day every weekend, and if he has to go back and forth twice in one day if he wants her to be with his friends there, half the time of the date will be spent on the train. He wants to call it off but doesn't know how to. Maybe he could just not show up, then send a letter as an excuse, that he got sick, too sick to call, with laryngitis and bronchitis plus some other throat and chest problems. But then she'll think why didn't he get someone like one of his parents to call for him if he couldn't talk himself? and if they both go back to the same camp next summer as CITs or camper-waiters, everyone there will think he was a liar and rat. Maybe his brother could call for him and say he's very sick. But his brother says that wouldn't be the right thing for either of them to do. "If you want to break the date, call her and say you're very sorry but you have to work at your job that Sunday and that you'll call her again soon for another date." "Suppose she says why don't we make a date now for the next Sunday?" and his brother says "Tell her your job's the kind where it might make you work every weekend for the next month. If your boss doesn't ask you to do that, which you'll know in a few days, you'll call her, and after that you don't have to call her and she'll gradually get the message or just not think of you anymore." Calls, says what his brother told him to, she says "I was really looking forward to it, I had so many interesting things to tell you, but I can understand. My father makes his workers work hard at their jobs too, and it's also a long trip out here for you." "The trip's not it. And it's not just the job but a ton of schoolwork to do. Reports, a big quiz at the start of the week, and because I'm working weekends, I have to study and do the reports at night." "You ought to be an orthodox Jew. Then you wouldn't have to work and study for school for a whole day. I also have lots of schoolwork to do, but I was going to get it done tonight and tomorrow afternoon so I could have time with you. Well, call if you want to, and if you don't call or don't want to, or something, you won't, I suppose. I think I got that right. It's what some people told me to say if this ever happened." "I know. You told me about it last time I called." "Did I? Then you must think I'm very stupid. Anyway, if you don't call, I won't be calling you," and she hangs up. He feels lousy. He made her sad, disappointed her, he could tell by her voice at the end; she might even have gone out and got special clothes for the date. And she was so nice about it. Didn't blame him, just accepted it. Maybe he should call her right back and say he just called his boss and told him he can't work this weekend, or can, but only Saturday. Even if he did call her right back he doesn't think she'd see him this Sunday or make a date with him anytime soon. Too sad and disappointed. He doesn't really know what she'd do if he called now, but it was probably the best thing not going out there, and she'll get over it soon. At least it was final. He thinks of her a few times after that the next few weeks, and a couple of times that he should call her. He doesn't know any other girls to go out with and she was so pretty and sweet and nice and, because she said she got such good grades in school, smart too, but doesn't. Next June he crosses the East River by subway on his way to his aunt and cousins in Coney Island and says to his brother "That's where Valerie, the girl I met last summer, lives; Williamsburg." He knows it's Williamsburg because he sees a lot of religious Jews in long beards and black clothes below the elevated station when they're pulling in and also when her father gave him directions he said "You ever come out to Coney Island? If you do, same way, same train, Williamsburg station's the first one over the bridge." She's not at camp that summer and next June when he's going to his aunt and cousins in Coney Island he looks for her in the street from the train windows, looks in the tenement windows the train passes in case by chance she's in one. If he does see her in the street he'll say to his brother "Go on without me; I'll meet up with you there later," and get off the train before the doors close and run down to say hello to her. Or if she's in one of the windows, then off the train at the next stop and run or subway back to find her, or call her from a phone booth in Williamsburg. He remembers her last name and street; he could get her phone number. And the coincidence of seeing her from the train and surprise of just running up to her or calling her from a nearby booth would make up for any bad feelings she still might have for him after almost two years, or could. He thinks of her every time after that when he's going to Coney Island by subway that way, but for some reason never when he's coming back. Then when he's around thirty the woman he's living with says she heard of a good cheap dermatologist in Williamsburg who could take care of her skin problem for half the cost of her Manhattan doctor. Would he go out there with her, since she doesn't know what kind of neighborhood it is? He doesn't think of Valerie then but does when they get off the train and look around for the doctor's street. "I once knew a girl here when I was fourteen or fifteen. Valerie Bubky. I wonder if she's still living here." "Hardly likely," the woman says. "She's probably married with children and long moved out, and her folks also, for look at this dump. I think we should forget the doctor, get back on the subway before we're robbed, and call him when we get home that we're canceling the appointment and that he should probably move away from here also before he gets killed. Why do people always talk about Williamsburg as if it's someplace special? It's a bleak shithole." They go back to the subway and during the ride home he wonders what would have happened if he'd gone on that date with her. He bets he would have seen her the next Sunday also, that they would have started to talk more, liked each other's company a lot and without needing other kids their age always around. And that Sunday with her would have been his first date. He forgets who his first date actually was. He might have seen her for a year, maybe years. Though her family was orthodox and she said she was too, he might have got her to let him pet her, in a few years to even make love with her. She could have been the first woman he had sex with, since he doubts he would have gone with his friends to prostitutes if he was dating her. He could have continued to see her in college, maybe even married her, had children with her. He could still be with her. She was so pretty and attentive and sweet, always with a smile when she saw him in camp, always glad to see him, and affectionate, a good kisser, and funny sometimes, he remembers—tickling him, once pushing him off a raft into the lake and trying to pull his trunks down in back as he fell, or maybe with both those she was just being flirtatious. Anyway, she could have been the first girl he really loved and who felt the same about him the same time.

Gwen. He's sixteen and they first meet at a dance at her girls' private school. Wearing the same perfume she wore every time he later saw her. It did what perfumes are supposed to, made him romantic, dizzy, want to kiss her neck, burrow his nose into her chest. She never let him. With another woman later on, Janine, it was carnation soap she bought by the twelve-box at Bloomingdales, which she and her bathroom and her apartment when the bathroom door was open, usually smelled of. Now he thinks Gwen was too young to wear perfume then. He once bought a box of that soap to remind him of Janine, after she broke their engagement. Once went to Bloomingdales to be sprayed with Gwen's perfume by one of the first-floor perfume ladies. First time in Paris he bought the smallest bottle there was of it, for his mother, so she'd wear it around the house sometimes and he'd be reminded of Gwen. "Mom, you never seem to put on that perfume I got you," and she would. On subways and buses or the street when he'd smell it he'd look around quickly, thinking it was she; same with the soap. Used to sneak into his parents' medicine chest and dab a drop of the perfume on his wrist and later in bed smell it. Always right before he went to sleep so no one would know he had it on and it'd be gone by morning. Goes to the dance with his friends. It's in the gym and one of the girls' mothers asks them at the door to sign in. All his friends are in private school. He makes up a name, Poly Prep, and says it's in Connecticut, and no, he left any kind of I.D. in his dorm but his friends will vouch for him. Sees her talking to some girls. He's immediately attracted, but how's he approach her? She's dressed like a rich girl, flouncy skirt, lace blouse, pearls, stylish hair. One of the girls she's with sees him staring, maybe is attracted to him—he never found out—and comes over and introduces herself, says this is what they're supposed to do with all the new boys, so don't think you're anything special, and asks what school he's at, then Gwen comes over and her friend introduces them. Two of his friends saw her when she walked over and made with the eyes and smiles to each other, but he caught their attention and pointed to himself and mouthed "Hands off, she's mine." "Poly Prep?" Gwen says. "Sounds like poly pulp. Can it be a real school or are you just a big fake—I won't tell." "Fake and a fraud, but don't get me tossed out; at least not yet." "Fake and a fraud" was what his father often said about various people he'd just met. The smell, was it coming from her? Bright face, inquiring eyes, good speech, dulcet—word he looked up from a book that week and used a lot—voice, long legs out of this stiff thing under her skirt— "What is that coming out, if I can ask?" pointing. "A crinoline. My parents manufacture them so whenever I step out socially like this I like to be a walking ad. Least I can do for all they're shelling out for me for this Easter society pri-school." "Easter what? I don't get it." "Try." Shuts his eyes. Get it quick, she'll admire it. "Something about Jewish and Gentile all in one?" "No, it's about what part of town this school's in. You'll get it in the end." Swan's neck, he thought then, or like a ballet dancer's. "Like to dance?" holding out his arms. Already giddy with her, saying and doing the wrong things, can't think straight, Easter society pri-school means what other than private? His hand feels hot in the small of her back, her hand hot on the back of his neck, her other hand smooth in his sweaty one. And it's from her, the smell. Sees himself nuzzling, kissing, their bodies in skimpy bathing suits on a blanket on a beach squeezed tight. Gets an erection and a big one and she must feel it because she backs up a bit. He wants to say excuse me, to show how sophisticated he is, and if she asks, to even say "For that," looking or pointing down, "and I truly apologize," but doesn't. It's a fox trot, thank God, only dance he really knows—he's tried to learn all the popular ones but once he gets out there it always ends up where he has to ad-lib—and during it she says "I had a dream last night I'd fall in love with and marry a proletarian, what do you make of that?" and he says, because he can't think of any way of making her believe he knows what it is and then later tonight looking it up, "What's a proletarian?" She says "Come on, don't kid me," and he says "Really, what, an iconoclast?" and she says "I know what that is and it's a good one but it's not that. No, if you don't know, that means you're probably one, though you're not the fellow in my dream, since this happens in college two years from now," and he thinks "Did I blow it? Of all the words I know, why couldn't that be one?" After the music stops and they separate he says "Like to do the next one?" and she says, glancing at his crotch—erection's gone down without him even noticing it—"In the beginning we're supposed to give each young man a chance—that's how it was put to us; I'm not quoting from the Bible. Maybe later, when all the young men are used up," and after she dances with a few other guys—he was lucky; next one was a lindy, which he's a real clod at—she disappears. He walks past the girls' bathroom on that floor several times, looks in some classrooms, goes downstairs to the school entrance, and outside. Oh well, he knows her name, thinks he can get her phone number from someone and if not he'll call up a few Wakesmans on the West Side where she said she lives or send her a letter care of this school, but he sees her in the gym as he's leaving and says "Sorry we couldn't dance again, but would it be OK to call you?" "Sure," and he says "I'll need your number," and she has a pen in her purse but nothing to write on but a dollar bill, he only has coins in his pockets but lies and says his paper money's in his coat downstairs, so she writes it on his palm and in front of the school he writes it in a friend's matchbook. He calls her that Monday, takes her to Radio City Music Hall by cab, they go to the restrooms downstairs when they get there and then sit in this big sitting room outside the restrooms while waiting for the next show to begin and he says "You know, I've had a dream over and over again about—" "A recurring one." "Yes. When I was a boy, you see, I went here a couple of times and since then have dreamt about the men's room here but where it has a hundred urinals in a row on both sides of the room. I just saw there weren't even twenty altogether—I counted them, but that's not including the stalls. Uh-oh, maybe I shouldn't have brought it up, for that's not very nice talk," and she says "No, it's good; conversation I like. So more like that, more. Tell me your deepest dreams; your darkest worries and thoughts. I hate all small talk; it's boring," but how does he produce more, for that urinal one might be all he has? He once had a dog he loved who jumped out of a car window and got permanently lost. Once got his tongue stuck to a popsicle and though a man told him not to he panicked and pulled it off. Once while fooling around he fell down a coal chute of an apartment building on his block and a fireman had to climb down and pull him up. Got lost in Central Park during a blizzard and for a while didn't think he'd make it out. Got hit by cars twice while playing ball on his sidestreet and both times ran home and into bed saying he thought he just came down with the grippe. His sister who's been so sick with cancer she almost died in the operating room a couple of times. His father who went to prison and now still can't get his dental license back. "Well, right now, nothing, but there's plenty of those in me, believe me," and she says "Then what do you want to do, even though you're not in college yet, after you get out?" and he says "Something good for mankind. A doctor, but not for money but for missionary work, though not connected to any religion. Unfortunately, I'm not good in the sciences. But my dad says I don't have to be and that he'll get me into dental school if I want, because once there it's all practical stuff." "But you don't want to be a dentist, putting your nose in people's mouths," and he says "No, a doctor, but medical school he doesn't think he can get me into with just a C average, which is all I've ever been, and also because he has no connections there, so I don't know what to do. But when you think of it, people have bad teeth everywhere and it causes so much pain and the relief of it's just as great as taking out a cancer, and I have to admit my father's a dentist, but not practicing these days. But just to go to Africa—maybe I'll learn French better and go to med school in Switzerland or someplace like I heard people do who can't get in here—and to work with poor starving natives and in the deepest bush." "That's nice. Money doesn't concern you. That's great, but you have such a long trek ahead. I'd like to be an artist of any sort—but a creator, not an interpreter—and right now I'm going about trying to determine which one. Maybe I'll be a triple or quadruple threat in several artistic fields, and with a number of hats on my head in each one." He doesn't get the hat expression, but nods, says it sound exciting, he once thought of art for himself too. Painting, which he used to do slews of as a kid and some of his school art teachers thought he was pretty good at, and even acting, which he thinks you can be a creator in, though maybe she's right, but he doesn't have enough talent for either or not compared to lots of people he's seen his age. "My feeling," she says, "and you know, I'm only starting out, but it's if you don't believe in yourself completely from the beginning in those fields, it's best to stay out of them. So you probably made the right decision, early as it was." The movie's about young concert performers—the reason he took her to it; classical music, maybe an intelligent story in it— and in the cab home he asks and she says she's grateful he took her but the plot and music were for the most part for people who only feed on sweets. "You noticed no Bartok, Stravinsky, Schoenberg, any of the modernists. You know why. Most people would run out of the theater, or worse, not go in." Stravinsky he thinks he heard of, but the others? but he says "There's something to what you say. But a little of it, I have to admit, like that Mendelssohn violin thing running through it, I kind of liked and think I'll get a recording of it. I got the name of the real player of it from the closing credits, which is why I made you sit through them. Francescatti." Oh, she says, she knows his Prokofiev and Bach. She lets him kiss her at the door. "Can I call you again?" and she says "Sure, call," and he says "Maybe we can make a date now—I've been invited to what should be a great party next Saturday," and she says "I don't have my calendar on me or know what my obligations at home will be next week. Best to call." He bends down to kiss her but she moves aside and says "One, for now, is enough." Next two days he thinks he can still smell her perfume on his sports jacket in his closet, but his brother takes a whiff and says he's imagining it. "Just sweat; you ought to get it dry-cleaned if you want anybody to go out with you." Calls that Tuesday; Monday would seem he was too much in a hurry. "Hi, I was wondering if you'd like to go to that party I mentioned," and she says it turns out she's busy all weekend, and when he asks, the next one too. He says he'll call again if she doesn't mind and she says OK. "By the way, how are you, what have you been doing?" and she says "Nothing much, and fine, there's little that ever gets me down, but you know how I feel about small talk. So I'll be speaking to you, Howard." Howard, his name, that she was saying it, he was going crazy for her. Draws her face and figure in that crinoline dozens of times, kisses his pillow several times pretending it's her. He loves everything about her. Looks, manners, mannerisms, intellect, clothes, tastes, gracefulness, cute younger sister who came out to see him that first date, that she and her sister share their own listed phone, her fancy East Side friends and school, fine old apartment building and apartment with a wide Hudson view, doormen, elevator men, flowers in the lobby, flowers in that little foyer right outside their front door, maid who wore a black and white uniform when there weren't even guests and called him Mr. Tetch, way the place was furnished and that Gwen brought him into the living room to meet her parents who were having coffee after dinner, father with a tie on and in what looked like a lounge jacket, mother also in elegant stay-at-home clothes and with this aristocratic voice and both getting up to shake his hand, paintings he was shown there, real drawings—with little frame lights above them—by Titian and Rembrandt, books she said she was reading, small poetry book she took to the movie in case, she said, she had a few extra minutes when let's say he went to look for a cab, thin soft lips and beautiful teeth, that she had a cat. Calls the Tuesday after the next and she says she's busy the following weekend, "Oh, that's too bad. Is there any weekend you won't be busy—in other words, maybe the first Friday or Saturday night where you won't?" and she says "I never make plans for more than the coming weekend—that last time was an aberration." "An aberration. OK," he says angrily, "an aberration," and hangs up, hoping his anger and hanging up and no good-bye will somehow interest her in him more; that he draws the line, has feelings, takes no crap, is like what she originally liked in him it seems, a strong proletariat. Right after that he gets depressed, doesn't know how he'll make it till next Tuesday or Wednesday when he'll call. Tuesday; Wednesday and she'll be busy for sure the next weekend or at least will have a good excuse: he called too late. And "aberration," and he writes it down way he thinks it's spelled, looks it up, it isn't in his dictionary, asks his mother what it means since she's known most of the big words he's asked her about before. "Why?" she says. "Because I heard someone use it." "In what capacity?" and he says "That knowing what you'll be doing two weekends in a row is an aberration." "That's not how it's used," and tells him what it means and spells it out for him and he finds it this time. He calls the next Tuesday and first thing she says is "Did you hang up on me last week?" and he says "No, I might have just said good-bye very softly, why?" and she says "Because if you did I'd think, boy, this fellow isn't worth answering the phone for if he's going to unload all his belligerence on me." "Not me," he says and asks her out and she says there would have been a definite possibility if she didn't have so many extracurricular activities this week like tap dance and singing lessons and an Italian class she's starting and she also models at the Art Students League one night a week, all of which means she'll be studying the whole weekend for her

610

midterms." "You model? Not in the nude." "Yes, it's for artists." "How do your parents let you? You're so young. Or even the art school?" and she says "I told the League I'm nineteen, since I feel I act it and could look it. As for my parents, they're both artists in their souls but business people to keep their souls alive and bodies fed, and they trust me. It's only the top part anyway, not that I wouldn't model the bottom part if they needed it. I was asked by an instructor there who sat on the stool next to mine at the health food lunch place near the League and thought I'd be perfect for the pose he had in mind." "Oh yeah, and God knows what he's going to ask you to do next," and she says "You really don't know what you're talking about." "You're absolutely right and I'm sorry," and asks her out for the weekend after next—"Anyone can repeat an aberration once, I'd think"—and she says "I'm afraid I won't be able to, but in a nice voice and when she says good-bye she says "So I suppose I'll be hearing from you," which gives him the confidence she'll say yes the next time. Calls the next Tuesday, she says she's sorry, she's busy that weekend, he says "Busy busy bizwax—with what, voice lessons, studying again, cooking school?" and she says "You sure sound cynical today," and he says "I'm not, or didn't mean to be; go on, tell me what your plans are, though of course you don't have to and I don't know why I asked," and she says "No, I'll be honest; I don't mind. I have appointments Friday and Saturday nights," and he says "You mean with guys, or just one," and she says "Yes, with two fellows I know," and he says "Guys you've been going out with, right?" and she says yes and he says "Then I guess I'll give up then, right?" hoping she'll say don't or he doesn't have to if he doesn't want to, and she says "If that's how you feel; excuse me, but good-bye," and hangs up. She was mad. That could mean a couple of things, one good, one bad. Somehow in her voice when she seemed mad it also seemed she was saying I'm mad because you made me mad but I'm not that mad where you don't have to call again. And if she's seeing two guys, it means she's not serious with one. No, he's crazy, what's he talking about, goddamn stupid idiot, and picks up the receiver and slams it down on its cradle, bangs the night table it's on with his fist, receiver jumps off and falls to the floor and he wants to grab it and smash it against the table, rip it out of the phone and wrap the wire around his neck and pull it tight till it hurts and cuts and leaves marks; puts the receiver down and grits his teeth and tears come and a sinking empty sickening feeling in his chest and he says "Oh shit, why the hell not, what the hell's wrong, why'd I even start, who the hell you think you are, you skinny rotten bitch?" and covers his face with his hands and digs his nails into his skin, and then his mother knocks on the door and says through it "May I come in now, Howard?—after all," since it's his parents' bedroom, and he says "Sure, sorry, I'm done here," and passes her with his head down and she says "Anything the matter, dear?" and he says "Well, you know, but I'll be all right," and to get to sleep that night after everyone's in bed he sneaks open the liquor cabinet in the living room and takes several swigs of Canadian rye and sits there till he starts to yawn. A friend tells him she's going out with two guys, a junior at Yale and a grad student at NYU. "The Yalie's very rich, not Jewish, an athlete and a scholar in English lit I think. The other guy's a poor Brooklyn or Bronx Yid and supposed to be real handsome and smart, always on total scholarship, and on his way to making a million in advertising or TV." "Him—both of them," Howard says, "have to be too old for her—I mean, she's barely sixteen," and his friend says "She seems to have her parents' permission, according to this girl who knows, so what can I tell you?" He sends her a letter saying "If you're interested in going to a movie one of these days, let me know," and gives his phone number and address. She doesn't contact him. He thinks of her every day, calls her three months after they last spoke, she says "Hello, how are you, it's been so long," and he asks her out to a movie the next Saturday afternoon and she says she'd love to. She takes a tomato from the kitchen as they leave her apartment, offers him the first bite on the street, he says it'd be too sloppy and he doesn't much like tomatoes, "I adore them," she says and bites into it without making a mess and eats it as they walk to the theater, holding it in front of his mouth when she's almost finished with it and says "Sure you don't want some? It's going fast," and he wants to, just to put his mouth where her lips did and to show he's not obstinate and takes chances, but says no. She smiles and chews the last of it and he thinks he loves everything she does; it's awful. She leans her head on his shoulder about fifteen minutes into the movie, he thinks should I? and decides to and kisses her hair and then her cheek and then very quickly her lips. She didn't stop him or look up at him and her eyes were closed when she kissed him so he waits what he thinks is about five minutes and then kisses her hair, cheek and lips and then a long kiss and tries to open her mouth with his tongue, thinking if she lets him do this then he really might be starting something with her, but she pulls away and says "Too fast, too far, let's just be kids," and kisses her finger and puts it on his lips and he says "Sure, whatever you like." Outside the theater he asks how she liked the movie and she says she's in a hurry to get home, can they get a cab? or just she'll get one, and he says "But it's only three blocks, and it's not raining," and she says "Don't worry, I'll pay." "That's not it; I'm working and I'm certainly not cheap," and hails a cab, tells her in it he had wanted to go for a bite after the movie but OK, maybe the next time, and she says, getting out of the cab, "It's a date." He says "Hey, I'm not taking this to my house," and pays, but she's already walking into her building, waving at him. He calls her when he gets home for a date next weekend and the housekeeper who answers says "She was only here but gone out." Calls her the next day and she says "What is it?" and he says "I wanted to take you up on what you said yesterday and make another date, maybe even an evening one, but I guess it's hopeless—somehow, your voice." "I think it is," and he says "I don't get it. You were so nice at the movie, we had fun, even walking to it—" and she says "Don't." "So it doesn't make a difference what I say or we did?" and she says "Not in the slightest, and please understand I'm not being malicious saying that. I like kissing and you're a nice fellow but I'm simply not interested in you the way you are in me." "How are you interested in me then?" and she says "Whatever way it is, it's not amorous, is that now clear?" and he says "OK, I got it finally," and slams the receiver down and feels miserable for a week. Calls her a month later and she says "Oh, hello?" and he asks what she's been up to lately and she talks a little about what she's been doing and then there's silence so he starts in about what he's been doing recently and then she says "That's nice, great, well, I'll have to say good-bye now," and he says "Any chance we can meet?" and she says "Howard, I'm still not interested. If you only wanted to be friends, that'd be a different thing." "OK, as friends, would you like to go to an art museum today?" and she says "Not this week, I'm busy." "Next week then?" and she says "I don't want to make plans so far ahead," and he says "Then you don't want to be friends; you don't want to be anything. All right. So screw you, friend," and hangs up. Oh God, that's it, that has to be it, for me, her, definitely for me and I'm sure she'll never talk to me again, and bangs his parents' bed with his fists and screams "Goddamn it, shit, shit," and starts tearing at his hair. His parents think he's going crazy and have his brother speak to him. It snows that night and the next day he walks in the park and kicks drifts in just a T-shirt and pants and shoes without socks so he can get a cold and pneumonia and die. Sees her on the street several months later and she waves to him and he waves to her as she goes down her block. She smiled when she waved. Maybe she's changed her opinion about him somewhat, wouldn't mind him calling her. Calls, says it was nice seeing her on the street and how is she? and she says "Listen, I'm busy this week, if that's what you were eventually going to ask, but thanks for calling." "Maybe next week?" and she says she's going away for the weekend, and for the month after that to Southern France for the Easter break. He's waiting tables in the neighborhood Schrafft's a year later when she comes in with two other girls and sits at another station. He pretends not to see her. Sees her in a mirror looking at him. All three have ice cream sodas and one of them has a sandwich. In the kitchen he tells their waiter "I know one of the girls at your four-table. Used to go out with her—the beautiful slim dark-haired one." "Her beautiful? Eh, so-so. But put the word in for them to give me a big tip." "No, it's all over and I have no influence with her, but she's got lots of family dough, so I'm sure you'll do OK." "Then get tight with her again. She's a good-looker, they all got juicy nookies, true? and if she's that rich and you can go into her dad's business, forget college; you've got it made." He's passing her table with a tray of dirty dishes, still pretending not to know she's there, and she says "Howard," he looks at her, "Oh hi, Gwen, hello," she introduces him to her friends and says "Since when do you work here?" and he says "It's a good place, lots of actors and writers working as waiters, so an interesting group, and it's in walking distance from home," and she says "I know that, but I meant for how long?" and he says "Few weeks. Look-it, the manager's a crab when I talk to personal friends who aren't my customers, so nice to see you," all in a voice and with an expression that he couldn't care less that he saw her, and smiles and says "Nice to meet you" to her friends. Watches her through mirrors or the kitchen door window from then on and after she leaves he asks her waiter how he did and he says "You didn't do your part well—almost a whiff," and he says "I'm really surprised. The tip must have been left up to one of the other girls, for she was always pretty free with her cash." Leaving the restaurant he thinks maybe she'll call him. For the next few weeks he looks at the restaurant door every time someone comes in, hoping it'll be she, alone or with her sister, parents or friends. If she does come in, he'll turn away, do his chores, ignore her even through mirrors, and then pass her table with dirty dishes, or with food for customers this time, and be surprised to see her when she speaks to him, or speak to her first this time and later, if she's alone or with her sister, maybe ask if she'd like to meet him when he gets off. About a half year later he sees her passing the standees' line he's on outside the Metropolitan Opera House. "Gwen!" "Howard," she says, "hi, I'm way in back, only came up to see how long the line is." "It's long; I don't know if you'll ever get in. You an opera buff? I didn't know that." "No, I like it; never saw Faust though and always wanted to." "Well come on, slip in here." She starts to, guy behind him says "Wait a minute, that isn't fair," and he says "I was expecting her; she didn't think I'd get here so early to get this far in front," and pulls her in. She thinks what he did—by her face—bold, and maybe what he said quick and clever. "You're alone I hope," he whispers into her ear. "Otherwise, I'm sure Charlie won't allow anyone else in." "I'm alone. You know him?" and he says "No, just based on his face and what he said, I was giving him a name. No meaning; just my usual nonsense, I suppose," and she says "I'm not sure you can gauge much from superficial contact with someone and only one expression on his face. And he's justified in how he acted, since I did cut in and what if they close him out right after us?" and he thinks Oh shit, here I go blowing it again, acting the snob, which I'm not. Think what you're going to say; make everything hit; for a few hours she's all yours and this might be your last chance. He asks and she tells: bit of fashion modeling, been learning Hindi, ice-skating a lot, was in an experimental film that got some attention—a western made in New Jersey if he can believe it—and is preparing to go to college. The line moves. They talk some more in the lobby during intermission. People stare at her she's so beautiful or maybe they've seen her in the movie and fashion ads. After the second act she says her feet are tired, she doesn't much like the opera and there are two more acts, so she has to go. "I'll go with you. I've seen it several times and I have to be at work early tomorrow. I'm starving besides, since I came straight here from night school. Like to have a bite somewhere nearby?" and she says it's really getting quite late. He says "Want to go by cab?" and she says she likes subways; so full of characters and life, especially at night. During the ride she says "No need for you to go with me all the way," and he says he wouldn't think of letting her walk home alone from the subway stop. She says "I do it all the time. It's reasonably safe and I can handle myself well. I carry a canister of mace and I've developed my diaphragm through voice and acting lessons where my screams would be heard for blocks." In front of her building she says he can't come up. Her folks are there and they object these days to midweek dates. "Wouldn't think of it, my dear, wouldn't think of it," and shakes her hand. She leans forward, her lips out, he hopes to kiss his and waits to see, and she pecks his cheek. Maybe if he'd leaned down to her she would have done it, but probably not. "Goodnight, nice seeing you again," and swivels around and walks away whistling and looking up at the sky and thinking what should be his strategy now? Don't call her for weeks; considering his history with her, she'll be mystified. He calls two days later and she says that was fun that opera night but what she neglected telling him is she's seriously mixed up with a Dartmouth man and has promised him she wouldn't see anyone else when they're apart. "Oh shucks," he says, "a little movie or something won't hurt." "I can't. I'd have to lie to him—he's very strict about this dictum, living like a celibate up there, all work and no women. And if I did tell him it's all innocence and old friendship between us, he'd still get incredibly jealous and mad." "Oh well," he says, "maybe some other lifetime. See ya," and gently hangs up. He cuts his hair short in front of the bathroom mirror, cuts his sideburns off, looking at the mirror over his shoulder, shaves the hair on his neck. He feels the hair on top and the sides, he can still grab some, and cuts it even more. Doesn't know why, other than it had something to do with her of course, but he suddenly felt prissy and like some fake artist with all those curls on his head and over his ears, and a little unclean. He asks some people in the film department at his college if they know of an experimental western made recently which which might have got some good reviews, but nobody can think of anything coming close to that other than *High Noon* and *Shane*. About a year later someone mentions a film like that and gives the title and he sees it at an art movie house and either she gave a different name for the credits and he didn't recognize her in it or this one wasn't it. He next sees her in a photography magazine. A friend shows him the full-page photo. Very high-fashion pose, and she's holding a smoking cigarette, though she never smoked when he knew her. Buys the magazine at a stand, though it's very expensive, cuts the page out and puts it in a book he's reading, and every now and then at school and work, takes it out to look at. Guy sitting next to him in the department store employees' cafeteria says "Who's the chick—some new actress? Never saw her before." "You want to hear something crazy? I used to go out with this piece of ass." "Yeah, me too, me too, was even married to her once." "No, it's the god's honest truth. Gwendolyn Wakesman. I even know her middle name, which it doesn't give here: Cora. Year and a half younger than I. When we were in high school, though she went to a fancy private and I to a junky public. And we were in love, or maybe I was more with her than she was with me, and I was the first to ball her also, and her second, third, fourth, all the way to maybe her fiftieth." "You're full of it," the guy says. "Knew you wouldn't believe it. Only thing wrong with her was that her calves were too fat and she smoked. I can't stand smoking. I get these physiological reactions to it—sneezing, trouble breathing, besides getting irritated; that 's why I'm sitting in the corner here, away from all those chimneys around us. And she smoked those smelly French cigarettes—she was kind of a phony also but not enough of one for me not to go out with someone so beautiful and to say no to screwing her, and I was sure that part of her personality would go away with age. Anyway, it was because of that smoking that I broke up with her. What a schmuck I was." "Good story, but I think you're still full of it." "What can I say that I haven't already? Kill me for it." Next sees her in the Metropolitan Museum. He's going up the big flight of stairs, she's coming down. "Gwen?" he says, for a moment, because of her shorter differently styled hair, not sure. "Well hi, how are you? My, we always seem to meet in the more cultural places. But I have to run. See you at Carnegie Hall next, yes?" Watches her go. Body fuller, face as beautiful, still the same perfume smell and artistic clothes. Maybe if it was just lunch she was going to he should have said "Want to go to the cafeteria here?" Follows her downstairs but at a distance of about a hundred feet. If she turns and sees him he'll say "Sorry, didn't want you to think I was following you, which

618

is why I kept at such a distance, but I realized I originally came here to see the Greek collection." She leaves the museum. He watches her hurry down the steps, hail a cab. Next sees her at Rockefeller Plaza. He's sitting on one of the long concrete planters, reading, waiting for Janine, when someone says "Howard." Looks up. "Oh my God. Gwen, Jesus, howaya, what's going on uh . . ." "You look great, Howard; different, natty, all the rage, and your face; blooming." "Not me, but—" "No, life's got to be going smooth for you. What have you been up to?" and he says "Nothing unusual, as usual. Actually, things are going OK, thank you. Job, personal life." "You just plunk down here to read on this gorgeous day or are you waiting for someone? For if you're not doing anything too important, we can talk while you walk me to Fifty-seventh Street where I've an appointment." "I'd love to but I am waiting for someone. My fiancée, as a matter of fact. I'm on my lunch hour. My job starts at noon, so it might sound peculiar saying lunch hour at four or so, but I'm a newsman." "So. Good luck then, in everything. I'm sure we'll bump into each other again, and my best to your fiancée." She puts out her cheek and he kisses it. "Before you go," he says, "and I know it's almost a mandatory question, or at least from one of the parties, when two people from the past meet after a few years, but you see any of the old people we knew?" "Who might they be? We didn't know anyone mutually, did we?" "Robin Richards? . . . The fellow who used to say 'The nose knows'? He had an unusually long nose, which now probably people look at as handsome, but he always had lots of gossip and social information to give out, so he made fun of himself with the nose line." She's still shaking her head. "I thought he crossed both our crowds. He went to Trinity. Then Ellen Levin? I didn't know her that well, really not at all, but I certainly remember her." "Her name's not familiar either," and he says "Ellen Levin, or Levine, or Levine," pronouncing it the other way. She was your best friend at school, I thought. Tall, pretty, bouncy blonde. Father had a hamper factory." "No," she says. "Then Helen? Evelyn? I don't think 'Eleanor.' Because I remember first talking to her at your school dance, night I first met you, and then she introduced us, or you just came over and introductions were made all around, because she thought we'd get along or saw I was mainly interested in you and not her." "Is that where we first met? I thought it was after a movie." "No. And maybe I got her last name wrong, but I'm sure her first name was something like Helen or Ellen." "I've never known a Helen or Ellen." "Everyone in New York's known an Ellen." "Then in high school or college. And I did always think we met after a movie. I still do. I even know what movie. *Modern Times*, at the New Yorker. You came up to me after it, in that lobby-entranceway where they have that enormous refreshment stand and long vertical box with movie calendars for the next few months, and asked what I thought of the movie and we had coffee or tea at a coffeehouse nearby, or you asked me." "I don't even think the New Yorker was the New Yorker when we first met. It was the Stoddard or something. And the only movie we ever went to—no, there were two, but the first was *Rhapsody*, with Elizabeth Taylor and Vittorio Gassman—the one about music. They're music students, concert performers. But young. And some other actor. John someone. A flash in the pan, pretty face, no talent, but the male romantic lead. Mendelssohn's Violin Concerto was also in it, I think, all over the place, and another schmaltzy piece—Rachmaninoff's Second or Tchaikovsky's First Piano Concerto. All I know is I loved the music then." "No, I never saw it." "At Radio City Music Hall. It was our first date. We sat for a while in the waiting room outside the two big restrooms downstairs." "I thought our first date was at the Metropolitan Museum. You showed me all the paintings you knew something about, talked nonstop about them, I guess to impress me. I was so young I didn't mind being impressed by a knowledgeable young man, especially about anything involving art." "No. We once met there—the last time, in fact— several years ago. We were going in opposite directions on the grand stairway there. It was very brief, hello, not even a how's-by-you, and then you ran as fast as anybody could run down those steps and I, I've got to admit, followed you out of the museum, or at least to the top of the steps, and watched you get into a cab." "Why'd you do that?" "Because, because, why do you think? A bitten smitten. I mean, maybe not then—at the museum. Then probably I was following you to see what had interested me—maybe even obsessed me—for so long about you." "You were that way about me?" "Are you crazy? Excuse me, but how could you say that? When I was sixteen, and then seventeen, eighteen and nineteen or so, I would have put my head under a speeding car's wheel for you. I in fact almost did do something like that for you once. I walked out of my house—no, I should shut up." "Go on, if you want. It's long ago—unless it embarrasses you. It doesn't me." "With only a shirt on—a short-sleeved—you know, not an undershirt—" "A T-shirt." "That's right, and pants and shoes too, of course, but no socks. To get pneumonia. In the freezing cold and snow, that's what I mean. So you'd hear about it later—from Robin Richards or through him to someone you knew—that I died or at least got very sick. And you'd be worried, concerned, upset, call me, want to see me—in the hospital room where I was recovering, for instance—then out of pity or something bordering on affection, start seeing me again but exclusively." "We never really *saw* each other. It wasn't even close to that." "I know. But that's how I felt. But all of that—the movie; movies, actually. I forget what the other one was but it was at Loew's 83rd or RKO 81st. And bumping into me not only at the Met museum but at the old opera house Met and standing in the orchestra standing room section with me to see *Faust*, plus my feelings for you then—none of it rings a bell?" "I remember the opera. I met you there by accident, I think, though whether I stood with you inside or sat alone or with someone else—and certainly whether it was upstairs or downstairs where we stood, if we did—I forget." "We stood alone. I stood behind you. We took the subway back to the West Side together. Before we took the subway I asked if you wanted to have a snack. Asked you outside or in the lobby after you wanted to leave after the second or third act. I stood behind you at the opera so you could see. I mean, that's not why I told you I was standing behind you, though I might have, but that's why I did it." "Well that was very nice of you if that's what you did. And whether it was *Modern Times* and at the New Yorker theater where I first met you, I could also be mistaken. My memory's never been one of the keenest. Though I do feel sure it was at an art movie house where we first met—the Thalia perhaps. And that you struck up a conversation about the movie, to get to meet me I realized and didn't mind, and we had coffee after or we didn't. Maybe I'm getting all the art movie houses mixed up with the art coffeehouses—and then you phoned me a few times. Unfortunately, or quite truthfully, I couldn't go out with you or wasn't interested. It could have been I was seeing someone at the time. Though I'm almost certain I did go with you once to the Metropolitan Museum. Probably just an innocent Sunday afternoon date. And then for the next few years I kept running into you at various palaces of culture in the city. Carnegie Hall, I believe." "No. Carnegie Hall is the place you said, when I bumped into you at the museum Met, 'Well, I suppose we'll next meet each other there.' Meaning, at another palace of culture." "Then the Modern." "Never the Modern. I would have remembered. Of all places, that's the one I most wanted to go to with you. And to also have a snack in the garden restaurant there, or if it was too cold, the one inside. Never the Modern. Never Carnegie Hall." "But places like that. As I said, my memory was never that sharp, but I never thought it was this bad. Anyway, it's been nice talking with you, Howard. Again, my regards to your fiancée. See? I remember I said that." "Listen, she'll be here any second. She's usually late, but not this much, and I'm sure she'd like meeting you." "I'm already very late." "You also might be interested in her. She was an actress, pretty successful at it from the time she was ten, but gave it up. She even did TV soap operas and a couple of drama shows and made Broadway three years ago, in a good play, as far as the critics were concerned, and she's friends with a couple of women who went to Sarah Lawrence and you went there, didn't you?" "I graduated last year, but I don't have the greatest memories of the place or the people in my class, so I'd rather not talk about it. Well,

Howard, I'll see you again I'm sure," and heads uptown. Years later he's living with a woman who once took a class at the Sarah Lawrence continuing ed school and for some reason was being sent the alumni magazine. He always reads the alumni news in it for the year Gwen graduated. She's never listed. Years after that he's seeing a woman and they're at the apartment of a friend of hers and he asks where the bathroom is. The friend says "I think the one off the living room's filled; there's another in my bedroom." He goes to it. On the night table is the latest Sarah Lawrence alumni magazine. He takes it to the bathroom, turns to the alumni news for Gwen's year and looks at it while pissing. Nothing about her. Puts the magazine back on the night table and sees a stack of alumni magazines on the radiator. He goes through about ten of them before finding something about Gwen from two years ago. She's produced documentaries on nature, done public television writing, "ghostwritten a poetical biography of a dying city," finished a "mastodonic novel which I decided would never get published and if published, never be received well, so I immediately trunked," took up residence in five cities in three countries in the last eight years "doing work research on I won't say what or with whom and I hope the finished results won't show," been married and divorced twice, no children and "because of all the undertakings I feel I still have to do and get done, I doubt I'll have any—my loss, not theirs," is now living and painting in a "saintly little town in the mountains near Santa Fe, something I'll most likely be doing for the rest of my life, for I feel I've finally found my art form." "She gives," the class correspondence secretary says, "no address, and no one should even attempt to reach her through New Mexico phone information, since for the next two years she's in self-imposed solitary without so much as a flush toilet, running faucet, mailbox or phone, refining her work for a solo showing at what I'm sure will be a prominent NYC gallery. Gwen also writes she's periodically gloomy because of her solitude but has never been more creative in her life—this from the one who was Ms. Creativity in our class for four straight years, and we had some winners. For companionship she says she has several sheep, horses, innumerable cats and a hundred-ten-pound Great Pyrenees named Fluffy to protect her from real mountain lions, bobcats and bears. Gwen only answered my inquiry—which came via a family member of hers, so don't think I have her address—to spare me the task of trying to track her down for the next ten years. Her parting words—and I apologize if she didn't mean for me to print any of them, even if I'm sure she doesn't get the alumni mag and wouldn't read anything about herself if she did—were 'Right now I'm solely and totally involved with my animals, artwork, and putting the finishing touches on my house' (which she built all by herself, I forgot to say, and without the help of electric screwdrivers and saws) 'but no people, and if all that sounds phony if not pathalogical, so be it.' It doesn't, Gwen. It sounds heavenly. From all of us: Follow your star." He reads art reviews and announcements of art exhibits in the *New York Times* for the next few years, but she's never mentioned, nor have any artists he knows heard of her work. During this time a friend who's a writer gives him a literary magazine with two of his stories in it. One's about a woman named Gwen Wakesman. In it the fictional character has a blind date with her when he's eighteen, French-kisses her on the first date, feels her breasts through her bra on the second, gets his hand in her underpants on the third, makes love with her in her apartment—her parents are in the Caribbean and her sister and the housekeeper went to the circus—on the next date. On the fifth date he teaches her how to go down on him without hurting him—she says it's her first time—and how to position her body so he can stick it into her behind—and they see each other for a year, having sex almost every time they meet, before he dumps her for her best friend. She becomes very upset over this, gets a room in a cheap hotel and calls him and says she's going to slit her wrists in the grubby bathtub, and she brought the razor blade to do it with, unless he spends the night with her there. He comes, undresses her, carries her to bed kissing her, then drops her on the floor and beats her up. "Now do you believe we're finished?" "Finished," she says.

"And you're not going to do anything stupid again? Because if you are I'm going to really mess up your face" "Nothing. I was wrong to threaten you." "Good. Now get dressed, clean yourself up and I'll take you home." Two days later she commits suicide. He goes to the funeral, gets on his knees in front of the open coffin and screams he's sorry for his heartlessness and prays for her to be alive again. He has a vision there that she steps out of the coffin and pats his head and says "Don't fret, my darling; it was more my fault than yours. I depended too much on our love affair going well. I was young and impulsive and ignorant and I forgive you with all my heart." That night he sleeps with her best friend, who was also at the funeral—they had dinner and saw a movie after—and he says "Don't ask me why but the sex just now was the best in my life. I thought I saw God. Maybe I did if he looks a lot like what the ancient painters depict him as in so much of their art." "I almost reached that state also," she says, "or maybe I did. I know there was a lot of clearing and light." "No, you're supposed to know a mystical experience when it happens to you, there is no probably or maybe. But it was good, right? You explain it, because I can't. And now I'm not only still feeling the buzz from my come but I also feel no remorse over Gwendolyn anymore whatsoever. I truly believe she forgave me today," and she says she still feels remorse just a little but she thinks she'll get over it in time, and they go at each other again. Howard calls his friend and says "You knew Gwen Wakesman?" and he says "Yeah, you too? I went out with her when I was around twenty. I changed my age a little for the story." "You know she's not dead, of course. She's living near Santa Fe, or was, up till about three years go." "She's still there but on a reservation now, learning how to make indianlike jewelry, silver and rugs. I'm in touch with someone who met her." "So how much of the rest of the story's true?" "You ask that of an author? You should be ashamed of yourself. Besides, you haven't said what you thought of it." "Some of it though, right?" and his friend says "What do you think? I went out with her for months and my libido hasn't changed since I was a sex-starved five." "But you're such a putz. What the fuck did she ever see in you and why in hell didn't you at least change her name? You can't use someone's real name like that. It's demoralizing; it's degrading. You're a total schmuck as a writer and the biggest shit as a person—no, the reverse. No, both, and I never want to see your scummy face again," and his friend hangs up. Couple of years later he's at a dinner party and the woman he sits beside at the table talks about herself, grew up in Lake Forest, boarding school in New Hampshire, summers in coastal Canada or Spain, graduated Sarah Lawrence—"Oh, what year?" "Sixty-two." "A year after Gwen Wakesman. Did you know her there?" "No I didn't. There were always two groups, academic-aesthetic and the finishing school types. She must have been in the other." "Which one were you in?" and she says "Are you belittling me? The academic-aesthetic." "That would have been the one she was in too." "If she was I would've known her, even if she was a year before me. We all interweaved." "She's been in the alumni magazine. I've read it. As an artist living outside Santa Fe." "I don't read that silly magazine. It's only published to raise money from the finishing school types in exchange for them telling us the names of their newest horse, boat or island and for the few a-a egotists in every class to talk endlessly about themselves and to promote their book tours and art exhibits and plays they're in." "I'm sure she would have been in the artistic group at school." He next sees her name in the obituary notice for her father. Surviving are his wife Gladys, daughter Gwendolyn Leigh-Balicoff, and two grandchildren, Olympia and Augustine. So she might have got married again and the kids could be hers or her sister's. She might even have adopted a couple of Indian children. But no mention of her sister. She die? Then it would have said "deceased." They disown her? Weeks later he looks up her father's name in the phone book; they've moved to Park Avenue, if it's the same Philip. Calls to find out where she's living. An older woman answers. If Gwen had he thinks he would have immediately hung up. "Hello, I'm trying to reach Gwendolyn Wakesman, now Leigh-hyphen-Balicoff. I have the right number?" "She's living in Munich," the woman says, "and I'm not allowed to furnish her address or phone number." "Munich. Well, nice city. And she has a phone now? Good. Could you possibly be the woman who worked for them then, Rose or Ruth?" "Ruth, yes." "You probably don't remember me, Ruth. My name's Harold Zeif. I used to date Gwen—just two dates, really—years ago, when we were in our teens." "I don't remember you, sir." "How could you, and there wouldn't be any need to. And God, you're still working there, unless you're only visiting for the day." "I'm still employed by the Wakesmans, though my chores have been reduced and I no longer live in." "Also, I was probably one of many young men Gwen knew. She was so pretty and intelligent and mature and charming, she must have had many suitors." "That she was and did, sir. I remember that." "How's Mrs. Wakesman taking the death of her husband? I mean, I didn't know her well either. I came in, her parents said hello, they were very nice—but it was a matter of seconds, maybe a minute I saw them and just one time. In the living room of the old Riverside Drive apartment, with all the paintings." "Same paintings are here now. Different furniture though." "I remember the furniture. Big elegant flowery couch, right?" "Vertical stripes." "I remember flowers. I'm of course wrong. But the chairs—soft easy ones—were flowered then." "Plain. A deep rich green one and a deep rich red one, if you're talking about the armed padded chairs. Both are gone now. They had a decorator in and out everything went. I got the red chair, cigarette burn-holes and all." "Then I'm thinking of someone else's apartment. But how's Mrs. Wakesman doing?" "Not well, as should be expected. They were tightly knit, at work and as parents." "I remember they were. From Gwen talking, and just for the minute I saw them they seemed like very fine people. Polite, generous, cosmopolitan. And Toby? It is Toby, right—Gwen's sister?" "Toby then but she changed it back to the original Dorothea when she turned twenty. She died many years ago." "Ohh, that's what I was afraid of. When the obituary didn't list her name as surviving. But no 'deceased,' it said, which puzzled me." "That was an error of the newspaper. It was asked to say she died and didn't survive." "I should have thought of that. I worked on newspapers and so know how they leave things out. But what a nice cute kid she was. Did she get sick?" "It's a story I don't want to go into, sir." "She didn't kill herself, I hope." "I shouldn't be saying anything, sir, and it doesn't seem you were close to the family." "Not with her wrists." "No, something much worse. Complete mutilation. They never got over it ever, neither Gwendolyn either. After all, there was only the two of them for the parents, and as sisters they were always little buddies." "I'm sure. I didn't know Dorothea well, but the times I did see her—I think she was there both times I went out with Gwen and then I used to see her walking on Broadway sometimes—she was a wonderful girl. Peppy, lively. Well, they're the same thing, but that's what she was. Double lively, chipper, energetic, I think—a real spark with a beautiful face and smile." "That's so. All of that. I loved her. Of the two, and I loved them both, she was my special little doll," and she starts crying. "I'm sorry," he says. "I didn't mean to bring it up." "That's all right. I like to cry for her." "I'm really sorry. Gwen, I suppose, was in for her father's funeral?" "I'd like to stop now, sir; I've things to do. May I ask why you called, so I can jot it down here? Is it to pay your condolences?" "In a way, yes. But especially to Gwen. And now for both her sister and father." "I'll try to convey it to her. Your name was how spelled?" "Harold. And then Z-e-i-f. It's been so long, she might not remember who I was." "I'll let her know, if she happens to call and I get on or if her mother writes to her." "Just one more thing, Ruth. Is Gwen now married?" "No." "So she married only two times?" "Three, but the third was annulled." "Then the last name Leigh-hyphen-so-on is her third husband's?" "It's a combination of her sister's middle name and her mother's maiden name which she decided to use when she moved to Europe. I think she said she wanted a new life in every possible way." "What's she doing there, working, painting?" "Nobody knows." "Surely you know but maybe you don't feel like saying or were instructed not to, which'd be OK." "No I don't know, sir, and neither

does her mother." "And the children mentioned in the obituary—
are they hers or Dorothea's or one of each?" "Dorothea's. They went
with the husband after the accident, you can call it." "It wasn't over
a man she killed herself, pardon me for asking. I shouldn't have;
I'm sorry." "I don't like answering that one way or the other, but it
wasn't, and it's none of your business as you said. If you don't mind
I won't give Gwendolyn your message. She once told me to screen
all the messages too." "You mean letters, packages, requests from
alumni magazines—things like that?" She doesn't answer. "I suppose
you're right. My condolences all around. That includes you too, of
course. I can imagine how you felt then, and now with Mr.
Wakesman after so many years, and I'm sorry if I sounded snoopy."
"Thank you," and she hangs up. He gets to Munich the next year
with his wife-to-be and looks up Gwen's name and then her maiden
name in the Munich phone books. She's unlisted or maybe not living
there anymore. His writer friend and he never speak after that last
phone call but he expects he'll bump into him one day and they'll
shake hands and eventually meet for coffee or a beer as they used
to about twice a year and he'll get around to asking him about his
relationship with Gwen and if he's heard anything new about where
she is and what she's doing.

Janine. Meets her at a New Year's Eve party. His brother invited
him to it but said not to get there too early; "That way they won't
think I invited everybody I know." Gone to a movie with friends,
drink and a hamburger after with them, they left for home to get
there before the real street reveling began and he walked uptown
for half an hour, stopped at a bar for a beer and then took a cab to
the party and was in it when twelve came. "Happy New Year," the
driver said when lots of horns and shouting went off around them.
"You too. May it be a great one for you." Seated on a couch, legs
crossed showing short muscular calves, seams running down the
stockings. Who wears seams? Doesn't like them, make her legs look
cheap. Holding a mug of something, coffee or tea, because it's
smoking. Blond hair put up in what she later says is a chignon,

animated pretty face laughing at something a woman in the chair nearest her says, catches him looking at her, he smiles and bows his head, she smiles back and turns to the woman. He walked into this reading or sitting or television room, since in addition to walls of books and lots of sitting furniture there's also a TV, looking for something to do or someone to talk to, foremost an attractive free woman, when he saw her, no men around, in a seated circle of several woman. He'll look at her till she looks at him again. If she seems interested, by her look, he'll smile and leave the room and make his move later. She doesn't seem interested—no smile back, a look of "So what seems so interesting?"—he'll still make his move later but less confidently. Other women are discussing a movie, she looks at him, raises her eyebrows as if saying "Something you want to say?" he smiles, she smiles back and then looks at her mug as if contemplating something inside it. Maybe the way the smoke twirls, milk in the coffee curls. He looks at his glass—what could she be thinking? that he make his move now?—it's half full but he holds it up and nods as if it needs refilling and leaves the room without looking at her again. Finds his brother; he can't even place the woman by Howard's description. "Actually, beautiful, little pug nose, sort of dirty blond kind of wiry hair up in a twisted pile in back, tweed skirt, I forget what color blouse or there might be a sweater over the blouse, seamed stockings, very lively face and plenty of hand motions, with not noticeably large breasts and seems a tiny waist. She could be a dancer." Looks around for her. While admiring the paintings in the living room of larger-than-life-sized nudes, the host says behind him "Something, huh? And they were done by my mother. It's an amazing story. She's only at the League for a year, took up painting for recreation after my dad died, never held a brush other than a scrub or tooth one, and look at what she can now produce: paintings that are both art and can give you a hard-on. The change in her, like her art, came almost overnight. Now she only wears dungarees and smocks, paints all day, dreams of painting and paintings all night, haunts the art museums weekends when she never went to any but Natural History and Historical Society before and only because they were around the block, and thinks of herself as a serious artist with a so-far unclear mission and her teacher's even thinking of solo-exhibiting her." Still can't find her so he goes back to the sitting room, she's on the couch, now in a corner of it because two other women have sat down, legs crossed same way, seams don't seem as bad, big knees, hairy thighs, bulging calves, sees them squeezing him and his breath puffing out, shuts his eyes and shakes the thought off, she doesn't look at him, at least when his eyes are open, and he leaves. If she had looked he would have gestured with his head to the door and then left. If she didn't come out in a minute or so he would have made another move, though he doesn't know what, some time later. Fifteen minutes later, after looking though the apartment for her, he heads for the sitting room to talk with her if she's there and not occupied or gesture with his head if she's busy, and sees her standing outside the sitting room talking to a man. Now or you'll never, and he says hello to her, hi to him, gives his name, "How are you, Happy New Year," and puts out his hand and shakes theirs. "I don't mean to be forward but I suddenly felt like talking to someone, and it's not out of mania or drink, so I thought I'd barge in on you two. Kind of awkward and awful, but do you mind?" She smiles as if what he's doing is funny, man's about to say something serious when he says "Don't worry, I'll be quiet, I'll just listen, won't contribute till my not contributing makes you nervous or I'm asked or obliged to speak." "No no, the man says, "please talk. Our conversation isn't really anything we can't continue next time we meet, since we're in the same class once a week." He asks and their names are Willie and Janine. Asks and it's an acting class. Asks and it's run by a well-known director in a couple of rooms in a dingy Broadway office building, but strictly for professionals. Asks and several prominent actors are in it. The most famous one sits in back in the dark in sunglasses and a fifty-thousand-dollar schmink, but is as sweet as can be. Want to hear a funny story? Janine's heard it from the source so don't cut in with the punchline. "One of the actors gets a call from her last week. She says hi, gives her first name and wants to do a scene with him. He doesn't know who she is, some older woman he recently met while bartending and who's making a play for him?—no pun intended and the actor said it with a straight face, showing how dumb he is. She wouldn't give her last name, didn't want to unnerve him I guess, just kept saying 'This is Marilyn, Marilyn,' and finally 'You know, from class,' and that they were all asked to pick a partner and do a scene for the class, weren't they? They're rehearsing it now. She serves him hot cocoa, it's all very nice and he says she's got talents up her ass." Asks and he's been in stock, on daytime TV, off-Broadway and some movie bits, while Janine here was on Broadway in a major role up to a month ago. Two months, she says. Asks and she says and he says he never liked that playwright's work, though he hasn't seen this play. Too traditional, homespun, unadventurous, with half the scenes around the kitchen or dining room table and half of those when the characters are in bathrobes getting ready for or having just got out of bed. There was a bathrobe scene in her play, she says, and her best scene too, but midway upstairs. "Oh boy you just blew it," Willie says, slaps his back, laughs, goes. Was there a signal between them? Looks to see and she seems annoyed, no doubt by his comments, apologizes, she says it's OK and he's probably a writer or wants to be one, and he says he's been doing little fictions and short plays but how'd she know? Because they're usually trying to negate a skillful older writer's work or just shoveling it into the grave. Asks and her father writes plays and television scripts and he even gets hate mail from young playwrights starting out or about to, damning the little success he's had, belittling what he's still very hard doing, praising only the not-written new. Apologizes and she says let's forget it but still looks angry. He did blow it. What could he do to make up for it? Mind, face, body, glamorous life, artistic father, probably her own apartment, says what she thinks, would love being close with her when that anger's for someone else. Says half his literary judgments are dumb and uninformed and he'll never shoot from the hip like that again. She says why's he making such promises to her? She's still angry. Afraid she'll say it's been nice talking to you but she's got to go. Asks and the mug only held tea because she has a cold and sore throat and what she really needed was honey in it which the host has but couldn't find. Wait and comes back with no tea because he couldn't find the honey when he thought he could but does have two aspirins and water if she needs. So kind and he says misguided overconfidence and he liked the way she was protective of her pa, not many people are. Suggests and they go out for sandwiches and tea with honey for her, she puts her arm around his on the way back, she's cold, didn't dress warmly enough tonight, but it still means something. Asks, if she doesn't mind, is surprised to find she's nine months younger than he, thought she was twenty-five. Looks that old? and says it's because of her maturity and range of experiences so he thought she was a very young looking twenty-five. Tries kissing her at the door, not that she wouldn't like to but someone might come out of the elevator or party, leads her around to where he thinks the service entrance is where they kiss, sit on the service steps and hold hands, stare into each other's eyes dreamily, hug, help each other off with their coats, stare, kiss, hug, kisses her hands, starts crying, says he loves her, isn't that crazy-stupid? and something never to be said so soon, she touches his tears, guesses she feels the same about him too, bizarre the way it started out or right after that went down and then so quickly changed. When? and she says when he told her to wait for she didn't know what and brought back aspirins and water. Wants to go home with her, she says someone brought her, anyway it wouldn't be a good idea, just a good friend who knows the host and lives a block from her and who'll be disappointed if he has to subway home alone. She giving him a line? Not something to ask. Could say it's because he loves her he's asking if she sleeps with this guy, she still might get offended and give up on him as fast as she got close. Here, take my sweater, when she's going, but she says she'll survive. Then his scarf, it's warmer than hers and that way he'll know she'll have to see him again to give it back, says she can always mail it but of course she'll see him, not tomorrow because she has scene run-throughs for class all day and things like that but the next night. Dinner at her apartment. Opens the door wearing an apron and lobster oven mitt she pretends to bite his nose with, framed impish photo of Churchill on her kitchen wall, Picasso boy with horse repro he doesn't tell her he dislikes above the couch, lots of poetry books, cookbooks, Nancy Drews and how to raise dogs, carnation soap smell from the bathroom though has to ask what it is, family photos all around, parents and siblings very handsome and animated then and now, louvered doors to the kitchen—louver, new word he learns—brought wine and napoleans—napoleans, she's always heard but never saw or had them—slips her hands into his back pockets when they kiss, holds his palm up when they're standing and rests her thigh on it, his look what're you doing? and says that's what Harpo always does, hasn't he seen their films? lets him sleep with her if he promises not to try to have sex, sleeps in what were then called baby dolls, he in pajamas too large her brother left when he slept over, later finds the same line in a recent play he reads from her bookshelf where the pajamas were the character's ex-lover's, sees her breasts through the baby dolls, says if he continues to peek she'll sleep with a bra underneath, her behind and a little trickle of pubic hair when she turns her back to him next day to dress, lets him hold but not rub her breasts in bed the third night, week to the day they first went to bed she says she's putting in her diaphragm, is it OK? he says he knows what that means, she doesn't want to have his baby, she says what in the world does he mean? holds her through the night, she says almost every man she's known has turned his back on her right after and slept by himself on his side of the bed and usually even after the first time they made love, remembers to fall asleep holding her every night even when he wants to curl up alone, she says they've had sex at least once a day for two weeks so tonight could he give her poor poopie a rest? After they say good-bye outside they keep looking back to wave and blow kisses, sometimes from more than a block apart, two abortions with a young playwright she wanted to marry or not marry but have kids with but he dropped her, that's why she left the play and was taken aback by his remark that first time, came pretty close to killing herself with poison over a much older actor two years ago, which was when she first thought of giving up the stage for something less frenetic and more cerebral, slit her wrists very slightly over a play director three years back, such a dumb profession where they're all only amateur therapists for the characters they play, wants to sculpt, pot, perhaps write poetry, learn Russian, German and French so she can read all their nineteenth-century literature, holds her tight when she spills all this, says he'll never drop or hurt her for what could ever stop him from wanting to be with her and making her happy forever, says same with her but they're probably a couple of naifs and they cry, kiss, hug and make so much love that night that next day they both ache. Two months after they meet he can't reach her. Said good-bye to her at her door, tried calling her that night, phone doesn't answer for days. Calls her folks and they haven't heard from her in a week but say don't worry as they're sure she's OK. Her friends have no idea. Tries letting himself into her place with the key she gave him but the cylinder's been changed. Something's up but doesn't know what. A guy probably but who could it be and when that she could have hidden it from him, so it's not possible. Waits in front of her acting class day she has it and she doesn't show. Calls the school next week saying he's from a flower store with a delivery for her and what day will she be in since she wasn't there last week to receive it and the receptionist says last week she was away but she notified them she'll be there today. Sees her leaving the building laughing and then putting her arm around the waist of the actor she said she used to date between the two men she nearly killed herself over but found him too rigid and Christian-religious so it could never have gotten serious and broke it off. Everything in him goes cold and drops. Wants to run away without them seeing him, get drunk in a bar and write her the bitterest letter he can and send it care of the acting school's address. But talk to her. Maybe it's just friendship with this guy, like actors are always behaving, so affectionate and full of bullshit, and the lock and not being in touch with him and all that is something she can completely explain. Lincoln sees him crossing Broadway to them and pushes her behind him and grabs her hand. "So I was right," Howard says. "To myself I mean. I mean between you two, I can't believe it. I hate saying the obvious, Janine, but I should have known—at least that you were screwing me good by keeping me on the hook and making me miserable while fucking some other guy." "Listen, Howard," Lincoln says, "you want to get it out, you probably have every right to, but it's not what you think at all. I don't know if she told you, but Janine and I used to see one another—" "You saying you now don't?" "No, we're together again, that's obvious as you said, but much closer than before, I'm afraid, and we wanted to tell you—" "What about her telling me? —How come you didn't? Come on, get out from behind him and speak to me, don't I deserve it?" "Of course you do," coming out from behind Lincoln and letting go of his hand. He tries grabbing it back but she cups her hands. "I'm sorry, very sorry, there's no excuse for the way I handled it with you." "She was wrong, Lincoln says. "She knows it, she admits it, I asked her to talk to you and she didn't know quite how to and I didn't want to do it for her, but I swear she was getting around to it and has felt rotten over it from the start." "Who cares what you have to say? I want her to speak. —Tell me, was the whole fucking thing with me an act? Were you acting for two months or only the last month or two weeks or what?" "That's not really a question, and I wasn't," she says. "Acting at the party I met you at with your stupid headache or whatever it was? Acting when you told me what a madwoman you once were but how with me everything changed?" "No, really no. I was serious. You were wonderful. But something just happened." "With what? Him you mean? When? How could it have? I was seeing you almost every day, fucking you just about every night." She shuts her eyes, seems to grit her teeth. "Don't get coarse," Lincoln says. "We understand how you feel, and your anger, but if you want to talk reasonably we can all go to a coffee shop and do it there." "I don't want to go to one," she says. "OK, we won't, but I don't know how good an idea it is to have it out here. It isn't a good idea, Howard." "So it wasn't an act with me, you're saying?" "No, never, but let's stop this on the street as Lincoln said. Now that we started talking, I'll phone you and we'll meet for a chat or talk on the phone about it some other time." "But it's all over, right?" "You're saying—wait, us two?" "Us, yes, That that's it, we're finished, done, 'Good-bye, Howard, you big fool, you stupid chump, you haven't a chance now and I won't say it but I don't give a shit what happens to you after this'?" "That's not it, and I'm sorry, deeply, but I don't know what else I can say." "Honestly, Howard, we should stop this," Lincoln says. "You want me to start putting on the act like you, Janine? To say it's all OK, easy come, go, good luck and all that crap and just walk away whistling so you'll feel better?" "No. And I truly do wish there was something I could do about it but I can't." "You can marry me. I want you to marry me and for you to have my babies. I always did. Do that, please." "I can't. I'm in fact actually marrying Lincoln, if you have to know." "What are you, kidding? You know him two weeks and a short while before a few years ago or whenever and you're getting married? Or maybe I did get it all wrong. That you were banging him for the two months I knew you. Saying 'I love you deeply, Howard,' and then turning around and saying 'But I love you even more' to him." "No. No. — Lincoln, really," as if they have to go and he should lead the way, she can't, she's about to get sick or faint or start screaming at Howard or just start screaming and he takes her hand, puts his arm around her shoulder and they head downtown. "Where you going? You running away? Can't take the fucking thing? It'll last a week with him, a day. A year, let's say. One great year, you rotten slut. Then who you going to act that you love next? What new putz?" Lincoln stops—that's what he wanted, them to stop—and starts back. "Lincoln, no," she says. "Now take it easy, Howard. I'm telling you, you're going too far and you're also being ridiculously unfair." "You're a witch," he says over Lincoln's shoulder. "I hate your guts, his guts, the fucking sidewalk you're on and phony fake school you go to—I hate you all." She's crying. "Go on, cry," moving around Lincoln to talk, who moves with him so he doesn't get right up to her probably. "Cry your baloney-living life out. And forget chatting. Oh chats, oh chats! No chats, calls, nothing. I never want to hear your ugly voice again." "You really don't have to act like this," Lincoln says. "Believe me, you're going to regret it later, but seriously." "You didn't have to see her. You knew she was seeing me and how I felt about her. Don't talk about natural forces either. You could have stayed away or waited till she dropped me if she did and then moved your big prick in." "That's not how it happened. Anyway, I'm sorry too as to the affect on you and I've said so and you simply have to believe me," and puts his hand on Howard's shoulders and for a few seconds rubs it. The director leaves the building with the famous actress and a few students, says "That the guy you told me to watch out for, Lincoln? What's he, drunk? coked up? Emily said she saw it from the window and is up there looking at us now, so if you want me I'll signal her to call the cops." "No, he'll be OK. He's just a nice guy in a tough spot." "Oh Jesus," Howard shouts. "Everybody," looking at Janine, "isn't Lincoln beautiful? Isn't he just wunderbar great? What a heart he's got, what a soul. I think we should all applaud him— come on, everybody, applaud," and claps. "I'd step away, Lincoln," the director says, with a hand wave getting one of the students to put the actress in a cab. "One swing from him and he'll spoil your gorgeous nose." "No, I'm fine," and puts his hands back on Howard's shoulders and digs his fingers in and starts massaging them and Janine comes up and holds Howard's hand and looks at him and smiles. "Fuck it, I give up on you," and pulls away and runs downtown, could make a right at the side street and disappear but runs across Broadway so they'll see him and down into a subway station. Gets drunk at a bar soon after and calls Lincoln's apartment from it. She answers and he says "It's me, don't hang up, I can't live without you, piesie, I can't," and starts crying. "I'm sorry, Howard,

I'm really very sorry. I told you why. So please don't call again. Then, if you still want, we can meet in about two weeks. Send a letter to my old address. I'm still collecting mail there or I have someone pick it up almost every day and I'll phone you and we'll meet and talk some more. Now I'm putting the receiver down, sweetie, and please, for both of us, do what I say," and he slams the receiver down before she hangs up. Tells himself not to but calls several times later and line's always busy. Gives up his modeling job at the League because he can't pose for twenty-minute stretches without going crazy thinking of her. Can't read or write or paint or draw or do any of the things he once liked to. Goes to movies, leaves after about fifteen minutes; museums, hoping he'll bump into her and she'll see how sad he is and one thing will lead to another and they'll start up again. Every time the phone rings at home he thinks it might be her saying she wants to see him, at least speak to him to see how he's doing, even that she loves him and didn't know how much till now, or just that she wants to explain some things she didn't so they can part as good friends. Calls in a week, Lincoln answers and says he doesn't think it's the right time just yet for him to speak to Janine and to understand he's upsetting her every time he calls and try not to again for a while. "But she told me to call her," and Lincoln says "If she said that then she's changed her mind." "Let her tell me that," and Lincoln says "She asked me to speak for her," and he says "How do I know you're not talking for her without her permission and that she might want to speak to me but doesn't have the chance to decide yes or no on it because you're not telling her I'm here?" and Lincoln says "You'll have to take my word, there's no other way." "Well, let's say it's so, how long's a while when you said not to call again before that?" and Lincoln says "Few months, possibly more. I won't spin out the reasons why it should be that long. And I also hate doing what I'm about to, Howard, since I actually like you and can appreciate your passion and I know this hostility is only anomalous behavior on your part, but I've got to go so I'll have to cut off," and hangs up. Anomalous. Would look it up but can't even stand these days opening a dictionary. Calls a few hours later hoping she'll answer. Lincoln does and Howard says "Listen, I'm sure she'll speak to me if you tell her I'm here and absolutely calm and peaceful and it'll only be for a few seconds and nothing nasty," and Lincoln says "Believe what you want on that, Howard—believe anything, if it makes you feel better, because all that can be helpful in a way—but I swear to you, it's not true," and he says "What isn't?" and Lincoln says "What you said, what you asked," and he says "I forget what that was," and thinks He's probably right, it's probably so, I can understand why she wouldn't, and says "You still there?" and Lincoln says "Still here," and says "Anything more you have to say?" and Lincoln says "Nope, you?" and he wants to curse him out and say the whole situation stinks and he still feels Lincoln's a pig but thinks maybe the moderate approach will help, for once he won't act on his first impulse, and Lincoln will go back to her and say "He seemed so polite, reasonable, pleasant, well adjusted the last time we spoke," and she might then think she can talk to him again and might even think better than that in his favor, that he was distraught before but for good reason, and also passionate, as Lincoln said, which she might like if Lincoln isn't, but now he's mature and congenial, gracious and calm, and says "So, nice talking to you, Lincoln, and thanks so much for your attitude through all this, and I mean it," and Lincoln says "Good," as if he doesn't believe it, and he says "You know that I'm being serious now. I don't know anyone who would have had the character, if you don't object to my saying this, to handle the whole thing the way you did. And best to Janine and much happiness to you both," and Lincoln says "I'll convey it," and hangs up. Few days later he waits across Broadway, sees them leaving the school, they don't see him and don't seem to be looking around for him, nobody at the second-floor window, ducks behind a parked car, looks through its windows at them, both with serious faces on, angry or peeved at something, maybe at each other or how they performed in a scene today or expressions that might seem like anger but are apprehension or alarm he might be around—he is seeing them from a distance and through two windows—holding hands, cross the avenue at the corner, he moves around the car as they get nearer the sidewalk till he's in front of the hood looking around it, follows them though he thinks he knows where they're going, they go where he thought, down the uptown IRT station, no doubt for Lincoln's place. Drinks a lot in a bar for a couple of hours, same subway station uptown, pictures where they stood, sat, stands in front of Lincoln's building, six stories, rundown, mangled garbage cans in front with no lids, first-floor apartment windows with gates across and towels on top of the lower windows' upper sashes to keep out the cold, vestibule has that dead roach or insecticide smell, never been able to identify it but most of the old tenements have it, maybe just mildew or wall rot, one of the mailbox doors ripped off and another almost twisted in half, first-floor hallway, through the front-door window, dirty, needing painting bad. So cheap rent probably, romantic little rooms he bets and which she'll give her special touch, roaches around and maybe mice but so what? Just bang them with paper or your hands or feet and the mice with a broom and make love under lots of covers, because probably insufficient heat. Get a cheap heater, sit by it while you work and stick it by the bed on her side or in the bathroom when you go to sleep. Lincoln's name on the bell roster and in the mailbox, 4C. Doesn't know if it's the front or rear. Her name taped above the regular name space in the mailbox but not on the roster. Goes outside and looks up at the fourth-floor windows. Shades up in two, down in the three others, lights on in all but never sees anyone. Gives up in an hour. Cold out, some people passing on the sidestreet look at him as if he's about to commit a crime. Calls up friends of hers who seemed to like him. Several say what can he do? She's in love, getting married soon, best thing is to accept it or forget her. One invites him for coffee. Lincoln's been a Christian Scientist since he was a kid, he's told. Janine used to be one when she was a girl, and her mother still practices it sometimes. Lincoln brought her back into the church. She's given up alcohol, little she drank, does the Mary Baker Eddy and Bible exercises every day, is already distributing old *Monitors* and religious magazines and leaflets to barbershops and places like that. She's never been happier or healthier. She not only says it but looks it. She's even given up coffee and regular tea. They've visited the mother church in Boston twice since they got together and for their honeymoon they're flying to Paris to see avant-garde plays for a week—Lincoln speaks fluent French—and then to study there for a month with what she guesses could be called a Christian Scientist guru. Lincoln's bought an Italian motor scooter and they zip around town on it like a couple of kids and they both got jobs on the same soap for this fall. The wedding date and place are a secret except to their guests, this woman says, "presumably to keep it from you and another of her past suitors. She certainly knocked off a few." Calls her at Lincoln's, she answers and he says "So how are you?" and she says "I'm fine, what do you want?" and he says "Oh God, gruff voice, I thought you said you wanted to talk to me in a couple of weeks," and she says "Lincoln explained it to you once; that should be enough," and he says "Please don't ride on motor scooters; they're dangerous. Oil slick comes, it'll skid and you'll crash or fall off. Get a helmet at least," and she says "You're probably right about the helmet; I'll get one for Lincoln too." "And you gave up coffee and tea that has caffeine, I heard. You used to love coffee, made the best I ever had. Ground it fresh every morning, mixed it with whatever you mixed it with—chicory, sometimes two different beans." "It became a fetish. And it's a stimulant. I happen to love herbal teas or vegetable broth first thing in the morning, at least as much." "Good, all that makes you feel better, live longer, you don't need doctors anymore, but he's twelve years older than you, someone said." "So what? I wasn't hiding it." "But when you're twenty-eight, he'll be forty. Thirty-eight, he'll be fifty, and so on. By comparison to you, he already looks old." "He looks as young and is probably in twice the physical shape you or any man your age is, including professional athletes. He never drank, smoke, did anything to poison his body, and because his principal theatrical interest is mime, just practicing it hours a day keeps him incredibly fit. He can stand upside down on a single finger and then walk on two—you know what it takes to do that? As for his mind, it's clear, imaginative, and youthful as they come." "Religion is the last refuge of a dumbbell or whatever someone once said. Who needs to bow? Who needs to pray? Like a bunch of beggars the way they hand around that dumb money tray. And who needs to read some wacko whose hip bones stitched naturally after a break but starts up her own religion from it." "You haven't read her. We don't bow. Other than for what we think are its practical benefits, praying can be like meditation, which you loftily once said you thought there could be some value to and you might want to try. You ought to witness a Science testimonial some Wednesday afternoon or night at any of the churches around town or go to a Sunday service. Everyone's lovingly invited, even tourists, and you'll see we're not robots and there are no ministers. It's entirely run by laymen and women, services and church. I could lead a service if I wanted to and knew enough." "You've been brainwashed. Your mind's hanging out to dry and is getting bleached by the sun and holes in it from the wind." "I knew you'd get around to that business eventually. Insults and ignorance. We've seen it before. Please don't call again, Howard. You were once sweet and caring but you're now a headache. Right after this I'm having our phone disconnected," and hangs up. Calls back a few minutes later to apologize and the phone's busy. Calls the next day and it's busy and day after that the number's been changed and new one's unlisted. It's an emergency, he tells the operator and she says "Not even for emergencies it says." Writes her letters, apologizes in them, says he was feeling crazy and depressed before, so because of it bitter and unloving, but he's now over it, pleads for her to meet him so he can ask her forgiveness in person, but they're never answered or sent back. Wants to get away from her, hitch and train around the country, have adventures, more experiences, meet lots of women, work at various places to make money to continue traveling. Goes to D. C. to say good-bye to his oldest brother. In an elevator at the Press Club an acquaintance of

Jerry's steps in, they're introduced, says "He the brother who wants to be a writer?" "Both," Jerry says, "but the older one's actually getting published." Remembers Jerry telling him Howard worked as a copyboy at CBS when he was in college, wonders if he'd like to fill in for a vacationing reporter for three weeks. Does, stays for two years. Year after he has the job he gets Lincoln's number from information. Calls a few times over the next months. Lincoln always answers and Howard always hangs up. Once though he says in a muffled fake voice "Hello, this is Balicoff Studios in Los Angeles, is Miss Austin in?" "Hold on, please," and in the background Lincoln says "It's fantasyland; what do they want?" and she gets on and says "Janine Austin speaking," and he says nothing and she says "Hello, what studio in L. A., my husband wasn't able to catch it so fast?" and says nothing and she says "Have we been cut off? Could you speak louder, if you're speaking, or do you want to call back? Yell yes and I'll hang up." Nothing and she says "I think I hear someone there; is anyone there?" and waits a few seconds and says "Oh well, if it is some studio, try to call back, thanks," and hangs up. She sounded the same, maybe a little artificial because she thought it was an important professional call. Pictured Lincoln seated beside her on the bed, holding her hand, ear near the receiver. Then them both waiting for the studio to call back and after a half hour or so dialing California information for Balicoff Studios or any name sounding like that, and then realizing it was a prank and maybe even Howard calling, or maybe they realized it right after she hung up or Lincoln realized it before, or there could be a new guy carried away by her and they thought it might be him. Calls her folks a couple of weeks later when he's drunk and depressed and says "Howard Tetch, you remember me," and her father says "Sure," and says "How's Janine?" and he says "Fine," and says "Good, any other news about her?" and he says "None we know of—take care of yourself, Howard, nice speaking to you," and says "That's great, and nice talking to you too, sir." Wrong thing to do, thinks next morning. They'll tell her, they'll all say how immature he still is and doesn't he realize how disturbing it is getting a drunken late-evening call like that? Writes her folks an apology, saying he'd gone to a party, too much to drink, got sloppily sentimental—doesn't know why, Janine hasn't been on his mind for a year—it'll never be repeated, wishes them well, doesn't hear back from them. He and another reporter quit their jobs to form their own radio news service, running it out of the radio-TV gallery in the Capitol. Month after they start it his partner has a stroke, partially paralyzed and can't type or speak on the air anymore and Howard can't run it alone or bring in anyone else as his partner was the brains behind it. Could go back to his old job but returns to New York permanently because just around then the freighter his brother Alex was on disappeared in the Atlantic and he thinks he should be near his sister and folks. Moves in with them, job, calls up one of Janine's best friends, doesn't mention her name but hopes she and her husband will and tell him something about her. They've heard him on radio several times, seen him on TV asking questions at the political conventions and of visiting dignitaries like Khrushchev and Macmillan and Mrs. Roosevelt at Washington airports and in the Capitol and such and once on a panel show on some news subject, glad he's found something he likes doing and is good at and he says he doesn't much like it, still wants to write and actually gets some lines down now and then. They invite him for dinner, wonder if they should invite Janine. "Why," he says casually, "she still in the city?" "You didn't know? *You're* some reporter. They got divorced. Incompatible. Nothing brutal. Simply couldn't live with each other after a while. Maybe it was sex, or with actors, more likely ego. And more with Lincoln than her, because she was never much that way, was she?" "Ego? No, not that I saw." "She's still very involved with Christian Science and they see each other at the same Sunday church service sometimes, but that's all. She got a Mexican quickie. So you wouldn't mind?" "Me? It'd be nice seeing her again, if she can stand being in the same room with me." "And why wouldn't she? She once told me she understood why you did what you did, though at the time found it unbearable, but harbors no ill feelings." Goes to their apartment, hopes she's been invited and comes, brings a good bottle of wine, expensive pastries, combed his hair this way and that to try to cover his growing baldness, tie? no tie, but shine your shoes, tried ironing his pants but his mother took over: "You're too nervous. Men can never do it right anyway unless they worked in a cleaner's. Where you going?" and when she hears Janine might be there: "Too bad about her divorce. I always liked that girl. Real lively, but how you let her get to you I never approved. Never be a fall guy. Sensitivity's fine, but make the women come to you. Remember what everyone knows and has told me: with your looks and brains you could have almost anyone. Give her our best." It's winter, old snow on the ground, sees her wet boots on the doormat. His pulse; number of other physical reactions which were also with him during his twenty-block walk here. She answers, big bright smile and loud hi as she used to open the door with when things were good with them. Happy to see him, says it, looks it. He pretends to be subdued: "Thank you, nice seeing you too," but sweat on his face a giveaway. "Look at me," wiping. "I ran from the bus stop for exercise, which I didn't get today, and because I thought I might be late. I hate hanging people up, and I see I'm not," looking at the wall clock. "Hope you didn't shake up the wine and cake too much." Oh God, how could he run with the wine and cake? "No, I held them both to me, cake straight," and demonstrates. "Anyway, hi and hello," putting out his hand. She shakes it and puts out her cheek. "This is fun," she says, "five minutes of greetings." Where's the couple? Hears them in the kitchen. They must have planned, or she said "Let me get it," so she planned, but why the plans if it wasn't that they were busy and she was just helping them out by answering the door? But why wouldn't they be out here by now? Maybe a good sign. No older, hair up and even blonder, as beautiful, body seemingly unchanged. She says "We're having champagne—I'm not but they are and I hope you will too— to celebrate a belated happy new year. I was supposed to go to a party with the Lipsatz's but never made it. The flu." "You OK now?"

"Of course, it was weeks ago." "Sometimes they linger on," knowing he's showing too much concern. How to undo that? Thinks; can't. Just says "You're right." Lipsatzes come out with hors d'oeuvres and the champagne and tray of champagne glasses, one filled with club soda and ice. "Happy new year," Janine says, holding her glass up and they all say happy new year and he intentionally starts the kissing by kissing Naomi's cheek first, then goes over to her and she puts her lips out and he gives what he thinks she expects, a peck, then kisses Mel's cheek and right after he does realizes Mel just wanted to hug. "It's really wonderful being here," he says—they're still in the foyer, he hasn't taken off his coat yet—"old friends, really," and thinks, taking off his coat, switching the glass from hand to hand instead of putting it down on a sideboard which seems new or highly polished and he doesn't want to stain, if he could only say something funny, true, untrite. He's still nervous, pulsing in spots; relax, try to avoid eye contact with her for most of the evening and see how she reacts. Much better at dinner: words there when and where he wants them and often big ones but where it's not obvious they're said to impress. "What's 'extrapolation' again?" she says at the table. Lipsatzes in the kitchen cleaning up, though the plates and utensils were throwaway paper and plastic and there was no salad or bread and the entire dinner came out of one pot. There to leave them alone? If so, only planned on their part. "Why," though he knows, "in something you read?" "You used it, don't you remember? When you were saying President Kennedy's a charming lightweight compared to Mike Mansfield who you said is the one senator there qualified to run the country." "Sure, in decency, dignity, speaking ability, modesty, intelligence, world experience and things like that. His face is pockmarked and he comes from little Montana, so maybe that's what killed it. But Jesus, I totally forgot using the word. Just came and went. At least you know I didn't say it to impress you. I won't even try defining it I'm so bad at that," and then gives one straight from the dictionary, as he'd looked it up last night for about the fifth time in a year. She says "Talking about impressions. I'm impressed the way you've changed in almost every aspect. It must be your work, people depending on you and all the interesting types you met, living away from home and in your own apartment, holding down a demanding position and what any two years would do to someone our still impressionable age." "I don't know. To me I'm just the same old schmo, but thanks." "Oh come off it." They leave together. Said at the table to her "I've got to go—work tomorrow—but you stay." She said no, the Lipsatzes have to get up for work too. In the elevator she says "I'll get the number 10 bus downtown." "Take a cab. It's late and your neighborhood I'm sure isn't the safest." "Money money money," she says, "but I'll be all right." "Here," and he fishes out a five. "I'm working and I don't want you going home except by cab." "Always so protective," she says. "I'd do it for almost anyone, honestly." Opens the cab door for her, tells himself not to attempt even an innocent kiss goodbye, says "May I call you?" "I hope so, if just so I can give you your five dollars back." "Precious cargo," he says to the driver, who nods, doesn't turn around, and thinks another trite familiar remark; when she's driving home she'll think I'm even a worse schmuck than I was. She waves through the back window as the cab pulls away; he gives a brief wave and then pretends to be fingering his coat and pants pockets for something, eyes where his hands are, anxious look. Before the cab left she said "Want to be dropped off on the way?" and he said he'd rather jog home— "exercise again"—but walks, interpreting all the signs he could remember and what she said, punching his palm several times, not believing his luck. Phones, they meet, kiss the first night, meet, doesn't want to sleep with him till she feels they're ready, he tells himself don't push it, ruin it, she's not saying she doesn't want to be with him. Takes a week. Night of the biggest snowfall in years. Maybe it contributed to it in different ways. They're walking home from a movie in the Village. Nonessential cars, radio says the next day, weren't allowed into the city. Several horses with sleighs down lower Fifth. Cross-country skiers, no traffic noises, so voices from blocks away. "Hiya neighbor," a stranger says. Throws snowballs at lampposts, lobs one at her and she quickly turns around and it smacks her back. "You-u-u," and comes at him with a handful of snow as if she's going to mash it into his face, drops it when she gets close and either he hugs her and she falls into his arms or she falls into his arms and then he hugs her, and they laugh, brush the snow away from the other's neck, nip at each other's lips and then kiss. "I'm going to get even with you one day for that snowball, mister," she says when they separate, and he gets down on one knee and says "No, please, have pity, don't," and makes a snowball down there and threatens to throw it at her and she screams and runs off. Arms around each other's waists rest of the way, kissing, saying things like "I'm gonna say it: I love you, always have, always will"; "I love you too, sweetie"; "You do? You mean romantically? Then I love you too-too." "Too-too what?" "Too-too much which isn't enough." "Never too-too much, never enough; by George, what do I mean?" "Never ever have I loved you more, never have I loved anyone more or as much. Seriously, I'm being serious, though I bet you don't want to hear it." "You're a darling and a dearie," she says, "and I mean it." "I'm gonna say this is the happiest night of my sappy life; day or night, happiest sappiest anytime, day, dusk, dawn or night." "It isn't mine but it's one of and that's sufficient, isn't it, or not?" "It doesn't always have to be equal so long as it's close." "It is; it's going along perfectly; we've lots more time." Apartment's warm, radiators knocking, windows steamed up, doesn't want to push, ruin it, though now isn't sure he could, still, she's a changeable sort, gets down to his jockey shorts as he does whenever he sleeps over—fresh pair every day; they're white, doesn't want her turned off by stains—kisses her goodnight, "So good night then, my dear, sleep well, pleasant tights," saluting her, bowing, shaking her hand, then the other, wants her—knows he's going too far—to pick up on the irony of their passionate kissing on the street and now going to separate beds, heads for the couch hoping she'll call him back if just for another kiss, when he gets there wonders if he shouldn't have tried necking with her just now, massaging her back, maybe curling his arm around to brush her breast, "Excuse me," somehow maneuvering her hand to his fly. No, but at least to have said "You know I'd love sleeping with you—perfect night, the snow, hissing radiators, rising risers, chained tires clanging outside, besides what I've said is the deepest besides the ruttiest kind of love I've ever had for anyone including you. But I can understand why you're not tempted—no, that's not the right word—so I'm not going to push it, ruin it. We've time as you say, right, so who's complaining?—not I," and then, as he did, to walk to the couch without looking back. She says, when he's making the couch up, pretending not to notice her going back and forth from bathroom to bedroom, trying to push his penis back between his thighs because it's sticking straight out, "Listen," in a short nightie, nipples and pubes seen through, "why don't you sleep with me tonight, if you promise to take off those godawful shorts." "You want me to wear boxer shorts instead of briefs?" "Anything. Nothing, under your pants, if I had the choice between those and no underclothes." Engaged in a couple of months. Proposes in her building's basement while they're taking clothes out of the washer and sorting them and putting most into the drier. "I know this is the wrong place but would you, if I asked, marry me?" and she says "Why, what other place would be more memorable to be asked that except maybe the toilet? and I'd love to." "Let me get it straight—for the record as we reporters like to say—I never did but I heard about it—you'd love to marry me?" "Yes, I would." "You will marry me then?" "Yes, I've said it." "We can tell people, we can start planning for it? I can start considering your apartment my home?" "We might want to get a larger one, but for the time being, sure, it's ours. As for telling people, let's digest it for now and, to mix it up a bit, sit on it for about two weeks, but don't you worry, I won't change my mind." Their folks meet at a restaurant and her father says "I can see who he resembles," looking at his mother, and she says "Oh, Simon was very handsome when he was Howard's age—all the women went for him and I felt fortunate he chose me. But he got plump and now you can't see the likeness except in the strong chin, but I'd say he resembles him." "Don't ruin it for the boy," his father says. "I was a born eater while he's mostly hated food and has stayed thin. But you're the bathing beauty—you know she was Miss New York, or was it Rockaway, before I met her and she danced in the Scandals?—so let them think he got his good looks and sleek physique from you." "With Ziegfeld. And I would have won the Miss America too if they had talent then as part of the competition. But it was all rear ends and no brains and they chose some Pennsylvania Slovak who everyone said slept with the two main judges when they couldn't get me." "You never told me about the hanky-panky," Howard says. Starts reading the daily Christian Science exercises from *Science and Health* and the Bible because he knows it'll please her, going to church with her almost every Sunday. She's usually one of the ushers: standing at attention at the door when you first come in, passing around the plate, always smiling because she believes it's infectious and in ways curing, white flower pinned to her dark collar; he can't stand looking at her she seems so fake and once thinks if she ever breaks up with him he'll use that image of her smiling and ushering in her ugly prim suit and pumps to lessen the pain. Says "I'm finding the readings very interesting, lot to learn from it, she's a very smart woman, and the Bible's such a beautiful book; I wish my folks had read it to me as a kid as yours did," though finds it all a drag, too much like school was, but will continue doing it enthusiastically; then he'll quickly give her a kid. She doesn't want one so soon, he'll inseminate her somehow: stick it in before she says "Wait for my diaphragm," all out of passion; then say let them do it that way a while, he never gets to be inside her without the smelly cream, he can control it till the last moment but he'll take it out long before that, while secretly leaking little by little in. She says "You don't have to read or attend any of it if you don't like, though of course if you really want to, it'd be very nice." Wedding set for May. They want a small city hall ceremony and the reception in a Chinese restaurant on 103rd and Broadway but her parents say their house. She'll be accompanied downstairs. Her favorite flowers everywhere and about forty guests. He'll be waiting for her and they'll walk the next few steps together to the judge in front of the fireplace, lit if it isn't a hot day. Two-day honeymoon at the Sturbridge Inn, which they'll get to by rented car. In April, morning after a lot of evening lovemaking, where it's so bright and crisp that he jumps out of bed an hour before the alarm's to go off, half hour of energetic calisthenics, shower, reads by the kitchen window while having coffee and toast, kisses her hand and nudges her instead of letting the alarm go off, from the kitchen catches her through the bedroom mirror getting out of bed naked, holding up her breasts to inspect and slipping into her bathrobe, he's dressing for work while she's putting on hose when she says "I have something to tell you." Way she says it. And doesn't look up at him. Immediately shouts "Forget it. Don't say anything, I'll just pack my clothes. Because it's happened again. But this time you drew me in nearer to give me even greater disappointment. You're cutting it all off, right?" "No. Don't jump the gun, Howard." "Ah, fuck it. Ah, screw it. The whole thing's obvious. You're never going to go through with it even if you say now you only want the wedding postponed." "I do only want it postponed. I've no doubts about my feelings for you but think we need more time to sanctify it." "Sanctify, horseshit." "It was the wrong word. And wrongly worded. I meant—" "You meant, you meant—we're over with, don't tell me. You're booting me the fuck out, for can you actually tell me you want me to continue living here?" "True, I do think it'd be better if we had separate living places for the time being. A month or two. Maybe through the summer, though we'll still see each other, of course; just a bit less. But this will give us time and room to think if we truly do want to go ahead with it." "I truly do. There's nothing I want more." "But I've been married. Getting divorced was devastating and I don't want to—I want to make absolutely sure I'm absolutely sure about marriage again. If we decide to go ahead with it, then it'll only have been a few months' delay." "Nah, you're soft-pedaling me out of here. It's always the same. Whenever you want something that bad, it never turns out OK.

Whenever *I* want—not you." "That's not it." "It is it. You know goddamn well we're done with, done with," banging the couch with his fists. His untied tie starts to slide off his neck when he bangs and he grabs and twists it and tries tearing it in two and then throws it across the room. "You know what you're doing?" she says. "You're making me think why have I put up with you so long and your terrible tantrums?" "That was the first with you ever. But excuses. I'll give you real ones. Our different religions. You're a Christian Scientist and I'm an idiot trying to please you by reading it till I'm sick and blind." "Well that's news." "I'll give you more. You think you don't love me enough or maybe realized you never did." "You know that's not so." "It is. You hate even being mentioned as my fiancée. I saw it on the street with that guy Weinberg or Weintraub or whatever his name is—Ned, my brother Jerry's friend. After I introduced you—" "I only said later—he the one by Rockefeller Plaza?" "Yes." "I didn't like being introduced as your appendage but by my name." "But I was proud of it, wanted to tell everybody—" "I still didn't like it. It's demeaning, outdated, a step away from 'my betrothed' or 'intended' or 'future slave.' Maybe not that bad, but do I go around calling you my fiancé?" "Do, I'd love it; then 'my husband, my beloved, the love of my life.' What the hell else is it for? But you didn't like it because it was the realization that by the designation people had the expectation we'd eventually get married, and at that moment it sunk in." "You're being silly. But we'll talk later, or we'll be late for work." "I'm being realistic. If I can see, then I say what I see, and I can see it,on the wall, the freaking end-of-getting-married and end of everything else between us, so stop hiding it to make it so-called easier for me. Because if I'm to start getting the jitters about you dumping me, I want to starting today." "All I can say—" putting on her coat, "Don't you want something to eat?" "No." "Is that you're acting all out of proportion to the situation. But after the way you acted, perhaps it would be best if you got your things together this weekend and moved out for the time being," "And you're saying you weren't going to tell me that before we had this rotten talk?" "I probably would have, if you didn't leave on your own in a week or so." "Bullshit. Horseshit. I could kill you. Sorry, I don't mean that, but I hate you for what you've done. Sucking me in, leading me on . . ." He's punching his palm, biting his knuckles now. "Go yourself. I'll throw my junk together while you're out and that'll be it for us." "No, I don't want you wrecking the place. Besides, I don't want to leave it like this. Come on, Howard, really; stick another tie in your pocket and let's go." Does, muttering "Fuck you, you bastard, go screw yourself," under his breath. They take the subway, don't speak. Didn't when they walked to the subway, he always a few feet ahead of her, "Boy, you really want to be rid of me," she said. "Why don't you just race on ahead?" I would, I would, if I didn't want to, he thought. Didn't know if he should stick the coins in the turnstile for her, as he usually does, but did, after he went through, without looking at her. She touches his hand while they stand hanging on to a pole during the ride, but he pulls it away, looks at the ads around, can't stand looking at anything and shuts his eyes. I hate her. I'm going to go crazy without her. If it's bad now, what'll it be when my stuff's all out of her place and I don't have an excuse to see her? I'll call, she'll be nice on the phone, but won't see me. Maybe in a few weeks, she'll say. She'll start with some other guy, probably one from her church. Seemed to be a lot of good-looking bright guys there and a lot more fun-making in the sense she likes than him. Jolly, healthy, gay. I'll drink too much to get to sleep, wake up a few hours after I pass out and feel even worse because I won't be able to get back to sleep besides being a little stomach-sick, so I'll just think of her, the bitch, hours before with her apron on, cooking dinner for some guy, later on top of him in bed, at the same moment he's thinking all this, that smile on her puss when she's up there doing it that way, taking this subway with him next day. Shakes off the thought. "Anything wrong?" she says. "No," closes his eyes again, recalls her as the smiling usher, escorting one of the elderly congregants down the aisle, that phony and fake. "Aren't the stained-glass windows here beautiful?" first time she took him. No, they're not, he thought, they're churchy, depressing, but said yes. I should be glad to be rid of her. If they had children, what fun would it be bringing them up if she led them to church every Sunday? This business with medicine. Dinner with her boring church friends, no wine, or a bottle only in front of him, and after, Sanka or herbal tea, though if he likes, real coffee. What'll I say to my folks, brother and friends? Who'm I going to move in with? I'll have to get my own place quick. That's not easy. Everyone wants a cheap place in the Village. But I want it to be near hers but not in the same neighborhood, so I can bump into her or plan it so it looks that way. Forget that. I'll get one, anywhere in the city that's cheap, show her I don't need her. Show her nothing. Tell friends it's over and you want to go out with other women and then go out with them, find someone else— that's the best cure, and staying away from her. Opens his eyes, looks at her. So goddamn beautiful, it kills him. Would love for it to be like it's been, handholding on the train, if they get seats each reading a different section from the same newspaper and occasionally commenting on it, parting kiss. "Listen," he says, and puts his mouth to her ear, "I love you too much, that's the problem." "That's not it," she says, "believe me." "Then what is?" "Let's talk about it later," as it's her stop they're pulling into, and she puts out her cheek, he says "Oh shove it. I'm not going to just take everything you dish out," and she shrugs and goes. He's at work but can't work, calls her after lunch and says "So where do I stand? Can I come by later to at least pick up the stuff I need?" "Hold it. Don't go to extremes again. We should talk, Meet me after work?" Meet, dinner out, grabs her hand when they walk to the restaurant, she clutches his, puts her head on his shoulder, over dinner she says she was much too hasty this morning and didn't think through lots of what she said, his reaction didn't help matters but she takes part responsibility for that, she still wants the marriage postponed, she doesn't know till when, but please stay, she's almost sure it can all work out. "I'll stay, no question about it," kisses her hands, she kisses his, stare at each other and cry. Few weeks later, while they're dressing for work, he

Frog

says "By the way, have you had any more thoughts, either way, about the marriage being postponed or anything regarding it and us? Just asking, you don't have to answer." "Truth is, after careful consideration, corny as that has to sound to you, and talking it over with some people good for that—" "Your practitioner?" "Among others. That's all right, isn't it?" "Really, what more important decision could you make, so anything you say." By her expression and she's looking right at him and that "corny as that has to sound" remark, he thinks everything's going to be OK. "Anyway, you asked, so I'm saying, though I hate for it always to be the first thing in the day—I don't know when the right time for it could be—" "Wait, what are you saying?" "You must have sensed something's been wrong between us since the last time." "No, nothing, what?" can hardly speak, "everything's been great." "It hasn't. Quite the opposite. I've been withdrawn from you, melancholic to downright depressed most times the last two weeks. It's because it isn't working, and I also knew what I'd be saying now would hurt you, which made me feel even worse." "Why? You've been happy, gay, moody occasionally, but not for long and no more than me—natural moodiness, comes and goes. And we've been fine together, same as ever whenever it's gone well, and it has, joking around, sleeping together—" "Not fine; not happy or gay. If I seemed liked it then it was an act not to show how I felt but one I wasn't even aware of. And sleeping with you is what you wanted so I gave in but not with any enthusiasm or joy. You had to know that too." "I didn't. That's not at all what I caught." "Then I'm not saying any more. We'll talk tonight. I don't want to ruin your day or mine as I did the last time." "You saying you definitely can never think of marrying me?" "I think so. Or at least that's what I think now. And without that direction, we shouldn't live together. Something isn't clicking with us, I don't know what. You've been wonderful, have put up with me and my moods, but I need time to be by myself and think things out. Maybe, but I doubt it, I'll discover—" He pushes her, wants to hit her, she sees it, fist up and his face, and backs away. "Don't worry, I never would. Never you.

656

Not that precious face. Oh no, I couldn't," and smashes his fist through a panel of the closet door. She says "Now who's going to pay for that?" "Fuck it, you moron, your goddamn door." "All right, I will fuck it. I'll fuck it, fuck it, fuck it, you fucking fucking curser. You crazy man. For the first time, though you've given signs, I'm truly afraid of you," and goes into the bathroom and locks it. He listens at the bathroom door. "You crying in there? Well if you are, cry all you want; just think of what you've done to me," and runs water over his hand, wants to put antiseptic on it but that's in the bathroom, wraps it with a dishtowel and leaves. Calls her at work and says "Sorry about the door. Tell Mrs. Young I fell with such force or something that my head went through it, but that I'll pay for it." "I saw blood in the kitchen. How's your hand?" "My hand deserves what I did to it, so don't worry. I also want to say, if it'd help things, and I don't think it'd be a bad idea for me—I'm interested in it and I need—you saw—some additional spiritual discipline in my life like this—I'll convert to Science." "Do it only for yourself, not me. It won't change anything between us. It's not the issue. Be Jewish; even be Orthodox Jewish." "But I need you to stay with me and guide me in it. I'm serious about it. It's not just for you." "Go to any Science church other than mine and ask them for advice. But nothing related to me." "Ah, you just don't love me, that's all. You maybe did a little once—now and then—but not enough." "Anyway, I'll stay somewhere else tonight and you can start moving out. I'll give you till around six tomorrow. But please go? And promise you won't wreck anything else or take whatever's not yours?" Gets an apartment. Gets drunk a lot. Calls her late at night a lot, for anything. "The Auden book I said I didn't want? I need it back. Not only because I'm starting to love his work again but there's something in it I have to find and copy down to go into my own writing." "I'll send it." "I have to have it by morning. Can I come right down?" She's on her stoop with the book. "Here. Please don't bother me with little things like this again. You want anything more of yours I might have, tell me now and we'll go upstairs and get it and that'll be all." They go upstairs. He grabs her on the third-floor landing to kiss her. She puts her hand between their mouths. "Please. I feel nothing but sympathy for you now." "Fuck you, you rat. You can have whatever I've left up there, or throw it out the window for all I care. Plus this book," and heaves it downstairs, kicks it out of his way as he leaves the building. Weeks later wishes he hadn't; one about Yeats and another about suffering he wanted to go to; also the shortie where children die in the streets. He was drinking and in a sad serious mood. Meets her two years later at an art gallery she's working at. Saw the review and that afternoon had nothing to do. "Fancy this," he says and she looks up from a textbook and that smile and big hi. "I didn't mean to just spring up on you. You're I swear a complete surprise." She's no longer a Christian Scientist, is living with an artist who exhibits here but nothing of his up this moment, courses in anthropology, paleontology, ancient Greek, given up theater for good. News quit him when the show went off the air and he's living on unemployment and writing a book. They kiss each other's cheeks good-bye. "Wait a sec, I haven't even looked around," does, says he wasn't disappointed and it's a nice walk back through the park. "By the way," and invites him for dinner. Accepts but hour before just can't see himself there, sitting, wanting, coming back, and calls to say he suddenly got a stomach flu. The artist answers, says she's in the can now, he'll relay the message. "Too bad, it would've been interesting. Most of our pals can't talk anything but dealers or painters, when they're not descanting on Chinese food and movies. In fact I've tried to bring some writers onto the scene to change that, but another time, hey? and feel good," and he says "That's very kind, thanks." Months later goes out of his way to pass their building. Looking through all the store windows around there just in case and sees her on one of the checkout lines of the supermarket on her block. Goes in, says he was heading for the subway, looked left just for a second and couldn't believe his eyes. "Watch out," she shouts as the conveyor belt moves her food and she jokes how she sometimes thinks her hand's going to move with it when she's thinking about something else and disappear under the belt. "Who knows what's under there; I imagine teeth." Laughs, at the same time realizing he's being phony since he doesn't think it funny. Invites him upstairs for coffee; Ricardo's in Germany for an opening of his work. Carries both bags, despite her protests, and remembers shopping with her when they lived together; always liked it. Coffee's rich, ground just for this brewing; king- or queen-sized mattress on the floor behind a screen. Very little furniture, all the lighting fluorescent except for two student lamps by their bed pillows, most of the place seems to be his studio. "Where do you work when you're home?" and she says in bed or at the kitchen table. "Ricardo pays the bills and is the at-home artist and it was his place so gets most of the space." Lots of expressionistic nudes, still lifes, sunsets or rises over some Mediterranean fishing village it seems with mountains in the back and big storms boiling behind them. None of the nudes look like her except a little in the face: heavier breasts, larger aureoles, bigger bushes, darker hair, thinner legs, squarer buns. "Interesting; nice; good; exciting; terrific color, any of you?" and she says "Zillions, in every kind of pose, clothed and unclothed, including some frankly pornographic ones and a few unerotic nudes with him—'Artist and His Model'—but they go straight into the gallery or on the road. These are all early works to hide the cracks." Books piled up against the walls, bunches of tiny dried flowers throughout the loft, bathroom smells from her soap; in it a life-sized mirror-image self-portrait, he supposes, looking as if he's about to break the mirror with his brush; dark, handsome, bearded, angry, long fat semierect penis; only painting so far he really likes. "That him in there?" and she says "It's embarrassing, that one. I like to tell people it's his nonexistent identical-twin brother, but maybe that doesn't help," and he laughs when she does, again thinks he's a phony. Wants to throw her down and rip her clothes off and rape her. Give her time only to put her diaphragm in if that's what she still uses—looked for the case in the bathroom but didn't find it—but to tape her mouth if he has to and flatten her to the mattress, grab her ass from behind with both hands and push her up to him as far as she can go and to come fast and for the whole thing to be over with forever. Maybe for them to stay locked like that for a few minutes but without him looking at her and then if he can to come again the same way or with her turned over. To go to jail for it, long as they'd want to stick him in it—he wouldn't give any resistance. Kiss on the cheeks good-bye. "We really should do dinner," she says. "Ricardo would enjoy meeting you." "Sure he would." "Why wouldn't he? He's interested in anyone with a serious purpose, dcesn't have to be art, and says the two of you are much alike. He's punched his hand through a door and wall a few times too." "I only did it that once and would like to forget about it." He calls and they meet twice in the next two years, for coffee, the next time lunch. Ricardo sold the loft and went to Paris to live and work and she's following him in a month. She's studying art history now, also figure drawing. He says he'll take her to the airport by bus; she says she does have a lot of luggage so it would be a great help. In the flat she's staying at when he picks her up he says he has something he doesn't know if he should tell her. "Paris has evaporated," she says. "I'm still madly in love with you, I'm sorry," and chokes up. She looks consoling while busily getting last-minute things together. "I didn't know that and wish it weren't true. We've become good friends and I'd hate for anything to spoil it." "Don't worry, nothing will; I'm not about to make a move on you." Kisses her hands, just before she's going to board he hugs her good-bye. She keeps her head stretched to the side so he can't get at her lips when he kisses her. "Oh, I forgot," though he intended it for now, and pulls out of his coat two gift-wrapped paperbacks and a jar of instant tea and she says "Gosh, where am I going to stash these? I haven't an inch of space left," and he says he'll send them to her and takes them back. They correspond about once every other month. Tells her he's coming to Paris to live, always wanted to and isn't it the thing for a young writer to do? and he can't take another day of substitute teaching in junior high schools but put away enough money from it; maybe he'll get to see her, take her to lunch. Who you kidding? he tells himself. He's going because she's there and in her last letter she said things weren't going well with Ricardo; their relationship's often been tempestuous but now it was getting uncivilized. He thinks: she's usually broke, has no job there, they've been living outside of Paris and not going in much, she's written, so maybe she'll want to move into the hotel with him and let him support her awhile. At the least, if she's living off him, she'll let him screw her from time to time and maybe eventually something deeper might develop and maybe right away. Certainly if he learns French fluently, which he plans to, and gets a job there with some American firm or French firm needing Americans in editing or news or something like that—just writing anything—things will even get better for them. He calls her day after he gets there and Ricardo says she left today for New York and is probably this minute at the Luxembourg airport. He calls Icelandic there, they get her and she says "I didn't leave because you were coming, though I knew you were and wanted to see you, but because Rick and I had the worst fight of our lives and I didn't want to be in France or even Europe another second." "Cash in your ticket, get your luggage off the plane if it's already on. And if you can't, don't worry, I'll buy you new clothes and reimburse you for your ticket some way if they don't refund it, but come stay with me at my hotel here or in your own room at the hotel—I'll take care of all of it for as long as you want and I won't make any kind of demands on you." "Write me," she says. "It'll give me surrogate pleasure reading about the wonderful experiences and people you're meeting in Paris." Doesn't know anyone there, writes a little, walks around a lot, studies French at the Alliance Francaise every morning but gets to meet no one in his classes—Bulgarians, South Americans, Israelis, who only want to be with one another, and Africans who only want to meet girls— goes to bars young Americans and Scandinavians hang out in but can never open a conversation and nobody starts one with him. Calls Ricardo a month after he gets there and says he got a letter from Janine "and she said what a great cheap area yours is to live in, so I'm coming out by train to look around and wonder if I could stop by to get advice on what the good blocks are and so on," which is all a lie: no letter so far and only wants to see where she lived, bed she slept in, guy she slept with, any new paintings of her, just any trace of her, and maybe Ricardo will also introduce him to some people, or give him names and addresses of Americans in Paris, who could become acquaintances or friends. Ricardo's short—he thought him tall from his self-portrait—muscular, rough looking, talks tough, New York, paint clothes, paint flecks in his hair and on his nose, place smelling of oils, polite, laughs loud, gives him a beer, bisquits, hard salami, the best chair, hovel a mess, parakeet flying in and out of its open cage, two pussycats she took in and left behind, says "She's a complex creature—we both know that—with no ambition or focus, which I didn't mind—did you?—since it meant she was always here for me when I was hungry or horny or hungover or boorishly talkative or things like that—but which other men might not like, her always waiting on or for them, and she hated. That the case, she should've stuck in acting; she could've made a potful and name at it with her magnetism and face—the eternal child-knockout—and she was superb at it I heard. Anyhow, years of my shit, she wanted someone gentler, quieter, she said, and who'd ultimately want to marry and give her little snotnoses and help her raise them, and I guess I fooled around on the side a little too much too, even giving her crabs once, but put that burning lotion on you and you get rid of them quickly enough, and she knew that part of me from the start but it all must've built up. She's something though, right?—great cook, great in the sack, intuitive and ethereal and bright as they make them and with that right zing of cheer and throaty voice that gobbles you up—no wonder men at bars punched one another out and in every language just to have the privilege of buying the next bottle of mineral water for her." No new paintings of her since for a year now he's only been doing old or decrepit nudes and mad people and idiots of both sexes when he isn't doing imaginary cityscapes. Wants to take Howard to a bar where she used to play darts and pinball and write poetry but he pretends to have a stomachache, "I think something to do with the water at my hotel which the *propriétaire,* if that's for the man, said was safe to drink, thinks why the hell don't I tell him I can't stand him and am immensely jealous because he knows all he has to do to get her back is phone her and act nice and apologize and say everything's going to be peachy-keen between them from now on in and that even though he understands her all right she's too fucking good for him and that she only lived with him and stayed in love this long and would go back to him because she's a bloody self-destructive schmuck. Every time he gets a letter from her he goes to the small fenced-in park across from the hotel to read it, and if it's raining, to the café a street away to read it over coffee and a brioche, even if it's delivered in the third mail. Gets a writing fellowship to California and she says she'll meet him at the ship when it docks in New York. She's not there. Calls her at the apartment she's sitting for and she says "I phoned your home for the exact arrival time and your mother asked me not to meet you, that I've done enough harm and shouldn't even try to see you because if I do you'll probably stay here and forget the fellowship. I'm sorry she feels that way but I can see what she means. My changeability has had a long string of messing things up." "You really think so? Ah, we're past that. Can I come over now?" "Love for you to." "Where you going?" his mother says and he says "Janine, I have to give her something somebody gave me for her in Paris and was too breakable to send," and she says "You're nuts," and his father says "A glutton for punishment; let him out of here, he won't listen to us anyway." Kisses her at the door. It was just to be on the cheek from his part but she puts her lips out, arms around him—he follows but lets his hands droop— and pulls him in, keeps him there. Gets an erection, backs away and says he's sorry, "thought I could control it though it used to happen all the time when I was a kid—could barely get on the dance floor with anyone," and she says "It's natural so who's worrying about it? And so many men are homosexual these days or letting it all come out what's always been hidden or stifled, that I'm glad to see you haven't changed. Just because it'd be so surprising, I think I'd become a nun if you became a homo, I mean gay." They go out for dinner, hold hands on the table, say little, gaze into each other's eyes, laugh about that, "What's come over us, monsieur?" and he says "Compression, dilution, shrinkage, the aging process, Irma the Girl in Wraparound Body Plastic, the Little White Cloud That Cried, good ole Yankee soil, light and loose summer clothes, but don't listen to me since I don't know anything, but probably nothing, niente, yenta," kiss hands (hers), rub cheeks against knuckles (his), knock off a bottle of Chianti, later make love. He thought it could happen and at the table devised a plan for the walk back and after to help it take place: act the way he did when he saw her at the Lipsatzes two years after their first big breakup: indifferent, distracted, uninterested, looking at everything but her (store windows, passersby, traffic, sky), talking—little he did and which had to be extracted—about uninteresting things: weather, world, hands in his pants pockets. At the door he said what he'd planned to: "Well, I'll see ya," waved (planned), turned (unplanned) to the elevator (if she didn't say anything he was going to turn back to her and say "Oh, good night,") when she said "This might be impertinent and maybe completely undesirable to you, but would you like to spend the night here?— you can," and he said "Where, on the narrow couch?" She was shaking her head and smiling but he said "No offense meant, but after that tiny bunkbed aboard ship for nine days I need a real box spring and mattress," and she said "With me; I wouldn't have asked otherwise, but if there's to be a discussion about it then we should forget it because I don't want to have it in my borrowed public hallway." "No problem, I'd like to," and went around her before she could change her mind, which he thought she was thinking she might, inside, said he was very tired, "I'm going straight to the bedroom if it's all right," she said "Good idea; I'm pretty tired and a bit tipsy too," no kisses, made sure not to touch her or smile, till she came out of the bathroom naked, turned on the fan and climbed into bed—he was already in it, wishing they'd shared a beer on the couch and he'd slowly taken off her clothes and then she'd helped him off with his. Thinks it's going to be just this one time: way she turned over after they were done, no good night kiss, and moved away during the night each time he pressed up to her or put his foot on hers. "Something the matter?" he asked once and she said "Nothing, why should it be?" and he said "I hope it wasn't my dis-interested attitude before we went to bed and possibly even on the street—I was just thinking about other things then: ship this morning, being back, flying to California in a few days—I don't even have a place there to stay yet or know how I'm going to get from airport to campus housing office, and she said "You were fine, everything's all right, and I can understand: moving around so much can do it." Nah, something's wrong: gaze and stuff at dinner were an act (not on his part) or the wine, or plus it, and going to bed with him, and he's being realistic here, not self-pummeling, was probably the first of her every-third-year gift to him for being such a dopey faithful friend. He should know by now nothing he does will work with her; even if she said she loved him he wouldn't believe it; he doesn't know what she'd have to do for it to take; if she said she wanted to come to California with him, he'd let her, but still wouldn't believe she'd stay. What would he care? She'd help him settle in, take away the jitters of a new place, few days' lays, fellow fellowists or whatever they're called would see he came with someone of substance or just beautiful and engaging and after she left there'd be other women out there: bigger, blonder, less something, more something, younger, fresh. If she said "Let's get married," he'd say OK and if she actually did it—he'd never push—only then would he say it took, but maybe even then he'd be suspect. So maybe after a couple of years of relatively untroubled marriage; probably only then, and also with a baby or when she was visibly pregnant with the first. So he tries making the most of it when he wakes up and she's still sleeping. If there's one time he's going to remember her, this is to be it, but that's never worked much either. Slowly pulls the sheet off of her. She's on her back, knee up before it settles and rests, eyelids for a few seconds fluttering. Loves

her body: hard, soft, no tan or extra bulge, light fuzz on her arms
and legs; never shaved, freckled chest. Gently puts his face up to
her pubic hair and skims his lips through it. Smells: no odor; inhales:
there's something, more of urine and vaginal cream, but not much;
wants to lick it but doesn't want to wake her. Could be she's awake,
curious what he's doing, peering at him through the thinnest eyeslits.
Maybe wants him to do what he wants to but doesn't want to show
she's awake for it might stop him. If they only had a signal. Inspects
her breasts, area around the aureoles, nipple tips, as much as he
can see inside her vagina without parting it, legs, neck, arms, armpit,
hair there, curves, midriff. To see if he can detect any change in her
body since he saw her naked years ago. No new lines, scars, bumps,
weight gain, gray. Face next to hers now; she's smiling while sleeping
but no fluttering. Is she up, maybe waiting for him to just get on
top of her and stick it in? He's ready and probably won't have another
chance, maybe ever. Her reasoning: doesn't want him to think she
wants it a second time when she does, long as he's here; then he
might think she wants him to stay. No, not how women feel or think.
Time he wanted to rape her; glad he didn't, her participation better
than any forced lay, and of course other things: stigma, prison, her
rage. And once in, which should be easy with last night's semen
and grease and if need be his spit, even if she objected and didn't
want it, he thinks she'd let him finish if he was quick. In a way rape
but all she'd have to do was say get off and if he wasn't coming at
the time or in a few seconds, he would. Oscillating fan lifting her
head hair up and moving her pubic hair every time it blows her way,
plus the horripilation on her legs. "You up, he whispers, "or just
your goose bumps and hair?" Smile doesn't turn smilier; she's asleep,
lids fluttering again, or is that a trick? Only that once last night, he
wanted it again but she said kind of drowsily "My poor pussy's
conked out before I have, so not possible." Wanted to say "You don't
have to do a thing, just stay there, asleep if you want," but caught
himself moment before he was going to say it, also dropped the grin.
"What do you mean 'poor'—I was too rough or went in too far?"

"I think I have the beginning of a yeast thing in there, but nothing that should spread." "Then maybe in the morning if you're feeling better," and she said "Fine...nice...what're we talking of?... really, sleepy, sweetie, OK?..." and then seemed to be asleep, that kind of breathing. Kissed her shoulder, erection jammed against her behind, hoping she'd make a little wiggling move or something suggesting he stick it in. Bet if he had, halfway or less, quarterway or just the head or tip, she wouldn't have noticed it. Should have, then moved the way he would and jerking it with his hand; probably so little left, wouldn't have been a mess. Six-thirty but bright out; puts his arm across her, sheet up and feels himself getting sleepy. Next thing: she's nudging him awake with her toes, sitting on the bed stretching, saying she's been writing a play these days, neglected to tell him because she didn't think he'd be interested, and is dying to get at it, so he'll have to leave right after a quick continental breakfast, and jumps out of bed. "You see?" he shouts and from the bathroom she says angrily "See what?" and he says "Nothing, something to myself how I should try to get some writing time in today too," and wonders what did I mean? but glad he caught himself again. Over coffee and rolls she says she's going to her folks later for a few days, but they'll write. At the door he wants to say "One question only; why'd you sleep with me if you were planning to give me the quick heave?" and going down in the elevator thinks "I hate being so fucking mature," and slams the wall with his palms, hoping she heard it and knows what the sound means. That night thinks of calling her at her folks and saying "One question only; why'd you even want to meet me at the ship?" Next day thinks of calling her there and saying "Listen, what are you doing that's so important in New York? You haven't your own apartment; you're living out of a suitcase; come to California with me. Not for loveydovemaking but because we're pals. We'll be around writers, you can write there and maybe even better than here. You say your play's about out-of-work stage actors? Well, distance does it, I learned in Paris, writing better than I ever did about New York." Goes to California. Lots of things happen. Comes back to New York for Christmas to be with his family, didn't plan to but calls her, they go to a party, dance, holds her close and moves them slowly though not that kind of music, pot passed around but she won't touch it or even pass it so neither does he, her head against his chest, eyes closed he sees, when out of nowhere he says "You of course know I've never stopped loving you since I met you, but didn't I say almost the exact same thing last time I was in?—I forget," and she looks up and says "Why do you?" and he says "Love you?" and she nods, kisses his chest, looks up again and nods and he thinks is he on to something here? maybe she wants to be convinced before she says she wants to go to California with him without him even asking her: personality, voice, looks of course, her hair, their sex, intelligence which he should have listed first, perceptiveness, humor, playfulness, even her changeability, her size, breath, shape, smells, kindness, gentleness, how she is with people, those she doesn't even know, upbringing, way she drives, folks, everything, he can't think of anything about her he doesn't admire or like very much or love, her searches, curiosity he means, all the things she's done and does, oh, they've had their differences, let's face it, but her background, foreground, middleground, she's laughing, "It's true, I just feel tremendously good with you, holding you like this, dancing, sitting, just knocking on the door here before, and things that can't be explained: biology, chemistry, psychopathology," she's laughing, prospect of babies, brushing her hair, cutting her toenails, sudsing her back, kissing the top of her head like this, does it, she's laughing, "You name it; the full gamut; that's why, now that you asked," and she says "Thank you, sweetie, all very nice, really, I appreciate it, needed it too, but I don't deserve it from someone so loving and good and after the way I've treated you," and he says "Ah shucks, ma'am," and she puts her lips up and they kiss and he thinks is this going to be it, tonight, tomorrow, she's finally decided on him or at least for the time being and who knows till when? don't say anything; no hopes up; just see. They dance some more, kiss, hold hands while sitting, woman she knows who wants to talk with her alone says "Boy, don't you two ever separate?" they laugh, later she says "Why don't I see myself home by taxi?" he says "No, I'll take you, but by taxi," when the cab pulls up to her building she says "You don't want to take it while you have one? They don't come around here much," he says "Nah, too expensive; I'll take the subway," she says "I have money upstairs if you need," "No, I'm happy with the subway," at her door she says "It's awfully cold out and the whole trip home for you an hour minimum if you don't take a cab, want to sleep on the couch here?" and he says "With you?— oh, I shouldn't have said that," and she says "If we keep our clothes on," "Then why not in bed if we keep our clothes on?—say, great idea, Howard," "Because I know you," and he says "Well, I know you too, so *there*—ah, I'm acting like such a kid," "Because I know what you'll want to do and why wouldn't you?" and he says "Well, why not then?—it's cold, we're warm, I love you, you don't hate me, we've made naughty-naughty together before and a couple of times swore we wouldn't do something and then did and enjoyed it—hey, I'm making a bit pitch here, baby, a really big one," and she says "Just the couch, with clothes, I'd love holding you all night," so they get on it, no pullout, blankets over them which keep falling off and she picks up and both of them put back on, he on the inside holding her tight for one reason afraid she'll fall off and then give up on it and sleep alone in bed, he can't take his pants off, though asks, because he has no undershorts, she just in underpants and bra and socks, once puts his hand down her pants, she slaps his wrist lightly and pulls his hand out, "Too bad, for I swear it'd be wonderful if you let it or just left my hand in there, I wouldn't let my fingers do anything," "I'm sure so but no thanks, let's go to sleep," breakfast, kiss before he leaves, says he'll call her, she says she'll be around all week, doesn't, not the next three weeks he's in New York, hated the horniness, his cornballness, didn't really sleep, tired entire next day, raised hopes though told himself not to, rest of it, no more, *forget* it, whole thing's such delusory nonsensicalness, seeing her, wanting to see her, dying to sleep with her, pining away for her, walking the streets thinking of her and hoping he'll bump into her, to have her love him, what shit, crock of, he could never understand her ever, *get that*, he's sure of it, so good luck to the next guy, and in a way a lucky guy, her face, shape and spark etcetera, for it could only be with a new guy, his with her is marked, and if she calls he'll tell her or politely as he can say to her to get lost, no, that it's best they don't see each other, for him, her, in the long run and no explanation if she asks for one, which he doubts she will—she won't, she'll just say all right if that's how he feels or what he wants—but thanks, he'll say, and after he hangs up: but no thanks, you little skunk, none. Goes back to California. Lots of things happen. Writes her care of her parents three years later when he's working for a big systems analysis firm in L. A. doing technical writing. Just to say how are you, been a long time, was thinking of her, what's been happening, curious. Gets a letter from her from some small town in Northern California saying she's been on the coast for a year, thought he might still be in California, wanted to write his old school on the Peninsula but wasn't sure what department or that if she got the right one it'd forward the mail of one of its former grad students, didn't want to ask his mother because of how she's felt about her contacting him, living with a logger/master woodcarver and never been happier: California's a dream state: the ease, people, nature, weather, opportunities and room—she doesn't see how she could live anywhere else. If he's ever around here, stop by; they've a guest cottage Milton built overlooking the ocean and mountains and she'd love showing him the area; though she can no longer stand the East, she still gets a craving for intellectual easterners with something to say, and he might like it so such he'd move up here. Few months later he's flying to San Francisco for a job interview and calls her, thinking he can rent a car and spend a day with her. Man who answers gives him another number to call. She says she got married last month—not to the logger-carver but to someone, if he can believe it, for it was the greatest mistake of her life, she'd only met a few weeks before, and left him a day after the ceremony and is now getting an annulment. She'd rather not see anyone now and once this is over she's driving straight to New York; she's already got a sublet and gives him the address and phone number. Years later his first book's reviewed in a New York newspaper; she sends him a letter care of his publisher, congratulating him on the book and being reviewed in such a prestigious place, "even if she impaled and then poleaxed you before dragging your body through the mud—the stinker; imagine doing that to a first book and one, between her lines, that sounds so promising," asks him to call her if he gets a chance. Calls: she's married, husband's a filmmaker, no kids but they're trying, renting a house in New Jersey, taking courses in botany and library science at a state college nearby, doing volunteer work for the town library which she'll become the paid librarian of once she gets her degree; since she hardly ever gets into the city, invites him for dinner out there. He borrows a car. Her husband's not home when he gets there and they sit on the grass in the backyard, beer and cheese and crackers, she tells him the names of all the trees, flowers and shrubs and even the grass and weeds around the place and what bird and insect sounds they're hearing, he says he always wanted to know things like that and about mushrooms and rocks and how to navigate a boat just by the stars, asks if she's read any good books or new poets or seen any plays lately and she says she ordered his book for the town library but it hasn't arrived yet so she hasn't read it. "Of course I could have ordered it for myself from the bookstore—I looked for it just to browse through but they didn't have it—but the price was a bit steep; we're always short so never buy new hardcovers, even by good friends." "I should have brought a copy for you and Braxton, but I felt that'd be pushing it on you." "Good news is there are already six people on the library reserve list for your book—four from my pep talks about you—but since I work there, my name's on top. After I read it I'll give you another review." "I don't know if it'll be favorable, since one of the pieces is about when our engagement busted up and is pretty close to the original." "I've been

written about before but nobody's come near to getting me the way
I see myself. I'd almost write about myself to get it right, but I found
out I'm a lousy writer. Anyway, so long as you didn't use my name
or my parents' names and disguised me a little—more to show you're
just not a reporter—write what you like." "I forget what I called you.
Jackson, and where the reader never knows if that's your first or last
name." Wonders how come she never changes? Face, manner,
temperament, same high pointy breasts and tiny waist and bouncy
gait and so on, while he's lost most of his hair since they first met,
jowls and deep face creases, little heavier and slower but not much,
less sensitive and responsive, darker, grimmer, more downbeat a
person—almost everyone says so—doesn't try as hard for good fellow-
feeling or jokes. Phone rings and she goes to answer it, comes back
with more beer for them and sits. For a moment he saw her white
panties and he thinks a patch of hair sticking out there; skirt's above
her knees; same fuzz on her legs. Braxton, asking her to extend his
apologies to him for being late and saying he's leaving the office in
half an hour and it takes him, she says, another half-hour to get here.
Wants the phone to ring again so she can get up to answer it and
then sit down opposite him again so he can again see her panties.
What if, no this is ridiculous. But what if she said now, though she's
given and is giving no sign of it, "You think we can quickly make
love?" Of course saying something a little before it. "You're probably
not going to like this idea, Howard . . ." "You wouldn't believe what
I've been thinking, Howard . . ." He'd do it, is sure of it, since almost
all he can think about now is putting his lips on her lips and then
on her legs. After, he'd say to himself he's such a bastard, she's the
only married woman he'd do it with who's trying to get pregnant
by her husband. He'd carry on with her in the city if she wanted,
and for as long as she wanted, but always asking her to divorce
Braxton before she gets pregnant by one of them—he wouldn't want
any doubt as to whose kid it is—and marry him. She did get pregnant
and wasn't sure whose it was but wanted to marry him, he'd say
to get rid of it or prove through some tests it's his. She didn't want

to get married but wanted to have the baby one of them had got her pregnant with, he'd have to assume it was Braxton's or if it wasn't that Braxton would be the father to it, and that would probably be the end of their relationship. Braxton's nice, polite, tall, broad shoulders, build of an ex-college swimmer, big mop of hair, plain-looking, little fat in the face, pinholes on the nose, pants keep sliding down because he has no behind, quiet—maybe because Howard's there and been so talkative—not very intelligent, it seems, though maybe he's holding back there too. But one knows: way he responds, lack of questions, choice of words, things he picks to discuss, flat expression, nothing in the eyes; it's surely what he'd like to believe. They seem close. Howard and she were inside by then and she rushed to the door when he came in and kissed him; before that, when she heard a car pulling up in front, she said "That's Brax, I recognize the muffler," and beamed, looked out the window, stopped their conversation cold. Braxton likes to skydive—"That's his biggest passion," she said; "we take vacations around it"—water-ski, rock climb, camp out, snorkel, chop logs into kindling, takes boxing lessons, used to fence, his reading's mostly work research and magazines about these things. "Do you play chess?" she said in the backyard; "I forget, but if you do I bet he'd love to whip through a couple of games after dinner." Go; "he's become something of a master at that game too." Writes and shoots industrial films and commercials for a New Jersey company but hopes to do serious film-making in the future. "Maybe you and Howard can team up on one of his stories or unpublished books." "You never know," Braxton says, "but it's got to be something you can play in. —I've never seen her in anything, so I want to get her back into acting one last time." "I've lots of things for women; mostly, though they're all pretty intriguing, they're not very nice." She tried skydiving once, she said; got so frightened that she felt she experienced death. "I saw myself splattering on the ground and everything after that, even my funeral, while coming down." "Was I at it?" Howard said. "Just faces and my family and Braxton, but it was just one of many things, so very quick." "It was a stupid question to begin with; I wasn't being serious, though the thought of it makes me shudder." She patted his knee. The house is small, simple, comfortable, but lots of art work she acquired when working in the gallery years before, some of it the painter's. One of her by him, he thinks, frontal nude, but doesn't ask and tries to keep from constantly looking back at it. If it were in the gallery or a museum and noboody was around he'd go right up to it to get a close look at the face and genital area. They have dinner. Time to shut up, ask a lot of questions that'll take time to answer and just listen. At least stop trying to impress her, which he knows he's been doing—"Publishing is an eleemosynary venture when it comes to my works. . . . The next book, which I've already got my advance for, promises to do even worse"—and by contrast trying to make Braxton look bad. It's hopeless and wrong. "How come so suddenly silent?" she says. "My food no good and you don't want to say?" "No, you're the same great cook. Could be I drank too much beer in the sun and I've also been working late a lot, so I'm tired and should probably go while I can still drive." They insist he stay the night; they don't want him cracking up on the road. They give him the guest room, which will be the baby's room, she says, "that is, if we ever have one." "Sure we will," Braxton says. "Three, four if you want. —We've gone in for tests, everything's clear, count's up to par, the doctor says it's a shoo-in—so don't be surprised if you're carrying in a year." "I know, and one at a time please, sweetie. — Braxton's family's noted for its twins and triplets every third conception. Both his sister and brother and also his parents with the three of them." "Triplets? Jesus, I've never met anybody who was one," and is sorry he didn't know sooner because he'd like to hear about it. They share a common wall. He listens through it—then his ear flat against it with his hand over his other ear—but only hears mumbling for speech, the word "filibuster" from Braxton very loud, a light switch clicking on and off several times, no sex sounds. He shakes his penis a little, thinks he should do it into his handkerchief—maybe there's even some good cheesecake in the magazines on the shelves above him—then thinks he'd only be doing it to say to himself he did it in their house, and goes to sleep. He has a quick dream of her coming into the room in a nightgown and holding a towel, sitting on the bed and jostling him awake: "Up, you up?" That was inevitable, he thinks, and wishes it had gone on longer. He goes to the bathroom late at night, when he comes back stands in front of their door thinking of them sleeping close, maybe a little entangled, after probably having made quiet sex—all the talk of conception and semen might have led to it or maybe they try doing it every night to up the chances of them conceiving. "Lucky fucking stiff," he whispers, low. Braxton's gone by the time he washes up in the morning and goes into the kitchen for coffee. She's reading the paper there, in her bathrobe. They talk a little more and then he kisses her cheek, hopes they can do this again some time, she says "Without doubt we will. Braxton really liked you, thought you a very stimulating person and would like to get to know you better." "I liked him very much too," and goes. That's the last time he sees her. Neither calls or writes again. Bumps into an actor friend of hers from when they first met who says he still speaks to her about twice a year and was out to her house a year ago; she and Braxton have two children and decided that'll be it, though he wants more. Braxton's still making industrial films and television ads but owns his own company; she's a language arts teacher in a private school and writing children's books, but none have sold so far and she's done about a dozen. "She read me one; about a horse and a cow who get married because of some dumb farmer's blunder; it was hilarious and ends with them producing some animal called a how." He'll give her Howard's regards next time he speaks to her, whenever that'll be. The gallery she worked at is having a twentieth anniversary party. He knows a woman—met and became friends with her at an art colony he went to that summer—who's represented by the gallery and she told him about the party. "Look out for a beautiful blonde woman named Janine. Maybe not as blonde and beautiful anymore, I'm sure lovely features still, an intelligent kind of dignified look, and about so high. She used to work there—receptionist, hanging up paintings, writing some of the catalogs—fifteen years ago—but became close friends with the owner, even stayed at her apartment when she couldn't afford a room or was between this place and that lover, and long weekends at her beach house, so I'm sure she'll be there. Last name was Austin but now it's Jameson or Jimson or Johnson—her husband's first name is Braxton—and I only remember one of those was her last name or something like it when I read an obit of her father last year and it gave that name as one of the deceased." The woman says "Maybe you'd like to go; I'm sure I can bring more than one friend," and he says "Nah, I don't know if I want to see her again like that—wangling an invitation. And I hate gallery parties; jug wines in fancy carafes and no chairs, and how would I tell it to Denise—that I'm going to a party where I'm almost sure to see an old girlfriend, love of my life till I met her?" The woman reports back to him. She did see a beautiful blonde woman, in her early forties but looked ten years younger, "asked about her, was told her name was Janine, went up to her and said I knew you. She was immediately all interest; asked me questions about you for an hour. In fact most of my talking time there I spent with her and was taken up by you. What are you doing? How do you support yourself? What do you look like? Where do you live? Is your mother still alive? Are you married or have you been since she last saw you and do you have any children?—somehow she felt you would by now, in or out of marriage. What's my relationship to you? When I said 'friend' she gave me this double take, for she didn't think you could ever know a single attractive woman long, as she put it, and just be friends. 'Well, he's changed—people do,' she said, and then she asked what's the woman like who you are involved with. She said you two were once engaged, but so many years ago that she forgets when. You never told me that. And that you were on and off with one another for a while after that and much in love as she was with you at times, it never seemed to work out. She obviously has a high impression of your intelligence and talent and character and thinks

676

you were the nicest man she ever was close with, other than her husband, who wasn't there, by the way, or never came over to her while we talked, and she never looked around for him. Never for no one, in fact. She wasn't one of those people at parties who are always darting their eyes about while you're talking to them or standing with their backs to the wall so they can see everyone and be seen by everyone too. That says a great deal about her. When I told her of all you've written and also got published lately, she said she was going out the next day to buy everything of yours she could. That she hadn't known you had stuck with it, but didn't see why you wouldn't, and what are some of the book titles and so on? I couldn't remember one, not even the newest. But you know me; I've little to nil interest in books except for the art ones and if I did ever read one of yours I probably wouldn't understand or like it, which is possibly why we stay friends—that I only talk about the covers." "What's she doing—she say?" "I think teaching. Or maybe she said she's the principal of an all-girls' school, or dean, or in admissions—head of it or assistant to head. I'm sorry, I forget. Also some artwork too, she's doing—besides devoting lots of time to her children, of course—which she seemed too embarrassed to talk about, the art, maybe because I'm a professional painter and she thought it presumptuous talking to me of it. I should have pursued it because I knew you would have wanted to know what exactly in art she was in." He wanted to ask about her hair, what style was it in and the color, but that would have sounded funny and he didn't quite know how to phrase it, though he tried a few times in his head. And her body—was it still slim, with that tiny waist and strong legs, and energetic, or had it grown, got a little fleshy and slowed down? but he's sure she would have said something like "You men—only interested in our bods, or mostly, and after we reach a certain age, go for the younger flesh and throw us away; I hate that," and not answered it. Also what she smelled like—from the carnation soap she was famous to him for? Doesn't remember even thinking of it last time he saw her, and forgets if it was in the bathroom of their house when he slept over? If it was, wouldn't he have thought of it then? He doesn't know. But he does remember that every time he did smell it—at her place or someone else's—after he hadn't seen her for a while, he thought of the smell and of her. But what's he talking about? That soap wouldn't smell on a person an hour or so after she washed herself with it; it's perfume he's thinking of, which he doesn't think she ever used, and it's someone else he's thinking of who always wore one particular identifying kind. He says "Did she show you any pictures of her kids or say what sex they were or how old?" and she says "No, only that she has them; two, but I said that. What else about her? Nothing, except that she's a lovely woman in every way. I felt immediately at ease and in rapport with her and could see myself becoming good friends with her if I had the chance, and of course why you were so attracted to her." "In love with her. I could have killed myself over her. I think I almost did once. No, that was over someone else, much earlier on." "Well, you were young, with her and all of them before her, and since no person's worth killing yourself over, good thing you didn't."

Says to his mother and brother "Well, I'm going now to get the deli and stuff and take care of the house before all the people come, so I'll see you." His mother says "Do you have enough money?" and he says "You gave me more than enough, but if I need more, I have some of my own." "No, I don't want you paying for anything," and reaches for her pocketbook. His brother says "He has enough—he told you—and if he doesn't, you'll give it to him later," and to Howard "No tongue or fatty pastrami or meat like that. Just simple stuff, trimmed well, and get more than you think we need, because more people might be coming than we think. Also, we could use it while we're sitting at Mom's the next few days." "By 'simple,' what do you mean?" and his brother says "Turkey, roast beef, lox, the best bologna, but nothing where the guests have to start picking off pieces because of the gristle and fat." "OK, but I don't want to be feeding and cleaning up after people the next few days. Making sandwiches, getting them drinks, people thinking it's a restaurant we're running, as Dad used to say," and his brother says "That's what you have to do when you sit. Not make things for them—they do that for you and serve you it and clean up after. But a lot come a long way and some around lunchtime and they're hungry, naturally, also from sitting there for so long, so there should be food and pastries and coffee for them to help themselves. So get another can of coffee while you're at it, and pastries too—little ones, big ones, but nothing with icing or that fluffy cream on it or goo in it. Coffeecakes and babkas— that's what I mean you should get. Two or three of them, but simple ones, with mostly walnuts and raisins in them," and hands Howard two twenties. "I told you, I have my own money and what Mom gave me," and his brother says "Take it, I earn more than enough to play the sport, and I don't want you holding back on what you buy." He kisses his mother, brother, sister-in-law, says "I'm going to pay my respects a last minute," his brother and sister-in-law nod, his mother seems to be off somewhere else, sitting erect, head arched back, eyes open but on nothing it seems, remembering, probably, maybe in a daze. Goes into the next room, sits on the front bench opposite the box, shuts his eyes, bows his head, folds his hands in his lap, hears the sound sonebody mentioned before and wanted to know what it could be: "There a pipe around that's leaking?" Dripping, from the ice his father must be on, probably into a metal pan, from the sound of it, on the floor under the platform the box is on. Holes through the platform so the water can drip through? How *do* they do it? Something the rabbi insisted on if he was going to conduct the service? No modern refrigeration, which would be against his religious tenets? So why'd they get an Orthodox rabbi if his father hasn't been Orthodox for forty years and they'd have to put up with this dripping? Going to be like this during the funeral? Then realizes; when the funeral home official—the salesman, really—showed them the caskets and then in his office asked lots of questions, like if they wanted their father embalmed, or rather "Of course you'll probably want your father embalmed," his brother and he said what for? He's going into the ground tomorrow, around twenty-six hours after he died, so why do all that to the body and pay a couple-hundred more for it too? So probably on ice to preserve him for the funeral, which the embalming fluid probably would do, and where he won't smell. Maybe that's it, maybe not. Says "So I'll see you in the morning," closes his eyes again, lets whatever it is come in—nothing does; it's all blank or flashing dots—and stands, moves his hand above the casket, then below the platform close to the curtain; doesn't feel any colder. Thinks of lifting the curtain to see what kind of pan and the water, but maybe he's got it all wrong; maybe it's blood dripping, maybe something worse, and goes. Outside the home he thinks why didn't he do what he was going to when he went into that room: hasn't seen his father since in the hospital this morning, so open the casket to see the job they did on him and maybe for his last look. Forgot, that's all, nothing deeper; got caught up in other things. Gets at the deli soda, seltzer, beer, coffee, milk, bread, sugar substitute, pound of this, two pounds of that, slice it thin, slice it thick, slice it regular, trim it a little more please, his brother says no fat, only the best, whatever's the best, sure, salami too, nobody asked but he's sure people will eat it and kosher salami's supposed to be the finest, but only half a pound, same with the bologna, Isaac Gellis, any good brand like that, ham he knows they don't have or nothing like it, right? sour and new pickles, lots of them, sour tomatoes, some of those pepper things with the long stems, couple of gefilte fishes, or fish for the plural, how do you say it? with plenty of carrot slices on them but not too much juice, it's going to be eaten in an hour, cole slaw, potato salad, whitefish, nova, gravlax, whatever that is, he was told by his brother to get it, some of that spread there—chopped liver; of course—he thinks that's it; maybe some roast turkey. Asks them to deliver but please make it quick, lots of hungry people will be flocking soon to his folks' apartment from the funeral home and the food should be there when they come, and the counterman says "Oh, someone in the family? My condolences, all around, and don't worry, our boy will be there before you, I bet, if you don't get a cab and take it home right after you step out of here," and he says "Don't make it that fast; nobody will be there to receive it," leaves, snaps his fingers outside, goes back and says "And could you throw in some of that nice deli mustard you prepare—enough for thirty people?" and stops off at a liquor store for several liquors, then at a bakery. At the apartment he opens the dining room table, puts a tablecloth on it—his mother told him which cloth—lots of paper napkins, no time to fold them into triangles, silver, plastic cups and paper plates—she told him where to find them—opens the liquor bottles and sets them on a side table with a pitcher of water and a few swizzle sticks, fills the ice bucket with ice, gets the cakes on dinner plates and puts them on the table with a bread knife between them, makes himself a drink, drinks it, makes another, pulls out two breakfront drawers of old photos his mother's kept there since they moved from Brooklyn thirty-five years ago, buzzer from the building's vestibule, forgot to get the coffee ready, buzzes the ringer in, deliveryman and lets him carry everything into the kitchen though his mother told him for what could be bugs at the store to have him leave the delivery at the door, gets the electric percolator going, slices the fish, pickles, tomatoes, puts everything on platters and into bowls, cleans a bag of radishes and garnishes the food platters with them, brings the platters and bowls to the dining room table, looks for serving forks and spoons. Arranges the table till it looks right to him. His idea, from right to left: tableware first, main food next, salads and accessories after, pastries last. Turns the kitchen radio on and is glad to get sad music: churchlike, possibly Bach, a cantata, maybe the Easter one or the Passion, for it's familiar and Easter's only days away. Makes himself a drink, sees there's one in the dining room he didn't touch and drinks it down, bourbon instead of scotch, starts on the new one. Soda and seltzer on the side table. Salt, pepper, mustard in a bowl on the main table. On the kitchen counter by the percolator: milk, sugar, sugar substitute in a dish, glass of teaspoons with the handles up, all the cups and saucers and mugs in the house. Phone rings. Doesn't want to answer it. It'll be somebody with his condolences but then it could be his brother about his mom. His mother's cousin from Florida. Her condolences. He was the most wonderful good-natured man. Brought people together who never would have been. Almost matched her up with someone after her husband died but she decided taking care of one sick man for years and then burying him was enough. Just like his mother did but for twice as long as she and with his sister and dad, but she's a saint. Which son is he, the oldest or youngest? Last time she saw him, but he wouldn't remember her, was at a seder his parents gave more than twenty-five years ago. Funeral at Riverside? She won't be able to come up for it, she never travels a mile from her home these days, but tell Mother she called. Beer he'll leave in the refrigerator but how will people know it's there? They'll just have to snoop around or ask. He leave anything out? Phone rings. His father's nephew. He couldn't make it tonight but he'll be there tomorrow. He knows it'll be in the paper but sometimes they don't get it right so what time's the funeral? And because he's not sure about these etiquette things, he's expected to get there to pay his respects a half-hour before? So, what can he say? Uncle Cy's the last one on the Tetch side from that age group and the oldest. Next it'll be their generation. What's he talking about, since they've already lost a few; both of them their sisters and his middle brother, right? Tomorrow, then, and love to Aunt Pauline. Toothpicks, for some of these people, and a few more ashtrays. But why encourage them? and last thing he wants after everyone goes and there's still a mess is to empty and clean ashtrays. Gets the garbage can from under the sink. Phone rings. Though it's only half filled, wants an empty can to start with. Takes it out to dump and then relines it. Newspapers; maybe now that his father's dead, plastic trash bags. Collects all the photos he can find of a certain time of his father. Phone rings, yells for it to go to hell, doesn't want to speak to anyone, no one, has enough things to do and is just plain drained and not in a talking mood, picks up the receiver, hand over the mouthpiece, presses the disconnect buttons and leaves the receiver off the cradle. Drinks, pours another, but doesn't want to get sloshed, his mother might need him and there might be all that cleaning up, so puts it to the side. Beeping from the phone, drinks while it's doing it, and then it stops. Leans about fifty photos of his father against the wall above the dining room mantel, tapes several to the wall above it. Graduation photo from high school he's been told, though looks five years too old for it. Bar mitzvah photo: hat for an old man and too big, tefillin, prayer shawl, mantilla, poncho, whatever it's called, face radiantly self-confident and mature while he in his official bar mitzvah photo looked like a shy kid. Rowing a boat. Swinging a bat. Feeding a duck. Throwing an apple down from a tree. Reading a newspaper on his favorite park bench. On their honeymoon cruise to Bermuda, back of it says. Sitting on bar stools at Sloppy Joe's in Cuba, sign on the interior awning says. Glasses raised, he raises his, here's to ya, pal, phone rings. When he put the receiver back on? What else he do he doesn't know about? Should go to the john so he doesn't have to when there's a line for it. Goes, makes sure to zip up. Phone rings, ah shit. Deliveryman came and left twenty-something minutes ago so should be back by now: delivered, gave him a tip, that was it. Standing on a diving board ready to dive in, one-piece swimsuit but looking good and fit. Dad and she or just him alone and lots of other people, relatives at family functions, friends or associates at professional or fraternal affairs, half with their heads twisted around or chairs turned. Between Alex and him during a summer camp visit, hairy gray chest, big belly, skinny legs, galvanizing smile, his dead brother looking so ungovernable, though his father's got them both around the neck in a good grip, with his wild curly hair and cocky face and dark suntan and budding build. Standing, if that's him, with his arms on the shoulders of two buddies, with his basic training unit. His mother and brother and sister-in-law come in, aunts, uncles, cousins, friends. Door never shuts. Outside buzzer and cigar smoke never stop. Opens a window but someone says too cold so he closes it. Phone always ringing or being dialed. They've been detained longer than they thought so go ahead with dinner. What's doing with gold in Hong Kong and Tokyo?

What's he think about Nixon's newest antics? someone asks him. Hasn't read the paper or listened to the radio in days, what'd he say? Food being picked at or wolfed down and wonders if he should start cleaning up now or just bring in the kitchen trash can if nobody's put something terrible in it or a couple of opened shopping bags and let everyone help themselves. His brother signals him with a finger, corners him. What's with these photos? Thanks for the great job getting the food and setting up the table, but he go out of his mind? People haven't said anything because they're too embarrassed to. Sorry, thought it'd be nice, seeing him as he was, not sick as he's been for years, and maybe his typical misdirected spontaneity and too much to drink. But this one he particularly likes: in his office bending over a patient, his dark hair, starched white smock, and look how rugged he looks and glittering his dental equipment is, and the photo seems professionally lit and taken, as if for a magazine. Was it? Brother shrugs, sort of doubts it, but it with the others if he can has to go. And look at this one of them in Paris, at the Café de la Paix of all places, which took them twenty years to get to once they'd planned it, and where he had what she called his first ministroke. Maybe that one should go right away because of its associations for her, and stuffs it into his back pocket. But he's tired and it's been a big one and last night at the hospital when he barely got a wink sitting by Dad's bed, so he's afraid he'll have to call it a day. Please do whatever he pleases with the photos himself. Kisses his brother, says good night to his mother; she doesn't seem to recognize him, then calls him Alex, corrects herself and calls him Jerome, then says of course it's her youngest child Howard—she means her youngest son; Vera was her youngest child—but then she's always been awful with names, and he leans over to hug her and she kisses his forehead. He'll be in the boys' room all night in case she needs him, he says, and good nights to everyone he passes on his way to his old bed.

The baby comes out and doctor says "Got it, it's a girl, and starts to hold it up but says "But you knew that, right?" and nose is suctioned again, eyes cleaned, umbilical cord's cut and quickly does some other things and hands it to the nurse who rushes to the warmer, pats the baby dry, says "Heartbeat's normal, color's a healthy pink," weighs and measures it and wraps it up and brings it to them and says "So who gets her, daddy first?" because his arms are out and he says "She's still a bit dizzy and weak, I'll hold it OK," and takes it in his arms, shows it to Denise, who's being sewed up while waiting for her placenta to pass, and breaks into such deep sobs that the nurse takes the baby from him and puts it on Denise's stomach. Breaks into sobs during his wedding ceremony. Rabbi smiles, says "Let's hold it a few seconds, people," looks at his watch because he has to officiate at a funeral in an hour, he told them before the ceremony, and it's a half-hour cab ride from here. Sobs when he hears a certain Bach cantata on the radio and the woman says "It's a beautiful piece and a very lovely interpretation, I know," and he says "It's not that. I should have turned the radio off when the announcer said what number it was, for I know what it does to me and I didn't want to screw up such a nice dinner." "It's done, so maybe if you want to eat, you should say," and he says "It reminds me of my brother. A few months after that ship he was on got lost and probably split up and sunk, I bought a record of this same cantata. Not for it but for the much more exalting one on the other side whose number I've since forgot—thirty-three, I think. I played it, after I played the one I bought the record for a few times, and right at that sad part just before my brother popped into my head and I started sobbing more for him than I had since he was lost. To top it off, for about ten years after that, whenever I wanted a good cry, I'd put that cantata on. Though first I'd have a couple of vodkas or half bottle of wine, and would douse the lights—it was always at night—or just keep a low-watt one on and sit in a chair with another vodka or the rest of the wine and often with some poetry books to turn to two or three of what I knew were particularly sad poems, and my brother would automatically appear about five minutes into it and I'd sob uncontrollably. It rarely failed and would probably work for me today if I had the record and there weren't too many scratches on it and the sound wasn't too inferior to what we have on records today." Sobs the first time he sees a certain Russian film. Went to the theater alone, it was about a year after his brother was lost, good reviews, a friend whose opinion he respected had told him it was a terrific film, interesting and moving and cinematographically near perfect, the second or third contemporary Russian film to hit the States since the new Soviet-American cultural exchange, sat in back, film was touching in places and light and a little trivial and dull in others and as far as he could tell very well acted and made. But the ending. Young soldier returning to the war front, never coming back, babushka'd mother seeing him off minutes after he got there, as he'd spent his entire leave getting home—powerful music, serious voiceover with a few words Howard could make out because of similar ones in German and English, closing shot of him on the bed of the truck that had taken him the last few miles to his village and will drive him back to the train, but before that shouting "There, there," and pounding the truck's cab and directing the driver down a country road, jumping out, kissing his mother—she was working in the fields with other women—soon the driver shouting "Come on, soldier, we don't have time, you'll miss the only train," and they hug and kiss and paw some more and the driver honks and he climbs aboard, his mother and he waving to each other as the truck gets smaller and smaller as it drives to the main road. He sat sobbing when the Russian word for "The End" appeared and then the music stopped and screen went dark and houselights came on. It was an art movie theater so almost everyone had seen it from the beginning and was now leaving when someone coming up the aisle said "Tetch?" Newsman he knew from Washington. Introduced his wife, said "This guy and I covered Congress at the same time, used to interview Kennedy together right in the Senate cloakroom sometimes, since we each had a 50-kilo station in Boston and my outfit one in Wooster. —Remember, Jack tapping his pen on your mike when he talked, then on his teeth while he was thinking till

you had to tell him to stop? Clink-clink, he was killing the tape. —
This guy was a maniac reporter, all over the place. Three to four
interviews going at once sometimes—his outfit just edited and aired
them separately—and who once boxed me out of a once-in-a-lifetime
interview with Nixon when he was veep and who no one thought
gave single radio interviews. But he catches him flying through the
halls and shoves the mike into Nixon's mouth and starts asking
questions, and when I see it and try to set up to join in, he says
'Stubbs, this is mine, back off.' Nixon's just laughing but wouldn't
give me one after his was over. But I got him back with an excluso
with Hoffa on some hearings and one with Lyndon on Ike taking
too many naps and golfing days that for a while had that town upside
down. But the real killer was when he gets one with Khrushchev,
if even only for two minutes and in translation, by breaking ranks
with the rest of us cordoned-off reporters and running with his tape
recorder and gear up the Lincoln Memorial steps. 'Who is this imp?'
we all later hear Nikita say through his translator on radio that day.
Nothing much of substance—he's sure he'll enjoy his brief stay. But
just to have got the first interview with English in it three hours after
he steps off the plane? And then quickies with Mrs. K. and his son-
in-law from *Pravda* or *Izvestia* and his wife—I wish they'd shot this
guy. And you really could have been shot by either of the secret
services for running up on them—you knew that, didn't you?" "I
knew but didn't think. My boss was hot on my getting beats and
I guess I liked the little notoriety that went with it. But listen, Mickey,
and excuse me," to his wife, "but I found the film so moving I still
really can't speak. I'm going to sit another minute." "Sure, the
movie?—I can understand," and said they'd wait for him in the lobby
for coffee if he was only going to be a few minutes, and he got up
in a minute when the movie started but they weren't there. Takes
the woman he's engaged to to the film a few months later. Doesn't
say what it did to him, just that it was a movie he remembers liking
very much, thinks she'll enjoy it and he wouldn't mind seeing it
again. At the end he's sobbing so hard his shirt's wet from where

the tears dropped and she says "What are you crying like that for? It was sad but not that sad and it certainly wasn't that convincing or great a film. Fact is, it was kind of schmalzty, if I can use that ugly word, and which hasn't almost applied to any movie I've seen in years till this. I'm sorry, I don't mean to belittle honest and open emotion, and I think it's wonderful the way you let it flow so freely, but that overgrown boy and girl with those half-witted innocent expressions and twinklings of what we know will never be consummated love? And the mother—holy Horace, get me a double vodka straight." "It just affected me, what can I tell you—maybe the music most of all." "Leave it to the Russians: mother patriotism with no faults." Calls his mother up every year on his sister's birthday, never says why he's calling, just "Hello, how are you, what've you been doing?" and she always says "Fine, I guess; you know me: not doing much. Today's Vera's birthday, but you probably knew that," and he says "I was thinking of it today too," and she usually says "What age would she have been?" and he gives the age and she usually says "It's hard to believe she would have been that old—she was twenty-six but so small and such a child," and by then he's feeling like crying and she usually starts in too till she tells him she can't speak anymore and she'll call him back later tonight if she can remember by the time it's not too late, or tomorrow, does he mind? and he says no, not at all and puts the receiver down and sobs where he's sitting till he can't anymore. Sobs when he comes over to her apartment and says he might have the same thing Vera had, or at least the doctors think so. First tells her to sit, they drink coffee, she says "Like me to toast you a bagel?—I just took them out of the freezer," and he says no, she says "What's on your mind, you look so worried," he says he has some bad news, she says "You and Dora breaking up again?" and he says "No, everything's fine between us, or as good as it's going to get, which ain't hot and not the way I want it but that's OK, we still have something and lots of good moments and I love her little girl and maybe it'll get better, anyway she's been wonderful about this," and she says "What?" and he says "I think—

the doctors think—I've seen two surgeons already about it, one of them Dora's father-in-law—she still has a nice relationship with him even if she's divorcing Lewis—anyway—she insisted I go to him when she saw the lump on my leg that wouldn't go away—they think I could have the same thing Vera did, a neurofibroma, though in all probability—at least it's as good a chance—it's a synovial cyst—" "A Baker's cyst?" she says, "Yes, and they're going to operate—he is—as soon as—not Dora's father-in-law but the other surgeon—he sent me to him, a neurosurgeon specializing in limbs—Dr. Michaels isn't; he strictly brains—but as soon as this Dr. Vinskint gets a bed for me in the hospital he's associated with, which is Memorial, I'm afraid, Vera's old place," and that's when he starts sobbing, not for himself he later tells her and believes, but for Vera, "the poor kid, because what she went through, nobody should. Me, I'll be all right, and I've lived past forty so, you know, I've at least had a shot at things. Though Vinskint did say—and don't get worried; chances of it are slight—that if it's what he hopes and generally thinks it isn't and it's really spread and is malignant, which it was with Vera but in most people it's benign, he might have to take off the leg below the knee, which is where the cyst or fibroma is, behind it, though not then and there. He'd want me to wake up and think about it a while but I'd have to make my decision soon." Vinskint wakes him during the operation and says "The biopsy report was just wired down from that window up there—you can't see it—and the pathologist said it's the cyst, which is what I thought and hoped it was, but we had to make sure, and I'm taking the rest of it out as long as I've got you opened up. You should feel very fortunate and relieved, Mr. Tetch, which I'm sure you are," and he says "Thank you, I do, I am," and they put him out. After, people say—a doctor cousin especially who berates him for not coming to him for a third opinion—"I could have told you over the phone what it was by your description of it and it could have been drained with a needle in any doctor's office for two hundred bucks"—that he should complain to the hospital and its medical board and some even say he should sue the doctors for malpractice—the one who first diagnosed it and referred him and the one who operated on him—but he doesn't like to sue and hates getting involved with lawyers and it's Dora's father-in-law and Gretchen's grandpapa and he doesn't want to hurt their relationship with the man and his own with them. Is dropped by a number of women over a period of about three years after Dora. Some in a week or two, some in a few months, and it hurts a little sometimes but no stronger reaction than that. But with the one months before he meets his future wife—the last woman he slept with regularly before her—he sobs when she tells him it isn't working out between them anymore and she's calling it quits. She asked him to meet her at a bar near her job after she gets off from work and he starts sobbing in one of the front booths. She looks around, seems alarmed, tells him to stop, please, this is a place she comes to almost every day for lunch or a beer and it's a good place to read and draw—the lighting and they don't bother her after they clear away her plate or glass—and now they might think she's afraid to think what, and what's all his blubbering for anyway? They never were that close. It was an affair of convenience—affair's even too weighty a word for what they had. He was coming from someone, she from someone else, they both had been given the ole heave-ho so felt good meeting up with someone nice so soon and someone who didn't give them each a hard time and want to spend all his hours with her or she with him, like the last one with her did before he kicked her out, and they had some fun, were companions, helpmates, bedmates, had similar interests—of course still do—and were even helpful in other ways like when she took care of his mail for two weeks when he was away and he helping her move into her new apartment and also helping her paint it with her—but now she feels it's gone about as far as it could or should, that it's sort of reached a point where it has to develop or just stop—he's still sobbing—and since it never can go any further—they both know that—and please stop crying, stop it, people are looking, it's too damn embarrassing and uncalled-for and unfair, because he couldn't have felt anything more for her up till now than a slight attachment, and look at their ages, he's almost twice hers and should want someone closer to his own, at the most ten years younger, just as she does with a man but the opposite way around, so please, cut the blubbering or will he at least just spit what it is out? and he says he was thinking he'd like to marry her and have a baby, so maybe that's why he's so sad and disappointed—says this when he knows it's out of desperation and a lie and he wouldn't know what to say or do if she said yes or give her time to think about it—but she says what? he crazy? Where's that come from? This some sick stupid joke on his part? It's a lie, she knows it, blubbering didn't work so now he's offering—suggesting—bullshitting to her about marriage and kiddies just to get her back for a week, maybe even just to fuck tonight, and let's face it, before he drops her dead flat because he'd be so frightened and perplexed if she ever said yes. For how can he think marriage and babies? How can he?—tell her, tell her. He says nothing, just looks at the table, and she says sure one day she'll want a baby, but when she's ready, which she's not and won't be for years—five, six—she has her education to finish, her art to develop and think about, some other experiences including other men to go through—just as sure one day she'll want a young husband as her children's or child's father—but also when she's ready, which she of course right now isn't. And why a much younger husband than he when she is ready? She'll tell him. He unloaded that bomb about marriage and babies on her, she'll unload this on him. Because of the personal energy-level thing, for one reason. Between him and someone much younger. And because she wants someone with the same or close-to-it cultural attitudes or values and interests rather than differences and different frames of reference or frame of references or frames of references or whatever the hell he called them—what he liked to talk about a lot, she should say: culture, morals, values. And just someone to look at who's younger and less line-ier in the face and who's hairier in the head and less on the body and not so gray there and firmer, solider, more athletic, less serious, less done in by life, less seen-it-all in life, just less a lot, she'll say, plus more juvenile in humor and spirits even. So anyhow, don't tell her it's the marriage-baby thing why he said he blubbered, because it's not, they both know it, so come up with something better or nothing, for all she cares now, and he says, wiping his face, maybe it's because so many women—he thinks this is it, because he'd like to get at it himself—women young and older but none younger than she even when it first started, have dumped him in the last few years that it secretly took its toll and culminated in that dumb what she called blubbering before. But OK, no marriage, forget babies, though he does eventually want to have them before he gets too old and weak to pick them up and carry them—maybe that's the problem too. But just leave him here—she should go—and let him figure out what it really is if it isn't what he just said, and she says she does have to be someplace now but he promises no more scenes here?—remember, this is her place almost every weekday and it's already been embarrassing enough for her here today, and he nods and she says he'll pay? for she's had a pie and two beers and there's his coffee, and he says he has enough on him, and she says leave a dollar as a tip too—two, even—that should smooth things over with the bar, and he says will do but just go, and he leaves right after she does, no thinking about it, there's nothing to think about it anymore, he could see she's had it with him, she's probably got another guy and didn't want to say it, she already gave him crabs a couple months back from some guy she met when he was away for those two weeks, but she at least told him when she found out she had it and gave him enough of her prescription medicine to cure it, and she calls that night, says he all right? he says yes, thanks, she says good, well that's all she wanted to say, and he says thanks for calling, that was very considerate, but would she like to do something tonight? and she says after that scene today and what she said about him he still thinks she'd want to screw with him? and he says who mentioned screwing?—just to go out, a movie, he feels much better, whatever she'd like to do—a bar, even, or someplace for a bite—and she says didn't he hear her today? She doesn't want to see him again ever. She only called out of concern because he was in such terrible shape today but she can see even that was a wrong move, another reason why they're so incompatible—that's the word she was searching for all that time in the bar—they're incompatible, because he takes things—looks at things—so differently than her—he looks at them as if he's not twenty but sometimes thirty or forty years older than her and not because she acts much younger than she is either, and he says thank you, that's very nice, what he wanted to hear, she's a sweetheart, really, but if she has a few seconds more he'd like to say this—something he just came up with but had thought hard about since the bar and nothing insulting, so don't worry—but the reason why he felt so bad about himself today and did that sobbing was because he thinks after her he'll never get anybody, that she was the last one or possibility of one, that he has no job, no prospects of one, no money besides, and at his age, well he must have felt his whole life was hopeless and still does in a way, foolish and hopeless and on a terrific decline, and she says is he pulling one on her again? and he says when did he ever? and she says come on and he says absolutely, he's not pulling anything, and she says then no, it's not hopeless, it's never hopeless, what's hopeless is getting into the bag of thinking it is, but with him it's probably just his thinking it is tonight, but tomorrow he won't think that, she assures him, or at least not to the degree of tonight, and the day after he'll think even less than like tonight, and he says maybe she's right, maybe he's wrong, she's got a good point, he usually makes things seem worse off than they are, so thanks, and now he also wants to say that if she ever changes her mind he'd certainly like to see her again and yes, if it resulted in that then to end up in bed with her anytime in the future she'd like, so if she ever reconsiders, though he knows what her feeling now is about it, give him a call, and she says did she hear right? yes she heard right, well she's going to tell him something now also, but something insulting but she also hopes constructive—if it keeps him from contacting her again that'll be constructive enough—and this will also be the last words she hopes to ever say to him, unless he's going to be one of those annoying-type schmos where she'll be forced to get an unlisted new phone number, and that's that an idiot—is he still listening or has he hung up? and he says go on, shoot—an idiot is someone who's never going to learn anything in life and, she wants to add, not because he's unwilling to either, and before he can say does she mean him? she hangs up. They never speak to each other again, he never bumps into her, sees her on the street, nothing like that, or meet any of her friends or hear anything about her till four years later, on a Broadway bus heading uptown, a woman waves to him from a seat when he's walking up the aisle, he stops, says hello, she says doesn't he remember her? he says he thinks he does but forgets from where, she says she's Aluthea, Carrie's best friend when he was going out with her a few years ago—she was in fact at the same party he met Carrie at—remember? she went out with his crazy friend Bernie for a while till she found out how crazy he was, and he says oh yeah, he remembers, asks how she is, then how Carrie is and she says Carrie's married, living upstate, on something like a farm, her husband has lots of money and bought it, and he says that's nice, he's married too and not only that his wife's two months away from having their first baby—a girl, though they weren't supposed to know but the obstetrician's nurse blabbed the results of the test—vindictively, they're pretty sure of, but that's over and done with and asks if he can sit and sits next to her and says is Carrie anything like that?—a baby, maybe two by now, even if it seemed she didn't want to get married or have kids for about ten years—her education and art, she used to say, and she says her art's not as important to her anymore and she'd like to get pregnant but hasn't been able to, and he says well, they'll go, if they haven't already done so, for pregnancy tests, and maybe a tube will have to be blown through with air or whatever the process is, or fertility pills, though one has to watch out with those because you can wind up with triplets, and she says oh no, her doctor says that as a couple they'll never be able to have children, that she's simply unable to because of some incorrectible malfuction with her ovaries—not even an implant's possible, it'll just reject, all of which has devastated her for she's been saying there's nothing she wants more than to have a baby, and he says he's sorry, it must be a hard thing to accept for somone so young, and hard for her husband also, and thinks how strange, for if anyone was built to have a kid and then nurse it, it was she, which was probably mostly what attracted him to her, her large tall shapely body, perfect but just bigger in every way, and she says it's been a lot more than hard for her—she's become a wreck over it, principally because her husband doesn't want to adopt a child, he only wants to have a natural one, and he says an adopted one is natural but he of course realizes what she means and doesn't know what he'd do if he were in the husband's position but hopes they can work themselves out of the dilemma, and then his stop comes and he sees someone's rung for it and he says good-bye and hopes they'll see each other on the bus again sometime and to give his best to Carrie and walks home feeling bad for her but doesn't say anything to his wife about meeting the woman on the bus and has never told her about that time in the bar. To her, Carrie's just someone he saw one day a week for a while till she gave him crabs or a short time after that and the last person he slept with, though months earlier, before he met her. He's thought of the sobbing scene lots of times since it happened, not for a while though till he bumped into Aluthea, and never could come up with what precisely brought it on and then kept it going for so long, since he doesn't think he ever sobbed longer as an adult, and was always ashamed of it and glad he never met Carrie again. He wonders if Aluthea recalled the sobbing scene, since she must have known about it from Carrie, and if anytime while she was talking to him she thought of him peculiarly. Anyway, the culmination explanation—that her dropping him so unexpectedly came after so many other women had dropped him or had refused to go out with him when he heard about them from a friend and called or met them at a party and asked and by someone he thought would be the last to do it—she in fact had said several times that if anyone dropped anyone it'd be he—probably comes as close to why it happened as anything he can think of. Thinks why again. Yep, that's about the best he can come up with. Sobs when his second daughter comes out but not as hard as he did with the first. "Wow," the obstetrician says while she's stitching up Denise, "I never saw a man react so emotionally to the delivery of his child." "You forget what he was like when Olivia was born—much much worse," Denise says she said when she later told him what the doctor had said, for he was sobbing too loudly and ferociously to hear either of them.

His brother comes back, walks through the door, says "So Howie, how are you, how's it going, what've you been up to?" "Alex, what is this? you gotta be kidding," pinches himself, slaps his face, "Still gotta be a dream," bites the inside of his cheeks, shuts his eyes for a few seconds, then says "It isn't, you haven't gone away, I still don't believe it but I'm gonna make the most of it," rushes over to him, hugs him, kisses his shoulders, keeps his arm around him while he yells "Denise, Olivia, Eva, the babysitter, hurry in here, meet someone you've never met before, my brudder Alex, lost at sea years ago, thirty years, in ten it would've been forty, in twenty it would've been fifty, thirty: sixty, and by then I'd be an old man but still I'm sure mourning several nights a year my dear lost brudder, crying some days too—jeez am I glad to see you, meet the family," and points to the staircase when he hears someone coming down, it's Eva, says "Babysitter's gone home, Mommy told me to tell you...who's this?" and he says "My brudder—*brother*," "But I know your brother—Uncle Jerry, and this isn't him," "This is my other brother, the one I've talked so much about—you know, on a ship, lost at sea, terrific storms in the ocean, the North Atlantic to be specific, ship probably split apart or by some fluke rolled over by the waves, life buoy washed up on the Irish coast, only thing of the ship ever found that they knew belonged to it, we thought him dead, sweetheart, but here the guy is—ask him something, tell him to say where he's been all these years and how he got here and that he's your uncle, my and Uncle Jerry's brother, your grandmother's middle son—God am I happy, and we got to call her up quick," and runs to the phone, dials, woman answers, he says "Is this LaDonna or Sojourner?," "Sojourner," she says, "Well hi, this is Howard, Pauline's youngest son, a fabulous practically unbelievable thing's just happened, get me my mother quick," and she says "She's napping—should I wake her?" and Alex's waving his hand no, and Howard says "One second please" into the phone and covers the mouthpiece and Alex says "I don't think we should spring it on her like this—the shock of it," and Howard says to Sojourner "No, tell her I called and will call back later and don't mention anything about the fantastic or unbelievable part of why I called—how is she, by the way?" and she says "As well as can be expected—you know, we took a walk down and back the block today—it tired her out—and not eating very much but not because she has no appetite—she only wants to stay slim, she says—she's quite a vain woman—while I tell her good eating shows good health and good looks, and she still won't listen when I say not to smoke so much—she says she's not inhaling but I see it—and also not to drink before she retires at night—scotch for sure not, but not even water, for it gets her up to void and if I'm not by her side right away she tries for the potty herself and sometimes falls," and he says "Thanks, thanks for everything—I'll call, and hangs up and says "Oh boy, Mom's in lousy shape, and of course Vera and Dad died," "No, I didn't know but by now expected as much" "Yeah, you were lucky not being here—both eroded so slowly—and also lucky in a way with Mom, avoiding the quick slide this time, but then there's all you kissed—missed—but see what he did before, Eva, about my not waking Grandma up?—he was almost all the time right, this brudder of mine, your uncle—Christ, what would I have done not having him around when I was growing up? and Christ, what I would've done if he hadn't disappeared—I was only twenty-four, hardly on my way, and he was my best friend and the serious drinking I fell into—really, why the thirty-year silence, Alex, unless the details are too disquieting for witty-kiddy ears?" "Do you mean me?" Eva says and he says "No, I meant cats, it's an expression, 'Here, kitty-witty, nicht disquiet bischen ears,' but one that's probably too far in the past for you to understand, like 'the bum's rush' is for me, which was Dad's—remember, Alex? and do you know if it meant fast and if fast then fast as you run away from the bum or fast as the bum rushes away after he puts the touch on you? another expression of his—'Don't put the touch on me in front of people,' when we wanted a dime for a comic book and saw the best opportunity to get it—a dime then, sweetheart, think of it," "What's a dime or a comic book?" and Alex says "Before we talk about my long silence, let me tell you your Eva's a doll—what I've missed and not kissed not being around from the time she was born—if you want, come and give your unc a juicy squeeze, my beautiful niece," and opens his arms and she shrinks from him, runs behind Howard and holds onto his legs while looking through them at Alex, when Olivia comes down, arms loaded with books, "I heard from upstairs but had to get these first— Alexander, your brother, impossible and you know it, Dada—a person can't swim up again after thirty years below and say 'Hi, I'm alive,' and spit some water out that might be gagging him"—Eva's laughing—"Oh, they can pump water out of some drowned persons when they haven't drowned for very long and make them breathe again, and sometimes even after an hour if they've been in very cold water, with ice floating on top and snow in the trees, because it lowers the body temperature and heartbeat and I don't know how but you're saved—I read that in one of my Nancy Drew books," and drops the books on the floor and starts looking through them—"I can't find which one it's in so you'll have to trust me—so who is he, Dada, a friend of yours impersonating your brother to trick us for some reason?—maybe it'll fool Eva but not me," and she sits on the couch with the books on her lap and starts reading, and he says "Olivia, show some respect—it's your uncle, my brother, this is a miracle till explained otherwise—even if you don't fall for it because you think you're so smart and have better things to do at the moment, please get up and kiss him," and she slams the book down—"If you make me lose my place!"—and goes over to Alex and puts her cheek out and looks pained, he closes his eyes and kisses her, looks content, says "Ah, another honeypot you got, you apotheosized kid, and with such a smooth cheek too"—"That's because she hasn't shaved yet"— Olivia clenches her eyes tight and hands into fists—"Only kidding, my sweetie—for some reason, Alex, she's never going to shave— only kidding, my sweetie, but by now you know me, though Alex doesn't—he stopped dead with me at twenty-four: easy with the jokes, not so with the other things," caresses her face, she looks up at him and pops him a kiss, "Oh this gal's bright, good, sensitive, imaginative, creative—sounds like a college reference I'm giving but she's gonna be the artist in the family—compared to her we're has-beens who never were, unless you've done something startling and long-lasting under another name since we last heard from you and it can be converted," and Alex says "Don't worry, all the material you've probably used about me the past thirty years is still valid and not dated, if it was done well," and he says "Me?—strictly fiction; only non-fict I've writ was called 'Why I Don't Write It,' which proved its point by reading unbeingable and where no magazine asked me for one again, but let's start unraveling the snarl as to where you've been so long and why all this time you didn't clue us in, but darn, here's Denise—just when I thought I'd get an answer from you— though wish you'd met her previous to her present condition—she had such lively eyes, like the sea," and she comes downstairs slowly—"Howard?," "I'm here, dear, just a few steps farther," "How many?," "Seven, not counting the floor"—clutching the rail with both hands, foot edging to the end of each step before going over and dipping to the next one till she nudges it, then, toe poised over a step: "I can't make it this way—I'm scared I'll fall," and he says "Just five more steps not counting the floor—for Alex," and she starts to cry, Alex says "Go to her," he says "No no, this'll help—I want her to learn how to do it or else we'll have to sell this place at a loss to buy a ranch house," "You can move her to the first floor," "I want to be with my wife in our bedroom upstairs—I'm a beast: I need my warmth, her smells, my sex and her breasts," she gets on her knees and crawls down the steps backwards, holding onto the balusters, stands at the bottom, "Watch when she smiles," he whispers to Alex, "nobody has one like her—it lights up blown bulbs even when they're not in the sockets, and if they are, even when the lamp's unplugged—our whole globe could run for a year on the electricity her smile gives off, our sun is a dark dewdrop in a deep cave at the peak of the Ice Age by comparison, our solar system could spin another min with a single glint of that facial detonation and if she had her old eyes back, for days," she grabs a cane off the bottom of the banister, "Where are you fellas?," "Over here," Howard says, "up two, down three and then weave around another staircase," and she faces them and says "Alex, what a delight finally to meet you and especially when we thought you'd perished, and what a change your being here will have on Howard and in turn on the children and me—you're the chief reason he sleeps so feistily at night and acts like a caffeine neurotic during most of the day," and she pokes the cane in front of her hitting a bunch of things and then getting the tip caught under the rug—"I can't use this rotten stick, she shouts, holding it above her as if she's going to throw it, "it's for cripples, not blinds," "Oh oh," Howard says, "now we'll never see her smile or not much of one—anyone got a match or flashlight?," "Go to her," Alex says, "stop pitching for laughs," and he says "No no, believe me I'm doing the right thing—she's got to learn to walk with it or else she'll stay in her room under the covers all day be it this place or a ranch house, and then why would I disrupt my life to give up this great place at a big loss to buy an overpriced ugly ranch house besides sticking the kids with new playmates and a different school?," "Because she's your wife and their mother and you're supposed to help, support and etcetera her," "Listen, happy as I am to see you— giddy's the word, rapt, ecstatic, beside myself, though I don't entirely show it—and much as I've missed you—agonizingly's how I'd put it, heartstrickenly, sickenly—you can't come back after thirty years and second or third thing—Olivia, have you been counting? for she's the math whiz here," but she doesn't look up from her book—"tell me how to ruin my life—run it, I mean, ream it, wreck it, rot it, rue it," "I can advise you when you're being a little too cruel where it hurts—you always had that streak in you but I thought by this time you'd have muzzled or domesticated most of it," "And if I always had that then you've always had the ability not to clam up or mind your own bizwax," "That can't be constituted an ability, even if I were a clam," "The know-how, know-too-much, know-it-all-how-do-I-tell-my-schmucky-bro-how-to-conduct-his-life, and knack's the word I meant, skill, trick, touch—but I have to live with her and have lived with her and in her absence do most of the things for the house and kids—shopping, mopping, slopping—nobody ever thinks of that, rarely, let's face it, unfairly, so why don't you just wise up or get lost?," "You said it, I didn't," and Alex goes over to Denise, takes the cane from her and puts it back on the banister, kisses her hands and leads her to the couch and sits her beside Olivia, squeezes in between them, whispers something into her ear, she slaps her thigh and smiles (she never did both at the same time with me, Howard thinks, or one after the other; thinks again: no, never, far as he can think back), the houselights go on when anyone who could have turned them on is in the living room several feet from the nearest light switch, and even if that person could have reached a light switch it wouldn't have turned on all the lights on the first floor and in the stairwell and on the porch right outside the front door, Alex whispers something to her again and she smiles and slaps her thigh at the same time: air conditioners, radios and television upstairs, washer, drier, humidifier and probably all the lights downstairs, toaster, dishwasher, food processor, juice squeezer, kitchen radio, stove light and fan, "Stop smiling," he shouts, "and Alex, stop whispering funny things to her—with so much power on at once we're bound to blow a fuse," Eva sits on Alex's lap and kisses his hand, Olivia kisses his hand and then puts his arm around her shoulder while she reads, "This is what I was most afraid of if you ever did come back," Howard says, "not only that you'd outshine me intellectually and perceptively and with general all-around sensibleness but that you'd outdo me as a writer with the work you came back with or were now working on, show me up in front of my kids with your gentleness and equanimity and all the rest of those things, make my wife enjoy herself twice as much in your company than mine—three times, four, five, jack up the utility bill in my house where I couldn't afford paying it, and start a kissing-hand habit in my family and maybe eventually on our street and in the neighborhood when before my family was doing just fine kissing one another on the cheek and head and lips and as neighbors we were doing fine also with a mere nod or hello—well, go on then, she's much better off with almost anyone but me, and maybe the kids ditto, and if she stays in the family with you, even better, since I'll get to see her at functions and such from time to time and also my kids," and he stamps out of the house, hoping Denise will call him back and the kids will run after him and Alex will say he's sorry and what does Howard mean and maybe something stupid besides, juvenile, injudicious, senseless, obscene, all the interior and porch lights of the other houses suddenly go on at once when the sun's straight up or an hour to the side left or right but bright, through the living room window sees his girls, turned around now with their knees probably on the cushions and their elbows on top of the couch's back—Alex and Denise smiling and talking continuously, one or the other or both at the same time, energetic talk, lots of face gestures, he can't see it but thinks from the way their arms are positioned that they might even be holding hands—waving at him forlornly, curiously, bewilderedly, for a few seconds Olivia staring him in the face with a look saying you know darn well what you're doing's totally wrong and absurd, he waves back and whispers "I'm your daddy, honey, don't look at me like that, and besides, you know how horrible I feel so don't make it worse," says loud enough for them to hear if they can hear him through the closed window and door and with all the appliances in the house going, for he didn't see anyone get up to turn them off, "I swear I never wanted to leave you two, it was the last thing on earth I wanted to do, in the world, the universe, whatever's more than that, for you mean everything there is to me and leaving you is like a death that's quick but pain filled and unforeknown and -foretold—I don't quite know what I meant by the last part of that but it sounded right and may be—that I've always loved your mother from the minute I set eyes on her, second, instant, and that instant to maybe a minute after it across a room filled with partygoers, chatter and tobacco smoke—some day if either of you want I'll tell you about it and exactly or as close as I can get to it and if my memory by then's still good, how I felt and what I remember her response to me was when I finally did get up the guts to go over to her to introduce myself—it's true she and I have had our spats and brawls but we seemed till now to have been able to talk them out, I don't like her illness any more than you do, condition, affliction, hate it, damn it, would kick its ass in if I could, but occasionally it gets to me in other ways, that she can't do almost anything she used to like helping with the cooking, cleaning and shopping and your homework and getting you kids to your various activities and schools and just seeing the things around the house that need picking up before someone trips over them and breaks a limb, so all the extra work I have to do, and while I'm at it all those tedious to good books with the horrible readers of them on tape she gets I also if I'm in the house have to listen to, I didn't want to storm out of here looking and acting like such a fool, I don't like pretending I know where I'm going now and what I'm going to do, I'm in fact trying to find out why I did what I did before by talking about it and related things here with you," they wave only their fingers this time and turn around, Olivia putting Alex's arm around her shoulder and holding it there and with her other hand holding her book close to her face, Eva back on Alex's lap and kissing his visible hand, Alex and Denise laughing now and jabbering when the laughing stops, they don't turn to the window once, he doesn't understand it, if he were Alex he'd look and see what he's doing out there and then tell her and then for them both to smile and wave to him that it's all all right and to come back in, he wishes he knew what they were talking so actively about, vigorously, spiritedly, he's glad his brother's back, nobody can hear him but if he said that aloud and someone could hear him he'd want that person to know he's happy as can be to see his brother after thirty years, happy he's alive, looking well, intelligent, everything intact, glad he's able to make Denise laugh, glad she's laughing, that his kids love their uncle, glad everyone there's happy and having such a good time, though wishes things could be switched around a bit to a lot—brother back, that unchanged, healthy, intact, etcetera, Denise laughing, smiling, animated, both animated but he seated between them holding their hidden hands and Eva on his lap and Olivia on the other side of Alex or Denise with her arm stretched behind whomever she's sitting beside so her hand's on his shoulder or neck, patting it, habit she got from him when he used to pick her up to comfort her before she could even walk or when he'd walk her to sleep, or just resting on or stroking it, goes to the dogwood tree in the front yard, only tree there, centered in the small lawn, doesn't know why he went to it or what he's going to do there, stare at it? walk past it and then where? snap a branch off and toss it over or into his hedge and then what? all the streetlights on the street and the cross one go on at once though the sun's still almost straight up and bright, never liked the tree even when it blossomed pink or gave on a hot day enough shade to sit beneath, which he never did, always preferred sitting in the rocker on the covered porch and close enough to the railing to put his feet up, little table by the chair to put down his newspaper or book and drink, its branches are sharp and have scratched his arms when he's tried to mow close to it and the top of his head once when he bent down under the low branches to get the mower right up to the trunk, is that it with all dogwoods or just pink-blossoming ones or just his: low branches and sharpness? all or most of the house alarms in the neighborhood go off, four or five of them, loud almost simultaneous hum starts up from what seems like all the air conditioners in the neighborhood, though it can't be fifty degrees out, fifty-five, he wasn't serious before about her smile and what it could do concerning electricity and giving off energy and moving solar systems and stuff, it was what literary people, even people with just literary pretensions, and of course some nonliterary people who happen to know the word, like to call, well, like to call, exaggeration for want of the fancier literary word he can't come up with now but which sounds Greek and has some part that sounds like bell or ball in it but always slips his mind when he wants to use it, bill, bull, boll, but he'll see: usually two days at the most, three, after he can't recall it he comes across it in a newspaper article or magazine when he hasn't seen it in one for months, sees an ant crawling up the tree trunk and immediately drops to his knees under the branches, resights the ant and squashes it with his thumb, then thinks why'd he do that? it wasn't in the house or heading for it and even if it were heading to it, it was just one, he probably wanted to take something out on something, let off steam, thinks of slapping his hand against the trunk for the same reason, beating it, then maybe both hands and then maybe his head, to take it in his hands, which would have to hurt by then, and slam it against the trunk till he gets too dizzy or tired to or collapses or his head opens up bad, but that would make no sense either unless he wanted Alex or Denise to come out to help his head, which he doesn't think he does, and though a gash wouldn't bother him much or the blood—his head got knocked around plenty when he was a kid, though never self-inflicted, with scars dotted along the sides and his continuing baldness revealing a few forgotten creases on top—he wouldn't stick himself with the pain that goes with those slams, flicks the ant off his thumb, sees several more crawling up the trunk, "You you-yous," holding his fist over them, crawls out from under the tree and goes into the house, doesn't know why, maybe to sit between Alex and Denise, put Eva on his lap, Olivia's hand on his shoulder or back and even patting it for her in case she doesn't, for one thing to finally find out where he's been for thirty years and how'd he get here, for another—well, lots of anothers but one's just to apologize to them all for his behavior before—nobody's

there, shuts off all the appliances and lights, looks out the living room
window to the lane of grass between his house and the shrubs that
belong to the next, out the kitchen door to the backyard and swing
set, shouts for them and then goes upstairs, shuts off Denise's
typewriter and all the appliances and lights, she could be showing
Alex his studio and the guest bed in the basement, even making up
the bed for him if he's bushed, for he might have come a long way
in a few days, not had much sleep—runs the two flights downstairs,
front door knocks, shuts off all the appliances and lights there and
the sump pump which continued pumping when there was no water
left to dump, upstairs, front door ding-dongs and knocks though
doesn't remember shutting it, looks through the small door window
to see if it's Alex or Denise—window's too high to see if it's the kids
if they're standing close to the door—a woman, shuts the porch light,
opens the door, strangely familiar, not strangely but queerly,
familiarly, family, it's—she's—he's sure what his sister would look
like if she'd lived another twenty-four—five—four years, "Hello," she
says, "How do you do, but I'm sorry, if this is for my wife, for she
doesn't seem to be here though she was a few minutes ago," "No,
I'm not here for her but would love meeting her and the children
eventually," "Then if it's for anything like some organization or
charity—a donation, something to sign, a petition, and then a
donation for the costs of printing and distributing the petition and
keeping the organization going—we don't do that here—it's my, not
my wife's, repudiation or reaction against or whatever you want to
call it of all door-to-door solicitations and canvassings, no matter
how—not 'important,' not 'good' in the sense of the right thing,
moral, virtuous, not 'upright,' not 'upstanding,' but a certain word
I'm looking for—," " 'Well-intentioned, well-meaning, high-
principled'?," "That's right—any of those, but we don't, much as we
might approve of what you're pushing—supporting—canvassing for
and want us to join, give to, support or sign, anyway, along those
lines, and you should see me—hear me—when I get them over the
phone—I'm rapidly—rabidly—against the private home phone being

used for solicitations and ads of any kind and the recorded ones—
you know, or maybe you don't, but the 'Hi, I'm Chuck Computer
and are you sure you have enough cemetery plots?'—the worst,
though I wouldn't go so far as to start or give to or canvass for a
campaign against them," same long straight dark hair combed the
same way though now streaked a bit gray, hollow cheeks like hers
the last few years but more like a model's high cheekbones so less
out of illness—"Vera?—I mean, it can't be but who else could it but
it can't, so excuse me," "Howard," she says, "even if I knew this was
your home, for a while I was undecided it was you," "But it's
impossible, I take back what I said, or if *Vera*, then you just happen
to have the same name as my dead sister, quite a coincidence I'd say,
seeing how you look a lot like I'd imagine her to at your age," "But
I am your sister Vera," and he says "But I was in the room with you—
her—when she died," "You went out of it for ten minutes at the end
when I supposedly croaked," "That's true, how'd you know? but she
was so close to death when I left her—her looks were of someone
dying, the darkness and paleness, the depletion and stress, and
they'd asked me to leave or else I left to go to the toilet or because
I needed a break from seeing her in that condition all night and early
morning or just for a coffee to revitalize me after a sleepless night
and maybe a bun because I was starved, and when I came back
minutes later the door was closed and a nurse behind it wouldn't
let me in—I'm almost sure that's how it happened, at least one of
those or a combo with the coffee and bun and definitely the nurse
not letting me back in and from what I saw through the door crack
before she shut it on me there were lots of people in white working
busily around her and calling out for things," "A nurse came in when
you were sitting beside me, took one look at me, felt my pulse and
told you to leave and then called in what I like to call the goon
squad—the emergency team of medical people and machines who
are there to revive you but also there when all your chances with
them are up and they're pulling out the plugs and cleaning you up,"
"Was that what happened with her, you're saying?," "Sure, they

pulled them out of me but I was alive and hale after, though my urethra and arms sore from the catheter and IVs, just as I was hale when all the tubes, needles and plugs were in," "That's ridiculous—she was in and out of a coma the whole night before and morning she died—I know because I stayed with her, swabbed her lips, mopped her brow—dabbed it and her lips and with water on a rag dabbed her tongue tip—she looked so sad, her eyes so weak and breathing so bad, hair so wet—I dabbed that too—all over her was this cold sweat—oh, the poor thing, why does someone so young have to go through so much woe and pain—anyone, old or young, but with her it was from when she was a little kid and went on and got worse and worse for twenty years—she even asked me—one of the last things I could make out because of her weak voice coupled with her trouble in getting her thoughts together and expressed—maybe an hour before she died when she all of a sudden jumped out of it and had unusually lucid speech for her at the time—why it had to be she who was sick for so long and had lived so abnormally and was now dying," "I never said that about dying," "That's true, she didn't, but what she said was, if my memory serves me right which it does rarely—variably, and locking me with her eyes while saying it—anyway, 'How come me, Howie?' or the old 'Why me, why me?' for she was, to illustrate how sick she'd become and what she looked like then, down to around sixty-five pounds from her usual hundred ten—'usual' meaning eight or nine years before, because her weight loss started long before the end, and sixty-five was just the doctor's educated guess—she could have been sixty, fifty-five, since there was no reason to weigh her and if they had wanted to she was too weak and frail to be moved—the gist of it is that from the moment she was put on the hospital's bed everyone knew it was going to be her last living place," "It was all an elaborate ruse, that last night and day—my decline at home, phoning the doctor what to do, ambulancing me to the hospital and so on," "A ruse, the weight loss and dying eyes?—I went to her burial—the funeral first and then the burial and a year later to whatever they call that ceremony where they put the monument up and say some prayers over it," "That's what I'm saying—it was all an elaborate ruse," "Lookit, for argument's sake let's say you are her, but she—Vera—you would never have pulled it on Mom—for years she worked like three nurses and suffered so much then and for lots of years before and after—we all suffered but those two were very close and she was her mother so she much more," "Mom was in on it—everyone was but you," "But why, just for argument's sake?" "To get me away from you," "Oh come on, if you're going to concoct some cock-and-bull story at least have it make a little sense," "You stuck your finger in me once and moved it around inside for a while and kept it on my clitoris when you thought you finally found it and pushed down hard on it till I felt I would scream and right after you took your finger out—my eyes were shut, I was pretending to be asleep, I was too young to know what to do, too frightened and confused to stop you—you threatened to kill me if I told anyone—you said even if it took ten years from the time after I told anyone you'd kill me when I wasn't looking or prepared for it with whatever means you had—a gun—you said you could get one—with a knife, a bat, a brick, an ice pick—with the belt you were wearing then by wrapping it around my neck and you took it off and held it tight by its ends and snapped it—by this time you must have known I was awake though I was still pretending not to be, looking at you through the thinnest eye slits, though you also must have been unsure if I was awake when you did it with your finger to me, because you said 'You've heard me warn you and speak about this for the one and only time and if you're really as asleep as you look, then OK, and if you don't have a clue what I'm talking about, even better for you,' so that's why it was all an elaborate ruse, nobody wanted me killed or for you to go through what they knew you would—remorse, prison, that you were an excitable guy so might be killed there or end up killing yourself—everybody believed your threats, even though they were made more than a dozen years before I told anyone what you did, and realized the consequences if you killed me, they said you had it in you to or to yourself or both because you could never take the shame of anyone knowing what you did to me with your finger and threat and then killing me, but they didn't want to ask you to go away to live somewhere else because they thought you'd come back on the sly to kill me or, away from them watching you, kill yourself, so they sent me away, Jerry knew where I was, Dad, they all saw me from time to time, I went to live with relatives of one of Mom's friends in Wisconsin, they weren't well off and could use the money for my room and board, the doctors and nurses all knew of the elaborate ruse, even the ambulance men who drove me that last time were in on it, the hospital orderlies and dietician on my floor who I only secretly got to use when you were away from the room," "Wait, let's say for argument's sake again in this cock-and-bull story that's at least a bit better than before—all the names and most of the facts right and things, so more believable but still with a few holes—I'd already been out of the house working for a number of years, and didn't they ever think of therapy to help me get over it?," "Everybody knew your views on it—you'd said plenty of times you had nothing against it for anyone but yourself," "I'm not saying I would have changed my mind but it's possible I might have," "As Dad used to say about you, you were always too much of a hard nut," "He said that to whom?," "To you, to me, and as for your out-of-the-house stuff, the folks got you to move back for a few years soon after I told them, didn't they?," "I came back from my Washington job with little money—no, that was after Alex died, which he isn't by the way— dead, but I'll tell you more about that later, or I won't, for who are you to tell it to? and California's where I came back from a month before she died and had no money and my father was sick so I stayed to have a place to live and to help my mother with him for what turned out to be a few years, but anyway, for argument's sake for the last time, and to me this is the clincher who you're not, let's say you weren't as sick as you looked in the hospital the day you didn't die, what happened to your illness? for you were diagnosed chronic progressive or some term by the time you were twelve, and after you didn't die but to me you did—and believe me I wouldn't be talking to you like this if you really were Vera, I'd be all over her in happiness if she were alive and miserable talking seriously to someone about her death—your doctors tried consoling us by saying you lived longer than they ever expected, though credited it mostly to Mom's meticulous unsparing nursing of you," "All part of the elaborate ruse, and the good country living might have had something to do with my complete recovery, and maybe just being away from the threat of you, or else I'd been misdiagnosed from the time I was five, repeatedly operated on when I never should have been, or some spectacular unaccountable remission that plenty of terminal people get and which eventually wiped away all my illness's signs except the surgery scars, but I'd been slowly getting better or not worse for years, you never saw it because of all your living here and there and only coming back for days or weeks and then paying little attention to me because maybe you thought I was so ugly and deformed or you worried I might allude to the finger incident," "Not true; the scars did scare me sometimes, especially when they were fresh and that tracheotomy one when it was still almost a hole, but I used to take you to dinner and movies—not many but some and especially when I lived in New York with Janine—your first Indian food at a place called the Bombay, those Shanghai somethings or another at 103rd and the other at 125th under the el—you defiantly ate with a fork and called Janine and me phonies with our chopsticks, which I loved you for doing and saying what you wanted," "So you did it occasionally, or irregularly, or biannually, but as for me then, I wasn't off crutches yet but no new flareups of the disease for years, so when I did have that last setback it was all part of the elaborate ruse, our aunts, uncles and cousins knew of it, most of my church pals and all our folks' good friends, we had a makeup artist come to the house when you were out for an hour that last day to make me look suddenly worse, and then the next days at the hospital to make me look comatose and then dead, she was dressed like an orderly and then like one of the nurses who rushed into the room to supposedly pull out the plugs, we even hired an out-of-work director to stage the whole thing, of course the rabbi at the funeral was in on it, I wanted a minister but Dad said 'Born a Jew, and since we're surviving you, die a Jew—if you outlive us you can have it the way you want,' the funeral home people knew of it—I was already on the plane to Wisconsin so couldn't see, much as I wanted to, your reaction and how everybody else acted, the body in the casket was around my weight in two fifty-pound sandbags, which is why Mom ordered the casket to stay closed, not because she thought people would be put off by my last looks, the cemetery owners, even the gravediggers there and all the guests, except the ones who only learned about it through the obit, at the funeral, burial and unveiling," "Unveiling, that's the word I wanted." "In the end it benefited you as much as me, as you didn't go to jail or anything like that and I didn't live around you with the threat of your killing me hanging over my head and you possibly even trying to diddle me again," "I never would have done either, ever, I was just a kid saying and doing kid things, I passed her room, or went to it intentionally to speak to her or catch her nude, her nightlight was on, saw her sleeping on her back or thought she was sleeping, but then probably woke her with what I did, nightdress above her waist or a few inches below it or right on it, anyway, her legs pretty much open and pubic area exposed, everybody was out, I was getting a quarter an hour to act as the sitter, I got excited at what I saw as I think would any guy my age, the line of hair above her crack like a short pencil-thin mustache standing up, the crack itself for the first time, I'd never seen one even on a baby at a beach, maybe mothers and nannies suspected me even at an early age and immediately covered their girls, once my mother nude from my room into theirs when they thought I was asleep if they thought about it but I was too young to understand what it was to get excited and she was all hair there and prancing around fast, so not good for an extended look, I felt horrible for years about what I did to Vera, for a few seconds at the funeral I was glad she was dead so the secret would go with her, since neither she nor anyone else ever gave me a sign she'd told or they knew, in fact on that last hospital day I whispered to her almost up against her ear how sorry I'd always been about it and said what it was explicitly, something like 'Your vagina that time some fifteen years back when I put my finger in, it was the most despicable thing I ever did in my life and I apologize a thousand times for it," "No you didn't, I was conscious every second you were there, except the night when I slept, but you say it was the last day, and I'm telling you you never said anything about it, if you had I would have stopped the elaborate ruse right then or soon after, somehow made a miraculous recovery, got the makeup artist in once more, been discharged, gone home, gotten much better under Mom's care and lived a normal life there with the family and you, all things forgiven, for it would have saved us all a lot of time and trouble and the folks a tremendous expense: fake hospital care, for no matter how hard Dad tried finagling it he couldn't get Blue Cross or Cancer Care to pay, the funeral, burial and unveiling ceremonies and gravestone, and my airfare to Wisconsin and living costs out there till I was able to get a job, and so on, even the regular postman knew, Mrs. G. at her bakery down the block, Morris the candy store man, most of the butchers at Gristede's, I became a dental hygienist thanks to Dad who heartbroken when none of his boys became dentists settled on the next best thing for me, married a vet who specializes in farm animal teeth and gums and help him run his practice, because of all the different treatments and operations I had when I was a girl I couldn't have any children that weren't stillborn, I'm a doting aunt to several of Ted's nieces and nephews and less so, since I never saw them as much, to Jerry's kids and now even their kids, do you finally believe me or do you want to phone Jerry or Mom for proof?— you once complained that my painting by numbers was for morons and bought me a real paint set and canvases I felt too unequal to to ever use, you once took me to Janine's Christian Science practioner because you thought as long as nothing else was working maybe that would, you once, because of the red and black plaid flannel shirt

I took from your drawer and wore—," "What made you come see me now?" "Why put it off longer? why not have done it sooner? one time I was all set to fly in to tell you when I got a bad flu and then changed my mind, what you don't know will hurt you? what you do know might kill you? why bring up old bilge or why not work it out before you're dead? for you might get hit by a falling brick tomorrow like I heard happens in the city or one in some punk's hand and then I'd always be sorry we didn't talk of it, or I could find I've had another kind of cancer for years and go in three days flat, so who knows? reasons for doing can be just as good for not, Ted said do and don't, Jerry said don't and do, Mom said 'What's best for you, what's best for you both,' Dad said to clam it since knowing you'd been duped for so long might give you even more reason for doing me in, Alex never said since he was drowned or his ship blew up or something before I told anyone, but now you say he's kicking, good, I want to reunion with him too, for one thing to explain why I stole his ship fare from his drawer which stopped his round-the-world trip for half a year which I guess ended up with him getting on a different one coming home that now never went down or did but without him—I liked having him around, didn't want to see him go or me be the last child at home, but mind if I use your bathroom?—tiny bladders run in our family—remember Mom dashing in from the street and leaving a pee line on the floor?" and he points the way, says "What am I saying, I mean doing, for it's not as if I see you every day?—oh Jesus, Vera, this is more than I can say, both of you back the same day," kisses her hands, says "I feel so bad what I put you though starting from that time in your room, I also want you to meet Denise and our girls, they're going to love having a blood sister-in-law and aunt from me—Denise is an only child and all of what would have been her relatives right down to the last second cousin were murdered or worked or frozen or starved to death during World War II, and also please, whatever you do, don't tell my kids what I did to you—no threats but I will feel rotten if they find out," and puts his arms around her and kisses her head, she says "You still retract like you used to because of the ugly scar down my back—for my sake try to get used to it if you're going to hug me," and he says "I always thought I did it in a way where you didn't notice, I'm sorry, and go to the bathroom, you're jumping around as if you have to," and she goes in, shuts the door, turns the faucet on, "Just like Mom," he says, "with the water going, so nobody will hear," "You say something?," "The faucet—Mom—I don't think I spoke about this with anyone in the family—used to even turn it on to teach us how to pee in the bowl—she thought the sound of it, which still gives me the urge to go if I'm in the john or at the kitchen sink and the water's on," phone rings, "It's Dad," he says, "has to be, the triumveral—which lots of people must have already coined—return, or march," and picks up the phone and says hello, "Will you accept a collect call from Simon Tetch?" a woman says, "Sure, put him on, I won't even ask how he's there, since I saw him right before my eyes die—no going-out-of-the-room-at-the-last-moment on my part—and then a day later get buried, and his body I saw at the funeral," "Howard," a voice like his father's says, "how's my boy, and good to hear you, and how I got back I'll level with you straight off—I wasn't dead or faking, just some look- and feelalike coma that even had the doctors and morticians fooled, and then I pushed and crawled out of the box and above ground like I've pushed and crawled out of every spot I've been in, whole and better and a lot smarter and tougher from it and ending up standing on two feet but this time in need of a little cleaning," "And this was when—yesterday or the day before after almost twenty years—how was the food down there?," "It was some time ago—you figure it out, you're the one who was always making with the plots and angles and complications, and you probably still are, if I know you, only because you couldn't turn up anything better to do—but I'm here and that should be enough," "You know, reasons have to satisfy me logically, plausibly—," "Oh plausibly, with your flossy words, well I got them too: abomination, ridicule," "All I'm saying is your explanation doesn't quite make it, but I'm glad you called," "Good, since my life's much easier when you're not being a wise guy, and listen, I'm sorry for the reverse charges, which shouldn't stand you much as I'll be brief, but I'm at a booth and had no change on me," "No problem, glad it didn't stop you from calling, and let's face it, Dad—do you think I can say this?—you were never one much for making calls from pay phones if you first couldn't tell the operator you lost your coin in the slot or got the wrong number, or even from the one at home, so maybe it is you on the phone," "Why you being so sarcastic? and it was you who was always the big sport with our phone—calling pals in California—that homely stringbean and her kid you once lived with out there—but you never picked up the tab for it, never even asked to see the phone bill," "I used to leave a couple bucks by the phone if I made a long-distance call and with a note saying for my California call at such and such a time, and I called from home because I was living there then, helping Mom take care of you, which was a promise I made her and OK, I wanted to do it too, and if I went out to call it would have cost me twice as much because of I don't know what implausible justifications the phone company gave—operator assistance for a while, but when I could dial direct from a pay phone if I put in the right change after a recorded voice told me how much?," "You never understood even with the local calls that it's extra charges after the first three minutes, and that piled up into big phone bills, but did you put money down for those?," "So the phone bill was a few extra bucks a month because of me, so what?—you knew you were never going to see your last buck and you had a free nurse's aide in me minus my room and board," "I wasn't made of money is what I'm saying," "And I'm saying you had enough dough stashed away to take care of the little extra a month on the phone bills, and I'll pay you back everything you still think I owe you for those calls, with interest and interest on the interest, for I've money, a regular job, not a tremendous salary but enough to get you back every last red cent of it," "Forget it, it's over and done with and I don't want to be petty, but you used to make me mad with that business and other things—my liquor, for instance, swilling it like a dozen drunken Irishmen at a wake but did you once bring a bottle home?," "Sure I did, probably more than I drank, booze for Mom, booze for me, wine, cordials, beer, soda when I was drinking brandy and soda," "When, if you didn't keep it in your room?—you never brought and you drank too much and the best stuff I had too, the scotch and my one bottle of rare Crown Royal I was saving for special occasions, and then you watered the bottles, don't tell me, ruining the liquor for me when I was finally able to have my one shot a month," "While you're at it why not bring up the refrigerator—," "Just tell me first, did you water my Crown Royal?," "Yeah, I don't know, I might have watered a bottle or two of something—it was late and I was probably exhausted but couldn't sleep or just keyed up from having taken care of you and needed a drink—one of your big fecal spills, for instance, which I'm not blaming you for—and I'd run out of my own booze and Mom's was empty too and I thought you might be checking the bottle level the next day, but if I took an inch of it it was a lot," "Three or four inches, if I remember, and not because I measured and checked it but because of its taste, but what about the refrigerator you started mentioning before—how you used to stand in front of the open door all day?," "That too, but I was thinking about your complaints of how much I ate," "You nearly ate us out of house and home, but you were fidgety from taking care of me maybe, which led to all your overeating, so like you I shouldn't blame you there, but with the open door you acted as if we had lots of stock in Con Ed—you also acted as if the refrigerator bulb and the food spoiling inside were replaceable for free," "Then you should have got a see-through refrigerator door, for how else could I have seen what was inside?," "You could have come to it the way I did, with an idea what you wanted to eat and what was inside," "Mom was constantly buying different foods, so I didn't kow what was inside," "And you were constantly eating but I don't think buying it," "You wanted me to set aside a special little section of the refrigerator for myself with just the food I bought?," "I wanted you, since you weren't shelling out for your own upkeep outside, to contribute something to the house—food, alcohol or money—for no matter how little you earned with your sub work at school you always still could have given in a small cut," "What about how much you were saving on nursing care with me and Mom?," "Listen, with my own mother—my father I couldn't do it for because he just keeled over one day and died—but with her when she was sick I paid for round-the-clock nurses in the hospital and then a live-in one for her at home till she died," "You were such a good son—that's what you liked to stress—and what lousy sons we were, or just me," "Not lousy, you just always thought you knew better than me so never did anything I asked, and you also never chipped in a dime to the house," "You became a dentist early and made much more than I," "I was paying half my parents' living costs when I was working two jobs while going to dental school, but it could be I had more incentive than you kids, coming from a background where we had almost nothing," "You went into everything else, why not my Gentile girl-friends next?," "I'll go into them—which ones?—you had so many, one uglier and skinnier than the next, and you lived with some, you brought them to the house for dinner so we had to entertain them no less, one Kraut you even had stay a week and don't let's forget again that especially ugly stringbean one and her kid you lived with at the house for a few months," "A couple of weeks—we were supposed to for a few months, while she went to some accelerated interior design school, but it was obviously upsetting you and in turn Mom and us, so we moved out, and I did ask your permission first— you forget that or just don't want to remember—I called from California and wrote and in both the call and your letter back you said though you don't entirely approve of the arrangement, you gave your permission," "I never gave anything, your mother must have even though I told her not to," "And that Kraut for a week was a Dane I met there whose parents put me up for a while, and she was a friend, that's all—we had similar interests in art and literature and looking at cathedrals and so on—and we slept in different rooms in her home and ours," "Oh, you were shtupping her, don't tell me—you thought you had a shlong ten feet long that had to be used every night or it would become standard size—well then you should have used it in your own home—I hated all your Gentile girlfriends, there was never anything to them, no looks or brains, with probably tight anti-Semites for parents if they had any money—you were throwing yourself away on them just to get laid," "You liked them well enough when they were around, and they were always pleasant to you, much more than you rated seeing what you thought of them—Janine, for example—she made you laugh, held your hand when she talked to you sometimes, treated you with plenty of respect, and if you thought she was ugly and skinny then you have less of an eye for beauty than I ever thought, for weren't you always boasting you married one? or maybe you only started keeping your glasses filthy when I met her," "I forget this Janine, most of them looked like the next one, maybe there was an exception some place, but rich, beautiful and Jewish is what I'm saying I wanted for you and you should have too and could have got, for if they have everything a Gentile girl does but also's Jewish, what's so wrong with it?—fewer problems, for one thing, because you're mostly from the same background so understand each other from the beginning, and Jewish girls are as sexy as any—more so most times—maybe it's in the religion or what's not in it or what they learn at home—to give a man who gives them a good life everything he wants—and you had the looks, height and brains to get one but you never took advantage of it—then you lost your hair like me—I told you you would—but not like me you didn't have any money to make up for it, and you were drinking too much and not taking care of yourself in other ways—clothes, even though I said if you were interested in a Jewish girl I'd buy you an entire wardrobe to date her—your beard sometimes, other times a mustache—nobody even knew who you were because of these quick-change acts with your face—and your old sneakers, no socks with them sometimes, you were getting to look like a street rummy with all of this, so then why would they want you?," "I still had a youthful face—it's genetic, from Mom's side—and I didn't shrink or lose as much hair as you at a comparable age or my brains, but I didn't happen to meet a Jewish girl I liked then, maybe just circumstance." "You didn't meet them because you didn't want to have anything to do with them—they were Jewish, so not as good as far as you were concerned—no small features, stick legs, no invisible nose or breasts—Jewish was trafe for some smart-aleck reason—you only wanted Gentile because they were different from what the rest of our families had and you could shove them into my face because you knew I hated it—consider yourself lucky one didn't foul you up for good by getting a baby from you and making you pay through the nose for it," "How do you know one didn't?," "First of all you had no money for payments to her if she did," "I'm only talking about the baby part," "That's just what they'd do—out of marriage, even when living with their own husbands but from someone else, and right after she screwed with you she'd screw with him and then with both of them smoking a cigarette after she'd tell him she's pregnant by you and he'd come with a gun after your head, but don't even insinuate to me you and one woman did, I don't want to hear it not even as a joke, because if it's true then you're finished in my eyes and because of your cavalier attitude to it, in the world's," "No, I'm sorry, it never happened, probably I was lucky, and now I'm married and have two wonderful girls and my wife couldn't be nicer, and she's Jewish, what do you know? though it had nothing to do with it—I just, well, met her, and she turned out to be that—in fact when I first saw her I thought she wasn't," "And it made you more attracted to her," "No, I was just attracted to her, Jewish or not—the smile, the face and hair, from across the room without her even saying or even looking at me, and her body," "A full body, what I've been talking about, one you can grab and that fills out a dress," "Some women I knew had full bodies," "You've had them all, I know—big, skinny, one with all legs, another with all neck, you said like a swan's, I said like a beer bottle—long hair another one had down to the floor and what a mess, one with hair like a marine recruit," "That's because it was burned in a fire and had to be cut short," "Blacks, whites, mostly WASP but a few Chinese thrown in," "She was Philippine," "Short and squat, like a baseball catcher, not to mention that greasy thick hair, though if I had my choice I'd take them over the blacks—you made me sick with what you did, but you at least showed the common sense for once not to bring the black to our house," "I didn't want to humiliate her," "And us?," "I didn't want to tamper with your sensibilities either, though I doubt Mom would have minded—the woman was a very well respected modern dancer, had advanced degrees in other fields and came from a fine professional home," "So why didn't you marry her if she was that good?," "She was too rigid sometimes, maybe we were both too self-conscious about our being together and the remarks and stares we got, I found her dull a lot and didn't love her though she said she did me, so that was why we broke up—I don't know for sure but I'm glad we did because of what I eventually got," "A sick woman," "When I married her she wasn't, but you'd leave her because she got a disease?—that's not what Mom did with you," "We were already thirty-five years married—with yours I would have found out better before I married that she was sick," "There weren't any signs," "Did you look hard enough, did you notice?—you just saw the great body and face and pretty blond hair and wanted to stick what you thought was your big prick in and she'd be impressed, and then you got hooked like all schnooks do with simply having a chunk of pussy always around for them and said 'May I?' or 'Would she?' and of course she does for by then she's over thirty and maybe knows she's got a little illness and getting worse and will probably need lots of taking care of later and her folks can't live forever and besides all that you finally landed a decent job and dressing better and so forth," "I was dressing just as badly, maybe better footwear because I discovered sneakers made my feet ache when I walked in them a lot and also now underpants and socks—I could afford them," "Anyone could afford them, you were just too much of a slob to wear them—pissing the last few drops into your trousers, you didn't notice but I did, the stains—anyway, I'm saying she was no dope, she knew that no matter how sick she was to become you were the kind of guy—you probably even bragged about it—to stick with her for life, which is all to the good but bad for you," "How so if I'm helping her? and let me tell you that sometimes I'm not such a nice guy about it too," "Maybe because you sensed something wasn't to Hoyle, because to throw away the rest of your life on someone who might have fooled you into thinking she was well when you met her or popped the question?," "That's not it at all, but you left out dentistry—just want to remind you," "What about it—I loved the field, yanking out stubborn teeth, fixing the ones that stayed, measuring and then finishing off the plates to perfection and people walking around with them in and complimenting me on how good they fit, besides all the money and the kibitzers who were always dropping in," "I'm referring to my not going into it," "You're proud of it, so you bring it up, but you broke my heart when you stopped taking the sciences in college—you had the personality like me for dentistry—outgoing, unassuming, a boy from the boys—you could have shared my office half time and done what you wanted the other half—write, painted, taken the piano— or we could have had two offices between us and once I retired and you bought me out you would have owned them both—one in the Chrysler building which I always wanted—imagine, that tall a place and so important in architecture, which you must have liked, and up till the last time I checked not a single dentist in it," "I was terrible in the sciences," "You could have ignored that you knew I wanted it so much and tried harder and passed and then forgotten them when you got into dental school because you don't need them there, once in it's all practical stuff—in fact you can still go back to college, get all the predental subjects out of the way in a year and then go to dental school, people have done it this late in their lives—that famous peaceful man who studied medicine in his forties, then went to Africa with his degree and I think his organ but unlike that guy, since he only wanted to be away from the world, you could make lots of money, take that tiny house of yours and triple it in size, or buy a new one, a ranch house so your wife doesn't have to walk up the steps and fall down them like in the old one, or a city and country one both, two cars instead of one, garages in the house for when it snows and to keep them from being swiped off the street, drive to your office and garage your car there too, and your girls could have their own ponies, not just dolls of ones, and go to the best of private schools, and you want to go on vacation you get another dentist to cover your practice, like you do for him, and off you go for a month with your wife and a special nurse for her if you want and a nanny to stay with the kids at home, and round-the-clock nurses all the time for her at home if it ever gets that bad, for who else is going to do it and now you haven't the means," "Me, I will, I teach college so I've time, also because I don't want nurses around and no nannies for the kids, I want us to bring them up ourselves, I don't even like a housekeeper in the house for more than a few hours a week—just to clean up in a way I can't, spots or clumps of dust I never see—I like my quietness, nobody around but the family or at least for extended stays, and if we have to move to a ranch house, which is what, the one-floor family house? then we'll do it since I make enough to live OK, but I don't want my girls spoiled with too many things they don't need, trunks stuffed with dolls, closets with party dresses and dressers with sweaters and hose, certainly not private schools at so early an age unless there are killers or idiot teachers in the public ones they're assigned to, and nothing to do with ponies or any of the horsey-set pets, just what I need are pony turds all over my yard and the cult of the equine inside, and as a teacher I get longer vacations than a month, we like going to Maine all summer to a simple rented cottage overlooking the ocean and doing our nonschool work there," "You can buy that ocean cottage and a piece of the ocean, then add a couple of out-of-the-house studios with bathrooms and little kitchens in them so you both can work to your hearts' content, but probably not in Maine for you want it to be a spot you can go weekends to summers when you have to be at the office and for skiing and short drives up all year," "If I make enough doing what I'm doing maybe I will buy a cottage on a Maine beach, two bedrooms, where we can each work in one, maybe a little room for a guest, but nothing big where we have to do a lot of furnishing and cleaning up, but look, you got to believe I once really wanted to become a dentist, not to make a great living, or so I sold myself the idea then, but to go to very poor areas here and abroad and work on rotting teeth, but after a few predent courses I knew it wasn't for me—truthfully, you loved working on mouths, which I admired you for a lot—I love people to have healthy and pain- and stink-free teeth—while I couldn't even cut up an earthworm in bio—I had to have this bright premed seated at the same lab table do it for me on the q.t. and I still only got a D," "You can get used to everything I found—I nearly fainted when they made me dissect a cadaver's head in my first year at dental school, but I wanted to become a dentist so much that I didn't let it stop me, and you don't have to be the kind of dentist I was—you like kids so much you can specialize in their teeth and hand out stickers and cheap toy trinkets after, or only work on gums, implants, adult braces—those guys make more than anyone alive except one kind or another drug or Wall Street thief," "Fine for you, which I also admired, pushing through with what you couldn't stomach, but I've no interest in making a bundle and since teaching only takes about thirty hours a week max I have some time to do what I really like to too," "And where's it all get you?—you have to check your checkbook every time you fill your tank with gas," "Not anymore, but what else you want to say to me while we're at it?," "What else could there be?—we just about covered it all," "Alex, what's got to be your thirty-year gripe against me but never expressed," "You're the one with the full head of guilt so you get rid of it—me, I don't let it bother me day to day," "But we're on the line, talking instead of yelling about things for once, so let's use the opportunity," "Forget it, arguments when you're desperate never get you anywhere, also because I don't want you paying too big a bill for this call," "What's the difference, it's my money, and what the hell's it for?" "The difference is you don't want to piss it all away on AT&T," "That's you again—chip chip chip, cutting back on the x-rays when you took care of my teeth and later with other dentists costing me three root canals," "I was no good with my kids' teeth—it took me a while to realize that—I didn't want to hurt them so knew I wasn't going to drill too deep," "Then what about winding through streets you didn't know rather than directly over the bridge to save on the toll, probably costing you another gallon of gas besides?," "That was before the higher prices—seventeen, eighteen cents a gallon so who cared? and you saw streets you never saw before and who says we always got to go the way they tell us or because it's straight and new? and I'm not talking here about anything but the actual gas, streets, bridges and such so don't make another meaning of it," "But if it's an important phone talk—like if you're ruining your kids' teeth with your sensitivity or wasting your passengers' time with your meandering route—I'm saying when something might just possibly come out of it to clear things up once and for all or smooth them out?," "Who could know what you're talking about from that? and I can't help it but we're running up a phone bill that's beginning to make me sick," "Look, give me your number if you can and I'll call right back—trick I should have thought of before to make you feel easier with how much this is costing me and which I picked up from you whenever you were going overtime on a pay phone—that and banging the side of the box same time you dropped the nickel into the slot which somehow recorded it as a quarter," "I didn't do those only to save—I got a kick putting one over on the system, something you should try more of to make yourself not so rigid, but OK, I can see you'll never let up, and somebody declared it truth day today and your pockets are burning and got to be put out, so Alex and that last call of his from England, right? and what you said in it, especially after I pleaded with you beforehand, knowing your fast mouth and mind of your own, to keep your trap shut," "I thought he'd want to be here if Vera died and not days after she was buried," "But she didn't die, which I knew she wouldn't—she'd taken a turn for the worse, something she'd done before after one or two of her operations and lived, so I told you if he called, which we expected since he knew she was going in and he was that kind of brother, and asked how she was to say 'Not bad, in fact pretty good,' for I knew he'd fly straight home if he knew the real shape she was in, but what does the big brain say?—he says 'Dad's not giving you the complete lowdown, the operation was a flop and it's possible she might die,' and I yell on the extension 'Don't listen to that jerk—he's just jealous you're away playing and he's working—she's fine, a little set back but she'll be OK, stay where you are, you paid through the nose for your trip so have fun while you can, get your traveling bug out of your system and then come back and be serious again with your life, just keep us posted with your address if we think, which I don't expect us to, you should come back suddenly and we need to telegram,' but he says you wouldn't lie to him on this, he thanks us both, me for trying to spare him so he could continue traveling and you for telling him the score and he's taking the next flight home, and then something must have lit up in you—misgivings or some serious thinking over that you were changing matters when they shouldn't for otherwise you never would have given in, but you compromised with me for once by telling him he doesn't have to run home so fast, that he could enjoy himself some more by taking a ship back, which were cheaper than planes then—maybe even a freighter which you said could be an interesting finishing experience for him, and I remember him saying 'You mean it about Vera?' and you saying 'Indubitably for sure,' which was a code saying between you two when you both totally went along with something, and that you had perhaps overdone her sickness to him somewhat and that he has that much more time—oh, I could have slugged you because if I was him you certainly weren't convincing me—but he fell for it— for a very bright guy he had a sudden dumb moment—and did what you suggested, found a cheap freighter in a couple of days and sent us a telegram that he was on his way and when in Boston it would get there, and then two weeks went by, we got worried, three—," "I don't know if you know or if this is the appropriate time to bring it up but I saw him just before—I forgot to mention it—Vera too, not together, one after the—," "Good, I'd like to see them too, but think of all those years your mother and I went through when you didn't see him—nobody did and all because you wouldn't listen to me—you thought you knew better—you wanted him back because you were gloomy over some floozy who dumped you that week he called so you wanted your best pal to talk about it with plus to take over some of the hospital-sitting chores you did in Vera's room then too," "Maybe that was part of it—a small part, the girl, who if I recall was nice, and my wanting his company—but I really did think Vera was that sick and would die," "Why, where was the evidence?," "Something about the way the doctor spoke and looked at me earlier that day told me she was even worse off than he said," "Come on, he was just another arrogant Mt. Sinai doctor—they all look as if they're about to spit on you," "No, it was something else," "What, his eyes? you didn't like his tie? the way his Adam's apple jumped up and down when he said 'no, yes, goddamnit'? because I was there too—right outside her room, right? and outside through the little window down the hall it was just getting dark—you asked if you should contact your brother overseas to get him home and he said he didn't think her condition was as grave as that right now," "If he used the word grave, maybe that was it," "He used the word serious, bad, urgent," "I still felt he was holding back—this business that a positive attitude on our part—and of course it's better if we actually believe what we convey and can get the patient to laugh about his condition—will make her feel good and possibly give her that little extra she needs to pull through," "So it's what did it, so why knock the guy?," "My attitude to her and often Mom's and her sisters' was usually dejection and pity, and you and Jerry only came to the hospital for a half-hour after work," "I had to make money for the medical bills and Jerry had his own family to support," "I wasn't complaining, just saying, though I will admit—not boast—that I took two weeks from work—future vacation time—to be there and help, and she was mostly in and out of sleep all the time so she hardly noticed us till she suddenly popped out of it one morning—we weren't even there, an aide was—and quickly got better," "So, good hospital care and the doctor urging us to a happy attitude with her helped her survive," "She survived because she was still young and relatively strong and probably had it in her not to give up so quick and the week's sleep and IV gave her the rest and extra strength she needed," "No, she survived mainly because she wanted to see Alex— she loved him like she did nobody but your mother—and the longer we kept him away from the hospital the better, for if he had flown back as fast as you first wanted she would have taken one look, smiled, given up now that she saw him, and died," "Ah, I could never win an argument with you or even make much sense to you in a discussion and I shouldn't have even started trying," "That's because I'm talking what you hate to hear most: reasonableness and speaking the truth," "The truth according to Dada—no, I'm Dada to my kids, and Daddy and Papa, while you were just Dad, which was all right, while Mom, now that I think of it, is still Mommy, Momma, Ma, but anyway it's just winning the argument, your truth, or drubbing your fellow discussant, while mine, which isn't a truth but conduct, is not," "You're way over my head there, sonny, and maybe even over yours, but where you like to be, alone, looking down, sarcastic," "But before you said I was a boy from the boys," "You once were but something happened and now you're not, but look it, this call's gone way past the point where I can tolerate it costing so much so I'm hanging up," "But I have the dough I told you and am willing to spend it for this so stop worrying," "I'm sorry but I just can't stand AT&T taking you for a sucker," and hangs up, "I also forgot to mention that if Alex hadn't taken that freighter he might have got the plane he was supposed to return on a couple of months later and it might have gone down, but you would have said 'Did one go down that we know of?' and I would have said 'We didn't check then but one could have and we wouldn't have known,' and you would have said 'The planes when they go down you hear about and I would have made the connection then no matter how much and how long after I was mourning him,' and I would have said 'You see, I can't win an argument with you or even hold even in a discussion,' and you would have said something that made me lose the argument or disgusted with the discussion even more such as 'Because your arguments aren't logical, you've drunk too much and maybe in the past took too much dope which has made your brains unsensible, you don't connect things intelligently the way intelligent people are supposed to so maybe you're not as intelligent as I thought and some people have said,' and I would have said 'Since when have you thought that, and what people, because nobody's told me?' and you would have said 'There you go again, trying to squirm out of it by putting yourself down—when insults and intelligence aren't working, try a little humility and self-hatred, right?' and I would have said 'Oh boy, you sure got me there, Charlie,' and you would have said 'Oh boy is right—you got yourself long ago, strung yourself up's more like it, and don't you by now know your father's name?' and I would have said 'I was just parroting one of your expressions, but your name, your name, your name—no, I don't want to say it, it's not nice,' and you would have said 'Go on, say what the hell you like, we're family,' and I would have said 'I suppose once in my life isn't too bad—your name, dear Dad, is gelt,' and you would have said 'What's with the 'dear Dad'—to make me feel better? but if that is my name, then you have none, which makes you and my relation to you what?' and I would have said 'Geltless?' and you would have said 'No, it makes you more but what, I hate to say,' and I would have said 'But you'll say it,' and you would have said and I would have and you and I and on and on like that till maybe I hung up before you did," and hangs up, knows it's useless but knocks on the bathroom door, no answer, says "Anyone in, for if anyone is say so or I'm coming in," nothing, goes in, empty, seat's up the way he left it last time he peed even though he told himself then to put it down after, puts it down, goes outside the house and runs to the back, side and front yards looking for Vera, Denise, Alex, his girls, sits on the rocker on the front porch, tells himself to wait, if he sits long enough one of them will come, never likes not to know where his girls are, hopes

they're safe, prays without praying they are, should he make himself
a drink and bring it out here with a book or newspaper? it's past
five so time, no, just stay seated and wait, how many moments of
quiet does he get like this? no mowers going in neighbors' yards,
cars zipping past, shuts his eyes, cups his hands over them to keep
out as much light as he can and to make it easier for him to think
if he wants to think, thinks one thing missing: Alex got away but
how?—Vera and Dad were explained OK or as well as possible for
now but Alex?—he got away as the ship was sinking but how?—the
ship was sinking or had sunk and he swam to a lifeboat or climbed
down to one from the ship, if he swam he had to swim fast and hard
because the water was so cold that one minute in it he'd die of shock
before he drowned, nobody else in the lifeboat or someone or several
other people in it but they all died, and it ended up on a remote
Irish beach in a week and he decided—he had lots of time to think
in the boat what he'd do if he survived—to fake his identity for a
year to be away from all his past obligations and ties—he knew how
much it would hurt his family but he wanted to have more time to
think about life and just do what he wanted to like write—something
might have happened in the lifeboat, too much sun, rain, being alone
for so long, the cold, always being wet, no food or anything to drink,
almost no chance he'd survive, patterns of the stars, he might have
hallucinated a lot, had a religious experience of some kind, some
deep change when he saw all those men on the ship and in the
lifeboat die—he'll work it out thoroughly when he has more time—
or Alex lost his memory when the ship crashed or the shock of the
cold water or in the lifeboat and the sun and cold and he wound
up on an Irish beach and wandered around for a while till he was
found, or it could have been drugs on the ship days before the
accident, some fall when the ship was hit or going down, a fight
one of those nights or he was breaking up one and someone
slammed his head with a bottle or club and his memory going that
way and thirty years later suddenly returning after he struck his head
against something or another fight or breaking up one or he simply

came out of it or through drugs or was in a coma for almost thirty years and only recently came to, or his lifeboat ghosted to shore, he walked to a village, faked an English or Scottish accent and convinced the Irish authorities he was a drifter or hiker, found a job, room, cottage, bought a typewriter or just used pencil and pen and lived alone under a fake name and wrote for what he thought would be a year but it stretched to two, three, ten, thirty, or he was picked up in the lifeboat by a passing ship, sort of a slave one which he only escaped from this year, or one from a Communist country he defected to if it'd keep it a secret for a year, when he planned to leave, but it stretched to thirty and somehow the authorities forgot, there could have been an Irishman or Norwegian in the lifeboat and Alex told him he wanted to escape his old life for a year and the man helped him get false papers, place to live and a job in his country, or the two had talked it over on the ship days before and happened to wind up in the same lifeboat alone or with others but the others died, or just with the man, no talk about escaping his old life, the man died and they looked alike and he took his papers, dumped him overboard and when the lifeboat landed or was picked up he passed himself off as that man, planned to do it a year but did it for thirty, married, children, grandchildren, wrote a number of books under the fake name or a pen name if he took someone else's name and always refused to be interviewed or photographed, especially for book jackets and publicity shots, till he had an experience—drug, religious, someone close dying, through another head injury or something he read in a newspaper or magazine or saw in a movie— and decided to see his family in the States and explain everything and ask their forgiveness, or he only did it a few months—maybe all he'd planned to—when he tripped and hit his head or got into a fight or was breaking up one when someone clubbed or punched him and he banged his head against the bar or floor and lost his memory and only came out of it this year, few weeks ago, days, their car pulls up, girls waving to him from the back seat and shouting "Daddy, Dada, hiya, hi," wife smiling from the driver's seat and saying "Hello, sweetheart, can you help me with some packages?," "Oh, you bought some more goodies again, huh?" and she says "Groceries, things we needed, and paint and brushes and stuff at the hardware store," and he says "Oh, you got some heavy work cut out for me again, huh?" and she says "In a way, but nothing you didn't say you wouldn't do," and he says "Wait a minute, wait—I didn't say? I wouldn't do?—does that mean I said I'd do it?," "Eva's room—we agreed on it, it needed a paint job years before we moved in here, and I'm not suggesting you have to start today—even this week if you don't want," and he says "Just kidding, and it'll look nice—that room needs some cheering up," and goes to the car while she's positioning herself to get out of it, kisses her through the window, "How are you?," "Fine thanks," she says, "and you?," "Fine also—some work done, a little thinking, a little rest, a gorgeous day," "Girls," she shouts and he turns around alarmed and sees they're at the curb, goes over, says "You weren't going to cross without one of us, right?" and Olivia says "No, we were waiting here like we're supposed to," and takes Eva's hand and he says "Good, my beautiful smart girls, but while we're here let's practice it—look both ways before you cross," "We already did," Olivia says, "You have to do it just before you're going to cross—also the side street in case a car's coming out of it or stopped—if one's there let it go where it's going to or park before you cross," "We know," Olivia says, "you've told us," "And of course, Eva, never cross the street alone or just with Olivia," "I know," she says, "can we cross?," "OK, coast's clear," he says, waving them across, takes his wife's walker out of the passenger front seat, brings it around, opens it, asks where she's been, "Out, shopping, you can see," pointing to the back of the car where the packages and paints must be, "But why didn't you tell me?—I assumed everything was OK, but next time," holding her arm so she can step out of the car and grab the walker, "no matter how steeped in my work you think I might be, whenever you're going out for more than a half-hour or so without my first knowing it, knock on my door or leave a note or later call me," and then stands in the street looking both ways while she crosses it.

Frog

"Great, we're in the car, all packed, ready to go, apartment's been raked, burners all off, windows up so no to little dust when we return, everybody buckled up? sitting back?—so let's get out of here," and he pats Denise's knee, starts the car, checks the street through the rear view and his side mirror, looks over his left shoulder, truck's coming, "Come on, come on, you're not supposed to be here except for a delivery and you're wasting our precious time, we've a long way to go," truck passes, checks the mirrors again, over his shoulder, all clear, same in front, even the light's green and with enough time to make it, and he goes.

"Where do you want to eat tonight?" he says to Denise at the first red light and she says "You made a reservation for the Breakwater, so do we have a choice?" and he says "I made it a while ago, but you said you might want to change things around a little and go to a seafood place in Cape Porpoise," and she says "We can do that coming home, for you didn't make a reservation for that night also, did you?" and he says "I was going to tonight—to be safe, since it'll be the Thursday before the Labor Day weekend; but then I was thinking the Breakwater's gotten so expensive and fancy with the candles and no wine carafes," and she says "Still, it's close to the

Green Heron, so you can walk the girls to it and I'll drive," and he says "You feel safe doing it?" and she says "What, the equivalent of two city blocks?" and he says "But your feet, you say they don't feel the pedals," and she says "Not right off most times but I'll go real slow, and back the car into the Green Heron parking spot so I don't have to pull out in reverse," and he says "I'll walk the girls, get them on the porch or inside and run back and drive you," and she says "That's a waste of energy and unnecessary," and Olivia says "Is the Breakwater where they have the rainbow sherbert I like?" and he says "Dot's de platz, hon," and Eva says "I want rainbow sherbert tonight," and he says "Only if you finish all our dinners—OK," to Denise, "we'll stick with the Breakwater—it's simpler—but maybe for the last time."

"Dinner, why we talking dinner?" she says, "we've got a few hours till lunch yet," and he says "Same place in Holland, Mass.— Goodalls, Goodwalls?" and she says "If we can make it before the girls starve," and he says "I packed a food bag just in case—those baby bagels, carrot sticks and such, even a tahini-spread sandwich for you, so we'll try for it?" and she says "Do we have to settle on it now?" and he says "You know me, I like to get most things done ahead of time so with a clear mind I can go at the few things I really like doing," and she says "Why don't you then get your gravestone made and engraved and obit written and invite the guests you especially want at your funeral and unveiling and related rituals?— perhaps a big blowout after," and he says "Nice premortuary talk in front of the kids, and please don't mention blowouts while we drive," and she says "Just asking but when did you make the Breakwater reservation?" and he says "To make or break the makewater breakavacation—when the Green Heron opened for the season, so around April," and she says "Don't you find that a wee bit something?" and he says "Maybe even March, but remember a few years ago in May when I tried for a room at the Heron and they were booked through Labor Day, so we couldn't even stay there coming back?" and she says "A small affordable unassuming room for a night in a chic summer resort is one thing, plus we had four cats then, but a large restaurant where there are many other restaurants of supposedly similar size, quality, prices and view?— the worst that could happen is we'd wait half an hour to an hour for a table which would mean the kids would play and bother us a little, I'd read and you'd get semibombed on two straight-up martinis at the bar," and he says "Well, I made it off the office phone, same time I made the Green Heron reservation, for the latter made me think of the other, and here it is today and we've nothing to worry or later be bothered or me tomorrow hungover about and no hour to lose," and she says "That is something, I suppose," and rests her head back, feet up on the dashboard, big sigh, shuts her eyes.

That a way, close yourself off and pretend to be tired when you want to get out of it—not fooling him. And what the fuck she going on about and got to be so tired over?—she sorted the bedding and clothes, that's all, and too much of them, meaning more than he needed to pack, while he did his own things and the rest of the work to get them on the road at almost the exact time they planned for: loading, cleaning, yesterday's pickup for UPS, scavenging the neighborhood for boxes before buying them at the store, car oiled and lubed, tank filled, tires, making all the calls for the paper delivery up there and cut off here, getting the phone in and utilities turned on, instructions to the post office here to forward the mail and there to hold it, last-minute shop, bringing the kids' library books back, all the necessary checks, monetary and otherwise, in addition to defrosting the fridge—worst chore there is, with that refrigerator, other than changing a tire, which he's done once a summer for years so will probably have to do this one too—and gassing and burning himself cleaning the oven. His father used to say to him "I work and you're bushed, no doubt from watching me." What's probably the case with her is she resents he can run around like that and do so many things so fast and efficiently so bitches or tunes him out. But for going back and next summer he'll say help him out some by taking care of everything she can do by phone and sitting at a table doing a few pen squiggles and she'll probably say she'll be glad to if he doesn't ask her to do it long before she has to or if he hasn't already done it. She's right on a lot of it—he likes to get things out of the way too much—and she does have her illness, but at least give him a little credit for all he did. It'd be nice if they had something else to talk about now. A book, Chekhov story he just read and she's practically memorized, an elaborately interpretable sociological subject or news events, something that could carry them smoothly through the next two tedious hours of the trip, or a string of those, some interesting part of his or her life the other doesn't know of or has completely forgotten and which would bring other things to mind. He was always awful at thinking up conversation starters while she's always been good at it, being that kind of teacher and more of a listener than he, but it's not something he can ask her to do: Think up some good hot topics for talks, otherwise we'll be bored.

She knows why she harped on him like that. Physically drained, leg muscles ache, right eye's not focusing right, not enough sleep, bad night with her bladder—you'd think he would have said something this morning she woke him up so often last night—but mostly him pressuring them so they could get out by the prearranged time: get dressed, finish your breakfast, this bag ready to go? the medicine chest cleaned out? pulling the half-eaten bowls and plates away from the girls so he could clean the dishes and table, sweeping up, then yelling crumbs, more crumbs, because Eva was eating a croissant and dropping a few flakes, without asking her shutting the radio off and packing it when she was cooking and listening to a piano piece she wanted to know the name of, nagging her how much longer she thinks she needs, half-hour she said, half-hour to her is always an hour he said, can she make a half-hour a half-hour this time? Another woman might think it not endearing, not amusing, ludicrous for sure, but something his advance planning, and he does take care of lots of things she hates to do but more likely is unable to, so, "helpful," though not quite that either. But his compulsiveness and occasional rudeness in carrying it through cancels his helpfulness. If only he could say that sometimes he does things just a bit peculiarly if not wrongly, she'd say let's open a good bottle of red wine tonight for she sees a start on his part of some sort of self-awareness. And please, to keep the peace, no more word games that make little sense—she hopes that fakeavacation was only an aberration and not the running mood of the trip.

She wants rainbow sherbert and she doesn't want to share it with Eva. She'll ask for her own cup, and if they say one cup with two spoons, she'll say Eva has germs, everyone has germs, she's been looking forward to it all year and she swears she can finish it all, and if they say if she finishes her portion they'll think about getting another cup she can share, she'll ask for her own flavor, lemon or vanilla or whatever there is except chocolate and coffee and anything with raisins or berries or nuts, since Eva will only want rainbow. If there's only rainbow and some of those other ones she doesn't like, she'll go along with them but ask them to promise for when they drive back and go to the Breakwater that she can get her own cup of rainbow. If they can't promise that she'll say just think about it then and tell her later but don't say absolutely no.

That man's so old. He walks so slow that his dog's going to walk away from him and never be seen again. She should shout to him to walk faster and catch up. Or to get a rope and tie the dog to it and hold on tight. They lost Kitty to coyotes last summer she heard them say when they didn't see her, which is why Olivia and she hate the house they call the black house they're going to. Where is he? Daddy drives so fast she can't almost see the man and his dog anymore. "Daddy, you're driving too fast." "No I'm not." "Daddy, listen to me, you have to slow down." "Please, sweetie, don't tell Daddy how to drive. —Listen to her, Denise: Eva the boss. —You forgot to order me when to floss my teeth and go to bed last night, Eva." "Daddy, I don't order you anything and I am not the boss. You're not the boss either." "I'm not the boss?" "Nobody is, but I want you to do what I say now—go slower." "Eva, I'm serious, you're distracting me, so pipe down." "Don't say pipe down. You said never to talk angry or to say shut up." "I said to pipe down, which is like a musical instruction because of your beautiful singing voice—to make the sound softer and the feeling behind it sweeter." "You said to shut up and I'm saying everything you say you say to yourself and not me and you have to slow down." "Look at that linguistic construction," he says to Denise, "when last year it was blur-blur-slow-blur-down." "Shh," Denise says to her, "don't bother the driver." Man, catch up with your dog or you'll lose him and then you'll be sad. She wishes she had a dog. A dog could kill coyotes or run away from them or get a bunch of dog-friends to gang up on them and chase them away. Not like Kitty who was old and blind and Daddy shouldn't have let her outside for air. But they won't get her one. He says they're dirty and full of kaka and their mouths stink, and Mommy said if he doesn't want one then she'll have to wait till she's old enough to get one for her own home. She can't wait that long. There might be more coyotes then and not so many dogs and she'll be afraid to lose it like Kitty.

"Look at this traffic," he says. "The world's ugliest expressway, the Cross Bronx, dividing the bloody borough in two." "Why bloody?" Olivia says. "Because there are murders in it?" "Because it sounded good. 'Bleak' would have been more appropriate, but could I have said bleaky? —Should I take the left thru-traffic or the right?" "Stay on the right," Denise says, "that's always been better, even at toll booths for some reason." "That so?" Considers. "Eh, I don't know." "I don't know why you don't, since you're the one who told me it and a few times proved it along with running commentary." "Well, if I said it then it's got to be true, right? Right." Stays right. Bad shot at conversation. Try to get something better going. "You know, when they were building this charnel house for cars I was dating a girl in the Bronx. It was a block or so from her building and we used to walk to it at night sometimes because it was quiet and unfrequented. Think of it: the Bronx, a walk, at night, not an Italian neighborhood, and we'd go there to look at the rubble and equipment and complain of it and of course to make out. But I knew even then what it'd do to this bleaky borough." "You can't say that," Olivia says. "I know, dear. —I remember—veddy social-conscious-head then—I used to get real hot under the collar as to what the city was doing to the Bronx. I was very anticar then. People, I used to say. What about the people? Well, I still say it, or think it, but not with the same fervor. Now it's children." "What's make out?" Olivia says. "To take a good look." "Like stare?" "Like stare." "Was that Sharon Hirshkowitz?" Denise says. "You told me about her. Where she wouldn't let you beep-beep or even close to it. And after a year you got so frustrated by it and other things in your life and the slow way things were going that you wanted to quit college and join the army reserves and get your service over with and they rejected you and so on. The one who married some big TV quiz-show producer and host after she worked for him as a secretary right out of college and later divorced him and got a few million plus his miserable expensive art collection." "She would only let us play with our hands—down there—you know, temporary relief—but for more than a year and a half? I swear, I almost forced her to once and everything was off and she cried and cried and said she understood and was sorry and I stopped. We used to see each other almost every day at college and weekends, write each other poetry and a week alone at her sister's house on Fire Island and that sort of stuff. What a waste. Imagine today?" "Oh, in some ways things are as prudish if not worse." "The religious right, states banning every kind of abortion, some textbook censorship, the NEA thing, right? I don't understand the particulars of that controversy but you're telling me some government institution's going to define *obscene* for me? Based on what the average person thinks—prurience, community standards and all that?" "I know; it's absurd." "But what do you think?" "Sharon? This expressway? The Bronx in general? The NEA?" "Yeah." "I wouldn't force myself on an expressway or want one, no matter how much I loved them, forced on me, but most of it the same as you." "The NEA?" "What I said—absurd, odious. Careful, we're coming to the Major Deegan turnoff on our right." "Who was the

Major anyway? —Not interested? Probably engineer corps. Maybe the guy who designed the Cross Bronx Expressway and the title's honorary or he got it in World War II for shooting his general. — Don't worry, I got it. My high school principal was a Deegan but that's about what I know of him. Two thousand boys. He had a crewcut. I forget with an A or an E."

Where'd she put her diaphragm? Doesn't remember putting it back in the case or the case into the cosmetics bag. No, she put the case into the bag and the bag into their overnight valise but doesn't remember putting the diaphragm into the case. Still in, she forgot. They should make one with a benign alarm in it to go off after the sixth hour or, if she knew she was going to be around anyone except her husband, to set it to just tickle her. Wanted...started...was playing with herself early this morning in bed when she couldn't sleep. Thought he might be interested. He usually is with a little prompting and if he hasn't done it in a day or since the previous night, and has joked it's his duty to serve her that way whenever she wants. Joke or not, he's usually done so except when exhausted or drunk. And if she tells him all she needs is a few minutes of vigorous fingering and him in her another few—this is mainly for sleep, no orgasm necessary on her part but be her guest on his— even better for him because then he's home away free—after he finishes fingering, quick as he likes which she thinks he likes best even if he's said slow way, long buildup, with her coming, is infinitely preferable. Got up to pee, put it in when she sat back on the bed, thinking better there than in the bathroom since it'd be a hint to him if he was awake and even a turn-on, that slapping sound, the jelly smell, and just watching her insert it. Kissed his shoulder, he didn't respond. Kissed his neck and back—he was on his side turned away fron her, didn't respond. Felt his thigh, penis—at first she was sure he was pretending not to notice her. He stayed soft so he probably was asleep, since she never knew him not to respond somewhat when she really rubbed it except when he was exhausted, etcetera, sick or it was too soon after they last did it. Young men. Some could do it three times in a row, when she was young, which maybe had something to do with it—her body then, to look at and what it could do and take—with only a few minutes to a half-hour needed between orgasms, and a couple of them could stay hard and in and start right over again and sometimes three times a night for several days in a row, which really made her ache. While she doesn't remember him more than a couple of times coming twice in a night and with probably a few hours between. Quality over quantity? Not really. Some of those young men were just as able and felt as good, but no doubt most of them have slowed down too. She played with it a bit longer and then didn't want to be a pest. Should have tried doing it longer to herself but her condition's made it nearly impossible for her to finish even with him in her. And this morning, girls still sleeping, he was in such a rush to get things done for the trip that he was up before six. She said in her head when he was dressing "Come back to bed, I want to have sex." Should have said it aloud, and if he just smiled and went on dressing, said something about what he's said is his duty and that they can make it quick. Strokes his leg, he smiles, takes his hand off the wheel and squeezes her hand and puts his hand back on the wheel. "So we're friends again?" he says. "When weren't we?" "Lots," and whispers "Come on, we've hated each other sometimes and a few times at the same time." "I guess that's true but yes, friends—you're a dear, and do we have a choice?" Whispers: "You can always leave me. I'd never leave you but I'd never make a row if you left me." "So you say about both." "What?" Olivia says. "Nothing," she says, "we're talking. — But didn't you once say a young woman—younger by twenty years than you—last one you were with for a while before you met me— said that about you: that you would and she would never and a month later she ended up leaving you?" "Who did?" Olivia says. "This is private," she says. "Just sit back, and you have a book there, read or look out of the window." "I'm bored." "So read. That's what we got you the new books for." Olivia picks up a book. He looks back at her, sees she's reading, Eva's playing with a doll, says to

Denise "She had a venereal problem with a D. Not with a, well, I can't find the right initial, but she wasn't a hot babe—not like you. Maybe it was just to me because of the age difference." "Don't be silly. Dozen years later, women that age must still be attracted to you. You're very X-E and you know it." "Sure I do, sure I am, sure they are. But I told you she gave me it, this V with a D. Actually with an A, for ailment—initials that crawled." "You did." "But by the time I met you I'd been disinfected. Actually, she was the next to last before you. There was the one I met at the U of C reading I gave and which five people came to. My only groupie. She'd read a story of mine once, one of the three she'd read in her adult life—she was an English major so didn't read much fiction—and since I was the only live writer of the three, she was impressed. After her I thought of going on tour—it was so easy. 'Are you married?' she said, after I signed the photocopy of my story she had. 'If you're not or you are but legally or mutually separated, I've a car outside if you want to go home with me.' Later I learned she was mostly a lesbian. Pre-AIDS by a few months, so no problem. Now who knows what I'd do." "So that's why you'll never leave me. I'm the only woman you're sure is virus free." "You got it. So, it's the Breakwater after all? Settled? Because it has become pretty expensive and so chichi. That whole town has." "It was always chichi but worse since the VP became a P." "Blueberry bagels, strawberry mustard, Kennebunkport air in a can. Farts, that's what's in them, a secret they're able to keep for they figure nobody's going to open the can. Fug 'em." "Don't curse," Eva says. "Don't say fuck." "I didn't and don't you. I said fug. It's a dance. To do the fug. Let's cut a rug with the fug." "Don't push it," Denise says. "It'll make it more memorable to her." "Hey kids," he yells, "a barge. In the water. So, getting closer to Maine. This river to that reach to that ocean. No cows or those immaculate clouds yet but I see them way off in the distance." "What else you see?" Olivia says. "Hey, Country View Drive-in. Milton, the owner, feeding his pet rabbits and geese in those cages next to the outside tables and then racing back to the kitchen to cook up a mess of fishburgers. We're on our way, Milton; see you for snacks in two or three days." "What else you see?" Eva says. "Well, through the rear view mirror there's grandpa leaving his building to walk to Zabar's to send us some of your favorite plain bagels and cream cheese—he doesn't see how we can live without them up there. And in front, but only as far as southern Maine this time—oh no, President B., his helicopters, landing in Bennyshlumpsnort just to crowd up the joint with reporters and secret servicemen and ruin our day—stay away. I really do hope he isn't in for the weekend," to Denise. "It's always twice as crowded, even at the beach I take the kids to where the voters jam the shore hoping to see him at the wheel of his speedboat. I don't know why they expect to sight him. Most of those Maine motorboat guys his age look alike—tall, gangly, angly, deepcheeked, peaked cap down to their long thin noses, but I guess no one else has gunboats preceding and following him and a flying gunboat overhead. 'Oh look, there he is.' 'No, I think that's him.' 'But they look exactly alike and same with their boats.' 'The first one's an impostor to take the heat off the real B.' Or how about what I heard on the beach last year: 'I just got word on my CB he's left the compound by boat ten minutes ago and is heading this way.' " "If he is in town I hope he jogs by the inn as I heard he does. It'll be exciting, especially for the girls to see him—or eats breakfast there tomorrow, which he's also done." "Tomorrow's Saturday, fish and zip-along-the-water day, so no jogging or breakfast away. Save that for after church on Sunday when the news cameras have nothing to do and he can wave at them. And I don't want to be frisked by the S.S. a dozen times before I even take my first coffee sip. But can you believe it, everyone? Breakfast at the Green Heron tomorrow, tonight some fresh-picked crabmeat hor-durvy and local grilled fish, the best night of the year for me. Maine to look forward to for two months. And no beds to make, clean sheets, a clean bathroom, nothing to clean up, taking the kids to the beach before dinner if it doesn't rain—please, dear God, no rain. Then back to the inn for a scotch with their rocks and reading the paper or a book while you bathe then. And after dinner back to the inn again, no noises outside but the distant shore banging and bugs busting their brains out against the screen. Beach and tree smells and those wild bush roses—and all this after a long car trip with only me at the wheel, no crit intended, so even better. And big comfortable bed with several fluffed-up pillows and at the restaurant a bottle of good wine between us or one-fifth you, four-fifths me, so from Major Deegan to major love, what do you say?" "You want it confirmed beforehand?" "Wouldn't mind." "If no major disturbances, I'll be ready. Was, this morning, if you didn't know." "I didn't. Why didn't you moan something, grab or nudge me?" "Oh well, but you brought scotch?" "Sure, in an old applesauce jar, about four shots' worth, but sealed with duct tape and then in a plastic bag and tied, so don't worry, it's with my things and won't spill." "Who was worrying? I just don't want you to get drunk or have too much of a headache tomorrow to drive well." "I also brought Alka-Seltzer and stuck a few aspirins into my wallet, wrapped in foil, just in case." "Our exit's coming up soon. Four or five, but you'll know it by the one right after the Yonkers racetrack. It's beside a big disorderly looking shopping center, and looks more like an exit to it than to 287. If I nod off for a nap now you'll get us off this and onto the expressway OK?" "I remember how. Cross County, aka 287, exit to it on the right—keep a sharp eye out for it looks more like a turnoff to the center than an entry road to the expressway. Then Cross County to Hutchinson north or east to the Merritt Parkway and all the way to the end of the Merritt where we can either make a right to a road leading to 95 or continue straight ahead to Hartford on the Wilbur Cross. But you'll be awake by then and if you're not I'll get you up to help make the decision between the two." "Wilbur Cross, why not? We've never taken it north but took it coming back last year and you said it seemed faster than our usual route: 91, 95 and so on." "But the unknown. Will we know how to get to 84 or 86 or whatever it is out of Hartford? They were changing the numerals last year and it was all screwed up and we made it right to Wilbur Cross just by chance." "It'll be posted; they'll have worked it out. After a year I bet there are signs still saying '86, once 84,' or '84, once 86,' or was it 84 or 86 to 184 or 186? No matter what, there won't be a problem. New England isn't New York City." "Are we in Maine yet?" Eva says. "No, dummy," Olivia says. "Don't talk like that," he says. "You'd want her to give that same crap to you? —No, darling. First New York, which we're still in, then Connecticut, Massachusetts, New Hampshire for not very long, California, South Oregon, North Oregon, Washington state and finally over the Piscataqua if that's the name of it Bridge—I think Mommy calls it Kittery Bridge because it ends up in Kittery and has a nicer ring to it and she never wants to chance spelling Piscatooey. Then about twenty miles on the Maine Turnpike to Wells and 9 or 6 or 1 or a couple of those roads till we're in Phlegmylunkpork, Lemonyjunkwart, Georgiepishpot, Bushyposhfort, over the quaint Water Street bridge with hundreds of under- or overdressed tourists gawking around where to spend their next thousand bucks, right at Ocean Avenue at the souvenir-shirt shop and about a mile on it past Whale Watch till hello Green Heron Inn and maybe the green heron itself sleeping by the pond there. Supposed to be good luck if you see it but don't wake it." "Then my luck the last few years should have been better," Denise says. "From today on the *Times'* travel section said. But lets hope no slip-ups, car-disrupts, torrential rains, wrong roads, souths instead of norths, wests instead of easts, or we'll be behind in time and we all want to get there on the nose to carry out our plans, correct? and which I expect will be," looking at his watch, "five-o-dot." "Coming to our exit," she says. "Slow down, stay right. You see it?" "I see it, I know it, now I got it—why you checking up on me so much? I could do it blindfolded." "I know how upset you get—either of these two dividing roads in front will do, since they come together soon—when you miss an exit on a long trip and have to go back for even a few miles. Every time we miss a familiar landmark—the Charter Oak Bridge, the truck or moving-van billboard with the real truck on top of it in Wooster or Lawrence I believe—you say we could have crossed or passed it ten miles ago, if we had to backtrack five miles, or ten minutes ago and we won't make it on five-o-dot and that sort of thing. Do you remember the worst one?" "Sure. You were at the wheel. I was navigating and the overhead Maine and New Hampshire and Cape Cod arrow-right sign wasn't up yet, nor the left one to Springfield. Maybe just little ones on the side we didn't see or just 'Mass Pike, East, West.' " "I was pregnant with Olivia then—seven months...July, August, September—well, six plus—but wanted to divorce you on the spot." "Good thing we weren't traveling with two lawyers, a judge and court." "I thought you'd never come out of it. The Big Pout I called it for a few years. For that wrong turn cost us about fifteen miles in the opposite direction before we could turn around, so thirty miles or thirty minutes or so and at the time you weren't this generous to admit who was controlling the map." "Forty minutes, ten of which I later made up by doing seventy-five to eighty over a long stretch without getting caught." "What happened?" Olivia says. "Daddy was being so nice to Mommy she got all confused and made a wrong turn." "No, what happened?" "You don't believe me? —She doesn't believe me." "What happened, Mommy?" "You read too many books, kid," he says. "You should be asking what's a pout or 'controlling the map' means." "I know what those are." "That's what I'm saying. You know all the words. But you should be asking what they mean instead of trying to find out the grimy details of every grim scene. Well, Ms. Drew, this case you ain't gonna solve 'cause you ain't gonna get all the facts." "What's a pout?" Eva says. "A pout's—oh, I'm lousy at definitions. Your mom's much better at it." "What's a debonition?" "An endearing—agh, there I am using that word again as if I didn't know it was a phony one and didn't know any other. A debonition's a real sweet pronunication of definition." "What are they, Mommy— endearing, pruncation and the ones I said?" "A pout is a grimace, a scowl," Denise says, "like this," and pouts. "And pronunciation, which is how you say it, is the way words are pronounced, spoken. And definition is the meaning of a word. For instance, grimace and scowl are other words for pout." "What's meaning?" and Denise says

"What I said—what a word means." "It can also be an interpretation of something," Olivia says. "Did you hear that?" he says to Denise. "Everybody—hey, fancy lady in the speeding Mercedes out there, did you hear that? My kid! Both of them, one for serious asking, other for her answers. What's that?" Cups his left ear. " 'Way beyond us' you say what she said? —And look, just noticed, hardly any traffic around—now we're going, now we're cooking with gas. And hey, everybody, Hay's Farmstand in Blue Hill—just remembered. I don't see it but I do smell it. Organic carrots and sugar snaps, seventeen varieties of red lettuce, blueberries with worms in them because they're not sprayed—can't wait." "They haven't worms," Denise says, "or few that do won't have live ones if you cook them, and don't scare the kids or they'll be more things they don't eat. And I'm going to conk out for about half an hour now, you have the route straight? Were coming up on Hutchinson—" "I saw the sign." "Left—it'll be a sharp one—good. Next, Merritt, which it goes right into, and why not Wilbur Cross, since both parkways are overgrown so with less sun on them." "Okey-doke. A shady journey. Say, good title for something, though nothing I'd do." "What about the one I gave you," Olivia says. "*Slow and Low*—you never used it." "It's good—who knows? *The Slow and Low Stories*; one character named Slow, the other Low; maybe one day." "And *The Lonely Bed*, Eva's title for you." "That's more for a single short piece or a children's book. A bed that can't find anyone to sleep on it because it's too lumpy or hard. Or it's in an old Maine attic or barn for a hundred years with no one to talk to but a mosquito or earwig before an antique hunter finds it, says 'Hey, pure oak, great bargain,' and goes through all sorts of purchases and fixings-up to make it sleepable. New mattress and box spring and designer patchwork quilt and sheets and maybe even a friend or two for it now that the insects are gone—a night table and bedlamp—before the bed's finally slept on to its delight, so much so its springs squeal. Maybe we'll write it this summer. Or I just gave you the idea, so you write and illustrate it." "No, you the words; something for the two of us to do." "OK, collaborators. But now you two rest back there. Mommy wants to nap, right?" to Denise. "Will music disturb you? "If it's not clashy-bangy-squeaky modern or even a Scarlatti sonata too loud." He looks in the rear view, sits up and adjusts it. Olivia reading, Eva looking at one of her books but blinking as if she's about to doze off. "Fix her pillow and she might get two hours." Denise does—"I'm not tired," Eva says—buckles up again, rests her head back and shuts her eyes. His beautiful wife who always looks better to him full face than profile. Nose, chin, now sacks under her eyes only seen from the side. And what happened to her breasts? Used to look at them from this angle and up till not even two years ago they were always fat or full and jutted out, even after the kids were weaned; now like anybody's; when they're hanging over him, two of them just about fill his hand. Diet, disease, maybe the drugs. And her calves: mottled, ankles swollen, when before like, well anything but like alabaster or marble, but for now that'll do: like the rest of her body except her buttocks: smooth, white. Her hair, always thick, wavier than usual today and with more ringlets; must have washed it when he was packing the car and leftover wetness and the humidity's doing it. Loves those curls. Like, well anything but like a young woman in a Renaissance painting holding a single pink or rose, but for now like one of those. "Don't ever cut your hair more than an inch or two—please; don't ask me why." Eyes him. "Speaking to me? It might fall out from chemo, in clumps or patches, so be prepared for that, but I won't cut or shave it—promise." Eyes close, back to the look she left; usually falls asleep in the car with a little smile, but over nothing he said. Fair unmarked face skin, not just pale; big broad forehead with a big broad brain behind, yellow-green eyes he loves the color of but can't look at very long. Maybe that's the way with all light eyes: pretty but they don't draw you in deep. Or they do draw but don't eventually stop you like dark eyes do. Oh who cares and what's she thinking? Probably just letting things come in or wondering why he brought up her hair. Why not her buttocks and neck? Well, he did think of her buttocks he'd tell her if she asked. Once fairly soft and large, now short and hard like a professional dancer's or athlete's because of all her exercise and weight loss, though pocked more than before: exercise? age? babies? not the drugs. Everything but the pocks he'd talk about. As for her neck, well anything but like a dancer's or swan's or a dancer dancing a swan, but for now that, and with her head arched back against the seat, even more. Or she could be thinking why's he keep looking at me while I'm trying to fall asleep? Worried about me? Or thinking of leaving me because he's afraid he'll be forced to take care of me completely in a few years? Help me up, help me down, turn me over in bed to avoid bed sores, dress me, undress me, bed pans, wiping my ass, feeding me, wiping my mouth, probably no sex, pads all during the day, diapers when I sleep and my pains and complaints and muddled talk? Also what I might look like then—shouldn't have mentioned the hair loss. But if he does leave, let him—just don't take the girls and she'll deal with it best she can: parents, friends, professional care. In other words: who needs the stiff if he's going to screw around with whatever she's got left to fight this fucking thing and make matters for her even worse? She wouldn't use fuck in any form, probably not even in her head. She's never said it around him except once when they had a big row and she said, after he said "Fuck you" to her, "Go fuck yourself too, you fucking prick." When she wakes he should ask about the car smile and maybe what she thinks before she dozes off. If she asks why he could say he just wants to know someone else's thoughts and thought process but his own. His work bag! Feels behind the seat on his right where he thinks he put it, feels Olivia's leg, bag of Denise's health foods, cooler, some books but nothing else on the floor. With his other hand feels on the left side but can't get back there very far. Doesn't like to take his eyes off the road for more than a couple of seconds but sits up, turns around and looks behind his seat. Bag's there, Olivia's reading, Eva's asleep. Should have asked Olivia to look but didn't think of it. Shouldn't have panicked the way he did because suppose there'd been an accident because of it? His two kids, his wife hurt, maybe killed, and over his work? Not there it'd be somewhere, in the apartment, or if left on the street when he was packing the car and was now gone, then a great loss but not something he couldn't eventually make up for most of it and for all he knows come out better than before. It's happened—page mysteriously lost, page mistakenly used for scrap paper and tossed out—probably because he wanted to make up for the loss so much that he concentrated and worked even harder on it. If he couldn't make up for it, if nothing came back and couldn't be reproduced and he lost it all or what hadn't been photocopied and put some other place, in the long run so what? But what's he gain by finding or not finding it right away or later, for think of the risk he took. Well, if he found just now he didn't have it in the car he'd stop and phone the doorman in their building and ask him to see if the bag was still in the lobby from when he took all the things out of the elevator and if not to go outside to see if it's where the car was parked. If it wasn't in either place he might drive back to see if he left it in the apartment, but he's sure he didn't. He remembers carrying it downstairs but doesn't remember if he set it down outside the elevator or took it straight to the car. Actually, just to make sure, he'd ask the doorman to go into the apartment and if he found it there or in either of the other places, he'd ask him to send it express and he'd send him a check for it plus about twenty bucks extra. But the risk he took looking behind the seat while he drove. Pictures what it could be like now, few seconds after. He'd be alive, Denise and the girls would be all over the place, screaming, maybe no screaming, stop. If one of the kids died from an accident like that or lost an arm or eye, it'd end his life. Or sort of, or close to it, certainly worse if he was responsible for it, or even that can't be predicted, but stop. And he said if his kids died, what if they didn't but Denise did? He'd suffer, more so if he was responsible for it, or equally so, he'd be miserable for months, for a year, for a long time and then would try to hook up with someone and get married and have a child or two by her and having the new children which he wouldn't have had with Denise would make up for it some he'd think. Suppose Denise asked him how much of her falling apart does he think he can take. Why'd he think that? Something from before, connected to his depressing thoughts, or even the cooler with her ice packs and cold cap for if it gets too hot for her in the car. He'd say—truth now, what? He'd say— Things are always difficult to predict, he'd start off with, how one would react to something like that. How does one know how accustomed one can grow? And by falling apart, how bad? If she said: on her back, couldn't get up, had to be spoon-fed or through tubes, body a bony mess, so on, he'd say he loves her, would never think of forsaking her under any circumstances—deserting, leaving—it'd be terrible for the kids besides: how could he face them, and if he couldn't face them, how could he see them, and if he couldn't see them, how could he live? Nah, getting too fancy and off the mark. What would he say after he said he'd never leave? That he went through this with his sister a little and a lot more with his dad and both of them for several years so he's familiar how bad things can get and used to them he can become, doing things he didn't think he could and being of some help. So, what's to add?—he's here to the end, no question about it, the end meaning till the end of their marriage, which means till one or the other of them croaks of old age as they used to say, and he hopes that works both ways. Scratch the last. She'd say he's just trying to make her feel good, for he knows he's as healthy as a horse. So was she, he could say to that, but that wouldn't be too good either.

He squeezes her hand, she squeezes his, eyes still closed, smiles a different smile, one for him, but her face still facing front, takes her hand out from under his and puts it with the other on her lap. Why didn't she keep it under his? Probably to tell him to keep both hands on the wheel. He turns on the radio. Damnit, Dvorak, dials around and back to the station he had it on, though it's fading now so next time he turns it on it'll be out of range, and turns it off. "Oh, I forgot to tell you," she says, looking at him. "Did the music disturb you?" "No. And we're nowhere near Wilbur Cross, are we?" "You kidding? You were out for what, ten, fifteen minutes? We're just about coming to Westport." "I spoke to Rosalie the other day and she said when were driving up we should definitely make a point of dropping in." "Was that a serious invitation?" "Rosalie; of course." "But the 'definitely make a point.' " ''That was my wording, not hers. She even said to come for lunch. That there's always something good there to quickly prepare and eat." "It means changing our plans, taking the Connecticut Turnpike instead of Wilbur Cross—you want that? What about the shade? And that's an hour, hour and a half at least at their place, even without lunch." "Hour and a half at the most. And if it's lunch, we got that out of the way, so maybe a half-hour's been lost. And we keep saying we want to see them—" "You do. I like them but, you know. . ." "What?" "Nothing." "We haven't seen them for more than a year, so here's a perfect opportunity." "Perfect. But if you haven't seen someone for a year when you could have, maybe that says something." "What does it say?" "It says what it says and how do we know they'll be in in about an hour or however long it takes? And they've a new place north of new Haven, so it might be tough finding even if she gave you specific directions." "She did. They're so easy I didn't have to write them down. Off an exit, then a road, lane by the same name, all lefts, last house and only shingled one and we're there. It's five minutes from 91 and then you get back on the next exit, so you lose, or possibly even gain if it's a shortcut, three to five miles of mileage. She said to call just before." "That means stopping and calling." "We could do it at the next service station. While you're filling up and the girls are urinating, I can call." "I don't have to fill up; besides, gas prices are usually much more expensive on the Merritt, and you're going to get out of the car to call?" "Why can't I? Just hand me my walker and some change, and if there are steps without a railing, help me up, and that's all. I'll have to stop soon for a ladies' room break anyway." "That I'll do, anything, but the Shostaks? She's lively and likable but he dominates everybody and has no sense of humor." "That's ridiculous." "Well, if he does have one it's always done with a French or Latin phrase or is so erudite in English everyone laughs because they think they understand it or are afraid not to because of what he'll think of them." "Not true. He's very generous and sensitive, maybe it's the occasional inflated fool he can't take, but he's one of the rare big minds who listens to what you say and usually has something to say about it. After all, that's one way of showing interest in your thoughts." "Still, the guy intimidates me with his conversations. Ancient law and politics, modern history and linguistics, painting, literature and music of all periods and the decline of culture and end of the LP." "You're as much for the LP as he is and you love art and literature and serious music of all kinds." "To see, read and listen to, not to talk." "You like doing that too, about literature, and we always come away stimulated by our conversations with them. It'll also provide us with some good road conversation, which I love doing with you. Unfortunately, that kind of talk doesn't happen enough with friends or you. It's movies, vacations, breakups, bodybuilding, running shoes, food." "He talks a few of those also, but OK, he is stimulating and I like talking about books I've read with someone who's read and remembered them, but not all the ibid.'s and op. cit.'s and minutay and stuff." "Minutiae." "Oh screw that word. When it's too tough to pronounce, spell and know the meaning of and then how to place it in a sentence, hell with it, and think if I'd have said it that way in front of him. The eyes! And later 'Did you hear that minutial brain? And he teaches?' Really I don't mean to put the guy down, for he is all the things you said if also a bit domineering and windbaggy and too much of the can't-abide-fools. And for an hour or two I can tolerate it for the stimulation and later the conversation it generates. But I just want to drive on, only make the natural stops. Pee, feed, gas. Maybe we can make more of a plan to see them on the way back." "You'll give a different excuse then if you remember you gave this one." "So we won't. But sometime after. In New York on our Christmas or spring breaks or invite them for a weekend in Baltimore if you like. But once moving, I'm a slave to getting there, not stopping off and frittering away our time." "Frittering? Is that a joke? Howard Shostak and it's frittering?" "Wrong word, not frittering. Schnickering, pelickeling, but we'll stick to the Wilbur Cross?" "Stick, stick," her head back, closing her eyes. Dvorak, when she was getting birth contractions with Olivia and was told by the hospital to continue to record them and wait, an all-night program of his music when he wanted to listen to almost anyone else while they stayed up in bed. When driving home from the hospital night Olivia was born, *Cosi fan Tutti* on the radio; knew it was Mozart but wrote the station and enclosed a self-addressed postcard to get the opera's name. "Do you want a rest stop soon?" "Now that Eva's up I could probably use one to avoid an unnoticed overflow." "Next one I see and probably to top off the gas tank too, no matter what it costs. That ought to hold us to Bumpylumppen or the first gas station over the Maine border." "Fine. Anything, right? to save time."

Mommy and Daddy are fighting again. It scares her because her ears are listening too much. Olivia doesn't care. She sits there only to read and doesn't worry if Mommy falls down and breaks her crown and cries from it or is yelled at. If he talks harsh to her again she'll shout for him to stop, don't dare do that, don't scream, be nice, don't be angry and mean, everyone here will hate you in the face and not talk to you ever, he has such a bad temper, gets mad a lot, Mommy only when it's right. Now Mommy's resting again it seems. That's good because she's tired and upset and before said her legs hurt. She wishes she could read because just looking at book pictures and the outside and into other cars except when they have kids in them and dogs and cats jumping around loose, gets boring. If they don't have rainbow sherbert there she'll make a fuss till they have to send away for it to a store. Are they in Maine yet? Probably not because she didn't sleep. There'll be a big bridge he said and the color of the road will change from dark to light and there'll be more trees and beaches to see and cars with people in bathing suits in them and the clouds will have fishes and porpoises and seals. What's a crown if she's not wearing one and why do they say upset and not down? One year he said "Look, a seal," and she did but he dived and stayed there and they waited but she never saw him. Daddy said he had a big mustache and glasses and waved to them before he dived. She wanted to know how come he said the seal was a he, did he see his penis? He just sprayed water on his window or it rained when she was thinking. It looks like the drops on top are racing down. She picks one with a baby's face to win, follows it against another she hates because it looks like a snake, but the wipers wash the drippings away before her favorite one could get to the bottom. She should have told Daddy not to before he did, but then he might have yelled at her does she want him not to see and them to get into a crash? She doesn't. If they died because they're in the front she doesn't want Olivia and she to ever go to different homes.

Look at the reflection of the house in the pond. She should have told Momma about it but now it's gone. Reflections are more beautiful than the real thing. They're like paintings. They're the ones that should stay, not the real thing. "Do you know what?" Olivia says. Here comes a gem, he thinks. I hope this isn't going to be long, Denise thinks. Maybe if she doesn't say anything. "Do I know what?" he says. "Reflections are more beautiful than the real thing." "That's a beautiful thought," he says. "Where'd it come from?" "It's not a thought; it's what I said." "I meant it's a beautiful idea, observation, and don't get so testy. But did it come out of nowhere? I'm always interested in where and how these inspirations or sudden impressions of yours come from." "It is beautiful, dearie," Denise says to her. "Reflections are like paintings." Olivia says. "They're the things that should stay, not what is real—the real things you see, I mean." "That's utterly amazing," he says. " 'Reflections are like paintings; they're the things that should stay.' Someone should write down some of the things you say. Actually, your mother has for years, about all of us." "I can write it down," Olivia says. "Do you have a pen I can use, Mommy?" "Not on me this moment." "You have one in your bag. I saw you put it there." "I don't want to try to reach it now. It's near my feet and it'd be sort of a struggle, to tell you the truth." "Then I'll lose what I said." "There's always another thought or expression and I'll remember it." "Quick, what was it she said?" he says to

Denise. " 'Reflections are like paintings. They're more beautiful than the real thing. They're the things that should stay, not the real.' " " 'Not what's real' or 'the real thing,' " Olivia says. "Close enough. And my guess is you got it by looking at a house or tree above a little pond we passed, am I right?" "Yes, did you see me?" "I didn't marry a dunce, did I, Olivia?" he says. "Her memory, way she figured out how you made the observation, which your daddy couldn't." "Mommy is not a dunce," Eva says. "Don't say harsh things about her." "I said I didn't marry one, sweetheart. Meaning she's a nondunce—smart. And I said it affectionately. I love your mother," and rubs the back of Denise's head. Denise smiles at him, takes his hand and kisses it. "Oh look, they're kissing," Olivia says. "And the palm," he says "that's big stuff." "What's a dunce?" Eva says. They all laugh. "Don't laugh at me." "We did because you were funny and silly," Olivia says. "I know you are but what am I?" "Funny and silly." "I know you are but what am I?" "Please, not that refrain again," he says. "Someone, save us." "I know someone save you, Daddy, but who'll save me?" "Hey, how could we have forgotten?—Fowler entrance to Walker Pond. Great warm lake swimming, and I'll blow up your tubes and you can play in the water long as you like." "How am I going to get down there this year?" Denise says. "The car. I'll back down it right to where the rear wheels are in the water." "It's too embarrassing. All the beach eyes on me as I tumble out of my seat and you run around the car to set up the walker." "Hell with what people think." "Easy for you but for me I'm not ready yet." "Do they call it Walker Pond because some people walk into it with a walker?" Eva says. "Did you hear that?" he says. "Where's she come up with them?" "I'm not going into that water," Olivia says. "There're leeches." "So we'll bring a salt shaker and go like this, shake shake shake, and the one in the thirty times we go there that might get you, will drop off. But I'll stick by you and catch them before they get you. Then heave-ho with a stick and I'll knock them out on land with a rock." "That's disgusting." "Why? You don't like them—*dead*. You know, when I was a kid in Miss Humphrey's camp in New

Hampshire—" "I don't want to hear that story again. Eva, he came out of the water every time with five to ten leeches on him." "Great, you don't want to hear it but you give away the ending. And not every time; just when the weeds were stirred up or something. Beaver Lake. Outside of Derry. I'd love to take a detour one time to see how the place has changed or stayed the same. I'm sure by the picture in my head and of the road and stuff from Derry I could find it. I even remember the cottage my mother stayed at when she came up to see us, Vera and me, for a day or so. And the toy she gave me—some pinball set—you know, where you pull a knob back and shoot the ball and it's supposed to land in one of those semicircles or cups. And taking us to Rockingham Racetrack and the amusement park nearby, I think. And looking so beautiful and big-citylike—dressed so stylishly, and same with her hair up, compared to the locals. Though maybe that image of her comes from the photo I have somewhere of us at the amusement park, Vera and I eating ice cream cones and my mother behind us with her jacket over her shoulders. I even remember riding in the back of a car with her and maybe Vera to her cottage for the night. And that it was night, probably August, and looking outside and seeing the houses passing, and being given the pinball set and tearing it open in the car. Maybe I didn't want to leave her for the night. I was so in love with my mother. She never struck me, rarely said anything but nice words in a low voice to us. And she must have only recently arrived that day if I was only then opening the gift. Though I suppose she could have had dinner with us at the camp and seen us swim and things like that and kept the gifts in her suitcase till we got in the car. But the leeches never bothered me in the lake. It was to your credit, even—Captain Bloodsucker they called you—the number of leeches you had on you over the next guy. And some man was always there with a lit cigarette—something good at last to say about cigarettes—and went tip tip tip and they all dropped off, one, two, three, ten. And after Walker Pond, well, hey, the Country View Drive-in again, or the Bagaduce this time for fried clams and a crabmeat or lobster roll and the best onion rings north or east or west or wherever it is of the Country View." "I want Country View," Eva says. "They put jimmies on your baby ice cream cones." "You remember the jimmies and that they have baby cones too? What else?" "The cows and kittens and rabbits in cages." "Cows in cages?" Olivia says. "Don't, Olivia darling, she's remembering." "In the country, I said," Eva says. "The kittens and rabbits and the geese that steal your hamburger buns." "Incredible. You kids didn't talk about it just before?" "No." "I always thought kids her age had little year-to-year memory of things like that. What else do you remember there?" "The dirty bathroom where Mommy didn't want to go in because it had flies all over the toilet seat and nobody flushed it." Frog. Oh my God, Denise thinks. "Frog," she says. "Frog?" he says. "At the Country View?" "Maybe they're in the geese and duck pond there," Olivia says. "We left Frog home unless someone miraculously brought him." "I didn't," he says, "and I'm the only one who loads and carries things." "None of that now. This is serious." "I'm sorry, I wasn't martyring myself again, I think, but he's back home? What should we do?" "We have to go back." "Go back? Maybe sixty miles along the way—did you check the odometer before we left? For I didn't but meant to." "No." "I think we're getting near Stratford and the Wilbur Cross," he says. "It's got to be more than sixty, which is a hundred-twenty-plus miles altogether. Two-and-a-half hours out of our way at least—more, since we don't do sixty, sixty-five in the city or on the Deegan or Cross Bronx and most of the times not even on this Merritt. And the Cross Bronx—did you see it going the opposite way? It was gridlock in the making, and later it gets, worse it becomes." "Then we'll go Saw Mill River to Henry Hudson," she says, "but we can't leave him. The windows are shut, his water will dry up, he has enough food for a day, he'll be eating his own excrement." "He's just a turtle." "But he's our turtle, our responsibility." "Why is his name Frog if he's a turtle?" Eva says. "Don't ask questions like that now," he says. "I already told her once," Olivia says, "and you did too." "I forget," Eva says. "Because Daddy didn't want any name for him, thought him

too simple a pet for one. If a pet can't answer to his name, he said—"
"Don't explain now, I said," he says, "we're thinking." "Then I'll
whisper," and she whispers into Eva's ear "And so when I said we
had to have a name, that I don't want to just call it Turtle, he said
not a long one. No double syllable—da-da, Eve-a, double, two
sounds, see? So I said Frog from the *Frog and Toad* book I was reading
you then." "Why not Toad?" "I said stop," he says. "Whisper," Olivia
whispers. "Because Frog was my favorite character of the two and
Toad sounds ugly." "Oh, now I know," Eva says. "I'm sorry, Howard,
I should have been the one to remember it," Denise says, "for you
were doing almost everything else. But we have to act now and that's
to go back." "No, listen, there's got to be another way. You don't mind
if he doesn't spend the summer with us—just that he lives?" "Yes."
"So we'll call the Matlocks and have them get our key from the
doorman and they can take care of him in their place for the summer.
And if they go on vacation for a while—I think they said two weeks—
give him to the Leventhals, and so on. We'd do that for them. We
have done things like that—looked after their plants, picked their
kid up at the school bus stop once. We'll explain our situation, that
we're an hour and a half away already—" "The Matlocks are at work
and who knows where their kids are—camp, probably, or with
friends. Even if we get one of them at work, you think it fair asking
them to take care of a turtle for two months—cleaning out its bowl,
feeding it, worrying that it might die in the heat?" "They've air
conditioners in every room. He'll be fine. And we'll say we'll pay
them for the extra electricity if it gets too hot for the turtle and the
air conditioner has to be on for him when nobody's home." "But
they should do this for two months when to get him it'll be two-
and-a-half hours out of our way at the most? Even if it comes to three-
and-a-half hours, so what? If you want to do the right thing you have
to pay for it sometimes." "Yeah, I know, you're right, but we have
dinner reservations for six-thirty, I want to go to the beach with the
kids for an hour before dinner and they want to too. I want to have
a drink after a long trip and read the paper—" "We could always

go to another restaurant there or Cape Porpoise for dinner as you said, and the rest of your entertainment you'll have to skip this once." "It's June 30th, Friday, no less, the beginning of one of the peak vacation weeks of the summer. Suppose all of Cape Porpoise is booked tonight? We know nothing about the place except it has a couple of fish restaurants. And with dainty and dapper Kennebunkport we know all the decent restaurants will be filled around eight. Especially at eight. That's when they finish their cocktails and want to eat after a long day in their gardens and on their patios and tennis courts and boats, and which is around the time we'd be getting there if we drove back now for the turtle." "So we'll stop for dinner at a nice place on the way." "I don't want to get off the road except for water stops and a quick lunch till we get there." "Then we'll find a drive-in or diner in Kennebunkport like the Country View, bring beer and wine to it in paper bags if we have to, because I know that drinking with your dinner's one of your main considerations—" "It is, I like it with my dinner but right now it's not the point." "Yay, please let's go to one of those other Country Views," Olivia says. "Nothing. I don't want to hear anything from you kids, now listen to me." "Don't shout," Eva says. "I already told you so." "And I told you. Mommy and I are talking." "You're shouting." "We're discussing. Now both of you, shut up. I'm sorry, but be quiet." "Don't scold them," Denise says. "They're not doing anything. Anyway, we can't ask the Matlocks— it's just too long—and Frog can't be left there and I can't come up with any other solution but going back. —We're coming up on an exit." "There are exits every mile or so on the Merritt and, if I remember, on the Wilbur Cross, so don't worry." "You're making it worse for yourself. Further we go, less you'll feel—there's a sign for the Stratford theater now." "I see it." "Less you'll feel like turning around." "We have to turn around, Dada," Olivia says. "We have to get Frog." "I got it," he says. "Your mother. She'd do it, wouldn't she, take care of him—your folks?" "I think so," Denise says. "But they're going to one of their Polish hotels for two weeks in August and middle of July she's spending a week with us." "Your father can take care of him when she's with us and we'll worry about the Polish hotel later. Their cleaning lady—someone, one of their neighbors, or the Matlocks then. I know it'll be a pain in the butt for them all and I'm sorry, but we'll try to make it as easy as we can. They can give it to the Matlocks for those two weeks if their vacations don't coincide. If they do, the Leventhals or someone, or I'm sure even my brother will drive down and take him for two weeks and maybe till the end of the summer if I really ask him and his vacation doesn't fall in with theirs. And we'll take care of the cab fare and everything else from our place to your mother's and back to the Matlocks and so on. She can get the keys from the doorman. Tobley—he's on till four today. If she can't pick up the turtle by then, we'll tell him to tell the doorman who succeeds him to give it to her. Or she can go up and get it herself with the spare keys, but we'll have to call Tobley first for I'm sure he won't give the keys to her unless we tell him." "I don't want her going upstairs and gathering up Frog and his bowl and food and carrying it to the cab; too exerting and heavy." "Then Tobley or the other doorman or one of the porters will do it. I'll tell him on the phone I'll send him something. And till then he can keep the turtle downstairs in their little office till your mother or father comes, or go upstairs and get it when they come." "Good, that's what we'll do. Stop at the next service station so we can phone everyone. You have the downstairs phone number?" "In my address book in my work bag. Or if I didn't transfer it to the new book, which I'm almost positive I did, we can always get it through New York information under 'Apartment Buildings,' I think. Something like that. I did it once. Wait—oh crap. The doormen don't have the spare set. We do, unless you took it out of the saucer on the piano and brought it down—remember?" "Remember what?" she says. "You forgot your keys—two days ago—and the doorman gave you the one spare set they have and you told me to bring it down yesterday and I forgot and last night you said for me to make sure to do it today, but you didn't when you were leaving?" "No." "So it's there. Don't the Matlocks have a spare set?" "They did but I asked for it back when I forgot my keys last week—I was upstairs when I realized it and rang their apartment and got them." "Where's that set now?" "In my purse probably." "So why didn't you use it to let yourself in the other day when you got the spare set from the doorman?" "I don't know if I had that purse with me, but anyway, I forgot it was in it till now." "Then I don't know what to do." "No, come on, we have to think of something—you've been great at it." "Then this. I'll call Tobley and have him get a spare set from management and even if it takes two days—we can tell him we'll pay for messenger or livery service of the keys to the building—the turtle will still be alive. After all, he's a turtle, and possibly a hibernating animal, or even if he isn't or only hibernates in the winter—built for surviving under uncertain or changeable conditions. And everything won't dry up or run out in a day and a half." "But you know with management it could take three to four days. And if it gets very hot and with the windows up except for an inch in the kitchen, Frog might die." "Turtles love hot humid weather." "But if it gets too hot and humid in the room over a few days the oxygen in his bowl could evaporate, or whatever oxygen does—disappear—along with the water. And he'll die that way and I don't want the doorman—well I first don't want Frog to die—but I don't want the doorman to have to deal with that. It wouldn't be fair. And suppose management can't come up with a spare set? You know they're totally disorganized and indifferent except for the first-of-the-month rent envelope in your box and an eviction notice if you haven't paid in five days." "Then break down the goddamn door, I'll tell them." "Fine if it's your door, but they won't do it for a turtle even if you say you'll pay for it. No, that's something where you have to slip the super some money and right on the spot and then later pay management for the door." "So let's stop off at a town near here and send the keys express through the post office to the doorman and then call Tobley to say it's coming. He or one of the other doormen will get it tomorrow." "Suppose they don't?" she says. "There could be any number of mixups. The wrong doorman might get it and not know what to do with it—a substitute,

which there often is and especially during vacation time and
sometimes they even have one of the porters take over for an
afternoon or day. Or maybe the doorman Tobley tells you will be
on and that's the one you address it to, might call in sick or the
schedule's been changed and Tobley doesn't know this fellow's off.
So it just stays around waiting for him." "Then I'll tell Tobley to have
tomorrow's doormen look out for the express mail addressed to
'Doorman,' and even for the porter-substitute, if there's one, to look
out for it." "That'd be too vague. That doorman or porter might not
want to deal with something he doesn't know about or that might
entail extra work for him. Or if it's delivered around four or five,
the evening doorman might just leave it for the morning one, and
the morning one, well I don't know—it might get lost by then." "It
won't. And I'll have Tobley follow up on it. And this is express mail
we're talking about, not regular, so no four or five delivery but usually
around noon." "Express isn't always express. And why are you so
sure a small town around here will have express mail? We could be
spending as much time looking for a post office as it would take to
get back to New York." "All towns of a certain size do, and if the
one we go to doesn't, we'll ask in that post office for a town that
does. It shouldn't take us very long." "Why are you so sure it'll get
to the city the next day and not Monday?" "It's delivered every day,
Sunday included I'm almost sure of—yes, Sunday too; in fact it's the
only kind of mail delivered that day, or maybe special delivery too.
And this is Connecticut, one state over from New York, so it has
to get there the next day." "Maybe not from one small town to a big
city. But look, what I'm reallly saying, Howard, is we shouldn't rely
on it completely, even if we called the Matlocks, knew they'd be home
tomorrow and Sunday and sent the keys to them to give to the
doorman to get Frog for my mother or to get and keep him for most
of the summer themselves. And if the keys don't get there by
Sunday—" "They'll be there tomorrow." "—the earliest Frog could
be rescued would be Monday. And if it's this hot and sticky today
and it's not even noon, and we're on a mostly shaded road with our

windows down and further north now and in the country, it's bound to get even worse in the city the next two days, so it could be too late to get Frog by then. So we have to go back, please." "Your argument's absurd, or pushing it, or something, but just words to persuade me, no matter how sincere you are about getting him." "We have to go back, please—also because I don't feel it fair to burden anyone about this but ourselves. Pay attention. Wilbur Cross ahead and the road to 95, so let's find a way to turn around now." "It doesn't make any sense to me, it just doesn't. I'm continuing on Wilbur but don't worry, if we decide on turning around the next exit should only be a few minutes from here and the one after that another few minutes and so on. But what I'm trying to say is three, if I exceed the speed limit a lot, but more likely four hours, and for a turtle? I don't feel anything for him. I'd say to forget the whole thing and leave him there for the summer except I don't want to think about the mess it'll make for two months and then have to come back to it and clean it up. Nor do I want his carcass and stuff stinking up the building and for the doormen or porters to have to deal with it—maybe even breaking down the door if they don't immediately find our keys, and then we'll be out a couple of hundred bucks. But he doesn't do anything but crap and eat and move around a little and occasionally snap at imaginary flying bugs and we shouldn't even have him. People shouldn't have pets period unless they need them for seeing-eye dogs or extreme loneliness or fighting off criminals and those aren't our problems." "All that we can discuss some other time." "But why did we get him? The girls were sad. Because it was him or a yapping bird because we lost the cats, which after a long enough mourning period I can say I never really liked and who were a stiff pain and I did most of the taking care of and cleaning up for—" "Another time." "OK. He's practically nothing to me. And why shouldn't he be? He's so insentient he wouldn't know he was being hurt and dying if I did it with my own hands, I think." "Right, and lobsters don't either. Which is why you drop them into boiling water so easily." "What are you talking? I don't even eat them

at other people's homes." "That's what I'm saying. You know Frog would feel pain if you dropped a drop of hot water on him and if there was no air, suffocation, and other things. That he's aware we're gone and not there to feed him, I don't know; but that there's nothing to eat, when that happens, and he's hungry and then starving— come on. But we'll improve things to make him more active and his life better. First, a bigger tank." "Oh, I'm sure along the way." "No, after we're up there a day or so—during our big shop. It's been on my mind a long time. We should let him walk around the room every day, in Maine or in the city. And in the country we said we'd let him go on the grass sometimes and in the lake, or salt water—whichever he can take; we'll have to find out." "I want to walk Frog on the grass," Olivia says. "I don't want him to die." "So do I," Eva says. "Frog shouldn't die, right, Olivia?" "Right." "Listen, everybody, please, hush for a minute," he says. "I'm thinking of some other solution but going back for him." "No other," Denise says. "Next exit, we have to turn around." "If we go back to New York will I miss my rainbow sherbert?" Eva says. "Almost everything will be the same except later," Denise says. "Probably at a different restaurant, so regular sherbet or ice cream instead of rainbow. Or so much later that we'll be eating on the way so we'll have to skip dessert tonight to get back on the road and in the Green Heron before your father gets too tired driving. But that means we'll get something like it or the same thing tomorrow or the next day at a different place—Dick's in Ellsworth, when we do that big shop there." "I don't want to miss dessert," Olivia says. "So you think we should let Frog die in our apartment because you want dessert?" "I didn't say that." "Then what are you saying? It's a long trip back to New York. And then a long trip back to where we are right now. And maybe even a longer trip to get right here because by then a lot more people will be heading out for the long weekend—" "Oh Christ, I forgot all about that," he says. "It'll be hell, and by the time we got to Hartford or New Haven, even worse, and when we got to the Maine border, the absolute pits." "And your father will keep saying we could have been here three hours ago or so, four hours, etcetera, even five—we might as well prepare ourselves for five—besides what hell he'll say it'll be when we pass Portsmouth and are getting close to the Maine border and that once wonderfully freeing bridge. But when we get to the Mass. Pike exit he'll really let me have it. For then he'll recall the up-till-then worst driving mistake we've ever made together—I made, he'll insinuate. But we can't let an animal die because it'll be convenient for us, can we? Sherbets over turtles—are we kidding? If Frog were a frog I'd say I don't know but I'd probably go back for it. If Frog were a worm I'd say let it go. It's small, it'd decompose fast, there wouldn't be that much of a smell, certainly not enough to break down a door for, and it's nowhere near as developed as a frog or turtle." "The turtle isn't so developed," he says, "at least on the brain scale." "It's developed enough. It sleeps, it feels fear, it makes love, it lays eggs, it sits on them and fights off predators, and when they're hatched it turns the little turtles around in the right direction to the ocean if that's what kind of turtle or tortoise it is. It doesn't come when you call or lick your fingers after you feed it but it's smarter than a lot of us think. I've seen a film—" "Public TV again, where we get all our learning it seems." "Don't be like that," she says, "you sound awful." "I saw that film program too," Olivia says. "Most of the babies couldn't find the ocean and the mother kept pushing, and one time a bird caught one of them." "I saw that too," Eva says. "The bird was ugly and mean." "You couldn't have seen it. Even I was small, so you were too young or not born." "How do you know?" "Stop it, both of you, all of you," Denise says. "The argument's over. All the arguments and justifications and I must have this and that and such. We're wasting time—*precious* time, Howard. Forget express mail and the Matlocks and the mother solution and everything else. I don't even want her going over there in this weather—either of them, my father too—and carrying Frog home. It'll be too heavy and sweaty and they're too old and might not know what to do with Frog and he could die from that also—that happened with my hamster when I was a girl." "What happened?" Olivia says. "Nothing. I'm also too old for them to do my dirty work for me. That's what you and I are here for each other and I wish you'd see that already; and when it's dirty work we have to do together, we do it without blaming and ridiculing the other. We'll all have to accept missing everything we planned to get—sherbets and scotch and newspaper and Captain Bush at the helm and the rest of it. If we make one phone call it should be to the Breakwater to cancel the reservation." "They will anyhow when we don't show." "Well, to do it right, we shouldn't have them hold it for even a half-hour if we know this long beforehand we can't make it. Dinner on the road. Maybe we'll discover a better place than we ever dreamed of and convenient, a minute off the road. No alcohol for you, or just one, but we might even like it so much and like coming to Kennebunkport already fed and ready for I don't know what—just things we haven't done there at night—that we'll want to do it this way from now on. It'll give us a few more hours in the city and where we don't have to rush out so fast to be on time for this and that and forget things like Frog. And if we leave after a good meal, the girls will sleep for two hours in the car. So, sound good? Relaxed morning, not going to bed so early the previous night? Lunch at home, newspaper read over your second coffee and thus a bit less to fill up the car? Leisurely jog through Riverside Park rather than the early-morning sprint you say you always do day we leave? We can even sleep later, do a wash rather than leave our dirty sheets behind, and then a less anxious drive— no need to speed—Green Heron, bath, maybe a short walk or ride for an ice cream or a beer for you or something like that after we check in. Then, the next day, breakfast and a couple of hours for the girls and you at the beach before we start off, since it's the shorter part of our trip. Anyway, who's to say we could have done everything we wanted to today—beach and such—since for all we know it might rain." "It's not supposed to." "You know? You didn't have the news on that I'm aware of, even at home." "The paper. When I was quickly going through it after I bought it to see if there was any mention of Bush planning to be there today and have dinner at the Breakwater.

There was nothing, though the weather report page said Portland would be fair and clear, high around seventy-five." "So, you've beached it with the girls every summer coming and going when the weather was good—one time they can miss it." "I don't want to," Olivia says. "Wouldn't you for Frog though? He's supposed to be yours. Think of the thought of his death troubling you if you let him die." "I'll miss the beach but I'll miss Frog more," Eva says. "You're only saying that for Momma," Olivia says. "No I'm not. I don't want Frog to die." "I don't either. But I've been wanting to go to that beach all week for its pebbles and tomorrow it'll rain or Daddy will say 'Hurry up, let's get out of here.' " "Believe me," he says, "if I thought the turtle was going to die I swear, no matter what I said, I'd go back for him. But what he'll have is two harrowing days—terrible ones, meaning—or maybe not even that bad. But two at the most if we make the calls today and send the keys express." "Don't try to bamboozle us," Denise says. "Frog could die or get very sick. Did you change his water today? For I didn't." "Let me think. No, to be honest, not since yesterday. But it's not my job or yours, even if I'm just about the only one who does it. It's Olivia's, not that I'm trying to make her feel bad or it makes things better for him." "I'm sorry," Olivia says. "I was going to but nobody told me and I was busy getting my markers and things together and I forgot." "Then we definitely have to go back," Denise says. "His water's old and he does his stuff in it, you know that." "I think we should go back too, Daddy," Olivia says. "If we do can you get a book from my room I left there and want to read again in the car? It'll be a long trip and I might run out." "Will do," Denise says. "You'll get it for her, won't you?" "OK, I've been overruled," he says. "I'm going to hate it all the way back and then all the way here again and to Georgiecraphole." "Why should you? Use it as an opportunity not to make a big demonstration about it—to just fume and rage through the trip how much you hate it. Rise above it for once. If anything, you'll get that out of it. Maybe it wouldn't be the first time you did that, but not letting things get to you the way you usually let them, and you might even end up thanking Frog for it." "You mean thanking you." "No, just Frog. And maybe he'll understand what you did for him and from then on come when you call him. It's a good example for the girls too. Please take this exit." "No, I can't change, not on something like this, but I will do it. Hey, we're going back. Everybody buckled up? We're all in the car, sitting back? Then let's go," and he takes the exit.